ADVANCE PRAISE

Not often does a writer manage to create a novel with a scope that is both sweeping and specific, broad and still focused. Don Jeffries has done exactly this with *The Unreals*. His story carries readers through an array of adventures, twists of plot, unexpected dialogue and events, and moments of redemption and angst. His expansive cast of characters grab hold of the reader's attention and manage to make themselves both believable and exciting to follow. ʃ but Jeffries' work reminded me of the  f which I am very fond, while managing a t d Jeffries for this evidently articulat tily recommend it to readers looking f

- Luke Reynolds, Author of *Imagine it Better* and *Break These Rules*

In *The Unreals*, Donald Jeffries has crafted at once a rollicking fantasy adventure with surrealistically bizarre characters, settings, and situations, a funny yet thought-provokingly serious social satire, and a contrarian anarchist manifesto that will often infuriate liberals and conservatives alike. Depicting a cross-country journey in 1987 from the Washington D.C. suburbs to a mental institution in Iowa by a band of quirky, unclassifiable eccentrics and free spirits, the story winds along roads and through areas plagued by what ufologists call the "Oz Factor" of an indefinably, oppressively weird, spookily quiet environment and feeling of total isolation. There are continual passing allusions to Fortean mysteries, unsolved disappearances, etc., throughout the book, as well as to the Kennedy assassination and conspiracy theories.

Conspiracy theories and Fortean mysteries pervade a surreal tale recalling H.P. Lovecraft, Vladimir Nabokov, and Thomas Pynchon, with echoes of Richard Fariña's *Been Down So Long It Looks Like Up to Me*, John Kennedy Toole's *Confederacy of Dunces*, and Voltaire's *Candide*.

- T. Peter Park, Historian, Librarian and Fortean researcher

The Unreals is an amazing display of erudition and wit. Don Jeffries is the real thing!

- Alexander Theroux , ex-Harvard Professor, multiple Award-winning writer, author of the acclaimed novel *Darconville's Cat*.

I loved this book. Mr. Jeffries knows how to tell a good tale. It's fun, fast-paced, and you really don't know what's coming around the next bend. It's on my bookshelf between my Rudyard Kipling and *Confederacy of Dunces* -- because I didn't know where else to put it, and honestly 'somewhere between Kipling and Confederacy of Dunces is probably the best way I could describe it as well.

-Robert Ben Garant, author of *Writing Movies for Profit*

The Unreals

Donald Jeffries

Pocol Press

Clifton, VA

POCOL PRESS
Published in the United States of America
by Pocol Press
6023 Pocol Drive
Clifton, VA 20124
www.pocolpress.com

This is a work of fiction. Names, characters, places and incidents are products of the author's imagination or are used fictitiously and are not to be construed as real. Any resemblance to actual events, locales organizations or persons, living or dead, is entirely coincidental.

Originally published by Stone Garden Press, ISBN: 1-60076-034-1.

Publisher's Cataloguing-in-Publication

Jeffries, Donald 1956-
    The Unreals / Donald Jeffries.
    p. cm.
    ISBN 978-1-929763-62-7

1. Missing persons --Fiction. 2. Grandfathers --Fiction. 3. United States --Description and travel --Fiction. 4. Fantasy. I. Title.

    PS3610.E385 U57 2015

    Fic --dc23   2014960160

Library of Congress Control Number: 2014960160

TABLE OF CONTENTS

DEDICATION

This book is lovingly dedicated to the memory of my mother, Anna Turvey, and my wife, the inspiration behind it and the REAL Jeanne.

CARRIED AWAY FROM OLD VIRGINNY

Dear Waldo,

I regret to inform you that I am leaving. This may come as a shock to you, but such things are inevitable byproducts of our confused little world. Do not doubt I would resist this, were it in my power to do so. There are, unfortunately, many circumstances beyond my control. Please be advised to disassociate yourself from my beliefs; find your own, less dangerous road to true knowledge. As far as those who are misguided enough to care are concerned, I am disappearing forever. I dare not say any more, even this may be too much. Perhaps we will meet again in a better place, with only the good and righteous allowed to inhabit it. You surely must be aware there are no such restrictions here. I always hated goodbyes, Waldo, and I would have preferred almost any kind imaginable to this one - I'm truly sorry. Remember me fondly and please be careful. I'll always love you.
Old Hoss

Waldo Billingsly stared at the note in his hands. What did it mean? How could his grandfather-his hero-the man who'd raised him since that other bleak and terrible day, leave in such a sudden unexpected fashion?

When Waldo had opened his eyes just a short time earlier, he immediately sensed something was wrong. Although the June day was warm and delightful with the birds singing merrily outside his bedroom window, the emotional 28 year old had awakened with an air of impending doom.

He'd been dreaming about Ambrose Bierce, and had felt, as all people do from time to time, the dream held some significance. His grandfather loved the writings of Bierce and was obsessed with the author's unexplained disappearance. Waldo knew Bierce had also been keenly interested in strange disappearances before he vanished himself. The irony had always fascinated Old Hoss, and Waldo shook his head in wonder at how magnified it became with his grandfather's own abrupt departure. Was it possible, he wondered, for an individual, as a result of an abnormal interest in the subject, to cause his own disappearance? Or, as Charles Fort playfully suggested, in one of his many outrageous musings on the subject, could it be that some humans are simply fated to vanish inexplicably? Fort had been the foremost iconoclast of the century, perhaps of all time, and Waldo was familiar with every unsubtle nuance of his outlandish theories, as his books on unexplained phenomena held a treasured place in his grandfather's voluminous library.

The old man was an early riser, and when Waldo had stumbled into the kitchen just after noon to find no empty cereal bowl with traces of granola in it awaiting him on the table, and no extremist broadcast blaring out of the short wave radio set in the living room, he really began to panic. He conducted a quick, superficial check of the entire house, his timid nature flinching at every turn in fear of discovering his grandfather's body, but it proved to be about as productive as the frantic dragnets set by bumbling, nineteenth century London bobbies for the elusive Jack The Ripper. Visions of little green men in flying saucers, noiselessly whisking his grandfather away to another world as he slept in the room across the hall, danced in Waldo's head as he read the contents of Old Hoss's farewell note over and over again. Finally, he threw the piece of paper down in frustration and ran his fingers through his long brown hair. Weary of speculating, he felt tears welling up in his green eyes.

The man whose apparent loss Waldo mourned so deeply was a truly unique individual. Abner Billingsly was a dynamic, original thinker possessing uncommon insight into the human experience. Waldo's grandfather had witnessed over three quarters of the twentieth century unfold before him, but in spite of his 81 years, his tall, sturdy frame was still vigorous, in large measure due to lengthy daily walks and a strict vegetarian diet he'd instituted well before it was in vogue. Even considering his robust constitution, however, it was difficult to imagine the elderly eccentric embarking upon any spontaneous journeys. He had never learned to drive, and although he enjoyed traveling all over the world during much of his life, for the past several years he'd confined himself within the Virginia, Maryland, and Washington, D.C. borders.

The old man's nonconformity was evident by his vow, which he'd honored since the days of the Great Depression, to never tuck his shirt tail in. He wore his gray hair long, and sported a thick beard on his open and friendly face. His looks were only slightly marred by a large, bulbous nose, which reddened easily from the strain of his hearty laugh and booming voice. As a child, raised on a farm in Warrenton, Virginia, Waldo's grandfather had been driven by a burning desire to become a major league baseball player. This dream was nurtured by numerous trips into Washington, D.C. with his father to see the Senators play. The awestruck youngster's father regaled him with tales of the old-timers who'd played in the 1880's and 1890's, and Waldo's grandfather took a particular delight in hearing of the exploits of one Old Hoss Radbourne, a legendary pitcher of that era. This interest in Radbourne led to his playmates christening him with the same nickname, and it stuck throughout his life. A dose of scarlet fever at the age of fourteen had weakened Old Hoss Billingsly considerably, and shattered his dreams of playing major league baseball. Four years later, Waldo's grandfather received a stroke of good fortune when his uncle, the notorious Mad Millard Billingsly, a very rich and marginally sane character, left a sizable inheritance to him. Shrewd maneuvering in the stock market, combined with a great deal of luck, left Old Hoss a millionaire at the age of 21.

Waldo's grandfather began creatively writing at this point, and fell in love with a fellow fledgling novelist during a trip to New York. Old Hoss never elaborated about the true love of his life, beyond the fact that she was incredibly beautiful and talented, and her name was Cora. Upon reading her completed novel, Old Hoss was so impressed that he lent his considerable financial support in an effort to find a publisher. Waldo's grandfather was able, through his influence, to arrange a meeting with a renowned publishing firm, and Cora's manuscript was well received and considered for publication. The following day Waldo's grandfather discovered Cora's brutally murdered body in her apartment. Her assailant was never apprehended, and Old Hoss, torn by grief, left New York City after the funeral, never to return again. He also vowed, at this time, to forego any future effort at publishing his own writings, which began to grow at an astonishing rate. The creative urge was gone, however, and he carved instead his own niche in the literary field by producing a steady stream of small pamphlets on unexplained phenomena, bizarre historical and political theories, and other matters unacceptable in polite society. Eventually, Old Hoss married pretty Barbara Jackson, twelve years his junior, but tragedy struck again when she died giving birth to their first child, a healthy baby girl. Old Hoss's only child was later killed, along with her husband, distant cousin John Billingsly, in a plane crash. Barbara's son, ten year old Waldo, moved in with his grandfather, who raised him in his kind, inimitable fashion. Old Hoss's attempts at indoctrinating Waldo into his curious methods of observation and reasoning were, not surprisingly, a smashing success. Waldo grew to share his grandfather's penchant for the odd and controversial, and began checking the bushes and glancing over his shoulder far more often than the average teenager. He became convinced, in a word, that there was a group somewhere orchestrating all, in an evil, secretive manner, capable of repelling all efforts to stop them. Some of the colorful titles of Old Hoss's unpublished pamphlets illustrate the fringes he patrolled quite vividly: *Are There Holes Instead of Poles?, An Agnostic Looks at Jewish Bankers, Baseball Died When the Dead Ball Did, O'Come All Ye Traitors, Orgone Energy and Secret Meditation Rooms, Fantastic Friends of the Founding Fathers.*

Waldo went into the bathroom and blew his nose, a compulsive habit he'd inherited from his grandfather. He brushed his long, unmanageable hair repeatedly, put down the brush at last, and sighed when it fell back into the same disheveled position.

Waldo was of average height, with an abnormally large chest that contrasted sharply with the rest of his slight frame. His finely chiseled, handsome features often went unnoticed, due to a general disregard for his appearance, and a lack of self confidence that caused him to bow his head around strangers and adopt an unattractive, stooping posture. The nervous, immature young man was the last person anyone would choose to find them, if they happened to become lost or displaced, and yet he was solely responsible for locating Old Hoss. There were no other close relatives, and his grandfather's few surviving friends were unlikely to be of much assistance. One was in a mental institution, where he'd been for a number of years, and Waldo wasn't even certain he was still alive. The other was an ex-college professor, who shared many of the same interests his grandfather did, and was thought to be mentally unstable himself.

Waldo realized, since he'd been left a note indicating that his grandfather was indeed missing, voluntarily or not, that the most logical course of action at this point was to notify the police. This presented a problem, however. Waldo, like his grandfather, detested the police and cherished the notion that their main function was to inconvenience, intimidate, and incarcerate law-abiding citizens. In spite of this firm belief, Waldo, shaking his head and second-guessing himself as he dialed the number, decided to phone the police department.

The brief conversation that ensued did nothing to change his opinion. After being informed that the missing person was of legal age, the police spokesperson curtly cut matters short by stating, "in that case, there's really nothing we can do." Waldo felt almost vindicated by this nonresponsiveness, and was starting to weigh his other options when someone knocked at the back door.

Waldo, who was in the kitchen, ran down the stairs leading to the sprawling colonial's finished basement. Old Hoss used the massive lower level of his home to pursue his investigations into those uncharted areas of inquiry he held so dear. There was a fully equipped laboratory, although the old man had never been capable of conducting an experiment in the strictest scientific sense; a vast room sectioned off which served as the main library, housing an unparalleled array of unpublicized and ignored books, magazines, and newspapers, as well as a large number of his own unpublished pamphlets; a photographic darkroom; a small projection area for private viewing of the few films Waldo's grandfather deemed worthwhile; and Old Hoss's vaunted "study", which contained the rest of his unpublished pamphlets, his 18th century writing desk, and the typewriter he'd purchased in 1930 and been too superstitious to replace.

Waldo unlocked the door and opened it to find, much as he'd expected, Professor Hiram Buckley, the aforementioned ex-history teacher, standing there. Of their infrequent visitors, only the Professor ever used this entrance.

"Ah, Waldo!" Buckley exclaimed. "May I-that is-is your grandfather in?"

Professor Hiram Buckley was always a spectacle to behold. He was a thin man in his late fifties with only wisps of hair on his rather pointed head, and a jet black goatee that should have made him appear sinister but somehow didn't. He wore thick glasses, without which he was legally blind, and his wardrobe, which never varied, consisted of a bright green and orange-checkered jacket, a yellow relic of a necktie, dating back prior to the yuppie power era, black and gray striped pants, and well-worn brown boots, which always seemed caked with mud. The professor looked the part of one obsessed with such things as U.F.O.'s, werewolves, the secrets of ancient cultures, and missing Kennedy assassination witnesses.

"Uh...well, no he isn't, actually." Waldo replied.

"Oh, is he-that is-when will he back?"

Waldo sighed and indicated that Professor Buckley should come inside. He proceeded to relate to the Professor the fact that his grandfather had disappeared, leaving only an enigmatic note behind; that he'd contacted the police, who were of no assistance, and that he was confused and would be grateful for any suggestions in the matter.

The Professor tugged at his yellow tie, one of his numerous quirks, and frowned. "Oh dear, what can be-that is-have you thought about where he might have gone?"

"Yes." Waldo responded wearily. "But the note seemed to indicate he wasn't going..."

"Excuse me..." The Professor interrupted. "But may I see the note?"

"Sure. It's upstairs." Waldo started walking towards the steps. "Come on, I'll fix you a drink."

The two of them found themselves in the kitchen a few moments later, and Waldo turned towards Buckley with a smile.

"The usual, Professor?"

Hiram Buckley grinned broadly, as well. "Ah, yes-that is-if it's not too much trouble, my boy."

"Of course not." Waldo answered, and mixed the Professor's standard Tom Collins, heavy on the lemon, light on the lime. Handing it to the grateful gentleman, he led the way into the living room.

"I say-that is-you don't think this is too early for ..."

"Not at all, Professor." Waldo knew before Buckley finished that he was, as usual, seeking reassurance that his drinking alcohol during the morning hours was a proper, acceptable form of behavior. The Professor was no alcoholic, yet he did enjoy the taste of liquor, and would most often partake of it at odd times, such as weekday mornings, while not imbibing at all during what are considered conventional partying hours. Saturday nights, for instance, were more likely to find Hiram Buckley at home immersed in the writings of H.P. Lovecraft or Ezra Pound than tipping his elbow in a bar.

Waldo sat down on the sofa and picked up the note, which was lying on the coffee table. "Here it is," he said, handing it to Buckley.

The Professor scanned it with a furrowed brow, expending many "hmmms" in the process. He laid the note down, at length, and daintily took a sip of his drink.

"Waldo," he spoke with an air of authority, "I will-that is-I love your grandfather. Please let me help you find him."

Waldo nodded in appreciation. "That's very kind of you, Professor. But, I don't know where to begin looking. Do you have any ideas?"

"Hmmm. Let me see the note again." Professor Buckley took the piece of paper and turned it over and over again in his hands, as if he were receiving some kind of psychic vibrations by doing so.

"The best-that is-the most likely place to begin searching is ..."

He began tugging furiously at his tie again.

"How about the museums? You know how Old Hoss loved them."

Waldo attempted to discard this idea politely, gently pointing out that the Smithsonian museums consisted of many buildings, and besides, the note seemed to indicate he was being abducted in some fashion. "You see, Professor Buckley, I really don't know much about his social life, other than he didn't seem to have much of one. Do you know ...?"

"Waldo, my boy," The Professor interrupted again, "the suburbs of northern Virginia are crowded with quiet corners where the unsuspecting can be hidden, and the unforeseen can occur. Despite our reputation for being a congested metropolitan area, there are places where one can wander to, on their own or otherwise, and never be heard from again."

Waldo groaned and hung his head.

The Professor realized how indelicate he must have sounded and moved next to Waldo on the couch, placing his arm around the young man's shoulder.

"Waldo, I'm very sorry. I was-that is-I didn't mean to sound so ... gruesome." Buckley's face suddenly brightened. "Is it possible-that is-he was quite a drinker when he wanted to be, Waldo, and he might very well be in one of his favorite watering-holes right now, in such a condition that he cannot return home."

Waldo shrugged. "I guess that's as good a place as any to start."

"That's the spirit, boy." The Professor patted him on the back and stood up. "I suggest we begin in Old Towne, Alexandria. He loved that section."

With that, Waldo and the Professor left the house and drove off in the latter's van, which was painted in a bright array of colors that meshed nicely with its sartorially splendid owner.

They searched every bar in Old Towne, as well as all the used bookstores, but Old Hoss was nowhere to be found. Eventually, tired and discouraged, Waldo and Hiram Buckley drove back to Annandale, where the Billingsly house was located. Waldo invited the Professor in and, as both of them were terribly hungry, they ordered a pizza.

While they were waiting for their dinner to be delivered, the Professor picked up a frayed, black briefcase, which he'd brought in from the van. Opening it, he held aloft several sheets of paper, which were actually copies of the obscure little newsletter he published, called *Force Of Habit*.

"Waldo...do you mind?" The Professor asked.

Hiram Buckley had once been a history professor at a local community college, whose transformation into a dapper, offbeat, and mostly unemployed philosopher had been abrupt. According to the tale he often told, which he invariably began with the lamenting line "ah, if only I'd never read *None Dare Call It Conspiracy*......,"

He considered himself a sort of esoteric martyr, who'd sacrificed everything for principle. Apparently that little book had set him on a course towards political extremism, culminating in the loss of his job at the community college, as well as the breakup of his previously stable marriage. By the time he met Old Hoss, a few years later, Hiram Buckley was one of those unfortunates the normal and untroubled point at in scorn and laugh at derisively; a veritable dog that's kicked while it's down. He was, under such circumstances, a perfect companion for Abner "Old Hoss" Billingsly, one of the few people who didn't consider him a prime candidate for St. Elizabeth's, the infamous mental hospital located in the District of Columbia. Since his career in education had been so rudely interrupted, the Professor had worked his way through a series of menial, low paying jobs, which he inevitably lost due to his proclivity for preaching unwelcome and unpopular political ideas to his fellow employees. He managed somehow to eke out, through the meager wages he earned from his various, short term positions, enough of a living to maintain a small efficiency apartment in nearby Falls Church. His small publication, which he'd been producing for many years, had a very limited circulation, but Waldo had always enjoyed reading the copies of *Force Of Habit* mailed to his grandfather, who was, of course, a faithful subscriber. The most popular part of the newsletter, if any part of a publication that is read by such small numbers of people can be referred to as such, was the "Letters To H.B." section, wherein loyal readers tested the wisdom of Professor Buckley. They also pontificated on various topics to such an extent that it was considered likely by all, including Waldo and Old Hoss, that the letters were written by Hiram Buckley himself. The Professor invariably managed to read a few of the letters aloud, during each of his visits, and Old Hoss was the perfect sounding board, providing the kind of positive reinforcement that Buckley and most of the rest of humanity seek but often starve for. Waldo normally enjoyed these performances, as the Professor would read them with great fervor, and they were often amusing and thought provoking, but with his mind full of horrible images of his grandfather's possible fate, he was merely able to lamely nod his assent to the Professor.

Hiram Buckley looked somewhat disappointed at Waldo's obvious lack of enthusiasm, but rallied quickly and picked one of his favorite selections from the October 1979 issue.

"If I may begin..."

Waldo smiled. "Please go ahead, Professor."

"Thank you." The Professor started reading:

Dear H.B.,
I have seen the term "fredneck" mentioned in your newsletter several times. Please explain what it means.
Former Flapper in Flushing

Dear Former:
A fredneck is an entity combining the worst characteristics of the freak and the redneck. The fact that they have not been officially recognized comes as distressing news to those segments of the population, which, while perhaps not affixing a colorful label on them, have become painfully aware of their less than charming presence. The whole fredneck phenomenon most probably began with the Hell's

8

Angel and similar types of localized motorcycle gangs that flourished in the 1960's. Marlon Brando, James Dean, and Elvis Presley laid the groundwork for this in the 1950's, establishing the kind of persona, which would develop into the full-fledged fredneck a decade later. In those early, innocent years, it was merely necessary to present the vaguely dangerous world of the Brando and Dean types as being sexy and desirable. I would venture to guess that more bad marriages were caused as a result of young girls absorbing that lesson in 1950's movie theaters, than by all the combined efforts of unqualified secretaries and friendly neighborhood milkmen. A message was sent out loud and clear to American women: it was not "cool" to be attracted to a nice, polite young man. It was better, instead, to risk everything to obtain the reckless, often unattractive ne'er do well. By the time motorcycle gangs started forming in the 1960's, the true fredneck was born with them. Then, as now, the fredneck specialized in violent behavior, usually chemically enhanced, administering liberal doses of verbal and physical abuse in their patented obnoxious fashion. Fittingly, today's frednecks carry on the traditional staples of their able predecessors: general uncleanliness, a totally incomprehensible line of reasoning, and surprisingly attractive female companions, riding astride the backs of their most trusted means of transportation. Predictably enough, they continue to enjoy great luck in their few encounters with the law, whose long arm never seems to apprehend them when they are participating in their favorite destructive pastimes. The fredneck is one of the great scourges of society, on a par with the inner city gang member and nearly as dangerous as the local Congressional representative.

Waldo expressed his approval, though not as demonstratively as he might have at other times.

"Thank you, my boy." The Professor beamed proudly. "Would you like me to read another one?"

Waldo didn't have a chance to respond to this, as their pizza arrived at that moment, and the scent of the sausage and pepperoni, combined with the fact they hadn't eaten all day, compelled them to forget everything else. Discarding his cherished briefcase, the Professor, who insisted on paying, tossed a large bill at the happy deliveryman, and they sat down and devoured their dinner.

Professor Buckley offered to stay the night, but Waldo finally persuaded him to leave, reassuring him repeatedly that he would be called back promptly should that become necessary. It was after 11:30 when the Professor departed, and the exhausted young man immediately lay down on the sofa and lit up a cigarette.

Waldo inhaled deeply, staring at the ceiling. It was at times like this that he was at his worst. His mind, while indecisive, was also capable of producing the most detailed, fantastic daydreams imaginable, and with the mysterious disappearance of his grandfather as fodder, his speculations grew even more intense and far-fetched than usual. On the other hand, the logical part of his brain, underdeveloped as it was, went almost entirely untapped in such a situation. Waldo was literally frozen into inaction by his chemical makeup, and this was apparent in the number of cigarettes he lit, the number of sighs he expelled, and the number of times his helpless fingers alternated between nervously tapping the coffee table and running through his unkempt hair.

All that night, Waldo remained awake, deep in unproductive thought, routinely walking back and forth from the living room to the front porch, where he would take a seat in the old-fashioned swing and smoke heavily. The blissful suburban setting, especially on spring nights like this, when the crickets chirped so lustily, and the porch swing creaked so reassuringly in the warm breeze, was perfect for conjuring up bold new fantasies.

Professor Buckley arrived early the next morning, and the two of them spent several hours scouring other unusual nooks and crannies of northern Virginia. They checked more of the smaller, atmospheric bars, the ones which opened at sunrise and catered to a few loyal, unconventional customers; they checked more used book stores; they checked Catholic churches and rectories, which the doubting oldtimer would sometimes wander into and debate the priests; they even gathered up the courage to enter the country's murder capital, Washington, D.C., to check some of the quaint little parks that dot its environs, as Old Hoss was known, on rare occasions, to take a bus into the city and wind up sitting like a tourist, admiring the wonderful statues in them. They looked, in all reality, about as thoroughly as one could look for someone who held very few acquaintances and seldom ventured out of doors.

As the Professor sat in an easy chair in the living room, sipping another Tom Collins and speculating about who and what Old Hoss might have encountered during his daily brisk walks about the neighborhood, Waldo, not having slept at all during the night, began to nod off.

"My boy, although I've never owned a flag, I feel as though my heart was at half-mast." As the one time pride of the local community college began an impromptu eulogy for an individual who may not have needed one, he suddenly noticed his young companion's drooping eyelids. "I say, Waldo-that is-are you sleepy?"

Waldo opened his eyes. "Huh? Oh... yes, I must be..."

The Professor stood up. "Forgive me, Waldo. I should really be more observant. I'm going now, but please phone me later." He downed his drink and straightened his bright yellow tie. "Now you sleep, my boy- you need your rest."

"Thank you, Professor, I will." Waldo wearily replied, closing the door closed behind the eccentric ex-history teacher.

Walking into the kitchen, Waldo poured himself a Coke and lit up a cigarette. His thoughts turned back to his missing grandfather. How could he find him? Where else could he look? Was it possible his grandfather had kept some part of his life hidden from him? The questions kept coming as he blew smoke rings in the direction of the refrigerator. If there was indeed a grim reality to face, and a corpse to be found, Waldo knew that in some cases the bodies remained undiscovered for a long time. The nervous young man shivered at this, and at the even more frightening fate accorded those rare missing persons who were *never* located. As he watched the smoke rings dissolve, Waldo realized he had to do *something*, and do it quickly. The more time elapsed, the more likely it was that his grandfather would become mere fodder for speculation, like Amelia Earhart, or even Ambrose Bierce.

Waldo gazed at the old man's room. To borrow a phrase from the Warren Commission, it was a "monument to clutter." There were books and papers strewn haphazardly on the bed, the dresser drawers, the night stand, and all over the floor. The decor resembled an esoteric precipitation, like the strange showers of frogs and fish described in the books of Charles Fort. Impressive cobwebs hung from every corner and the walls were filled with posters of non-academy award winning movies. The large walk-in closet was overflowing with Old Hoss's massive comic book collection which, had more care been shown it, would have been worth a small fortune. Stepping carefully, Waldo made his way to an old wooden chair, picked up a thick volume which was lying there conspicuously, brushed some papers aside and sat down.

The book he held was merely a thick stack of notebook paper, loosely bound together with string. Written on the cover page was The *Journal of Sam Hancock*. Waldo frowned. What was Old Hoss doing with Sam Hancock's Journal? Being high-strung and far from level-headed, Waldo had waited an inordinately long time to thoroughly comb his grandfather's bedroom.

Could his belated discovery of a seemingly innocuous private diary actually be of significance?

Waldo remembered Sam Hancock quite well, even though he hadn't seen him for nearly twenty years. Hancock, a year younger than Old Hoss, had been Waldo's grandfather's best friend from the moment they first met as spectators at the Army-McCarthy hearings in the 1950's. As a youth, Waldo had often been left with various nannies during the times Old Hoss and Hancock journeyed about the globe quenching their mutual thirst for knowledge of the world's most bizarre mysteries. Of course, Waldo's grandfather was so loving and attentive when he was at home, that the youngster was able to handle the not infrequent separations better than he might have otherwise. Waldo had genuinely liked Sam Hancock, and he recalled with fondness how the old man would muss his hair and tell him that if he had been lucky enough to have children he would have wanted them to be just like Waldo. Waldo had, in fact, felt rather sorry for him, as he seemed to have no one that cared about him other than Old Hoss.

Sam Hancock had been a short and stocky man, with slick, dark brown hair, who always appeared much younger than he was. He was blessed with extraordinary health, and was responsible for influencing Old Hoss to adopt a vegetarian diet. Although Waldo's grandfather was the closest friend he ever had, much of Sam Hancock's past remained hidden even from him. His apparent financial independence was derived from some unknown source, in that he was never known to have held a job. After meeting and forming a fast friendship, Old Hoss and Hancock, in addition to traveling together on numerous occasions, founded T.O.T.E.N.O. (The Organization To End National Organizations). They were the only members. Working closely together over the years, their research into certain unexplored areas yielded two books: *Untold Stories From American History* and *Bizarre Events and Vanishing Virtues*. Naturally, no effort was made to publish either one. In 1969, Hancock inexplicably and without warning fired his recently purchased shotgun into his television screen, then ran outside, shooting wildly at passing motorists. Firing and re-loading until his ammunition was gone, Hancock collapsed on the front porch steps of his Annandale, Virginia home and stared blankly into space until the police arrived and took him away. Fortunately, Hancock had never fired a gun before and thus was a poor shot, so no one was injured during his outburst. Old Hoss's best friend was declared insane and sent to The Last Chance Relaxation Home in Cornoil, Iowa. Hancock refused to comment on his actions, to Old Hoss or the authorities, and at last report was entering his nineteenth year of absolute silence in The Extremely Unreachable Ward of the Iowa mental institution.

When the incident occurred, and suddenly Sam Hancock stopped coming around, Waldo, not unnaturally, questioned his absence. Old Hoss explained that Mr. Hancock was very sick, that he'd been transported to an asylum in far away Iowa, and that it was unclear when he would be better. Waldo was hardly satisfied with this explanation, and was rather frightened by the name of the ominous sounding ward he'd been placed in, but eventually, as a budding teen with hormones to respond to, he ceased wondering what had happened to Sam Hancock. Actually, until he'd found the book he now held in his hands, Waldo hadn't thought of Sam Hancock for many, many years. He turned the pages of the journal and randomly stopped to read an entry:

The Journal of Sam Hancock, May 1, 1967

Liberals, especially those who fancy themselves to be scientifically inclined, love to preface anything that can't be explained within the narrow parameters of their push-button belief systems with the inane statement "we don't know." This is usually followed by a long and confusing, but ultimately successful argument proving their total uncertainty.

Today is May Day, their glorious anniversary; and thus I am preoccupied with liberal axioms. There will be no flags lowered today for the untold millions slaughtered by the communists over the last fifty years. No reporter in this "Christian" land will expose the savage murders of priests and nuns in every place the red devils have come to power. But no one wants to spoil their holiday, so I will mumble to myself in a secluded corner.

Our young men continue to fall in Vietnam, led to their graves by the hand of the great conspiracy as surely as they were ushered into the undeclared war by their draft boards. And L.B.J., the "accidental president", stands there like the comic caricature he is. He smiled the same way on Air Force One that day, pleasantly drawling the oath of office as Jackie politely remained devastated in a dress still dripping her husband's blood. But enough about Johnson, he is not alone by any means. This republic is falling fast in every direction; in politics, in culture, in architecture, in sports, in every area of human endeavor America is dying. Athletes and movie stars care nothing for the fans that pay their outrageous salaries. Not that they ever did, of course, but at least in the past they had the propriety to disguise their ingratitude with a show of public politeness, or what Ambrose Bierce termed "the most acceptable form of hypocrisy." Instead of feeling fortunate and at least feigning a degree of graciousness, these pampered laborers at leisure have come to actually believe their scripts.

But now the night grows darker and the drums roll in the

distance. Here's the pitch- *swing*...and another thousand vibrant youngsters dead in the jungles, another thousand wide-eyed socialists and campus fanatics patrolling the streets and terrifying the authorities who finance them. But it's all okay because Martin Luther King has a dream, and the Cartwright boys are as near as the next Ponderosa, just beyond the hills, riding slightly behind J. Edgar Hoover and the Untouchables. Sure...and the Great Depression was an accidental occurrence, and the Rockefellers are kindly philanthropists, and U.F.O.'s are spacecraft from another planet, and thousands of slaves toiling over the centuries built the ancient pyramids, and Lee Harvey Oswald killed President Kennedy, and U.F.O.'s are figments of the imagination, and the Soviet government can be trusted, and J.D. Salinger must be interviewed, and someday there will be nuclear war, and the U.S. government can be trusted, and the Washington Senators will win the American League pennant.

This tirade of Hancock's appeared near the end of the journal, and Waldo, his curiosity piqued, continued flipping the pages, stopping to read one of the last entries:

The Journal of Sam Hancock, August 19, 1968

Gore Vidal is not afraid of death. This surprising information was just relayed to the public on one of those fascinating talk shows. Undoubtedly, Norman Mailer holds the same opinion. Well, isn't it only logical, you might ask, that the best and brightest among us should not fall victim to devil-with-the-pitchfork type fears? Or garden of paradise hopes? Perhaps.
But what about a theory so dangerous, so mind boggling, and yes, so irrational, that it must be referred to only as The Viewpoint That Dare Not Speak Its Name?
"Golden lads and girls all must
As chimney sweepers, come to dust."
You can read every book ever written in any language at any point in history, and you will not find a hint of it.
"Now I lay me down to sleep..."
You can watch all of the talk shows, pore over transcripts of "Meet The Press", and follow the adventures of Jacques Cousteau, but you won't hear a word about it.
"I pray the Lord my soul to keep..."
You can speak with every person on the face of the earth, even the more imaginative mental patients, and none of them will mention it.
"If I should die before I wake..."

14

From the moment any of us utter our first goo-goo's and ga-ga's, we are as good as gone. At that precise instant, any possibility that It will ever arise in us is irrevocably crushed. If any proof is needed, consider how immune to strong emotion our society has grown. At your next visit to the local funeral parlor, glance at the mourners, who can more properly be defined as spectators. Notice how they smell, how well-dressed and dignified they are. This is because viewing the dead has become overwhelmingly acceptable as a social function. Yes, even the corpse is part of the festivities, lying there as the guest of honor, laid out in his best clothes, pumped full of chemicals and smeared with make-up as the patrons file by and nurse their long buried consciences with silk handkerchiefs. Their grief is controlled by outside forces; they will be heartbroken for as long as it is socially acceptable. Thus, if the deceased is a spouse or close family member, periods of depression and deep longing for the past (not to exceed sporadic outbursts thereof) may continue for up to a year, although most "normal" persons will be fully recovered in half that time. Society has taken care of everything; those few left among us with passionate, loving hearts would obviously never totally rebound from this horrible, unexplainable phenomenon called death. It has provided for those unfortunate souls, through its all-encompassing empathy, by building mental health facilities, where they are always welcome.

Waldo could see, as he continued skimming through the bulky tome, the steady progression, or perhaps regression, of both the journal's content and the author's state of mind. The vast majority of the opening pages consisted of accounts detailing Hancock's numerous trips, most of them with Old Hoss, to locales connected in some manner to one strange mystery or another. These encapsulated descriptions of his travels gradually diminished in number as the journal wore on, superseded by scathing social and political commentary, until by the closing pages every entry was an increasingly bitter attack on some facet of the modern world.

Waldo eventually reached the last page and was surprised to find a Post-it note stuck there. Pulling it off, he trembled as he read, written in his grandfather's distinctive scrawl, the words:

Room Five.

An idea was beginning to form in Waldo's mind, that perhaps Sam Hancock's journal had been left there on purpose, to be easily discovered and, more importantly, sifted through. Could the simple little note, fastened unaccountably to the final page, be a clue from his grandfather? Was it possible that *Room Five* referred to the number of the room Sam Hancock occupied in the Extremely Unreachable Ward at

The Last Chance Relaxation Home, and that Old Hoss Billingsly had decided, on the spur of the moment, to visit his old friend in Cornoil, Iowa?

2
THE RAIN, THE POLICE, AND OTHER THINGS

From *More Unanswered Questions*, an unpublished pamphlet by Abner Billingsly, pg. 25:
"Who originates the latest slang terms that are, seemingly overnight, known to every black youth across the country?"

On a street corner in southeast Washington, D.C., The Afro-Anarchists, a trio of doo-wop protest singers, were rehearsing their latest unrecorded number, *Ghetto Executive*:

"Here in the inner city-slum-ghetto
I'm the man with the briefcase-the C.E.O.
I make sure that everyone
Has their kids and totes their guns
My people never walk, they dance
Like bona fide victims of circumstance
Some of them fast, some of them tall
All of them crazy about basketball
And I make sure they always choose
The most expensive tennis shoes
Gangs and money laundering
Unemployment, redistricting
Across this land, not many live
The life of a ghetto executive."

A small crowd applauded their efforts, then drifted away into the night.

"Man, you were off-key!" exclaimed Woodrow "Bucktooth" Johnson. Bucktooth, who derived his nickname from a prominent overbite, a condition that went untreated in his youth due to the fact his single mother's paycheck left little room for expensive orthodontia, was short and stout with a pliable, friendly disposition.

"You can't even spell off-key." Fontaine Washington, Jr., against whom this accusation had been leveled, chuckled in reply.

Fontaine was of medium height, with a rather powerful frame, and was a great admirer of the black radicals of the sixties, which was apparent by the massive, outdated Afro hairstyle he wore so proudly.

"Gentlemen, I beg to differ." The voice of reason belonged to their lead singer and songwriter, Phosphate Jefferson. "I believe we sounded quite proficient."

Phosphate Jefferson, a brilliant thinker possessing a variety of talents, was a native Washingtonian born to poverty stricken parents. Phosphate was the youngest of eleven children, and grew up a bright, studious boy who consistently performed well in every endeavor he undertook. Although his outstanding scholastic record earned him a college scholarship to a prestigious Ivy League university, the obedient, well-mannered Phosphate turned it down to stay at home and care for his elderly parents, who were unusually old when their youngest child was born. Phosphate, a truly devoted son, did everything for his beloved mother and father, supporting them financially by working at menial jobs, and never complained about the lack of assistance from his siblings. After his parents' death, Phosphate discovered Christianity, not in some extravagant, "born-again" manner, but in his own low-key style. Adhering to a strict interpretation of the teachings of Jesus Christ, Phosphate sold the modest house he grew up in, in an effort to rid himself of all material possessions, and became voluntarily homeless, utilizing the proceeds from the sale to feed and clothe himself. A short time later, he formed The Afro-Anarchists with two career street people, Woodrow "Bucktooth" Johnson and Fontaine Washington, Jr. The three of them sung where they could for what they could, which mostly turned out to be on street corners for nothing. Phosphate, despite the deep religious beliefs which led him to discard what few material belongings he had, and adopt an attitude of tolerance towards his fellow man which would make a cloistered nun proud, rarely expressed his faith to others, and even his fellow Afro-Anarchists were unaware of his convictions.

The other two members of the doo-wop protest trio were not, unfortunately, like their leader, and shared in common with millions of other African-American youths a startling lack of education, technical skills, and parental guidance. They were, like many a non-African-American as well, perfect bit players in the great melodramas surrounding them.

The Afro-Anarchists had actually been paid the night before, for performing at a local high school dance, and this was such a rare experience for them that it was agreed a celebration was in order. They had planned, therefore, after a strenuous after dinner practice session, to venture into one of the nicer, upscale sections of the city and hop, as far as their finances allowed them to, from bar to bar.

It was growing late, into the prime partying hours, and the streets were becoming crowded with merrymakers of all sorts. The doo-wop trio agreed to end their rehearsal at this point and, feeling they should begin their night on the town in suitable style, hailed a taxi.

They were fortunate that a taxi happened, at that moment, to stop at their street corner, as most cab drivers avoided that area of town entirely. The driver was a recent arrival in the country, and thus hadn't yet developed an adequate sense of discrimination regarding potential fares. He even smiled at them as they entered the vehicle.

"Hallo. Where to take?" He asked politely.

Phosphate, settling into his seat, produced a cheap bottle of champagne from under his light windbreaker and responded, in a voice mimicking a pretentious aristocrat's, "Onward, my good man, to the most expensive spot in the city."

Waldo awoke with a start. He'd fallen asleep while reading more of Sam Hancock's journal, and shortly thereafter found himself entangled in yet another nightmare involving flying, his favorite phobia. He had reluctantly boarded a plush modern airliner, something which in real life he was one of the few Americans under the age of 100 to have never done, and, of course, it wasn't long before the engines failed. Along came Charlton Heston, with a grave announcement over the loudspeaker, and a screaming Shelley Winters, then finally...his parents.

Waldo thought of them often. He'd only been ten years old when the tragic event occurred, and yet he still dreamed about them nearly every night. The vast majority of people, who are fortunate enough not to have experienced this kind of loss, cannot fathom the impact of such a blow on a young child. Waldo had been devastated, as any ten year old would be, and all these years later as a grown man he still felt the residue of that enormous pain. During his brief lapses of consciousness, when his tortured mind reluctantly surrendered to fatigue, Waldo would often wind up tossing and turning in remembrance of the farewell kisses at the airport and the look on Old Hoss's face when he'd answered the telephone. In other unpleasant dreams, such as the one from which he'd just awakened, Waldo writhed in agony over the mere contemplation of the whirring propellers, the loading ramp, and the smiling stewardesses.

With a sigh and a Kennedyesque brush of his hair, Waldo got up and lit a cigarette. He picked up Sam Hancock's journal and walked to the living room. Staring out of the large picture window, the memory of his troubling dream was gradually replaced by other, more immediate concerns.

Was it logical for his grandfather, after nearly twenty years, to suddenly trek all the way to Iowa to see his old friend? In that case, why not simply say so in the note, instead of penning such a dramatic, cryptic farewell message? As Waldo mulled all this over, he reached for his cigarette and was disgruntled to discover it was no longer lit, the result of a quantity of spilled soft drink, sufficient to put it out, that was in the ashtray. Waldo softly cursed himself and picked up the pack, seeking a replacement. He was even more upset to learn that the cigarette pack, his last one, was empty.

It was well past the conventional dinner hour, and Waldo's stomach started growling. As an off-the-wall sort of fellow, as well as a chronic insomniac, Waldo was used to sleeping sporadically and at odd times, and it was entirely in character for him to fall asleep, as he had, in the late afternoon, and wake up at a time when most fast food establishments were closing for the night. It had been, in Waldo's disorganized itinerary, a kind of loose plan to eat at a fast food place for dinner, and he was nearly as disappointed over being unable to purchase his patented two double cheeseburgers and large order of fries (unlike his grandfather, Waldo was no vegetarian) as he was at running out of cigarettes. Shaking his head in disgust at himself, as he often did, Waldo grabbed his car keys and left the house in search of cigarettes and whatever monthly special on non-health food the local convenience store had to offer.

Jumping in his car, he selected an appropriately obscure tape and popped it in the cassette deck. Waldo truly hated to drive, not because he had any difficulty in handling an automobile, or felt uncomfortable behind the wheel, but because of his general distaste for modern devices. Of course, the car could hardly at this point in history, nearly a century after its invention, be properly termed modern, but Waldo's view of the world was often out of focus and behind the times. His romantic, daydreaming personality held a natural affinity for the past and disliked the negative aspects of modernization. He also cared deeply about the environment, as any sensitive, poetic spirit must, and his heart ached over the pollution and congestion left in the wake of the fantastic scientific advances. Waldo longed to have his own horse to travel about on, and loved to look at old photographs and daguerreotypes of Washington, D.C. and the suburbs flanking it taken before they, like nearly all populated areas, were branded with the stamp of cold, concrete uniformity. His imagination often led him galloping through those old pictures, dust flying from the heels of his chestnut stallion, down the wild romantic roads of an unsold world. Waldo, however, as a card-carrying member of the A.S.C.P.A. and friend to all creatures, was adamantly opposed to using animals as a form of transportation, and thus was in a quandary about the issue and had to temper such fantasies accordingly. It was impossible for him to conceive of such a world right now, as he headed for the capital beltway, the ultimate monster in the ongoing campaign to cement the remainder of the countryside.

Waldo owned an old, beat-up red Datsun which ran well enough, but was unable to attain a speed exceeding fifty miles per hour. It was just starting to rain as Waldo approached the entry ramp leading onto the beltway. He despised using the beltway at all, but it made no sense to travel side roads when he could get somewhere in half the time by taking it. As Waldo started to turn right at the ramp, a Trans Am suddenly cut in front of him, nearly running over a Volkswagen Beetle in the process. Waldo felt the anger rising up within him, and his hand went instinctively for the horn, but, swallowing hard, he slammed his fist on the dashboard instead. He had discovered long ago that despite the county's demands that it function in order to pass the safety inspection, the horn was totally useless. It was also potentially dangerous, as the only reaction it ever brought was a flying middle finger and a continuation of whatever it was that caused the horn to be honked in the first place. There were even rare cases where the offending driver being honked at had slammed on the brakes, run from his car towards the one who had dared to question his driving ability, and actually attempted to start a physical altercation. Sometimes this was more than an attempt, as actual punches were thrown. On a few occasions, these eligible voters had worked themselves into such a frenzy that they'd pulled a gun, which was apparently being carried with them for just such a purpose, and killed the poor unsuspecting motorist who'd been foolish enough to utilize a device that was not only legal, but mandatory. As he watched the Trans Am swerve perilously from lane to lane until it finally sped out of sight, water spraying from its big, bad tires, Waldo took a page from Professor Hiram Buckley's book and immediately labeled the driver a typical fredneck. *That fredneck must be in a hurry to beat up his "old lady"*, thought Waldo, who now, as always, was daydreaming as he drove.

Waldo's daydreams were different from Walter Mitty's, but they were just as vivid and persistent. Sometimes he imagined various lovely women swooning before him, or great crowds gathering to hear him spout out radical opinions, but most often Waldo simply pictured some forthcoming event, of an everyday, trivial nature, and how it might unfold. Various insignificant images were in Waldo's mind at that moment, of convenience store half-price specials and the like, and they melded with his worries about his grandfather to create a mosaic of inattention that was hardly conducive to being behind the wheel of a vehicle moving at fifty miles per hour.

Suddenly Waldo was jarred out of his stupor by the sounds of horns honking and tires skidding. He slammed on the brakes at once, and saw that it was too late to avoid crashing into the pile of vehicles clustered before him. Waldo felt the impact and instinctively flung his hands up to protect his face.

Fortunately for Waldo, he'd been able to slow down enough so that although he was thrown across the passenger seat, banging his head on the door handle, he was not seriously injured. Had an official authority of any kind been there to note it, some mention would surely have been made of Waldo's failure to wear his seatbelt, which he refused to do as a misguided matter of principle, and how it would have saved him from sustaining the few minor bruises he did.

Waldo, after berating himself, with his usual passion, for not having paid attention, lifted his head cautiously to peer over the dashboard at the accident scene. What a scene it was: there were automobiles literally everywhere, strewn about in all directions, some flipped over, some badly damaged. Others, apparently like his own car, seemed relatively unmarred. The rain was pouring down heavily, and there were figures scurrying around, shouting and gesturing at each other in the collective glow the headlights cast in the darkness.

"My God! Alda time! So many problem!" A wiry little Korean man, dressed in a brown and white striped shirt that clashed with his gray checkered pants, was waving his arms above his head as he encircled a badly damaged BMW, which was near the front of the whole accident scene. "Alda time!"

Waldo sunk back down in the passenger seat, reluctant to leave the car and face an unreal situation like this one. Unreal was perhaps Waldo's favorite word, and he used it liberally, in conjunction with his favorite adverb, "ridiculous," to refer to those persons, things, or, in this case, situations he found objectionable. Professor Hiram Buckley spoke of "ridiculous Unreals" himself, much as Waldo borrowed the Professor's pet term "fredneck" whenever he felt the urge to. This passion for obscure reference sharing, renowned in political fringe circles, had been handed down to Waldo by his grandfather, who utilized it to great effect. Basically, Waldo considered those who stare back blankly and refuse to answer when a greeting is extended to them; or operators of motor vehicles who dart dangerously out into the flow of traffic but then proceed along at a snail's pace (thus he was undoubtedly planning to brand someone involved in the present fiasco an unreal); or strangers who strike up weird, confusing conversations in public places; or figures sneaking silently through the dark who approach you, know your name, yet decline to explain how; or men and women who ignore, abuse, and cheat on their loyal, loving spouses; to all be primary examples of Unreals.

There were countless other examples, some growing out of personal experience, others from the author's fertile imagination, in Waldo's own unpublished pamphlet, and the definitive work on the subject, *Real To Unreal: A Practical Guide For The Uninformed.* In Waldo's most delusional moments, he even dared to suspect that the Unreals were manufactured somewhere, perhaps a picturesque plant in the secluded mountains, and programmed to enter society in order to interact with and harass real people like him. Of course, given his own penchant for the eccentric and unconventional, Waldo might well be defined as an unreal himself, by his own rigid standards.

I've got to stop daydreaming... Waldo thought as he sunk even lower in the passenger seat, like a little child hoping that the deeper he burrowed into his comfortable cushion, the easier it would be to make the unpleasant situation go away. *Could I have caused it?*

He was snapped out of his stupor by a loud pounding on the car window. Looking up reluctantly, he saw the nightmarish figure of the law enforcement officer, sporting that friendly, helpful expression that has made them famous the world over. Feeling queasy, Waldo fumbled his way out of the car.

"What's wrong with you? Are you on something? I've been knocking on your window for a good minute and you just ignored me."

The policeman's grating, drill sergeant-style staccato delivery hit Waldo like a machine gun as soon as he opened the door. *And they never start anything,* he thought to himself.

"Alright, I don't have all night. Let's see your license."

Waldo felt a knot growing in his stomach. He'd always been terrified of police officers, and he did everything he could to avoid all contact with them. He would sooner face a group of disgruntled frednecks, or a pack of mischievous Unreals, than have to deal with a police officer enforcing the law.

"I said where's your license?" The policeman snarled, displaying the kind of patience and understanding inherent in all government employees.

"Oh...I'm sorry, officer." A nervous Waldo grabbed so quickly for his wallet that it flew out of his hands, whizzing past the policeman's head and skidding across the wet pavement. His partner had just emerged from an excited group of Asians, which included the little man with the unfashionable outfit Waldo had seen waving his arms and yelling desperately in broken English, who were apparently the occupants of one of the cars involved in the accident. This other officer, as nondescript as his partner, glared at Waldo as the wallet came to a stop against his well-shined shoe. This policeman was young, probably younger than Waldo, yet by the painstaking manner in which he bent down to pick up the wallet, and the expression on his face which advertised his disgust at having to do so, he might have been confused with a paraplegic ordered to kick a game winning field goal. After finally lifting the heavy object, with visible difficulty, the officer walked over to where they were standing and began tossing the wallet up and down while staring a hole through Waldo. Unnerved by the lawman's steady gaze, Waldo attempted a feeble smile and tried not to look suspicious. He grew increasingly uneasy as the policeman continued staring at him as if he were a mass murderer, while the cluster of Korean voices wailed away over his shoulder. Finally, after a minute or two, the apparently satisfied eyes left their unsettled target and turned towards the other officer.

"Looks like the Kims over there started the whole thing." The staring lawman's voice was unemotional and monotonous. "From what all of the others involved say, Mr. Kim suddenly moved over into the fast lane. I talked to the young guy that was behind him, and he said the oriental maniac couldn't have been going more than forty. When he suddenly changed lanes without even a turn signal, the young guy-that's his old Dodge over there-beat up pretty good, huh? Anyway, the Dodge couldn't slow down in time and smashed into the back of the Kim's BMW. That started a chain reaction and, well, you see what happened. Lucky there wasn't more traffic, or it'd be twice as bad. Shit, can you imagine something like this during rush hour? Doesn't look like anybody's hurt bad, but the first few cars, the young guy's and the Kim's, are pretty well dented up. Most of the vehicles had enough time to slow down and just kind of bang into each other at low speeds. Well, I'm gonna go back and try to talk to the Kims again. Can't understand hardly anything they say, but they sure are upset. I'll see if I can calm them down."

"Alright, Bill." His partner turned to Waldo. "What did you see, son?"

Waldo was used to being referred to as "son" despite his 28 years of age. He surprised himself by spitting out an un-stuttered and simple "nothing really, officer."

"Okay. But stick around for a while longer."

Waldo nodded and looked at the policeman's face. Somehow the water that was dripping from the bill of his cap made him appear almost human. *Nah*, Waldo thought, *it would take a lot more than water to wash that look off.*

"Man, is this fucked up or what?"

Waldo turned around, as this probing question seemed to be flung in his direction. He expected to find an obnoxious fredneck standing there, eager to engage in some inarticulate conversation.

He wasn't disappointed- it was a fredneck.

This fredneck, however, was truly different. The pudgy figure with thinning, dirty-blond hair, dressed in a flannel shirt that was at least a decade out of style, and a pair of faded blue jeans with an ever-present dog-eared copy of Lord Byron's collected poems protruding from the hip pocket, was, unlike most frednecks, a friendly, easygoing fellow.

"Hey man, my name's Brisbane Wrock." The fredneck's face burst into a surprisingly genuine smile.

Brisbane Wrock was born and raised in Boston, where his ancestors had for generations lived, toiled in obscurity, and died. His parents were no exception, mired in the same dismal working class existence. Brisbane's father was an alcoholic, like most of the men in the poor district where they lived, and abused his middle child and only son both verbally and physically. As a youth, Brisbane was quite heavy and the object of much ridicule. The young, future fredneck loved all sports passionately, and despite his size, was able to perform well at them. Eventually, however, his weight presented enough problems that he decided to go on a crash diet during the summer months preceding his entrance into high school.

Brisbane lost fifty pounds on that diet, but became curiously disillusioned with sports and turned to other pursuits, such as abusing drugs. As a result of this, combined with his poor grades and increasingly anti-social behavior, Brisbane was constantly in some form of trouble, and finally dropped out of school at the age of sixteen. After roaming aimlessly up and down the east coast for several years, Brisbane had recently wandered into the suburbs of Virginia. He anticipated remaining in the area for a brief time, enjoying his bohemian lifestyle, sleeping under the stars in open fields, and avoiding steady employment until a new, unknown destination beckoned him.

"I'm Waldo Billingsly." Waldo cautiously smiled back.

"Glad to meet you, man." Brisbane thrust out his hand and Waldo accepted it. "I was right up near the front of all this."

"Oh, is that your car?" Waldo pointed towards a badly dented 1965 Dodge Dart.

"Yeah. It's not as bad as it looks, though. I've brought it back from a lot worse."

The rain had gradually diminished into a light sprinkle. There were still a number of people yelling, in various languages, but their voices weren't quite as loud, and there was little sense of pandemonium left. A group of construction workers, who had been busy blocking one of the lanes on the beltway, left the job they hadn't appeared to have started yet, and observed the proceedings.

There was a growing crowd of motorists, who always seem to gather and gawk at accident sites, stopping their automobiles to gaze at the carnage. Since there wasn't much carnage to see, most of them didn't remain for very long. The two original policemen on the scene had been joined by a large contingent of officers, enough to apprehend all the violent criminals wreaking havoc at the time in other, unpatroled areas.

Waldo began to feel relaxed enough by the fredneck's pleasant demeanor to venture an opinion. "Does it seem to you that Asian drivers are involved in a disproportionate amount of traffic accidents?"

Brisbane's face lit up. "Man, that was goin' through my head as soon as that BMW switched lanes. I said to myself I bet that fucking driver's an Oriental. I've been in two other wrecks, both times with Orientals."

"That doesn't surprise me. Most every Asian I've ever known has been a terrible driver." Waldo paused, realizing that he was sounding more than a little bigoted. "But, of course, that doesn't reflect on them as human beings."

Brisbane chuckled. "Shit, man, I'm not judging anything about them accept their driving ability."

Waldo nodded. "After all, if one were to generalize about whole races of people, then, well, you'd have to credit Asians with being a thrifty and hard-working group."

"Yeah, dude, you're right." Brisbane reached into his shirt pocket for a cigarette. "But no one's testing your political correctness here. And it is a fucking fact that when they get out on the road, it's like they're all, well...unreal or something."

Waldo's heart skipped a beat at the sound of that magical word. This was one unique fredneck, alright. Not very many people used his favorite term in that way. "My sentiments exactly." He nodded in agreement.

"Man, it pisses me off," Brisbane spoke with his cigarette between his lips, "I don't think it'll be too hard to bang out the dents in my car- shit, as old as it is, it had plenty already- but I was getting ready to stick a really rare bootleg Dylan tape into my cassette deck when that fucking Oriental cut in front of me. Believe it or not, when I hit his car, somehow the tape slipped out of my hand, and my window was open..." Brisbane gestured towards a bit of debris on the road. "...and it landed on the highway." The fredneck shook his head sadly. "One of the cars behind me crushed it to pieces."

Waldo expressed his sympathy. "I'm sorry. Are you a big fan of Dylan's?" Bob Dylan was one of the few living entertainers the absurdly discriminating Waldo liked.

"Shit yeah, before his accident he was awesome."

Waldo was growing excited now, as the fredneck was starting to trod into his familiar fringe territory. "Yes, I've studied his lyrics and they do seem to be quite different after the accident."

"They sure do. I've always suspected that, well, maybe it wasn't an accident."

Waldo asked Brisbane for a cigarette. "What do you mean?"

The fredneck handed him a cigarette and grinned conspiratorially. "I think he might have been politically silenced."

Waldo could barely contain himself. "I think you may be right."

"Yeah, I'm into some pretty strange things, esoteric politics, mainly." Brisbane said. "I don't know if you're familiar with anything along the lines of *The Yipster Times*, or that kind of shit."

Waldo threw his cigarette into a puddle on the road. "Listen, Brisbane, how would you like to come over to my house tonight after we're through here?

I was going to get something to eat, and some cigarettes, then maybe we could drink some beers and talk some more. There's a lot of interesting things at the house you might like to see."

"Like what?" Asked the fredneck, as if he was about to turn down an offer of free beer.

"Well, I live with my grandfather, and he was-is-a very brilliant man, with a collection of writings like nothing you've ever read before. I'm sure you'd find them interesting. I also have a great assortment of video tapes of my favorite television shows. I love the classics from the old days: *The Andy Griffith Show, Leave It To Beaver, Green Acres, The Beverly Hillbillies.*"

Waldo's adrenalin was pumping over the prospect of making a new friend, especially one that shared his own rather unique interests.

"Sure man, I'd love to. I'm a Barney Fife freak. And you can't have too much knowledge."

"No, you can't." Waldo replied quietly.

3
FREDNECKS HAVE MORE FUN

At Snortin' Reformatory, a notorious Washington, D.C. jail located in the northern Virginia suburbs, The Afro-Anarchists were being thrown into a cell. It was a situation that the three of them, like many young black males in the D.C. area, had long ago come to expect as a rite of passage.

As the door slammed shut behind them, Bucktooth spoke. "Man, Phosphate, they didn't read us our rights or nothin'."

"Yeah, Phos," Fontaine chimed in, "I didn't think they had to beat us, neither. And whoever heard of being charged with singing too loud and off-key in a public establishment? I don't believe there is no kind of law for that shit."

"Well, excuse me, my faithful companions in crime." Phosphate smiled calmly. "I really should rectify this injustice by utilizing some of my many powerful connections. Let's see, what shall it be? Why don't I contact my uncle, the noted federal court judge? Or perhaps my cousin, the chief of police? I am sure they would be most happy to deliver us from the clutches of this nefarious dwelling."

"Oh shit, Phos!" Both Fontaine and Bucktooth laughed heartily at the top doo-wopper's wry sarcasm.

"As I've said so many times before, civilized behavior on the part of law enforcement officials only occurs on television." Phosphate now bore the earnest countenance of an Abraham Lincoln solemnly intoning the Gettysburg Address, which he seemed to do whenever he hopped up on his soapbox. Needless to say, Phosphate had spent a large portion of his life resembling Old Abe. After a pause suitable for dramatic effect, he continued in a lighter vein. "Gentlemen, I believe a song is in order." Clearing his golden vocal chords, the top doo-wopper began singing:

"We is in jail, we got no bail
We don't know why we're here
There is no doubt when we get out
We probably will be queer
We will not fight, we got no rights
We promise to obey you
All your laws are here because
No evidence will sway you
We knew when we were apprehended
Our sentence would not be suspended

We've seen the inmates and we're nervous
We want our community service
So do your best when you arrest
Another coon or spade
And sure as shit we know we'll get
Justice in these jails you made
We got no grammar in the slammer
We won't let you down
I know some whiteys who isn't mighty
In my part of town
So shoot the breeze and aim to kill
Impress the boys up on the hill
We'll make new friends while we wait
For others to counsel and deliberate."

Just then a couple of service-minded guards, bored with watching the homosexual escapades in the adjacent cell, decided that The Afro-Anarchists had been, once again, singing too loudly. In perfect stereotypical fashion, they were cajoling and elbowing each other in the ribs as they carted off the unlucky threesome to a quiet place to administer another pre-trial beating.

After the police had finished with them, Brisbane climbed into his decidedly un-fredneck-like '65 Dodge Dart, which was still operational despite the body damage, and followed Waldo to the nearest convenience store.

Standing in front of the store as they drove up were two rough-looking characters. One of them appeared to be some sort of skinhead, and his tee shirt, with "Satan Never Sleeps" emblazoned across the front, did little to conceal his impressive collection of tattoos. The other man was much older, and his dark complexion, bright scarf, and dangling earrings all combined to convey the classic gypsy image.

Waldo eyed the men suspiciously as he left his car and cautiously approached the store.

"*Grrreetings*, gentlemen." The gypsy-like man's elaborate rolling of his r's parted his full red lips, revealing two gold front teeth. "How arrre you this evening?"

"Fine, thank you." Waldo responded in a slightly nervous voice. "If you'll excuse us..."

"Gentlemen, please" the gypsy laughed lustily, and Waldo noticed that the skinhead had moved in front of the door, blocking their way. "We desirrre to ask you a few questions."

"Hey, dudes, what the fuck do you think you're doin'?" Brisbane was obviously adopting a typically fredneck-like, defiant posture.

The gypsy's black eyes glared at Waldo. "I underrrrstand that you arrre going to be heading out west..."

Waldo's mouth was agape. "H-h-how did you know...?"

At that moment, an older model black Cadillac suddenly roared into the parking lot and pulled up in front of the store.

"Goodbye, gentlemen, and good luck." The gypsy smiled at them and climbed into the back seat of the car, followed by the skinhead.

The black Cadillac sped off as abruptly as it had arrived, and left Waldo and Brisbane staring at each other in astonishment.

"Shit man, what was *that*?" The incredulous fredneck asked.

Waldo shook his head. "I-I don't know."

Brisbane lit up a cigarette. "What did that gypsy-type dude mean by you going out west?"

"Well, I don't really know that I am going out there." Waldo replied.

"Did you know the dude?"

"Of course not. I've never seen either one of them before."

"Then how," the fredneck inhaled deeply, "did he know you might be going there?"

"Good question." Waldo ran his fingers through his hair. "I wish I had an answer." He then opened the door to the convenience store. "Come on, let's go inside. I'm really hungry."

As they perused the variety of unhealthy items offered by the store, Waldo recounted the story of his grandfather's disappearance to Brisbane. When he mentioned his discovery of the post-it note on the last page of Sam Hancock's journal, the fredneck whistled.

"Shit man, then you might really be goin' out west!" Brisbane had decided on two chilidogs and an order of nachos with cheese. "How could that gypsy-dude have known that?"

Waldo's fertile imagination could have conjured up many wild and paranoid hypotheses to explain the stranger's remark, but he merely shrugged and placed his own selection of a large frozen pizza and a couple of ice cream treats in front of the cashier. "A pack of Camel Lights too, please."

They left the convenience store, and Waldo was careful to check the back seat of his old Datsun for whatever other odd persons might be lurking about in the dark.

When they arrived back at Waldo's house, Professor Hiram Buckley's brightly colored van was parked in the driveway.

"Waldo, my boy, where in the world have you been?" The Professor, who had been sitting on the front porch, came rushing down the driveway. "I tried to call you..."

"Relax, Professor." Waldo turned the engine off and exited the car. "Come on inside, my dinner needs to be heated up and I'm awfully hungry."

Waldo turned and waited for Brisbane, who had just parked his car behind him, and couldn't help noticing the peculiar look on the Professor's face as the fredneck approached them.

"Shit man," Brisbane exclaimed, with a mouth full of chilidog, "this house is fucking humongous!"

Professor Buckley visibly winced. "Waldo," he spoke in a snooty tone, "who is this?"

"Oh, excuse me, Professor," Waldo placed his hand on the fredneck's shoulder, "this is Brisbane Wrock. We were both involved in an accident tonight, on the beltway..."

"Waldo! Are you alright, my boy?" The Professor tugged at his yellow tie with obvious concern.

"Yes, I'm fine, Professor. Fortunately, no one was seriously hurt." Waldo started walking up the quaint cobblestone path which led to the front door. "Brisbane and I had a nice talk while we were waiting, and I invited him back here..."

Professor Buckley grabbed Waldo and pulled him aside, out of earshot of Brisbane. "Waldo, have you thought-that is-did you tell him about your grandfather?"

Waldo smiled. "Yes, Professor. Why?"

The Professor sighed and shook his head. "Well, it's none of my business, I suppose, but a...*fredneck*?"

"Professor, please," Waldo whispered, "he seems like a very nice guy."

Hiram Buckley threw up his hands in defeat and followed Waldo up the steps and onto the front porch, where Brisbane was waiting for them.

"Shit man," the fredneck pointed towards the paper bag in Waldo's hand, "your ice cream's melting."

Waldo looked down and saw by the quantity of milky white substance on his shoes that the fredneck was right. He hurriedly produced his key and opened the door, then ran for the kitchen.

"Make yourselves at home, I'll be right back." He called as he raced down the hallway. After placing his ice cream in the freezer, and depositing his frozen pizza in the oven, he returned to the living room to find the fredneck and Professor Buckley pacing about in an awkward silence.

"Please, have a seat, both of you." Waldo lit up a cigarette and sat down in the recliner. "Professor, did you know that Brisbane is very interested in esoteric politics?"

"Indeed." Professor Buckley gazed at the fredneck. "Such as?"

"Well, shit man, lots of stuff- C.I.A. abuses, secret military weapons, subliminal advertising, U.F.O. cover-ups..."

"Where do you get your information?" The Professor interrupted.

The fredneck shrugged. "I read a lot of far-out things."

The Professor was holding his battered briefcase in his hand, as he almost always did, and he seized this opportunity to open it and hold aloft a copy of *Force Of Habit*. "This, young man, is one of the world's most exclusive periodicals. I write, edit, and publish it myself. Have you, by any chance, read *it* before?"

The fredneck shook his head. "No, man, I don't think I've ever seen that one before."

"Perhaps you'd like me to read a brief excerpt?" The Professor asked.

"Sure, man, go ahead."

"Waldo, if there are-that is-may I?"

"Please, Professor, by all means." Waldo replied. "Will you excuse me for a moment, though? I have to check on my pizza. Can I get either of you something to drink?"

Hiram Buckley, as it was late at night, simply asked for a glass of ice water, while Brisbane predictably requested a beer.

As Waldo walked to the kitchen, Professor Buckley began reading from the March 1986 issue:

Dear H.B,
Recently I was watching a television special on battered women. During the course of the broadcast, a reporter interviewed an expert on the subject (how, by the way, does one become an expert on battered women?) who said, and I quote, "it is estimated that two thirds of all instances of battered women syndrome go unreported." Now, I ask you, how do you compute or estimate a figure that is not reported?
Muddled in Midlothian

Dear Muddled:
Wow! Do you mean that the probing reporter didn't ask the "expert" that? Come on, I fail to believe something that preposterous could occur under the guise of a free press.

Dear H.B:
I have been working at the same company for 12 years. I have been passed over for promotions time and time again in favor of those

*I feel are less qualified than I am. Many of these people were trained
by me, and their performance in management has mirrored their
previous record as lower-level personnel: dull, uninspired, and non-
productive. I know many others who have suffered the same injustice.
My question to you is: is it really a fact of life that the wrong people
always get promoted? If so, why?*
    Ralph Kramden, Jr.
    Jamaica, New York

    Dear Ralph, Jr.:
    *Unfortunately, it is true all too often. For some mysterious
reason, corporate America seems to prefer close-minded,
unimaginative, and incompetent leaders to oversee its hapless,
stagnant work force. This kind of person is a scarce commodity. After
all, how many people do you know whose powers of over-reaction are
strong enough to permit them to care whether a laborer tucks in his
shirt or not? This is the kind of rare bird that upper management
wants to govern its mishmash of comedy and corruption. It is
obviously more important to American business leaders that the lowest
paid employees wear their name tags correctly or not be three minutes
late arriving for work than that they do their jobs efficiently. I say
that because they have proven they support real employee
incompetence. For whatever reason, it seems that legitimate
deficiencies are always ignored by management and trivial ones
emphasized. The sidesplitting spectacle of a group of over-paid, non-
producing executives toiling over how to add yet another "assistant
director" to the company payroll while stressing fiscal restraint must
amuse those whose lot it is to vacuum their carpets to no end. It
probably isn't quite as humorous, however, when the hard-working
producers' generous annual 25 cents an hour raises are due, and they
discover to their chagrin that their mere pittances must be sacrificed in
order that the boys in the executive washroom have a fresh face to
banter with around the urinals. This, my friend, is why "good old
American know-how" cannot produce an automobile, a television, a
pair of shoes, or any other real item of industry to compete with Japan
and many other rapidly advancing nations. Rest assured, however,
that we lead the world in non-productive fields of endeavor such as
"consultants", "analysts", "directors", "vice-presidents in charge of
production", etc., etc.*

    "Ooowww!" Brisbane expressed his approval of the Professor's
typically lengthy diatribe with the screeching salutation popularized by
frednecks and adopted by all attendees at rock concerts. "That was

awesome, man!"

"Thank you, my boy, thank you." Professor Buckley was beaming with pride, and had obviously overcome his initial hostility towards Brisbane.

Waldo, who had returned from the kitchen in the middle of the Professor's observations regarding the shortcomings of American management, and quietly handed the spellbound fredneck his beer, applauded enthusiastically. "I don't think I've heard those before, Professor."

"No, my boy-that is-did you like them?"

"Yes, they were great." Waldo handed the Professor his glass of ice water. "Here you go, Professor. I didn't want to interrupt you."

"Oh, thank you, Waldo." Professor Buckley sipped the water slowly, as was his wont. "Would you like to hear some more..."

"Shit yeah!" roared Brisbane.

Waldo smiled and nodded in agreement, aware that it was liable to be another long night.

A few hours later, when Professor Buckley had fallen asleep, evidently exhausted from a marathon reading of "Letters To H.B.," Waldo asked Brisbane if he would like to view some video tapes.

The fredneck belched his approval, requested another beer, and followed Waldo into the kitchen.

Waldo opened the refrigerator, handed Brisbane a beer, and pointed towards the adjoining room. "Why don't you go ahead into the family room and look around, while I make some popcorn."

"Sure, dude, sounds cool to me." The amiable fredneck replied, and meandered into the family room.

When Waldo carried a bowl of popcorn into the room a short time later, he found Brisbane sifting through his massive assortment of tapes, muttering the titles aloud in awe.

"Gerald McBoingBoing, Amos 'n Andy, Laurel & Hardy" The fredneck was as flushed with excitement as a youngster in a candy store. *"Freaks!, Plan Nine From Outer Space!, Never Give A Sucker An Even Break!, Mars Needs Women!"*

Waldo smiled. He was proud of his extensive collection of offbeat movies, television shows, documentaries, and cartoons. The large family room was lined with bookcases full of videotapes, all neatly arranged by subject matter. Waldo approached a shelf and ran his fingers down the row of tapes there.

"These are some of my most prized possessions." He said.

The fredneck glanced at the labels and whistled. "Shit man, you must have every *Andy Griffith* there is!"

The Andy Griffith Show was Waldo's favorite television series of all time, and since the advent of home video recorders in the late 1970's, one of his greatest pleasures in life had been propping his feet up late at night and watching several episodes in a row.

"I thought you'd like them." Waldo said. "Listen, Brisbane, I was wondering- since we'll probably be up all night watching *Andy Griffith*- why don't I show you some of my grandfather's writings first?"

"Okay, dude, but I want to see some classic Barney Fife afterwards."

Waldo led the way downstairs and opened the door to Old Hoss's huge library. When he turned on the light, the fredneck whistled loudly.

"Shit man, you and your grandfather sure believe in collecting things, don't you?" Brisbane gazed at the reams of rare books, magazines, and papers, none of them likely to be stocked by the local public library.

Waldo picked up a few unpublished pamphlets and handed them to the fredneck. "My grandfather wrote hundreds of these things. You might like reading a few of them."

"Sure, man." Brisbane took the pamphlets. "By the way- where's that note he left you?"

"Oh, I completely forgot to show it to you." Waldo reached into his pants pocket, where he'd absentmindedly deposited the note early that morning, and produced the crumpled piece of paper.

Brisbane laid the pamphlets down and read the note. When he finished, his brow was furrowed. "Man, this is weird. What the fuck does this mean?"

"I have no idea. It's really strange."

The fredneck appeared to be entering a reflective state of mind. "Much as I despise them, man, don't you think you should call the police about this?"

"I guess I forgot to mention that I did call them." Waldo sighed out loud. "And they reacted just like you might expect them to."

"What'd they say?"

"Well, they gave me the runaround." Waldo replied. "They told me there wasn't much they could do unless I had more for them to go on."

"In which case you wouldn't need to pay their salaries because you'd do the job yourself." Brisbane was going into his famous anti-police bit. "You ever notice how the cops are never there when something serious happens? Shit, there's no money in that for them. If you were illegally parked, instead of trying to find your missing grandfather, you can bet that a whole fleet of pigs would be on your ass to stop you before you park again. There's no fucking revenue in fighting serious crime! If they catch a rapist or murderer, they can't make anything off of it, like they can with traffic citations. Plus, a violent criminal is gonna be much more dangerous than a traffic offender. The law is totally fucked up."

Waldo basically agreed with all the points in Brisbane's soliloquy. "I know that their priorities are out of whack. That's why they never cut down on the rate of serious crime. If they did, there wouldn't be any need for their services."

"Just like if people stopped getting sick, there'd be a whole lot of doctors looking for new careers." Brisbane chuckled at his own astuteness. "You know, man, just looking through some of this shit," the fredneck had picked up one of the pamphlets and was leafing through it, "it seems to me like maybe your grandfather didn't disappear at all. Have you considered that... maybe *they* got him?"

Waldo set his features in that classic James Stewart-Gary Cooper look of determination he wore whenever the situation merited it. "Of course, that's a real possibility. But... I just know he's alive somewhere-I can feel it in my heart."

"Sure, man. There's no proof he's not." Brisbane sat down with a pile of unpublished pamphlets in his lap. "That old dude must have been... interesting."

"Yes, he certainly was-I mean is-that."

Brisbane's attention was drawn to a bulkier than average product of Old Hoss Billingsly's entitled *Political Schizophrenia*. The fredneck opened it to page 23:

THE DEATH ROW - THE MOST RENOWNED VICTIMS OF OUR MASTERS
The Right-Wing Lineup- Primary Suspects: The International Communist/Satanic/Globalist Empire

1865 - Abraham Lincoln U.S. President: Victim printed currency without resorting to banker indebtedness. A London newspaper actually printed an editorial hinting that his death would be a welcome event shortly before he was assassinated.

1913 - Ambrose Bierce U.S. Writer: Victim saw what lay ahead and did not like it. Infuriating his powerful adversaries, he decided to disappear. He was successful.

1923 - Warren G. Harding U.S. President: Victim died in San Francisco after eating spoiled shellfish. No autopsy was performed. The official cause of death was said to be "a sudden stroke."

1935 - Huey P. Long U.S. Senator: Victim's populist appeal was too powerful a threat to F.D.R. and the New Deal gang. Despite the usual lies of the court historians, there is little doubt that victim would have been elected President of the United States in 1936.

1937 - H.P. Lovecraft U.S. Writer: Victim's politics were confusing but his delving into certain *verboten* areas in his strange short stories evidently went too far.

1945 - James Forrestal U.S. Secretary: Victim had stumbled upon some very important information. Although a long time member of the elite crowd, he was apparently possessed with a latent trace of patriotism, and made the mistake of assuming his reputation would shield him from harm. He "jumped" out of a window at Bethesda Naval Hospital.

1945 - William Seabrook U.S. Writer: Victim, friend of the evil Aleister Crowley, among others, committed "suicide" after becoming possessed with the occult while writing the book *Witchcraft*.

1952 - Eugene E. Cox U.S. Congressman: Victim headed a committee in Congress investigating tax-free foundations. He died suddenly and the probe faltered.

1957 - Joseph McCarthy U.S. Senator: Victim refused to give up after an unprecedented smear campaign against him, and, like Gary Cooper in *Meet John Doe*, came to believe in the role he was selected to play. Unlike Frank Capra films, his ending at Bethesda Naval Hospital was neither happy nor explained.

1970 - Vince Lombardi Pro Football Coach: Victim represented the ultimate in the old-school style of football. Times were changing and he wouldn't. He developed cancer.

The Left-Wing Lineup- Primary Suspects: The International CIA/ Mafia/Military/Banker Consortium

1944 - Joseph P. Kennedy, Jr. Aspiring Politician: Hatred of the Kennedys dates back long before they were a national fad. F.D.R. didn't like his daddy (neither did Winston Churchill or any other members of The Inner Sanctum) and there were strong indications victim's plane was tampered with prior to crashing, facts were concealed, etc.

1957 - Wilhelm Reich Psychoanalyst/Author: Victim's orgone theories were very controversial, and all his data on the subject were burned by the Food and Drug Administration. Thrown into jail by the U.S. government, he died there shortly afterwards.

1959 - Morris K. Jessup U.F.O. Investigator/Author: Victim had knowledge of the top secret Philadelphia Experiment and quite probably had discovered the true origin of U.F.O.'s. After his "suicide", his papers were never found.

1962 - Marilyn Monroe U.S. Actress: Victim was apparently in love with then Attorney General Robert F. Kennedy. Her "suicide" was a warning to J.F.K. to change or else. He didn't.

1963 - John F. Kennedy U.S. President: The Big One. So much is known about victim's death being the result of an obvious conspiracy that it makes one wonder exactly what he did to warrant such an elaborate crime and cover-up.

1965 - Malcolm X Black Muslim Leader: Victim was visited in jail by one of the infamous M.I.B.'s, or Men In Black. This alone makes his death worth looking into. The fact that he was subsequently assassinated during the decade of the assassination makes it more interesting still.

1967 - Frank Edwards U.F.O. Investigator/Author: Actually victim also investigated other unexplained phenomena and had a fine curiosity which led him into many significant areas of inquiry. It finally killed him when he chose to have a fatal "heart attack" on the 20th anniversary of the first modern U.F.O. sighting.

1968 - Martin Luther King, Jr. Civil Rights Leader: Victim was a mild threat to the power structure, but the main reason for his assassination was as a warning to R.F.K.

1968 - Robert F. Kennedy U.S. Senator: Victim was zealous in his desire to avenge his brother's death. He too failed to heed his warning and followed J.F.K. into Arlington National Cemetery.

1973 - Graham Parsons U.S. Rock Star: Victim was not known as a threat, but his death was too strange to overlook. He died while rehearsing in the desert. A friend then burned his body, hence no autopsy and no explanation for his sudden death while still in his 20's.

1980 - John Lennon British Rock Star: Like all the Beatles, victim had a big following in the U.S. His shooting was no different from all the others- a lone deranged gunman killing a public figure for no apparent reason. His alleged assailant, like most of the others in modern times, was referred to by all three of his names and was never heard from publicly in regards to his motive, or whether he in fact admitted killing the victim.

Brisbane put the pamphlet down. "Vince Lombardi?"

"Well, sometimes my grandfather could get carried away." Waldo replied. "What did you think of it?"

"It's pretty wild, alright." The fredneck replied. "I haven't even heard of some of those people. But I like your grandfather's style." Brisbane drained the remainder of his beer and handed the empty can to Waldo. "Could I have another cold one, dude?"

"Sure, Brisbane." Waldo said. "I'll be right back."

"Thanks, man." The fredneck picked up another pamphlet and

settled back in the easy chair. "I'm gonna look through some more of your grandfather's stuff."

Brisbane settled on a pamphlet entitled *Why They May Actually Count The Votes*, flipped it open to page 16 and started reading:

"What about the nauseating cultural excrement, such as disco music, that seems to capture the dim imagination of each generation? This latest rage, with its elementary lyrics and blow-dried practitioners gyrating aimlessly to the hypnotic beat, is perhaps the penultimate example of the tastelessness of the marketplace. Once disco had been officially recognized as a national phenomenon, television executives toiled tirelessly to slip some reference to it in their shows. These mighty capitalists prodded their stable of creative talent to produce a series of insipid disco theme songs for every splendid show they produced. The rebellious rock stars kowtowed to this passing fad and lowered themselves to insert its monotonous beat into their songs. Movies have been made about it, catch phrases coined, and wardrobes designed for it. This is all quite common with popular momentary amusements, for disco is, after all, just a fad and will eventually go the way of streaking. However, Disco as a state of mind, with a capital D, appears to have become more influential, and to have more staying power than the sickening music itself. Persons afflicted with Disco, commonly known as Discoers, are invariably successful in any field they choose to enter. This is due to the fact that they are tailor-made for modern society; they are superficial, unsympathetic, and trendy. They are narrow-minded and easily controlled, and appear to possess magical powers over forces the average person is helpless against; their clothes never wrinkle or spot, they never have anything hanging out of their noses, they never have to go to the bathroom at the wrong time, and they never fart in public. They make perfect employees; everyone has seen them- young executives brown-nosing (most of the time this isn't necessary, since Discoers are instantly recognized as such and automatically liked by those in positions of authority) their way to the top; young social workers dispensing advice culled from textbooks and seminars; clean young men and women screwing the average citizen with inflexible attitudes and the robotic smiles that come with their respective diplomas. They swallow enormous amounts of propaganda, and on those rare occasions when they are exposed to a different viewpoint, they vomit on cue. They wholeheartedly follow the admonition of one of their earlier anthems: *Don't Rock The Boat*. Although this mentality has been around for ages and is responsible, to a large degree, for the mess we're seemingly always in, it never had a name before. Well, now it does, and I christen thee of the cold hearts and dark spirits as the new but actually Ancient Order of Disco. I trust that what few honest historians may be left a hundred years hence will judge more fairly than I the extent of the cultural filth that permeates the 1970's. I, in my biased fashion, prefer to label this horrible decade as the worst in recorded times. That's quite a statement to make, considering the worthy competition."

Waldo returned to the library to find Brisbane repeatedly uttering "remarkable!", in a manner reminiscent of the youngster in the unforgettable Little Rascals' short *Forgotten Babies*.

Handing Brisbane his beer, Waldo smiled. "I guess you must have liked..."

"Liked?" Brisbane exclaimed from behind his tipped beer can, looking very much like the truly generalized fredneck. "Shit man, I love your grandfather's writing. I wish I could meet him."

Waldo shook his head sadly. "Well, maybe someday..."

"You really think he might have gone to see that crazy dude..."

"I just don't know." Waldo answered. "Do you want to see the journal I was telling you about? It's upstairs, in my grandfather's bedroom."

The fredneck was agreeable to this, and in a few moments they were in Old Hoss's bedroom, and Brisbane was staring around in wonder again.

"Wow!" He cried out when he saw the number of comic books piled in Old Hoss's closet. "Shit, Waldo, your grandfather was something else! You gotta find him, dude."

Waldo nodded. "Well, I certainly want to, Brisbane."

The fredneck saw Sam Hancock's journal lying on the bed. "Who the fuck," he asked, picking it up and glancing at the cover, "is Sam Hancock?'

"That's the journal I wanted to show you." Waldo replied. "Sam Hancock was my grandfather's best friend for many years..."

"He's the dude in the insane asylum in Idaho?"

"Iowa, not Idaho." Waldo corrected him. "It's a long shot, I know, but that Post-it note on the last page..."

Brisbane turned to the back of the journal. "*Room Five*. Hmmm. So you think your grandfather might have left that as some kind of clue for you?"

"Like I said, I don't know. I've looked everywhere I can think of, and I haven't found anything else. It doesn't seem to make much sense, that he'd travel all the way out there after all these years, but..."

"Shit, dude, let's go there then." Brisbane attempted to light his cigarette without success. "Damn disposable lighters. You got a light, man?"

Waldo was taken aback. "You mean you'd actually go with..."

"Shit yeah. I'm a roamer, man. I've spent most of my life on the road, and I've never been to Iowa. I'd like to go." Brisbane lit his cigarette and handed Waldo's lighter back to him. "Besides, I really want to meet your grandfather."

"Well, I haven't decided for sure whether I'm going..."

"That's okay, dude." The fredneck interrupted again. "If you do go, I'll go with you. Shit, I'll even drive."

"That's very nice of you." Waldo replied. "But what about your car?"

"I told you, man, it's looked a lot worse than that before. It's just body damage- we could make it there easy."

"That does sound..."

"Don't worry, man." Brisbane apparently was not going to allow Waldo to finish any sentences. "Think about it. Now, how about some Barney Fife?"

"Sure, but...first could I show you something else?" Waldo asked hopefully.

"What is it?"

"Wait here for a minute." Waldo ran to his own bedroom across the hall, grabbed some papers, and returned. "Here are some of my own writings." With an effortless bit of modesty, he handed a small pamphlet entitled *New Fairy Tales For The Immature And Maladjusted* to the fredneck.

Brisbane grinned and opened the pamphlet, taking a long swig of his beer as he hit page 19:

"Sooner or later, someone must question the validity of certain professions, and, more specifically, the practitioners thereof who parade before the public in emperor's clothes.

For instance, how did Ann Landers or her real-life sister Dear Abby come to have advice columns of their own? What could they possibly have studied in order to qualify them as "advice-givers?" Is this not a legitimate question to ask? Well, then, why hasn't someone asked it? I won't flog that dead horse any longer, but it is important for those who would like to have a position similar to the simplistic sisters to ask themselves that same question.

Gossip columnists patrol their mundane arena with the same sort of mysterious merit the advice-givers do. Plainly put, how does anyone become a gossip columnist? I can't simplify it down to a lower scale than that. Are there universities that offer courses in gossip writing?

How about plain old Gossip 111? Are there that many literate people who could not write a gossip column? What then, qualifies the chosen few above the rest?

Turning, if possible, to an even easier occupation, how about movie critics? Now, let's simplify again. Just what does a movie critic's job entail? Unless there's something I'm missing, a movie reviewer simply attends lots of movies (for free!) and informs the public, in a written column or by way of television, whether he likes them or not. I am aware that there are classes in movie criticism, and that, if nothing else about our sorry educational system does, should worry everyone. What can they teach other than how to give an opinion? All a person requires to be a movie critic is an attention span of two hours or less and a public school literacy level. That's it! Before this page becomes inflamed, I will say only that it is imperative for anyone desiring to join this well-paid fraternity to inquire into what criteria employers use to weed out prospective movie critics. Almost the same rules apply in regards to music critics, except that the sense of vision is not necessary. I refuse to believe the rumors that there are courses in rock criticism at institutions of higher learning. Rock critics are the most mystifying group we've examined so far. I can't pretend to know what one must do to be allowed to review records for *Rolling Stone* or countless other smaller publications, and I become even more paranoid than usual just thinking about it. Moving as far away as possible, how can one become a wine taster? This is perhaps the most illegitimate job imaginable, as it requires merely the ability to lift one's arm to one's lips, swallow an alcoholic beverage, and give an opinion. The sense of taste is, of course, mandatory. Along the same general lines, but perhaps a tad more physically demanding, is the position of food or restaurant critic. Just think- who among us wouldn't want to eat free food for a career?

I could go on and on, and probably will, asking more questions like: how did Dr. Ruth Westheimer become an expert on sex? Or Dr. Joyce Brothers, former boxing "expert" on the scandal-ridden game shows of the 1950's? How does one get to publish a book about how to win at Pac-Man, how to beat Rubik's Cube, or even less serious subjects? What did Richard Simmons study in college? How about Phil Donohue, Sally Jessy Raphael, Oprah Winfrey, and the slew of other talk-show hosts that force us to ask again- who picked them and why? Doesn't it seem that hosting a talk show in other words, talking for a living- is something that millions of people across this country could handle at least as effectively as those lucky and very, very rich ones do? Why are "psychics" such as Jean Dixon permitted to continue making predictions when year after year they are almost always wrong? Remember the little green men from Mars capturing earth's teenagers,

Jean? Why is Don King, convicted murderer, a millionaire boxing promoter? How could a murderer place himself in a position to become one? What are the requirements to be a promoter? One would need a lot of money, I imagine, for starters, yet it is unlikely that King, a poor black sitting in prison, had enough. How did Jimmy "the Greek" Snyder become the recognized expert on odds-making? What degree does one require to become an odds-maker? Certainly accuracy is not necessary, as Snyder's track record is abysmal. How does one become a fashion designer? Finally, who is Dick Clark, and what talent does he have? How can someone be discovered who does nothing?

That's enough of this subject. It is some kind of release to be able to say things that will never be said elsewhere, and perhaps some unsatisfied soul will find the solace of a kindred spirit in these unpublished pages."

Brisbane burst into a fit of maniacal laughter, rolling off the edge of the bed, where he'd been sitting, and onto the floor. When he had regained his composure to the extent that he could speak, he merely gasped "remarkable" over and over again.

"Are you alright, Brisbane?" Waldo, although intensely pleased with the way his work had been received, was mildly concerned that the red-faced fredneck might actually harm himself by laughing so strenuously.

Brisbane struggled several times to respond before finally replying, in fragments, "Man...that was...great...please...I can't...take anymore...this stuff...is...too much..."

Waldo agreed that they had probably read enough extremist tracts for one night, and suggested a Barney Fife festival was in order.

The fredneck gradually recovered and followed Waldo back to the family room, where a bowl of cold popcorn, which they had inexplicably failed to carry downstairs with them earlier, awaited them. Waldo cued up one of his favorite *Andy Griffith* episodes, and soon he and Brisbane were guffawing their heads off to the antics of Barney Fife, Gomer Pyle, Otis Campbell and company. Before that episode was ended, the fredneck, inspired by more beers, adamantly requested something prominently featuring Mayberry barber Floyd Lawson. "Floyd, Floyd, Floyd..." he chanted drunkenly while Waldo scanned his video index and inserted a six-hour tape, all of it containing vintage Floyd Lawson. Brisbane became ecstatic over this, laughing at every subtle nuance of Howard McNear's in the loudest possible way, and shouting various things at the screen.   In no time Waldo forgot his troubles and joined his new friend in yelling and whooping it up, even to the point of crying out exuberantly "this is some good shit!" After that burst of fredneckesque enthusiasm had flown out of his mouth, Waldo wanted to take it back, but took his beer can instead and downed the remainder. He got up unsteadily, and murmuring a slurred "I need another beer," staggered towards the kitchen.

"Waldo, what-that is-how did you let me fall asleep?"

Professor Buckley, with his colorful attire suitably wrinkled, rushed into the family room.

Waldo looked up at the comical figure, and smiled in the manner of one whose senses were greatly dulled by alcohol. "Oh, I'm sorry, Professor."

One of Hiram Buckley's more notable quirks was his steadfast refusal to sleep unless it was completely unavoidable. It was his fervent desire, in fact, to join those odd, unexplainable freaks of nature who have proven it is actually possible to live without it.

He would often speak of one Al Hepin, a New Jersey handyman who lived to be 94 years old, in glowing terms and relate to anyone within earshot how he'd claimed to have never slept in his entire life. This seemingly impossible feat was supposedly documented by a team of medics who observed the old man for weeks and never saw him close his eyes. Whenever the Professor allowed his exhaustion to overcome him he took it as a personal failure, and would walk around muttering, "I don't understand it" over and over again until he was distracted by another of his nonsensical interests.

"My boy, we didn't even discuss, before I chanced to-that is-did you make any progress today at all?" Professor Buckley asked. "In reference to your grandfather's disappearance, that is..."

Waldo lit up a cigarette and noticed that Brisbane had passed out on the sofa. "Uh, well, let's see..." He attempted to clear his head. "Yes, I did find something." Waldo realized he hadn't told the Professor about discovering the Post-it note in Sam Hancock's journal. "Come on, Professor, and I'll show you."

Hiram Buckley followed Waldo to Old Hoss's bedroom, and appeared to be somewhat flabbergasted, when shown the Post-it note, at the notion that *Room Five* could refer to Sam Hancock's room number at The Last Chance Relaxation Home.

"Come, my boy-that is-why would you make that assumption?"

Waldo shrugged. "Well, I know it's kind of illogical, but I've been in this room a million times, and I've never seen Sam Hancock's journal sitting out before. And since I don't have any other clues whatsoever..."

"Hmmmm." Professor Buckley tugged at his tie thoughtfully. "You may have a point. Perhaps I shouldn't discount your theory so hastily."

"Professor," Waldo looked at the eccentric ex-history teacher. "I have to tell you... I haven't decided for sure yet, but... I may go out there to look for him."

"Do you mean travel all the way to Iowa- to the mental institution? Waldo, that's a bit-that is-it's quite a distance from here. What if your grandfather's not there?" Professor Buckley shook his head worriedly. "You'd have wasted a great deal of time and money, my boy, and the trail would be even colder than it is now by the time you returned. What then?"

"I don't know, Professor. But what else can we do here?" Waldo placed his hand on the older man's shoulder. "I respect your opinion, but this is something I have to decide."

"Very well, my boy." Professor Buckley replied. "I'm going home now- I have some experiments to work on." The "experiments" the one time pride of the local community college was speaking of bore little similarity to any being conducted in conventional laboratories. Presently, having given up his recent efforts to invent a device to trace phone calls from the dead, the Professor was engaged in a thorough analysis of data confirming that the overwhelming majority of joggers wildly exaggerate the distances they actually cover.

"Okay, Professor." Waldo motioned towards the family room. "I'm going to watch some more *Andy Griffith* tapes."

Hiram Buckley frowned. "Waldo, how can you waste your time on such worthless junk? I can't imagine-that is-I threw my television set out the window in '59. Did I ever tell you...?"

"Yes, Professor." Waldo responded.

Professor Buckley had indeed reiterated his belief, on numerous occasions, that all Americans should emulate his dramatic gesture and similarly rid themselves of what he considered the foremost disaster of modern times.

"Yes, well, I'll be dropping by tomorrow-that is-" Professor Buckley glanced at his wristwatch, "later this afternoon."

Waldo waved goodbye and watched from the doorway as the odd little man in the bright, clashing wardrobe walked down the driveway and stepped into his equally colorful van and drove away. He then locked the door securely, as he always did, and returned to the family room for more sitcom shenanigans from the land of Mayberry.

Waldo opened his eyes. The sun was peeking in through the Venetian blinds, and its strips of illumination were cast about the room, reflecting off of the empty beer cans and lined in precise rows across the slumbering figure of Brisbane Wrock. The fredneck hadn't moved a fraction of an inch from his position on the sofa, and if it hadn't been for his loud snoring one might have been tempted to place a mirror under his nose.

Waldo's head was throbbing as he slowly walked to the kitchen and poured himself a Coke. Drinking cola always helped his infrequent hangovers, and he took a long and leisurely swallow of the heaven-sent beverage.

Returning to the family room, Waldo sat down in his favorite chair, propped his feet up on a hassock, ands lit a cigarette. Inhaling deeply, he studied the prone frame on the couch.

What was he to make of Brisbane Wrock? Waldo was hopeful they might become good friends, but was cynical about the whole idea of friendship. Waldo had never been a social butterfly, but he'd made his share of acquaintances over the years. Whenever he contemplated the high turnover rate among those he'd associated with during his lifetime, he became depressed and would wind up sifting through the volumes of old poetry in his grandfather's library, taking solace in some suitably sorrowful verse. His memory often raced back to his eleventh-grade English teacher, Mrs. something-or-other, and her thoughts on the subject. Although Waldo remembered little or nothing of his twelve years of public school instruction, he did vividly recall her words that day: *"You students, every one of you, will be extremely fortunate if, ten years from now, you're still in contact with any of your present friends. Most of you will have an entirely different set of friends in five years."* Waldo, like every other student in the class, had chuckled at this with the all-knowing air of a high school junior; now he realized just how right she'd been. All of the close friends Waldo had ever known had long since gone their separate ways. In some cases the parting had been mutual, but far too many times Waldo felt he'd been deserted for no apparent reason. He invariably took these commonplace events as a personal betrayal, and his sensitive nature did not permit such wounds to easily heal. Waldo clearly felt that, in friendship as in love, his emotions were different from the rest of humanity's. He never could concede that he might, on occasion, have unknowingly trampled upon others' feelings, or walked away from a friendship by choice. Thus it was with hesitation and not a little fear that Waldo gazed at the sleeping fredneck. Would this new acquaintance turn out to be like all of his other friends? Or worse, would he turn out to be like all of the other frednecks?

As Waldo mulled over these sobering thoughts, Brisbane began to show some signs of life. The young fredneck slowly stirred, then engaged in a luxuriant stretching routine. As he raised his arms above him, Brisbane opened his mouth and bellowed like a wild animal.

Eventually he raised himself to a sitting posture.

As soon as he sat up, Brisbane seemed to become instantly awake, jumping to his feet with a cheerful "hey, man!" Noticing Waldo's soda, the energetic fredneck requested one.

"Sure, help yourself. There's more in the refrigerator." Waldo didn't feel like leaving his comfortable position.

"Okay, man, thanks." Brisbane said over his shoulder, already heading for the kitchen.

Brisbane returned with his Coke a few moments later, and as soon as he sat down it was evident to Waldo that he wanted to get high. Waldo perceived this because the friendly fredneck pulled a joint from his pocket, stuck it between his lips, and lit it up. Following an especially long hit, Brisbane exhaled his words along with his smoke. "You don't mind if I catch a little morning buzz, do you?"

Waldo was tempted to fling a clever reply back, reminding the fredneck that it was actually early in the afternoon and pointing out that the non-fredneck world was unreasonable enough to require that a request be submitted prior to its approval, not afterwards.

His wit failed him, however, so he shook his head and weakly smiled.

It was obvious that Brisbane, over the years, had spent a great deal of time with his head bent over rolling papers, pipes, and bongs. Like a combat tested veteran, he seemed to devour the illegal substance in record breaking time, sucking expertly on the thin little joint until the final remains disappeared in a pile of ashes. The marijuana seemed to work wonders for Brisbane's intellect. Immediately after consuming the joint, he stared at Waldo with a new coherence and said, "Ever hear of Clapham Wood, man?"

Waldo shook his head. "No, I don't believe so. Why?"

"It's a forest, on England's South Downs, where weird things have happened for hundreds of years." The fredneck's eyes seemed redder to Waldo than the dope could have made them, and his whole persona appeared to be rapidly changing. "Dogs, horses, all kinds of animals, and people-like your grandfather, Waldo-have vanished there without a trace. The church rector disappeared in there in 1979. U.F.O. sightings are frequent there, and mysterious footprints have been found."

Waldo felt a slight chill. "That's all very interesting, Brisbane, but..."

Brisbane placed his Coke on the end table, wiped his lips, and took another joint from his shirt pocket. "Did you know that in Owensville, Indiana, the children once arrived at their school to discover that someone had painted *Remember Pearl Harbor* in huge letters on the sidewalk there? The strange thing is that it happened on December 7,

1939- two years to the day before Pearl Harbor was actually attacked by the Japanese. How do you explain something like that, Waldo?"

Waldo's spine was really beginning to tingle. "I-I don't know, Brisbane."

Holding the joint out towards Waldo, the fredneck, now looking very strange, spoke softly, "Look man, this stuff is really special. It's my own homemade mixture, guaranteed to open clogged brain cells and raise consciousness." Sounding like a renegade Amway distributor, Brisbane continued, "This ancient recipe consists of seven different herbs, with a few very secret ingredients thrown in to..."

"Alright, I'll try it." Waldo interrupted, surprising himself with his reply. Waldo's lengthy abstinence from smoking marijuana had been based entirely on a desire to obey his grandfather's wishes. When Waldo was a teenager, and like nearly every other member of his generation, at least casually smoking the substance, Old Hoss had discovered his bag one day and flushed it down the toilet in a dramatic display, issuing a dire warning to stay away from anything which made the human mind even more malleable than it already was. Now, smelling the substance in the air, and watching the fredneck smoke it so merrily, Waldo evidently rekindled some pleasant memories and astonished himself by his desire to once again ingest it.

"Yeah?" Brisbane raised his eyebrows. "That's a very wise decision, man."

Brisbane lit the joint, took a lengthy hit, and passed it to Waldo. Waldo's hands were trembling as he maneuvered the joint to his mouth. He hesitated for an instant, then inhaled deeply. It felt good to taste the reefer; he'd always liked that taste, and now he realized just how much he'd missed it. Momentarily ignoring Brisbane, Waldo took a few more long hits before his fredneck pal cleared his throat to get his attention. Waldo grinned stupidly and handed the joint to a visibly amused Brisbane.

The fredneck's bemusement lasted only for an instant, however, and gradually the differences Waldo had noticed earlier became more apparent. Brisbane's eyes grew so red that they hardly seemed human, and they peered at Waldo with a frightening intensity. There was a new, authoritative presence about the normally rumpled fredneck, and even his voice sounded deeper.

"How can it be that a baby was born in New York City's St. Vincent's Hospital in 1935 with no brain whatsoever? For 27 days, Waldo, this baby lived and ate and cried just like any other. In fact, it appeared to be so normal it was only at the autopsy, following its sudden death, that the startling discovery of the total absence of a brain was made." The fredneck was speaking in a bizarre, robotic monotone,

48

and he seemed anything but friendly. "A noted German brain specialist, Dr. Hufeland, once performed an autopsy on a paralyzed man who had been in full possession of his faculties to the very end. Instead of a brain, he found eleven ounces of water in the man's skull. As far back as 1788, Waldo, there was a report of a baby girl being born to an Englishwoman who was revealed, through an autopsy, to have had no brain. What can all of this mean, Waldo? How can someone function at all, let alone normally, if the organ supposedly governing all of our functions is not present? And how is *your* brain feeling, by the way, Waldo?"

Waldo instinctively knew that he had consumed some very powerful dope, even before he felt the tingling sensation at the back of his head. Within a very short period of time, his whole head was buzzing and he was unable to move. Waldo's heart was pounding away an erratic tune, gradually increasing in volume until he thought his eardrums would burst. All the while Brisbane kept glaring menacingly at him and the only noise he could hear was the horrible sonic boom of his palpitating heart. Then, all at once, the noise stopped. This really terrified Waldo, as he couldn't be certain whether or not he had a heartbeat. The nervous young man had been periodically addicted to checking his pulse for years, and thus he now experienced a brand of fear that only those possessed with such things can understand. Thinking he was probably dead, Waldo looked at the strange new figure before him. Gazing hypnotically into his eyes, Brisbane began to speak in an even more monstrously different voice.

"Are you Waldo Billingsly?" He asked in a prosecutorial style.

Waldo now felt his Adam's apple bobbing in time to the flow of his saliva, so he attempted a response. "*Yup.*" He heard a weak and barely recognizable Gary Cooper-like voice emerge from his lips.

"Do you believe in the romantic ideal- the bright fields and streams of heaven- the innocent figures of beautiful young girls romping naked through the rain forests- the validity of the concepts of right and wrong- the purity of the virgin soul?"

Waldo blinked his swollen eyes and replied "*yup*" in the same strange voice.

"Do you suffer from the pangs of incurable nostalgia and is your sympathy activated whenever a person, an animal, a building, an idea, or an institution dies?"

"*Yup.*" Waldo's new voice answered easily this time.

"Do you believe in the sanctity of the Constitution, the incontestable sovereignty of the United States, the inalienable right of each person to freedom on earth and a heaven or hell afterwards?"

"*Yup.*" Gary Cooper-Waldo Billingsly firmly responded.

"Do you subscribe to Thoreau's concept of 'simplify, simplify'?"

"*Yup.*"

"Do you believe in the sentimental version of the 'good old days' and would you willingly return to them?"

"*Yup.*"

"Do you believe in the sacredness of childhood- the angelic glow of little faces playing games of nonsense? Do you observe a plot to kill off this magical period completely?"

"*Yup.*"

"Do you believe there is an inherent difference between the sexes? Do you wish to find a beautiful virginal female to share your traditional fantasies and satisfy your idealistic desires? Do you deplore the lack of such creatures in the present age? Are you left with a lump in your throat when you consider the trend towards more feminine men and more masculine women? Do you want a girl just like the girl that married dear old dad?"

"*Yup.*" Waldo-Gary was nothing if not consistent.

"Do you feel shivers running up your spine when the national anthem, *The Battle Hymn Of The Republic*, Christmas carols, or other such songs are played; when film clips of John and Robert Kennedy are shown; at pertinent points, especially the ending, of old movies; when hearing about appealing American legends and folklore; or when reading certain sad, poignant poems?"

"*Yup.*"

The strange new Brisbane leaned forward and said, "It's obvious, Mr. Billingsly, that you are suffering from old fashioned romanticism and the only way to cure this despicable disease is to confront it head-on. Therefore, Mr. Billingsly, I would like you to meet your medicine-your prescription for well-being, as it were."

Brisbane waved his hand like a magician and into the family room walked a beautiful woman. She was a perfect cross physically between Jane Fonda and Gloria Steinem, managing to combine the most attractive attributes of each. She was dressed in a conservative blue dress suit, complete with a spotless white necktie. Sauntering sleekly over to the sofa, she sat down next to Brisbane, adroitly crossed her legs, and smoothed her dress.

Brisbane turned to Jane-Gloria and said, "Why don't you tell our friend Mr. Billingsly something about yourself?"

Flashing a dazzling, professional smile, Jane-Gloria looked at Waldo-Gary and began a soliloquy: "I'm a career woman, first and foremost. I don't care to comfort, submit to, or buoy the spirits of any man. My God is mammon, and I'm *very* religious. Women have been second-class citizens for far too long, and we're not going to stop fighting until we get what we deserve."

Brisbane interrupted her. "What would you say that she deserved, Mr. Billingsly?"

Waldo-Gary stared back blankly, so Brisbane said, "Okay, you better continue for awhile. I guess he's not quite ready."

Jane-Gloria then continued: "We need more women in higher places. I don't mean small-time positions, I'm talking about heads of corporations, bank vice-presidents, military officers, directors and producers of everything. In all of these fields, it should be mandated that a large percentage of females be promoted on a strict quota basis, with an accompanying special feminist task force created for purposes of enforcement. This would enable young girls to have productive role models to emulate like young boys have always had. I feel perfectly comfortable in saying that having children is not on my personal agenda. I seem not to possess the vaunted motherly instinct, and in the unlikely event I should be trapped into giving birth, I would feel compelled to enter the child in a day care program at the earliest possible date. I think that women should stop trying to live up to some unrealistic traditional ideal and instead start concentrating on becoming movers and shakers. Frankly, I'm only interested in how successful a man is; I won't be seen with some loser just because he happens to be nice and polite. I want the challenge of a dynamic man who knows what he wants and goes for it. Let me say also, that I believe pro athletes- who, by the way, really turn me on- are actually criminally underpaid when you consider what kind of revenue their talents bring in. I believe in the law of the jungle, and feel no remorse when some more fit survivor swallows up a weaker, inferior rival. I have no trouble with the theory of evolution or the adversary system of justice, I think that all people claiming to have seen flying saucers are either crazy or lying, and I also accept without reservation the Warren Commission's conclusion that Lee Harvey Oswald acted alone in..."

"That's enough!" screamed Waldo-Gary. "I know exactly what she deserves."

Brisbane smiled broadly. "Alright, Mr. Billingsly, then by all means give it to her."

Suddenly they were transported to an outdoor arena, which former season ticket holders such as Old Hoss Billingsly would have instantly recognized as old Griffith Stadium, home of the late, lamented, original Washington Senators baseball team. The next thing Waldo-Gary knew, the three of them were standing at home plate, where an old-fashioned wooden chair had appeared. Brisbane took Jane-Gloria by the hand and presented her, like some medieval victim of ritual sacrifice, to Waldo-Gary.

Waldo-Gary grabbed Jane-Gloria by the wrist. He then led her over to the wooden chair that was located directly on top of home plate and sat down.

"Alright, young lady, you're going to get a good, sound spanking." Waldo-Gary's voice, like Longfellow Deeds's and Long John Willoughby's, was quiet but forceful.

A chant of "*spank, spank, spank*" began emanating from above them, and Waldo-Gary looked up at the stands and realized they were full. The spectators in the seats did not seem quite defined, and swayed about in a slow, fuzzy motion in their outdated attire. In Waldo-Gary's eyes, the figures resembled some fifty thousand vague, cheering ghosts. Spurred on by the crowd, and feeling like Babe Ruth, he pulled Jane-Gloria across his lap.

"I think she's been so naughty that she ought to receive her spanking on the bare behind." Brisbane helpfully suggested.

At the mention of this, the stands erupted into hoots and cries of "*take her panties down!*" Waldo-Gary eagerly nodded his agreement and raised Jane-Gloria's skirt up above her waist. He then slowly pulled her pink panties down, revealing her shapely bottom to fifty thousand probably unreal fanatics. Waldo-Gary then began spanking her, all the while telling her to mend her ways and modify her opinions in a voice that was somehow loud enough to be heard by all of the howling maniacs in the stadium. These odd, unfashionable, and nearly certain illusions reacted to every reprimand he gave her with further cheers and epithets. Soon Jane-Gloria was kicking her pretty legs and crying like a baby as Waldo-Gary meted out fifty hard smacks to her upturned behind.

When Waldo-Gary counted out the fiftieth spank, the people and/or spirits in the stands went completely berserk, and their wild applause was climaxed by a spontaneous standing ovation. Brisbane exclaimed euphorically, "The Committee of Discipline is very pleased, Mr. Billingsly, *very* pleased!" He then pointed behind Waldo-Gary.

There, to Waldo-Gary's amazement, standing along the third-base line, were the apparent members of the heretofore-unknown Committee of Discipline. The five hazy, almost transparent figures were all easily recognizable. As Waldo-Gary's mouth dropped open and his frying mind whirled, Brisbane made the formal introductions.

"Mr. Billingsly, allow me to present the members of the Committee. Starting from your left, they are: Mr. Patrick Henry, Mr. Charles "Old Hoss" Radbourne, Mr. Edgar Allan Poe, Mr. Lewis Carroll, and the grand poobah himself, Mr. Huey Long." (It may be pertinent to mention here that the reason Old Hoss Radbourne was easily recognizable to anyone, let alone a very stoned Waldo-Gary, was because his grandfather had for years kept an old daguerreotype of his namesake hanging in his laboratory.) "They are quite pleased with your efforts, Mr. Billingsly." With that, a very beautiful and stirring rendition of *Battle Hymn Of The Republic* began playing off in the distance somewhere, and gradually increased in volume until Waldo- Gary was moved to stand up (the humiliated Jane-Gloria had vanished without his even realizing it, leaving her pink panties behind her in the batter's box) and triumphantly salute the Committee, whose members all smiled in response before slowly melting away into the base paths.

Then, in an instant, Just Plain Waldo was back in his family room, and the old Brisbane was sitting on the couch with a puzzled expression on his face.

"Hey man, are you alright?" The fredneck asked.

Waldo felt his head. No tingling. He spoke. "I don't know. I guess so." No Gary Cooper.

"Shit man, I just asked you if you wanted to get high and you act like you're in a catatonic trance or something. I guess that means no, huh?"

"Yes, I suppose it does." Said Waldo with a sigh.

The Afro-Anarchists were waiting at a bus stop, just outside the gates of Snorting' Reformatory. Phosphate, Fontaine, and Bucktooth were preparing to head back to the violence, poverty, and comedy of southeast Washington, D.C.

"I sure am glad to be free again!" Bucktooth innocently exclaimed.

"Sheeet!" Fontaine was famous for lengthening his expletives. "Buck, you ain't never been free, and you ain't free now."

"The starving throngs of intellectually emaciated citizens might disagree with you, Fontaine." Phosphate appeared to be inching towards his soapbox. "After all, no one who is not a multi-millionaire seriously questions the right of all individuals to the basic protections guaranteed by our Constitution. At least not in theory. However, at a time when aliens, legal and illegal, continue to flood all ports of entry to our country; in an age where the media and the public figures fondle each other to the subliminal delight of the unwitting audience; and when poor white bigots are relegated to whispering racist jokes to each other in the backs of deserted rest rooms, I submit to you that no one is free." The top doo-wopper held his little finger up in the air and stared into space, as if searching for an imaginary debating opponent. "To put it indelicately, Fontaine: freedom is nothing more than having the right to say "nigger" whenever you damn well please."

Fontaine frowned. "Damn, Phos, I always thought it meant

53

something a lot different from that."

"In other times, and other places, indeed it did, Fontaine." Phosphate patted his fellow Afro-Anarchist on the back. "I always make it a point to try and consider those views which are most odious to me, and to fight for their right to be heard. That is hardly an original philosophy of course, but it has seldom been practiced over the centuries."

"Where the hell's our bus?" Bucktooth interrupted the head Afro-Anarchist's sermon. "It shoulda been here ten minutes ago."

"Gentlemen, I sense something in the wind." Phosphate looked all about him with a peculiar expression on his face. "I wouldn't be surprised if we were about to embark upon a great adventure."

Fontaine and Bucktooth chuckled at the top doo-wopper's dramatic, foreboding words. "You sound like a character in some bad movie." Fontaine observed.

"You just never know." Phosphate smiled. "Life imitates art, my friends."

"There it is!" Bucktooth pointed towards their bus, which was slowly approaching in the distance.

Phosphate's cryptic speculations were left behind them as they boarded the bus and headed back to their crime ridden community and the world of doo-wop protesting.

Waldo studied himself in his bedroom mirror. His open, expressive face clearly advertised a package that few in modern day society would find appealing: immature, emotional, and extremely vulnerable. He was searching for something specific in his reflection but the image before him stared back blankly and held its silence. Had his incredible dream/drug/sexual fantasy earlier in the day been merely a product of his overactive imagination? Or was it actually caused by Brisbane's special mixture of weed? The elements involved in the events that probably didn't transpire at old Griffith Stadium held no special significance for the nervous young man, unless they were buried so deep in his subconscious that only a master psychoanalyst could extract them. Waldo had never been the baseball fan his grandfather once was, and he abhorred violence of any kind. He was, in fact, a firm opponent of corporal punishment, and thus was baffled and ashamed of the sadistic nature of his dream/fantasy. Feeling about as close to an answer as the search party that boarded the desolate, abandoned *Mary Celeste* in the nineteenth century waters of the Atlantic ocean, Waldo finally managed to turn away from the mirror and walk into the family room, where he sat down in his favorite chair and routinely swung his feet up on the hassock.

Brisbane had left shortly after Waldo's apparently illusory experience with Jane-Gloria at long demolished Griffith Stadium, saying he would return later that evening with some writings of his own. Waldo didn't know whether or not to suspect Brisbane of playing a typically sadistic fredneck-style trick on him by spiking the dope with a more powerful substance. That sort of thing, along with the ever-popular practice of slipping something potent and illegal into unsuspecting non-users' drinks, was among the most cherished of fredneck traditions. To take his mind off the subject (and the growing, frightening realization that it *would* be fun to spank either Jane Fonda or Gloria Steinem), Waldo turned on the television.

The local news programs were just starting, and Waldo would often watch them through some masochistic urge to torture himself and raise his blood pressure. The smiling anchorwoman was about to interview a special guest, which was a popular daily feature that all three competing stations, by the same clever sort of coincidence that enabled them to simultaneously air sports, weather, and traffic reports, happened to broadcast at the same time. Usually the special guest was some celebrity in town to promote their latest venture or an "official spokesperson" for some momentarily popular cause. Today a representative from G.G.A.D.D. (Great Grandparents Against Drunk Drivers) was being asked to field a handful of sophomoric questions. Waldo rolled his eyes and inhaled a little deeper. The spokesperson for the group, an elderly lady pushing ninety, answered all of the leading questions coherently enough, although she did keep rubbing her face, which had probably been irritated by the heavy amount of makeup utilized to make her more palatable to the hip viewing audience. After a very predictable exchange lasting about two minutes, the anchorwoman thanked her guest and turned to other important topics. Waldo realized that a great number of drunk drivers were frednecks, but he was also aware that drunk driving had been prevalent for many years without being declared a problem of paramount importance. The sudden intense focus on the subject paralleled, albeit on a smaller stage, the recent surge of interest in the homeless and the outcry about nuclear weapons a few years back.

Waldo's suspicions were aroused early on in the "debate" about drunk driving and how to combat it. His observational skills were finely honed and he knew how to recognize such "debates" for what they really were. "When only one side of a supposedly controversial issue is allowed access through the media- *watch out!*" Old Hoss used to counsel him. Of course, Waldo's grandfather adamantly held that the press was manipulated and controlled by the government, and thus found its reporting on all matters to be unreliable. It was only natural for Waldo, so heavily influenced by his grandfather in all respects, to instinctively feel this issue was one of those to "watch out" for.

Waldo had been raised to believe that when the personal liberty of the individual conflicted with the interests of the general public, only in rare and carefully defined instances should the state's welfare be considered a higher priority. Therefore Waldo, who considered it his duty to hold an opinion on all topics, felt he had no choice but to rise to the defense of a group that included a substantial number of undesirable elements, many of them frednecks.

"Even frednecks have rights." He mumbled to himself. Meandering slowly out into the main hallway, his attention was caught by the faded world atlas hanging on the wall there. Waldo sighed and ran his fingers across the map of the United States, trying to picture in his non-geographically inclined mind the shortest possible route to Iowa.

4
BARNEY FIFE SLEPT HERE

Waldo, after studying the map in the hall with about as much understanding as the average citizen has of quantum physics, wandered into his grandfather's bedroom. He laid down on the bed and stared at the ceiling. As he fretted over whether or not to embark upon a long journey that might well prove fruitless, he drifted off to sleep. This was no small accomplishment for Waldo, but when he awoke he did not feel rested. Rising slowly out of bed and stretching his arms, he noticed that the room was even messier than usual. There were a bunch of his grandfather's pamphlets lying about everywhere, as Brisbane had cut a real swath through them. Waldo aimlessly picked one up and started reading. It was a spoof of the old local Washington, D.C. news show "Agronsky And Company," entitled *Billingsly And Company:*

MR. BILLINGSLY: Good evening and welcome to "A Few Minutes With Billingsly & Company." We have a very distinguished group of guests on our show tonight. Allow me to introduce them to you: first, there is that cynical master of unhappiness, known to wander off in his advanced years to allegedly assist revolutions in Mexico- Mr. Ambrose Bierce. Next we have that bastion of independence and illumination- Mr. Thomas Jefferson. To his right is the man many consider to be the greatest baseball player of all time- Mr. Ty Cobb. Also tonight, ladies and gentlemen, may I present to you the brilliant and reclusive poet- Miss Emily Dickinson. And finally, a man who specialized in causing sleepless nights for scientists everywhere- Mr. Charles Fort. Good evening, panel. I offer my sincere thanks to each of you for being (or not being) here with us tonight. I would like to open our discussion with Mr. Bierce. Mr. Bierce, you were the most vicious critic of your time- probably of all time- and condemned nearly every facet of society during your long and illustrious career. Would you say that the world is a better place to live in today than at the time you disappeared?

MR. BIERCE: *Well, Abner, I feel it would certainly be difficult not to have improved upon the terrible conditions of my day. What is obvious is that technological advancements have made the disorder more noticeable.*
MR. BILLINGSLY: Do you think any changes for the better have been made?
MR. BIERCE: *Yes, the progression from strips of rags to sanitary*

napkins has certainly made life easier for women. Had it not resulted in a coinciding change of temperament, whereby they suddenly realized there was more to life than waiting at home in the pantry for their alcoholic, abusive husbands, the lot of man might also have improved.

MR. BILLINGSLY: What's your opinion on this, Miss Dickinson?

MISS DICKINSON: *Well...I don't really know.*

MR. BILLINGSLY: Oh, I see. Because of the fact you stayed in the same house for nearly your entire life, you don't feel capable of judging your own age, let alone ours. Am I right?

MISS DICKINSON: *Yes.*

MR. BILLINGSLY: What about politicians, Ambrose? Any changes there?

MR. BIERCE: *Yes- they have increased their life expectancies.*

MR. BILLINGSLY: Any more or less corrupt?

MR. BIERCE: *I rarely quote the Bible, as you know, but one of its more enlightened passages says something about there being "nothing new under the sun."*

MR. BILLINGSLY: Do you agree with Bitter Bierce's bleak assessment of our modern political leaders, Mr. Jefferson?

MR. JEFFERSON: *Well, the present day politicians may, as the eminent Mr. Bierce suggests, be totally corrupt, or- perhaps just as tragically- they may be irreparably incompetent.*

MR. BILLINGSLY: Do you think, Tom, that in the course of these past 200 years America has continued the form of government that you and the rest of the founding fathers envisioned and set into motion? If not, has it been improved upon or debased?

MR. JEFFERSON: *I am sad to say, Old Horse, that it has been destroyed.*

MR. BILLINGSLY: That's Old Hoss, Tim. But how has it been destroyed?

MR. JEFFERSON: *Well, I haven't been around for the last 160 years so I may not be the most accurate observer. Be that as it may, from what I can determine, by a gradual process begun in earnest in 1913, the leaders sworn to uphold the Constitution have usurped the power and majesty of that document- which is almost as timeless a piece of work as my own Declaration of Independence, I might add- until it is today an unnoticed and virtually worthless piece of paper.*

MR. BIERCE: *Bravo!*

MR. DICKINSON: *I think that was the longest sentence I've ever heard.*

MR. BILLINGSLY: I agree with both of you. What are the major problems facing the land of the formerly free at this time, Tom?

MR. JEFFERSON: *I have to concur that America's freedom should be referred to in the past tense. The great educational system that I envisioned would narrow the chasm between the common man and the aristocracy has merely produced powerless wards of the state, not free and sovereign citizens. It is highly improbable that this largely ignorant population could ever learn to think even minor matters through for themselves, let alone petition their government for a redress of grievances. When this ignorance and apathy is coupled with the fear of official reprisal, the probability factor of any workable solution arising plummets to zero.*

MR. COBB: *When are we going to talk about astroturf, Abner?*

MR. BILLINGSLY: In a minute, Ty. So you don't see any use in exposing the problems until there is some capability of solving them, Tom?

MR. JEFFERSON: *Those of us who fought the War of Independence- not, by the way, a revolution by any definition- were faced with the most powerful enemy in the world at that time. Should modern-day patriots plan a revolt similar to ours, the adversaries they would face constitute a power infinitely greater than George's England.*

MR. BILLINGSLY: Well said, Tom. Miss Dickinson, let's turn to you for a moment. The world is well aware that you spent most of your lifetime inside your house, greeting your infrequent visitors from darkened hallways. Given the changes that have occurred since your death, would you be just as willing to lead such an outcast existence today?

MISS DICKINSON: *Yes.*

MR. BILLINGSLY: Okay... Mr. Fort, you've been uncharacteristically quiet. Let me direct a few questions your way. Since your research into unexplained phenomena paved the way for all of the subsequent investigation in that field, I think our viewers would like to know if you approve of the present day ufologists and, in particular, the so-called "forteans" who've adopted your name?

MR. FORT: *I detest the term "fortean" and deny any affiliation with those who have deemed themselves as such. If I were still around, I would either slap a fat lawsuit on them for unauthorized use of my name or try to hire them at outrageous salaries to trample the forests of strange uncharted areas for data. To believe that U.F.O.'s are alien spacecraft is just as illogical as denying their existence. It is also just as logical. I held my own opinions about all of these things, and were I alive today I would be burying my head in piles of obscure old reports ignored by established science and no more willing to convey to the laughable world my absurd, private views.*

59

MR. BILLINGSLY: Charles, if you were living, would you be inclined to believe what a few mostly deceased individuals have whispered: namely, that we never went to the moon?

MR. FORT: *I would be more than willing to waste many hours looking into it.*

MR. BILLINGSLY: Turning to a more serious subject, Mr. Cobb, what do you think of modern-day baseball?

MR. COBB: *It stinks! I ranted and raved about those boys in the 50's, but I sure as hell didn't think it could get any worse.*

MR. BILLINGSLY: Be specific, Ty.

MR. COBB: *First of all, you have astroturf. And indoor stadiums. And softball uniforms. It isn't baseball! I said it about the players in the 50's, and it's twice as true today: they can't bunt, they can't field, they don't even look for the walk, they won't play hurt, and you can't call them ballplayers! Why, there isn't a player in the big leagues today who could've made any minor league team in my day. Nowadays they play with a lowered mound, a juiced-up ball, and a smaller strike zone, but they still can't approach our batting averages. There's too many teams, they've diluted what little talent is out there. Hell, Canada has two teams but the nation's capital, Washington, D.C., which supported an American League club that was almost always a loser for over 70 years, doesn't have one. It's just not right! And the salaries- don't get me started on that! Whew! You got .210 hitters who are millionaires! It's insane!*

MR. BILLINGSLY: Ty, when, in your estimation, did the quality of major league baseball begin going downhill?

MR. COBB: *Well, it was a different game when I played. We played with a dead ball, you know. I think players in my era were as a whole the hungriest, had the most desire. We scrapped and fought, anything to win. We played hurt, too. I mean really hurt, not like today when they put you on the critical list if you break a fingernail. The players of the 20's were more of the slugging type, and swung a little too much from their heels, but they played circles around today's pampered sissies. In the 30's and early 40's, play had deteriorated somewhat, but was still at a major league level and I recognized it as such. After World War II it just kept going, and by the 50's it was gone. Also, they say today it's a lot harder on them, taking long plane flights, night games and all that. Hell, we had to ride on stuffy, cramped trains and we stayed dirty and drunk. You mean to tell me that riding in luxurious comfort on a modern aircraft, watching movies, ogling the stewardesses, is tougher than what we went through? I'll admit it's harder to hit at night, but what about all the games we had to play into the dusk, without lights, until they were called on account of darkness? And, if it's really true what they say about night baseball and hitting, doesn't it stand to reason that the Chicago Cubs should hit better than the other teams? They play half their games at Wrigley Field, which is the only major league ballpark left without lights, and it probably won't last much longer. Yet, look at their record. The Cubs have been worse than just about anybody else in the majors over the last 40 years, and they haven't been to the World Series since 1945, longer than any other team in baseball.*

MR. BILLINGSLY: Well, Ty, is it fair to say that you think all modern day major leaguers are overpaid, feminized, softball players?

MR. COBB: *That's fair enough.*

MR. BILLINGSLY: You've convinced me, Ty! You've also taken up most of the show with your tirade. So we'll have to sum it up now. I'd like each of you to answer this question: is there any hope, however remote, that the condition of our country will ever improve?

MR. BIERCE: *Ha! Ha! Ha! Ha!*

MR. JEFFERSON: *No.*

MR. FORT: *No.*

MISS DICKINSON: *No.*

MR. COBB: *No.*

MR. BILLINGSLY: It's unanimous! Well, I'd like to thank our distinguished panel for a most enlightening conversation. Certainly you're no less depressed, but perhaps a little wiser for sitting in with us on "A Few Minutes With Billingsly & Company." Goodnight.

Just as Waldo put the pamphlet down, he heard Brisbane burst in through the front door, unannounced and without knocking, in traditional fredneck style.

"Hey Waldo!" The fredneck shouted in his casual, friendly manner. "Where the fuck are you, man?"

"Back here, Brisbane." Waldo responded. "In the family room."

Brisbane walked into the room with an acoustic guitar slung over his shoulder. "Shit man, I brought my guitar. I thought you might wanna hear some of my songs."

"Oh, sure." Waldo smiled. "I was just finishing writing something myself."

"Great- I'll read it later- but I brought some of my shit like I said I would. Look at this!" Brisbane handed Waldo a sheet of paper containing the lyrics to his song *Let's Kill All The Arabs And The Jews.*

Brisbane flipped his guitar around to the proper position and began strumming:

"Let's kill all the Arabs and the Jews

And read all about it in the news
We'll fill up all the obituaries
And piss in all the cemeteries
And finally let the world know of our views
When you're talking prejudice
You're talking to the very best
The Arabs and Jews can drop their bombs
And move their asses to Vietnam
And let the world finally get some rest
Scream hate and say that I'm no good
I don't want you in my neighborhood
You seem to think I give a shit
Well, I need another bong hit
You won't stand where my granddaddy stood."

Brisbane finished with a flourish, repeating the last line several times before putting his guitar down and looking anxiously at Waldo. "Well?"

Waldo didn't know what to say. "Brisbane, the tune is nice, but the lyrics...were you being sarcastic or what?"

"Shit man, it's a fucking parody!" The fredneck seemed offended that Waldo hadn't caught on to his clever satire.

Waldo wasn't completely convinced that there wasn't a grain of true fervor in the sentiments Brisbane had so passionately sung about. He was aware that, along with their other attractive traits, a sizable percentage of frednecks were bigots. Not as great a percentage, perhaps, as among plain old rednecks, but a large number nonetheless. Waldo himself had inherited his share of prejudice from Old Hoss. The old eccentric always became defensive whenever his grandson gently suggested that maybe there was a trace of racism or anti-semitism in some of his writings. Waldo tried not to be intolerant in his attitude towards others, but he was a product of his environment as much as anyone else, and that environment had been dominated by his grandfather. Thus, Waldo wasn't appalled at the nature of Brisbane's lyrics, just taken aback. He could tell that the effervescent fredneck had a whole concert planned for his benefit, and Waldo wasn't exactly looking forward to sitting through what would most likely be a series of similar songs. Thus, he attempted to distract the fredneck into changing his itinerary.

"Listen, Brisbane," Waldo possessed little natural salesmanship, and it was quite an effort for him to avoid the pratfalls that have crushed the careers of many a telemarketing representative, "why don't we watch the two-part *Andy Griffith* where Barney comes back to Mayberry and Warren worships him?"

"Yeah!" The fredneck exclaimed. "And in part two, he finds out that Thelma Lou is married to someone else." Brisbane flipped his guitar pick, which he'd been using to dislodge the dirt under his fingernails, onto the cocktail table. "Shit, that scene at the high school reunion, when Barney is so heartbroken, I mean, there's almost nothing that can make me cry, man, but..."

"Okay..." Waldo tried not to appear smug, "let's go watch it then."

"Hey dude, you cue up the tape and I'll get us some..." The fredneck checked himself, a slight worried expression on his face. "We drank pretty much last night. You do have more beer, don't you?"

"Yes, plenty."

Actually Waldo seldom drank alcoholic beverages, but he was a smart shopper and purchased large quantities of beer whenever the sales price was irresistible, presumably on the pretense of someday developing a friendship with a heavy drinker.

As the fredneck grinned broadly and, humming some nondescript heavy metal tune, headed for the kitchen, Waldo silently patted himself on the back.

All afternoon and into the evening, the tapes whirred, the beer flowed, and Brisbane expounded upon his infamous H & D Theory. This theory held that the best looking females, for unknown reasons, are invariably drawn to unattractive males. It further postulated that the less personable the male, and the worse his financial situation, the more attracted to him the good looking females were likely to be. H & D stood for honeys and derelicts, Brisbane explained, and with each additional beer he drank, the fredneck unleashed a bit more of the sexual frustration within him. "Shit man, all you have to do is go out to a mall, singles bar, or any public place where young people gather, especially rock concerts, and tell me my fucking theory isn't right!" Brisbane chugged his beer.

"The D's treat their H's like shit, and the H's love it! And almost every time you seen an H & D in a car together, the H is driving. They even chauffeur them around, dude! Think about that shit! Would you be turned on by some ugly, mean bitch who treated you like shit?" The fredneck shook his head in disgust and went to the kitchen for another beer.

Waldo was receptive to the fredneck's bizarre hypothesis, but felt it his duty to play the devil's advocate. "I think your theory is interesting, Brisbane, and I hate to say it but... sometimes you sound like you hate all women because, well... you don't have any."

Brisbane wore a quizzical look when he returned to the family room. "Really? Well, for all you know I might have a harem somewhere. And I don't hate women. They seem to hate me. By the way, dude, where are all *your* women?"

Waldo had always been self-conscious about his lack of success with the ladies, and he felt a slight blush coming to his modest cheek. "Uh... look, Brisbane, I didn't mean to hurt your feelings. And you're right, I haven't been very lucky when it comes to romance. I guess I lashed out at you because of my own... well, anyhow, I'm sorry." Waldo sounded as contrite as he had as a youngster trembling in line at St. Phillip's, awaiting confession. Had Brisbane been raised a Catholic, as Waldo was prior to his parents' death, he might very well have been moved to order a penance for the apologetic young man.

"That's okay, man." Brisbane had felt so obliged to defend himself that he hadn't opened his beer can yet. Quickly rectifying this, he plopped down on the sofa and took a long swig. "You guessed right too, dude: I'm no Romeo. No girl ever called me back, or passed me notes in class. I never admitted it before- when we were in school all the freaks had to pretend that kind of stuff wasn't cool- but I never had a date for any of those Sadie Hawkins-Homecoming type of dances. Before I dropped out, that is."

Waldo, with a look comforting enough to qualify him for membership in any self-respecting support group, nodded in total understanding. "I know what you mean, Brisbane, but at least you didn't have to sit home alone the night of the senior prom, imagining what your classmates were doing. Well, I mean, I guess you might have been alone, but you weren't really a part of it by then."

Brisbane winced sympathetically. "That must have been fucking awful. Especially when you knew those lucky dudes were taking their chicks to the beach afterwards and most of them were gonna get laid."

"Sometimes it seems like...I don't know, certain guys have a power to attract women that defies rational explanation." Waldo remarked ruefully.

"Shit yeah!" The fredneck exclaimed. "It starts when they first reach puberty, and the chicks are all over them from then on. Unlucky guys like you and me, man, might as well face it- if the women don't begin liking you when you're young, they're never going to. Unless you become a millionaire or something. You can't figure love out, dude- it's a mess."

Waldo sniffled and lit a cigarette. "I think I can tell you something, Brisbane, that no one else knows: I've never...well, I haven't...uh, I'm still a virgin."

Brisbane's mouth dropped open. "No shit! Damn, man, you're even worse off than me! But not too much, I guess. I haven't had any

64

since... let's see, I think it was..."

Waldo and Brisbane's maudlin recital of self-pity was interrupted by a knock at the back door.

"Oh, that must be the Professor." Waldo wiped his nose with his sleeve. "I thought he'd be here sooner."

Brisbane remained in the family room, deeply absorbed in painful memories of his past, while Waldo ran downstairs to let Professor Buckley in.

Following the Professor's arrival, the discussion turned to more productive matters, such as the pursuit of missing grandfathers.

"Shit man," Brisbane belched loudly, "I think we ought to be heading for Idaho..."

"Iowa." Waldo corrected him.

"Yeah, Iowa. Have you decided if we're gonna go or not?"

Hiram Buckley, who seemed to have grave reservations about such a trip, gazed at Waldo intently, awaiting a response.

Waldo downed the remainder of his beer and ground his cigarette butt out in the ashtray. Standing up a bit unsteadily, but with a theatrical flair, he replied, "Yes, Brisbane, I have decided to go to Iowa. Professor, you're welcome to come, of course."

The dapper ex-history teacher frowned in obvious disapproval. "Waldo, my boy, I don't think-that is-if you must go, then...I will too."

Waldo smiled. "Thanks, Professor, I really appreciate that. Brisbane, I was thinking that maybe we could leave tomorrow."

"Okay, dude. Let's all sleep a little and book when we wake up."

Professor Buckley appeared offended by such a suggestion. "Young man," he intoned solemnly, "I *never* sleep."

Brisbane finished his beer and cuddled up cozily on the couch. "Good for you, dude, but *I* do."

"Waldo," Professor Buckley asked, "I would like-that is-could I read some of Sam Hancock's journal?"

Before the Professor had completed his sentence, the fredneck was sound asleep.

"Certainly, Professor." Waldo responded, and led the way quietly, so as not to disturb Brisbane, to his grandfather's bedroom.

Hiram Buckley sat down on the edge of the bed and Waldo handed him the thick journal.

"Here you are, Professor." He said. "I think I'm going to try and sleep a little myself, if you don't mind. You can stay the night if you like."

"Since I've just gotten here, my boy, I believe I will." The Professor took off his glasses and polished them with the tail of his coat. "If it's alright with you, I'd like to read some of this. After all, I think I ought to know something about the man we're traveling so far to see."

"Sure, Professor." Waldo smiled. "If you need me, I'll be in my room across the hall."

Hiram Buckley opened the journal and scanned a few pages until he found an early entry which grabbed his attention:

The Journal of Sam Hancock, June 16, 1934

I have just returned from Hollywood, California. This fascinating city of dreams has always intrigued me, and my pulse beat a bit faster the entire two weeks of my visit. It was quite a treat to observe members of the beautiful and famous set in the flesh, and in fact celebrity watching became the favorite aspect of my trip. I make this admission to counsel others, like myself, who deem themselves above such maddening activities as ogling actors and actresses, to proceed with caution when you're a tourist in Tinseltown; the scent of fame is *very* alluring. I was fortunate in the number of movie stars I was able to spot. For instance, in the renowned Brown Derby restaurant alone, I saw Clark Gable, William Powell, Helen Twelvetrees (I just love that name!), and Loretta Young, who was even more lovely in person than she is on screen. I was a bit disappointed in not seeing Bela Lugosi, who is my favorite actor. Apparently he does not spend a great deal of time there, and in fact has not done a film that fully utilized his enormous talent, in my opinion, since *Dracula* three years ago. The highlight of my trip, however, was a chance encounter with another player from that film, leading lady Helen Chandler. This entry will be devoted primarily to relating that meeting in detail, as it was both fascinating and disturbing.

I was out on the town one night during my second week in Hollywood, at a night spot called The Roaring Lion. It isn't a place usually frequented by celebrities, nor is it owned or sponsored by the studio whose image is reflected in its name. On this night, however, Helen Chandler was there, although no one would ever guess she was a movie star, judging by her sad and solitary presence at a corner table. Being fairly knowledgeable about the motion picture industry, it didn't take me long to recognize her. As I sat there by myself drinking a whiskey and soda, I observed her carefully. She was drinking quite heavily and appeared to have little regard for her symbolic status in the public eye. She also wore a very real, un-celluloid-like troubled expression on her lovely face. After I'd been there for over an hour, and no one had approached her, I decided, with a little assistance from the alcohol, to try and strike up a conversation with her. I struggled to appear confident as I strode towards her table.

"Excuse me, madam, but aren't you Helen Chandler?" I asked cautiously.

She rolled her eyes in an obviously drunken manner. "And who are you- some producer that wants li'l' ole me to star in your movie?" She gulped down the remainder of her drink. "Do me a favor, mister, and buy me another, will ya?"

Seeing an opportunity if ever there was one, I smiled roguishly at her. "I'll buy you as many drinks as you like, if you allow me to sit down and have the pleasure of talking with you, Miss Chandler."

"Suit yourself. It's a free country."

After signaling a waiter and ordering another Manhattan for her, I offered her a cigarette. She readily accepted, and I lit one up for myself as well. I began the conversation by telling her how much I'd enjoyed *Dracula*.

"Yeah, that was kind of fun, but that's probably where it all started." She was staring at me for the first time with semi-focused eyes.

I dared to question her further about her curious statement.

"Exactly what do you mean by 'where it all started'?"

She laughed out loud. "Oh, I don't imagine you're in this business, are you?"

"No, I'm afraid not. To be perfectly honest about it, I'm what you movie people probably hate almost as much as critics- a starry-eyed fan on a two week vacation out here." I felt, as I usually do, that being candid would work to my advantage.

"Well, I'll be glad to give you my autograph- you're the first one who's asked for it in quite a while." She started rummaging through her purse for a pen.

"No, wait. I don't want your autograph."

She looked sad, almost tragic. "No? Oh well, join the crowd. What do you want, then?"

I took a long swallow of my cocktail. "Please don't be offended- I'm not interested in anyone's autograph. If you were John Barrymore or Mary Pickford, I'd feel the same. I am, however, a lover of film, and I am frankly fascinated at meeting a star. I would just like to talk with you, if you don't mind."

"I don't mind, dear, but there are a lot more famous actresses than me to talk to. Of course, they probably wouldn't talk to you, though. So, you know my name and have an unfair advantage on me. What's yours?" She seemed less smashed now.

"Sam Hancock. I'm pleased to meet you." I held out my hand and she shook it limply. I was surprised at how cold and delicate her skin felt. I wouldn't go to the lengths of not washing that hand, but it's likely that I will break down and tell people about it. "I haven't seen you in any movies for some time now, Miss Chandler. Are you purposely staying away from them?"

She laughed again as she put out her cigarette. "You're very observant. There aren't many people out there who would know if I ever made another film or not. But, ever since it started, no one's asked me to be in one."

She had made the same cryptic reference to "it" twice now, and I counted that as one too many times to be dismissed as drunken babbling. "If you don't mind my asking- and I realize I already have, but you didn't answer me- what do you mean by 'ever since it started'?"

Her eyes roamed all about the place, which was not very crowded, and, seemingly satisfied that no one was eavesdropping, she leaned towards me and whispered in my ear. "Tell me, do you believe there are things that can't be explained?"

I had to remain noncommittal, seeing as how she wasn't being specific. "That depends. What sort of unexplained things?"

She grasped my hand firmly and looked me straight in the eye. "There are those out here who share the supposed fictional appetites of the title character in my most famous picture."

I thought for a minute before I spoke again. For some strange reason, I found myself growing slightly nervous over this preposterous notion. The fact she had starred in a highly acclaimed horror movie that I had seen a great many times certainly lent credibility to the ghostly quality in her voice. "Are you talking about real...vampires?"

She answered in the same frail tone that had frightened audiences so much in *Dracula*. "What do you think I'm talking about?"

I lit up another cigarette. "Do you mean to say there are really such things as vampires, and that some of them are here, in Hollywood?" I'm sure my incredulity must have been visible on my face.

She smiled sadly and nodded. "I can see that you don't believe me, and I don't blame you. I thought it was nonsense, too, at first. But then one of my friends... oh, I've told you too much already! I need another drink." She began frantically searching for a waiter.

She had whet my curiosity too much now, however, and I didn't intend to let her stop until she'd quenched it. "Miss Chandler, I can see that this is painful for you to discuss, but you did bring it up and I'm a very inquisitive man. Please, tell me more; I'd like to help you, if I can."

The poor creature surely appeared as if she needed someone's help as she smiled back politely. "Would you really help me, really and truly? Oh, but no one can." Her cocktail arrived and she drank half of it before continuing. "I don't see that it makes any difference now; if you must know, I suppose it can't hurt to tell you. But I won't be held responsible for anything that happens."

I frowned. "I can't imagine what you mean by that."

She sighed in response and smoothed her clinging dress, which accentuated her lithe form. Taking a deep breath, her words flowed melodiously: "It all began just over a year ago, when I met this young, struggling actress. Well, I'll never forget what it felt like to be one- it hasn't been that long- and I always try to help them when I can. Anyway, to make a long story short, this actress- well, actually the poor thing never did get to act in anything, never became anything more than an extra- anyhow, we became friends. She started confiding in me, like friends do with one another, telling me about all the problems she was having with her boyfriend, who was the strangest egg you'd ever want to meet. Well, eventually she just came right out and told me that he was a vampire. Now, I can see by your expression that you're skeptical; I was too, until I met *him*. He looked more like a perfectly cast vampire than Bela Lugosi ever dreamed of, dear. A few weeks after she'd told me this, she knocked at my door in the middle of the night, in a perfectly hysterical state. She begged me to kill her because her boyfriend and some of his fellow fiends were hounding her to join them, and she was terrified at the thought of spending eternity in the undead state, always on the hunt for fresh blood. At that point, I still never believed she was in any real danger, but I made her stay there in my apartment until she'd calmed down. Shortly before sunrise, she suddenly announced that she was leaving. She said, as she walked out the door, and I'll never forget her words, 'I must go now- I can hear *them* calling.' After she left my house that morning, she hasn't been seen again, by me or anyone else."

Completely captivated by her tale and her charming, visibly theatrical style of telling it, I reluctantly interrupted her. "Excuse me, Miss Chandler, but how do you know that? Did you check with the police, or her family?"

"Certainly I reported it to the police- not the part about vampires of course, they'd never believe that- but they were unable to help; there wasn't any evidence of foul play, she was of legal age, and, like they told me, 'there are lots of missing persons in California.' As for her family, as far as I know, they're back in the Midwest somewhere. Like a lot of people in this business, she changed her name as soon as she came out here, so I don't even know what her real name was." She finished her drink and stared at me expectantly, probing for a reaction.

It would be difficult not to react to such a story. Growing rather protective of this famous woman, I boldly ventured to pat her hand. "What about this odd boyfriend- maybe we could question him."

69

She laughed again. "You must go to the movies a lot. This is not *Dracula*, and the villain isn't Bela Lugosi. They took a good friend away from me, and they know *I* know. But, at any rate, I did try to find her boyfriend the day after she disappeared. I knew where he lived and I went there. His landlord said he'd left unexpectedly and he didn't know where he'd gone. Lucky for me he wasn't there, I suppose." She took another deep breath and squinted at her watch. "Oh, my Lord. I didn't realize it was that late. I really must be going."

By this point, I was completely smitten with her and overcome by a sense of chivalry that was compelling me to help her. I implored her to stay a while longer.

She took my hand and squeezed it. "I really am sorry, but I do have to go. It was very nice to have someone to talk to." She arose from the table unsteadily.

"Hey, Helen!"

A young man was striding towards us with an earnest expression on his face. I recognized him instantly as Dwight Frye, another member of the cast in *Dracula*, who'd portrayed Mr. Renfield.

"Oh, Dwight! Am I glad to see you!" Helen almost fell towards him, and he caught her in his arms.

"What are you doing out in this condition? You haven't been talking again, have you?" Dwight Frye stared at me. "And who is this fellow?"

"Sam Hancock. I'm a great admirer of your work, Mr. Frye." I extended my hand.

He ignored this overture. "How do you know my name?" He demanded.

I lit up a cigarette. "Why, I'd know you anywhere, Mr. Frye. I think you're one of the best character actors in Hollywood."

"Don't worry, Dwight. He's only a tourist." Helen assured him.

"Hmmmm... well, anyhow, we better leave." Dwight took her by the elbow and started to lead her away.

"Wait, Miss Chandler, why did you tell me all of this? Aren't you afraid?" I exclaimed.

"Listen, I'll tell you what, let's meet back here tomorrow night at nine o'clock. Same table, okay?" She stumbled as she leaned towards me and grabbed my arm to steady herself.

"Do you want me to call you a cab?" I asked.

"Don't be silly, there's lots of cabs around here, and I'm not too drunk to stand and wait for one."

"I'll be with her, she'll be alright." Dwight Frye said.

I stood up and started following them. "Before you leave, there's one thing I have to know. Have you told anyone else about all of this?"

She laughed louder than she had all night. "Why do you think I'm not working?" She replied, as she sashayed out of the place on the arm of the diminutive character actor.

She never showed up the next night. I wasn't really surprised, and when I tried to look her up, I discovered her phone number was unlisted. Since she wasn't a very big star, none of the tour guides knew where she lived, and I was left without any means of contacting her again. Her mind-boggling story still haunts me, and I shudder to think of the fantastic implications should it somehow be true. It would change one's perspective on everything. I might add here that the manner in which this entry was written, recounting exact conversations and intimate details, was not meant to be perfectly accurate. I am just beginning this journal, and I want to make it as interesting as possible to read. From time to time, I intend to describe all my experiences in the same fashion, and hopefully this will provide a greater degree of readability, for myself or any others who might chance upon it.

As for the rest of my trip, after meeting Helen Chandler and spending an evening drinking with her and listening to her relate such an incredible tale, any movie stars I saw during the remainder of my stay were of secondary interest.

Hiram Buckley whistled to himself in admiration. *I'm looking forward to meeting this Sam Hancock*, he thought, and settled back to read some more. It was going to be, undoubtedly, another sleepless night for the one-time pride of the local community college.

5
WHEN THE DOO-DOO WOPPERS COME PRO-PROTESTING
ALONG

From *More Unanswered Questions*, an unpublished pamphlet by
Abner Billingsly, pg. 14:
"Is there actually some written documentation somewhere verifying
the claims that historical figures such as Alexander the Great,
Michaelangelo, Socrates, and Leonardo Da Vinci were homosexuals?"

While Professor Buckley spent the night poring over Sam Hancock's
journal, his two erstwhile fellow heroes slept. They were not resting
peacefully, however.

Brisbane, although he certainly wasn't an insomniac, had, like
Waldo, long been plagued by recurrent nightmares. The fredneck was
presently tossing and turning his way through "Brisbane Wrock's 500th
Fat Boy Nightmare":

Fade to a junior high school gymnasium. It is the day of the annual
tryouts for the Rimrockers, the school basketball team. At least a third of
the eighth grade boys are attempting to win one of the highly coveted
spots on the squad. One of them is 13 year old Brisbane Wrock. He is the
fattest kid in the school, but is determined to defy all the odds and make
the team. The fat kid is slow, but has great hand-eye coordination in all
sports, and in this one his deadly aim makes him a superior outside shot in
comparison to the other boys. Young Brisbane is a lover of all sports and
is naturally talented at most of them, but his ballooning weight is
becoming an increasing handicap, especially in the way his peers perceive
him.

The tryout begins and chubby Brisbane excels in all areas. He
makes a higher percentage of free throws than anyone else, converts more
layups in the allotted minute than anyone else, and during the intrasquad
games he scores more points than anyone else. The coaches soon cease
their asinine postures of barely-controlled hysteria, and actually notice
that he can play the game better than most of the others there. Brisbane is
definitely one of the 12 best basketball players at the tryout by any
standard.

In the locker room after the tryout, the head coach calls out the
names of the 12 boys who have been selected to represent the school as
this year's Rimrockers. Young Brisbane holds his breath as each one is
announced until finally his dream comes true- his name is called out as

72

one of the Rimrockers! Some of the boys aren't laughing now, and a few of the more humane ones actually congratulate him. He remains on cloud nine throughout that wonderful Friday evening, and the weekend that follows is one of the most pleasant he has ever experienced.

On Monday morning, several people come up and congratulate Brisbane on what they all recognize as a monumental accomplishment. Then, during his regular gym class, he notices that the physical education teacher, who is also the Rimrockers' head coach, is ignoring him completely. Brisbane plans to talk to him after class anyway, to thank him for looking past his plump body and basing his evaluation on merit. When the class ends and Brisbane approaches the coach, he motions the fat youngster into his office. Trying to appear unhappy with his task but betraying a certain sense of sadistic relish, the coach tells Brisbane that there was a mistake, he'd confused him with another boy with a similar last name, and that he was sorry to inform him he wasn't a Rimrocker.

Needless to say, the chubby 13 year old is crushed. He knows that the coach called his name- he certainly recognized his own name when he heard it. And what about all the boys who knew it and had been congratulating him the past three days? But he doesn't argue with the coach- after all, there were many methods that gym teachers used to embarrass fat kids, and Brisbane had heard enough derisive taunts in his life.

Something positive grows out of this episode; Brisbane is propelled by the terrible humiliation to go on a diet and lose a great deal of weight. Although he remains a bit chunky, no one will ever call him names again. He'll weather his share of adolescent catcalls, but will be spared any further exposure to those vicious, time-tested words which have long been utilized to great effect, in countless variations, by fine upstanding men, women and children everywhere. Unfortunately, the incident causes another, less wholesome change in Brisbane. He swears off sports completely and never tries out for any team in high school, despite being much slimmer and faster than before. Fade out.

Waldo was not being bothered by nightmares that night, due to the fact he wasn't remaining asleep long enough to have one. Actually, Waldo's insomnia was a much more frequent malady than his odd dreams were. The problem had begun in his childhood, long before he lost his parents, when little Waldo would lay awake all night but pretend to be asleep because his parents would scold him if he didn't. Waldo's mother and father were basically good parents, and felt, as most people do, that a good night's sleep was both normal and necessary, particularly for a growing child. He remembered distinctly how every year, on the last night of summer vacation, he would become so excited about returning to school the next day that he would not sleep at all. In adulthood, Waldo would engage in a bit of self-analysis and theorize that his anticipation at such times, which was curious since he generally hated school, was but a childish precursor of his adult tastes. Waldo was a lover of hype; his powerful imagination found more joy in the expectation of things than in their actual fruition. Each Christmas eve, Waldo's restlessness reached a peak; he never in his life had slept a wink on that most magical of nights. Of course, many, if not most kids who sleep normally during the rest of the year become insomniacs on Christmas eve, but Waldo carried this a step further. Even now, at the age of 28, and with no more toys awaiting him, he could not sleep at all on Christmas eve.

Waldo, sitting in bed with his eyes opened as wide as a farmer's at a flea market, put out another in a long line of cigarettes and tried to stop thinking about the trip he was on the verge of undertaking. His sense of apprehension, at all times a powerful facet of his personality, was apparent in the sweat on his palms and the acceleration of his heartbeat. Before he'd retired, or at least attempted to, Waldo had taken some of his grandfather's unpublished pamphlets from the library downstairs and brought them back to his bedroom. Tossing them absentmindedly on the floor, where they lay like some idiosyncratic, non-Persian rug, he'd left them there to provide a sense of security, as if they were a bottle of tranquilizers or a favorite old blanket. Waldo's sleeping problems, however, were not about to be cured by such whimsical devices, and eventually he signaled his capitulation to the forces of insomnia by throwing off the covers and turning on his bedside lamp. Sifting through the pile of papers with a series of loud, frustrated sighs, Waldo eventually picked up a satire entitled *An Unauthorized Playboy Interview With Abner Billingsly*, which seemed a promising one to relax, or even dose off to, and began reading:

PLAYBOY: In glancing through your voluminous collection of unpublished material, the question must be asked: why haven't you published anything?

A.B.: *I'm afraid I can't give you an adequate explanation for that. Let's just say that there are reasons why, and they are quite logical.*

PLAYBOY: Couldn't get anyone to publish them, eh?

A.B.: *You men at Playboy are certainly qualified to judge literary talent, so I won't quibble with you.*

PLAYBOY: Hmmm. Well, let's go on. From poring over your works, one may come to the conclusion that you are an angry man who despises society and all who populate it. Is that a fair assumption?

A.B.: *Yes.*

PLAYBOY: Is there anything about this world you don't hate?

A.B.: *Certainly. If I didn't find something to give me a semblance of pleasure, I would have beheaded myself long ago. I enjoy, much like your playmates, long wet kisses, gentle sushi bars, modeling and/or acting, and men with lots of money. Just kidding. I love reading many different poets and writers, most of whom, unfortunately, are no longer with us. I am grateful for the financial independence which allows me to pursue my investigative work and the writings that emerge from it. In spite of myself, I still receive a wonderful warmth at Christmas time. And of course there is my grandson Waldo, who is the greatest gift anyone could have and brings me the most satisfaction of all.*

PLAYBOY: Well, it's comforting to know that you're capable of feeling enjoyment, but most of your writings reflect the intense negativity you seem to harbor about almost everything. Why do you project such a pessimistic view?

A.B.: *Anyone who has a heart and even a shadow of common sense cannot help but feel that everything is wrong. Further observation yields the unflattering picture of cohesive design, not misguided happenstance, behind all of the undeniable atrocities. Pessimism is a forced condition; one would love to be bubbly and upbeat. I am probably one of the last permitted pessimists; they are rumored to be perfecting some incredibly advanced drugs in their secret laboratories. In the future, perhaps they will nab potential naysayers in infancy and prescribe one of these, and where pharmacology fails, surgical alteration always remains an option. They desire a population of pep squad members, cheering every injustice heaped upon them as if it were worthy of a bonfire rally.*

PLAYBOY: Just who are "they?"

A.B.: *They are the crux of the paranoid biscuit. Intrepid right-wingers and left-wingers have chased different portions of them over the centuries without success. It is only within the last 50 years or so that a great deal of suppressed literature has been produced by many dead paranoid writers. The right-wingers monitor the misdeeds of the communists, the Federal Reserve system, the I.R.S., the Council on Foreign Relations, the Trilateral Commission, the United Nations, the Masons, international bankers, and of course the Jews. The left-wingers, on the other hand, are more subdued these days and much less interesting. They prefer to watch the actions of the C.I.A., the F.B.I., the military industrial complex, the Business Roundtable, and the major oil companies. Neither group connects any of their favorites with those in the opposing camp, thereby eliminating whatever slight possibility may exist of overthrowing them.*

PLAYBOY: Let's discuss some other issues. What do you think of television today, in the late 1970's?

75

A.B.: *I think that it has reached a point where it is impossible to parody it- it is self-parody.*

PLAYBOY: So you see nothing worthwhile in the present trend of t.v. shows tackling relevant subjects, instead of the standard comedy and dramatic fare?

A.B.: *There's certainly nothing wrong with relevance, but I hardly think that requiring every program to bear the stamp of some quasi-liberal authoritative body is an improvement.*

PLAYBOY: What do you mean?

A.B.: *I mean that it's as predictable as 1930's-era Hollywood was. At that time, the few black characters in movies were either dancers or housekeepers. You could depend on them to be harmless, comforting caricatures and of course it was wrong and also quite absurd. Now, however, if you see a black character, you can safely guess that it will be a ludicrous, angelic portrayal bearing as little resemblance to reality as the old negative stereotypes. Now television has determined it will handle issues that the establishment, of which t.v. is an integral part, has permitted it to discuss. These issues always center around a buffoonish white male who is ignorant, bigoted, and oftentimes criminal. Countering this image is the intelligent, understanding minority or "career woman", who is childishly opposed on some topic by the white male ignoramus. A debate ensues, and the minority or woman totally devastates the white male, whose pitiful, ungrammatical arguments could have been more credibly waged by the average preschooler. It's interesting that those who call themselves liberals want to bring these topics to t.v. and claim this as a breakthrough against censorship, while at the same time demanding that no Black, no Jew, no homosexual, no minority members of any kind are ever to be presented as saying or doing something as ostensibly fictitious characters that could possibly be construed in what these liberals consider a demeaning light. Unless, of course, they are minority members with no powerful lobby, such as Polish Americans, Arab Americans, and Eskimos. In modern lingo, the liberals' objection appears not to be with the justifiably denigrated Steppin' Fetchit type roles, but rather with anything that shows a minority to be capable of wrongdoing. Some of us would recognize such frailties as part of human behavior. If that's not censorship, I don't know what is. They've even attempted to rectify the sins of the past by mutilating old films and television shows that feature what they think to be inappropriate depictions of minorities. Splicing out scenes of Buckwheat's hair standing on end or Stymie expressing a liking for watermelon, as has been done in regards to the wonderful old Our Gang shorts, reveals the liberals' irrationality more than any shortcomings on the part of the films' creators. Those films could only offend those who* want to control free artistic expression, and such people do not deserve to be labeled liberal or open-minded in any true sense of the word. No, I don't think Norman Lear's world is any more significant than Jethro Bodine's, and nowhere near as interesting.

PLAYBOY: Well, how do you feel about Blacks, and minority rights in general?

A.B.: *What do you mean by Blacks? Am I supposed to know the millions of black people in the world, or even all those in the United States, well enough to cast judgment on them as a race? What do you want me to say- what the typical phony celebrity would? Of course I oppose real discrimination against them, or any other group. I think that no one should be treated any differently than anyone else because of their sex, skin pigmentation, religion, or their high-pitched voice, for that matter. But at the same time, it is absurd to label any criticism of Blacks as racist. This has fostered an attitude of fear among Whites, even at the top of the corporate ladder, where highly paid leaders in luxurious offices quake at the prospect of discrimination suits. I don't believe that being scared of someone because they're a certain color will solve the very real racial problems in this country.*

PLAYBOY: What are your views on sex?

A.B.: *Let me turn that around. When is Playboy going to have a plain, average looking girl as a centerfold? Why must you discriminate yourselves?*

PLAYBOY: Uh...do you think nudity should be allowed on network television?

A.B.: *I just happen to have a theory regarding that, as I seem to about nearly every subject known to man. I think that, to improve the quality of network programming, the executives in charge should force the females that star in their shows, whom they hired for one purpose only, to finally reveal those reasons in front of the cameras and stop the titillation. I believe that after watching a few performances in the nude, the frustrated male audience, at any rate, would realize there was nothing of substance to be tuning in for and might even be moved to demand more meaningful entertainment. This would include the female newscasters, who amazingly enough all share the same vacuous look that propelled their counterparts on the sitcoms and soap operas to fame. Isn't it remarkable that feminist leaders, who constantly whine about trivial things that set the sexes at each others' throats, never complain about this? Although I'm hardly the candidate to do so, I'll ask the question for them: why are all the most qualified women, assuming that a personnel office exists at those television stations to read their resumes and sort their credentials, who graduate from journalism school sexy and desirable? Wouldn't it be logical to think that at least one ugly, or* even average-looking woman could earn high enough marks to qualify? Or are the women chosen for television jobs evaluated in some other manner? Oh, well...

PLAYBOY: Don't you think that's a little extreme?

A.B.: *Don't force me to quote Barry Goldwater.*

PLAYBOY: Do you believe in God?

A.B.: *I wish I possessed the faith that some people do; unfortunately I don't. But I'd never be idiotic enough to maintain there is no God; creation proves some type of creator exists. Whether it's omnipotent, or even sane, is open to debate. I do find, however, that the forces behind it all seem to have a certain enmity for Jesus Christ. How many movies, for instance, can go five minutes without some character taking his name in vain? Why, they're probably the two most used words in film, and as my pappy once told me, if they're on the wrong side of everything else...*

PLAYBOY: How about evolution?

A.B.: *Come on, now. Surely you cosmopolitan types here at Playboy don't believe in such superstitious nonsense. But let me ask you—how about bullet holes in ancient fossils? Ever hear of plaster of paris?*

PLAYBOY: So you distrust science?

A.B.: *What is called science today, yes. I subscribe to the ideal of science: knowledge through experimentation. Scientists have, however, through the course of history, refused to follow this simple ideal. Instead of correlating and investigating all data, science keeps whatever fits in with its preconceived notions and discards everything else. If a Charles Fort uncovers evidence of little frogs falling from the sky, science is compelled to reject the reports immediately on the logical grounds that there are no frogs in the sky and thus none to fall from it. In this way are the thousands of unconnected U.F.O. witnesses dismissed as mistaken because there are no unexplained objects flying in the sky. That kind of reasoning reminds me of the Warren Commission counsel who wanted to use as evidence of Oswald's guilt in the Kennedy assassination the "fact" that he'd shot a Dallas policeman. No, I don't think I care for science.*

PLAYBOY: So you're an assassination buff, too?

A.B.: *If a buff is one who objects to a giant falsehood, yes. If a buff is one who believes that finding the real murderers of President John F. Kennedy is the pressing problem facing America today, yes.*

PLAYBOY: You don't accept that Oswald acted alone?

A.B.: *The evidence is so overwhelmingly obvious in exculpating Oswald and, in fact, proving it impossible for him to have shot anyone, that I am beginning to believe the main thrust of the cover-up was not in suppressing things, but in leaving it all like a tantalizing trail of breadcrumbs for various official defenders to compete with each other to invent the most humorous explanation refuting the exposure of it. The fact is that most of the media have not merely ignored this issue, which would be bad enough, but have joined the cover-up in a partisan role, spewing out the fabrications that are scripted for them. It is totally inexcusable and the only conclusion one can come to is that all of the major media know who killed J.F.K. and are in their employ.*

PLAYBOY: Now, you've made a serious accusation here. Do you consider Playboy to be covering-up?

A.B.: *From what I've read, it has followed all the official guidelines devised by the establishment.*

PLAYBOY: Thank you, Mr. Billingsly.

Waldo, his eyelids growing heavy, tossed the pamphlet aside and turned the light off. It was nearing dawn and whatever sleep he got could only assist the weary, inexperienced traveler in preparing for the journey ahead of him.

By mid-afternoon, Waldo, Brisbane, and the Professor were conscious and moving about. A few hours later, in unseasonably chilly, overcast weather, the three of them packed themselves and their meager belongings into Brisbane's decidedly un-fredneck-like 1965 Dodge Dart. Stocked with an ample supply of beer, a few changes of clothes, some eclectic music, and far more extremist writings than seemed necessary- like a briefcase full of Hiram Buckley's *Force Of Habit*, Sam Hancock's journal, and a number of Waldo's grandfather's unpublished pamphlets- they were just preparing to leave when suddenly a figure came rushing towards them, shouting and waving his arms desperately.

"Waldo! Waldo! Wait! Don't go!"

Waldo, sitting in the passenger seat, rolled down his window. "Big Abdullah! What's the matter?"

Big Adbullah was a chubby Iranian barber whom Old Hoss held a rather distant friendship with. Waldo hadn't seen him in quite some time, and it hadn't crossed his mind that Big Abdullah might have any information about his grandfather's disappearance. The fact that he'd run all the way from his place of business, which was over three miles away, was evident by the sweat rolling down his bright red face as he thrust his hands against the passenger door. His barrel chest heaving in agony, Big Abdullah attempted to speak.

"Waldo...I...must...tell...you..." The Iranian barber was trying mightily to catch his breath. "I...just met.....and they..."

"Who the fuck is this dude?" Brisbane, who'd just started the engine, demanded impatiently.

79

"This is Abdullah Hassan, a friend of my grandfather's." Waldo explained. "Please, Big Abdullah, go on. We were just about to leave..."

"I know...Waldo, I know." Big Abdullah had nearly recovered. "You see, Waldo, I was...workin' just this afternoon, when these two...gentlemen came in and gave me a message for ya."

"What kind of message?" Waldo nervously asked.

"Well, Waldo, it don't make much sense to me, you see, but they said- that is one of them said, the other didn't do any talking- that you wasn't to be traveling out west." Big Abdullah scratched his balding head. "And, if you did, I hate to tell you this part, Waldo, but he said, and these was his exact words, *tell him it'll be the last trip he ever takes.*"

Professor Buckley was tugging furiously at his tie. "Oh, dear. Waldo, what the-that is-who would say such a thing?"

Waldo shrugged. "I don't know, Professor. Big Abdullah, what did the man who left this message look like?"

"Can You Believe? Well, he was...I think I'd say he was a gypsy. At least he looked like one to me."

Waldo glanced knowingly at Brisbane. "Was his friend a skinhead?"

"Yeah, with *Satan Never Sleeps* on his tee shirt?" The fredneck chimed in.

Big Abdullah nodded. "Do you know them, Waldo?"

"We met them once." Waldo softly replied. "Listen, Big Abdullah, I want to thank you very much for rushing over here to give me the message, but I'm afraid this is a trip that must be taken."

The chubby barber grimaced. "Waldo, do you know what you're doing? I wouldn't want anything to happen to you."

"Yes, Waldo, do you?" Hiram Buckley echoed from the back seat.

"I know what I have to do." Waldo responded firmly. "I'm not really sure what's going on here, but this only strengthens my belief that the answers to my grandfather's disappearance lie in Cornoil, Iowa."

Big Abdullah threw up his hands. "I can't stop you from doing what you got to do, Waldo. Good luck to you."

"Thanks, Big Abdullah." Waldo grasped the Iranian barber's beefy hand.

"Okay man, are you ready now?" Brisbane asked.

"Yes." Waldo lit up a cigarette.

"So long, Waldo. I'll be praying for you." Big Abdullah sadly waved at them as Brisbane's car backed out of the driveway.

Professor Buckley was anxious to learn the details of their encounter with the gypsy and the skinhead, and Waldo related them to him.

"Waldo, my boy," Hiram Buckley struggled to sound old and wise, "this is too much. When the gypsies become involved..."

"What do you mean, Professor?" Brisbane asked.

"Such strange creatures as-that is-have you ever heard what happens when a gypsy dies?" The Professor adjusted his thick spectacles. "All gypsies, wherever they may be, somehow know it when one of them passes on. They'll travel hundreds of miles to attend the funeral. No, when you start encountering gypsies, it can only mean trouble."

Waldo was tingling with anticipation at the prospect of traveling all the way to the far flung fields of Iowa in the quest to find his missing grandfather. Up until this point, with a cross country sojourn staring him in the face, Waldo had unintentionally followed the advice of Ambrose Bierce, who defined a road as merely "a strip of land along which one may pass from where it is too tiresome to be to where it is futile to go."

In a matter of minutes they were on the capital beltway. Traffic was surprisingly sparse for a late Friday afternoon, and Professor Buckley was quick to note it.

"I say-that is-have you ever seen so few cars on the road?" He asked, still tugging at his yellow tie.

"Shit man, this is a fucking weekday." The fredneck agreed. "I know I haven't been in your area long, but don't you have a rush hour?"

"Washington D.C.-that is-this area is renowned for its rush hours." Professor Buckley informed him. "And I find the absence of one today to be most perplexing. Particularly, Waldo, in light of that terrifying message the barber brought you."

Waldo inhaled deeply. "Professor, I know something really peculiar is happening, and the lack of traffic might even be connected to it. That message certainly was. But, don't you see, all this means that my grandfather really must have gone to Iowa."

"I'm sorry, dude, but I don't see that." Brisbane said.

"Brisbane, that gypsy mentioning to us, and then leaving a warning, about going out west..."

"Can only mean," Hiram Buckley interrupted him, "that we may be on the verge of a personal introduction to the forces we've long suspected were out there somewhere. I've written about Them, speculated about Them, for a good many years, my boy, and I'm not certain I'm ready to meet Them face to face. Are you, Waldo?"

"I don't know." Waldo answered quietly.

The sun eventually peeked out from behind the clouds, just in time for its setting, and seemed in doing so to lighten their mood and lift their spirits.

Waldo pulled a pen and pad from his jacket and suggested they pass the time by thinking of lists that would never make it into the best-selling "Book of Lists" series. This idea might have been scoffed at by more conventional types accustomed to playing license tag poker as they

81

traveled, but Waldo's two off-beat compatriots voiced no objections to it. Brisbane, popping open a can of beer almost simultaneously as he did so, accorded it a proper fredneck salute by belching his approval.

Utilizing their cumulative reserve of twisted creative juices, they soon were cracking themselves up with such lists as: *10 Comedians Who Are Actually Funny, 5 Citizens Who Understand The Theory Of Relativity, 10 Television Shows Not Set In New York Or California, 5 American Carpet Stores Not Run By Iranians,* and *5 Multi-Millionaires Who Actually Paid Taxes.* Eventually, they came up with *The 10 Favorite Words Of Country Bumpkins* and *The 10 Favorite Words Of Inner-City Youth*:

Bumpkins	Inner City Youth
1. Turkey	1. Motherfucker
2. Nigger	2. Nigger
3. Ain't	3. Ain't
4. Bad (former inner-city term)	4. Yo (former Goober Pyle term)
5. Cent (as in 50 cent)	5. Cent (as in 50 cent)
6. Funky (former inner-city term)	6. Aunt (pronounced correctly)
7. Distributor	7. Homeboy
8. Alternator	8. Bitch
9. Pickup	9. Nike
10. Cashmoney	10. Cashmoney

While formulating these lists, Waldo, Brisbane, and the Professor held a lengthy discussion on the topic of slang terms. All agreed that, whatever the expression, if it originated in black circles it would eventually find its way into the waiting mouths of the country bumpkins. Waldo remarked that it must give the inner-city youths a certain vicarious satisfaction to watch the bumpkins parrot phrases that they had grown tired of.

Picking up steam, the hysterically funny threesome culminated their efforts with *The Minutest Of U.S. Minorities*:

1. Poor professional athletes
2. Rich U.F.O. contactees
3. Unemployed Orientals
4. Vegetarian rednecks
5. Infertile poor women
6. Old black musicians who aren't legends

7. Unsuccessful offspring of the successful
8. Successful offspring of the unsuccessful
9. Jewish janitors
10. Elected third party political candidates
11. White people under 45 who dislike the Beatles
12. Neo-Nazi celebrities

While partaking of their innocuous fun, Waldo and Brisbane had also been consuming beer at an alarming rate. To Professor Buckley they seemed like a pair of nearly drunken anachronisms, scoffing at the inferior world outside; oblivious to shadowy figures appearing periodically along the hillsides of the beltway, oblivious to Dylan, warning of heart attack machines over the back seat speakers, oblivious, finally, to the blue and white patrol car with the flashing red lights.

"Uh, oh...shit!" Brisbane was jarred out of his stupor by that most fearsome of all sights in his rear view mirror.

Waldo drained his beer and hurriedly stuffed it under his seat, the Professor let loose with a number of "oh dear's" and tugged a little harder on his tie, and the fredneck pulled over to the side of the road and waited, sweat pouring out of him as rapidly as the beer had gone in.

The policeman sauntered up to the driver's window. "Sir, do you realize that you were weaving all over the road?" He asked, with the self-confidence that stems from the public perception of infallibility.

"No, uh, I thought I was driving alright." Brisbane's tone was much milder than usual.

"Well, you weren't and you're very lucky not to have injured yourself or others. Have you been drinking any alcoholic beverages, sir?"

Brisbane swallowed hard. *How do you answer a question like that,* he wondered. The frightened fredneck solved his dilemma by refusing to respond. He also could not hold back another loud and satisfying belch. This apparently sealed his fate.

"Sir, would you step out of the car, please."

Brisbane hypnotically obeyed, as if he had an option not to, and in an efficiently short period of time he was handcuffed and in the back seat of the patrol car. The fredneck was still awaiting his Miranda rights as a towing company was called to gingerly transport his decidedly un-fredneck-like vehicle to a safer place.

After forcing them all to wait anxiously while he scrutinized his clipboard for ten minutes, the officer hustled Waldo and Professor Buckley into the police car, without a word of explanation. As Waldo sat there between his fredneck friend and the trembling ex-history teacher, he was as stunned as most middle-class Americans are in such situations. He knew not to vocalize his astonishment, however, as there were no t.v.

83

cameras rolling (and thus no rights being read), to afford them protection from a trumped up charge of resisting arrest with a matching set of bruises.

Well, if I ever had any doubts about the seriousness of the crusade against drunk drivers... Waldo, who was unsure of what it was he was being arrested for, closed his eyes and battled the temptation to speculate about the potential interaction among corrupt policemen, strict judges, vengeful lobbyists, lackadaisical guards, and crowded jail cells.

The Afro Anarchists, having returned to their favorite corner of southeast Washington, D.C., were relaxing there as the last bits of burnt orange sunlight disappeared below the horizon. Fontaine and Bucktooth were engaged in a heated dispute over whether or not Bucktooth had consumed more than his share of the dope they'd been smoking. Phosphate, the erudite leader of the doo-wop trio, leaned against a lamppost and finished off the reefer as he watched the two verbal combatants with more than a trace of amusement.

"Gentlemen, please." The top doo-wopper, with a style epitomizing what some anonymous trend-setter had meant decades earlier by the term "cool," allowed them to bicker back and forth sufficiently before interfering. "Does this disagreement seem to be a suitable one for civilized parties to become involved in? Isn't it just a bit capricious? Why not shake hands and settle the matter amicably?"

Fontaine and Bucktooth, both strongly influenced by the head Afro Anarchist, melted almost immediately into sheepish, apologetic figures falling all over themselves with remorse.

Like a demanding headmaster, Phosphate nodded his approval. Reaching into his windbreaker, he pulled out a sheet of paper. "I've written a new song, gentlemen. Why don't we rehearse it?"

Counting to three, he began crooning *The Watermelon Blues*:

"Brother, if you listen to the N.A.A.C.P.
You're lucky 'cause they never speak to me
They tell me how to talk and vote and act
But I like watermelon and that's a fact
I like it juicy and I like it ripe
Don't tell me I'm a stereotype
If I want chicken, if I want ribs
Then tell Col. Sanders where I live
Now, I believe in rights, don't you doubt
But it's just food we're talking about
If I could ask for something from the N.A.A.C.P.
Black history month isn't what it would be

And as for the folks at the United Way
They haven't helped me out today
My stomach's growlin', turn off the news
And cut into these watermelon blues."

A rather large crowd had gathered, and puzzled by the song, began eyeing the trio suspiciously. As Phosphate's voice faded into the stillness of the night, their less than appreciative audience circled the hapless lads and edged in closer. The gang of young black males was obviously irked at the content of Phosphate's lyrics. While scores of unconcerned motorists whizzed by in their locked automobiles, faces hungry with anger glared at the vulnerable threesome from all sides.

Being surrounded by such potential danger left Fontaine and Bucktooth, as it would any lost, unsuspecting tourists, shaking in their sneakers. Phosphate, however, was capable of analyzing the situation from a bemused distance, even as he stood in its explosive center. After a frightening period of suspense, a short teenager with a brown stocking cap pulled down halfway over his eyes elbowed his way to the front.

Staring directly at an unmoved Phosphate, he broke the silence loudly. "Hey motherfucker, what kind of motherfuckerin' shit you doin'?"

Phosphate calmly replied, "Ah, the spokesman for the mob. Well, my young friend, your question is quite complex. It merits an in depth response, and thus I hesitate to offend you with my humble superficiality."

A tall, bony youth jabbed his finger in Fontaine's chest. "Look, motherfucker, we gonna cut your black asses!"

Fontaine attempted to reply, but ended up looking like a second-rate imitation of Barney Fife. Except this wasn't Mayberry, and they weren't on television.

Phosphate now spoke with a restrained anger. "First, may I remind you that you outnumber us ten to one, and your threats therefore display a startling lack of courage. Second, I wish I had a dollar for every 'motherfucker' you fellows spit out. Third, why don't you be more specific in your criticism of our song?"

The short teenager who'd spoken first seemed a little intimidated by the top doo-wopper's forthright attitude, and wasn't as cocky now. "Yo, moth...uh, man, we don't like the shit you was saying."

"What particular shit are you referring to?" Phosphate asked, realizing that he'd gained the upper hand.

"Well, I don't know exactly, but you sounded like you was saying you ain't a nigger or somethin'." The one-time leader of the pack's lack of confidence was visible as he self-consciously tugged his stocking cap down to his nose.

"Young man," Phosphate began lecturing in his earnest, Ward

Cleaver-style monotone, "I do not want anybody to call me a nigger. I do not want to call myself a nigger either. The point of this song- if there is one- and the point of my philosophy in general, is that we who are known as 'Blacks', or 'African-Americans', or whatever it is we label ourselves collectively as, must stop confronting our complexion at every turn, and injecting concern over it into disinterested areas."

The bony finger-jabber was quieter now, too. "What you mean, man?"

"Well, as the song says, I don't base my life on what the N.A.A.C.P., or the United Negro College Fund, or whichever celebrated black reverend happens to be the star of the moment has to say." Phosphate's melodious voice was increasing in volume. "We cannot afford to dwell on the terrible injustices suffered by our ancestors. It is not enjoyable for me to picture my great- grandparents sweating in the cotton fields. Is it for any of you? Then let us move on to more productive matters. Like trying to clean up the neighborhoods we were herded into by greedy politicians, or learning to speak the language properly. How can you be certain you've been discriminated against when you constantly utter profanities and engage in unsundry activities that decent people of all colors and sizes find objectionable? It is only natural for prejudice to exist against ignorance, violence, unfriendliness, and dishonesty. I prefer to believe that the majority of white people dislike the behavior of the most visible Blacks, the ones featured so prominently on nightly newscasts, rather than their skin pigmentation. Citizens of this country who happen to be Black must, in my opinion, learn to assimilate before they disintegrate. As you can see, I have a great deal to say about a lot of crucial issues, and I choose to express myself through the avenue of song. Have I dispelled your concerns, or do you still take offense at anything I've said?"

The crowd of inner-city youngsters had become increasingly captivated by the soaring oratorical brilliance of Phosphate Jefferson. When he finally finished his rambling speech, all those youths who'd so nonchalantly wanted to carve him up only a few minutes earlier were as spellbound as if they'd just heard Martin Luther King, Jr.'s last speech, the stirring and emotional "mine eyes have seen the glory of the coming of the Lord" one.

With his voice slightly quavering, the formerly bitter youth with the stocking cap raised it up to a point where he could see clearly and gazed at Phosphate with tears in his eyes. "Shit man, that was beautiful. I never had a father, and I ain't never heard no black man talk like that before. You ought to be a senator or somethin'."

"Yeah, he's right, holmes."

"You know it, homeboy."

"You'd be one brother they couldn't shut up."

These and other laudatory remarks were being shouted out so enthusiastically that the top doo-wopper found it hard to resist bowing in appreciation. Then some members of the crowd actually began yelling for them to sing *Watermelon Blues* again, the song they'd so adamantly disliked only moments before. Smiling broadly at his new fans and his two greatly relieved partners, Phosphate led the entire group in a rousing encore.

Sometime later, after all the official niceties had been taken care of, Waldo, Brisbane, and the Professor found themselves in a small, filthy cell at Snortin' Reformatory.

Snortin' was a Virginia jail with a notorious reputation, known for its cold-blooded inhabitants. Some of them wore uniforms and carried guns. It was also a substantial nuisance to members of the local community, who were so bold as to raise objections to the amazing numbers of escapees that romped through their neighborhoods with startling regularity.

Since neither Waldo nor Brisbane had anyone to be released to, and Hiram Buckley's wife and kids, rumored to still be living somewhere in the state, had avoided contact with him for many years, the authorities at the county detention center had kindly offered to escort them personally from the congested drunk tank there. This was not out of some latent sense of mercy on their part, however, or due to the lack of available space at all penal institutions. Instead, they had determined that the only way to protect society from such dangerous criminals as Waldo, Brisbane, and Professor Buckley was to send them to Snortin' Reformatory.

Undoubtedly, this even more unreasonable than usual decision of theirs was a result of Brisbane's persistent Lee Harvey Oswald/Bruno Richard Hauptmann-style protestations of innocence. Waldo shuddered to think that, thanks to both the law's and the fredneck's predictable antics, he was in danger of being anally raped for nothing more than drinking a beer in the passenger seat of an automobile.

Waldo was not alone by any means in trembling over an unjust plight. With the recent uproar over drunk driving, arrests had skyrocketed and detention centers all around the country were overflowing with bewildered motorists. Many of these dumbstruck, inebriated souls had been transferred and thoughtfully placed behind the same bars that held back murderers and rapists. Unfortunately for our heroes, they now joined the ranks of these luckless citizens.

Unbeknownst to the plastered pair and the befuddled ex-history teacher, the Afro Anarchists had been arrested once again, for disorderly conduct, shortly after their encounter with the gang of angry youths. Apparently, the trio of doo-woppers had wandered over into the Virginia suburbs, which they were known to do on occasion, and frequented a bar that was appropriately named *Hick Heaven*. After a predictable verbal altercation with the unfriendly customers, they wound up singing their protest songs, loudly and off-key, on top of the tables. A brawl ensued shortly thereafter, and Phosphate, Fontaine, and Bucktooth were among those apprehended and brought to swift justice. As possibly might have been surmised, the Afro Anarchists were about to be thrown into a cell at Snortin' Reformatory containing three prisoners recently arrested on drunk driving charges. Actually, exactly what Waldo and Professor Buckley were being incarcerated for had not been established, although it was clear that a thorough thumbing of legal precedents would result in the discovery of *some* infraction to charge them with.

As the shackled trio of dangerous doo-woppers were led towards the cell containing Waldo, Brisbane, and the Professor, a jet black raven suddenly alighted on the landing outside the barred window there. Staring directly at Waldo, or so it seemed to the unnerved young prisoner, he opened his beak and spoke a single word: *"nevermore"*, then flew away as abruptly as he'd come.

Waldo, an admirer of Edgar Allan Poe's, would normally have found such an occurrence more fascinating than frightening, but after the gypsy's portentous warning, the strange absence of traffic on the highway, and an intricate baseball/spanking fantasy, even those less instinctively paranoid than himself might begin to question their sanity.

"Waldo-that is-oh dear, what is happening?" Professor Buckley was not the ideal person to alleviate anyone's fears.

"Man, you *do* attract some bizarre shit, don't you?" Brisbane, lighting up a cigarette, actually seemed to be enjoying himself.

At that moment, a friendly pair of guards arrived with their latest prey in tow, and, after removing their handcuffs, shoved the three doo-wopping disorderly offenders into the cell.

Waldo scrutinized his new cellmates, and the trio of songsters eyed the allegedly intoxicated duo, as well as the colorfully dressed Professor, with a comparable level of curiosity.

Phosphate eventually made the first overture, extending his hand to Waldo and introducing himself. This friendly gesture broke the ice sufficiently, and within seconds Brisbane was meeting Fontaine, Professor Buckley was greeting Bucktooth, and so on.

"Well, to what grave infraction of the law do you gentlemen owe your incarceration?" Phosphate asked, once the maddening festival of hand-shaking was completed.

Waldo started to respond, but the top doo-wopper's sarcastic query had stoked the radical fires that burned within Brisbane. "For the terrible crime of drunk driving! These asshole cops suck!" The fredneck obviously relished every opportunity to criticize the law enforcement profession. "How the hell can you have a fucking free country when you're subject to arrest for operating a privately owned vehicle while drinking a legally purchased commodity? And then they move us to *jail*? Shit man, there wasn't any reason for Waldo and the Professor to even be arrested. They didn't break any fucking law, and they sent them here with me without charging them with anything! It's fucking ridiculous!"

Waldo was amused to note how the fredneck, while his vocabulary broadened the more incensed he became, was also flinging out the "fucks" like a madman. Apparently, like most frednecks, Brisbane resorted to using an even more profane tongue than usual when he was especially perturbed.

Phosphate eloquently echoed the fredneck's comments. "I couldn't agree with you more, my friend. Any society that allows the citizen to assume financial responsibility without concurrently bestowing upon him the liberty that must naturally follow is false and cannot endure."

Waldo was awestruck by the doo-wopping intellectual's words, which would have sounded at home in the old Virginia House of Burgesses or on the fields of Bull Run. He was also struck by the contrast of the figure speaking them, who looked little like Patrick Henry or Abraham Lincoln.

Brisbane, meanwhile, seemed to take immediately to the sage-like leader of the Afro Anarchists, with the kind of glow in his eyes that had previously been reserved only for the pre-accident work of Bob Dylan.

While Brisbane listened with a rapt attention to Phosphate express his extremist opinions, Waldo tried to converse with Fontaine and Bucktooth. The two Afro Anarchists seemed to be competing against each other for the Most Perfect Stereotype of the Year award, and Waldo, exasperated over his game efforts to engage them in conversation, was grateful when the top doo-wopper finally turned towards him.

"Your friend Brisbane has told me how your grandfather recently disappeared, and that all of you are participating in the effort to find him. He also mentioned that he was a most amazing man of many interests, an intellectual purist who delighted in chronicling his observations in brilliant, unpublished tomes. Do you, by any chance, have some of his writings with you?"

Waldo smiled in appreciation. He reached into his shirt pocket and extracted a folded, well-worn pamphlet. It was a mystery to Waldo how the ever-alert police officers had missed it when they confiscated everything from his comb to his lucky cigarette lighter. The emotional young man had taken a rather romantic vow to keep one of his grandfather's unpublished pamphlets next to his heart at all times during the journey to Iowa, almost as if the scent of the ink would activate any bloodhound instincts within him. Never one to bypass a chance to showcase the work of his beloved grandfather, Waldo proudly handed it to Phosphate.

"Thank you for your kind words about my grandfather. This pamphlet is one of his best, I think."

Phosphate took the pamphlet gingerly and with almost a display of reverence for it. It was entitled *Asylum Is Not Something The Insane Seek*. Unfolding it carefully, the top doo-wopper opened it and began reading:

The Latest, Most Outlandish, Most Fashionable Diseases:

1. *Post Traumatic Stress Syndrome*- I must admit that I am not a veteran. I could never summon up the necessary enthusiasm to trot off mindlessly on a bureaucratic whim, for the glory of losing my life in a faraway land for no discernable cause. That said, the present trend towards the beatification of Vietnam vets disturbs me. I simply can't see the heroism in an individual who is unconstitutionally ordered to fight a senseless war against a decidedly weaker opponent. What I feel for them is pity over their being born at the wrong time, and thus drafted into the whole sordid mess. But now they are out there with all the other pressure groups, demanding their "rights." This is interesting, in that they share the curious ability of all special interest groups to remain oblivious to the very real governmental denial of every citizen's rights. They have taken their complaints to the ultimate degree of absurdity: they have created an emotional illness for themselves. It has been christened *Post Traumatic Stress Syndrome*, and it equips the Vietnam vet with a convenient crutch to dismiss any personal misconduct. Now, I don't believe in veterans being discriminated against, but I think the very nice benefit package which they, like all members of the military, now enjoy, compares favorably to nearly all such benefits that average working men and women are presently receiving. In my mind, anyone who fought in Vietnam certainly went through hell, but no more so than youngsters at Valley Forge or Normandy. What the world needs is an end to this transparent financial racket called war, not another mental illness.

2. *Post Partum Depression Syndrome*- This is a brand new term which serves to erase the guilt of mothers who drown their babies in bathtubs and/or throw them off of bridges. Yes, you read that correctly. Now it is possible for a woman to kill her baby (and no need for a messy abortion-like debate over it) and claim her actions to be the result of this recently discovered "illness." As far as I can determine, no father has yet been able to contract the disease, but it is likely to prove contagious.

3. *Anorexia*- Because of television and its constant glorification of

thinness, a "disease" of this nature was inevitable. Again, it appears to be almost exclusively a female affliction. This may be because not every male on t.v. and in the movies has to adhere to one patently unrealistic ideal standard. I do feel sympathy for those who permit themselves to perform the rather distasteful rituals of this "illness", but I still must question its validity as a real disorder.

4. *Severe Gambling Disorder*- I'm not sure they're going to call it that, and neither are they at this point, but there is a strong effort underway to include uncontrollable gambling along with other destructive social actions, such as drinking excessive amounts of alcohol, in the pantheon of "diseases." At the time of its official acceptance (in other words, after "victims" suffering from it have appeared on enough talk shows for the public to identify with it), it will probably be given a classy, scientific name. I will say, as I've said before, that I don't find the notion that one's behavior is uncontrollable to be a very credible one. I never have believed the A.A. nonsense about a heavy drinker not being responsible for his actions, and I certainly have to scoff at the very thought of a gambler being granted permission to blame his losses (it seems a near certainty that those who win will not be affected) on yet another fancy "disorder."

5. *Homophobia*- The concept of "gay rights" has been gaining credibility to such an extent that homosexuals are now firmly entrenched in the special interest sphere, and a brand new malady has been invented to accompany their newly respected status. This *Homophobia* is apparently not just the fear of homosexuality, as the name would imply, but some kind of warped desire on the part of bigots everywhere to hinder the free pursuit of the homosexual "lifestyle." This is only the beginning of an inexorable onslaught of "diseases" infecting those who refuse to be tolerant and open-minded. In the future, such afflictions as "Afrophobia", "Zionophobia", "globaphobia", and "femiphobia" may be commonplace, thanks to this unhealthy precedent. Let us hope that the "illnesses" themselves prove more pluralistic than those suffering from them, and that "Christophobia", "Naziphobia", "Arabphobia", and "monogaphobia" will be just as easily detected.

6. *Alzheimer's Disease*- Why didn't elderly people contract this "disease" until recent times? Where was it hiding? Could it be that this illness was "discovered" in order to further the cause of nursing homes, thereby making it palatable for the minuscule number of children who still find it morally repugnant to abandon their parents to surrender and join the crowd? Until a few generations ago, the aged in this country tended to be cared for by their families. This arrangement was not unique, and still is the norm throughout most of the civilized world, particularly in the orient, where the elderly are virtually idolized. In this lovely land of ours,

91

however, so rich in folklore and tradition, the vast majority of young people today would no sooner give shelter to their parents than they would harbor a rabid animal. They must be heaving a giant collective sigh of relief at the introduction of such a convenient "ailment", and the gold plated excuse for their negligence that it represents.

7. *Battered Women Syndrome*- A newly labeled "illness" that strikes disproportionately at those women in the lower economic strata whose husbands suffer from alcoholism, it provides the perfect subject matter for the various daytime talk shows. Most disinterested observers can identify its future "victims" well in advance, through a casual encounter with their mean, unreasonable, and often intoxicated mates. Apparently the "disease" is a powerful one, however, and can only be diagnosed after the "victim" has reproduced, usually more than once, with the germ carrier, and borne its symptoms on her face and body for many years. I gently suggest to these unfortunate women, who are certainly suffering, that what is afflicting them is not a "disease" but the end results of a poor choice in marriage partners.

8. *Executive Burn-Out*- A very serious thing, this is. It was only a matter of time until the strenuous activities of the executive set endangered their health. Just imagine being forced to labor all day by attending constant "meetings", committing adultery with your young and able secretary, straining your memory to retain the punchlines of the latest topical jokes being bandied about the water cooler, driving to a leisurely luncheon engagement with your car phone at your ear so the other motorists will think you're discussing something important, and scheduling at least one brief visit to your office. Whose constitution could withstand such punishment? This condition nearly always befalls men, but an increasing number of female executives are developing it as well. Their only problem is that there are, as yet, not enough young and able male secretaries to go around, but I expect in time the situation will be rectified.

9. *Stress*- The father of *Executive Burn-Out* and other illegitimate fads, like the once wildly popular *Workaholic* craze. I find it humorous and insightful that this "disease" is only to be found among members of the upper-middle class. Apparently no porters, dishwashers, or construction workers suffer from it. Its "victims" always seem to be the great non-producers of society, who are drawing large salaries and doing little or nothing to earn them. In that vein, one would expect such people to fall prey to an ailment associated with guilt, but certainly not with tension. If this "illness" indeed existed, it would logically strike most often in the aching, fatigued members of the working class, who actually have to worry over such things as rent, food, car payments, and medical bills. Their concerns are entirely different from the "victims" of this dreaded

"disease", to whom a capital gains tax increase or negative leading economic indicators can mean the difference between high blood pressure and peace of mind.

10. *Sex Addiction*- This one is not officially labeled yet, but is already being whispered about in all the smart circles. One can imagine the adulterers of the world to be licking their chops at the prospect of contracting this "disorder." I, for one, refuse to believe that this "disease" is anything more than a rumor. It is one thing to call the American people gullible, misinformed, and unconcerned, but to think that they could allow such self-serving fluffery as this to be diagnosed as an "illness" is beyond my powers."

Phosphate lifted his eyes from the paper. "That," the top doo-wopper's voice was pregnant with awe, "was brilliant."

"Thank you." Waldo's chest expanded a few inches.

"If I may," Phosphate said, "I'd like to offer my assistance in the search for your grandfather."

"What?" Waldo asked. "You mean go to Iowa with us?"

"If you have the room." Phosphate replied. "Unfortunately, in addition to being homeless, we are without any means of transportation."

Waldo was stunned. "Well, I certainly don't mind the extra help. But, frankly I'm amazed. I mean- you just met us."

"We can all fit in my car." Brisbane said. "Shit, it'll be pretty cramped, especially on a long trip, but I had nine people riding in it to the Stones concert in '75." The fredneck chuckled. "Of course, we lost a couple there so it wasn't as crowded on the way back."

"Well, then, as soon as we get out of here," Waldo gripped the bars of the cell, "I guess we'll all be heading to Iowa."

Phosphate smiled. "I would consider it a personal honor, as well as a service to humanity, to accompany you, and I'm sure my fellow Afro-Anarchists agree, don't you, gentlemen?"

Fontaine and Bucktooth normally agreed with their leader about almost everything, and their fervent nods revealed that this was no exception.

Brisbane, who was obviously impressed by Phosphate, seemed pleased at the prospect of commuting to Iowa with him. Professor Buckley, meanwhile, was sitting on one of the two bottom bunk beds in the cell with his head in his hands. All four beds (the six of them were still too distracted to fret over any questions about sleeping accommodations) were barely padded and had obviously held many an illegal carcass. The Professor had preferred to remain in a silent, fearful stupor since the doo-wopping trio arrived, with his mind too preoccupied to be sociable.

"Waldo," Phosphate stroked his chin in contemplation, which he

93

often did, unintentionally adopting a psychiatric pose, "you're journeying to Iowa in an attempt to locate your grandfather's friend..."

"Sam Hancock." Waldo interrupted. "There's a mental institution there, The Last Chance Relaxation Home, in a place called Cornoil. He was committed there almost twenty years ago."

"Yes, I see. And this note you found in his journal..."

"Leads me to believe my grandfather may have gone to visit him." Waldo explained.

"At any rate, it appears to be the only clue you have." The top doo-wopper observed. "In fictional cases, at least, there are mysteries which have been solved with less evidence."

The six new friends, or at least five of them, considering that Professor Buckley was maintaining a worried, silent vigil, talked for the remainder of the night. As dawn approached, they were all wide awake, pacing back and forth nervously within the confines of the cell. None of them wanted to face the thought of sleeping with one of their cell mates, and the imagined risks inherent in such a situation. Thus they waited, sleepless and afraid, as the prison gradually came alive with the sights and noises of its staid existence, for the wheels of injustice to grind in their particular direction.

6

NOTHING TO FEAR BUT FEAR ITSELF

At an appropriately early hour, the guards strolled into their block and awakened the prisoners sleeping in the other cells by banging their clubs against the bars.

Fontaine, who'd previously served a stint in the Army, forgot where he was for a moment, leaped to attention, faced the sadistically smiling guard who'd stopped in front of their cell and accorded him a rusty salute.

The guard merely let out a crude, burning-cross-kind of chuckle. "At ease, private spearchucker." He sounded rather disappointed as he opened their cell door. "You're all free to go. Someone decided to play the great benefactor. He bailed you out a half hour ago."

"What?" Brisbane spoke for the incredulous group. "None of us know anybody- at least Waldo, the Professor, and I don't- that would place bail for us. Who was he?"

"How the hell should I know?" The guard possessed a voice that would make a piece of chalk scratching its way across a blackboard envious.

"Come on, dude," Brisbane pleaded, "can't you tell us anything about the guy? I mean, did you see him?"

"All I know," the guard rolled his eyes resignedly, "is that an old man came in here early this morning and said he could vouch for your reliability. He placed bond for the six of you."

"What was his name?" Waldo asked with a shiver slowly beginning to creep up his spine.

"Andy, Amber..."

"Ambrose!" Waldo shouted excitedly.

"Yeah, I think that was it." The guard had dropped his intrinsically antagonistic posture for the moment. "Shit, what the hell kind of a name is that, anyway? Some kind of saint or something, ain't it?"

"Yes, among other things." Waldo responded cryptically.

"Was he an old man?" Professor Buckley had left his cot and was growing interested.

"Hell, I already told you that! He was real old." The guard snickered. "Crazy looking old coot. Had long white hair and a beard that to see it would make you think he was a Rip Van Winkle or something- you know, asleep for, what was it- twenty years?"

Waldo smiled knowingly. "We might be talking about a much longer period of time than that." Only those with a bent of mind such as Waldo's could possibly have conjured up the notion that a writer born

95

nearly 150 years ago was alive and busily placing bail for strangers such as himself.

Leaving the guard scratching his head over Waldo's Twilight Zone-style remark, the six newly emancipated inmates were remanded over to the custody of another guard, who indicated they were to follow him.

Eventually, they were led to a room that was evidently the magistrate's office, which was inexplicably located there. There was a middle-aged, gray haired man sitting behind a desk there, and he motioned for them to sit down. "Warden!" He called out. "They're here."

A few seconds later, a very tall, thin man with dark brown hair that didn't appear to have been washed in quite some time trotted, literally, into the room. Diving into a chair on one side of the desk, he twisted himself into an impossibly uncomfortable posture, then continued to cross and uncross his long legs over and over again.

Glancing at each of them in turn with his dark, beady eyes, he eventually directed his attention exclusively on Waldo. "I am Warden LaFlaha. I understand that someone bailed you boys out this morning."

At the mention of his peculiar name, Brisbane, Fontaine, and Bucktooth burst into laughter simultaneously. LaFlaha ignored this completely, and it quickly subsided.

"Did you enjoy your stay?" The strange warden casually thrust a long, skeletal finger deep into one of his nostrils and left it resting comfortably there, with an expression on his face that seemed to defy anyone to point out the impropriety of such a thing. "I imagine you've all been rehabilitated."

Brisbane, Fontaine, and Bucktooth struggled to keep from laughing again.

"Someone has to weed out the unjustly accused from the unpunished repeat offenders." The weird warden used his free hand to pull a crusty, well-worn handkerchief from his coat pocket, which he placed nonchalantly on top of his head, evidently to sop up some of the excess grease from his hair.

"Man! I don't believe this!" Fontaine shook his head in bemusement, as if to privately confirm yet another example of the idiocy of all white authority figures.

"I must be on my way." LaFlaha suddenly sprung to his full enormous height. "Congratulations on your release. Remember, it's a dangerous world, and it always pays to obey the law."

Then the absurd, gangling figure galloped off, like some overgrown child impersonating a horse, and slammed the door behind him.

Waldo and the others, astounded by this odd man who'd entered and left so quickly without any discernable purpose, stared at each other with dazed expressions. As they recovered from this perplexing interlude, and waited for the magistrate to guide them further through the due processes of law, they were subjected to the popular psychological ploy of delay. Much as doctors make their patients sit in waiting rooms until they've read all the interesting and current magazines there, and banks, stores, agencies, and other businesses guarantee crowded lines by injudiciously using their personnel at the busiest times, this magistrate was intent on gazing down at his paperwork until their frustration simmered into total submission.

Finally, he brought his eyes up from the desk and stared at the six impatient, nearly ex-prisoners in a theatrical, menacing style. "Well," he eventually said, "which one of you is Mr. Wrock?"

Brisbane nervously raised his hand like the schoolboy he once was, desiring permission to leave class and play *Wipeout* with his fingers on the paper towel holders in the boys' bathroom.

"Young man, your blood alcohol level was .012. The legal limit in the state of Virginia is .010. That means you were legally intoxicated when the officer stopped you, and you were operating a motor vehicle at the time. Do you understand?"

Brisbane's heart dropped to his knees. He understood perfectly. In this day and age he'd be better off admitting to a series of child molestations. At least then he could plead insanity. He bit his lip as he spoke. "What happens now?"

"Well, you're free to go, since bail has been posted for you. Normally under these circumstances, a court date is set and I advise contacting an attorney to discuss your options." The magistrate suddenly smiled in a most peculiar manner. "However, in this case, I'm going to make an exception. Mr. Wrock, let this episode serve as a warning to you to be more careful in the future. At this time, I see no reason to press any charges against you."

Brisbane's eyes grew wide. "Huh? You mean that's it?"

Waldo was astounded. *How could this be?* he wondered. "You mean that he doesn't have to go to any classes? Or pay any fine?"

"That's correct, son."

Fontaine elbowed Bucktooth and whispered, "Shit, Buck, I guess that boy must be related to somebody."

Waldo was still attempting to figure the purpose behind this unprecedented act of leniency when the magistrate spoke again.

"Are you Mr. Billingsly?" he asked Waldo.

Waldo nodded.

"Well, son, it seems that the officer made a mistake in bringing you in. He really had no reason to do that and he is being severely reprimanded because of it. On behalf of this institution, as well as the police department, I want to offer you an apology for any inconvenience this has caused you."

Waldo was really flabbergasted now. The kind of sane, merciful attitude this magistrate was displaying was virtually unheard of in the American jurisprudence system. He might have ranted and raved, fredneck style, about the abuse of his rights, but Waldo remained silent. Despite being full of the old protest spirit, and certainly entitled to it in this situation, Waldo had never felt the inclination to join the ranks of those litigants cluttering up the courts with whiplash lawsuits. He was grateful just to be leaving prison.

The magistrate then looked at the Afro Anarchists. "I assume you fellows are the ones charged with disorderly conduct. Am I right?"

"Sure you're right." Bucktooth replied.

"Bucktooth, please." Phosphate interjected. "Yes, sir, we are the Afro Anarchists, a vocal group. I must stress that we feel our arrest was unnecessary and that the charges were completely frivolous."

The magistrate gave Phosphate the kind of look that is usually given to citizens who speak their peace. "Well, this is the second time this month that you gentlemen have been brought in for the same thing. Am I right?"

"Sure, you..."

Bucktooth's automatic slang reflex was cut off even more abruptly this time by Phosphate. "Sir, we felt the same way about the other incident a few weeks ago, but no one would listen to us."

"That's what they all say." The magistrate suddenly smiled in the same odd fashion as before. "But, you may be right. Perhaps you were simply being harassed. It wouldn't be the first time that's happened. I don't see any reason to make a big deal over this..."

"Shit, this is unbelievable!" Brisbane exclaimed.

The magistrate tapped his fingers on the desk. "Well, that appears to take care of everything."

Hiram Buckley spoke up unsteadily. "Excuse me, but-that is-I don't believe you mentioned me."

"Oh, of course. What's your name?"

"Buckley. Professor Hiram Buckley."

"Alright, let me look at your file." The magistrate shuffled the papers on his desk. "I don't see anything here about a Hiram Buckley. Perhaps you were brought here mistakenly as well. At any rate, you're free to leave, of course."

Waldo couldn't resist approaching the magistrate's desk. "Sir, I want to thank you for your...unusual..."

"You know, son," the magistrate interrupted Waldo, "all of us here at the prison wish you the best of luck in Iowa."

Waldo now felt a major league chill trotting up and down his spine.

"Wha...wha...what do you mean?"

The magistrate unleashed a blood curdling laugh. "Be careful where you look for your grandfather, Waldo." Then, abruptly switching gears, he adopted a crusty-but-kind-hearted-1950's-style demeanor. "Alright, all of your personal belongings are on the table by the door, and your car, Mr. Wrock, is in the prison parking lot. Now get outa here, all of you, before I change my mind!"

Waldo and the others didn't protest this order in the slightest, doing a fair impression of the Keystone Kops, bumping into each other repeatedly as they left Snortin' Reformatory, quickly and eagerly.

None of them spoke until they'd left the prison gates behind them and entered the parking lot.

"Shit man, what the fuck is going on?" The fredneck was shaking his head in befuddlement. "First that gypsy you don't know mentions you going out west, then leaves a warning for you, and now this magistrate dude you don't know says something about you looking for your grandfather. And how did he let me off like that? Shit man, you know as well as I do how hard-ass they've gotten about drunk driving."

Waldo didn't know the answers to a lot of questions. "I-I-I just can't explain any of it, Brisbane. But it's really starting to scare me."

Fontaine, seemingly unfazed by it all, chuckled. "Sheeeet! I don't want to know!"

Bucktooth concurred with these sentiments. "Damn right. Just be glad we got our asses out of that place before they turned to candy."

Brisbane then gasped and pointed in wonder at his decidedly un-fredneck-like '65 Dodge Dart, which was parked a few rows in front of them. "And why is my car here? Shit man, they towed it! Have you ever heard of the law bringing your car back after it's been towed? And allowing you miss out on the inconvenience of picking it up? And not even making you pay for it? No fucking way! I tell you, dude..."

"Wee Willie Keeler- lifetime average: .345"

Brisbane blinked his eyes. The voice belonged to a thin young boy who was clad only in a pair of bright flowered shorts. There was a giant pentagram on his scrawny chest, and it appeared to have been branded or carved into his pallid white skin, rather than tattooed there. He was wearing a pair of mirrored sunglasses, and sported a rainbow of colors in his spiked punk hairdo. He was seated on the pavement directly in front of the fredneck's car, where no one had been only seconds before. Sitting next to him was a plump, middle-aged woman with a dull brown scarf tied tightly around her head.

Bucktooth started laughing when he saw the bright, conspicuous figure, a reaction the odd youngster was undoubtedly accustomed to.

Without looking up, the boy turned to his female companion. "Ask me another."

The plump woman glared at Bucktooth. "You heathen." Patting the boy on the leg, she spoke to him sweetly. "Who holds the record for the most runs scored in a season?"

"Before 1900 or after?" The boy asked.

"Both."

"Oh, Doctor, you're so mean to me!" The boy smiled and stared down at the pavement in contemplation. "Before 1900, the record is 192, set by Billy Hamilton in 1894, and the modern mark, after 1900, belongs to Babe Ruth, who scored 177 in 1921."

The woman looked up with a satisfied expression on her plain, spectacled face. "Do any of you want to try and stump him?"

Phosphate spoke up. "Stump him on what, madam?"

"Shoestring knows more about baseball than any living person." The woman's pride was obvious in her voice. "Go ahead, ask him anyone's batting average, earned run average, who was in what World Series, who had the most stolen bases in 1924, anything at all."

Brisbane had been quite a sports fan in his youth, and he scratched his head in thought. "Shit, how about Walter Johnson- what was his lifetime earned run average?"

The boy scoffed. "Come on, at least make it challenging. His lifetime earned run average was 2.17, everybody knows that. He also, of course, holds the record for the most career shutouts with 113."

Waldo turned to Brisbane. "Is he right?"

Brisbane shrugged. "How should I know?"

"Of course he's right. He's always right." The woman patted the boy lovingly on the back.

Professor Buckley grasped Waldo firmly by the arm. "Waldo, my boy," he kept his voice low, "these are-that is-we must leave immediately. I know it's useless to dissuade you from what I consider to be a dangerous, foolhardy mission, but I beg you to at least not dawdle with all the *unreal* obstacles someone is so generously placing in our way."

Waldo nodded. "Yes, well, we really must be going now. It was...nice talking to you both."

"My name's Dr. Xmaster." The woman thrust her hand out towards Waldo. "And this is my prodigal patient Shoestring."

Brisbane started walking around the unusual duo, followed by the Professor. "Come on, you guys." The fredneck exclaimed. "Do you want to spend all day talking to some nuts in the parking lot? Let's get the fuck out of here."

Dr. Xmaster smiled at Brisbane. "Please don't let us delay you." She leaned over and placed her head on Shoestring's shoulder. "Perhaps we'll run into each other again on the road."

"Yes, perhaps we will." Phosphate had been studying the odd pair intently, and appeared to be entering one of his introspective moods.

"Aren't they a pitiful sight, Shoestring?" The good doctor kissed the youth's gaunt shoulder blade with an uncomfortable amount of ardor and sneered at Waldo and the others.

"As pathetic as Ed Delahanty teetering near the edge of Niagara Falls, Doctor." Her colorful companion replied.

With that, Shoestring and Dr. Xmaster slowly rose to their feet and shuffled away aimlessly, in no particular direction.

Only Brisbane realized this obscure reference was to the mysterious death of Hall of Famer Ed Delahanty in 1903, but he didn't allow his interest to slow down his pace as he raced to the car alongside his flustered compatriots.

They all managed to squeeze into Brisbane's decidedly un-fredneck-like vehicle, and as they passed through the gates of Snortin' Reformatory a few moments later, none of them cast a single look back.

Since none of the Afro Anarchists had any worldly possessions to speak of, nor any address to forward their mail from, there was no need to delay leaving for Cornoil, Iowa. All that was necessary was a quick stop at a local convenience store for more beer, as there were now three additional thirsts to satisfy.

It took Brisbane less than thirty seconds behind the wheel to open and begin drinking a can of beer. Like nearly all people arrested for drunk driving, the fredneck learned no lesson and sought the solace of more alcohol at the first opportunity. Soon the beer cans were popping open in rapid machine-gun fashion and Brisbane steered his car onto the interstate.

Phosphate asked the others if they would like to hear a little road music, something more substantial and not as long as *99 Bottles Of Beer On The Wall*. Everyone was amenable to this, so the top doo-wopper snapped his fingers and led his comrades in *More Tar Babies For Congress*:

> "America, please vote for me
> I'm from your vicinity
> I've been called a jungle bunny
> But I still think the name is funny
> You won't touch my bank account
> Unless it holds a large amount
> I got no credit, and can't withdraw
> What the tellers never saw
> I'll show up and stay awake

101

You won't call me a mistake
I'll love the job, just wait and see
And worship my incumbency
I'll say 'nay' and start to laugh
When they mention greed and graft
Sure, I'd like a Cadillac
But first I want my license back
Listen to me, citizens
'Cause you won't get this chance again
I will work my ass off for you
Register to vote if you want me to
I flunked the standards for admission
But I'll mop up the competition."

Waldo and Brisbane complimented the Afro Anarchists on their beautiful harmonies, which echoed through the crowded confines of the old Dodge Dart like a quadrophonic stereo system. Waldo, however, was a bit curious, as most listeners were, about Phosphate's constant obsession with racial themes. Hiram Buckley kept his praise to a bare, unenthusiastic minimum, as his tastes in music ran from ragtime and Tin Pan Alley to the pre-World War II-era big bands.

While Waldo had been suitably impressed, and the Professor merely polite, Brisbane waxed rhapsodic over the talents of Phosphate Jefferson as they drove past miles of standard highway scenery: scattered hills and trees, concrete bridges, and green mileage and exit signs. He continuously raved about the top doo-wopper's "awesome" lyrics while chugging beers in rapid succession. The fredneck was, in fact, directly on course for another encounter with the law and Phosphate, for one, recognized this and gingerly suggested that he allow someone else to drive. The extent of Brisbane's growing admiration, even worship, of the head Afro Anarchist was reflected by the fact that he unhesitantly pulled the car over on the emergency shoulder of the road and relinquished the driver's seat without an argument or a single expletive.

"Shit, you're right, man." Brisbane stumbled out of the car unsteadily with a glazed look in his eyes. "I am pretty fucking wasted."

Professor Buckley, as the only occupant of the car who wasn't drinking, was the logical choice to take the wheel, and he did so with a great deal of fanfare; adjusting and readjusting the rear view and side mirrors, carefully checking the few gauges on the dashboard like an airline pilot, and wiping his thick glasses on the tail of his coat. Eventually, just prior to Fontaine unleashing a torrid critique of his fastidiousness, the one- time pride of the local community college gently eased the automobile back onto the interstate.

They'd traveled a fair distance, and were in the midst of simultaneously discussing the mysterious Oak Island money pit and the legend of St. Germain, when Bucktooth suddenly pointed upwards. "Look! On the bridge!" he shouted excitedly.

Waldo and the others looked up, but the car was already passing under the bridge and they could see nothing.

"Damn, Buck, what was it?" Fontaine demanded.

"Yes, please tell us what you saw." Phosphate urged.

Bucktooth, like so many witnesses to U.F.O. sightings over the years, quickly realized there was no advantage in reporting something no one else had observed. "Uh...well, I'm not really sure what I saw."

"Shit man, the way you shouted, you saw *something!*" Brisbane said.

Bucktooth threw up his hands, refusing to elaborate. Eventually the others forgot about the incident, and passed it off as the result of an overactive imagination and/or massive alcohol consumption.

As he slowly sipped his beer, Bucktooth contemplated the bizarre scene in the magistrate's office, especially the remarks alluding to the search for Waldo's grandfather, and considered his decision to remain silent a sound one. Combined with their other strange experiences, of which he'd only heard, Bucktooth felt certain that Waldo and the others would find any mention of familiar figures with colorful hairdos leaning over bridges and staring down at them to be unwelcome and distracting news.

As the hours went by, it was decided that, due to a critical shortage of funds, driving duties would be divided up equally among everyone. Since even the cheapest of motels required some form of payment, the six unemployed travelers reluctantly agreed to sleep in the car, and rotate four hour shifts behind the wheel. They were forced, however, to work around the fredneck owner of the vehicle, who was becoming increasingly incapable of driving at all. Brisbane was downing beers at an astonishing rate, usually with his free arm draped around Phosphate, as he rambled on incessantly and incoherently about everything he could think of.

As they traveled farther west on the interstate, the lanes narrowed from four to two, and the landscape became dotted with farms and roadside stands, providing a more scenic setting. The decidedly un-fredneck-like '65 Dodge Dart plodded on past the grazing cattle and horses, and the fresh vegetable and fruit stands, through the evening and into the middle of the night.

Waldo looked at the clock on the dashboard. It was four a.m., and he was in the middle of his driving shift. Brisbane had just passed out, and the others in the car were also asleep, even the Professor, who'd finally succumbed to fatigue after remaining awake for nearly 60 hours. The nervous young man, having listened to the fredneck's nonsensical alcoholic jargon for longer than he would have liked, was grateful for the silence, which was broken only by the soft hum of the engine and the periodic snoring of his comrades.

Reaching into his pocket for a cigarette, Waldo discovered that he didn't have any left. As he was so frequently forced to do, Waldo administered a good tongue lashing to himself. His forgetfulness had long been a chronic problem, but no amount of self-chastisement seemed to alleviate it. He gazed out at the lush countryside, with its bales of hay and pastoral fields gleaming in the pale glow of the crescent moon, and found it easy to picture the many U.F.O. encounters which occurred in just such an atmosphere. But at this moment, his main concern was locating a place that sold cigarettes.

Waldo was about to wake Fontaine, who was seated next to him, and ask him for a smoke, when he suddenly noticed a small purple sign up ahead. His attention was drawn towards it due to its unusual color. He slowed down considerably, as there was no one else on the road at that hour, and could see, in the weak beams cast by the old car's headlights, that it said, "Open All Night - Beer And Ice - Next Exit." Waldo breathed a sigh of relief and took the next exit, which he found to be curiously unnumbered and unnamed, with merely a single little sign labeled "Exit" to mark the spot. There were no streetlights to illuminate the unnamed road the exit led to, and Waldo turned right-the only way he could- with a bit of trepidation.

After a couple of miles, the road suddenly turned to gravel, and then a mere dirt path. Waldo's nerves grew ever more jagged as he contemplated the likelihood of an unlit, unpaved road being situated such a short distance from the interstate. He was about to turn around when he saw a dilapidated wood frame building with a dim neon sign that flashed its "Beer And Ice" message like a proverbial candle in the darkness Waldo was about to curse. Waldo swung the car off the dirt path and parked in front of the pathetic little store, noticing the rotting boards and dull gray paint, which was thoroughly cracked and appeared to have been slapped on by someone long since departed from the scene. He was somewhat disappointed that there were no atmospheric characters out front gathered about the ancient soft drink cooler enjoying a late night bottle of pop. No one stirred as he turned off the engine, so Waldo went inside by himself.

There were no other cars outside the queer little establishment, but Waldo didn't find that particularly unusual, considering it was four o'clock in the morning. He did, however, find it a bit unsettling that no one appeared to be inside either. The place was extremely dirty, and Waldo had to brush away the cobwebs as he opened the door. It was a small, typical country store, but it seemed to be terribly outdated. There was a picture of Charles Lindbergh hanging on one of the walls, a small table by the entrance with a checker board on it, which appeared to have been abandoned in mid-game, and a glass case labeled "Live Bait", that Waldo peered into and saw was full of petrified, long dead worms. There was even an old fashioned pickle barrel on one side of the counter, and a yellowed canister of jelly beans next to the outmoded cash register. In addition to the abundance of cobwebs, which spread from every corner and hung motionless in the air, the items on the shelves were all covered with dust. It didn't appear to Waldo as if anything in the place had been touched for quite some time.

Waldo was about to call out for some assistance when he noticed a small shelf containing magazines and paperback books at the rear of the store. As it was next to impossible for Waldo to pass by any reading material without perusing it thoroughly, he made a beeline for the back of the place. Quickly scanning the reading matter, Waldo was perplexed to discover that all the magazines were at least fifty years old. The books dated from the same era, and were priced at ten cents each. Waldo, gradually becoming accustomed to the weird and unexplainable, was preparing to leave in bewilderment when suddenly his heart began racing. There, on the lower left hand corner of the magazine display, was an issue of Hiram Buckley's *Force Of Habit*. Waldo now felt certain that any establishment offering such an obscure and controversial newsletter for sale, one that probably had fewer subscribers than *The Flat Earth News*, was no mere general store. Reaching down, he picked up the extremist periodical, and tried to imagine what sort of ridiculous Unreals must be employed by this anitquated place. Glancing at the cover, Waldo frowned. It was dated February 1969, but he was almost certain that the Professor hadn't started *Force Of Habit* until the mid-'70's. Waldo found the "Letters To H.B." section and started reading:

Dear H.B.,
Am still recovering from the Super Bowl. Send your new issue pronto!
Zeke Sopolski
Baltimore, Maryland

Dear H.B.,
I thought I'd seen it all with the "miracle" Jets being allowed to get to the Super Bowl, but this is too much. What's next- the "miracle" Mets winning the World Series? Earl Morrall was apparently the only person at the stadium who didn't see a wide-open Jimmy Orr waving his arms in vain. Joe Namath, talented playboy and mediocre quarterback, will

105

now be assured of a place in history. I predict that Morrall and coach Don Shula, especially, will be rewarded for throwing the game. The defense put on a clinic of flailing arms and missed tackles. Even my former hero Johnny Unitas must have been in on it, since he too could not solve the invincible Jet defense when Shula put him in late in the game. The same legend who could beat the Sam Huffs and Willie Woods couldn't fool the Verlon Biggs and Randy Beverly express? Is nothing sacred? My young son was so demoralized over the defeat that he deflated his genuine league football, which was autographed by members of the Colts, and fed it to our killer German Shepherd. We are now seriously considering taking him to a psychiatrist, due to the fact he refuses to eat (he has lost 38 pounds since the game) and speaks to no one except his imaginary ballet teacher. He used to want to become a Baltimore Colt, but now his ambition is to dance ballet professionally, and we are forced to watch him, an emaciated youth darting about on tiptoes and giggling in secretive conversations with his invisible instructor. What can we do? Please tell me why the Super Bowl was fixed.

 Fulton X. O'Crater
 Baltimore, Maryland

 Dear Mr. Sapolski and Mr. O'Crater: I feel for both of you. Your case in particular, Mr. O'Crater, is similar to dozens of reports that I've received. It is even rumored that a certain farmer in Frederick was so bereaved over the outcome of the game that he devised a giant slingshot and aimed it at the moon, intending to propel himself there and presumably spend the rest of his days staring at craters and foraging for green cheese. The attempt failed and he was imbedded head first in his tomato garden after hurtling a few hundred yards. We may imagine him to still be there, with his feet pointing skywards as a living testimonial to the seriousness of the American sports fan. But, to answer your question, it was imperative that the A.F.L. team win this Super Bowl to establish its credibility, after the first two games between the league champions had produced lopsided victories by the N.F.L.'s Green Bay Packers. To pave the way for a lucrative merger with the N.F.L., something drastic had to be done to alter the widely held view that the A.F.L. was a demonstrably inferior league. That is why the event was staged the way it was, and the fact the winners were from the media capital of the world, and quarterbacked by the sport's most "glamorous" and overpublicized player, only amplified the effects of an A.F.L. "upset." And, of course, a lot of money was made from heavy wagering by those in the know. This also serves as a reminder to the unwary that the conspirators have reached into the world of sports and claimed it as *another of their possessions.*

Waldo looked around the store. It didn't seem likely that any employee was about to return from a coffee break, so he was faced with the sort of decision most people are faced with at one time or another: Should he leave the money for his cigarettes and the *Force Of Habit* issue, which he was anxious to show the Professor, on the counter or steal away into the night without paying? Torn between the potential comfort of a nurtured conscience and the illicit thrill of theft, he eventually made a bold move in the later direction. As he rummaged through the cigarettes which were stored under the counter, he was only mildly surprised to find just older, non-filtered brands stocked there. Except for, oddly enough, a single pack of Camel Lights, which was Waldo's brand. Not one to be half-hearted about anything, Waldo took a few six packs of lukewarm beer from the barely functioning, elderly cooler in the middle of the store, along with several kinds of nutrition-less but filling snack foods from the shelves, carefully blowing the thick dust off in the process, and placed them in paper bags he found stored under the counter next to the cigarettes. He packed the bags as well as any young grocery boy and, gathering them up in his arms, scurried out of the strange place with his adrenalin pumping. As he passed the ancient soft drink cooler out front, Waldo tossed some bottles of soda into one of the bags for good measure.

When Waldo returned to the car, he discovered that the previously intermittent snoring of his companions had turned into a veritable symphony of indelicate, masculine sounds. He could hear them clearly through the closed windows of the automobile, drowning out the distant noises from the interstate and enlivening the abnormal stillness in the air. Waldo deposited his booty in the trunk as quietly as possible, so as not to disturb anyone, grabbed a beer and his pack of cigarettes, and peeled away like a real gangster.

Waldo opened his stolen beer, and despite the fact it was flat and tepid, it tasted better than any he might have purchased. The basically honest young man relished it, along with a thoroughly satisfying stolen cigarette, and chuckled to himself. *Who says crime doesn't pay?* he thought, a smile curling about his lips as he accelerated over the speed limit.

Waldo stopped the car. He'd been driving back and forth on the dirt road for nearly two hours, in an unsuccessful attempt to find his way back to the interstate, and was now totally frustrated. He was also frightened, as it should have been an elementary matter, even for someone like himself, who was cursed with a notoriously bad sense of direction, to locate the exit. When Waldo had turned off the interstate and onto the unnamed road, he'd only traveled a few miles before discovering the eerie little store. Therefore, the laws of reality would seem to dictate that a trip backwards in the same direction should lead, after a similarly short distance, to the elusive highway exit. Such laws did not appear to be presently operating, however, as the nervous young man felt as if he were driving in circles, instead of a straight line. There were no markers of any kind along the road, and the surrounding landscape was nondescript and unchanging, like the background of a cheaply produced television cartoon. The strangest thing of all, and it caused the hair on the back of Waldo's neck to stand up, was the fact that as he drove aimlessly up and down the unnamed dirt path, not only did it never turn back into the paved road he'd originally been on, *he never passed by the curious old store again.* Thus Waldo sat there, his mind reeling in confusion, having apparently slipped into some under-publicized version of the Bermuda Triangle.

Although Waldo didn't share the attitude of most males, who refuse to admit they're lost as a matter of pride, he hadn't awakened any of the others to seek their assistance out of fear they'd think him stupid, incompetent, or insane. He reluctantly decided that at this point they should be apprised of the situation, and he reached over Fontaine to shake Phosphate and inform him of the dilemma they appeared to be in. Waldo felt the top doo-wopper would be the calmest one of his companions in a crisis, as well as the most helpful.

Phosphate opened his eyes and stared semi-coherently at Waldo. "Yes...what is it?"

"I hate to wake you like this, Phosphate, but I have to tell you..." Waldo took a deep breath. "I think we're lost."

"What do you mean, Waldo?" The top doo-wopper yawned. "How can we be lost?"

Waldo then proceeded to tell him of the series of events which had placed them in the midst of this surrealistic locale, which they seemed unable to leave.

"Well, Waldo, my first suggestion is to move the car off the road." Phosphate said. "We don't want to block traffic."

"Don't worry about that," Waldo reached for a cigarette, "I've been on this road for a couple of hours and *I haven't seen another car.*"

"Hmmm." The top doo-wopper reverted to his patented stroking the chin routine. "It does appear, my friend, as if some powerful, mysterious forces don't want you to find your grandfather."

"Waldo, I say-that is-what's going on?" Professor Buckley, being the light and infrequent sleeper he was, had been awakened by their voices. "And why did you let me fall asleep? I don't understand it..."

Waldo explained things to the Professor, and as he did their conversation, particularly the ex-history teacher's plaintive cries of alarm, roused the others in the car.

"Shit man, where the fuck are we?" Brisbane unconcernedly stretched his arms, hitting Professor Buckley and Bucktooth in the process.

The dawn was breaking, and the land on either side of the dirt path became even colder and bleaker in the light. The sky was full of threatening gray clouds, gathered in strange, fleeting shapes, that cast a suitably portentous atmosphere.

"Oh dear," Professor Buckley solemnly intoned, "I knew-that is-we must get out of here."

"Sheeet!" Fontaine patted his stomach. "I need something to eat, man. I got a terrible craving for some doughnuts."

"Shit man, so do I!" The fredneck exclaimed. "Why don't you drive around and try to find a place, dude?"

"I told you that there isn't anything around here." Waldo started the engine. "But I'll humor you. I want to show you all what I mean anyhow."

They hadn't traveled half a mile when a purple sign, like the one on the beltway, popped up in front of them, standing out incongruently amid the lifeless surroundings. It read: "Katy's Delightful Dippin' Donuts - Next Right."

Waldo shook his head in disbelief. "Huh? I must have passed by this spot twenty times, and I *know* that sign wasn't there before."

"Sure, dude, sure." Brisbane goaded him. "Let's eat now and talk about it later."

Waldo turned right at the next street, which he also hadn't seen previously. He was certain of that, because one of the oddest things about the dirt path he'd traversed so extensively was the complete absence of any side streets whatsoever. It even had a name, albeit a predictably curious one: DeMohrenschildt Lane.

DeMohrenschildt Lane was even narrower than the unnamed dirt path, and just as unpaved. It was graveled, and the old car's shocks revealed their age in the way its occupants were bounced and jostled as it maneuvered along. A short distance later, they came upon a cheerful looking place, with its bright pink facade standing in stark contrast against the stormy, swirling horizon. A large billboard sign proclaimed "Katy's Delightful Dippin' Donuts - The Best In Town." The building sat in the middle of an inordinately large parking lot, which was completely empty.

"Alright! It's empty!" Bucktooth cried out exuberantly.

"But is it open?" Phosphate wondered. "And, assuming it is, where are the employees' vehicles?"

"Let's pull in, man," Brisbane suggested, "and find out."

Waldo, numbed by his recent experiences, mechanically parked the car and they all climbed out.

"There you go!" Fontaine pointed to a "Yes - We're Open" sign hanging in the door.

They entered the place and were greeted by a buxom blonde in her early forties, who was wiping down a table and whistling the country standard *Take This Job And Shove It* as she did so.

There was a pleasant aroma of fresh dough in the air, and the entire place seemed, from the neat little tables with their formica tops, to the red and white checkered floor tiles and the sparkling chrome ovens which were visible in the back, to be uncannily clean. "Hi there, fellas. Ya'll came at a good time."

The woman had a friendly smile and a pleasant manner, that combined with her looks and her heavy drawl to impart the impression of an archetypal southern waitress. "I just made a batch of doughnuts. They're as fresh as the boys that hang out at the pool hall on Saturday nights."

They all laughed politely and settled down on the counter stools. The woman hustled behind the counter and took their orders. There were many kinds of doughnuts offered, including some eclectic varieties none of them had heard of, and it was difficult to choose between them. Eventually they did, however, and the patient, cheerful blonde swiftly placed their food before them, initiating a light banter as they ate.

"How ya'll like my doughnuts?" She asked. "Most folks around here think they're the best they ever tasted."

All of their mouths were full, so they answered with a chorus of "hmmmms" and nodding heads.

The blonde looked outside at the empty parking lot. "It's good you fellas got here when you did. Nothin's better than a fresh doughnut."

"I'm inclined to agree with you, madam. It's a pity there aren't more customers here to enjoy them." Phosphate took a big bite of his unusual pineapple-seaweed doughnut.

The waitress wiped her hands on her apron. "Yeah, well, there ain't a whole lot of folks that live in these parts. Are you boys from around here?"

Waldo finished swallowing some of his delectable coconut jelly doughnut. "No, we're not. The Professor-" he pointed towards Hiram Buckley, who was engrossed in a garlic and butterscotch cruller, "and I live in Northern Virginia..."

"And we-" Fontaine laid his chocolate chip eclair down and threw an arm around each of his fellow Afro Anarchists, "are from the nation's capital."

"Oh...Washington, D.C." The buxom blonde was impressed. "It must be excitin' livin' there, around all them monuments and everything."

Bucktooth giggled, a few crumbs from his banana jawbreaker doughnut tumbling out of his mouth as he did. "Yeah, it's a thrill a minute."

The woman looked at Brisbane. "What about you, son? Where are you from?"

The fredneck spoke with a mouth full of raspberry wheat doughnut. "I'm a free spirit, man. I travel from place to place."

The telephone on the wall rang and the waitress excused herself and walked over to answer it.

While the waitress was busy chatting on the phone, Waldo seized the opportunity to relate to everyone in detail how he'd taken the exit last night in an effort to buy cigarettes, turned onto the dark, unnamed road which quickly became a dirt path, and found the aged, seemingly nonfunctioning store.

"You wouldn't have believed that place." Waldo wiped his lips in his usual dainty fashion. "There were cobwebs hanging all over, and everything in it was covered with dust. I felt like its first customer in fifty years."

"Shit man," Brisbane whistled. "I don't know if I can make it all the way to Iowa, if this stuff keeps happening."

"And guess what, Professor?" Waldo turned to the one time pride of the local community college. "There was a copy of *Force Of Habit* there! I took it with me," Waldo lowered his voice, "along with some other things."

"What things, man?" Fontaine inquired.

"I'll show you later." Waldo replied.

Professor Buckley finished eating his second doughnut, an outlandish oatmeal peppercorn concoction which was advertised as the monthly special. "My boy, this is most-that is-I can't understand such a thing, even with my proclivity to imagine..."

"Of course you can't understand it- who could?" The fredneck interrupted. "How could an issue of your newsletter show up on the shelf of a country store, in the middle of nowhere? Did you distribute it anywhere other than through the mail?"

The professor shook his head. "There's no way that could happen. My circulation is *very* limited."

Waldo ran out to the car, opened the trunk, searched through the bags, and raced back in with the copy of *Force Of Habit* in his hands.

"Here- see for yourself." He handed it to Professor Buckley.

The ex-history teacher's mouth dropped open as he stared at the periodical. "W-W-Waldo..." he stuttered, "what are-that is- the date on this is February 1969. The first issue of *Force Of Habit* was published in April 1975."

111

"Shit man!" The fredneck exclaimed. "You mean..."

"*I never wrote this.*" The Professor stated. "Waldo, there is something very strange afoot."

Phosphate had picked up the issue and was perusing it. "Professor Buckley, the writing is very similar in style to yours." "Yes, I know-that is-it's a damned good imitation." Professor Buckley sipped his ice water. "By the way, how do you know anything about my writing style?"

"I must admit," the top doo-wopper smiled at the Professor, "to being a former subscriber of your delightful periodical. I didn't mention it earlier for fear of embarrassing you with my praise."

"Imagine that!" Waldo was amazed. "But how did you, I mean, if you're a street person, you have no address. How was it mailed to you?"

"I wasn't always homeless." Phosphate replied. "I received it years ago, when I was living in my parents' house. I imagine I was, like Waldo's grandfather, one of your charter subscribers."

Professor Buckley frowned. "I'm sorry, Phosphate, but I don't recall your name. I really should, too-that is-there weren't many names to remember."

"I'm certain you had more important things on your mind." The head Afro Anarchist reached for a napkin. "It's quite a task to try and inform the public that it's being increasingly oppressed."

"How could we be any more fucking oppressed?" Brisbane asked.

"There are things you can't even imagine, Brisbane."

"Man, we're used to being oppressed." Fontaine chuckled.

"We're not talking about separate bathrooms here, Fontaine." Phosphate counseled in his inimitable fashion. "If they decided to press all the levers at their disposal, they would have the lot of us begging for a return to the cotton fields."

"Damn, these doughnuts are on time!" Bucktooth was concerned with more important matters.

"Excuse me for overhearin'," The buxom blonde had completed her phone call and she placed her strong, overworked forearms on the counter and leaned towards them, "but you fellas sound like you're in an Alfred Hitchcock movie or somethin'. What are ya'll talking about?"

"Nothing of significance, madam." Phosphate smiled at her. "But, I'm sure we must sound like a group of irregular windbags. Why don't you tell us something about yourself?"

The waitress seemed eager to do just that. "Alright, don't mind if I do. My name's Peggy Polk. I been workin' at this here doughnut shop for 16 years and I love it. You get to meet all kinds here, different types of folks. There ain't a whole lot to tell- my life's pretty borin'. I been married twice, got three kids, two girls and a boy. Probably the only interestin' thing about me is that I'm a direct descendant of the President, you know,

112

James K. Polk. Ya'll ever hear of him?"

"No shit!" Brisbane was impressed.

"Well, that makes an interesting exception to the theory of inherited power among the elite." Waldo noted. "I mean no offense, ma'am, but how did a descendant of a President of the United States come to work in..."

"A dump like this?" Peggy Polk lit up a cigarette. "You make it sound like I was a criminal or somethin'. I told you I like this job just fine. It meets my needs. My folks was always poor and so was theirs' before them. I guess old President Polk musta had some money, but if he did he sure didn't pass any on to me or none of mine." She brushed some blonde strands of hair from her overly-made-up face. "There- now ya'll know all about me. Why don't you tell me somethin' about yourselves?"

Phosphate responded for them. "Well, I don't know about the others, but I certainly don't have a President in my family tree. You should be very proud of that, Ms. Polk. I think I can speak for everyone when I say that we are six newfound friends who happen to be on an especially important mission."

"What, are you boys answering the call?" Peggy inquired.

"Not that kind of call." The top doo-wopper explained. "Actually we are endeavoring to locate Waldo's missing grandfather, who recently vanished without a trace from his home in northern Virginia."

"Which one of you is Waldo?" Peggy asked.

Waldo identified himself.

"Don't you have no idea what happened to him, honey?"

"Well, I have my suspicions." Waldo lit up a cigarette.

Peggy poured herself a cup of coffee. "You don't think nobody did nothin' to him, do you?"

Waldo stared down at the counter. "I hope not."

"Where was he when you last seen him?" The blonde waitress was an indefatigable interrogator, rattling off questions like a small town Perry Mason.

"At our house, back in Annandale, Virginia, the night before he disappeared."

"Well, honey," Peggy smiled understandingly at Waldo, "if you don't mind me askin', why are you lookin' here for him?"

"We're not looking here. We just happened to stop for doughnuts." Waldo was growing tired of being questioned.

"Tell her about that crazy road, Waldo," Bucktooth interjected, "and how you drove around for hours trying to find the highway exit."

"Huh?" Peggy looked flabbergasted.

"Nothing, madam." Phosphate frowned at his fellow Afro Anarchist. "Bucktooth tends to exaggerate. Our destination is Cornoil,

Iowa. That is where Waldo believes his grandfather may very well be. We have just started our journey, and we will be stopping at various places along the way in order to satisfy our appetites. Your fine establishment is one such place."

"What's so special about the corner of Iowa?" A puzzled Peggy asked.

"No, that's Cornoil, Iowa." Waldo corrected her. "The Last Chance Relaxation Home happens to be there."

"The what?"

"The Last Chance Relaxation Home." Brisbane spoke up. "His grandfather's best friend is presently residing there, or at least was, and Waldo figures he might..."

"I say, Waldo," Professor Buckley interrupted, "don't you think we should be going?"

Ignoring the Professor's remark, Peggy looked at Phosphate. "You colored boys say you're some kind of singing group?"

"Yes ma'am! We's from de nation's capital and we all sing good there! Dat place is full of us, you know!" Fontaine was touchy about his status as a member of a dispossessed minority group, and easily prone to sarcastic outbursts.

"Alright, Fontaine." The top doo-wopper was not bothered by such subtle indications of prejudice. "The use of such antiquated terms is not uncommon among the inhabitants in these sort of climes." Phosphate flashed his charismatic smile at the blonde presidential descendant. "Madam, it appears that we have finished our delicious breakfast. I regret to report that it is time for us to take leave of your delightful company."

"You sure use a lot of big words." Peggy observed.

"Kinda smart for a colored boy, ain't he?" Fontaine slyly remarked.

Phosphate stopped his fellow Afro Anarchist before he antagonized the basically well-meaning waitress. "Fontaine, don't you think Ms. Polk would enjoy hearing one of our compositions? Am I correct in assuming, madam, that you like country music?"

"I sure do!" She replied. "How did you know?"

"Just a guess." Phosphate said. "You're going to love this song, Ms. Polk. It possesses a bit of a country flavor."

The top doo-wopper then began crooning their new number, *You Ain't White Enough For Me*, with an uncharacteristic twang in his voice:

"There are no degrees of whiteness
Or so the purists say
But still I wash my skin in milk
Every Christmas day
They're laughing hard in Russia

114

At immigration quotas
They want to drink their vodka
And dance with Negro voters
I know there's no more riots
'Cause now the nigger's free
But if I owned a store I bet
They'd come and pick on me
If only they'd obey the law
And behave the way they should
We'd cheer their boxers even more
For bleeding so damn good
I ain't got no rhythm
But I'll listen to their songs
And admit that every single Whitey
Everywhere is wrong
If they would kindly keep their asses
Away from my address
And stay inside their neighborhoods
They've made into a mess
The Blacks are takin' over
I see them everywhere
But I'm still white- I got my rights
I'll never curl my hair!"

Peggy was tapping her foot as the song ended. "That was really good! Did ya'll make that up yourselves?"

Fontaine patted Phosphate on the back. "Yeah. Phosphate here writes most all of our songs."

Peggy smiled at the top doo-wopper. "Well, Phosphate, you sure got a heap of talent."

"Thank you, madam." Phosphate modestly replied. "Your gracious sentiments are duly noted and much appreciated."

"You fellas oughta be some kind of big music stars." Peggy said admiringly.

Phosphate shook his head. "Ms. Polk, I must confess that I share the view of Waldo's grandfather that it is sometimes in the best interests of all concerned not to seek financial gain through artistic endeavor. In addition, there is cause to doubt whether any of our material would be commercially viable."

Peggy sipped her coffee. "Whew! I didn't understand a dang word you said, but it sure sounded good!"

"Thank you, madam, and now we really must depart." Phosphate slid off the stool.

"Well, I wish ya'll luck in finding Waldo's grandfather, and may the good Lord bless you and yours."

"We return your wishes tenfold, and bow to your hospitality." As he spoke, the top doo-wopper really outdid himself, actually executing a flawless bow to the blonde waitress. "Never let it be said, madam, that the south is dead."

Peggy was visibly moved by the head Afro Anarchist's dramatic posturing. "You're a regular charmer, you are. Ya'll come back and see me sometime, ya hear?"

"Okay, Peggy. So long." Waldo was the last to walk out the door of the doughnut shop.

In the parking lot, Phosphate led the way briskly to the decidedly un-fredneck-like '65 Dodge Dart.

"Shit man, those doughnuts made me fucking tired!" Brisbane, who'd been awake for nearly an hour, stretched his arms.

Waldo handed the car keys to Bucktooth. "It's your turn to drive."

As they piled into the car, Fontaine turned to Phosphate. "Damn, Phos, why were you kissin' that bleached blonde's ass? She'd probably make you use the back door of her house."

The top doo-wopper's grin was as mischievous a one as his scrupulous features could form. "Quite possibly she would, Fontaine, but I happen to subscribe to the Golden Rule. And you surely must have noticed, did you not, that we formed such a favorable impression on her that she neglected to ask us to pay for our food."

"That's right!" Waldo exclaimed.

"Phosphate, you're fucking brilliant!" Brisbane declared.

"Please, I was simply taking advantage of a situation. When one is accustomed to living on a limited budget, it is sometimes an unfortunate necessity to resort to dishonest means in order to obtain sustenance. I do not like it, but I have become rather adept at it." Phosphate was clearly uncomfortable, as his humble nature found praise difficult to accept, particularly when he was being admired for actions that were illegal, if not immoral.

"I'll say!" The fredneck said.

Bucktooth steered the car back onto the graveled surface of DeMohrenschildt Lane.

"Waldo, you mentioned that you took some other things from the strange establishment you visited last night..." Phosphate was hoping to deflect some misguided admiration his way.

"Yeah, man, what else did you take from that crazy store?" Fontaine asked.

Waldo lit up a cigarette. "Well, it's all in the trunk; I can't remember everything, exactly. I just grabbed some snack food, beer, and sodas, you know- stuff like that."

Soon after they turned back onto the unnamed dirt path, a light rain finally began falling from the increasingly ominous looking sky. A gradual fog was creeping in as well, wrapping the bare, stark surroundings in a funereal pallor.

Against such a background, it was hard to picture a more vulnerable object than Brisbane's dented old vehicle, as it chugged along faithfully, its fuel supply dropping dangerously low, for miles and miles and encountered nothing, least of all a gas station.

"That tank," Bucktooth pointed at the gas gauge on the dashboard of the decidedly un-fredneck-like '65 Dodge Dart, "is almost empty. We ain't going much farther."

"Indeed it is." A solemn Phosphate agreed. "I suggest we stop the car and weigh our options."

"What options?" Professor Buckley asked. "Why do-that is- we've been traveling up and down this path for over an hour without seeing anyone or encountering anything. Even the doughnut shop cannot be relocated. In light of this, what options do we have?"

It was difficult to argue with the ex-history teacher's typically alarmist position. Brisbane's reliable old automobile had indeed been expending its remaining fuel supply in what seemed to be a hopeless effort to exit the unnamed dirt path. After leaving the doughnut shop and the blonde presidential descendant who worked there, they'd been unable to find DeMohrenschildt Lane again, or any other side street.

The rain was falling lightly but steadily, and the fog remained thick enough to add an air of gloom to an already desperate situation, but there was enough visibility for everyone to clearly observe the austere, unchanging nature of their surroundings.

Bucktooth stopped the car and turned off the engine. "Okay, what now?"

Waldo lit a cigarette. "I don't know. I suppose we could walk..."

"Hey you! Don't you know better than to stop in the middle of the road like that?"

They all turned their heads and saw that a tow truck, from out of nowhere, had pulled up alongside them. Behind the wheel was an unshaven, middle aged man with a bandage over one ear.

"Hell, I coulda run into you in this fog." There was a hard, unfriendly expression on the man's face. "What are you all doing out in these parts, anyhow?"

"Shit man, we don't know where the fuck we are." Brisbane replied. "We've been driving back and forth on this road for a long time, and we can't seem to get anywhere. How do we get to the interstate from here?"

"Before that," Bucktooth reminded him, "we need to find a gas station."

"Are you headed back to a service station?" Waldo wondered.

The man ignored the fredneck's question about the interstate. "Yep. It's about a mile from here. If you think you can make it, come on."

The tow truck abruptly roared off ahead of them, and Bucktooth quickly followed. After a mile or so, true to the driver's word, there appeared a well-lit, modern service station on the side of the road.

Professor Buckley shook his head. "This just gets curiouser and curiouser."

"How the hell," Fontaine echoed the Professor's sentiments, albeit without quoting Lewis Carroll, "did we miss that?"

As Bucktooth pulled the car up to one of the pumps, and everyone speculated about their passing this exact spot several times without seeing the gas station, Waldo noticed a group of five men standing in front of the men's room, which was located on one side of the building.

Something about the men sent a chill up Waldo's spine. Perhaps it was the tattooed arms, or the chewing tobacco being sprayed out sporadically. Or the chains hanging from their pants, which were worn just loosely enough to reveal the cracks of their asses when they bent down. Waldo knew in an instant that they were not likely to be cordial to a lost and pathetic interracial group. He turned to nudge Phosphate, who was seated next to him in the back seat, but the head Afro Anarchist was already cognizant of the potential danger awaiting them.

"Bucktooth," The top doo-wopper gritted his teeth, "please pump the gas quickly. *Very* quickly."

Bucktooth nodded and jumped out of the car.

"Damn!" Fontaine saw the five men, who were now slowly and menacingly approaching the car. "I knew I shoulda stayed in D.C.!"

"Gentlemen, I believe we are about to be officially greeted by some of the local citizens of this unnamed and mostly invisible jurisdiction." Phosphate tried to remain calm. "Fontaine, do not speak. If we sit here quietly, they may presume us to be illiterate and unthreatening. Perhaps then we will be allowed to proceed."

Waldo could see inside the small office, where oil, antifreeze, cigarettes, and other necessities of the road were sold. The unfriendly looking man with the bandage over his ear was sitting there behind the cash register with a malicious grin on his face.

One of the five men, apparently the leader, placed his hands on top of the car. He opened his mouth and smiled hideously, tobacco juice dripping from his few yellow teeth. The other four men were circling the car, laughing and cursing, punctuating their pleasure with blows to each other's arms.

Bucktooth was so frightened that he withdrew the pump from the gas tank, but continued pressing the nozzle down, so that gasoline poured out onto the pavement.

One of the men sneered at Bucktooth. "Hey, boy, what you think you're doin'? Take your goddamned hand off that nozzle before you waste

119

all the gas!"

Bucktooth simply dropped the nozzle on the ground and stood there shaking.

The leader placed his ugly face against the back window and stared in directly at Phosphate. "Well, lookey here, boys." He said, in the manner of many a badly stereotyped Hollywood villain. "Five niggers in one car. Of course, a couple of 'em are high yellers. By the way, I'm the manager here. And I say you boys was tryin' to make off without payin'."

Waldo could see Brisbane smoldering. "We don't want any trouble, sir." The nervous young man realized his mistake as soon as he'd spoken.

Another of the men, a short fat fellow bearing no small resemblance to Curly Howard of Three Stooges fame, yelled to his leader, "Hey, Cal, she's got manners - she called you sir!"

"Yeah," Cal snickered, "she sure did. I think her and the other nigger gals need a good screwing."

Waldo had long distrusted managers and employees of gas stations, but even his bold imagination couldn't have conjured up a scenario this preposterous.

Phosphate, revealing admirable courage, if less than his usual intelligence, stepped out of the car and walked right up to the leader. "Cal- I believe that is how your friend addressed you-for your information, I am a black male. There are two other black males in the car, as well as three white males. This should be obvious, and I'm not certain why you're having such difficulty grasping it. There are no girls in the car with us. Now, I can understand how, through ignorance, you would dislike someone because of their skin color. A great many people do. However, to fantasize about us sexually, even to the point of misidentifying our gender, indicates latent homosexual tendencies in you. Are you a homosexual, Cal?"

"Hell, no!" With one hand, Cal grabbed Phosphate by the throat and hoisted him into the air. "Now, coon boy, when we're through with you and your friends, you're gonna wish you had been screwed!"

In a compulsive, uncharacteristic display of bravado, Professor Buckley, who was seated in front on the passenger side, flung open his door in desperation and it rammed into the back of Cal's legs, causing him to drop the top doo-wopper. Brisbane, getting into the heroic act, leaped from the back seat and pulled Phosphate into the car. Bucktooth snapped out of his terrified stupor and jumped behind the wheel, and was able to accelerate out of the station before any of the dirty, frightening men could react.

As they roared away down the unnamed path, with its dirt flying in all directions, Waldo glanced back and saw that the gas station was no longer visible behind them. This didn't really surprise him, and he felt confident that if they turned around that very instant and returned to the spot, they would find only bleak, lifeless trees shrouded in mist there.

His hands trembling as he lit a cigarette, Waldo mulled over the sobering possibility that his trip to Iowa had been permanently derailed, and that he may have already joined his grandfather in the land of the lost.

They drove on in the rain and the fog, trying unsuccessfully to find *something*, for another hour when Brisbane, who was sobered by their dilemma and taking a turn behind the wheel, spotted another of the weird purple signs up ahead. This one read "Hidell Street - Next Left."

Everyone agreed that they'd better turn while they were able to, and the fredneck swung the car left at the clearly marked sign which they'd somehow missed on their many previous occasions passing the spot. After only a short distance down the sloping, graveled Hidell Street, Brisbane pointed excitedly to his right.

"Look!" He cried. "Let's see what the fuck *that* is!"

The fredneck was referring to a building with a neon sign flashing its name: "The One Year Wonder And All-Around Oddity Bar." Fontaine squinted at the sign. "Sheeet! What the hell kind of name is that?"

Brisbane turned his decidedly un-fredneck-like vehicle into the parking lot, which was slightly smaller than the doughnut shop's, but full of shiny, older model cars. The place bore an eerie appearance, despite its bright neon sign, as the sickly green paint on its shingled exterior was peeling, a window in front was broken, and there was an overturned dumpster on one side of the building. Trash was overflowing out onto the parking lot, and a putrid smell hung in the air. It didn't require much effort for Waldo to imagine giant rats charging them from the shadows.

"Young man, I say-that is-you can't be serious about going in there!" Professor Buckley exclaimed.

"Yes, Brisbane, it doesn't exactly look inviting." Waldo   cautioned.

"Shit man, what else can happen? It's not like we're any safer on that fucking dirt path." The fredneck pulled into a space between a Volkswagen Bug and what appeared to be a 1920's era car. "Damn, man! Look at that- a Model T!"

Waldo was, of course, incapable of differentiating between various makes of automobiles and unversed on the subject of cars in general, but even he could determine that it was unusual to find a Model T in a parking lot in 1987.

Brisbane hurriedly left the car and explored the parking lot with the enthusiasm, if not the vocabulary, of a small child. "Shit man! There's a fucking DeSoto!" The fredneck was gesturing towards certain vehicles and talking excitedly to himself. "And look at *that*- I haven't seen one of those

121

since the early '70's!"

All the others stood there nervously in the parking lot of extinct cars, waiting for Brisbane to finish his gawking and lead them inside. Eventually the fredneck wandered over to them with a flushed look of excitement on his face.

"Can you believe this shit? This parking lot is fucking awesome! Just imagine..." Brisbane nodded in the direction of the entrance, "what's behind *there*."

The fredneck then walked over and opened the door leading into the building.

"Come on!" He cried out to his hesitant companions. "Where's your sense of adventure?"

"Sheeet!" Fontaine responded. "I left my sense of adventure back on the highway...wherever that is."

"We might as well see what's inside." The top doo-wopper sighed. "We obviously aren't progressing much out here."

Holding hands, the five frightened friends inched forward behind Brisbane into The One Year Wonder And All-Around Oddity Bar.

The door opened into a dark, cool, narrow passage which evidently served as some sort of unorthodox foyer. There were no people about, no smoke in the air, no sounds of music or voices, none of the normal bar ambiance. The first thing they all noticed upon entering was the pungent aroma, much more powerful than the smell from the trash outside, wafting throughout the place.

"Damn!" Bucktooth held his nose. "I ain't never smelled no shit like that before!"

Waldo had to agree. The odor was overpowering and he staggered to one side from its effects. Throwing his hand against the wall to catch himself, Waldo discovered that it was both wet and slimy. He was thoroughly disgusted at this and was searching about for something to wipe it off on, when a door opened to their left and a large man in an outfit resembling what an upstanding member of a barbershop quartet might wear darted out into their path.

"Welcome, gentlemen! Oh, I'm sorry about that, sir." The rotund man produced a towel from under his red vest and handed it to Waldo. "I simply *must* have a talk with Weitzman about cleaning these walls!"

"Thank you." Waldo, even under these circumstances, was not one to forget his manners as he wiped the sludge from his hand.

The powerful stench seemed to dissipate with the arrival of the man, and they all resumed their normal breathing with a great deal of relief.

The place was only dimly lit, by some weak, unseen source of illumination, and they could barely make out the man's features as he spoke in a booming baritone. "My friends, we're *so* pleased to have you!"

He was twirling his fingers about his large black handlebar mustache. "Follow me into the lounge, please."

There was something in his manner that suggested compliance was in order, so they all obligingly followed him as he closed the door through which he'd entered, before any of them could see what lay behind it, and proceeded on down the dark, narrow passage.

After they'd walked a short distance, the strains of dixieland jazz began to be faintly detected, gradually growing louder until they melded with the unmistakable sounds of laughter, flirtation, posturing and clinking glasses that were so dear to the hearts of bar patrons everywhere.

The man with the handlebar mustache stopped abruptly and waved his hand to the right, and there appeared, as if by magic, a set of lustrous red velvet curtains on the wall.

"Damn man!" Fontaine exclaimed. "Are you some kind of magician or something?"

"I'm *something*, alright." The man flashed a peculiar smile and slowly pulled back the curtains. "May I present The One Year Wonder And All-Around Oddity Bar. Stay as long as you like- we *never* close."

They gazed into a large room that was overflowing with people. It was obvious, at a glance, that everyone there was as outdated as the cars parked outside. The women wore the bobbed hairdos and short skirts of the roaring twenties, and some of them were doing the Charleston on a makeshift dance floor. A charmingly scratched version of *Varsity Drag* was emanating from a pair of powerful loudspeakers that hung over the entrance and clashed with the old fashioned decor. Most of the men in the place were dressed in what appeared to be very, very old baseball uniforms.

Brisbane's eyes were as wide as a first time voter's as he stared around the room. "Shit, man! Look at those uniforms- the old Baltimore Orioles, the Boston Pilgrims, the Cleveland Spiders!"

"Gentlemen, this appears to be a most unusual establishment." Phosphate said. "I propose we obtain some refreshments and observe matters for awhile."

"Yeah, man! I'm thirsty!" Bucktooth agreed.

Waldo and the Professor were reluctant to stay, but the others quickly seated themselves at an available table, leaving the nervous duo little choice but to join them.

A pretty young redhead, clad in the typical flapper style, approached their table. "Hiya, keeds. What can I get ya?"

All of them ordered beer, except for Waldo, whose selection of a Manhattan was probably subconsciously influenced by the waitress's New York accent.

The waitress wrote their orders down, furiously chewing gum as she

123

did so. "Twenty three skidoo," she laughed, kicking her heels up in the manner of a more innocent age, and danced across the room.

"Ah, *Vagabond Lover*." Professor Buckley had temporarily forgotten his concerns as he listened to his favorite kind of music. "Rudy Vallee- the original crooner himself. What a voice!"

A slim, boyish brunette in a skimpy green dress evidently noticed how much the oddly attired ex-history teacher was enjoying the song and she walked over to their table and tapped him lightly on the arm.

"How's about a dance, boy?" She asked.

The Professor, unaccustomed to any advances from the opposite sex, sat there dumbfounded with his mouth open. "Well, I don't-that is-y-yes." He finally stammered.

"Ya know, boy, you really should change your outfit. Where'd you find it- at the circus?" The brunette laughed heartily as she led the one time pride of the community college out to the makeshift dance floor and threw her arms around him.

Professor Buckley looked ridiculous as he stumbled his way through the rest of the ballad, his bright clothing appearing even more conspicuous due to his startling ineptitude as a dancer.

Fontaine nudged Bucktooth and laughed uproariously. "Damn, Buck, I know white boys can't dance, but this shit is too much!"

Eventually, the song ended and another period piece, *Beyond The Blue Horizon*, began. Inexplicably, the pretty flapper remained on the dance floor with her pathetic partner, whose consistently ungraceful moves finally ceased to amuse Fontaine and Bucktooth.

"You know, you almost gotta feel sorry for somebody who's that bad." Fontaine shook his head.

The red haired waitress arrived with their drinks, dancing about the table as she placed their orders in front of them. "Hiya, keeds. Peachy place, ain't it?" Before anyone could respond, she kicked her heels in the air and flitted off again.

Waldo lit up a cigarette and tasted his drink. "Listen, I don't think we ought to stay here very long..."

"No shit, Sherlock!" Brisbane chortled. "But first I want to have a little fun. I think I'm gonna talk to some of these guys."

The fredneck left the table and walked over to a group of five men, all of them clad in the old baseball uniforms that were apparently quite popular at The One Year Wonder And All-Around Oddity Bar. They were huddled together on one side of the bar, and Brisbane broke into their conversation with a burst of fredneck chutzpah.

"Hey, dudes. I couldn't help noticing your uniforms. Would you mind telling me where you got them? I'd like to..."

"Excuse me, son." The fredneck was interrupted by the shortest member of the group. "I don't recall ever meeting you. Do any of you fellows know this boy?" The diminutive man wore an ancient Cubs uniform and spoke with a clipped New England accent.

The four other men shook their heads.

Brisbane started to open his mouth, but was interrupted again.

"Who'd you play for, son?" The tallest member of the group asked the puzzled fredneck.

"Huh?" Brisbane was growing increasingly uneasy. "Shit man, I don't know what you're talking about. I mean, I don't play for anybody."

"Don't you, though?" The lanky figure scowled. "You sure look like the athletic type to me."

"Lay off him, Buzz." One of the men spoke up in a southern dialect. "He's probably an outsider. We still get them every once in awhile- you ought to know that."

The man with the friendliest expression on his face smiled at Brisbane and held out his hand. "My name's Irv. Irv Waldron." Pointing at the tallest man, he introduced him. "That there is Buzz Arlett. The big guy hit .313 with 18 homers and 72 runs batted in for the 1931 Phillies. He's a relative newcomer and has a right to be bitter. Standing next to him is Jocko Flynn, who had a record of 24-6 with the 1886 Cubs and led all National League pitchers with a winning percentage of .800. To his right is Ray Jansen, who had 4 hits in 5 at bats for the St. Louis Browns in 1910. That's a lifetime average of .800, son. Never been topped. And the good old Texas boy next to him is Henry Schmidt, who had a 21-13 record as a pitcher for the 1901 Washington Nationals."

"Go on, Irv- tell him about yourself." Ray Jansen urged.

Irv drained his glass of beer. "Well, yes, I split the 1901 season with Milwaukee and Washington, batting .301. I also led the American League in number of times at bat."

Brisbane was having a difficult time comprehending what was being said. "Wait a minute, are you guys telling me that you were major leaguers?"

Waldron smiled and nodded.

The fredneck scratched his head. "But, I don't understand. You said that one dude played in 1886- that's over a hundred years ago, man- and yet he looks pretty young to me. And I know pretty much about old-time baseball, but I've never heard of any of you."

"I have."

Brisbane turned around to find the odd couple from the parking lot of Snortin' Reformatory standing behind him. The kid with the weird hairdo and the pentagram etched in his scrawny chest, whom his plump mentor referred to as Shoestring, had a curious grin on his face.

"I *said*," he repeated, "that I have heard of all those players."

His plain female companion, Dr. Xmaster, patted his bony back. "That's right, he has indeed. Shoestring knows the names and statistics of every player who ever appeared in the big leagues."

"The reason you probably haven't heard of these players," Shoestring explained, "is because they were only in the major leagues for a single season, or, in Jansen's case, only one spectacular game."

Brisbane rubbed his eyes. "I don't believe this shit. If they played so long ago, how can they still be so young, or even alive?"

Jocko Flynn laughed. "That's the magic of this place, my boy. We've been here for a long, long time. It's the only place that welcomed us after we were so unceremoniously dumped by major league baseball. Most of us here don't know any other home."

Brisbane shook his head vigorously. "No, this shit can't be happening."

Dr. Xmaster grinned mechanically. "Come, let us introduce you to some of the other patrons..."

With that, Brisbane was whisked along by several of the players into another room behind the bar. It was overflowing with more men dressed in outdated baseball uniforms. Some of them were playing darts in one corner, a few were gathered about a billiard table in the center, but most were sitting quietly at their tables nursing their bleak, depressed countenances with alcohol. The old tearjerker *I Wonder Who's Kissing Her Now* was coming from a player piano in the back of the room.

"Shoestring, tell our friend about some of these gentlemen." Dr. Xmaster urged her protegee.

"Yes, Doctor." The rainbow coiffed boy began pointing at various men and spouting off their statistics in a robotic fashion. "Over there is Ernie Sulik, who hit .287 for the 1936 Phillies. That's Tex Vache, who batted .313 for the 1925 Red Sox. Sitting by himself at that corner table is Harry Moore, who finished third in the batting race at .336 with the old Washington Nationals in his only season. All of these players share one thing in common: they performed very well in the major leagues for a single season, then never played again." There were tears welling up in Shoestring's eyes. "Others here do not quite fit the category of one-year wonder, but had careers that were just as strange. There's Cuckoo Christensen, who batted .350 as a rookie with the Reds in 1926, missing the batting title by only three points, and played just 57 games the next season before disappearing from the big leagues forever. Then there is Bill Keister, over by the dart board, who in a major league career from 1896-1903 never played for the same team or at the same position two years in a row. He was released by the Phillies, then the worst team in baseball, after leading them in runs batted in and hitting .320. Look at poor Len Koenecke, a Brooklyn outfielder who was slain in the air over Canada after skyjacking a plane late in the 1935 season. He was one of the Dodgers' leading hitters the year before, but he went berserk after manager Casey Stengel farmed him out. There's two more one-year wonders sitting together at the table in front of the rest rooms- Glenn Gardner, who was 3-1 with a 3.29 earned run average for the 1945 Cardinals, and his fellow pitcher John Gaddy, who had a 2-0 record and a sparkling 1.69 earned run average for the 1938 Dodgers. And we mustn't forget the unsung men who belong in the Hall of Fame but aren't even remembered at all today, especially by anyone on the Veterans' selection committee. Consider Ed McKean, the fellow with the huge pile of peanut shells on his table, who was in the majors for 13 years, from 1887-1899, and compiled a lifetime average of .302 with over 2000 hits, or his fellow shortstop George Davis, sitting at the table next to him with the big cigar in his mouth, who played from 1890-1909- 20 years- and finished with a .297 lifetime average and 2688 hits. Compare their stats with any shortstop's in the Hall of Fame, except Honus Wagner or Arky Vaughn, and tell me they're not superior. Pee Wee Reese indeed! Finally, there is the tragic figure leaning against the wall with the pool cue in his hand, Pete Browning. He played from 1882-1894, had a lifetime average of .343, won three batting titles, and was universally recognized as one of the greatest, if not *the* greatest hitter of his era. He died in a Louisville insane asylum in 1905. These men were all destined to come here for one reason or another, and they will remain here forever."

"But..." the fredneck was trembling, "how can he be standing there if he died in 1905?"

"Brisbane!" Waldo shouted above the din of the player piano's rendition of *That Old Gang Of Mine.* He and Phosphate, concerned over their friend's absence, were standing a few feet away in the doorway.

Brisbane rushed over to them. "Oh shit, uh, listen guys, uh, well...let's get the fuck out of here!"

The fredneck rushed from the room, with Waldo and Phosphate right behind him, leaving Shoestring, Dr. Xmaster, and a large group of mistreated and probably unreal baseball players to continue their curious pursuits.

Brisbane kept running through the bar, adroitly sidestepping the flappers who were dancing merrily from one spot to another, tearing part of the red velvet curtains down as he stumbled out of the entrance into the dark, narrow passage with the slimy walls.

"Brisbane, wait!" Waldo cried, as he stopped to grab Professor Buckley, who was still cavorting about the dance floor with the cute brunette, by the shoulder. "Come on, Professor. We have to leave!"

The ex-history teacher lifted his head from the girl's shoulder and peered at Waldo through his thick glasses. "What-that is-my boy, can't you see I'm busy?" There was a look of pure contentment on Hiram Buckley's face.

Phosphate had quickly rounded up his fellow Afro Anarchists, who were miffed over the absence of black flappers in the place, and they ran up breathlessly.

"Let's go, man," Fontaine exclaimed, "before they lock us in."

"Are you experiencing a problem with the Professor?" Phosphate asked.

Waldo sighed. "Yes, he doesn't seem to want to leave." Cupping his hand, he whispered in the top doo-wopper's ear, "I think he's in love."

Phosphate shook his head. "Well, that won't do. I have the inescapable feeling that if we don't depart from this establishment immediately, we may never be able to."

Let A Smile Be Your Umbrella was just ending, and the Professor's dance partner excused herself and went to powder her nose. Seizing the opportunity, Waldo took one of Professor Buckley's arms and Phosphate latched ahold of the other. Fontaine and Bucktooth each lifted a leg and they started carrying him off.

"Professor, I'm sorry, but this is for your own good." Waldo admonished, sounding like many a twentieth century parent.

"This is an outrage!" Screamed the Professor as he writhed and twisted his thin frame in a desperate attempt to break free. "I want to-that is-I'm well over 21, you know. Unhand me and allow me to stay!"

The large man with the handlebar mustache, who'd led them to the bar and apparently served as its unorthodox maitre de', came charging out of the back room waving a bill in his hand. "Stop, you hoodlums! You haven't paid! I'll call the police!"

Fortunately, they managed to struggle out into the hallway, and as soon as they did a great gushing sound arose. The red curtains disappeared behind them, and there was only wet, mucky drywall where the opening had been. The One Year Wonder And All-Around Oddity Bar was no more.

All of them stood frozen for a few moments in their astonishment before proceeding rapidly down the corridor with the protesting Professor in tow.

"No! Take me back!" The ex-history teacher cried. "She said I was *debonair*!"

Brisbane, no longer any kind of athlete at all, was huffing and puffing as he barreled out the door and into the parking lot. He was bending over and gasping for air when his companions exited the building and finally placed the Professor gingerly back on his own feet.

"I don't-that is-Waldo, especially you- how could you treat me in such a manner?" Professor Buckley was aghast at being handled in such an undignified fashion. "I want to go back in there." The ex-history teacher smoothed out his rumpled, colorful clothing.

"Professor Buckley, I offer you a humble apology for treating you so harshly. However," The top doo-wopper pointed upwards, "it is apparent that your desire to return to the company of your female acquaintance cannot be fulfilled. Please observe..."

The Professor turned around. The neon sign, flashing "The One Year Wonder And All-Around Oddity Bar", was gone. Gazing around the parking lot, he saw no vintage automobiles, no cars of any kind except for Brisbane's decidedly un-fredneck-like '65 Dodge Dart. The building was crumbling and obviously deserted.

Brisbane opened his car door and climbed in behind the wheel. "I'm leaving." He announced matter of factly. "Get in now, all of you, if you want to come."

They didn't hesitate to heed the fredneck's request, and it wasn't until they'd driven along Hidell Street long enough to know they were lost again that Brisbane related the details of his bizarre encounter with the denizens of The One Year Wonder And All-Around Oddity Bar.

"Shit man, it was unbelievable." The fredneck had opened a beer and was downing it rapidly. "Those ballplayers all looked so young...and that Doctor and her fucking Shoestring..."

"How could that be?" Waldo, who very rarely found anything he believed couldn't be, wondered aloud.

"I'm beginning to feel like a character," Phosphate stroked his chin, "in an episode of *The Twilight Zone*. I suggest we stop the car and conserve our fuel. It will be dark soon, and this place seems much less imposing by daylight."

Apparently they had been inside the bar for quite a while, as the night was rapidly descending upon them. All at once, the light rain turned into a torrential downpour, and an angry wind began to howl, causing the fog shrouded trees to appear less stark and harmless as they swayed violently back and forth.

"Damn man, all we need now is some thunder and lightning." Fontaine exclaimed.

As if on command, a sonic peal of thunder shook their car and a terrifying bolt of lightning crackled across the sky.

Brisbane stopped the car and turned off the engine. "Lock your doors. I don't know about the rest of you, but I need another beer."

The violent storm lasted throughout the night, and the six displaced souls huddled sleeplessly together in their cramped quarters, discussing their fate in terrified, foreboding tones. They also consumed a great deal of beer, and nervously munched on the vitamin-less snack foods Waldo had pilfered from the curious old general store.

As the first rays of dawn started peeking over the horizon, the rain abruptly ceased, and the wind stopped howling. A flock of bluebirds flew out of one of the bare, lifeless trees and brightened the cold, gray sky.

Waldo lit a cigarette. "You know, I have a funny feeling that, I don't know why, but if we drove back out to the dirt path..."

"We'd suddenly be able to find our way out of here?" Phosphate interjected.

"Yes, exactly." Waldo replied.

"An interesting theory." The top doo-wopper remarked. "The environment certainly seems less threatening now. I see no reason not to follow your suggestion."

Neither did anyone else, so Brisbane started the car and headed down Hiddell Street. Less than a mile later, they came not to an unnamed dirt path, but a modern, paved road with a marker indicating it was Edberg Avenue. There was also a sign, and it was a dull, conventional blue, not purple, that said "To Route 95" with an arrow pointing right.

"Alright!" Everyone shouted in unison.

It was indeed alright, as they encountered no more presidential descendants, bloodthirsty gas station attendants, ancient ballplayers, or even inclement weather, as Brisbane swung his decidedly un-fredneck-like vehicle back onto the interstate, in the general direction of Cornoil, Iowa.

"DeMohrenschildt. Hidell. Weitzman." Waldo ran his fingers through his hair. "I can't believe I didn't recognize those names right away!"

Brisbane diverted his eyes from the highway, to the distress of his fellow passengers, and turned towards Waldo, who was sitting next to him. "What the fuck are you talking about, man?"

Only a Kennedy assassination aficionado such as Waldo could have discerned a common thread in the names of DeMohrenschildt, Hiddell, and Weitzman. Having spent many nights in his life poring over all the available works on the subject, including the most obscure, privately published material, he was thoroughly familiar with all its maddening minutiae.

"I mean," Waldo explained, "that the name of the gravel path we turned off onto, where the doughnut shop was- DeMohrenschildt Lane- was the same as Lee Harvey Oswald's mentor in Dallas, the mysterious George DeMohrenschildt. Alex Hidell was Oswald's supposed alias, one he allegedly employed to order the ridiculous rifle they claimed was used to kill Kennedy and the pistol they claimed was used to murder police officer J.D. Tippit. And the name that man with the handlebar mustache referred to, when we were walking through that passage to the One Year

Wonder And All-Around Oddity Bar- Weitzman- was the name of one of the two deputies that found the rifle on the sixth floor of the Texas School Book Depository building after the assassination. Seymour Weitzman first swore that it was a German Mauser, but later identified it as an Italian Mannlicher Carcano, saying he had been mistaken. Don't you understand?"

Fontaine was staring at Waldo with the kind of vacant, unretentive expression normally worn by those struggling to comprehend the expanding universe, big bang, trickle down, single bullet, or any other equally absurd and widely accepted theory. "Who in the hell could understand *that*?"

"Waldo, wasn't DeMohrenschildt the one who shot himself just before the House Assassinations Committee could question him?" The top doo-wopper asked.

"Yes, and his was only one of many, many mysterious and timely deaths." Waldo clearly enjoyed displaying his superior knowledge about the case. "Did you hear about the reporter who was killed by a karate chop to the neck as he stepped out of the shower? Or the stripper..."

Hiram Buckley, familiar with the details of such disquieting incidents himself, opened his battered briefcase. Waldo, his own seldom used suitcase filled with a few personal effects and reams of his grandfather's unpublished pamphlets, had asked the Professor to carry Sam Hancock's journal in his old briefcase, and the ex-history teacher had managed to find room for it alongside all the precious back issues of *Force Of Habit*. The eccentric ex-history teacher had resigned himself to the fact that his brief romantic interlude with the pretty brunette flapper had been illusory in nature, much as he'd been forced to accept the finality of his wife's sudden departure some years previously.

As the discussion about murdered witnesses, umbrella men, and lethargic secret service agents raged on all about him, Professor Buckley opened the journal of Sam Hancock and settled back in his seat:

The Journal of Sam Hancock, February 14, 1954

Cupid didn't strike me with his arrow again this year, so I won't write about sweethearts and valentines today. What I want to recount here are the highlights of my recent excursion to Brazil. I was accompanied, as always, by my stalwart friend Abner "Old Hoss" Billingsly. We went there with the intention of picking up Colonel Percy Fawcett's trail. Fawcett disappeared in its deep, inhospitable jungles, along with two others in his expedition, a few decades ago. It is the belief of a few on the political fringes that the Colonel was murdered by some strange tribe in order to stop him from revealing what secrets lie in that

131

mysterious and still mostly unexplored region of the world. Others speculate that he fell victim to a bizarre magnetic force that sucked him away into another dimension. Although we did not locate Colonel Fawcett or his remains, nor even find any clues regarding his fate, we did make the acquaintance of another interesting character.

It is a curious fact that on most of our numerous trips, we do seem to meet someone unusual, and they often prove beneficial or serve to enlighten us in some other manner when our investigative work has proven unfruitful. Homer Clambahan was one such individual.

Homer happened to be staying at the same hotel we were. Old Hoss and I were enjoying a few cocktails in the lounge there on our first night in Brazil, when an odd-looking fellow in a white lab coat walked up to our table. He later told us that he was forty years old, but he appeared to be much younger. He was small and frail looking, with thinning blonde hair and thick eyeglasses. Actually, had a movie director been searching to cast the role of a mad scientist, Homer Clambahan would have been the perfect choice. He was quite personable, and introduced himself to us, explaining that he had overheard a few words of our conversation and was aware we were fellow Americans.

"You know, I haven't met anyone here who speaks English fluently in over a year." There was a nasal quality in his soft, timid voice.

"Well, we're pleased to meet you, Homer. We didn't expect to run into many Americans here. This isn't exactly a tourist trap." Old Hoss spoke in his warm, friendly manner.

"What brings you gentlemen to this part of the world?" Homer asked.

I smiled at him. "I doubt if you'd understand our reason for being here." I certainly must have sounded snobbish.

"Try me." He dared.

Old Hoss lit up one of his large, foul smelling cigars. "Homer, have you ever heard of an explorer named Fawcett?"

"Sure, the Colonel vanished not all that far from here about, oh, I don't know, it must have been sometime back in the twenties."

"That's right. Well, Sam and I are kind of explorers ourselves, in a sense. So we've journeyed here, as we do to various other locales, in order to try and solve a very intriguing mystery. In this case, we're going to attempt to follow his last known path and see if we find anything." Old Hoss blew his pungent cigar smoke high into the air. It hovered over the bar like a thick cloud, and must have proved unpleasant to the few other patrons in the place.

"So you fellows are interested in the unknown, eh?" Homer was wearing a wide grin on his thin face.

"Yes, why?" I inquired.

132

"Because I just happen to have something in my room which I'm sure you'd find fascinating."

"What is it?" Old Hoss and I asked in unison.

"Come with me and I'll show you." He grinned again, apparently enjoying the look of anticipation on our faces.

Homer got up from the table and we followed him upstairs. We came to his room and the three of us entered. I must confess that my generally suspicious nature had me thinking him to be a potential homosexual or even worse. Old Hoss seemed to harbor no such reservations, however, and as soon as we were through the door he was questioning what and where it was.

"Relax," Homer said, "I'll be right back with it." He then went into the bathroom and closed the door behind him.

I was a bit apprehensive of his being out of our sight, remembering all too well the saga of the strange inventor who earlier in this century had come up with a liquid substance that, when added to water, produced gasoline. He had been persuaded by the man he'd mysteriously picked to demonstrate it on to take it to a major company, and when he did they were mightily impressed with his invention. They asked him to leave the room for a moment while they held a private discussion. The mysterious inventor stepped out into the hall and was never seen or heard from again. Despite a world wide search, he could not be found, and his magic liquid was never understood or duplicated. At any rate, such are the things I remember, and when Homer left the room, that story came to mind. It was ironic that I should be comparing him with an inventor, because it turned out that was exactly what he was.

When Homer came out of the bathroom, he was holding a small machine in his hands. It was really a nondescript device, and I would have a hard time finding anything about it that struck me as being unique or memorable. If it could be described at all, I'd say it was akin to a hot iron with lots of tiny wheels on it.

He gave the wheels a spin and requested that we keep our eyes on them. We sat there observing them for a good five minutes and the wheels did not lose any velocity.

"You ingenious rascal! It's perpetual motion!" Old Hoss exclaimed.

The crusty skeptic then asked Homer to let us examine the device in order to rule out what is usually found in such so-called perpetual motion machines- hidden batteries, strings, pulleys, etc. We searched it with a fine tooth comb without being able to unearth any chicanery on his part. There honestly didn't appear to be anything generating its energy.

"Go ahead, search all you want. I can assure you it's real. I've devoted many years to this project, and only recently perfected it. I based my studies on the work of Keely in the last century. Are you familiar with him?" Homer was challenging us to be informed about someone even more obscure than Colonel Fawcett.

"Certainly. John Keely of Philadelphia." Old Hoss knew something about nearly every eccentric who'd ever lived. "But didn't he destroy his machine after the powers of his day succeeded in suppressing it?"

"Yes. You really do know your history. However, he left some written data behind with a grandson whom I was able to track down, and he was gracious enough to allow me to study his grandfather's records."

"Well, what are you planning to do with your invention?" I wanted to know.

"I'm not sure yet. I'm well aware of what happened to Keely and even lesser known inventors who delved into this area long before me."

"I hope you're able to market it, but you surely must realize what damage such a product could cause to the fuel industry. Do you actually think they would allow such an advance in technology, which would make it possible for everyone to heat their homes and run their cars at little or no cost?" Old Hoss knew the extent of corporate greed if anyone did.

"I know, but what else can I do? I have nowhere else to take it." Homer looked fatigued and I tried to ignore the uneasy feeling that he possessed the aura of a man already beaten.

At that point, it was growing very late so we departed. We agreed to meet again in the morning for breakfast. It came as no real surprise to either of us when he didn't show up. Just for the fun of it, Old Hoss checked at the front desk and asked if Mr. Clambahan was still registered at the hotel. The clerk scanned his records and informed him that Mr. Clambahan had checked out that morning. Both Old Hoss and I have learned to find humor in such situations. We knew that the world would never hear of Homer Clambahan again. He had mentioned to us that the remote area was perfect for his work, and he intended to stay there indefinitely. And so we drank an early morning toast to him and his machine. It could have been a boon for mankind, but as in Mr. Keely's case and countless others, someone apparently felt otherwise. So I devote this entry in my journal to you, Homer Clambahan, wherever you are. Rest assured that *we* will remember and admire you.

"Most remarkable." Professor Buckley mumbled aloud.

"What's that, Professor?" Waldo asked.

"Oh, nothing, my boy. Have we-that is-I was just reading a bit of this Hancock's journal." The ex-history teacher gave his yellow tie a few obligatory tugs. "It's quite interesting, you know."

"Professor, when you've finished, I'd like to browse through it myself." Phosphate requested.

"Certainly, Phosphate."

They were approaching the point where interstate 95 branched off in another direction.

"Look- there it is, Brisbane!" Fontaine pointed to the exit sign. "Route 250- One Mile."

"Wait a second..." Phosphate said. "Unless I'm mistaken, route 95 branches off into route 270, not 250. That's the exit we're supposed to take."

"I don't think I've ever heard of route 250." remarked Waldo.

"Relax, all of you." Brisbane chuckled. His nervous system, numbed by years of drug usage, was quite resilient, and he had already left his experience in the One Year Wonder And All-Around Oddity Bar far behind him. "That's the exit we want."

"Are you sure, Brisbane?" Waldo asked.

"Waldo, you told me yourself about how bad you are at directions." The fredneck took a swig of his ever-present beer. "I know what I'm doing."

Indeed, it was hard to disagree with him, as the sky, no longer bearing a single sinister cloud of doom, was now a bright, reassuring blue, and the sun sparkled off the chrome of the other automobiles. As Brisbane veered right onto route 250, everyone felt comforted by the fact the sign was a perfectly legitimate green, not purple.

8
ON THE FUNNY SIDE OF THE STREET

From *More Unanswered Questions*, an unpublished pamphlet by
Abner Billingsly, pg. 15:
"Why is it that special news bulletins never interrupt commercials?"

The rest of that day was uneventful, and the six of them reveled in
the lack of excitement by drinking heavily and holding numerous heated
discussions on all manner of subjects close to the hearts of extremists
everywhere.

By dusk, whatever doubts any of them had about the legitimacy
and/or reality of route 250 had been dispelled. They were becoming quite
proficient at switching drivers, resembling a non-athletic relay team, and
Fontaine took Waldo's place behind the wheel in a minimum amount of
time, maneuvering the decidedly un-fredneck-like '65 Dodge Dart back
onto the perfectly normal looking highway in a smooth and orderly
fashion. Brisbane had reentered the familiar world of inebriation and was
inundating Phosphate with his theory about the Pavlovian effects of
"southern rock" music when he suddenly sat up straight and pointed to
the side of the road.

"Okay man, pull over!" He yelled at Fontaine, sounding like a law
enforcement officer with visions of illegal u-turns dancing in his head.
"Pick up that hitchhiker."

"Sheeet, man!" Fontaine objected. "It's already more crowded in
here than a bathroom at a Michael Jackson concert. Why in the hell do
you want to pick up a damn stranger?"

Brisbane belched. "Rules of the road, dude. It's my fucking car, and
I say we stop and give him a ride."

Fontaine shrugged in resignation and slowed the car down until
they came abreast of a man standing in a gray trenchcoat.

Brisbane ordered Bucktooth to climb in back and squeeze in
somehow alongside Phosphate, Professor Buckley, and himself. Although
older cars were generally capable of accommodating more passengers
than their modern brethren, it was hardly reasonable to expect four people
to be seated comfortably in the back seat of any automobile, and they all
joined Fontaine in protesting this illogical idea. The fredneck, however,
apparently felt strongly about the issue, and quelled any opposition by
pointing out the indisputable fact that it was *his* car.

The hitchhiker climbed in the front seat next to Waldo. "Thanks a
lot." He said as he settled in.

Waldo scrutinized the man carefully. He tended to share Fontaine's trepidation about picking up strangers thumbing rides. The hitchhiker was older than they were, probably around forty five or so, thought Waldo. He looked to be abnormally average, if such a thing were possible, in his bland gray suit, matching fedora, and colorless tie, as if he'd just stepped off a stage appearing in the title role of *Death Of A Salesman*.

"So what are you doing out here in the middle of nowhere?" Waldo realized that his words sounded as if they'd come from the opening of an old Universal horror film.

The man removed his nondescript felt hat, exposing a head of neatly parted brown and gray flecked hair. "Is this nowhere? I wasn't aware of that."

Waldo grew more suspicious at the stranger's flippant reply. Why would a middle-aged man be hitchhiking out on the interstate?

Phosphate seemed to become aroused as well, and addressed Waldo's concerns with a more logical question. "Did you have car trouble?"

The hitchhiker smirked. "I don't drive. Never have."

"Then how did you arrive," The top doo-wopper asked, "at this rather remote location?"

"I like the area." The man seemed unflustered and lit up an unfiltered cigarette, carefully moistening the tip before he stuck it in his mouth. "I hitchhiked here- it's the only way I travel."

"From where?" Phosphate was as relentless in his questioning as an overzealous law student.

"From anywhere." The stranger's responses were as curt and deceptive as an experienced intelligence agent's. "Or everywhere."

What is with this guy? Waldo wondered, becoming slowly alarmed. He tried to nonchalantly inch farther away on the car seat.

Brisbane, however, obviously wasn't bothered in the least by the hitchhiker. "My name's Brisbane Wrock, man, and that's Waldo Billingsly sitting next to you. You'll have to excuse him, he's got a lot on his mind. His grandfather recently disappeared without a trace. The guy driving is Fontaine Washington. Back here with me are Professor Hiram Buckley- in the bright outfit, Bucktooth Johnson, and Phosphate Jefferson- the one who keeps asking you all the questions."

The man glanced briefly at each of them and uttered a barely audible "how do you do?"

Phosphate didn't deter easily. "You know our names. What's yours?"

The man smiled faintly and said, "Fillmore. John Fillmore."

"You ain't related to Millard, are you?" Bucktooth asked.

The man laughed slightly. "No, I don't believe so."

"Oh, I just thought since we already met a Polk..." Bucktooth tried to explain his absurd reasoning.

"Where are you headed, John?" Brisbane was concise and to the point.

"I would be grateful if you could drop me off at the corner of Oak Cliff Drive. It should only be a couple of miles from here."

"But this is the interstate, Mr. Fillmore." Phosphate reminded him. "There isn't going to be a corner of anything here."

"You'll see." The man rolled down his window and, in reckless disregard for the laws against littering, flipped his cigarette butt out. "There'll be a corner of Oak Cliff, alright."

"And what's waiting for you there?" Waldo knew that he sounded like the anxious mother of a teenager, but he didn't care at this point whether or not the stranger found out he was suspicious of him.

"I don't think that's any of your business." The hitchhiker glared at Waldo for a split second with an angry pair of eyes, but just as rapidly his expression lightened and he flashed a broad smile. "Forgive me. I meant that in the most polite way."

"Sure man, we understand. Don't we, Waldo?" Brisbane chided in a paternalistic tone.

Waldo normally resented all advice, and he found it particularly difficult to accept any coming from a mere fredneck. He was too frightened to defend himself, however, as the image of the stranger's briefly flashing eyes-such a bright, blood red that they might have been mistaken for a wild animal's-burned vividly in his mind.

Waldo held his tongue for the rest of the short ride, which was spent in almost total silence. It was clear the hitchhiker was not going to reveal anything about himself to allay their apprehensions.

All at once, a construction crew appeared up ahead and Fontaine slowed the car down. There was a sign with a light flashing "Detour" and an arrow pointing right.

"Damn, man!" Fontaine commented as he followed the detour sign. "I hate being re-routed!"

Waldo was beginning to hyperventilate, as he was prone to do during his frequent anxiety attacks. He closed his eyes and wasn't at all surprised when Bucktooth screamed a few moments later.

"Look- it's another one of them purple signs!"

Waldo slowly opened his eyes and saw the sign, so distinctly and frighteningly conspicuous, looming on the right side of the road.

"Ah, there it is." The hitchhiker said smugly. "My street is next."

The purple sign did read "Oak Cliff- Next Right," and at length Fontaine stopped the car obligingly when the stranger announced they'd reached his destination. They appeared to be in a desolate stretch of countryside, hardly what one would expect just a short distance from the interstate, and various unidentified sounds of the wild echoed chillingly in the air.

It was nearly dark as the man got out of the car. He murmured a quick thank you to Brisbane and began walking briskly away. When he'd gone only a few steps, he turned around abruptly and stared directly at Waldo with an unearthly grin on his face.

"You'll notice, of course, that no one lives around here."

With that he let out an awful, piercing laugh and started moving at an even faster pace than before down the unpaved country path marked Oak Cliff.

Waldo, paralyzed with fear, recognized the name Oak Cliff as the section of Dallas where police officer J.D. Tippit was shot shortly after John F. Kennedy was assassinated on November 22, 1963. The stranger's bone chilling laugh was familiar to Waldo, as well. He'd laughed in the same identical manner as the magistrate back at Snortin' Reformatory.

"Oh dear, oh,dear." The Professor had torn himself away from Sam Hancock's journal and was now vying with Waldo for the title of most worried passenger. "This is so-that is-oh dear, *oh dear*."

"Waldo, what do you make of *that*?" Phosphate sounded amazingly calm.

Waldo, extremely upset, tried to keep his voice from trembling as he spoke. "I...I don't know. He must have been another ridiculous unreal."

The top doo-wopper, despite his erudite reputation, did not know what an unreal was. As Waldo attempted to brief him on the subject, he recovered somewhat from the unsettling experience.

Phosphate's fellow Afro Anarchist, Bucktooth, had witnessed something that the others apparently hadn't. Waiting for an appropriate pause in the infernal political chatter among Waldo, Brisbane, Phosphate, and Professor Buckley, Bucktooth spoke up.

"Hey, listen, everybody. I don't care if you all believe me or not, but I saw some weird shit back there!"

"Yeah, who didn't, Buck?" Fontaine replied.

Waldo's spine began warming up. "Oh... what was that, Bucktooth?"

Bucktooth's eyes grew wide as he blurted out, "When that strange dude got out of the car and walked away, I kept my eyes on him. Even when you was driving off, Fontaine, I was watching him. You're not gonna believe me but... I swear, one second I was looking at him and the next... he was gone!"

Brisbane chortled. "Sure, Bucktooth, sure."

"I ain't shitting you, man!" Bucktooth was adamant. "He disappeared right in front of my eyes, as I was watching him walk."

Phosphate made some sufficiently introspective and paranoid comment, but Waldo wasn't listening. He was shaking.

From the notorious diary of Mad Millard Billingsly, July 31, 1899:

These are grand times, indeed. I went to a lovely concert in Montrose Park this evening, and Georgetown never saw a more beautiful night. I can still hear *Wait 'Til The Sun Shines, Nellie* ringing in my ears. However, all is not bread and circuses here. We have experienced a mysterious epidemic of persons bursting into flames in our fair city lately. From acquaintances who are privy to such things, I have learned that this phenomenon is not unknown and is usually referred to as spontaneous human combustion. The first case here was reported about two months ago, and since then there have been at least seven more. Oddly enough, most of the incidents have occurred while the unfortunate victims were riding on our streetcars, which used to be renowned for their safety and comfort. In each instance, the person involved suddenly and inexplicably became engulfed in flames. There is never any outside source for the fire that the authorities can uncover, and in a few cases queer facts have emerged. Upon examination of one victim, it was discovered that his clothes were not even singed. This is extremely strange, and it is such information that is causing me to become much too concerned with the whole situation. And so it was nice to take a stroll and attend a concert tonight. It served to relax me and hopefully I can now take some time off from those long nights of alcohol, tobacco, and the rarely-read books that deal with the subject of persons unexpectedly igniting into flames. Until next time, I remain the eccentric one on the Potomac.

"But how do you explain his saying that no one lived around there? Or that horrible laugh?" Waldo had calmed down considerably and was in the midst of a searing debate with Brisbane over whether there had been anything strange, even otherworldly, about the hitchhiker they had picked up a few hours earlier.

"Shit man, you're too fucking paranoid! I've picked up hundreds of hitchhikers before and that dude was no weirder than half of them." The fredneck, certainly a verifiable paranoid himself, seemed to feel compelled to defend the honor of the hitchhiking set.

Waldo was just as determined to tie the encounter in with the unexplained incidents of the past few days. "Have you ever heard of the Men In Black, Brisbane?"

The fredneck thought he had, but couldn't recall precisely when or where.

Phosphate was only too happy to supply a definition. "The Men In

Black, or M.I.B.'s, as they are commonly referred to, are well known to most U.F.O. researchers."

"That's right." Waldo politely continued. "M.I.B.'s are men, obviously, usually dressed in black and in groups of three, who seem out of their element, acting in a peculiar manner..."

"Excuse me, Waldo," Phosphate cut in, "from everything I've read, your description of M.I.B.'s is most accurate, but I was under the impression that they specialize in visiting U.F.O. witnesses and harassing them."

"They do. And they usually claim-falsely most researchers agree-that they are representatives of some official organization, most often a branch of the military. They also tend to issue warnings, urging the witnesses not to tell anyone about them. However, Phosphate, they are also involved in other interesting areas. Did you know, for instance, that some people think the phony secret service agents in Dealy Plaza when J.F.K. was killed were M.I.B.'s?" Waldo sounded like the granddaddy of all Forteans.

"Hmmm. I've never heard that theory. It's just bizarre enough to be possible." There weren't very many theories Phosphate hadn't heard, and he was naturally curious to learn more about the subject.

Brisbane burst into the conversation. "Okay, man. All of that shit sounds fascinating, but what are you saying? That the hitchhiker we picked up was one of those M.I.B.'s?"

Waldo lit a cigarette and inhaled deeply before responding. "I'm not sure. I know he was very strange, and acted like an M.I.B. might be expected to, if you study some of the reports. And if he really did disappear..."

"Yeah, man, but that dude wasn't dressed in black and there was only one of him." Brisbane sounded unnatural in the role of a debunker. "And none of us has seen a U.F.O. lately. At least I haven't."

"I said they are *usually* in black and in threes." Waldo was bothered by his fredneck friend's attitude. "I don't understand why you're being so skeptical. You certainly seem to be interested in a lot of other peculiar things. And what about those old baseball players in that bar, or whatever it was, that you insisted on stopping in?"

Brisbane smiled. "Okay, I guess I'm being too argumentative. I'm sorry, man. It's just that I respect hitchhikers. Maybe that dude was an M.I.B." With that, the fredneck reached down and pulled a can of beer from the small cooler on the floor. Lifting it towards Waldo, he proposed a toast. "Here's to my good friend Waldo Billingsly. And to all the M.I.B.'s, wherever they may be."

"Gentlemen," Professor Buckley suddenly spoke up, "I can assure you that I am as interested in M.I.B.'s-that is-haven't any of you noticed that we appear to be back on the same sort of strange road that we had so much trouble leaving before?"

"Yeah!" Fontaine echoed. "I've been driving around for almost half an hour, and I don't know where the hell we are. I ain't never seen a detour that lasted this long."

"And there ain't no signs saying anything about it..." Bucktooth observed.

"Or how far we are from being back on the highway." Brisbane shook his head. "We have to face it- we're back where we were before."

"Well, it's not exactly the same." Waldo remarked. "I just saw a deer running across the road, and the weather isn't bad. But it *is* just as eerie."

"I'm afraid we've allowed our mutual interest in the paranormal to distract us from what should obviously be our main concern at the moment." The top doo-wopper admitted sheepishly. "Sometimes, it seems that those of us who are preoccupied with such things are capable of conversing about the odd and unexplained under *any* circumstances."

The decidedly un-fredneck-like '65 Dodge Dart found itself proceeding down yet another unnamed road, although this one was paved. The night sky was overcast, but not frightening, and the open, grassy terrain around them boasted a wide array of plant and animal life. From time to time, Fontaine could dimly discern, in the old car's headlights, a rabbit, a squirrel, or a raccoon scurrying quickly out of the way. With only Hollywood as a guide, it was impossible for any of them to positively identify the cry of a wolf, but *something* certainly was howling off in the distance. The new unnamed road, unlike the previous one, was liberally intersected by side streets, which the scared and weary travelers were understandably hesitant to venture onto.

"Shit man, you know how long it's gonna take us to get to Iowa at this rate?" Brisbane belched. "Waldo, when we find our way back to the interstate... I hate to say it, dude, but maybe we ought to, you know... turn around and head back to Virginia."

Waldo stared at the fredneck as if he'd suggested they don leather jackets, arm themselves with knives and chains, and terrorize some senior citizens. "Brisbane, I appreciate the fact you wanted to help me look for my grandfather. I'm especially grateful for the use of your car. But, if you've decided you don't want to help any longer, I understand. It's been a strange trip so far, and it probably will get stranger. I don't like it any more than you do, believe me. If that's what..."

"Okay, okay!" Brisbane tossed his empty beer can over his shoulder, Henry the Eighth-style, and reached for another. "I've had a lot to drink, it's been a long day, and I don't really know what I'm saying. Besides, I'm not sure we *could* find our way back to Virginia, or anywhere else, right now."

As the gas gauge on their trusty old means of transportation dipped a bit lower, none of his companions could disagree with the fredneck's bleak assessment.

A short time later, Fontaine suddenly went berserk when he saw yet another purple sign, this one reading "Mama Petunia's Bingo Parlor- Next Left."

"Oh, man!" He cried out in near orgasmic delight. "I love bingo!" With that, the eager Afro Anarchist turned left at the next side street, before anyone could utter a word of protest.

"Fontaine, what do you think you're doing?" Phosphate admonished his doo-wopping cohort. "Whether any of us share your affinity for bingo or not, you've exhibited a great deal of gall, as well as poor judgment, in turning onto one of these side streets, which will in all probability prove to be nefarious in nature."

"Damn, Phos, how do you know that?" Bucktooth attempted to defend his fellow Afro Anarchist. "I mean, we weren't going nowhere on that re-routed road."

"Bucktooth, that may be true." The top doo-wopper patted Fontaine paternally on the shoulder. "And I did not intend to unduly criticize Fontaine, I simply feel we must all begin to display a degree of caution; we are obviously dealing with elements of an extraordinary character."

Fontaine hung his head in disgrace, apparently steering the car by some extra sensory method. "I-I'm sorry, Phos. I don't know what came over me..."

"That's quite alright, Fontaine." Phosphate adopted the tone of a benevolent schoolmaster, which he did far too frequently when communicating with his two fellow Afro Anarchists.

"Excuse me, young man, but could you please keep your eyes on the road?" The careful ex-history teacher, a fervent disciple of defensive driving, reminded Fontaine.

"Oh yeah, man. Sorry." Fontaine lifted his head and proceeded to guide the car in a more conventional fashion.

"You know, we might as well go ahead and play a little bingo." Brisbane suddenly said. "With all the wild shit that's been happening, it might be just what we need..."

"What?" Waldo replied incredulously. "I thought you just said you wanted to turn around and go back to Virginia?"

The fredneck lit up a cigarette. "Yeah, and I still do. But I doubt if we'll be able to do that anytime soon. And in the meantime, I just thought a little diversion might relax us..."

"I don't need that sort of diversion." The Professor was tugging

143

furiously at his tie, a sure indicator that they were in dire straits.

"The brand of bingo played at any establishment around *here* is liable to be, as Waldo might describe it, unreal." Phosphate stroked his chin philosophically. "However, at this point I can raise no real objection to at least approaching the place. I don't see what we have to lose by doing so, and it will certainly please Fontaine."

Waldo threw his hands up in defeat, realizing that he and Professor Buckley were outvoted. "Like they say- the majority rules."

Having received a mandate of sorts, Fontaine drove on excitedly. After they'd traveled quite a distance, with no bingo parlor, or any other signs of civilization in sight, Waldo was about to suggest they conserve their remaining supply of gasoline and turn back, when a green glimmering light broke the darkness of the remote countryside.

"That must be the place!" Fontaine shouted.

As they drew closer, his suspicions were confirmed, as the light was in fact a neon sign, almost identical to the one they'd seen in front of The One Year Wonder And All-Around Oddity Bar, and it was flashing "Mama Petunia's Bingo Parlor" in big, bold letters.

Fontaine was as full of anticipation as a South American drug addict awaiting the arrival of a C.I.A. plane, and he pulled into the parking lot so haphazardly that he undoubtedly would have hit any pedestrians, real or otherwise, that chanced to be there. Fortunately, everyone must have been inside, engrossed in the game, and Fontaine met no bodily resistance as he sped to the back of the building, which was approximately the size of a fire station, and pulled the decidedly un-fredneck-like '65 Dodge Dart into a parking space.

As Fontaine rushed from the car and left the others far behind, Waldo wondered where all the people had come from, as there was a plethora of automobiles in the parking lot, yet they had passed no houses or stores, not even an unreal, outdated one, since they'd been detoured from route 230. The place in fact appeared to be packed, and the parking space Fontaine had found in the back had been one of the last, if not the last one available. As they walked towards the front entrance, past all the empty vehicles, Waldo felt more uneasy with every pickup truck and motorcycle he saw, as they definitely seemed to be unduly represented there. With his stereotypical notions about the owners of such modes of transportation, the sensitive young man became as fidgety as a grandmother on a rollercoaster.

As they rounded the corner of the building, a large man in overalls, bearing a striking physical similarity to Junior Sample of *Hee Haw* fame, came thundering down the front steps like some heretofore unidentified breed of bouncer.

The crude looking man stopped just in front of them and spat a giant wad of chewing tobacco their way. Bucktooth had to duck quickly to avoid being hit in the head. He then gazed at them with a dense countenance. "You boys from around here?" He drawled his words so slowly that it seemed impossible to believe it was his natural voice.

Phosphate spoke up immediately. "No, sir. We are on a cross country excursion and happened to be passing through your lovely town. We thought that perhaps we might partake of a little innocuous gambling and decided to frequent your place of business for that purpose."

The man who looked so much like Junior Sample still wore a blank expression on his face. "Well, I don't know now. Down here in Lovelady we don't exactly get a lot of tourists."

Waldo twitched at the mention of the town's name. "Did you say *Lovelady?*"

Junior Sample, Jr. nodded. "That's right. Let me see if Mama Petunia minds if you boys play with us tonight. Most of the time we require a reservation, you know, but she might be willing to make an exception. You all wait right here."

"Reservation?" Fontaine mumbled to himself with a frown on his face. "Is this a bingo hall or a fancy French restaurant?"

While Junior, Jr. walked inside, curiously picking up speed, despite his Humpty Dumpty-like frame, as he bounced up the steps, Waldo turned to the others. "Look, let's get out of here now. Did you see get a good look at that guy? Imagine what's inside." His trembling hands required several attempts before they succeeded in lighting a cigarette. "And what about the town's name- Lovelady?"

Brisbane looked puzzled. "What about it, man?"

"Billy Lovelady was an employee of the Texas School Book Depository on November 22, 1963." Waldo impatiently recounted. "When the famous Altgens photograph was published, and it was pointed out that a man closely resembling Lee Harvey Oswald could be seen standing in the doorway of the Depository at the moment the shots were being fired, supposedly six floors above him, the Warren Commission explained it away by identifying the individual in the doorway as Billy Lovelady."

"That is very interesting, Waldo. I'm not quite grasping the connection, however." Even Phosphate was struggling with Waldo's outlandish notion.

"Like I said before, DeMohrenschildt, Hidell, Weitzman, and Oakcliff are all names associated with the J.F.K. assassination." Waldo was like a man possessed. "What do you think the odds are that we'd keep running into all those uncommon names by mere coincidence?"

"Shit man, there's a lot of names connected with *that*." The fredneck responded.

Waldo, now thoroughly convinced that someone, aware of his inordinate interest in the Kennedy assassination, was providing names endemic to it for his exclusive benefit, inhaled deeply on his cigarette and felt as misunderstood as an adolescent with a set of car keys.

Professor Buckley was standing somewhat apart from the rest of the group, muttering "oh dear, *oh dear*" over and over again under his breath.

Just then, Junior Sample, Jr. came back outside accompanied by an old man and a little girl. He maneuvered his tremendous girth down the steps with surprising ease, but decelerated down to a more sauntering, rural gait when he touched level ground.

"Boys, Mama Petunia asked not to be disturbed, but her two assistants here, Mr. Nix and Mrs. Muchmore, give you their permission to go inside." Junior, Jr. spat another disgusting black wad of chewing tobacco out onto the pavement and turned to the little girl, who looked to be about ten years old. "Mrs. Muchmore, why don't you show our guests some pictures of your children. You fellas would like to see some nice pictures, wouldn't you?"

Waldo's response to the *Hee Haw*-star look-alike was to take off running, at a faster clip than any white man since the dawn of moving film. In seconds he was back at Brisbane's car, and he jumped in and locked all the doors.

The others were flabbergasted by Waldo's speedy exit. Desensitized somewhat by recent events, their reaction to such bizarre characters as ten year old married mothers and Junior Sample doppelgangers was not as rash or extreme as the nervous young man's.

Ever the diplomat, even when dealing with Unreals, Phosphate smiled at Junior Sample, Jr. and explained that their friend was sick and must be attended to. Without further ado, he strode off and the others followed him back to the car.

When they arrived there, they found a very pale Waldo sitting in the back seat, shivering and shaking like a pudgy girl at a high school dance.

"Shit Phos, why do we have to leave without playing..."

"Please, Fontaine." The top doo-wopper interrupted his disappointed crony. "Waldo is very upset. There will be plenty of other opportunities, hopefully, for you to play bingo."

Everyone piled into the decidedly un-fredneck-like '65 Dodge Dart, despite Fontaine's vociferous objections, with Phosphate sliding behind the wheel. As they drove away in silence, Bucktooth glanced back at Junior Sample, Jr. and his two companions. If he saw any of them disappear, he kept it to himself.

Phosphate had only driven a short distance when he softly said, "Waldo, I recognized those names myself. Nix and Muchmore were two of

146

the people who were taking home movies of the Kennedy assassination, correct?"

A thoroughly crazed Waldo, bearing an outward appearance guaranteed to eventually earn him a private, padded room somewhere, responded through a set of chattering teeth. "Y-Y-Y-Y-Yes. H-How d-d-did y-you know that?"

The top doo-wopper reached into the back seat and patted Waldo reassuringly on the knee. "My friend, I may not have immediately connected the other names to the assassination, but those two are familiar to any serious student of the case."

"Well, I-I'm glad *someone* agrees with me." Waldo, partially recovering his composure, obviously was directing his comment at Brisbane.

"I didn't say that I completely believed there was any significance to it, either." The top doo-wopper gently reminded him.

"Come on! How else do you explain it?" Waldo's voice grew higher-pitched, as it often did when he was defending one of his numerous controversial positions.

"I'm not implying that there isn't any significance to it, either." Phosphate sounded like a combination party loyalist and zen philosopher.

Waldo shook his head in frustration. "I can't believe you people. Like I said before, what are the odds of our running into all those names associated with the Kennedy assassination?"

"Waldo, what do-that is-it does appear evident that the events of November 22, 1963 are playing a prominent role in whatever it is that's transpiring here." Hiram Buckley, masking his emotions more successfully than his nervous young friend, tugged at his faded yellow tie. "If someone were to-that is-this particular subject, the Kennedy assassination, was a favorite obsession of Old Hoss's, and I'm not surprised to find references to it popping up so often. What we need to do-I mean he called that child *Mrs.*, my boy- is to somehow reconcile ourselves to-that is-define, if not identify *Them*. Oh dear, if only I'd never read *None Dare Call It Conspiracy*."

Waldo had composed himself enough to perform important tasks like lighting a cigarette. "That big man at the bingo parlor, who I thought looked a lot like Junior Sample- he was on *Hee Haw*, remember- I wonder why he didn't introduce himself? Who knows what name they picked for him..."

"Junior Sample! Hey, that's a good one!" Bucktooth evidently had seen *Hee Haw* a time or two.

Phosphate stared introspectively out of the window. "I'm sure that his name suited him well, like Otis or Emmett." The top doo-wopper crossed his fingers as he spoke. He didn't have the heart to tell Waldo that

147

he had observed a small nametag on the shirt pocket of the man who looked like Junior Sample, which the rotund figure had taken off and abruptly pocketed only seconds after they'd met. Although the man had moved quickly, the head Afro Anarchist was able to spot his last name. It was Ruby.

Later on, in the dead of the night, having long since parked the car in order to conserve their remaining fuel, and with their beer supply dipping dangerously low as well, Waldo and Phosphate somehow found themselves discussing the strange story behind the writing of the classic tale *Frankenstein* by Mary Shelley.

"But if they were in some kind of competition to see who could write the best, or scariest ghost story, what has made me wonder is how she defeated two of the most brilliant poets of the romantic era." Waldo was referring to her competitors, husband Percy Bysshe Shelley, and close friend and noted deviate Lord Byron.

In yet another example of their common interests, both Waldo and the top doo-wopper had long been fascinated by this legend of two dynamic muse masters on sabbatical in a dark and spooky manor, with its hint of sexual shenanigans, and the penultimate gothic novel borne out of it all.

"Unless I'm mistaken, wasn't there another fellow there?" Phosphate wondered aloud. "I believe he was a doctor or..."

"Yeah, his name was Polidori, and he wrote what is considered to be the first modern vampire novel." Brisbane reached into the back pocket of his faded jeans, which wasn't an easy task in such cramped conditions, and produced a dog-eared paperback, which he waved at them.

"Take a good look at this, guys. It's a copy of Byron's collected verses."

"My dear Brisbane, you appear to be somewhat perturbed." Phosphate observed.

"Yeah, I am. In case you haven't noticed, I carry this book with me all the time, and I probably know more about Byron than both of you combined, and yet you two continue with your fucking pseudo-intellectual bullshit like I'm not here, even on a subject like this, that I'm an expert on!"

Phosphate turned around. "My friend, I'm sorry if we neglected to formally ask you for your thoughts on the matter." The top doo-wopper's tone was soothing and persuasive, like a salesman's before the contract is signed. "We weren't having a closed conversation, and you were certainly free to join in at any time. You seem not to have been reluctant about participating in prior discussions."

"If I may interrupt," Professor Buckley looked up from Sam

Hancock's journal, which he was sifting through again, "I have a suggestion. While we're on this topic, why don't-that is-wouldn't it be challenging for all of us to produce an unpublished pamphlet of our own, similar to the way those long dead poets wrote ghost stories for each other?"

"Hmmm." Phosphate stroked his chin. "There certainly wouldn't appear to be any more appropriate method of honoring the man we seek to find."

"Shit man, we could hold a competition, like Byron and the Shelleys did, to see who can write the best one!" Brisbane had returned the well-read copy of Byron's collected verses to its usual place in his back pocket, his typical fredneck enthusiasm supplanting the anger of a moment before.

While Fontaine and Bucktooth reflected on the similarities or lack thereof between nineteenth century ghost stories and ideas from the political fringes, Phosphate stroked his chin some more.

"I don't think we should compete. The concept is fine, but I dislike the entire competitive process."

"Well, shit, then let's just do it for the fun of it." Brisbane, although a tad disappointed, still looked to be nearly as electrified as an executive in a slow pitch softball game. "Besides, what the fuck could we compete for?"

"Yeah, you're right about that." Bucktooth lamented. "None of us brought much money- shit, I know I didn't 'cause I don't have any- and when the stuff Waldo stole runs out, I don't know what we're gonna do for food."

There was no response to Bucktooth's pertinent observation, as the distracted and disorganized group remained predictably oblivious to the state of their dwindling finances which, once they returned to the corrupt, stable society they'd left behind, would have to rectified in one way or another.

With the decidedly un-fredneck-like vehicle parked on the side of the unnamed road, they turned a deaf ear to the howling outside their locked doors, ignored their sorry and unfathomable plight, and concentrated on more important matters, like composing unpublished pamphlets.

The lost and pitiful band of would-be rescuers worked diligently on their creations, deep into the night, sharing the two pens they possessed between them in a spirit of camaraderie that would have warmed the heart of the old maestro they were all trying to mimic. Professor Buckley thoughtfully provided some blank paper from the supply he always stored in his battered briefcase for just such occasions.

Waldo, having produced a substantial amount of unpublished material in his own right, whipped up a dandy entitled *Call Me Old Stone-*

Faced:

"I have a great sense of humor. There is nothing, in fact, that I enjoy more than a good laugh, but I simply don't find much of what presently purports to be comedy to be very amusing. I have never, in particular, found any standup comedian, other than Steve Martin in his heyday, who could even make me chuckle. They are truly pathetic; every family I have ever known has an uncle or aunt that is funnier than any of them. They are indistinguishable from one another; they all adopt the same obnoxious, wise-acre style, make it clear that they're liberal democrats, and spend much of their acts discussing the hilarious differences between New York and California. The people that actually pay to watch these shows are even more absurd, applauding like mad at every stupid and derivative joke, and appearing to be in an advanced state of hysteria, almost at the point of collapsing, whenever the camera pans over the audience. Of course, modern comics are hardly worse than their untalented predecessors, such as Milton Berle, George Burns, Bob Hope, Jan Murray, Joey Bishop, Red Buttons, and even lesser luminaries.

Even some of the few television comedy shows I like, such as the original *Saturday Night Live*, possess their share of distasteful aspects. For instance, how many viewers chuckled each week, during the program's first year, at "Weekend Update" anchor Chevy Chase's repeated references to Generalissimo Francisco Franco being still dead? I would venture a guess that no more than one percent of the audience had the vaguest notion who Franco was, yet they apparently found this curious catch-phrase to be humorous. Perhaps if they knew that General Franco, in addition to being the President of Spain for many years, was also an avid anti-communist, and led the loyalist Catholic faction during the country's civil war of the 1930's, they might be less apt to giggle so compliantly. Of course, during this same period, most of Hollywood's creative community were paying dues to the Abraham Lincoln Brigade, a pro-Soviet group that ardently supported the rebels who were methodically slaughtering priests and nuns and desecrating churches. So, the next time a rerun of Chevy Chase so snidely ridiculing Franco's memory airs, it might behoove interested fans of *Saturday Night Live* to ask why this pro-Christian, anti-communist leader was singled out for such scorn. Wouldn't it have been more appropriate to pick a brutal mass murderer such as Mao Tse Tung or Josef Stalin, and inform the audience that they were still dead each week?

Of course, I am all too sadly aware that the same people who laugh at standup comics, and fail to question why an obscure dead figure is mentioned in a derogatory manner every week on a popular television show, also waste their voting power on such worthies as Lyndon Johnson,

Richard Nixon, Alan Cranston, Dwight Eisenhower, Adam Clayton Powell, Ronald Reagan, etc., etc. Every four years, they allow themselves to be corralled into choosing their president from a small pool of dishonest candidates of the only two political parties that are permitted access to the media. They re-elect their congressional representatives, flying in the face of their own best interests, at such a high rate (usually anywhere from 96 to 98%) that even members of the Soviet Union's Politburo cannot match it. They bestow millionaire status upon largely illiterate and unappreciative pro athletes, by paying the exorbitant prices to attend their games, falling all over themselves to cheer them in the process. They still buy tickets in droves when the multi-millionaires go out on strike, refuse to sign autographs for youngsters, and express a negative view of fans in general, some of them even taking their disdain so far as to attack physically any fan who dares to boo them. They attend the concerts of rock stars who are multi-millionaires as well, and perform the same rituals of tribute the sports fans do. They swallow the rock stars' working-class image, their lyrical jibes against the "rich," and their expressions of concern for the poor and homeless. So much more could be said on the subject of public gullibility, but this leaflet has already strayed too far from its intended purpose. Perhaps I'm just too discriminating in my tastes, but I simply don't understand why, when there are scores of talented artists who are capable of producing timeless, original works of comedy, the Billy Crystals of the world receive so much publicity (and money), while some of the stars of the classic show *SCTV*, for instance, are relegated to bit roles. But then, if there's one thing the American public has proven time and time again, it's that they prefer their culture to be banal and that they have no collective taste. We live, after all, in a country where Michael Jackson is more popular than Elvis Costello. The vast majority of citizens respect the poorly educated and immature "stars" who perform such vital functions as stuffing a ball through a hoop, strumming a guitar, or grabbing their crotch and shouting expletives from a stage, far more than the lowly paid, by comparison, medical researchers and air traffic controllers who meander about their meaningless business in obscurity. This is a society that not only grants celebrities an undeserved, exalted status, but literally worships them. Now *that's* funny."

Phosphate called his brief but cogent offering *A Taxative Laxative*:

"Whenever I hear of a politician handing out an award for the most outrageous waste of taxpayer's money, I become confused. It all boils down to the paradox that has baffled the enlightened for years: *are they ignorant or are they evil?* As I see it, when a citizen of this country discovers that his money is funding a study on the ecology of subsistence pastoralism in Kenya, or the main cause of tricycle accidents, or the underlying reason why people fall down in bathtubs, or countless other examples equally as mind-boggling, he is left with three possible reactions:

1. The situation is disastrous; how can elected representatives allow my hard-earned money to be spent on such trivial things?
2. The situation is understandable; in a complex world all things should be considered and scientific progress must continue on all fronts. And who is to say that someone, somewhere, in this land of ours may not benefit from knowing what a study of bathtub mishaps has to report?
3. The situation is absurd; my representative graduated from a prestigious university, so he is not stupid. I cannot envision anyone studying tricycle accidents, why people fall in love, etc. If they honestly did, how would such an investigation be conducted? By hiring tots to have tricycle accidents, or maybe just hiding in some convenient suburban shrubbery and observing them as they happen? It seems obvious that the money allotted for such "studies" is actually being used for other, more mysterious purposes."

Brisbane produced a lively entry, which he aptly chose to title *What The Fuck?*:

"I can spot an ex-cheerleader even if she's wearing dentures and a blue wig. They all have this fucking look that they never lose. It's a look, I suppose, that could best be defined as one of total self-confidence. I've made a study, in fact, of cheerleaders, and what I've discovered is that the best-looking girls are not always picked to be cheerleaders, although most of them are very cute. Whatever talents they possess in order to be chosen for this most high honor, they certainly lead a charmed existence. They float and flutter through their various high schools like combination queen bees and screen goddesses. Of course, it isn't the cheerleader alone who makes high school such a wonderful place for the rest of us. The immortal jock is the true star of the public education show. It is fucking ridiculous that the schools in this country allow a system, where a small minority of the boys in each class are celebrated and worshiped like royalty, to continue year after year, generation after generation. They even have a ritual, kind of a time honored tradition, where each Friday during football season, the boys on the team wear their jerseys to class and the girls on the cheerleading squad wear their hot little outfits. Doesn't anyone on any local school board realize how this kind of blatant favoritism affects the 95% of the students who aren't football players or cheerleaders? I don't know about the other kids, but when I was in high school every teacher I ever had kissed the asses of the jocks in their classes with such passion that they appeared to be under the illusion that those asses belonged to some exalted, powerful group from whom they could win favors, and not mere teenagers. In every instance, and at all times, the jocks are treated differently from average students. When a jock gets into trouble, which is often because their giant egos are so fragile, the administration of the school, *any* school, goes into overdrive to protect this corrupt system that has come to be considered as part of American lore. Maybe if all the people who're so concerned about "education," and love to toss that word around like a sacred cow, would start to question the preposterous social class structure at these public schools they have such a fucking infatuation with, then test scores might rise. Maybe if the heavy importance and funding that is placed on male athletics were instead channeled into teaching kids basic skills, the rate of illiteracy would decrease. I know I'm the last fucking person in the world to be lecturing anybody about education, but if the schools had been run differently when I was a student, who knows- I might be sitting in an office somewhere with my feet propped up, staring at my Ivy League diploma hanging from the wall, instead of writing ridiculous shit like this that no one will ever read."

Professor Buckley's work was entitled *Poles, Pols, And More Polls*:

"What exactly is an exit poll? And why are they always correct in their projections? In fact, let me be totally irrational now and ask why polls are needed at all. Their only function appears to be to sway public opinion in one direction or another. In a free country, one that boasts so loudly about its unfettered elections, why should it be of any importance to know a particular candidate's level of support, even assuming it's an honest representation, prior to the voting? Doesn't this dramatically alter public perception, and cause votes to change from one candidate, who the media has declared has little chance to win, to another one who is ahead in the polls? The networks start relaying the results of various polls before the first primary, in New Hampshire, has even been held. Thus, at that time, a few carefully chosen candidates, acceptable to the establishment, are repeatedly referred to as the "frontrunners." This is nothing less than fraud, but still the media persists in its ways, declaring winners in races where 2% of the vote has been tabulated, yet never erring. Of course, there is really nothing to worry about, because the officially sanctioned guardians of democracy in all electoral matters, The League of Women Voters, will always be there to look out for *someone's* interests. They provide the vital function of "sponsoring" presidential debates which always exclude those candidates other than Democrats or Republicans. They also make sure that the "journalists" asking the questions at these shindigs are drawn from the same ranks as those who are invariably called upon at presidential press conferences. All of these intrepid news hounds have proven their mettle in the line of fire, and revealed themselves to be incapable of ruffling any powerful feathers. Thus, there is no reason for the establishment to worry about a representative of the "free" press bringing up something worthwhile, or even unrehearsed, at one of these ballyhooed extravaganzas. So, if you're a disenchanted (and disenfranchised) voter like me, don't listen to those solid citizens who perform their "civic duty" and then chastise nonparticipants by scolding, "if you didn't vote, you have no right to criticize." Of course you do! You are merely exercising the harshest option available in a free country: not participating because there is never anyone with a chance of winning who is worth voting for."

Bucktooth, whose real first name was Woodrow, while not exactly adhering to the established format for unpublished pamphlets, produced a surprisingly clever piece entitled *Woodrow in Wonderland*:

"Once upon a time there was a young black man whose name was Woodrow. He was very bored one day. And so he went outside and sat in the alley. So who shud walk up but this half-white sister. She was fine-looking to, I must say. She looked alot like Whitney Houston. She smiled at Woodrow and he says whats your name? She says Alice, whats yours? He says Woodrow please to meet you. She ask Woodrow if he wants to play a game. He says sure. He is by the way, checking out her fine body. She swings her ass as she walks and Woodrow follows her like a puppy dog. All of a sudden she stops and points to the ground. What is it Alice? It is a hole that we can jump down and enter wonderland. Wow! Woodrow is happy but skared. What if he cant get back up? So they jump down the hole and they are in Wonderland. First they see a cat that sings to them like James Brown. Then a big dog comes up and barks. His name is Louis Carol. He wants a piece of Alice. But Alice runs away and so does Woodrow. Then they see a queen that looks like a poker card. She keeps yelling off with their heads! Then ther is the guy who looks like Jesse Jackson. He is trying to move all these giant cheese peices around. Then all of a sudden Louis Carol runs up and bites Jesse Jackson right on his but. Alice and Woodrow cant help laughing but the queen yells off with their heads and they have to run reel fast. They make it back to the alley where Woodrow wakes up and discover that he was dreaming. He notises that he is holding a magazine in his hands. Whitney Houston is on the cover."

Finally, last and probably least was Fontaine's contribution. He did not want to leave an effort like Bucktooth's, with its similarity in grammatical style to a belatedly discovered lone assassin's diary. Instead, he totally ignored the boundaries devised by the missing master of the genre, and produced a rap song in honor of Abner Billingsly, *The Old Hoss Rap*:

"My name's Old Hoss and I'm the boss
I went somewhere and I got lost
I forgot to notify my next of kin
I don't know when I'll be back again
Well, I am white and I used to write
Faster than a Soviet satellite
I pull no punches, tell no lies
I never won the Pulitzer Prize
As you may know, I'm a gigolo
And all the women love me so
Whenever I say 'conspiracy'
They drop their underwear for me
So come on down and look around
You might find me in an Iowa town
I'm not saying what it's all about
That's for me to know- and for you to find out."

When they'd each completed their sure-to-remain-unpublished pamphlets, or in Fontaine's case his initial effort at rapping, everyone read and critiqued one another's work. Generally favorable reviews were received all around, although Bucktooth was ribbed good naturedly about his punctuation and his spelling prowess, and Fontaine was chided for not producing a pamphlet at all.

As morning approached, and no storm reared its awful head, everyone but Waldo and Professor Buckley eventually drifted off to sleep. None of them had slept much since embarking upon their journey, and the series of wild, improbable events that followed, so it was certainly a much needed and well deserved rest.

From somewhere off in the distance, Waldo thought he heard a rooster crow. For someone who'd never been near a farm in his life, and whose familiarity with the matter stemmed mainly from frequent viewings of Foghorn Leghorn cartoons, it was a questionable identification. However, such formalities seldom bothered Waldo, and he felt certain that it was indeed a rooster crowing, and was thus able to shiver slightly at the prospects *that* presented. What might they encounter on a farm in *these* parts?

Lighting a cigarette, and gazing at the Professor to reassure himself that he wasn't going to fall asleep either, Waldo kept watch over his innocent, dozing comrades. The way they were snoring, it appeared likely that the nervous young man would have ample opportunity to explore every nightmarish option his mind could manufacture as they pressed on in their irregular, haphazard course to Cornoil, Iowa.

9

THEY KNOW NOT WHAT COURSE OTHERS MAY TAKE

It was early afternoon, and Brisbane and the Afro Anarchists were still fast asleep. Waldo and the Professor, weary of swatting odd, obscure facts and theories back and forth, decided to step out of the car and stretch their legs.

"Waldo, I say-that is-aren't you tired, my boy?" Professor Buckley, suppressing a yawn, was unaccustomed to others matching his wakefulness wink for wink, as it were, and seemed jealous of the competition Waldo presented in that regard.

"Who can sleep?" Waldo replied. "We're on another of these crazy roads, we can't find the interstate..."

"Yes, I suppose you're right." The Professor interrupted, taking off his thick spectacles and polishing them on his bright tie. "I, on the other hand, *never* sleep, as I'm sure you're aware."

Waldo smiled. The Professor had little in life to be vain about, and he wasn't going to stop him from expressing a little pride now and then.

"Professor," Waldo neatly changed the subject, "why don't we take a walk? It'll help break the monotony."

Hiram Buckley, apparently growing immune to fear due to its constancy in recent days, shrugged resignedly. "At this point, my boy, I know-that is-why not? I need the exercise."

They shuffled off, rather tentatively, down the unnamed road. The setting was peaceful and serene, with the rolling, pastoral fields flung out on either side of them for as far as the eye could see. As they slowly trekked along, Waldo noticed, with a trace of discomfort, that everything seemed unusually quiet.

After only a hundred yards or so, the road abruptly ended and they found themselves facing an enclosed area that was brimming with assorted plants and grasses, and was literally overrun by a dazzling array of the largest, reddest strawberries imaginable.

"Oh dear, this is..." Professor Buckley nearly collapsed, grasping ahold of Waldo's shirt to keep from falling.

Waldo looked all around him. He was no horticulturist, but felt sure no berries *that* size had ever been grown on planet Earth. Some of them were over ten feet tall and thicker than a Japanese sumo wrestler. They were everywhere, reaching almost to the tops of the crumbling, gray stone walls that flanked either side of the small plot of land that appeared to be some kind of unconventional, monstrous strawberry patch.

Both Waldo and the Professor turned around, preparing to make a mad dash for Brisbane's car. Considering all they'd been through lately, they might have foreseen that neither the unnamed road nor the decidedly un-fredneck-like '65 Dodge Dart would be there, but they managed to delude themselves one more time and held onto each other like two abandoned toddlers at the sight of the empty field that now stood behind them.

"What ya'll doin'?"

At the sound of the strange voice, Professor Buckley, no threat to members of the high jumping fraternity, managed somehow to execute a beauty that would have made the world's record holder proud.

"Don't be so darn jumpy! I ain't gonna hurt ya."

Waldo and the Professor turned around towards the strawberry patch again, to find a short old man with a ruddy complexion, dressed in typical rural garb standing there. The man, who looked to be around seventy or so, grabbed his belt and hitched up his loose fitting blue jeans, which must have seen many a harvest moon, and extracted a toothpick from a mouth that had gravy stains all around its edges.

"Well, what ya'll lookin' at? Ya act like ya seen a ghost or somethin'." The old man pulled the tail of his faded blue flannel shirt out of his pants, brought it up quickly to his mouth, and deftly wiped away the stains.

"W-w-where are w-we?" Waldo managed to stutter.

"Ya'll are lost, huh? I knew it!" The old man slapped his knee as he chuckled. "Well, come on with me, then, back to the house. I'll rustle ya up some grub. Ya must be hungry."

Waldo and the Professor stared back over their shoulders at the silent, open field, and felt they had little choice but to comply. The old man, who moved sprightly for someone of his advanced years, led them through the giant strawberry patch, which wound around to the right, and stopped shortly thereafter at a rusted iron gate, beyond which were merely normal sized specimens of daffodils and buttercups. They were, however, forced to fight their way through some sprawling flora, which the Professor thought looked suspiciously like poison ivy, before emerging into a clearing where a bright, lovely white cottage stood. The charming little building was a comforting sight, with its deep blue shutters and quaint weather vane quivering slightly in the soft breeze. The grass was extraordinarily green and rich along either side of the well-swept path that led directly to the friendly welcome mat on the front porch step. Despite their trepidation, Waldo and the Professor couldn't help but feel a bit more relaxed in its presence.

The old man trotted up the path and waved them on. "Don't just stand thar! My wife's the best durn cook in all of Berrytown!"

Waldo felt an all too familiar tingle. "Did you say Berrytown?"

"Sure did, son. Ain't ya never heard of it?" The man paused on the front step and scratched his posterior with a great deal of fervor before opening the door.

"I've heard of it, alright." Professor Buckley mumbled under his breath to Waldo. "It's the town, in Pennsylvania, where the notorious religious sect known as the Moonies were born."

"It's also the title of a great song by Steely Dan." Waldo whispered back.

"What ya'll gabbing about?" The old man's grin revealed a set of teeth that obviously held the dentistry profession in low regard. "Ya wouldn't be keeping no secrets from me now, would ya?"

At that point, Waldo felt a strong pair of hands grab him from behind, and he could see that the Professor was being handled in the same rough manner. An enormous figure, with a human face but covered with hair like an ape, hoisted the Professor in the air, grunting contentedly as he did so. Waldo was lifted off the ground almost simultaneously, by an identical creature, who uttered *"here, boss"* in a comical, high-pitched voice and tossed the nervous young man forward, like a beach ball, so that he landed at the old man's feet. Professor Buckley rolled up next to him a few seconds later, and they both lay there shuddering in anticipation of what might happen next.

"Alright, Toofgib and Itey, git back to yer work now." The old man shook a gnarled finger in the direction of the two giant man-beasts, and they lumbered off submissively.

Waldo was alert enough to unravel the strange names, rapidly deciphering that they spelled Bigfoot and Yeti backwards. As he watched them disappear back into the giant strawberry patch, Waldo had to acknowledge that they certainly resembled most eyewitness descriptions of the legendary creatures.

"Come on inside now, and eat somethin'!" The old man's tone contained few traces of southern hospitality in it, and both Waldo and the Professor took it as an order, not an invitation, and quickly scrambled to their feet.

As they gingerly entered the cottage, a frail, hunched over woman in her twilight years hobbled towards them with the assistance of a cane.

"Bea! Is it ready?" The old man bellowed.

The old woman's head was shaking from side to side, as if she suffered from a form of palsy. "Y-y-y-yeah, B-bertram. F-f-food's on the t-table."

There was a small, tidy kitchen off to their right, and the old man swept Waldo and the Professor in, signalling them to sit down at a table by the old fashioned wood burning stove. The table was set for four, and there was a single pot in the middle, from which a great deal of steam was emanating.

The old man threw his head back and inhaled as he took a seat at the head of the table. "Mmmm. There ain't nothin' better than a good stew."

The old woman spooned a healthy portion of the liquid substance, which was of a beige color and an uneven, chunky consistency, into each of their bowls before sitting down next to her husband.

Waldo stared down at the food and stirred cautiously with his spoon. He could see out of the corner of his eye that the Professor was doing likewise.

"Come on, now!" The old man shouted. "Eat yer stew! Ya don't want to offend my wife, do ya?"

Professor Buckley summoned up some inner resolve. "Excuse me, but, I must-that is-exactly what kind of stew is this?"

The old man snickered and slapped his knee. "Settle down, will ya? But ya got a right to know what ya eat, I suppose. It's..."

"Ma! Whar's my ice cream?"

The old man was interrupted by a teen aged boy, evidently his son, who came bursting breathlessly into the room. The lad was tall and gangly, with long, greasy blonde hair. His clothing precisely matched that of the old man's. He was clutching a glass jar in one hand.

"Calm down, Master!" The old man reached out and whacked the boy in the side. "Don't ya be yellin' at yer Ma like that."

The teenager doubled over in pain as he received the blow to his side. "I-I-I'm sorry, Pa. I jest wanted..."

"H-h-here y-you are, h-honey." The old woman, without leaving her chair, leaned over and opened the obsolete ice box, which stood beside her. She produced a bowl of ice cream and held it towards her son. "I-it's y-your f-f-favorite- c-chocolate."

The young boy grabbed it eagerly and ran over to the counter next to the sink. While Waldo and the Professor watched in stunned silence, he opened the glass jar he'd been holding and emptied its contents into the bowl of ice cream. Even to a non-apartment dweller like Waldo, it was obvious that the insects scurrying out were roaches.

Waldo and the Professor blanched at this, and turned a few shades paler.

The teenager than slid the bowl, along with its unusual topping, into a microwave oven, which was fasted securely under one of the cabinets, and was the only modern thing about the entire kitchen.

The boy squealed with delight as the curious mixture cooked, dancing about excitedly to the awful sounds of the bugs popping, and when the timer went off thirty seconds later, he opened the door and dug right in, not bothering to use a spoon.

"Mmmmm." He raved half intelligibly through a mouthful of food.

"Pecan crunch- my favorite!"

"Master Plaster!" The old man yelled at the boy. "Whar's your manners? Ya don't eat no dessert in front of company without offerin' them some."

"'Scuse me." The teenager savored an especially juicy "pecan", rolling it lovingly around in his mouth before swallowing. "Ya'll want some?"

"No!" Waldo realized it was probably sound strategy to cloak his true feelings of repulsion and terror, and quickly softened his tone. "Thank you, anyway."

"Ya sound a little agitated, boy." The old man grinned wickedly at him. "But yer friend here, was askin' me, before young Master Plaster came in, what was in the stew. Well, as I said, ya got a right to know what yer puttin' in yer stomach. It's a recipe that's been in the family for a long, long time, and thar's a special ingredient what makes it so tasty." The old man took a heaping spoonful and held it out towards them. "Take a wiff of that! Ya ever hear of a little spice called *epidermis of homo sapiens?*"

Waldo reacted instinctively, flipping the table over, and the ghastly cannibalistic concoction flew into the air, splattering all over the old man and his wife.

"Run, Professor!" Waldo shouted, and was on his feet and out the door in a flash.

The overwrought, middle-aged Professor wasn't quite as fast, but managed to avoid the lunging teenage boy, who dove desperately at the ex-history teacher and banged his head nastily against one of the kitchen chairs in the process, and dart out of the little cottage several paces behind the galloping Waldo.

Waldo kicked open the rusted iron gate, which someone had thoughtfully closed, and dashed into the giant strawberry patch. He hesitated for a moment, allowing the gasping Professor Buckley to catch up, and conducted a visual search which unearthed no evidence of the two Bigfoot-like monsters.

With a single glance back over his shoulder, revealing that their bizarre pursuers hadn't even left the cottage yet, the nervous young man hurried through the rest of the patch, and was greatly relieved when he'd successfully traversed it without being attacked by any of the giant specimens of fruit.

Waldo was also amazed, at that point, to discover himself standing back on the pavement of the unnamed road again, with Brisbane's decidedly un-fredneck-like '65 Dodge Dart calmly resting a short distance away.

Turning to the Professor, who chugged up alongside of him and doubled over in agony, a common reaction for someone in such poor physical condition, Waldo's mouth dropped open. "Professor... was that all unreal?"

Hiram Buckley rose up unsteadily, to his full five feet seven inches of height, and pointed to the right. "A more appropriate question, my boy, would be- what is *that?*"

The Professor was gesturing towards another one of those disturbing purple signs, which was prominently positioned only a few yards from them. Waldo had inconceivably failed to notice it, and although it bore no relevance to the Kennedy assassination, it held a pertinence all its own. It read *Old Hoss Highway- Next Left.*

"Giant strawberries! Sheeet!"

Fontaine's reaction was typical of those Waldo and the Professor received from the others when they returned to the car and related their most recent unaccountable experience.

"Shit man, I want to go home!" Brisbane's ardent plea, spoken like a hapless soldier in some far off foxhole, couldn't really be answered of course, as he hadn't known a home for many years.

"Relax, my friends." Phosphate, who was standing next to the open rear door on the driver's side, placed his hands on top of the old automobile. "We should be growing accustomed to these things by now. I propose we cease rehashing these incomprehensible occurrences and discuss instead what we intend to do about *that.*" The top doo-wopper gestured towards the ominous purple sign that stood only yards away from them.

All of them had been eyeing the sign repeatedly, with varying degrees of anxiety, fully aware that its significance could not be overestimated.

Bucktooth was pacing about worriedly. "Damn, Phos, you can't mean...you want to turn onto that road?"

"Indeed, Phosphate, I am inclined at this point, to almost want-that is-to suggest we click our heels and repeat *there's no place like home* as a last resort." Professor Buckley gazed about him with a wild, bewildered expression.

The top doo-wopper smiled, as always a beacon of strength. "What have we to lose by turning onto Old Hoss Highway? Isn't it obvious, to all of you, that whatever has been happening thus far holds relevance only for us? Finding a street with such a name is entirely consistent with all the other unfathomable events." Phosphate stroked his chin. "Actually, I wouldn't be a bit surprised if that highway led us directly to Cornoil, Iowa."

"What?" Waldo stared at him incredulously. "I may be terrible about directions, but I do know we're a long way from Iowa."

162

"My friend," The top doo-wopper patted Waldo on the back, "none of us has any idea where we are. But, I've made my suggestion and I rest my case. I must reiterate, however, that I don't see how the situation can be any worse than it is now; we are lost and will soon be out of food and gasoline. Under those circumstances, we will starve to death. On the other hand, Old Hoss Highway might just allow us to reach our destination, and by a must faster, albeit supernatural route."

Brisbane lit up a cigarette. "Shit man, I'm with Phosphate. What the fuck can we do here? At least, if we take that road, maybe we'll find out what all this is about."

Neither Waldo nor the Professor, given their present predicament, could argue seriously against the head Afro Anarchist's proposal, so they seated themselves next to the others and waited with bated breath, like youngsters at an amusement park, for the next turn of events.

Phosphate took the wheel and slowly eased the car forward. When they came abreast of the sign, they could see that Old Hoss Highway was a harmless looking, four lane, paved road, and that other vehicles were traversing it in the distance.

"But where, " Waldo asked of no one in particular, "can those other cars be coming from? The road ends here."

"That's correct, Waldo." The top doo-wopper felt obligated to respond. "But how plausible has anything been lately? I feel confident now, my friend, that your hunch about Iowa and the mental institution was correct. Perhaps this route is the one possible way there, and thus represents the only chance to locate your grandfather."

Waldo shook his head. "I don't know what else to say, or to think. Brisbane, is there any beer left?"

"Now you're talking." The fredneck, who'd been so distracted he'd allowed nearly five minutes to elapse between beers, opened the cooler and produced two cans, handing one to Waldo.

The afternoon sky was overcast, and a few intermittent drops of rain fell against the windshield. As they drove along Old Hoss Highway, they eventually caught up to the other cars and joined the flow of traffic. This was surely strange, as they didn't appear to be traveling at a faster speed than anyone else, but no one in the decidedly un-fredneck-like '65 Dodge Dart seemed to notice. They were simply pleased to be progressing *somewhere*, and the trademark signs of civilization-the stores, houses, sidewalks, and billboards that had sprung up all around them- served to assuage their fears and provide them with a tiny sense of security.

"Yes, Waldo," Phosphate declared emphatically, "I do indeed feel like Robert Frost, on *The Road Not Taken*."

Waldo did not mention that he felt more akin to Thomas Gray, writing an *Elegy In A Country Churchyard*.

"But what about those fucking Nazca lines? They must have been used as some kind of landing strip." Brisbane remarked.

"It is seemingly an inescapable conclusion that they were." Phosphate paused to take a dignified hit from the pipe that was being passed around. "Of course, that has never stopped the intrepid scientific community and their illogical refutations. The pyramids seem to point, in the same fashion, towards some sort of superior civilization in the distant past that must have unearthed the power of flight."

Brisbane blew out marijuana smoke along with his words. "And don't forget the entrances at the poles that lead to the hollow earth. Or the crystal skull and the dancing wee people that carry off babies to their subterranean lairs."

They had driven for several miles, their fuel supply mysteriously remaining constant, when the fredneck produced a bag of weed from his boots and warily asked if anyone objected to his consuming it. When the Afro Anarchists replied by fervently requesting that he share it with them, Brisbane was happy to oblige.

Waldo, in spite of the seriousness of their situation, found himself amused at the impact dope seemed to have on the fredneck's intellect. He and Professor Buckley were the only ones not partaking heavily of the substance, his recent illusory experience with Jane-Gloria and old Griffith Stadium serving to strengthen his resolve to stay away from drugs. The nervous young man, with only a few beers to dull his senses, had taken over the driving duties and was straining to see through the smoke that filled the car.

"Brisbane," Waldo coughed, "weren't you the one I was arguing with over M.I.B.'s? You think they're unbelievable but the earth being hollow and fairies stealing babies aren't?"

Brisbane finished drawing on an especially long hit and his blood-shot eyes seemed to cut through the smoke like two small red lighthouses. "Shit man, when I'm high, I *want* to think about far out stuff like that. Talk to me about M.I.B.'s now, dude."

Waldo ignored this attractive offer and tried vainly to see out of the windshield. It was dark outside, and only the headlights of the oncoming vehicles were visible. Brisbane was being his usual stoned fredneck self, Phosphate was rapidly losing his composure, and Fontaine and Bucktooth were in a state of ecstasy, giggling constantly and spitting out gibberish that resembled no language known to man. They were smoking some of the same homemade concoction developed by Brisbane which had given Waldo such memorable moments without his even consuming it.

Fontaine, his excursions into the world of rap music apparently blossoming from unpublished odes about missing, elderly white men to striking, caustic paeans about the black experience, was now speaking in rhymes, when he could be understood, and Bucktooth was playing the part of his D.J. Suddenly Fontaine raised his voice, literally shouting in an off-key manner:

> "My name's Fontaine, I'm a dancing man
> Every step of the way
> And Fred Astaire, he ain't nowhere
> When I come to play
> If you know just who was great
> And who was a pretender
> Look at film of Peg Leg Bates
> And tell me you remember
> When they talk about Irving Berlin
> It makes me wanna holler
> He couldn't hold a candle to
> Nothing by Fats Waller
> Dolly Dawn and Mildred Bailey
> Peggy Lee? Shit!
> If that's what you call jazz
> Then you ain't gettin' it
> At least they let us dominate
> At running back and flanker
> But some of us would like to be
> Your friendly local banker
> I got big feet, they like the beat
> They always ask for more
> When I'm in town, all the girls around
> Show up on the dance floor."

Startled by Fontaine's loud outburst, Waldo ran the car off the road. Luckily, an aptly termed convenience store happened to be on that side, and instead of a ditch the decidedly un-fredneck-like vehicle pulled into its parking lot.

Waldo heaved a mammoth sigh of relief, and gathered himself enough to issue what he considered, as their driver, to be an obligatory warning to the others. "Look, I know I'm the only one here, besides the Professor, who isn't high, but I think you guys ought to take it easy on that stuff. I'm not trying to join the Nancy Reagan fan club, but I can barely breathe, let alone see, because of the smoke. Haven't you all had enough?"

Brisbane started to react in a typically fredneck-like fashion, but the top doo-wopper was not quite high enough to have lost his common sense.

"We're sorry, Waldo. We certainly never intended to make it difficult for you. I suggest we all go inside the store here and purchase some Super Big Gasser soft drinks to clear our heads."

Phosphate uncharacteristically started laughing when he said the words "Super Big Gasser", as if he found the name so amusing he couldn't contain himself. Neither, apparently, could the others, who followed the top doo-wopper's lead and stumbled, guffawing all the way, into the store. Waldo watched them and hoped that some hungry law officers didn't happen to drop by for their doughnut fix just yet.

As Waldo sat there behind the wheel, beside a pensive Professor Buckley, who appeared dangerously close to falling asleep, he lit up a cigarette and rolled down the window to ventilate the car.

"Waldooooo... don't go to Cornoil."

Turning to his left, Waldo was startled to find three very odd-looking little men standing next to the car. They seemed to intone the dire message in a single mechanical voice.

For once Waldo's nerves, numbed by so many weird experiences, did not fail him and he mustered up the courage to actually speak to the probable M.I.B.'s.

"Who are you and how do you know my name and where I'm going?" He demanded.

"Waldooooo... have you enjoyed your trip so far? May we introduce ourselves?" The three men were all of the same short stature, no more than five feet tall, with olive complexions and facial features that were slightly oriental in appearance. And they were, naturally, dressed in black. They continued talking in a foreboding tone. *"We are Hargis, Rowland, and Walther."*

With that, they began laughing in a most hideous manner, and Waldo, his nervous system kicked into overdrive by now, put his hands over his ears and tried unsuccessfully to drown out the sound. As he soberly reflected that Hargis, Rowland, and Walther were three more of the apparently inexhaustible supply of names connected with the events in Dallas on November 22, 1963, the odd little men vanished into thin air.

"Oh dear, *oh, dear.*" Professor Buckley moaned. "What..."

"Waldo...Professor...are you alright?" Phosphate exclaimed. The top doo-wopper was standing, along with his compatriots, in front of the convenience store. They all had smiles on their faces and Super Big Gassers in their hands.

After they'd climbed into the car, Phosphate turned to Waldo. "I saw those three small gentlemen." The head Afro Anarchist sucked heartily on his straw. "M.I.B.'s?"

Waldo nodded and started the engine. "I think so. They certainly looked like M.I.B.'s."

"Shit man," Brisbane was alternating between guzzling his Super Big Guzzler soda and the remnants of his latest beer, "did you notice the dude behind the counter? He was wearing a fucking masonic ring!"

"Damn, Bris, a whole lot of people wear those." Fontaine observed.

"Yeah, man," the fredneck finished his beer, enabling him to devote all his attention on the super big soft drink, "that's true, but what about them? Do you all know anything about the masons? Shit man, I could tell you some fucking stories! Washington, Jefferson, Franklin, Roosevelt- all those dudes were masons..."

"I once heard, somewhere, that Kennedy was the first non-mason to become President." Waldo remarked, somehow managing, as usual, to fit his favorite historical figure into the conversation.

"Shit yeah, he probably was!" Brisbane replied. "Did you know their oath, that they all have to take to become one, says some shit about tearing out their tongues and throwing them in the ocean if they ever reveal any secrets? I read in a fucking book once that Harry "33rd degree" Truman held a kind of mock masonic ceremony in the oval office to swear in the first heads of the intelligence group that later became the C.I.A."

"Very interesting." Phosphate said, more credibly than anyone on *Laugh-In* ever did. "I confess I'm not as familiar with this topic as I should be."

"Actually, I must-that is-it all goes back much further than that." Professor Buckley had been stimulated out of his stupor. "The influence of freemasonry began to be felt during the French Revolution, with figures belonging to the order, such as Rousseau and Voltaire, providing the inspiration for the carnage that followed, and others like Robiespierre, Marat, and Cagliostro, playing the most prominent roles in the events themselves."

The decidedly un-fredneck-like automobile trekked onward, still unaccountably maintaining its gasoline level, as the talk turned from one off-the-wall subject to another.

"Lots of people have vanished, and of course-that is-some of them were relatively well-known."

Professor Buckley was holding court, a couple of hours later, as their discourse strayed into an area that was particularly appropriate; the mysterious disappearances of human beings.

"Of course, everyone knows the story of the Lost Colony of Roanoke, and how not a single member was ever found; the man who allegedly shot John Wilkes Booth at Garrett's farm, although those of us who have-that is-the evidence indicates Booth wasn't there- at any rate, the man was a religious fanatic who'd castrated himself, one Sergeant Boston Corbett, and he later escaped from an insane asylum and disappeared without a

167

trace; socialite Dorothy Arnold, who was last seen at a bookstore in downtown New York City, and could not be located again despite an extensive search by her rich, well-connected family; Michael Rockefeller, who never returned from the African wilds, and no one can question *his* family's wealth and wherewithal to find him; who even remembers today that there were-that is-the handsome young twins, heirs to the throne of England, were playing one day, back, I imagine it was in the late 1300's, on the grounds in front of the Tower of London, and history records simply that they were not seen again. The list goes on and on..." The ex-history teacher paused to catch his breath. "Old Hoss knew more about all this than I do; he must have had every book ever written on the subject."

"He certainly did. He was very interested in the kidnapping of the Lindbergh baby, and used to point out all the unexplained aspects of it: how he could have been abducted, when both parents, as well as a nanny, were in the house; the lack of evidence against the man eventually electrocuted for the crime- Bruno Richard Hauptmann-and the terrible way he was framed for something the authorities had to know he couldn't have done; the strange role of Dr. Condon; how the body of the infant that was found and claimed to be the missing baby couldn't possibly have been that of Charles Augustus Lindbergh, Jr." Waldo's eyes began to grow a bit misty, as he reflected on the questionable status of Old Hoss himself. "My grandfather felt that the Lindbergh case was actually another mysterious disappearance, and not a murder or kidnapping. I heard a lot about it when I was growing up."

"Indeed you must have." The Professor concurred. "Your grandfather was fascinated by any kind of incident that featured a missing person whose fate remained unknown."

"Which explains his interest in Ambrose Bierce." Phosphate observed. "But what about the cases involving less prominent persons? I seem to recall something about an entire village of Eskimos vanishing some time ago."

"You're right, Phosphate." Professor Buckley replied. "A most curious occurrence that was, too. It happened in 1930, I believe. Of course, there are stranger reports; have you heard of the two English RAF pilots who crash landed in the Iraqi desert in 1924? Their footprints were clearly visible in the sand some distance from the aircraft, then suddenly stopped. They were never found. Can there be a rational explanation for *that*?"

"Shit man, I'm hungry!" Brisbane abruptly declared. "We haven't eaten anything for hours. Let's stop somewhere."

The fredneck was right. They'd been so preoccupied, first by their piteous plight and then with their eerie, endless discussions, that only now were their stomachs signaling how empty they were.

"Yeah, Bris is right!" Bucktooth agreed.

"I say we pull into the next place we see, even if it's a sushi bar!" Fontaine stated, only halfjokingly.

Everyone else recognized, all at once, just how hungry they were as well, and unanimously concurred that this should be remedied as soon as possible. It was past nine o'clock at night, and thus unlikely that many of the eating establishments they might encounter along Old Hoss Highway would still be open, if they shared anything in common with those in Northern Virginia. So it was an attentive group that dropped their controversial conversing for the moment and stared out into the light fog that had rolled in from somewhere, hoping to discover a place that hadn't closed its doors yet.

A surprisingly short time later, Brisbane excitedly pointed to the left hand side of the road. "Look, over there, man! A fucking Taco Bull!"

There indeed, just ahead in the distance, was the friendly logo of the fast food restaurant chain, beckoning to them like a large, leaking breast to a newborn infant.

Waldo turned into the parking lot, which was quite crowded, considering the hour, and found a space on the side of the building.

Brisbane, Fontaine, and Bucktooth exited the car before Waldo turned the lights off, yelling excitedly, making demonstrative gestures indicating how hungry they were and how much they intended to eat, and generally creating such a commotion that several of the patrons sitting inside could be seen gazing out the window with disturbed, intolerant looks on their faces.

"Come on, you two," Waldo quickly turned the engine off, "we better hurry in there before they cause any trouble."

Phosphate slid out of the car, closed the door behind him, and reached into his pocket. He withdrew his wallet and opened it up, producing two dollar bills. "I'm afraid we'll need to pool our resources prior to their ordering anything. I doubt very seriously if we can afford the repast they seem to be anticipating."

Professor Buckley nodded solemnly at this, handing Phosphate a single dollar, two quarters, and a dime. "This is all I have, Phosphate. When we left, I should have considered-that is-I'm not independently wealthy, you know."

Waldo, who'd never had a bank account of any kind due to his grandfather's distrust of such institutions, and thus had no way of drawing out money from whatever branch might have been in the area, began his stock ritual of self-chastisement. "I can't believe how stupid I am! I brought exactly ten dollars with me, for a cross country trip! What kind of planning is that?" The disgusted young man threw two five dollar bills at the top doo-wopper. "Here, Phosphate- you keep it. I don't deserve to

169

eat."

Phosphate draped his arm about Waldo's shoulders. "Come now, Waldo, you really must stop this annoying habit of criticizing yourself. If it makes you feel any better, none of us appear to have possessed any more financial foresight than you."

"Yes, Waldo, you know-that is-I was just like your grandfather, my boy- never dealt with a bank in my life." Professor Buckley patted down the few wisps of hair on his head, as if anyone would notice the difference. "We'll manage."

Waldo had to smile at this upbeat appraisal, coming as it did from one of the world's foremost worry-warts. "Okay, I'll stop brow-beating myself, for now anyway."

They walked into the fast food restaurant, with the top doo-wopper holding their grand total of thirteen dollars and sixty cents in his hand. Immediately they were treated to the unlikely sight of Fontaine, Bucktooth, and Brisbane cavorting about in front of a small crowd of onlookers, by the jukebox, rapping away an undistinguished tune:

"Yo, there folks, make this selection
Take extra napkins for your protection
Wipe your mouth and blow your nose
You got the right to, I suppose
I don't like Hunts, I just like Heinz
Don't mess with that steak because it's mines
This Mexican diet warms my heart
Makes me dance and sing and fart
Do you wanna know a secret?- the Beatles did
I went in the kitchen and opened the lids
Of all the pots and pans back there
And what I saw would curl your hair
I ain't gonna comment, I ain't no voyeur
If you got any questions, talk to my lawyer."

A short, thin young man with hair so slick and glistening it might have been combed with the proverbial "greasy kid stuff," came rushing out from behind the counter with an embarrassed expression on his flushed face.

"Hey, you three!" He jumped between the intrepid would-be rappers and their audience. "Folks, please go back to your meals. These...gentlemen were just about to leave."

"Shit man, we're not leaving." Brisbane said adamantly. "We haven't even ordered our food yet."

"That's right." Fontaine cautioned, with a sly smile on his face.

170

"You better get your scrawny ass back to work before I make a kiddie burrito out of you!"

"I happen to be the manager here, young man!" The small figure declared, with all the pomp inherent in the title.

"The manager!" Bucktooth roared with laughter. "How little is the assistant manager?"

"That's it," the manager responded, "I'm calling the police!"

"Excuse me, sir." Phosphate stepped forward, settling into his habitual role of diplomat. "I apologize for the atrocious behavior of my friends. Please allow us to order our food and be on our way."

The manager stared at the top doo-wopper and straightened out his clip-on bow tie, which had gone askew. "Well...I suppose that would be alright. I don't want any trouble."

"Thank you, sir." Phosphate replied, taking Fontaine and Bucktooth by the arms and leading them bodily to the counter. "I won't comment on your actions, I'm sure you realize how ridiculous they were. Our funds are extremely limited, so you will only be able to order a single taco each."

Waldo merely shook his head at Brisbane, and the fredneck sheepishly followed the Afro Anarchists without defending himself.

They each ordered a taco, permitting Phosphate to retain more than half their money in his wallet. As they were walking towards the door, munching their food as they went, the diminutive manager suddenly stepped into their path.

"Did I mention, gentlemen," he stated, adjusting his bow tie again, "that we're running a special at Taco Bull this evening?"

Waldo eyed him warily. "What do you mean?"

The small man smiled. "Well, for each order over...let's see, how much was your order, anyhow?"

"Five dollars and ninety seven cents." Phosphate replied.

"What a coincidence!" The manager exclaimed. "For all orders over five dollars and ninety six cents, we provide the customer with a room for the night, at the motel behind us."

"What?" Waldo's mouth flew open. "How...I mean, who ever heard of a fast food place..."

"Yeah man," Fontaine interrupted him, "how do you know we need a room, anyway?"

"Just a hunch." The little man softly answered. "You ought to at least look at it. It's very comfortable."

For everyone except Waldo and the Professor, curiosity proved stronger than fear, and Phosphate led them out of Taco Bull, immediately proceeding towards the back of the place.

"Please, I beg you," Professor Buckley intoned, "don't go any farther! We don't know-that is-oh dear, *oh dear!*"

Waldo and the Professor found themselves reluctantly following behind the others, remembering the old proverb about their being safety in numbers, and calculating that it might still apply in this situation.

There was indeed a building behind them, with turquoise shingles on its roof, a long row of doors along the front and around the sides, and the bulwark of all motels and hotels everywhere, at least in english speaking countries- a "vacancy" sign above the entrance.

"Phosphate," Waldo pleaded with the top doo-wopper, "why do you want to go in there? You know how illogical this all is- we've been doing okay sleeping in the car."

"Sheeeet!" Fontaine exclaimed. "You and the Professor don't care, 'cause you all don't ever sleep. Well, the rest of us do, and we prefer a bed."

"Especially when it's free!" Bucktooth echoed.

They entered the lobby, which was very small, furnished with an imitation brown leather sofa and matching chair, a floor lamp with a low wattage bulb in it, a single, forlorn palm plant, and a black and white television set tuned, with poor, snowy reception, to a typically insipid network drama.

The front desk was deserted, so Phosphate rang the bell which was sitting there for just such a purpose. An instant later, a rotund oriental man emerged from a door behind the television set, his short gray hair disheveled.

"Yaaah!" He shouted, like an out of shape samurai warrior. The man looked to be in his sixties, and his dirty white undershirt hardly concealed his massive belly, which would have been an impressive sight in the most redneck of neighborhoods. "You crazy or something?"

"I beg your pardon?" Phosphate asked, a bit taken aback by the elderly man's aggressiveness.

"Doesn't matter, man." The oriental chuckled heartily, his stomach bouncing up and down. "No can do! No can do! You want room?"

"Yes, I suppose so." The top doo-wopper replied. "I believe we are entitled to one, at no cost, according to the gentleman at Taco Bull..."

"You crazy or something?" The old man reached into his hip pocket, pulled out a moldy piece of white bread, and woofed it down in one piece. "Hmmmm. Doesn't matter, man. You say no charge? No can do! No can do!"

"Damn man, that's what the manager said!" Fontaine complained.

"Well, perhaps we misunderstood him." The top doo-wopper said. "I trust we didn't inconvenience you, sir."

The Oriental man patted his huge stomach. "Doesn't matter, man. If Taco Bull say you stay free, then okay. No can do."

Brisbane looked puzzled. "Which is it, dude? Can we stay for free or what?"

"I say okay!" The old man produced a paper cup from under the counter and downed its contents in a single gulp. "I forget- they have some special deal tonight. Here- room fifteen."

The chubby gentleman handed Phosphate a key and abruptly turned his back to them, focusing his attention on the television set.

Waldo was shaking his head as they walked back outside. "I don't like this. That guy was just like all the others we've met on this trip- *unreal!* Who knows what will happen if we spend the night here?"

Phosphate stopped. "All of us, particularly you, Waldo, would find a night's sleep in something other than a moving vehicle to be most refreshing. Our minds will be much clearer tomorrow."

Hesitantly trudging along behind the others, Waldo and the Professor exchanged worried glances. There were only a few cars in the unlit parking lot, and both of them made certain to check behind their backs every few steps.

"Ah, room fifteen!" The top doo-wopper stated as they came to one of the doors, painted turquoise like the shingles on the roof, which was located in the middle of a uniform row on the right side of the building. Phosphate inserted the key in the door, turned the knob, and entered.

When everyone was inside, the top doo-wopper closed the door. "Well, this looks quite inviting, wouldn't you say, Waldo?"

Waldo gazed at the twin beds, the walnut dresser, and the end table with a Gideon's Bible laying conspicuously upon it, and took a seat in the imitation red leather chair by the window. "You all go ahead and sleep..."

"Waldo, please." The lines in Phosphate's forehead revealed the extent of his concern. "If you don't relax, my friend, I fear these ongoing, bizarre experiences will affect your emotional stability. I've tried all my life to steer clear of paranoia, and that's quite difficult when you're capable of independent thought, but I sense that you're drifting dangerously in its direction. I don't imagine we've seen the worst of things yet, and I'd feel personally responsible if you were to develop some sort of long-lettered mental affliction before our journey is complete. I'm no psychiatrist, and I generally disregard the advice the members of that profession dispense, but I'll risk being labeled hypocritical by advising you, unofficially of course, to lay down and rest. Even a short period would prove most beneficial to you."

Waldo shrugged resignedly. "Okay, I've never been much of a sleeper, and I don't see how I can now, but I'll try."

The top doo-wopper grinned broadly and, in the best tradition of non-professional hospital employees, assisted the nervous but healthy young man into one of the twin beds. Without a second thought, or a fear that the other males observing him might hiss nasty comments his way,

Phosphate tucked Waldo in as tidily as any mother might have. Fortunately for his reputation, he did not kiss him lovingly on the forehead.

"Shit man, how the hell are we gonna sleep? I mean, *who with who?*" Brisbane's question raised the issue everyone was wondering about, with anxious hearts and fragile egos.

After a few minutes of unproductive debate, Brisbane jumped under the covers next to Waldo, and Fontaine chuckled as he fluffed the pillows on the other bed.

"Sheeeet!" He turned to Bucktooth and Phosphate. "Well, it looks like Jim Crow isn't dead after all!"

"Yeah man, separate but equal!" Bucktooth pulled back the covers.

"I'm extremely tired, gentlemen," Phosphate kicked off his shoes and climbed in beside them, "and both of you are far too sensitive. Some things *are* coincidental."

Brisbane turned out the light, and everyone forgot about the Professor, evidently taking it for granted that the one time pride of the local community college would forego another night's sleep in his customary fashion.

Indeed, Professor Buckley didn't have the slightest intention of falling asleep, and he waited until he heard the others snoring before he walked softly over to the end table and turned the lamp back on. No one stirred in response, so the ex-history teacher settled back in the imitation red leather chair by the window, opened his battered briefcase, which he'd naturally carried with him into Taco Bull, and pulled out Sam Hancock's journal. Avidly flipping the pages, he stopped to read an interesting entry:

The Journal of Sam Hancock, August 28, 1955

I returned yesterday from a week's visit to the military academy at West Point. Of course, we didn't stay at West Point itself, but we did obtain lodging at a hotel which was within five miles of the academy. By we, I refer to myself and Abner "Old Hoss" Billingsly, who is my customary companion on these frequent excursions and, need I say, my very best friend.

The reason for traveling to such an unlikely locale was our obsession with an ongoing mystery that occurred there just five years ago, the strange and unsolved disappearance of a West Point cadet, 21 year old Richard Colvin Cox. Both Old Hoss and I followed the case closely in the newspapers, and were well aware that, despite an intensive manhunt launched by the police, the F.B.I., and the Army's vaunted investigative division- C.I.D. (Criminal Investigative Detachment), no trace of the young man had been found. As there appeared to be no real clues to his fate, such a case was bound to attract veteran devotees of the unknown like Old Hoss and myself.

We arrived there on the twentieth, and once our belongings were unpacked in the hotel, we began our investigation as we always do- by drinking whiskey and sodas in the lounge downstairs. As is often the case, we made the acquaintance of a young man who was at the table next to us. Probably due to the fact that we usually discuss things of a more interesting nature than the weather or the latest local gossip, we are often eavesdropped upon in such settings by other patrons. This time was no exception, and the close proximity of our relative positions made it impossible for the young man not to have heard our conversation, even if he'd had a mind to.

Eventually we noticed the short, stout young man with thinning brown hair smiling pleasantly at us. Sliding his chair over towards our table, he spoke with a barely detectable British accent.

"Excuse me, gents, but I have no one to talk with, and I couldn't help listening to your conversation. I must confess it sounded interesting. Do you mind if I join you?"

Being friendly sorts, we welcomed the company. "By all means, sit down. We were, as I guess you know, discussing the cadet that vanished from West Point five years ago. Are you familiar with that case?" I asked him.

He looked at us with a peculiar expression on his round, ruddy face. "Familiar with it? I was at West Point at the time."

Old Hoss puffed a little harder on his trusty cigar, a sure sign of his undivided attention. "Were you?"

"Yes, indeed. And let me tell you, the Cox incident is one that I think about every day of my life." The young man seemed sincere. I had forgotten my manners, and moved quickly to rectify that. "My name is Sam Hancock, and this is Abner Billingsly. We're very pleased to meet you."

"Likewise. I'm Richard Gumbrecht."

I was anxious to pump him for more information, but felt it wise to conceal my eagerness. "Richard, and I trust you don't mind me calling you by your first name..."

"Of course not."

"Why, if you don't mind my asking, do you still think of the incident? Did you know Cox?" I inquired.

He took an agonizingly long sip from his drink, which appeared to be a gin and tonic. "Yeah, Dick and I were friends. But, I really should start at the beginning. Maybe I can help you all."

"By all means, please go ahead." I urged him.

"Well, okay." He lit up a cigarette. "How much do you know about what happened?"

"Not enough to be able to solve it." Old Hoss cleverly replied. "Why don't you just retell the whole story? We may have read a lot on the case, but I, for one, could stand a refresher course."

"Alright, I'll tell you everything I know." Gumbrecht took a deep breath and began. "Well, I was at the Point for two years. I can't give you any of the details about my own stay there, only as to how it relates to Cox. Anyway, Richard Cox was a nice chap and a good cadet. He and I used to hang one on together every so often, and I think I knew him better than most of the cadets there. It was on January 14, 1950- I still remember the date- that Cox was visited for the third time by a strange man named George, whom I feel is probably the key to the whole mystery."

"A third time?" I interrupted him.

"Yes, the first two times had been a week previously, and Cox had supposedly gone to the hotel Thayer with him, even though no one recalled seeing him there." Gumbrecht paused to sip his drink. "At any rate, on that night, after going out with George again, Cox had apparently had a few too many, and I can tell you from experience that it didn't take much to make Dick tipsy. Well, the weird thing about it was that his roommates took a picture of him that night. They found him asleep on his bed, and thought it would be funny to snap a photograph of him while he was sleeping one off. Well, when they did, Cox jumped up a few seconds later in a completely disoriented state of mind. He didn't seem to recognize his roommates, and behaved generally in a most peculiar way. Finally, he bolted from the room and into the hall, screaming incoherently. The two roommates had to drag him forcibly into the room. They were baffled by his hysterical outburst, and the next day they questioned him about it, but Dick seemed to be frightened of something. His roommates later told the authorities that they believed the mysterious George to be the cause of Cox's fear. The next night was a Saturday, and Dick requested a special d.p., or dinner privilege, to go to the Thayer hotel again, evidently with this George fellow. Well, if he did go there, no one saw him again, and he left behind $60.00 in checks in his room. As I'm sure you know, he hasn't been seen or heard from since."

"I wasn't aware of his behavior after the picture was taken." Old Hoss signalled the waitress to bring us another round of drinks.

"Neither was I, although I have seen the photo." I said. "Don't you find the fact that a photograph was taken of him sleeping on the eve of his disappearance to be a bit bizarre?"

"Indeed I do." Gumbrecht agreed. "It almost reminds one of the old Lincoln inauguration daguerreotype, where you can spot John Wilkes Booth and some of the other members of his band of conspirators in the crowd surrounding the President. This may not be that ironical, but it is certainly odd."

"Yes, it is." Old Hoss puffed on his cigar. "Tell us, Richard, why did you leave West Point? I don't mean to pry, but I sense that you left ahead of schedule and perhaps not of your own volition. Am I correct?"

Gumbrecht smiled. "You're quite perceptive. No, I didn't leave voluntarily, but I really can't discuss that. What I would like to do, and then I have to be going, is to give you the name of an official at the Point who will assist you. He is the only one there with any influence that will."

"How do you know that?" I wondered.

"Because I once was very interested in solving the mystery myself. As I told you, I really can't talk about it, but I will say that I ran into a lot of obstacles there. I'd still like to know what happened to my friend Dick Cox, so I'm trying to help you avoid some of the same mistakes I made." Gumbrecht handed me a slip of paper.

The name printed on it was Major John Hurley. "Are you sure this fellow is still there?"

He rose from the table. "I'm positive he is. I'm sorry to leave you so abruptly, but I have another engagement." Gumbrecht shook hands with us. "I wish you luck. Maybe you can succeed where I failed." He then strode off, with what both of us categorized as a distinct military bearing.

After he'd gone, Old Hoss and I speculated on the possible fate of cadet Richard Cox. Several whiskey and sodas later, we were no closer to an answer.

The next day, we were allowed into West Point, for the first and only time, as it turned out. The U.S. Military Academy is a stupendously impressive pile of gothic fortress buildings. When we first saw it, perched on the banks of the Hudson River, we couldn't help but be impressed by this visible reminder of America's obsession with pomp and power.

We attempted to justify our presence there by claiming to be representatives of the magazine Toteno (an inside joke, since those are the initials of The Organization To End National Organizations, an extremely exclusive group that Old Hoss and I founded recently). We were doing a piece on the Richard Cox disappearance, we explained.

To our astonishment, we were granted access to the files in the Registrar's office. The size and scope of the material from the Richard Cox investigation that was available to us was, however, predictably small and not even as informative as our chat with Richard Gumbrecht. We decided to go over the enrollment records while we were there and look up a few names. The first was Major John Hurley, whom we intended to try and contact. To our chagrin, we could find no mention of a Major John Hurley, past or present. Ignoring this momentary setback, we did find some record of the other party we were interested in, Richard Gumbrecht. What we discovered caused our knees to buckle. There had indeed been a

Richard Gumbrecht at West Point in January, 1950, but the records listed him as having died on January 20, 1951! Old Hoss and I exchanged startled glances, and we quickly left the office. Having momentarily lost our appetite for adventure, we halfheartedly questioned a young officer as to the whereabouts of a Major John Hurley. He checked another file and verified the records we had seen; there was no Major John Hurley listed as having been at West Point at any time in recent memory.

We left the Point and Old Hoss and I could think of nothing but what the enrollment records had said about Richard Gumbrecht. This started us on an extensive conversation about ghosts, and we sat up most of the night drinking and discussing things that go bump during those hours.

The next morning we acted somewhat more rationally, and checked the front desk to see if a Richard Gumbrecht had been registered there in the past few days. The bald stereotype of a desk clerk shook his head and showed us the list of guests for the last week. There was no Richard Gumbrecht there.

We didn't know what to think at this point, having experienced our share of strange phenonema, but never actually meeting a ghost before. We felt there were only a few possible explanations:

A)Richard Gumbrecht was not the young man's real name, and he had been using an alias for some unknown purpose; B)he was indeed a ghost; C)the records at West Point were in error, either through mistake or by design, and Gumbrecht was the living, breathing young man we had spoken to; D)the whole thing- the meeting with Richard Gumbrecht and then the discovery that he was recorded as having been deceased for over four years- was somehow connected to our investigation into the Cox disappearance; E)Old Hoss and I had imbibed too much and had imagined the whole episode.

Both of us felt confident we could discard the final alternative right away, having consumed quite a bit of alcohol over the years without hallucinating, especially in concert with each other. Of the remaining choices, we felt that D was probably the most likely, judging by our knowledge of the world's power brokers and their secret machinations.

For the next few days, we attempted to revisit West Point, but were refused admission. Our efforts to check the records at the local F.B.I. office turned up nothing, mainly because we were denied access to their files. The police were predictably unhelpful, and our questioning of local citizens introduced us to some colorful characters but failed to provide an answer to the mystery of cadet Richard Cox's abrupt disappearance.

There was one final curious thing. As we were leaving the hotel, standing in front of the entrance awaiting our taxi, both of us swore we saw Richard Gumbrecht drive by in a long black limousine. He was sitting in the back seat and was only visible to us from the right side, but I have no doubt, and neither does Old Hoss, that it was him. This incident merely underscored the frustration we felt at having learned so little about what really happened to Richard Colvin Cox on the night of January 14, 1950. We never accept defeat, however, and our file on this case remains an open one, in spite of what the authorities say. We can only assume that it will stay as unexplained as all the rest of the numerous mysteries Old Hoss and I are forever chasing after. Until then, goodnight Richard Cox, wherever you are...

Professor Buckley raised his eyes and stared out of the motel window. Satisfied that there were no representatives from the forces of evil lurking about in the darkness of the parking lot, he resumed his battle against slumber and persisted on with his reading.

The next morning, following an almost unprecedented eight hour
slumber, Waldo awoke to the sounds of live rap music. Blinking his eyes
and yawning lazily, the abnormally well rested young man turned over and
stared foggily at Fontaine and Brisbane, who were alternating on lead
vocals, while Bucktooth danced around and made appropriate
accompanying noises in the background. The fredneck and Fontaine had
co-written the song earlier that morning, and entitled their first
collaboration *Rappin' Joe Idaho*:

"You know we're just out on the road
Making our way to Idaho
All of their potatoes bruise
Maybe that's why I'm so confused
I look for corn and just say 'huh?'
I thought I was headed for Iowa
Whichever way I stop and stare
I didn't know either one was there
The Midwest and the wide open spaces
Are perfect homes for all white faces
Everyone speaks the English tongue
Believes in God and marries young
No minorities for rapes and looting
What the hell's a drive-by shooting?
Except, of course, at the local college
Where certain brothers display their knowledge
On the basketball courts and football fields
Alumni, fraternities, and sweetheart deals
They ain't no students, can't really read
As good as the average unemployed hayseed
Do your homework, find an occupation
What a friend we have in higher education!"

Waldo politely applauded and rose to a sitting posture.
"Shit man, did you like it or what?" Brisbane impatiently
demanded.
"Yes, it was...very nice." Waldo replied hesitantly, not certain he was
qualified to differentiate between good and bad rap music.
"Nice?" Fontaine snorted. "Man, you don't know..."

"Fontaine, you must learn to accept lukewarm praise and even criticism if you plan on branching out into this new field." Phosphate interrupted. The top doo-wopper was drying his hair, having merely caught the last few lines of their song after enjoying a long and leisurely shower. There appeared to be a none too subtle trace of jealousy in the head Afro Anarchist's tone, which might have been understandable considering the number of backup doo-wop protest singers available for hire should Fontaine and Bucktooth decide to pursue rapping full time.

"Well, damn, Phos, how much of the song did you hear?" Fontaine asked.

"Enough." The top doo-wopper answered curtly. "I suggest that all of you follow my example and shower. If this establishment is similar to most other motels, we'll have to check out in an hour. That doesn't leave much time, so I propose you start immediately."

"I don't think this motel *is* like any others." Bucktooth remarked to no one in particular, in a soft and timid voice. "But then, I ain't really been in many."

The Professor, also oblivious to the loud rap music, was still engrossed in Sam Hancock's journal, as he had been all night. No one else seemed overly enthusiastic about the prospect of bathing, so Waldo walked towards the bathroom.

"A shower would be just the thing, especially after that good night's sleep." He smiled at Phosphate.

"I detest it when someone says 'I told you so', my friend, but..." Phosphate toweled off his long angular arms once again.

"I know- I don't like it either. But you sure were right." Waldo replied as he closed the door.

"Excuse me, Professor." Phosphate slipped the sole shirt in his wardrobe on once again, his refusal to change it being a declaration on his part that even while he remained homeless, it would always have a place on his back, and approached the ex-history teacher, who was reclining comfortably in the imitation red leather chair by the window, his attention focused exclusively on the thoughts of Old Hoss's former best friend. "I thought that I might peruse a few of Waldo's grandfather's writings while waiting for the others to shower. Would you mind?"

Hiram Buckley lifted his head and stared about the room semi-coherently, as if unsure of his whereabouts. "What's that? I don't really- that is-of course, Phosphate, please be my guest."

Professor Buckley reached down under the chair and lifted his battered old briefcase onto the bed closest to him, opened it and produced a pile of papers.

"Here they are, at least some of them." He handed them to Phosphate. "Waldo entrusted them to-that is-they ought to keep you occupied for a while."

"Thank you, Professor." The top doo-wopper smiled and sat down on the edge of the bed. The unpublished pamphlet on top was entitled *Where No Man Treads*, and Phosphate began reading:

"What exactly is meant by the quaint and popular term *professional*? Does not the very word imply a superior class of people? Couldn't we apply this definition to farmers, or truckdrivers, or janitors, or factory workers, or butchers, or bakers, or any of the other anonymous classes of laborers? By bestowing such a title on certain fortunate groups such as doctors and lawyers, aren't we suggesting that what they provide is of a special importance? Aren't more imagined responsibilities being attributed to them in order to justify the undeniable reality of their superior rights and perquisites? Or are we simply recognizing the fact that they are paid far more than what we kindly refer to as 'employees?'

I hereby boldly state, from these secluded walls, that 'professional' could more accurately be defined as 'non-producing.' Every working man and woman in this country accepts the general notion that their superiors don't seem to do much of anything to earn their salaries, but few of them realize how accurate such time-honored blue collar folklore is. To put it bluntly- the more money one makes in our society, the less work one does. This is crystal clear to everyone except those who benefit from such an illogical arrangement. This fundamental truth is the reason that communism was born, and the slogan 'workers of the world unite, you have nothing to lose but your chains' must have lit a spark in the heart of many a manual laborer as he observed the various misdeeds of his managers.

Of course, the elitists who rule everything else either invented this apparent godsend for the working man themselves, or subverted it soon after its birth. Either way, what was a crying need- the redistribution of wealth- never materialized, only an even more oppressive despotism. The whole labor movement in this country was controlled in the same fashion, with its leaders persistently prone to raiding their union's coffers and forming business ties with organized crime figures. Despite their penchant for busting the heads of those nonconforming workers who, with mouths to feed, saw little choice but to cross one of the sacred picket lines, these fat and happy union bosses, unprincipled and unproductive to the core, have from their inception enjoyed a cozy relationship with their enemies in management. So the great majority of people, struggling to meet the necessities of life, tolerate an antiquated system in order to receive a minuscule yearly raise, if they're fortunate, that places them in a perpetual position of continuing usurious payments on the various debts they've incurred, without ever being able to pay them off. When one listens to such things as federal judges pleading with Congress for large salary increases because they aren't able to afford their childrens' college tuitions on $89,000 per year, one marvels that all working people aren't alcoholics.

In this country, we have actually come to think that certain persons, by virtue of their occupations and educational achievements, are entitled to a larger share of 'the American dream.' That 'American dream' means different things to different folks: to an inner-city youth, it may be merely an apartment and a nice used car; to a college graduate, particularly from a university with a prestigious reputation, it may mean a job sitting at a desk and attending lots of important meetings; but to someone unfortunate enough to be without a college degree, it might be working two physically taxing jobs for far less cumulative money than the college graduate's one position pays him. There is something monumentally unfair about all that, but whenever one raises this specter of massive disparity in standards of living, one is accused of being a communist.

Anyone familiar with my writings (a rather limited group, as there is little market for unpublished pamphlets) knows that I am violently anti-communist, and have in fact exposed many of the communist tendencies of our own government. Were I to espouse the moral necessity of a true redistribution of wealth, however, I too would be smeared as a subversive by my friends on both the left and right-wing fringes. The 'professional' is, as I stated earlier, in reality a non-producer. They produce nothing tangible, they simply are paid the largest amounts of money. If justice truly prevailed, the persons performing the hardest, least desirable tasks would earn the biggest paychecks, while those specializing in long business luncheons and leisurely golf games would be paid their commensurate worth. Toilet cleaners would be permitted to relax after hours in opulent mansions, catered to by a devoted staff, while executives would find it difficult to rise above the minimum wage salary, and would be the ones pounding their fists in frustration over the relentless rent increases inflicted upon them by their merciless landlords. Huey Long, one of a handful of honest twentieth century national politicians, had formulated a viable solution to the redistribution problem with his 'Share the Wealth' program. Unfortunately for the Senator from Louisiana, and those who might consider following his example, he was not the first, and certainly not the last, to be accorded what George Bernard Shaw termed 'the most extreme form of censorship.'"

"What a unique perspective this man has." Phosphate observed as he continued leafing through all the neglected, politically incorrect material.

While the top doo-wopper scanned over some of Old Hoss's

183

unpublished pamphlets, and Professor Buckley remained immersed in Sam Hancock's journal, Waldo finished showering and walked back into the room.

"Okay, somebody else can use the..."

"Out! Disja time!" The rotund oriental desk clerk abruptly burst into their room, with a red, sweaty face and a piece of moldy bread hanging out of the corner of his mouth. "Out! No can do!"

"What the..." Bucktooth resembled Buckwheat, of Little Rascals fame, as his mouth flew open in amazement.

"Shit man, who the fuck do you think you are, barging into somebody's room without even knocking?" Brisbane stepped forward belligerently.

"A better question would be: who do you think you are to shout profanities at our night manager?" A tall, gangly man with greasy brown hair, whom everyone instantly recognized as the Warden from Snortin' Reformatory with the curious name of LaFlaha, stepped into the room behind the overweight oriental. "Besides, why complain when you didn't even pay?"

Waldo stood there without a shirt, and was so startled to see the odd figure from the Virginia prison that he didn't bother to cover his large chest, which he considered to be feminine and was terribly self-conscious about.

"B-b-but y-you're..." Waldo tried to speak, but found himself shivering, as much from fear as from the goose bumps which had arisen even more rapidly than usual, undoubtedly due to the fact he'd just emerged from the shower. The nervous young man did, however, have the presence of mind to modestly cover himself with the same unwashed shirt he'd been wearing.

"I've recently made a career change." LaFlaha slowly raised a gnarled finger and, just as he had in the magistrate's office at Snortin' Reformatory, thrust it up into his nostril. "I find this field to be *very* rewarding."

Before the lanky ex-prison warden had a chance to say or do anything of an even more peculiar nature, the Professor latched ahold of his battered briefcase and darted out the door. With no opposition from LaFlaha or his aged oriental underling, the others rapidly followed, and found themselves panting like insurance salesmen in the parking lot outside Taco Bull shortly thereafter.

Waldo cast a look back over his shoulder and discovered that neither LaFlaha nor the roly poly night manager/desk clerk was pursuing them. He was able to reflect, even in his agitated state of mind, upon how similarly baffling this situation was to the one he and the Professor had so recently experienced, when the old man and his bug-eating son had

184

proven just as inexplicably reluctant to chase them through the giant strawberry patch.

"Waldo, my boy, I know-that is-*oh dear!*" Hiram Buckley rushed off to Brisbane's car and jumped into the back seat.

Everyone else was just as anxious to depart, so the decidedly un-fredneck-like '65 Dodge Dart was soon filled to capacity, without anyone expressing their astonishment, or a single paranoid comment.

They drove along Old Hoss Highway for a good five minutes in almost total silence, with the extra gasps of air from Waldo's hyperventilating and the flicking of disposable lighters being the only sounds in the car.

"Shit man, that dude with the finger up his nose..." Brisbane eventually commented, "how could he be here? What the fuck is going on?"

"My friend, I suspect that when this aptly named road ends," Phosphate answered matter-of-factly, "we shall all have a better idea of what is going on."

Everyone nodded in agreement, if not in understanding, and gradually they resumed their unusual discussions, on a far ranging set of topics from the Loch Ness Monster to the prospective merits of the Articles of Confederation and the Constitution.

As the debates raged on and passions blazed fiercely, Waldo stuck his head out of the window for some fresh air. He inhaled deeply and wondered if it was just another delusion or if he really did detect the faintest scent of corn.

"There it is!" Brisbane, who was driving, pointed excitedly to a sign indicating Cornoil was only five miles away. "Shit man, I can't believe it! How did we get to Iowa that fast? Talk about a fucking shortcut!"

"What if it's not the right Cornoil?" Bucktooth wondered.

It was early in the afternoon, and apparently they were only a short distance from their destination, with Old Hoss Highway proving to be a most remarkable thoroughfare from the east coast to the Midwest. The sky was crystal clear, providing little dramatic atmosphere, but this hardly pacified them, and their hearts beat faster as they drew ever closer to Iowa and the Last Chance Relaxation Home.

At this point, something very curious happened. Even when viewed in the context of their trip, with its bars full of dead baseball players, giant strawberry patchs, vanishing hitchhikers, and unnamed roads leading nowhere, what transpired that afternoon was very, very odd. Like so many alleged U.F.O. abductees before them, the six protagonists experienced a memory lapse. One moment, they were bantering about Kaspar Hauser and Atlantis, and the next found them blinking in astonishment on the side of the road several hours later, in the middle of the night, without any explanation for the missing time, or how they'd arrived there.

"Whoa, dude!" Brisbane exclaimed, with the tone of someone undergoing a dramatic head rush. "What the fuck..."

"H-h-h-how c-could it b-be night?" Waldo wondered, with his spine tingling in its typical fashion.

"Could it be," the erudite top doo-wopper was seemingly capable of postulating an outlandish theory during any situation, "that someone or something abducted us, perhaps even experimented upon us, during the hours that have elapsed since we last consciously recall anything?"

"I say-that is-of course, such reports are common in the U.F.O. literature." Professor Buckley was remaining unusually calm.

Brisbane started the engine. "Shit man, that sign said we were only five miles away from Iowa. I want to know what the fuck's waiting for us there. The suspense is killing me."

"Ah, 'tis harder knowing it is due than knowing it is here." The Professor was fond of quotations that few people would recognize, and often injected them into the conversation when it seemed appropriate.

The fredneck maneuvered his trusty old automobile back onto Old Hoss Highway, and everyone silently reflected upon this latest anomaly-what might have occurred during the missing hours, how it could be connected to the other bizarre goings-on, and what the future might hold in store.

Apparently they were still not quite in the midst of the normal time-space continuum, for the next few miles took the rest of the night to traverse, and the sun was just rising when they slipped past the welcoming billboard and into Iowa.

They were greeted by a chorus of crowing roosters, as they found themselves immediately passing through a town that resembled such video graveyards as Mayberry or Hooterville. The road narrowed to a single lane, and possessed an aggregation of potholes that would have made any elite, east coast suburb proud. Judging by the dry cleaning, barber shop, hardware store, and drug store signs, it was apparent they were in the middle of the business section of a distinctively Midwestern community.

The anticipation over having, in the most inconceivable manner imaginable, reached their destination, had caused the alcohol to flow freely. Indeed, the beer in the car seemed to be as strangely immune to depletion as the gasoline supply. All of them, except the Professor, had been drinking steadily for over an hour (if any estimation of time at that point could be trusted), and they must have been a peculiar sight to any citizens peeking out from between their venetian blinds. In that part of the country, if judged by the media through which the five wayward easterners had seen it filtered, milking the cows or attending sunrise services at the local protestant church were the sort of activities engaged in at that time of the morning. It was certain that an old car crammed full of Afro Anarchists, a colorfully clad ex-history teacher, a trembling twenty eight year old virgin, and a highly animated fredneck would be apt to draw attention, and that their imbibing in intoxicants at such an hour would be frowned upon.

Fontaine vividly demonstrated the effect that such early morning binges could produce when he began picking up empty beer cans off the floor, where there was quite a collection, and hurling them out the window at the quaint little town structures.

Phosphate quickly grabbed his fellow doo-wopper's arm. "What are you doing, Fontaine? Attempting to arouse the sleeping farmers, who I'm sure would be delighted to be awakened by the sounds of you desecrating their town?"

"Oh hell, it ain't like that, Phos." A minute degree of embarrassment shone through Fontaine's inebriated outer shell. "I was trying to see if these buildings was real or just some props. You know, like in that *Twilight Zone* show, where everything in the town is really part of a giant's dollhouse."

Phosphate smiled condescendingly. "I see. Well, in the future please try and show some restraint when you are conducting metaphysical experiments."

They drove through the town's limits, where it abruptly ended and the road became unpaved, an ominous sign in recent days, and one that created quite a bit of frenzy in the decidedly un-fredneck-like vehicle.

Suddenly Brisbane, who as always had led the others in alcohol consumption, announced loudly that he had to relieve himself. As there appeared to be no available rest room imminent, the fredneck pulled over to the side of the road. All around them, in every direction, were golden stalks of corn, a breathtaking sight in the dull orange glow of sunrise, pointing majestically towards the heavens. Waldo didn't bother to turn around, and if he had he'd become much too jaded to gasp at the disappearance of the town they'd left behind them.

"My, it appears as if the general impression about Iowa and corn is a highly accurate one." Phosphate observed.

"Talk about factual stereotypes!" Waldo agreed.

Brisbane didn't add to the anti-heartland comments being flung about in the car. "Shit, dudes! I really gotta go! I'll be right back." Being a fredneck, he was not averse to urinating in public, and he hurriedly slid out from behind the steering wheel, one hand on his zipper, and raced into the cornfield to the right of the car.

"Hey, maybe he'll be like that farmer you was telling us about,

Professor-the one that disappeared right in front of his family and friends-and never come back." Bucktooth's voice carried a hint of "Sunshine" Sammy Morrison, token black member of the East Side Kids.

"I don't think-that is-that was over a hundred years ago, my boy." Professor Buckley attempted to adopt an unfamiliar tone of reassurance.

However, when several minutes went by and all they could see were cornstalks dancing in the early morning breeze...

Brisbane rubbed his eyes. There, standing in the middle of an Iowa cornfield, were the two most beautiful girls he'd ever seen.

They appeared to be teenagers, each of them nearly identical physically, with chestnut brown hair, green eyes that twinkled at him impishly, and small, petite figures.

"Hello!" They chirped in unison, their vitality and vivaciousness evident in the way they literally bounded towards him.

The fredneck stood there flabbergasted. Fortunately, he'd been able to relieve himself before the girls suddenly materialized, out of nowhere, only yards away from him. Finally he smiled nervously and introduced himself.

"Well, Brisbane, we're pleased to meet you." One of the girls stepped forward and shook his hand as well as any businessman might have. "I'm Jeanne O'Sullivan and this is my twin sister Janie."

Jeanne and Janie O'Sullivan were sixteen years old, and lived with their parents, who were struggling against almost insurmountable odds to maintain their family farm in the midst of foreclosures, crop failures, and governmental indifference. The cornfield in which the fredneck had chosen to urinate was in fact a very special one, possessing the power to transport others back in time. Jeanne and Janie had discovered years ago that at certain points in their large cornfield, it was possible to slip back into the past. After a great deal of experimentation, the twins grew adept enough to correlate specific dates with various parts of the cornfield. This privilege seemed to be reserved solely for them, as their parents had walked through these "wrinkles in time" (Jeanne named the magical spots after the title of one of her favorite books, by Madeleine L'Engle) on numerous occasions with no effect. Neighbors and friends had as well, without disappearing into a previous point in history. The magical cornfield seemed only able to work in reverse, however, and penetrating the future was something the O'Sullivan twins had been unable to master.

"How did you come to be here?" Jeanne asked. "I don't think we've ever seen you in our cornfield before."

"Huh?" Brisbane was hesitant to divulge the real purpose of his visit to their cornfield.

Jeanne and Janie were not shocked to find a stranger on their land.

Because of the time-traveling aspects of the magical cornfield, it wasn't unusual for them to encounter persons from the past wandering aimlessly on their property. Apparently, whatever forces enabled them to travel back in time also allowed an occasional historical figure to arise in their midst. Since Brisbane happened to be standing in the general area that the O'Sullivan twins had long since identified as being the Civil War "wrinkle," they naturally assumed he was some sort of lost soul from that era. With his hairy, unkempt appearance, the fredneck actually wouldn't have looked out of place on the fields of Antietam or Gettysburg.

Janie smiled at him sympathetically. "Ah, you poor thing. We'll get you back, don't worry."

"Were you a yankee or a rebel?" Jeanne eyed him curiously. "Your uniform doesn't look like either side's."

"What are you talking about?" Brisbane was baffled.

Jeanne glanced at her sister. "You mean you're not from the Civil War period?"

The fredneck laughed. "Civil War? Come on, what do you mean?"

"Where *are* you from, then?" Janie asked.

"Well, actually I travel quite a bit, but I was staying in Virginia before I came out here." Brisbane lit up a cigarette.

"You mean you're not from the past at all?" Janie wore a startled expression.

"Shit, no. Uh, excuse my French. I mean- why, or I should say how, could I be from the past?"

"Are you interested in history?" Janie gazed intently at Brisbane.

"Yeah, sure." The fredneck responded, captivated by the charms of the lovely Irish lasses.

"Do you think we should tell him about it?" Janie turned to her sister.

"Please excuse us for a minute." Jeanne said, taking her twin by the hand and leading her a suitable distance away for a private conference.

Evidently the discussion revolved around whether or not to permit an outsider to know of their ability to bend the rules of time and space. Janie wanted to reveal everything to Brisbane, having been instantly attracted to the fredneck. Jeanne, on the other hand, was behaving more cautiously. They had never told their secret to anyone, and she didn't understand the great necessity of doing it now. The girls hadn't made a conscious effort to conceal the abilities of their cornfield, it simply had worked out that way. The O'Sullivan twins were very close to each other, with only a small group of relatives scattered across the country and few friends. Thus, there had never really been anyone, unless they'd decided to be unlike most American teenagers and confide in their parents, in a position to be told of its fantastic powers. The fredneck was about to

189

change all that, however, as Janie eventually prevailed upon her sister to trust her instincts.

Brisbane was lost in wonderment as he exhaled his cigarette smoke into the crisp morning air. Watching two cute girls whispering and aiming quizzical looks in his direction was not something he was accustomed to, and he was enjoying it immensely. At length, the twins walked back towards him.

"Well, we've decided to make you the first." Janie informed him.

"The first what?" Was Brisbane's predictable response.

"Why, the first person besides us to use this farm to travel back in time!" Janie giggled, relishing the stunned expression on the fredneck's face.

From the notorious diary of Mad Millard Billingsly, May 1914:

...The world demands that I do something-history demands it! How to stand idle whilst those dark forces creep ever onward? I fear an even greater calamity than what has transpired in this dying nation over the past year will soon befall the world. They need more light and...they are bloodthirsty in quest of it. I should like to visit the Himalayas while there is still time-*if* there is time. What will be next? Was Darwin not enough? There are strange aspects about every word being muttered in the colleges. Bah! Let us instead discuss more tales of fantastic comets that arrive and depart unexpectedly. Or *Popular Delusions And The Madness Of Crowds*. And yet they tred onwards, in search of what has never been theirs and never will be, so long as certain wild men breathe. Bring me my graham crackers, darling, and let us consolidate our dissidence...

Brisbane felt a sudden intense pressure throughout his body. Like the stomach reacts to the steepest drop of a monster rollercoaster, however, it subsided just when he thought he could take no more. He opened his eyes and recognized the figure of Franklin Delano Roosevelt, sitting behind his desk in the oval office. There were four other men with him, one of whom the well-read fredneck was able to identify as a young J. Edgar Hoover.

"What the fuck?" An excited Brisbane wondered aloud.

"We're witnessing a scene that took place in the White House in early 1935." Jeanne adopted the air of a museum tour guide. "President Roosevelt and F.B.I. Director Hoover are meeting with three others. They are, or rather were, John D. Rockefeller, Felix Frankfurter, and Bernard Baruch."

"J.P. Morgan and Jacob Schiff called in sick." Janie giggled at her own politically astute humor.

"Shhhh...they'll hear you!" Brisbane whispered desperately, beginning to feel that tingle of terror familiar to all sufferers of paranoia.

"Relax, Brisbane. Contrary to popular belief, we can only view the events of the past. F.D.R. and his cronies can't see or hear us and we can't change anything that they or any other historical figures have done." Jeanne explained, with the vocabulary and self-assuredness of someone much older.

"Let's listen to what they're saying, Brisbane." Janie urged:

F.D.R.-*Look, J.D., if this keeps up, we're in real trouble. His silly shenanigans are made to order for the bourgeoisie. He'll sweep the south without question, and who knows about the rest of the country?*

Rockefeller-*You ought to know that I, more than any of you, have reason to despise that cracker barrel demagogue. I agree with you, Frank, but can't the press do the job?*

F.D.R.-*No! They've done all they can do. This sort of thing is often necessary- you've certainly ordered enough of them in your time, J.D.- we've tried everything and he refuses to play ball with us. Can you imagine what the rest of this century might be like if he were elected?*

Frankfurter-*I'm with you all the way, Mr. President. That little rabble rouser from Louisiana must be stopped!*

Hoover-*Can we hurry this along, fellows? I have a date this evening.*

Baruch-*Are we all agreed then?*

Rockefeller-*Excuse me, I have to make a few calls.*

Brisbane and the twins continued staring intently at a gathering not meant for public viewing or school textbooks. The fredneck shot a glance in the girls' direction and noticed that they both were crying. It was then that he felt a tear on his own hardened cheek.

Waldo stared at the empty cornfield. "Where could he have gone?"

"Perhaps he did vanish." The top doo-wopper attempted to rationalize. "You of all people could not be blamed for suspecting that. As the Professor indicated in one of our earlier discussions, mysterious disappearances have been reported throughout history. If I'm not mistaken-and I certainly don't claim to be the expert Professor Buckley is on the subject-there was a high ranking military officer- Benjamin Bathhurst was his name, I believe- who walked around his horse and vanished before he reached the other side. Then there was a prisoner I recall reading about-I'm embarrassingly sketchy about the details-but he disappeared from the exercise yard in the prison, in full view of the guards and other inmates, leaving his irons behind on the ground. And the most baffling of all might be-again I must confess to not remembering any details-the case where a runner stumbled on the road, during a race against another individual, and vanished in front of scores of onlookers. Am I correct, Professor?

Hiram Buckley tugged at his tie and adjusted his spectacles. "Well-that is-I am, of course, familiar with those cases you mentioned. I must compliment you on your wide breadth of knowledge."

"Thank you, Professor. That means a great deal, coming from someone as esteemed as yourself." Phosphate smiled. "Actually, Waldo, in your grandfather's case, there is a much stronger possibility of a logical explanation than when someone goes into a cornfield to..."

"Maybe this cornfield didn't like him trying to take a leak in it." Fontaine, alert and no longer attempting to knock over buildings with beer cans or other similarly nonsensical stunts, interrupted with a feeble interjection of humor that fell flat on its face.

Phosphate started to lecture his fellow Afro Anarchist, as he so often did regarding real or imagined improprieties, but instead merely sighed resignedly. "I apologize for raising the supernatural specter so hastily. I recommend we wait a bit longer before we consign our companion to the land of Bishop Pike and D.B. Cooper."

For the first time, Waldo lit up a cigarette in Iowa. He stared at the hypnotically swaying stalks of corn and hoped that he wouldn't have to search for two missing people.

"We better get the cops." Bucktooth looked anxiously at Phosphate.

They had been waiting in the cornfield for over an hour, and the extent of their concern was reflected in this desperate suggestion to summon assistance from the law, which no self-respecting Afro-Anarchist would have dared to verbalize under normal circumstances.

"Say what?" Fontaine snickered. "Damn, Buck, you been watching *Hill Street Blues* again?"

"I think perhaps we should retreat to the car and seek some liquid refreshment before we undertake such a drastic measure." Phosphate's proposal was eagerly agreed to by all, and the five frantic friends hurriedly left the cornfield. As they emerged from the tall, abundant stalks, Fontaine raced to the decidedly un-fredneck-like '65 Dodge Dart and started to open the back door. As soon as his hand touched the handle, however, he relapsed into his "Sunshine" Sammy Morrison impersonation, and began pointing into the back seat with his eyes popping and his voice stammering incoherently.

"What is it, Fontaine?" A puzzled Waldo drew abreast of the manic East Side Kid-lookalike, peered into the car, and saw Brisbane calmly sleeping in the back seat.

"Man, what kind of stuff is goin' on here?" Fontaine was acting totally ridiculous now, dashing around in circles, calling out "lawdy," and generally conveying an excellent impression of a black vaudeville performer.

"Fontaine, I think you may have missed your calling. Did any of your relatives appear as extras in Tarzan films?" Phosphate's embarrassment over his fellow Afro-Anarchist's behavior was only partially masked by his light, bemused tone. "I'm just glad that the American Nazi Party isn't here to witness your histrionics."

"Vanna bet?"

The top doo-wopper turned around and saw, to his astonishment, two young men in German Reich uniforms exiting the cornfield.

"Man, these Iowa cornfields are too much!" Bucktooth exclaimed.

Waldo couldn't believe it. What were Nazis doing there? "Not even Simon Wiesenthal would think of this." He murmured to himself.

Apparently it was an audible murmur, for the larger and older-looking Nazi marched up to Waldo and snarled, in a perfectly menacing, Hollywood-Germanic tongue, "vut vas you sayink about Viesenthal? Is he a Jew?"

Waldo struggled to maintain his frequently lost composure. "What are you...I mean, this isn't Germany, you know."

To his surprise, instead of exiling him to a concentration camp, the large Nazi appeared bewildered. "I know." He replied in a meek, un-Nazi-like voice.

At that moment, Brisbane woke up to find himself laying in the back seat. Looking out of the window, he bolted from the car. "Hey!" He yelled, grabbing a Nazi with each hand, like a flustered mother might take hold of her wayward youngsters, "you guys need to get back! You have a war to lose!"

With that, the fredneck and the brown-shirted duo darted away together and dissolved again into the cornfield.

"Where," Waldo began in a slow, flabbergasted voice, "*were* you, Brisbane?"

"Man, if I told you, you'd think I was smoking some of my special stuff." The fredneck looked exhausted.

After witnessing Brisbane's startling exit into the cornfield with two Nazis in tow, the others had followed him. Despite an extensive search, they were unable to locate the slippery fredneck. But then Bucktooth, of all people, happened to wander off on his own and find Brisbane lying just beyond the farthest edge of the cornfield, next to some thick woods. Bucktooth's attention had been drawn to the area by a strange and very old oak tree, which stood proudly at the base of the woods, like a vigilant guard, and was all the more noticeable because of the words *The Forest Of Injured Egos*, which were carved into its aged trunk. The letters looked more natural than precise, as if they'd developed over the years along with the bark and sap, and were clearly visible from a distance. Bucktooth was puzzling over their possible significance when he discovered Brisbane laying prostrate only a short distance away. His preposterous reaction, much like Fontaine's had been moments earlier, was outdated and stereotypical in the worst sense, and had someone been there to videotape it, it unquestionably would have proven to be a popular feature at white supremacist gatherings. Nevertheless, his screaming did serve to draw the attention of everyone else just as well as a clear and unwavering "over here, guys" would have. The others reacted as quickly as they could, and dumbfounded upon seeing Brisbane there on the ground, began immediately badgering the fredneck.

"Yeah, man," Fontaine chirped in after Waldo's initial question, having been transformed back from ex-serial sidekick of the 30's to street wise doo-wop protester of the 80's, "who were those Nazi dudes and how did you know them?"

"Yes, my friend," Phosphate joined the interrogation, "we didn't know whether you'd become another Judge Crater or had somehow met the Iowa cornfield patrol. Then, immediately after we actually contemplate seeking the aid of the police, we find you asleep in the car. And what about the brown shirts, and the ensuing disappearance afterwards? Was that some kind of distorted encore performance? Would you care to explain?"

"Alright, *alright,* if you give me a fucking chance!" Brisbane looked as befuddled and helpless as Sirhan Sirhan in a hotel pantry. Taking a deep breath, he told them how he'd encountered the O'Sullivan twins and been introduced to the magical properties of their farm. "Shit man, they took me to the White House, and we heard F.D.R. and some other dudes planning Huey Long's assassination."

"What? Huh? Come on!" Were some of the exclamations his companions responded with.

"Wait a minute, there's more." Brisbane took another deep breath and rose to his feet. "They took me somewhere else, a couple different places. I witnessed a masonic meeting that included guys like Franklin, Washington, Hamilton, and that French dude- he was a writer- I can't remember his name."

"Voltaire?" Waldo guessed. "But...he must have been very old."

"Yeah, I think that was it." The fredneck continued. "There were other famous people there, but I don't recall, or I should say I don't want to. What they were doing...shit, you wouldn't believe it! And then, the last thing I got to see was a group of Union soldiers murdering this southern family, little kids and everything, when they refused to give up their land after the Civil War. I told Jeanne and Janie to take me back after that, but they still wanted to go on some more. I guess that's why they're not here."

"What about the Nazis?" Phosphate reminded him.

"Well, I don't really know. I think the girls said something about people from the past accidently coming back through time warps. I was just so fucking amazed by it all that I wasn't listening to a lot of what they said about how the whole thing works."

"But you jumped out of the car and grabbed those Nazis like you knew them." Waldo pointed out, with the guile of an ambitious district attorney.

The fredneck appeared confused. "I-I just don't know, man. To tell you the truth, I don't even remember being in the car or seeing any Nazis."

"Then why did you act like you did?" Waldo seemed determined to look for loopholes in Brisbane's story.

"Yeah man, what kind of shit are you pulling here?" Fontaine joined in on the attack.

"Waldo, my boy, please try-that is-why don't you give him a chance to respond?" Professor Buckley broke his long silence, which he'd spent by taking typically exaggerated deep breaths and soaking up the Midwestern atmosphere, with an attempted defense of the embattled Brisbane.

"Perhaps you'd care to explain why your memory seems to be failing you." Waldo ignored the Professor and continued his relentless and inexplicable cross-examination of the flustered fredneck.

Brisbane threw his arms up in frustration. "Okay! Shit, what do you expect me to do? I just had this wild experience that was stranger than any drug I've ever done. I still don't know what the fuck's going on."

Waldo was stunned by his own unreasonable attitude. He felt trapped in some uncharacteristic mood swing, with a touch of ugly mob mentality thrown in for good measure. Then all at once it came to him- he was jealous of the fact that Brisbane, one of the few men on the face of the earth who'd been as unsuccessful with women as he had, was the one who'd been lucky enough to discover two beautiful girls and travel through time with them.

Now that he'd diagnosed his own problem, Waldo attempted to effect a cure, with an apology as humble as any ever made in the most chaste and holy monasteries of the middle ages. "I'm really sorry, Brisbane. I didn't mean to sound like Iowa's answer to Clarence Darrow. Why don't we all relax and enjoy the view from here? It's really beautiful." Of course, it was the nervous young man's unspoken wish that two certain little ladies would appear to enhance the scenery.

Bucktooth looked at him as if he had suggested they all go on a cross-burning binge. "I don't know about nobody else, but I ain't had any food all day!"

Fontaine nodded and elbowed Bucktooth in the ribs, muttering just loud enough for Waldo to hear, "Sheeet, is he crazy or what? Who in the hell wants to sit in a damn cornfield? I ain't seen so much corn since Bob Hope's last t.v. special, and that's plenty for me!"

Phosphate and Brisbane agreed with Bucktooth as well, with the top doo-wopper diplomatically noting that although Waldo's idea was tempting, their stomachs had to have first priority. It was a curious fact that everyone suddenly noticed their hunger simultaneously, while never previously complaining about the lack of proper nutrition that had plagued them during the entire trip. Evidently their bodies were finally protesting the vitamin-free diet plan which had been foisted upon them, consisting of a few artificially preserved snacks, consumed on a highly irregular basis, washed down by large quantities of beer.

Brisbane recommended that they look for the twins' house and ask them, in the interest of saving time, where the nearest fast food establishment was located. Waldo suspected that the real reason his fredneck friend wanted to track down the girls had nothing to do with food. But then Waldo had an ulterior motive of his own, so he quickly agreed with Brisbane's suggestion.

"I'd sure like to meet those twins." Waldo ventured rather dreamily, always a sucker for a pretty face, particularly ones that knew the secrets of time travel.

"I think we all would." Observed Phosphate, and Fontaine and Bucktooth nodded as well. "By the way, Brisbane," the top doo-wopper continued, "do you have any idea which direction the house is in? I must confess that from this angle all I can see are corn stalks."

"Well, I know we're on their property and I don't think they're exactly plantation owners, so we can't be that far away from their house. I say we try over there first." The fredneck pointed straight ahead, to where the terrain appeared to slope downwards. "That looks like it's downhill. Shit man, I can't imagine it being anywhere else, since the horizon seems to be flat in every other direction. Unless they own the land on the other side of the road, which I doubt. Let's check down there." He then began striding off forthrightly, and the others followed.

While Fontaine and Bucktooth had started to accompany Waldo and the others on their mission to find the O'Sullivan house, they soon decided to turn back and smoke some reefer instead. As neither of them was carrying any dope on them, they were forced to trek back to the car to obtain some. Brisbane possessed a seemingly limitless supply of the substance, which he kept hidden behind the old cassette deck in his glove compartment, where it had, incidently, eluded the half-hearted efforts of the police officer to find it, when he'd stopped the fredneck for drunk driving several days previously. Of course, with all they'd been through since then, it was terribly difficult to believe that encounter with the law, which had resulted in the six of them meeting and embarking on the trip to Iowa together, had occurred so recently.

Brisbane's entire stash consisted of his very powerful, special homemade recipe, and after smoking an amount sufficient to the task at hand, the two Afro-Anarchists left the car and returned to the cornfield. Fontaine had informed Bucktooth of the well-known fact that ingesting marijuana in exotic locations intensified its effects. They both realized that an Iowa cornfield probably wasn't considered exotic by the majority of people, but it seemed exciting to them nevertheless.

They wandered to a spot, near the far edge of the cornfield, which was very close to where Fontaine had found Brisbane just a little while earlier.

"Shit, let's really make some munchies!" Fontaine shouted, forgetting that their dire financial situation would not permit them even a single meal a day, let alone any indulgences. Lighting up his trusty pipe, which he'd purchased prior to dropping out of tenth grade and was sentimentally attached to, he took a long hit and passed it to Bucktooth.

When they had nearly finished the bowl, Fontaine suddenly noticed a weird look in Bucktooth's eyes. It was somewhat akin to the look that Farina/Stymie/Buckwheat used to sport when something "spooked" them and their gang of fellow Little Rascals. At least Bucktooth's hair stayed in place. But his eyes were staring at something behind Fontaine, and his fellow doo-wopper was forced to turn around and see what it was. Needless to say, he wasn't anxious to. But, if he didn't look, his curiosity would remain unfulfilled, and few things were worse than that, so Fontaine gulped like a man upon whom a harsh sentence was being passed, and slowly lifted his gaze in the same direction as Bucktooth's.

Fontaine shouted out "ahhhh!" and Bucktooth joined in on the chorus as the two excited Afro-Anarchists ran away. What they were fleeing from was a very large being, at least twenty five feet tall, who closely resembled the renowned green giant of frozen vegetable fame. They were moving at world-class speed, in the manner popularized by film heroes being chased by creatures from lost worlds. But, like many a damsel in Hollywood distress, they also were sliding and tripping constantly. After traveling a good distance, zigzagging their way across the outskirts of the cornfield and the narrow grassy area leading to the deep woods which bordered it, they came to rest by another large oak tree, identical to the one Bucktooth had seen previously, which also seemed to guard the path into the woods. Neither of them noticed the words carved into it this time.

As they caught their breath, Bucktooth lifted his head and, instantly regaining his frightened Our Gang look, started pointing and jumping in the air. Seconds later came the glass-breaking screams and they were off and running again. Bucktooth had observed what looked suspiciously like a werewolf- and he'd certainly seen his share of them on countless late, late movies during his youth- prowling hungrily about the entrance to the thick woods. Fontaine had opted not to look this time and merely followed his fellow doo-wopper's lead without verifying that a real threat existed. They didn't stop, or even fall, until they arrived back at the car. The two of them scrambled into the welcome un-fredneck-like vehicle and locked all the doors.

Trembling much like Waldo was so often prone to do, Fontaine stared at his friend. "S-s-s-shit, B-Bucktooth, I ain't getting high in any more cornfields!"

Bucktooth shook his head. "I don't know about you, Fontaine, but I ain't getting high no more at all."

They made sure the windows were closed tightly and squeezed down like small children, huddled together on the backseat floor.

Meanwhile, Brisbane had been right- the O'Sullivan house was located just out of their line of sight, down a dirt embankment. Indeed it was hard to avoid categorizing it as the epitome of the expression "off the beaten track" due to the fact the other sides of the land surrounding it were raised as well, so that it appeared sunken, as if it had been built in some large crater left by a wayward meteorite. If there hadn't been a gravel path running down the slope on one side, and leading back to the road, more questions about the odd manner in which it was situated, and the way its occupants traveled back and forth to the society it seemed so isolated from, might have been asked by the intrepid group of adventurers.

Waldo was burning with anticipation as he stared at the lovely old place, a comfortable looking two story ranch house nestled almost exactly in the middle of all those golden waves of corn, which seemed to extend indefinitely off into the distance. The notoriously un-mathematically inclined Waldo estimated that the O'Sullivan land, at least that which was covered with corn stalks, must consist of fifty acres or more. Of course, he was admittedly incapable of computing with any accuracy the difference between five and fifteen miles, or fifty and one hundred feet, so any figure he estimated in regards to acreage must be deemed of questionable value. There was a well on the side of the house facing them, and an empty clothes line in back, with a charming little gazebo lying at the foot of the embankment there.

As Waldo walked slowly towards the place, his mind was laboring mightily at producing fantasies about the teenage twins. Brisbane had described them as the most beautiful girls he'd ever seen, and despite the fredneck's lifelong lack of contact with members of the opposite sex, and thus his questionable credibility in judging their relative physical gifts, Waldo found no difficulty in accepting his assessment. He was even able to picture himself in a variety of exciting, romantic scenarios with one or both of them. The nervous young man was overanxious to meet them, and yet he possessed all the self-confidence of a fifteen year old with a prominent pimple on the end of his nose.

Brisbane led the way to the front door. He knocked like any fredneck would be expected to- loudly and in a childish rhythm. They all waited patiently, but a minute went by and no one came to the door.

"Knock again- harder this time." Waldo realized his suggestion was preposterous, as both he and Phosphate had visibly reacted to each other, wincing at the force of Brisbane's pounding. But he was infatuated with the image his daydreaming mind had produced of the young girls, and thus was thinking even less rationally than usual.

Brisbane knocked again, and made even more noise in doing so, if such a thing was possible. Again they waited, but there was still no response. Eventually a curious Phosphate wandered off on his own and began peeping into various windows as he slowly circled the house.

"Is there-that is-do you see anyone inside, Phosphate?" Inquired Professor Buckley, whose high strung nature was forcing him to keep his eyes focused on the ground, for fear of what he might see. This did, however, enable the eccentric ex-history teacher, who was guardedly following the top doo-wopper, to retrace his footsteps more conveniently.

"Hmmm. I don't see any people, but there are some rather curious things about the place." Phosphate, so consistently keen and observant, would almost certainly have made a more believable Sam Spade than tiny Humphrey Bogart.

"Yeah, like what?" Brisbane asked as he finally left his post at the front door.

"Come here, and I'll show you." The top doo-wopper motioned to everyone. He was leaning against the kitchen window with his nose pressed up against it, a traditionally favorite posture of children everywhere. "First of all," Phosphate pointed inside, the only thing missing from his detective persona being a *My dear Watson* and a deerstalker cap, "you will notice that the calendar on the wall is dated May, 1971. And yet, if you will please follow me," the head Afro-Anarchist led them around to the living room window, "you'll see that there is a v.c.r. on top of the television set."

"And video recorders weren't around in 1971!" Waldo exclaimed, instantly latching on to Phosphate's irregular line of reasoning. "I mean, at least not in peoples' homes."

"Wait a minute!" Brisbane was having a hard time grasping the top doo-wopper's logic. "What fucking connection is there between 1971 and v.c.r.'s?"

Phosphate stroked his chin philosophically. "Well, perhaps none. But I do think it's peculiar that there should be a 1971 calendar hanging in anyone's 1987 kitchen, don't you?"

"Yeah, man, but what are you saying- that the O'Sullivan house is trapped in 1971 or something?" The fredneck was searching for an explanation too.

For once Phosphate's razor-sharp intellect failed him. "I don't know the reason, Brisbane. I am merely questioning what appears to be an anomaly."

"What other things were there that..." Waldo broke off in the middle of his sentence. He suddenly noticed a figure inside the house. "Look-over there!" He cried, pointing towards the dining room table. Someone was sitting there. Waldo was puzzling over why they hadn't seen the person before when the figure at the table abruptly spun around and revealed its face. The nervous young man screamed with even more passion than Fay Wray in her prime, for the face was that of the mysterious hitchhiker they'd encountered earlier in their journey. In an instant, remembering the man's peculiar manner, his blood-curdling laugh, and the way he'd vanished in full view of Bucktooth, Waldo was transformed into his version of the Flash and made a beeline for the car.

"There he goes again!" Brisbane, recalling Waldo's previous mad dash outside Mama Petunia's Bingo Parlor, seemed almost amused at the sight of his emotional friend running wildly across the cornfield, his long hair flying and his arms flailing, leaving a trail of bent stalks behind him. He turned to the pensive Afro-Anarchist leader. "I didn't see anything in there, I mean other than the outdated calendar, to make him act like that, did you?"

"No, I didn't." Phosphate replied quietly.

Waldo arrived at the car out of breath and nearly pulse-less. He was as deranged as a scarlet fever victim with a 106 degree temperature, and his heart jumped when he looked in the backseat and observed the two almost as frightened Afro-Anarchists shivering on the floor. They quickly picked themselves up when they saw Waldo, and not a green giant or werewolf, standing there. Fontaine unlocked the door and Waldo pushed his way in before either of the startled doo-woppers had a chance to make room for him.

"Damn, Waldo, what the hell's wrong with you?" Bucktooth protested.

"Yeah, man, you trying to crush us or something?" Fontaine was still shaken by his harrowing, drug-related experience, and Waldo was fortunate that the lifelong inner city inhabitant didn't respond to this unforeseen impact from another male body in the physically aggressive manner one might have expected.

Waldo, totally unresponsive, was staring straight ahead with a blank, vacuous look in his eyes. Had there been a fly buzzing about his head, he might have been mistaken for Anthony Perkins in the closing scene of *Psycho*.

For the first time, Fontaine and Bucktooth realized their nervous friend was in an even more crazed state than they were. Fontaine ventured a gentle question. "Say man, are you alright?"

This produced no reply, so Bucktooth tried his hand. "Hey Waldo, you look like you seen a ghost, man!"

At Bucktooth's rather carelessly chosen words, Waldo shot him a glance that clearly indicated his displeasure. He then turned his gaze back towards some unmentionable imaginary direction; one of ominous gypsies, abandoned general stores, incongruous highway signs, displaced hitchhikers and the like.

"Hey man, I don't know what happened that's making you act like this," Fontaine remarked somewhat tactfully, "but I *know* you couldn't have gone through no more terrifying shit than we did."   The doo-wop protester went on to recount their spine-tingling sightings of a jolly green giant and a probable werewolf. As he recounted the details, the distraught Waldo started to show gradual signs of interest. Apparently Fontaine's inadvertent attempt at psychology was working. The more Waldo heard the Afro-Anarchists' unbelievable tale, the less traumatized he felt over his own experience.

Finally, after Fontaine finished relating their encounters (Bucktooth had almost blown what little credibility they had by embellishing things in order to make Waldo's story pale by comparison. For instance, he threw in little yellow men from the planet Uranus, an escaped water buffalo with its fur on fire, and an evil motorcycle gang of homosexual zombies), Waldo lit up a cigarette, which was a sure indication that he was becoming semi-coherent, and stared pensively at them.

"You would not think," he spoke slowly, "that one person could possibly witness so many weird things without being on some kind of drug." The nervous young man then revealed how he had seen the hitchhiker in the O'Sullivan house.

Fontaine whistled. "Damn! I swear this shit is getting to be like *The Outer Limits*."

Bucktooth frowned. "Hey man, did Phosphate and them see that hitchhiker too?"

Waldo opened his eyes a little wider. "Why, I've been so wrapped up in my own crazy world that I completely forgot about them." His ever-present conscience then began bothering him, as it so often did, over the way he'd left the others in a literal cloud of dust back at a house that may or may not have been lost in a time warp, with a strange hitchhiker that may or may not have been lurking within it.

Gathering up all of the microscopic amount of nerve remaining inside him, Waldo told Fontaine and Bucktooth that he was going back to look for Phosphate, Brisbane, and Professor Buckley. The two almost as cautious Afro-Anarchists reluctantly agreed to accompany him.

Waldo wasn't surprised that their companions were nowhere to be found when they reached the O'Sullivan house. In light of everything that had transpired since they'd left northern Virginia, he was beginning to anticipate such supernatural twists at every turn. Running his trembling fingers through his unkempt hair, he gazed back at the swaying stalks of corn as if they could answer him.

"Shit, Waldo," Fontaine expressed the concern that the three of them shared, "you think they could have gone back into the past?"

Waldo stared down at his feet, the way he used to in high school whenever he spoke to a girl. "I-I don't know, Fontaine. I guess I don't know much about anything anymore."

With that, Waldo began wandering around the house. As he passed by the kitchen window, he remembered the calendar with the antiquated date and ventured to obtain a better view of it. As he strained his eyes through the window, Waldo's heart skipped once again. As might well have been predicted, the calendar now read 1987.

Fontaine and Bucktooth, who'd paused by the well to splash some water on their faces, heard a noise and ran to the other side of the house. There they found Waldo sitting on the ground under the kitchen window. He was sobbing uncontrollably.

"Ah, come on, man." Fontaine tried to be comforting. "Please don't start that running shit again. They'll turn up, you'll see. It ain't that bad."

Waldo glanced up at him. "You both probably think I'm crazy, and I'm starting to wonder myself. But I swear, that calendar did say 1971!"

Fontaine and Bucktooth, not having been apprised that anyone had observed such an outdated calendar, stared blankly at each other. Then Bucktooth peered inside the kitchen and spotted it on the wall.

"Oh yeah, I see a calendar, man. But shit, Waldo, it don't have 1971 on it."

Just then, they heard a strange humming noise coming from somewhere off in the distance. They also noticed that the wind was suddenly picking up.

"Damn, daddio!" Bucktooth exclaimed, lapsing, as he sometimes did, into the lingo of a cool 1950's era youth.

Waldo's gaze was transfixed upon the now wildly blowing stalks of corn, when all at once he saw Brisbane, Phosphate, and the Professor materialize in their midst. But they were not alone. They were being escorted by two very lovely young girls.

"*Wow! What? Shit! How?*" Were some of the ways in which Waldo, Fontaine, and Bucktooth verbalized their reactions to this astonishing sight.

Waldo, however, was more intrigued by the beauty of Jeanne O'Sullivan than with any scientifically impossible shenanigans. He just couldn't take his eyes off of her, and for that inexplicable reason which is essential to a belief in the theory of love at first sight, Waldo instantly preferred Jeanne to her equally pretty, nearly identical twin. Everything he found attractive in the female sex was condensed into her petite package. He didn't even bother to listen to Brisbane, Phosphate, and Professor Buckley recount their tale of time traveling intrigue. All Waldo wanted to do was to stare at that beautiful little face.

"Man, where the hell were you all?" Bucktooth inquired.

Phosphate took a deep breath and started to relate their adventure. "My friends, when Waldo ran off so abruptly, Brisbane, the Professor, and I started to follow him. One second we were walking up the embankment after our fleeing comrade, and in the next we found ourselves in a fourteenth century French village. Needless to say, we were quite alarmed and began racing around the small town like madmen."

"Yeah, it's a good thing no one could see us." Brisbane added.

The top doo-wopper nodded. "Indeed it was. But, to continue, apparently we happened upon a rather uninteresting time and place, at least from our modern perspective. If not for Jeanne and Janie, we might have been stuck there forever."

As Phosphate further explained, the girls had been using the farm for time traveling purposes for so long that they were familiar with virtually all its operating mechanisms. The most important of these were the various areas of the cornfield, or the "wrinkles," as the girls referred to them, and the specific time periods they represented. Only an instant before Brisbane, Phosphate, and the Professor were swallowed up and transported back in time, the O'Sullivan twins had just returned from some history hopping of their own. By a stroke of great fortune, they happened to witness the fredneck, the head Afro-Anarchist, and the one time pride of the local community college vanishing. Sensing that the three were novices (in their brief glimpse, neither girl recognized Brisbane), they immediately followed after them. Thus, by the slender thread of coincidence, Waldo's companions were saved from spending eternity watching a boring set of events framed by dull, unknown characters reciting their forgettable lines in a language none of them understood.

Waldo, after staring at her for at least five minutes, was busy making his fluttering heart's intentions painfully obvious to Jeanne. "Uh, uh, uh, uh, my name is...Waldo Billingsly."

Jeanne smiled sweetly. "I'm Jeanne O'Sullivan. Pleased to meet you."

Waldo attempted to initiate a conversation. He'd never known what to say to girls, and was always tongue tied around them, but he managed somehow to ask Jeanne, in a relatively normal manner, about herself- her likes and dislikes, etc. Their dialogue began awkwardly, but it soon became apparent that they shared an amazing array of interests. In fact, the starstruck Waldo was moved to proclaim subconsciously that destiny appeared to have brought them together. Such idealized, romantic notions were common to the nervous young man, but even the most skeptical philanderer would have to admit the two of them were quite compatible. For instance, their discussion, which Waldo found surprisingly easy to engage in after the first few moments, uncovered some remarkable similarities in taste. Waldo's two favorite movies of all time were *It's A Wonderful Life* and *Meet John Doe*, and he was astounded to discover that they were Jeanne's as well. The pretty teenager mentioned that her favorite *Leave It To Beaver* was the one in which Beaver falls into a giant soup bowl. So was Waldo's. Both of them liked the classic episode featuring Danny Thomas, aliens without thumbs, and a lot of walnuts better than any other *Dick Van Dyke Show*. They enjoyed the same musical artists, even the same books. After a while, Waldo, finding himself in a most unfamiliar situation, began feeling a bit frightened by the magnitude of their suitability for each other.

Jeanne, a most unconventional and mature sixteen year old, was even more tender-hearted and non-violent than Waldo, and her amiable personality, perplexed by the obsession so many of her female peers held for sweat and muscles, was bound to be attracted to the nervous, introspective young man. The beautiful teenager held a sense of humor in the highest regard, and felt not the slightest infatuation for money or status. Waldo became so excited when he heard the lovely youngster scoff, in her gentle, polite way, at the classmates who gasped in awe at the "hottest" and "sexiest" cars that some very fortunate boys drove to high school each morning, that he could barely contain his applause. Waldo was famous for falling in love at the drop of a hat, but he shattered all his previous records with Jeanne O'Sullivan.

"Waldo!"

Waldo turned dreamily towards the voice shouting his name. It was Brisbane.

"What the fuck are you doing?" The fredneck demanded. "Seeing M.I.B.'s again?"

Waldo was so enraptured with young Jeanne that he completely ignored Brisbane's rather belligerent remark. "Brisbane, please don't interrupt us."

With that, the formerly unsure Waldo grasped the underaged but delightful Jeanne's eager hand tightly and they strode off together up the embankment and into the cornfield. Apparently Jeanne felt none of his male companions' reservations about enjoying the view there.

Brisbane turned to Phosphate. "You believe that shit?"

The top doo-wopper smiled knowingly. "Do not be too harsh on our young friend Waldo. From what I have been able to determine, he has led a somewhat unsuccessful romantic life. How can we deny him such lovely companionship?"

Brisbane grumbled out a reluctant affirmation of Phosphate's point and then he quickly remembered that the other O'Sullivan twin, whom he'd mysteriously ignored following his rescue, in which she'd played an instrumental part, from the clutches of a boring fourteenth century village, had seemed interested in him. Janie had been standing there patiently observing the fredneck going through the transparent throes of jealousy, and now she displayed that disarming Irish smile that was one of the girls' most charming features.

"Come on, Brisbane." She led him by the hand and they too disappeared among the tall stalks of corn.

At this point Fontaine was feeling oppressed (partially due to the fact that it was 1987, and yet he still had no legitimate chance to win the hand of either fair white maiden), and he decided to express his

205

frustration with an improvised solo rap number, *Whitey Took Flighty Rap*:

"Black is beautiful, black is fine
If you're into sports and inexpensive wine
Black is strong, black is mean
Buy a big supply of Afro-Sheen
I used to think that if my hair was straight
They'd let me in, I could participate
But the Man don't like me 'cause I'm cool
I don't need his flag or his public schools
His skin is lighter 'cause his shit is weak
And we know now not to turn the other cheek
I ain't gonna smile or read no library books
We all know what counts is how a brother looks
It used to be hip to have a big afro
Now you go jerri-curls, I don't know
Whitey keep his women under lock and key..."

"Alright, Fontaine!" Phosphate usually didn't interfere with any of his cohort's individual musical projects, but he felt very strongly that Fontaine was being mean-spirited, if not vicious, in this latest rap song. "I do not wish to discourage your ventures into this popular field, but I must confess that those H.Rap Brown-kind of lyrics are offensive to me. Imagine how the Professor must feel listening to them, or what Waldo and Brisbane would think of such sentiments."

Fontaine wore a sheepish look on his face. "You're right, Phos. I guess I just get kinda carried away with that radical shit sometimes. I hope I didn't offend you, Professor."

"No, my boy-that is-I suppose we all have our latent militant tendencies." Professor Buckley, not one to anger easily, smiled reassuringly at the embarrassed Afro-Anarchist.

"Why don't we return to the car," The top doo-wopper proposed, "and figure out an agenda for the rest of the afternoon?"

Evidently, the madness of the last few hours, which had witnessed some members of the Old Hoss Billingsly search party being rescued themselves from a dire fate in fourteenth century limbo, and others experiencing wild visions of green giants and the like, had caused them to temporarily forget their hunger, and thus fail to inquire of the O'Sullivan twins just where the nearest fast food establishment was before they marched off into the cornfields with Waldo and Brisbane.

"Sheeet, let's find out where we can eat!" Fontaine exclaimed, quickly regaining his composure as well as his appetite. "I still ain't had no food, and if I get any hungrier, I'm gonna take a bite out of Bucktooth's ass!"

Bucktooth roared with laughter, and the four of them walked back towards Brisbane's decidedly un-fredneck-like vehicle.

With Waldo and Brisbane somewhere in the cornfields with their underaged Irish lasses, the Afro-Anarchists and Professor Buckley decided to wander back towards the quaint little business district they'd passed through earlier that morning. They were all famished, and their painful condition propelled them to gather what meager finances they possessed, without a thought for their two infatuated companions' welfare, in quest of satisfying it.

As they passed through the cornfield, there was no sign of Waldo, Brisbane, and the O'Sullivan twins, but no one considered this unusual in that it was taken for granted that the four of them would utilize the powers of the property to travel back in time together. After five minutes or so of trudging through and trampling over the fragile stalks, they arrived at the dirt path where Brisbane's trusty old car was parked. To their surprise, they saw a small wooden structure sitting by itself, directly across the road from them. Painted over its doorway in green lettering were the words *Grandpa's Place*.

"You figure that's a restaurant, Phos?" Bucktooth asked.

Phosphate scratched his chin in contemplation. "I really don't know, Bucktooth, but I recommend we find out." With that, the top doo-wopper strode unhesitatingly towards the place.

There were no cars in front, but then there didn't appear to be any parking lot for them. The grass didn't look as if it had been cut in a long, long time, and was high and thick enough to slow them up considerably as they waded through it. The only signs of life came from the hum of a loud fan which had been placed in one of the open windows in front. All that stood between the interior and a swarming band of yellow jackets and flies, that were hovering about the entrance, was a half unhinged screen door that was riddled with holes.

"Sheeet, I don't know about this place, Phos." Fontaine remarked. "It don't exactly look like it's doing a lot of business."

"You're correct, Fontaine." Phosphate walked up the creaking step and held open the door for his comrades. Then, lowering his voice, he winked. "If it *is* a restaurant."

The three hungry doo-woppers and the Professor entered the probable restaurant with a great deal of trepidation. There were several middle-aged men sitting at various tables, eating and drinking beer. The lighting was dim, as it is in most such establishments where men cluster about during the daylight hours, and the boisterous noise being made, which curiously enough hadn't been audible outside through the open window and the screen door full of holes, suddenly stopped the moment the foursome stepped inside. From the looks they received, which registered vividly through the smoke and the low wattage, it didn't appear that very many African-Americans had eaten there before.

A young oriental man dashed up to them from behind the bar, where he'd been watching a daytime talk show on the small color t.v. set bolted to the wall above it.

He smiled at them and spoke in a breathless manner. "What can I do for you gentlemen?"

Phosphate smiled back at him. "Well, we weren't certain that your enterprise was a restaurant. However, since it is clearly evident that is the case, we would like to order what I imagine, at this hour, would be considered a late lunch."

A short, fat man with a steel gray crewcut abruptly barged past the Oriental and thrust his ruddy face within inches of the top doo-wopper's.

"I'll handle this, Chop-Chop. What do you boys want to eat?" He turned towards some of the men who were drinking beer. "Chitlins?"

Phosphate shook his head and ignored the snickering customers. "No, actually I don't believe any of us enjoy eating the internal organs of animals. We would like to see a menu."

The man threw back his head and laughed. "You want to see a menu? Okay, here you go." He reached into the pocket of his multi-stained apron and handed a crumpled piece of paper to Phosphate.

The top doo-wopper scanned it briefly. The only thing printed on it were the words *we do not like serving strangers*. He showed it to Fontaine, Bucktooth, and Professor Buckley, then looked the crewcut man straight in the eye. "Sir, we have not eaten a proper meal for some time now. We are attempting to locate a missing person who may be in these parts, and we do need nourishment. If you don't want to serve us, we won't waste your time threatening to contact the local affiliate of the A.C.L.U.- just please inform us where the closest restaurant is that will."

The man's demeanor brightened instantly. Patting Phosphate on the back, he yelled out, "okay, Chop-Chop, bring them three specials. On the house! And don't be cheap with the portions!"

The head Afro-Anarchist was astounded. "Excuse me, sir, but didn't you..."

"I was just testing you, son." The crewcut man explained as he produced a handkerchief from his apron and wiped away some sweat from his forehead. "You see, we've had a lot of problems lately with escaped prisoners from the state penitentiary. You just can't be too careful, you know."

Fontaine snorted. "And you thought at least three of us were

208

prisoners, right?"

The man smiled. "It ain't a racial thing, son. I can see that's what you're thinking."

"Oh yeah? Then what about the chitlins crack?" Fontaine demanded.

The crewcut man wiped his mouth on the dirty apron. "Just part of the game, son."

"But if you thought we might be escaped prisoners," Phosphate frowned, "what made you realize we weren't? After all, we only asked to see a menu. Unless I'm mistaken, reviewing the cuisine before making a selection is common practice all over the world."

The crewcut man spoke as he wiped down an empty table for them. "Well, let's just say you passed the test, okay?"

An incredulous Bucktooth stared at the others. "Damn, I don't care about no explanation when I can get a free meal!"

"Did I hear-that is-are you really providing us with food at no charge?" The Professor asked, with a comparable expression on his oblong face.

"That's what I said." The crewcut man replied. "Now here, have a seat and relax. Chop-Chop will bring your meals out shortly."

Phosphate was deep in thought, as he usually was. "Sir, if I may ask you a question- as I mentioned earlier, we are in this area to search for a missing individual. We anticipate that he may be at a facility called the Last Chance Relaxation Home. Would you happen to know where it is?"

The crewcut man tore off his apron in obvious anger and flung it on the floor. "Forget what I said about the free meal. Get out of here right now!"

The four startled would-be diners had no chance to respond to this swift turn of events. A group of burly patrons temporarily left their beloved beer mugs and promptly tossed them through the door, where they landed in the overgrown grass outside, in a scene reminiscent of George Bailey and his guardian angel Clarence being thrown out of "Nick's Place" in *It's A Wonderful Life*, Waldo's favorite film. One of the oafish men actually called out "and don't come back" in true cliched Hollywood tradition.

Fontaine, Bucktooth, and the Professor ran off without a single glance behind them, but Phosphate paused at the edge of the dirt path, where Brisbane's decidedly un-fredneck-like car was parked, and observed *Grandpa's Place* carefully for a moment. There was no doubt in his mind that something about the place, and its analogy to deserted country stores covered with cobwebs, or doughnut shops with presidential descendants behind the counter, or gas stations with savage rednecks poised to attack unwary motorists, seemed to hold a great deal of significance for all of them. It was a testament to the oddity of the circumstances they had been finding themselves in over the last several days that Phosphate wasn't totally flabbergasted by the crewcut man's bizarre and mercurial changes in attitude.

Phosphate felt no bruises from being hoisted and lifted airborne into the tall grass in front of the place- which admittedly helped to break his fall- but he was growing increasingly concerned with the fact that none of the assorted oddball characters they'd encountered thus far had actually harmed them. Gazing at the dilapidated structure for a little longer, the top doo-wopper eventually walked away with a thousand questions racing unanswered through his mind, puzzled and still hungry.

Waldo and Jeanne were lying in the cornfield, in a bed of crushed stalks, staring up at the late afternoon sky. The nervous young man just couldn't believe that someone as kind and lovely- albeit underaged- as Jeanne O'Sullivan could actually care for him. They'd discussed their astonishing compatibility in great depth, and were sharing a cigarette and murmuring contentedly together when the beautiful young girl finally steered the easy flowing conversation into another direction.

"So what brought you to Iowa?" Jeanne inquired.

"Well, you see, my grandfather recently disappeared without a trace." Waldo was struggling to maintain his train of thought in his enthralled state of mind, but he managed to feel a tinge of embarrassment over neglecting to mention earlier the essential reason for his being there. "And, well, I decided that the best place to look for him would be in Iowa."

"Why here?" The Irish teenager asked. "Did your family come from these parts?"

Waldo's concentration continued to be centered on her pretty face. "Huh? Oh, yes, I looked for him as well as I could, but as there weren't any real clues..."

"But why did you come all the way from Virginia to here?" Jeanne semi-wiggled her cute little nose in a *Bewitched*-like manner.

"You see, my grandfather's best friend was committed to an institution in Cornoil, Iowa back in 1969, and, I don't know, for some crazy reason- I did find, the only clue, was a little note in his friend's journal- anyway, I think he might know what happened." Waldo looked all around him for a spot to extinguish the cigarette butt he held in his hand, and seeing nothing that wasn't flammable, he crushed it out on the bottom of his shoe. "By the way, we saw a sign back there that said something about Cornoil being five miles away. Do you know where it is?"

Jeanne giggled and nodded.

"Well, is it very far?"

"We're *in* Cornoil, silly!" She laughed.

Waldo breathed a deep sigh of relief. "Well, that's pretty convenient. At least now I know I might be close to an answer. Of course, with everything we've been through..."

"What do you mean?" Jeanne interrupted with an expression of concern crossing her pretty countenance.

Waldo went on to relate, in all their intricate details, the strange adventures of the past few days. When he was finished he raised his eyes from the ground, as he'd reverted back to form by focusing them there during the recounting of his admittedly bizarre story, and half expected the kind hearted teenager to be staring at him in disgust. Instead, the lovely girl threw her arms about him and kissed him more passionately than he'd ever been kissed before.

"You poor thing." Jeanne ran her fingers tenderly through his long hair. "I don't really know what you went through, it sounds pretty odd, but I'm pretty good with intuition, and I have a feeling you're going to find what you're looking for here."

It was all Waldo could do to resist responding with a quick affirmation that he indeed had found what he'd always been searching for, when he discovered her. He managed to control himself, however, and merely flash her a grateful smile.

"You didn't say where this friend of your grandfather's was. I know Cornoil pretty well, I could probably give you directions." There was an impish twinkle in Jeanne's green eyes.

Waldo was slightly embarrassed. "Well, he was, you know, committed. I mean to a mental health institution, called the Last Chance Relaxation Home."

"What?" Jeanne sat up. "Are you sure?"

"Of course I'm sure. Why, is there something wrong?"

"No, not at all." Jeanne answered with a lovely smile. "My sister and I just happen to be volunteer workers there."

"Shit, Phos, what the hell was *that* all about?" Fontaine was rolling a large joint.

The Afro-Anarchists and Professor Buckley were standing next to Brisbane's car. Fontaine and Bucktooth were still unnerved by their experience at *Grandpa's Place*, and were turning, as always, to their leader for guidance. The Professor, meanwhile, was growing increasingly detached with every new incomprehensible event, and was busily poring through his briefcase, consoling himself with massive amounts of extremist philosophy.

"Yeah, man, that shit is the final straw!" Bucktooth exclaimed. "Why in the hell are we here, Phos? I knew we shoulda turned around after I saw that hitchhiker disappear."

211

There was a trace of befuddlement on the normally unflappable top doo-wopper's face. "I really don't know why we've been encountering such characters as that crewcut man in the restaurant. I am as baffled by such happenings as you are. I can only surmise that they are connected, in some as yet undetermined manner, to the disappearance of Waldo's grandfather."

Fontaine lit up the joint, which he'd pilfered from the generous fredneck's ample supply in the glove compartment, and passed it to Phosphate. "Phos, I'm with Buck on this one, man. You're our leader, but I say we get our asses outa this damn place before some really dangerous shit happens."

Phosphate drew deeply on the joint. "Gentlemen, I ask your patience. If you will consider carefully for a moment, you will realize that despite some very nasty, unexplainable occurrences, we have not been harmed in any fashion."

"So you think we should just wait for some of this weird shit to hurt us?" Bucktooth asked.

"Remember, man, you didn't see a green giant or a werewolf." Fontaine reminded Phosphate. "I know damn well we were in danger there."

The head Afro-Anarchist patted Fontaine on the back. "Fontaine, I know you two have seen even odder things than I have, but remember that our reason for being here is to assist our friend Waldo in his noble mission." Throwing his arm around Bucktooth's shoulder, Phosphate spoke like a big brother. "I beg your indulgence, both of you. Who knows-the absurdity of recent events may have been magnified by the fact we haven't eaten regularly and have consumed a large amount of marijuana."

Fontaine chuckled. "Shit, Phos, that's just about what the cops would say if we reported any of this stuff."

Phosphate had to laugh himself. "I must admit you're right, Fontaine. I apologize for that."

The three doo-wop protest singers then decided, inasmuch as they had long since passed the hunger stage, and were only a few stages away from developing the bloated physiques of starving Ethiopians, that they would pass the time until Waldo and Brisbane returned with their under-aged girlfriends by smoking even more of Brisbane's dope. Of course, they vowed to replace it at some unspecified future date. The Professor was politely asked, as always, to participate in the illegal festivities, but once again demurred, preferring to shuffle through unpublished fringe material instead.

As the sun slowly sank down over the expansive O'Sullivan cornfields, Fontaine started rapping again:

"I don't eat much, for heaven's sakes
I don't go to the local house of pancakes
And sit on my butt with a plate of flapjacks
But I love-I love-I love to relax
Sometimes I feel so energized
I like to stay up late and socialize
I don't always have a pillow under my back
But I love-I love-I love to relax
I'd like to believe in working hard
I ain't been feathered, I just been tarred
I got no income, so I pay no tax
But I love-I love-I love to relax
We ain't all the same and we ain't all free
We're the most oppressed group in history
I don't carry weapons and I don't do crack
But I love-I love-I love to relax."

"I really am a volunteer at the Last Home. Janie and I work there every weekend and most afternoons after school."

It was nearly dark in the magical cornfield, whose powers they'd unaccountably allowed to remain untapped thus far, and Waldo was still expressing his amazement over the remarkable coincidence of her affiliation with the Last Chance Relaxation Home.

"Waldo, you never asked me about the house." The pretty teenager changed the subject. "They told me, I don't mean to embarrass you, something about the kitchen calendar."

Waldo felt his face turning red. "Well, I did think that, uh, I saw a date on there that said, well, uh, 1971. But I wasn't the only one-Phosphate saw it first."

Jeanne touched his hand lightly. "Ah, don't worry. I know you didn't imagine it. You see, sometimes our house, which is on the same land as the cornfield after all, gets mixed up in what I guess are the crazy magnetic fields or whatever that allow us to time travel. All kinds of kooky things happen around here. Sometimes people from the past just appear in our dining room when we're eating dinner."

This reassured Waldo somewhat, as it tended to verify his sighting of the Hitchhiker there. "Uh, Jeanne, that wasn't all I saw."

"Why, what else did you see?"

Waldo lowered his eyes to their customary position. "I know it sounds crazy, but I thought I saw the guy we picked up hitchhiking-remember I told you about him before- that, you know, Bucktooth saw disappear, sitting at your dining room table."

213

"Whew! That *is* weird!" Jeanne seemed suitably perplexed. "If he was a figure from the past, that's not so unusual, but if he was a hitchhiker you picked up in the present time then I can't explain how..."

"I can't explain much of anything that's happened since the morning I woke up and found my grandfather gone." Waldo glanced nervously all about him, as if checking for bugging devices amongst the corn stalks. Sighing, he tried his best to introduce the young Irish beauty to his theories regarding conspiracies, Unreals, and the like, with the air of an off-beat instructor in an extremist philosophy course. "I realize that you probably haven't heard many people talk like this before, but I can't help believing this stuff. Like Barney Fife used to say, *facts is facts.* I just thought that you should hear, I mean what can you possibly think when someone tells you about bars with dead baseball players in them, or giant strawberry patches, or disappearing men in black, or interstate exits that turn into deserted dirt paths? Anyhow, it's only fair that you know this about me, and I'll understand if you're like everybody else and decide to..."

Rather than beat a hasty departure, which was the traditionally accepted procedure at such points in Waldo's past conversations, Jeanne politely listened to his lengthy speculations, which she eventually interrupted by reaching out and hugging him.

"You poor thing. You sure have been through a lot, and you haven't really even started looking for your grandfather." She gave him a tender kiss on the cheek and reached down into her purse, fumbling around for a cigarette. Finally finding one, she lit it up and inhaled deeply. "I'd like to help you, if I can."

"You already have." Waldo replied dreamily. The underaged girl was so sweet and understanding, so patient, that he lost the desire to expound any further about his countless complaints against the establishment, or his crusades to reform it, and actually changed the topic himself. "Jeanne, what about your parents? Do they travel through time with you?"

"They don't know about it."

"But you said that sometimes people would just pop in and out while you were eating."

Jeanne blew smoke-rings high into the air, which was growing cooler with the onset of night. "My parents don't seem to be able to see them, or if they do, they don't say anything about it. Unless they're doing it in secret, and just don't want to tell us, they have no idea what the cornfield can do."

Waldo, now almost entirely free of his normal inhibitions, stroked her hair lovingly. "I just want to, well, thank you for still, uh, liking me after everything I told you."

Jeanne lay down on her back and pointed up at the crystal clear sky,

214

and the full moon and numerous stars which were becoming visible within it. "Isn't it wonderful?"

Waldo was staring at her when he responded. "It sure is."

Meanwhile, Brisbane and the Afro-Anarchists were partying like a group of fraternity brothers. The fredneck and Janie had spent an enjoyable time together, and the lovely underaged girl had insisted, once she'd discovered that they hadn't eaten properly in days, on bringing them some food. Apparently the O'Sullivan pantry was plentiful, for the Irish beauty returned to the car in no time with her arms full of cold chicken, wheat bread, apples, and two-thirds of a coconut cake. It was fortunate for Janie that she set everything down quickly on the hood of Brisbane's decidedly un-fredneck-like '65 Dodge Dart, or else she might have been seriously injured by the ravenous males descending upon her. After she left a few minutes later- which the starving fredneck acknowledged by grunting gratefully in her direction- to enjoy her own dinner at home, the five of them rapidly demolished almost all of the entire hearty feast. Professor Buckley ate only a single drumstick, as another of his unusual quirks was his penchant for subsisting on nearly as little food as sleep. The eccentric ex-history teacher munched slowly on his small portion as he sat by himself on the incline leading from the cornfield to the dirt path, and strained to read his beloved writings as the sun set and darkness arrived.

No one knew when Waldo might return, or thought to look for him in the cornfield, and it was only at the behest of Phosphate that they saved a few scraps of chicken, a piece of bread, and a thin slice of cake for him. Brisbane, not noticing that a substantial portion of his supply was missing, suggested they smoke some of his homemade concoction as they lay scattered about on the ground, full and satisfied. They'd been drinking beer as well, as the fredneck had found a warm six pack left from Waldo's take at the curious old general store, which had fallen unnoticed out of one of the bags at the back of the trunk. As a result, they soon found themselves enormously high.

"Shit, dudes, what the fuck do you think Waldo and Jeanne are doing?" There was more than a trace of envy in Brisbane's voice.

Phosphate exhaled a large quantity of smoke. "My friend, I am sure Waldo is safe and in good hands. He and the lovely Miss O'Sullivan seem to care for each other, so I find it not surprising that they would want to spend as much time together as possible."

The fredneck snorted. "Yeah, but it's getting late and she is only 16, you know. And what about Waldo's grandfather? That *is* the reason we came out here, isn't it? I just..."

All at once, a commotion started in the back seat of Brisbane's trusty old car. Fontaine and Bucktooth had begun stumbling around in some sort of ridiculous dance, and literally fallen in there, unnoticed by the others. Both of them were chemically enhanced to near peak level, and were jumping up and down, rocking the automobile from side to side as they rapped out an inconsistent, pseudo-comprehensible song:

> "Man, we're the greatest in the U.S.A.
> But no one pays attention to what we say
> We just don't say no, but we passed the test
> We lead the league in false arrests
> We ain't got no car, ain't got no clothes
> But at least we didn't die from an overdose
> We just want to have fun and feel a lady's touch
> But we got no home, so they don't like us much
> They like the way we look and the things we've said
> But they'd much rather have a roof over their head
> So come on girls, and make a small donation
> To the Fontaine and Bucktooth celebration."

Brisbane, intrigued by the haphazard hip-hop sounds, walked over to the car, stuck his head in the back window, and passed the joint he'd just lit to Fontaine.

"Shit man, that was alright, but I thought you and me were gonna write some more stuff." The fredneck was slightly offended.

Fontaine, who'd taken to being called F.W. Cooljay by his dutiful partner Bucktooth, waved at Brisbane with the insincerity of a Hollywood movie star acknowledging an adoring fan. "Yeah, sure baby. Love to work with ya sometime."

F.W. then passed the joint to Bucktooth, who was giggling so hysterically that he was compelled to hand it back to Brisbane. The fredneck was forced to laugh himself as the two erstwhile rappers started in on another number, which was garbled to such an extent that it was impossible to decipher any of the words.

Brisbane grabbed the last warm beer and returned to the grassy slope leading down from the cornfield, where Phosphate was stretched out next to the Professor, staring up at the spectacular, star-studded sky.

"Shit, Phosphate, do you really think we're gonna find Waldo's grandfather out here?" The fredneck sat down next to the head Afro-Anarchist and handed him the joint.

The top doo-wopper was feeling even mellower than normal, and he hardly needed to smoke any more reefer, but he took a nice, lengthy hit nevertheless. His attention was riveted on the full moon which shone down brightly on the Iowa countryside. Phosphate was so stoned that he

216

momentarily forgot his elementary astronomy and confused the lunar surface with the planet Mars. On that basis, he was studiously searching it for canals, like some sort of heir to the officially discredited theories of Percival Lowell. This was a perfectly natural activity for someone who'd been steadily ingesting a substance as potent as Brisbane's homemade herb.

"Hey, Phosphate, are you okay, man?" The fredneck asked, as his friend's unresponsive eyes remained fixed on the moon.

"I don't know, but judging by what has transpired thus far, it appears as if the search will be highly interesting." The leader of the Afro-Anarchists belatedly replied.

While Brisbane left Phosphate to ponder over his misidentified astral body, the Professor continued turning the pages of Sam Hancock's journal- as the unimpeded Midwestern moonlight cast as much illumination as any crackling fire had for pioneers like Abe Lincoln- until he came to a most interesting entry:

The Journal of Sam Hancock, April 30, 1959

I have just returned from Topsham, a tiny village of Devonshire, in the southwest of England. I undertook the journey, along with my trusted companion Abner "Old Hoss" Billingsly, in order to investigate a remarkable event which happened there just over one hundred years ago. Of course, both of us realized there was little chance of solving any mystery that occurred in the distant past, but we are old hands at lost causes, and find such things especially challenging.

Actually, we arrived in England originally to inquire into the murders committed by the notorious, never apprehended Jack the Ripper, but found the authorities suspiciously tight-lipped about the matter. Thus, we were forced to leave the Whitechapel area in the east end of London, where we'd arranged to stay at a dingy flophouse, ahead of schedule and without examining a single document in the case. As Old Hoss so cogently noted, what could be the possible reason for withholding anything from the public about a series of prostitute killings? That sort of suppression only serves to revive the rumors of Royal involvement. With time on our hands, we decided to visit Devon, an area both of us were familiar with due to the bizarre visitation by someone or something there on a snowy night in February of 1855.

On the morning of February 8, 1855, the citizens of the small village of Topsham had awakened to find a single series of footprints in the snow, which continued in a perfectly straight and unbroken line, over fences, walls, and rooftops. There was the general feeling at the time, due as much to the religious sentiments of the day as to the cloven-shaped appearance of the hoof prints, that the marks had been left by the Devil himself. As no scientific personage was ever able to adequately explain the footprints, and as they clearly were made overnight and couldn't be denied because of the scores of villagers who saw them the next morning, Old Hoss and I considered it to be one of the greatest enigmas of all time, and were naturally drawn to it.

We found our way to Topsham, which proved to be a sleepy, antiquated place, populated by traditional, hard working men and women. No hotels existed there, but a clean, tidy boarding house stood in the center of town, and fortunately a room was available. As our investigations customarily begin in a cocktail lounge, and as there was none in the boarding house, we settled on purchasing a bottle of whiskey at a nearby liquor store, and a liter of ginger ale at the local grocer's, and sat down shortly after sunset in a couple of rocking chairs on the old fashioned porch in front of the place. It wasn't long before a pleasingly plump, fiftyish woman left her own rocker, which was located a short distance away, and approached us with a nervous, timid expression on her face.

"Excuse me, gents," she said softly, in a barely audible tone, "but may I move next to you?"

There was indeed an empty chair directly across from us, so Old Hoss turned it around so it faced in our direction, and pointed towards it with a friendly smile. "Of course. Please sit down."

"T-thank you." The woman glanced all about her, as if she feared something that might be lurking nearby. "I-I hope you don't mind my saying it, but I couldn't help overhearing your..."

"We don't mind." Old Hoss interrupted, pausing to light up one of his patented large, foul smelling cigars. "What exactly did you hear that interested you?"

There were only a few others on the large porch, a mother contending with two small children who were repeatedly attempting to jump over one side, and an elderly man who appeared to be asleep, but the woman nonetheless leaned in towards us and lowered her voice to a whisper.

"You're here about...the *prints*, ain't you?" Her eyes opened wide. "I have to warn you, others have been here before, not in a while, but, they...well, let's just say they never left."

I sipped my drink as I listened very attentively. "What do you mean by that?" I asked her.

"Look, I ain't got long to talk to you." She declared, looking anxiously back over her shoulder. "How much do you gents know about what happened here?"

Old Hoss expelled a mouthful of cigar smoke into the night air.

"Just what we've read in books; that some unknown creature came here during the night and left behind a trail of very peculiar tracks."

"Did you know that they went along for over a hundred miles? In a perfect line, mind you. The world's full of nasty things; nasty chaps, nasty gals, nasty... Why, the townspeople was so excited about it afterwards that they didn't leave their homes at night for weeks. Can you imagine what they was afraid of?"

"Well, the legend is," I chuckled, "that the Devil walked in Devon that night."

The woman abruptly stood up and peered intently out into the darkness. She seemed to see something neither of us could, and turned to walk away.

"Wait!" Old Hoss called. "Where are you going?"

The woman was visibly shaking as she simply replied, "I've said too much. I wish you gents luck."

With that, the middle-aged lady planted her hands on the porch railing and flung herself over it, handling the ten foot drop like a youngster. She then dashed away without another word, leaving Old Hoss and I to speculate about her deep into the night.

As it turned out, everyone in Topsham seemed reluctant to talk about the events of February 8, 1855. Old Hoss and I spoke to several citizens, who all steadfastly refused to comment on the subject, every one of them wearing identical expressions of horror the moment it was mentioned. The mysterious woman was not seen again, and during a walk through town the following afternoon, it was all the two of us could do to keep from fleeing on foot when we listened to the local townspeople conversing among themselves. All of their discussions revolved around the discovery of a body, which by all accounts matched the description of the strange woman we'd spoken to on the porch of the boarding house, floating in a nearby pond. We quickly and unceremoniously left after that, with regrets over our failure to elicit much new information, but without a single look behind us.

And so, one mystery gives way to another; next month we will be traveling to Portugal, to inquire further into the miracle of Fatima, wherein three poor shepherd children are alleged to have seen and conversed with the Virgin Mary, and thousands of others supposedly witnessed the sun spinning out of control in the sky. I will provide full details in a later entry.

Hiram Buckley set the journal back down in his battered briefcase. There then transpired one of the most fantastic events yet; the one time pride of the local community college curled up in the grass and willingly drifted off to sleep.

A few hours later, Waldo was still nestled in the cornfield, looking up at the moon and blowing cigarette smoke towards it, lost in his own little sea of tranquility.

He was in love. But then again, he'd always fallen in love with absurd ease, and would certainly have found the custom of marrying young and quickly, which was such a popular practice among previous generations, more to his fancy than the long, drawn out, trial and error method finding favor in the present age. Due to his eccentricities, girls had very seldom been interested in Waldo. However, on those rare occasions when an attractive female seemed the least bit fond of him, the nervous young man never failed to overreact, writing poem after poem and song after song to sing the lady's praises. Needless to say, the fairer sex found such behavior, along with his habits of arriving punctually and phoning on schedule, to be odd and confusing.

But this time was different; Waldo was no longer a virgin. His emotional nature and decidedly different perspective on life in general had contributed to his exclusion from all of the promiscuousness which flowed so freely among his peers. Certainly, he was one of the very few living specimens of manhood over the age of sixteen without a disfiguring disability, or an honest vow of chastity, who'd managed to avoid sexual activity. And yet, the manner in which he'd finally escaped this condition, with the able assistance of the underaged beauty, somewhat served to redeem his reputation. Waldo and Jeanne had done *it* in 1865.

When their natural interest in each other had suddenly started moving at a warp factor in their bed of broken corn stalks, with the bold, romantic night burgeoning above them, Waldo had become frightened and felt compelled to confess his unlikely status as a virgin. Jeanne was just as understanding as he might have guessed, somehow managing to convey the dual images of wily sex kitten and blushing Catholic school girl simultaneously. Flashing a dazzling smile that carried equal parts of innocence and seductiveness, the teenager asked Waldo if he'd like to travel back in time and have his first sexual experience in a historical setting. Being a student of history, Waldo was enormously attracted to this idea. Thus, through the magic of the O'Sullivan farm, they were transported back to 1865 and delightfully consummated their brief relationship on the rear lawn of the White House, as Abraham Lincoln paced the floors above them.

Following his wonderful introduction to the joys of womanhood, Waldo found a perverse pleasure in leaving his after-sex cigarette butt glowing on the lawn of the executive mansion. Despite Jeanne's repeated assurances that it wouldn't actually be visible to any nineteenth century passers-by, Waldo preferred to picture his discarded cigarette butt being the center of much scrutiny, with puzzled Civil War-era Washingtonians reacting to it in the same way Brazilian farmers would react to U.F.O.'s a century later.

After their return to the bland and boring present, Jeanne had, like her sister, offered to alleviate his intense hunger. Waldo consented to her proposal, and she served up a similar repast to that consumed by the others. Unlike Janie, Jeanne ate with the young man she was so interested in, providing a nonsensical explanation that her distracted parents accepted without question. When Waldo had eaten most of the food, and Jeanne had nibbled on a few things in the perfect feminine manner, they went for a quiet, reflective walk through the cornfield. The moon had shone on Jeanne's hair in such a picturesque way that Waldo couldn't help feeling that he was living out a dream drawn with the poignant pen of a John Keats. Eventually, she told him that her parents must be growing worried, and it was with great reluctance that Waldo kissed her goodnight. After proceeding a few steps, the lovely girl had turned around and inquired as to where he and the others were going to sleep. For an instant, Waldo was tempted to reply with a personally uncharacteristic but typically macho response such as "next to you, baby," but as the extremely sensitive sort of fellow he was, he'd merely assured her that they would be fine spending this night, like most of the others since they'd left Virginia, in the decidedly un-fredneck-like vehicle. She'd then rushed back into his arms and kissed him passionately, and they had promised to meet back at Brisbane's car the next morning. She had left him then, and watching her stroll across the moonlit cornfield was just about the most poetic sight Waldo had ever seen.

Now, as he lay there stargazing and sighing contentedly, Waldo replayed the exciting events of the evening over and over again in his mind. He knew that Jeanne O'Sullivan had given him a very special gift, and he didn't mean sex. Closing his eyes, the nervous young man felt more at ease than he'd ever been.

12

OVER THE CORNFIELDS AND FAR AWAY

Waldo felt something warm and moist on his cheek. Opening his eyes, he was pleasantly surprised to find Jeanne O'Sullivan's lips planted there. She looked just as beautiful as she had yesterday, and was obviously more than a gorgeous manifestation of a particularly vigorous bout of fantasizing.

"Good morning, sleepy head." Jeanne whispered into his ear.

Waldo smiled dreamily. "Hi. I guess I must have slept all night in your cornfield. I hope your parents wouldn't mind that."

Jeanne placed her head on his chest. "Of course they wouldn't mind. I just hope you weren't too cold or uncomfortable out here."

The pretty teenager referred to the fact that the previous night had been unseasonably chilly for June.

"No, that was the best I've slept in well..." Waldo was about to declare that he hadn't rested that way for years, when he remembered the night they'd spent in the motel behind Taco Bull, and the resultant slumber there, "uh, it's just pretty unusual when I don't have insomnia. I almost always have trouble sleeping."

"I'm glad you got some rest then." Jeanne had an impish look on her cute face. "What did you guys have planned for today?"

"Well, I'd like to start searching for my grandfather. I really should have done something yesterday. Do you think you could take us to the Last Chance Relaxation Home?" Waldo sat up slowly and reached into his shirt pocket for a Camel Light.

"Sure, but I was hoping you could wait 'til tomorrow, since Janie and I are scheduled to work then."

Waldo found it difficult to concentrate on mundane matters like missing immediate family members as he held her close against him. "Well, I guess we can wait. I mean, if Sam Hancock is alive, and if somehow he knows something about my grandfather's disappearance, then what difference can a day make?" Waldo lit up his cigarette. "Why did you ask if we could wait? Was there something special you wanted to do?"

Jeanne giggled. "Yeah. I thought we could get the whole group together and do a little time-traveling." After her initial reluctance to reveal the powers of their farm to Brisbane, the Irish teenager now apparently harbored no reservations about including all of them in on their adventures.

Waldo drew deeply on his first cigarette of the day, which always tasted the best. "That sounds like fun. But we really do have to get to the Last Chance Relaxation Home tomorrow."

"Sure, we can all go together. That is, if you guys don't mind giving Janie and I a ride."

"Well, of course, but we're already crowded with six people, and I'm not sure if we'd all fit."

Jeanne ran her fingers through his long hair, which was more unkempt than usual from resting several hours amid the corn stalks. "I don't know about my sister, but I volunteer to sit on your lap."

With that, they decided to walk to the car and see if the others wanted to join them in a group excursion through time.

Strolling hand in hand, Waldo and Jeanne were beginning to increasingly resemble one of those totally unrealistic, Clark Gable-Myrna Loy 1930's-style couples; introduced in reel one, in love ten minutes later, married in reel two. Like a dream from a Hollywood script writer's pen, they melted into the bright yellow cornfields and ice blue Iowa sky. Had they been living in an earlier era, or had Jeanne been a few years older, everyone-even the law- might have considered them to be an ideal match.

"Well, what do you all think?" Jeanne asked in the bubbly manner of a pep rally organizer.

Waldo and Jeanne had arrived at the car and after some general and forgettable banter, she had told the others of her notion that they spend the day "history-hopping," as the twins sometimes so cutely described it.

"I find that to be a capital idea." Phosphate borrowed an expression from Gomez Addams to convey the extent of his approval.

"Yeah man, I could get into that." Brisbane spoke with one arm around Janie and the other grasping an early morning beer can, which he'd ardently requested, and had been fetched by his youthful companion from her parent's refrigerator only moments before. Janie had stolen up a brief time earlier and awakened the fredneck, much as her sister had awakened Waldo, but with a good deal less passion involved.

"My dear, what a-that is-I *would* love to go back in time." Professor Buckley remarked wistfully, having recovered from his rare full night's sleep, and the resultant fusillade of "I don't understand's" to explain it.

Fontaine and Bucktooth, as the only others besides the Professor who hadn't tested the time-traveling waters yet, were anxious to do so as well and completed the unanimous endorsement of Jeanne's proposal. Apparently no one was thinking of Old Hoss Billingsly that morning, nor heeding the famed capitalist creed that *time is of the essence*.

"Okay, then, where shall we go?" Jeanne was itching to start the festivities.

It was agreed at this point that everyone would have the opportunity of placing into nomination their individual choices for times and places to visit. Each of them selected three historical dates, which they wrote down on slips of paper thoughtfully provided by the Professor. These selections were then handed to the top doo-wopper, who read them aloud with great fanfare and counted the raised hands for each one. The one garnering the most votes would be the starting point for their time-traveling, followed by the runner up, then the third, and so on.

The nominees were many and when the votes were tabulated, since everyone tended to choose their own picks and thus offset each other, a surprising winner emerged. Fontaine had inexplicably selected July 31, 1969 in Appletree, Maine, and when he coaxed Bucktooth into supporting him, this nomination became the only one with two votes.

Waldo spoke for Brisbane, Phosphate, and the Professor, as well as himself. "Now wait a minute. With all of the great events from history we could witness, why should we waste our time with this? Tell me, Fontaine, what was so great about July 31, 1969 in Appletree, Maine?"

Fontaine seemed stunned that no one else was aware of the significance of the date. "Man, don't you all know? A bunch of real acid heads got together and held the greatest concert of all time there- they called it Outofstock. I thought you fellas, with all the weird shit you know, woulda heard of that."

Brisbane laughed. "Shit man, get real. What the hell are you talking about?"

Fontaine tried to explain. "Man, this event was so cool that the stars didn't let hardly anybody know about it, and it was such a secret thing that it never did get reported."

Waldo was skeptical. "I don't know why I've never heard of it. If it really happened, then there must be some information about it somewhere. I've spent most of my time looking for obscure, hidden stuff like that and I can't believe I wouldn't have..."

"Alright then, shit!" Fontaine, upset and beginning to feel oppressed again, interrupted Waldo's convincing claim that he was the greatest authority in this area. "If you all don't want to go by the voting, then what can I say?"

Jeanne, even at her tender age, was moved by the spirit of democracy to recommend a reasonable approach. "Why don't we go ahead and travel first to Appletree, Maine and see if there really was this big concert? I mean, at least we owe Fontaine a chance to see if he's telling the truth."

The others could hardly disagree with her logic, so they marched off together into the cornfield, and watched in awe as the O'Sullivan twins scoured the stalks for the appropriate date and location. It wasn't easy for the girls to find it, as they had never had much reason to journey to that particular place at any time, let alone on a specific date. After arduously sampling various areas of the cornfield by their secretive methods, which even an immensely curious Waldo was unable to decipher, and which they seemed strangely unwilling to divulge, Jeanne and Janie finally discovered the correct spot. The pretty teenagers then instructed the six males to join hands, and in an instant Waldo saw the Iowa landscape disappear and found himself in a small outdoor arena in Appletree, Maine.

The wind was whistling through the creaky wooden stands where they were seated. The few spectators there were scattered in different sections, and appeared oblivious to the thunderstorm raging above them. Waldo was astounded to feel no rain landing on him, as it was pouring from the sky. He turned to ask Jeanne about this, but she anticipated his question.

"Remember, silly- all we can do is watch. That's why nothing, not even this kind of weather, can effect us." Jeanne squeezed his hand. "It's kind of neat, don't you think, sitting in the rain without getting wet?"

Waldo had to admit that it was. The scene was breathtaking: a desolate little stadium with only a handful of onlookers witnessing what was undoubtedly the musical event of the century, as the thunder crashed violently and the rain came down in sheets. The lightning served to further illuminate the legendary figures performing on stage, who were showing an astonishing amount of bravery in playing their electric instruments under such conditions. Waldo could only surmise that their reckless behavior had been heavily influenced by the mind-expanding substances which were all around them.

It was hard for Waldo to fathom why this concert wasn't known as the unparalleled "happening" it clearly seemed to be, and even more difficult to believe that he had never heard even a rumor about it. All of the biggest names in rock and roll were there: the Beatles, the Rolling Stones, Bob Dylan, Elvis Presley, The Who, the Beach Boys, the Byrds, and many others.

Brisbane was really in his element, yelling out his favorite epithets with a ferocious enthusiasm. The fredneck seemed to forget that none of the people in attendance were able to see or hear him, and every time Waldo looked in his direction he saw him futilely attempting to converse with some member of the audience.

The eight time-travelers were apparently the only ones in the petite New England arena who weren't under the effects of some kind of hallucinogenic drug. From what Waldo was able to see through the driving rain, the small crowd was as busily engaged in passing these substances among themselves as they were in paying attention to the events on stage. *Long live the flower children,* Waldo mumbled cleverly to himself.

Fontaine was beaming with pride as he rocked back and forth to the music. "See, I told you all this shit really happened." The smug Afro-Anarchist, seeking to "get into" things totally, decided to emulate the ragged band of hippies who were altering their minds in the best tradition of the sixties. Holding three pills aloft in his hand, he took one himself, offered another to Brisbane (who grabbed it and popped it into his mouth without glancing at it), and handed the last one to Waldo.

Waldo had never shown an inclination to "expand his consciousness," even during his early youth when he smoked marijuana regularly. He turned to look at Jeanne, but she merely shrugged. At that moment, a brainstorm suddenly hit Waldo: he could ingest whatever he wanted since this was 1969, and he would never feel any effects from it back in the present time. Before he gave himself a chance to re-examine this line of reasoning, Waldo swallowed the pill courageously and sat back waiting for something wild to happen.

A short time later, during the incredible duet by Elvis Presley and John Lennon, Waldo began noticing some strange things. Like puffy pink elephants selling peanuts and miniature green garbage men dropping from the roof of the place, with their bright yellow parachutes. He closed his eyes, but they were still visible, and growing more complex, being joined by a bearded amputee chorus line and a giant spoon which was stirring the gray storm clouds in the sky like a thick soup. There was also a voice coming from far off in the distance which was calling his name, except that it was not quite accurate, referring to him as Waldo-Jimmy.

The nervous young man opened his eyes again and felt his young love's fingers lightly caressing his knee. Turning his head, he discovered that he was no longer seated next to Jeanne. Being a childhood fan of D.C. Comics, of which his grandfather had a substantial collection, he recognized the woman whose hand was on his knee as none other than Lois Lane. She batted her cartoon eyes and edged closer to him. Brisbane, meanwhile, had been transformed into Perry White, complete with gray hair and a big cigar. He was a realistic character, too, spouting out *Great Caesar's Ghost!* every few seconds. The ex-history teacher Hiram Buckley had been dipped in the fountain of youth, with a head full of curly hair and the look of an eager young scientist destined to have some secret experiment stolen from him. Phosphate, Fontaine, and Bucktooth were all gone, probably due to the fact that there were no black heroes, best pals, bosses, or girlfriends in comic books when Waldo was a youth. Waldo-Jimmy rolled up his sleeve, revealing both his newly freckled arm and his special wristwatch. With a simple touch, he activated its supersonic signal, and the next thing he knew Superman was sitting next to him in the stands.

"Hello, Jimmy! How is my pal? I've been out in space taking care of some errant meteors! They've been safely detoured! Are you enjoying yourself? Sorry I was late getting here! I hope you're still my best friend!" Superman was, as always, full of exclamations.

Waldo-Jimmy was so proud to be the Man of Steel's best friend that he couldn't resist embracing his pal. When the superhero hugged back, however, he forgot his own super-strength and Waldo-Jimmy felt himself being crushed. He attempted to cry out but Superman's powerful, vice-like grip made it impossible to do so. Struggling desperately, he began to lose consciousness...

"Waldo!"

Waldo opened his eyes. Jeanne was crouching over him with a look of extreme concern on her lovely countenance. "Are you okay?"

He saw that the others were huddled all around him. The sky was still dark and stormy, and he could hear the strains of *Chestnut Mare* being played by the Byrds.

"Shit man, he flipped out again!" Brisbane, initially feeling, like the others, that the nervous young man had been the victim of an early heart attack, was relieved to find Waldo's fainting to be the result of his unique emotional system instead.

"Wh-what happened?" A flabbergasted Waldo inquired.

"Sheeet, you passed out right after I handed you the acid." Fontaine, also pleased that his friend hadn't succumbed to a sudden physical ailment, was almost laughing.

Waldo felt the pill still clutched firmly in his hand and groaned.

"That's right, sweetheart, you did. I was so worried about you." Jeanne kissed him on the forehead.

Waldo's mood brightened instantly. For the first time in his life, an unrelated female had called him sweetheart.

"Was that the kind of thing you were talking about earlier?" Jeanne was lying with her head in Waldo's lap. They were alone once again in the magical cornfield. The beautiful teenager was referring to his performance at the star-studded, unreported concert in 1969 Appletree, Maine, and whether it might be related to the bizarre occurrences he had already mentioned to her, such as vanishing hitchhikers and names related to the Kennedy assassination which keep popping up in unlikely places.

"Yes, well, it's along the same lines." Waldo was staring off into yet another gorgeous Iowa sunset. "At least I think it is, I don't know."

"Well, maybe you should talk to someone about it." Jeanne gingerly suggested.

"Great, now you think I need to see a psychiatrist."

"No, I was thinking you might want to tell me." The lovely

227

underaged girl was being typically sympathetic and understanding.

"Well, okay, I guess you're right." Waldo felt so close to Jeanne that he decided to reveal his odd and embarrassing hallucination of spanking a composite Jane Fonda-Gloria Steinem at old Griffith Stadium.

Jeanne smiled. "Ahh, that's not so weird. Lots of people have those types of fantasies."

Waldo had been blushing ever since he brought the illusory incident up. "You see, I don't know what happened there, but it was more like my fainting at the concert than any of the other wild things." Lighting up a cigarette, the nervous young man continued. "Both times, I was offered drugs and thought that I accepted them..."

"And both times, you passed out without taking them." Jeanne interrupted.

"Yes, and on each occasion I had a bizarre fantasy." Waldo had told her, and no one else, about his imaginary transformation into Jimmy Olsen.

Waldo then lapsed into one of his frequent bouts of self-pity, calling himself names, downgrading his emotional stability, and questioning his own sanity. He even suggested that, in view of his erratic behavior and a belief system at odds with most of humanity, perhaps he might be better off committing himself to the Last Chance Relaxation Home when they finally arrived there.

Jeanne sat up and grabbed him by the shoulders. "Now look, you. I think that you're just about the most original, brilliant, best looking, nicest guy I've ever met. So you just stop worrying so much and I'm sure you'll be just fine."

Waldo was so touched by Jeanne's display of affection and the series of compliments she'd so lovingly flung his way, which he was entirely unaccustomed to, that he had to summon up all of his fortitude to keep from crying. Instead he took her in his arms and held her with all his might.

"Remember, I have confidence in you." She whispered in his ear.

Waldo couldn't hold back the tears anymore. No one had ever said that to him before.

Meanwhile, back at Central Headquarters, as Brisbane now referred to his decidedly un-fredneck-like '65 Dodge Dart, the other fellows were reflecting on the day's events. They were also getting high again. The fredneck's special homemade herb, of which a large quantity somehow remained, was helping them pass the time pleasurably as they waited for Waldo to turn his attention away from his sixteen year old girlfriend, and concentrate on finding his missing grandfather.

It had been quite a day, starting with Waldo's performance at the suppressed Outofstock extravaganza, which outshone some of the lesser artists there. Following that, they engaged in a full schedule of time-traveling, with stops at all of their nominated choices, from Waldo's long awaited view of Dallas on November 22, 1963, to Bucktooth's comical, childish selection of "way back there in ancient Rome." They had returned shortly before sunset, exhausted but filled with the kinds of memories that historians can only dream of.

The Professor was off by himself again, with his battered briefcase beside him, near the entrance to the deep woods that surrounded the property, whimsically absorbing more extremist thoughts by the pale light of the moon.

"So, when do you think Mister Waldo is going to grace us with his presence again?" Brisbane was taking an increasing number of bitter swipes at his erstwhile friend.

"Come now, Brisbane." Phosphate's voice of reason was more reassuring than ever, assisted by massive amounts of marijuana.

"Shit man, I don't mean to sound like I'm talking behind a friend's back or anything, but it just seems like he's getting a little hung up on this underage chick and forgetting why we all came out here in the first place."

"I understand your concern, my friend. However, before you say anything to Waldo, remember that we only arrived here yesterday morning. It is rather obvious that Miss O'Sullivan, whatever her age and legal status, has taken his mind off of all his worries. Surely you don't think that can be a bad thing?" Phosphate was exhaling equal amounts of doo-wop philosophy and marijuana smoke into the night air, which was unseasonably cool again.

"Well, yeah, I guess you're right, man." Brisbane took one of his patented mammoth hits from the trusty pipe with the red sparkles on its base, which always accompanied him on the road.

"Hey Bris, why you being so cold to Waldo?" Fontaine burst into the conversation. "It couldn't be that you're mad that you ain't got your twin and he has, could it?"

Brisbane turned as red as he could considering how dulled his senses were. "No, that's not it at all. I just want to get started searching for his grandfather. That's why we drove all the way out here, and went through all that mysterious shit, isn't it?"

Fontaine laughed good-naturedly. "Shit, Bris, what's your hurry? What in the world you got to rush back for?"

Brisbane had to chuckle at that himself. "Alright, dude, I see your point. But keep cutting on me and I'll cut off your supply of weed."

Fontaine looked aghast. "Oh no, Master Brisbane! Anything but that! You can take our women and keep us in the fields, but don't stop giving us our drugs!"

Phosphate became annoyed whenever Fontaine flew into one of his sarcastic outbursts. "Alright, Fontaine, if we want to be inspired by radical humor, we can always watch old film clips of the sixties riots."

Fontaine, as usual, heeded the top doo-wopper's admonition, and the bickering buddies allowed the effects of the powerful dope to fully kick in. They proceeded to collaborate on several new rap songs, which they performed under the bright Iowa moon. The two of them (Bucktooth was too stoned to participate) were quite a sight, rocking and sometimes reeling to their tunes, backed by rows and rows of corn stalks and an inattentive audience of three.

After Jeanne had brought him more food to eat, some of which he charitably saved for the others, they'd talked and snuggled until the hour was late enough so that all self-respecting underage girls were expected to be in doors. Thus, the beautiful teenager reluctantly left Waldo alone in the cornfield, still glowing over her expression of confidence in him.

Waldo had now reached a point where he'd almost completely forgotten the reason why he was there. Truly magnanimous souls would have forgiven him for this uncharacteristically selfish attitude, taking into consideration his past failures at romance and the undeniable allure of young Jeanne O'Sullivan. Of course, such understanding and empathy was presently, as always, frowned upon by most of humanity, and thus it should have occurred to Waldo that the others who had volunteered to help him find his grandfather might be growing annoyed with his persistent absences from them. Certainly the fredneck, at least, was showing signs of impatience, and everyone else, even the Professor, was wondering just when the search would begin. Waldo, however, wasn't the least bit concerned with such things as he happily drifted off to sleep almost as easily as normal people do every night.

Shortly after falling asleep, Waldo was awakened by the sound of voices singing somewhere off in the distance. They were of a soft, ethereal quality, yet strangely masculine, and bore no resemblance to the noise Fontaine and Brisbane were making in another part of the cornfield. The nervous young man's curiosity was aroused to the extent that he lit up his prerequisite cigarette and listened more intently. Oddly, the voices seemed to stop once Waldo started straining to hear them. Now wide awake and fully intrigued, he felt drawn to them somehow, and instinctively set out for the deep woods bordering the O'Sullivan cornfield, which *something* appeared to be telling him was their point of origin.

Waldo was not the most adventurous of souls under normal circumstances, but in light of all he'd encountered recently, his venturing into such a dark and potentially dangerous area was particularly perplexing.

At any rate, the nervous young man proceeded slowly through the tall stalks of corn. An unseasonable chill remained in the air, and he shivered slightly as the wind suddenly gusted and a fierce howl echoed over the countryside. As Waldo walked out of the cornfield and down a small grassy slope, the trees at the outer edge of the woods were swaying dramatically, and it wasn't difficult to imagine ominous forms in the shadows they cast. With a final glance back over his shoulder, Waldo entered the deep woods without noticing the sign on the two hundred year old oak tree that proclaimed: *You are now entering the Forest Of Injured Egos.*

The Forest of Injured Egos had been founded twenty years previously by bitter ex-bus driver Brady "Fred" O'Grady. O'Grady, dejected after being fired from his job, where he had toiled in splendid obscurity for eighteen years, and further disenchanted with the world when his better or poorer wife left him for something not quite so bad or poor, decided to find a peaceful spot to ponder his sorry plight. Apparently other men who thought of themselves as failures had emulated him, and as a result O'Grady presided over a thriving male community which was growing nearly as fast as the national divorce rate.

An owl hooted. At least Waldo assumed it was a hoot, not having actually heard one before. Creeping hesitantly along, all at once he noticed that everything had grown completely silent. Since there had been a chorus of crickets chirping only a few footsteps before, he found this most unusual. *That's strange,* he was whispering to himself when a figure suddenly darted out into the open and blocked his path.

"Are you an outcast or intruder?" Demanded the dark shape.

The startled Waldo sensed that he was indeed intruding but, having his iconoclastic pride about him, boldly replied that he was an outcast if ever there was one. The short, stooped, obviously masculine figure, in a voice sounding curiously like a combination of Walter Brennan and Edgar Buchanan, cackled for Waldo to follow him. Ever the trusting and inquisitive dreamer, the nervous young man readily agreed, defying the delicate emotional system which had caused him to run away madly from such things as outdated calendars.

As they walked slowly through the forest, whose blackness was pierced only by stray rays of moonlight, which filtered through the branches of the sturdy, ancient trees in surrealistic bits and pieces, Waldo began hearing noises again, but not ones normally associated with nature. It was then that he started to feel the familiar tingles racing up and down his spine. They were not the Francis Scott Key-type, but the Bermuda Triangle-Flying Saucer-Vlad The Impaler-Lee Harvey Oswald-variety.

They finally came to a clearing, a large open area that was well lit by what appeared to be old fashioned gas streetlights. These lights were hung along intermittent branches, and emitted a faint yellow substance which drifted slowly upwards and settled on the leaves of the trees, leaving a similarly colored tinge there. There wasn't a lamplighter in sight, but the devices certainly bore the mark of late nineteenth century authenticity. In the middle of the clearing, a huge campfire was burning and gathered around it were a large number of ragged-looking men singing a song:

"We're the ones who've been thrown out
The ones they never talk about
We wouldn't agree or give applause
To crooked men or rules and laws
We knew that we could never win
With coats and ties and shirts tucked in
Our brides they took their wedding vows
They're doing it again right now
A single word they didn't mean
They learned it from the silver screen
And so we gave it all away
And wandered here to laugh and play
It's later than you really think
So take a seat and have a drink!"

As they sang the closing line, every head turned directly towards Waldo. Swallowing hard, the nervous young man observed his now visible guide, who was small and fiftyish with long graying hair and matching beard, dressed in a frayed white tee-shirt, brown polyester pants, and a bright red pair of suspenders. His physical appearance, much like his voice, instantly brought to mind Walter Brennan and Edgar Buchanan, although his rather stooped posture and ragged clothing invoked comparisons to Ernest T. Bass as well. Beneath the hair and a sizable amount of dirt, Waldo saw a kind face, however, and he heaved a sigh of relief when the man smiled and extended his hand.

"The name's Brady O'Grady," he said, "but everybody calls me Fred."

"My name is Waldo Billingsly. Pleased to meet you." Waldo shook his hand, a bit surprised that the man's name bore no connection to the events in Dealy Plaza on November 22, 1963.

Fred indicated that Waldo should accept the invitation so fervently expressed in the campfire song's final line and join them in a drink. There was a big pot with a ladle hung on the side that was propped up against a tree, and Fred went over and poured some liquid into a cup, which seemed to materialize out of nowhere.

"Try this." O'Grady smiled. "It's the only thing we drink. It'll warm

232

your insides."

"What is it?" Asked the ever cautious Waldo.

"We call it the Forest Flaming Special. Go ahead-drink up."

"Well, okay..." Waldo lifted the cup and nearly dropped it when saw his name printed clearly on the side.

"We've been expecting you." explained Fred, beginning to laugh.

Brisbane was tired of rapping with Fontaine. He was also very, very high. As often happened when he was in such a condition, he felt a sudden, overpowering, irrational urge. The fredneck had abruptly determined that Waldo was in grave danger, and was in fact transmitting telepathic S.O.S.'s to him, which he hadn't quite decoded.

"Hey dudes, come on!" He exclaimed in a manner which reminded the others of an updated Hardy Boy. "Waldo needs us!"

Phosphate was just as stoned as Brisbane, but he was still in complete control of his mighty mental faculties. "I do not normally feel comfortable exploring unfamiliar territory at night on the strength of a hunch."

"But I'm telling you- Waldo is in trouble and he needs our help! And it is not a hunch, it's a fucking unexplained phenomenon!" The fredneck quickly explained the messages he'd been receiving from Waldo, which he admitted had not been completely deciphered.

The top doo-wopper was not one to leave untapped any of the mind's potential powers, but he couldn't let his tacit acknowledgment that telepathy might exist override any more or less reasonable possibilities. "Brisbane, I really must advise..."

"Shit then, stay here- all of you! I'll go myself!" With that, the fredneck started weaving in a zig-zag fashion towards the general direction of that part of the deep woods where Waldo, by coincidence, happened to be.

"Oh dear, I trust Waldo isn't...oh, dear." The Professor's attention had been diverted from the world of unpublished pamphlets and the journals of midwestern mental patients, and he was tugging at his yellow tie with a great deal of concern.

Phosphate looked at his two fellow Afro-Anarchists. "We can't very well allow Brisbane to walk around alone in the dark in his condition- he may hurt himself."

"Shit, Phos, I don't see Bris nowhere." Bucktooth had turned to watch the fredneck when he departed. "I ain't saying it was like what I saw that hitchhiker do, but..." Bucktooth's teeth were chattering and his blistered mind was growing more coherent with each shiver. "One second I was looking at him walking, and the next..."

With a long sigh, Phosphate marched off along the same path

Brisbane had, and indicated that Fontaine, Bucktooth, and Professor Buckley should follow him.

The three intrepid Afro-Anarchists and the eccentric ex-history teacher formed a most unconventional search party. They combed the cornfield and part of the woods bordering them without, unfortunately, nearing the significant section, but it was soon obvious they had lost Brisbane and could find no trace of Waldo, either.

"Man, how come every time Brisbane or Waldo go anywhere without us they disappear?" Fontaine brought up a surprisingly insightful observation.

"Yeah man, you figure both of them had to take a piss?" Bucktooth chuckled, referring to the fredneck's original disappearance following his entrance into the cornfield to relieve himself. Both he and Fontaine continued, for some reason known only to them, to find amusement in the incident.

"I don't believe I've ever heard of any evidence suggesting a correlation between urination and dematerialization." Phosphate's reply was appropriately flippant.

"Does anyone-that is-doesn't it seem rather cold for this time of year?" The Professor wrapped his thin arms around himself, and drew his colorful orange and green coat a bit tighter.

Fontaine provided the one time pride of the community college with the only answer he was going to get, as he suddenly began careening from side to side in another of his chemically unbalanced dance routines. This triggered Bucktooth into action, and he rapidly matched his fellow Afro-Anarchist step for step. In a few moments, their infernal rapping began again, as the two supposed doo-woppers bounced up and down between the rows of corn stalks, shouting their words with an inebriated passion:

"Yo, here we are in the cold moonlight
I have a feeling it's gonna be a long, long night
We are looking for friends who have disappeared
We are all as high as the stratosphere
There must be something in the soil
'Cause everyone vanishes in Cornoil
I look at the stalks in front of my face
I say something's magic about this place
Homeboy, you ain't never been alive
'Til you travel back to 1865
You gonna say there ain't no place like home
At the Coliseum in ancient Rome
You ain't gonna think that hell is war

When you're face to face with a dinosaur
So let your eyes roll and your fingers snap
While we break into the mystical cornfield rap!"

Neither the Professor nor Phosphate was listening. The eccentric
ex-history teacher had wandered back to the car to peruse more
uncirculated writings from the overhead light inside, as the night sky was
growing overcast, and even those with better eyesight than his would have
found reading in such conditions to be most uncomfortable. Phosphate,
meanwhile, was all "rapped" out by now. Disgruntled with this new form
of urban expression, which he associated with violence and ignorance, and
considered to be symptomatic of the failure and poverty his people seemed
destined to remain forever entrapped in, the leader of the Afro-Anarchists
was propped up under a tree at the mouth of the big woods. He looked for
all the world to be just as introspective as Issac Newton, except it was
unlikely that a big fat joint ever protruded from Sir Isaac's mouth. Slowly
smoking the reefer, the top doo-wopper looked upwards and, despite the
clouds which drifted back and forth across its surface, and made his work
more difficult, started searching the moon again for canals.

"Look around you, Waldo," Fred O'Grady spoke slowly and
succinctly, "and see the shattered lives and busted dreams, the aching
hearts and squelched tempers that are our only legacy to the world. Young
man, there are here among us tonight men who were and are qualified to
serve as lawyers, doctors, judges, congressional representatives, even
President of the United States. But alas, it was their misfortune to wear
their honesty on their shirt sleeves. They were naive enough to believe
what their Sunday school teachers and Boy Scout leaders taught them, and
had they been placed in positions of responsibility and influence they
would have carried out their duties with humble integrity and common
sense. That, of course, could never be permitted, and thus all these poor
souls have found their way here. At least in the Forest Of Injured Egos
they can speak the truth and not have to worry about losing a wife, a job,
or a friend by doing so." O'Grady paused to catch his breath and continue
his lengthy soliloquy. "We determined that you were akin to us, and
bound for the same destiny. Because of this, we made our hiding place
accessible to you, something we do only for those we deem to be pure of
heart and mind. That's why your name was on the cup- it was prepared
especially for you, Waldo. We want you to join us."
Waldo felt both flattered and offended to think that they judged him
worthy to join their kind but rather depressing ranks. The general
atmosphere of the place was one of hopelessness, and it resembled a sort
of graveyard full of men waiting to climb into ready-made holes. His

sensitive nature was touched by their offer, however, and he was aware that his eyes were growing damp. "Uh, Mr. O'Grady..."

"Please, I told you to call me Fred." O'Grady implored, then waved his hand in the direction of the circle of figures encamped around the fire, whose dancing flames illuminated their hapless, haggard faces. "Every man here, Waldo, has a story to tell. Take that fellow there, for instance- Narley Butterfields. He was once the finest toy salesman in all of Philadelphia, but he ran afoul of his superiors by complaining about his industry's lack of safety precautions. He wasn't satisfied with the reforms that were made, and eventually resigned to found his own unusual consumer organization, The Society For The Elimination Of Pointed Edges. His passion for rounding the corners on nearly every product made, however, was not conducive to earning a good living, and he was unable to support his family, who finally abandoned him. Blackballed by the only profession he knew, he arrived here ten years ago, and is one of our most upstanding members. Sitting to his right is Thomas "Tarzan" Whelps. "Tarzan" had a burning ambition to be a television weatherman, but during his first week studying meteorology in college, he suddenly realized that the entire field was a fraud, and only slightly more scientific than numerology. He confronted a local t.v. meteorologist, who was highly paid and renowned in the community, with the dreadful inaccuracy of his own "extended" forecasts for the past two months, and that eminent professional merely smiled and suggested that perhaps another career might be more appropriate for the young student. "Tarzan" was disillusioned to such an extent that after a few more years of aimless wandering from menial job to menial job, he found his way here. We are very proud of him. Then, over there, eating the Reese's peanut butter cups, is old Ebeneezer "Lucky" Chesterfield. "Lucky" is older than anyone else here, and he has spent his entire life defying the medical community by refusing to eat anything but sweets. He maintained for years that sugar was the true staff of life, and he proved it by consuming whole cakes and pies for dinner, and gallons of ice cream just before bedtime. One of his favorite sayings was that he never met a vegetable he liked, or a cookie he didn't. As he grew older and older, without a single health problem, he became more difficult for anyone to explain, and so it was easier for him to settle here, where no one finds his diet questionable or ridiculous, and he can enjoy it. When he last visited a doctor's office, just before he came here, his blood sugar level was found to be over 400. He still chuckles about that. By the way, Waldo, "Lucky" will be 105 next month. All of these men-like you-were destined to enter the Forest Of Injured Egos."

"But...how did they all find you?" A spellbound Waldo inquired.

"How did *you* find us?" O'Grady replied.

"I-I guess it was the sound of everyone singing." Waldo stammered.

"Precisely." O'Grady threw a few thick branches onto the campfire. "You see, Waldo, only those who are tuned in, so to speak, to our wavelength, can hear us. Those voices can be *very* loud, and carry a great distance. Everyone in these woods tonight heard them once, and responded just as you did."

"Yes, well, Fred, I'm honored to think that you want me to be a part of your group, but..." Waldo, who was becoming alarmed that O'Grady and his fellow failures might not permit anyone who'd visited them to leave, struggled to tactfully reject their offer, "I'm afraid, much as I'd like to, that I really can't join you."

"Why not, Waldo?"

"Well, you see, my grandfather disappeared without a trace recently and I came to Iowa to try and find him." For the first time in many hours, Waldo remembered the reason for his being in Cornoil. "I haven't even started looking yet. And besides, I've met this girl and..."

"I see." O'Grady's grizzled face took on an even sadder countenance. "Well, we're not tyrants here- no one is forced to stay against their will. Perhaps we've made a mistake; it wouldn't be the first time. I must request, however, that you not tell anyone of our presence here. If the authorities ever found out about us, we'd be right back on the assembly line."

"Don't worry, your secret's safe with me." Waldo's voice was breaking as he started to edge away from the campfire.

"Wait, I'll show you the way." O'Grady called out. "You'll never find it yourself in the dark. We're very well secluded here."

Waldo glanced back over his shoulder at the pathetic band of unshaven, unfashionably clothed figures- the men who comprised the membership of the Forest Of Injured Egos. Some of them were sadly waving goodbye to him as he quickly turned around and followed Fred O'Grady out of the clearing.

They traveled through the woods in a silence marred only by the sporadic sounds Waldo had heard on the way in, but they seemed far less threatening now. Eventually they reached the grand old oak tree that bore their society's name, and O'Grady uttered a simple farewell.

"Wait." Waldo grasped the Injured Ego's leader by the arm and looked into his eyes. They were full of tears, and the emotional young man had to wipe his own away before he could speak. At length he managed to compose himself. "Mr. O'Grady- I mean Fred- I want to tell you that I admire you and your ideals. It's just that it's all too depressing for me, even if I wasn't searching for my grandfather. I know you're probably right about the world, but I guess I'm still young enough to think I can change things. Who knows, maybe I'll be back here, but I have to tell you that I hope that never happens, as much as I like you. I'll remember where

237

you are, just in case. It was a pleasure to meet you, and I want you to know that you all have at least one person out here who's on your side."

O'Grady seemed genuinely touched by Waldo's rambling bit of sentimentality. "It's not often that I'm wrong about potential Injured Egos. By the way, I forgot to let you have the cup. After all, it's yours. Wait here and I'll..."

Waldo shook his head. "No, you keep it. As a kind of memento."

O'Grady looked like a lost puppy, and it was easy to imagine him wearing the same forlorn expression when he'd been fired after 18 loyal years as a bus driver. "Well then, here's to our never meeting again. Goodbye and good luck, Waldo." With that, he turned and vanished into the strange forest from whence he came.

Waldo heard singing again. This time, however, the voices belonged to Fontaine Washington and Bucktooth Johnson. After departing from the Forest Of Injured Egos, and sauntering about the moonlit cornfield in a rather melancholy mood, he'd approached its edges and been jolted from his thoughts by the latest musical effort of the two junior members of the Afro-Anarchists. Turning to his right, he walked a short distance and discovered the amateur rappers plying their wares in an open spot of land next to the main road. Their work was being performed in front of an occasional vehicle that drove by with its headlights serving as the poor man's version of a spotlight. They were just beginning a number as Waldo approached them:

"My name's Fontaine, his name's Woodrow
You don't want to meet either one of us, though
'Cause we're awful big and we're awful bad
Especially if you happen to make us mad
We'll pick you from our teeth like a Baby Ruth
Remember to call Woodrow 'Bucktooth'
We'll hit you with a left and hit you with a right
And for once you'll be sorry that you are white
My name's Woodrow, his name's Fontaine
We don't look alike, we are not the same
We don't carry a knife, don't carry a gun
But we can kick the shit out of anyone
So leave us alone if you don't want trouble
'Cause when you see us, you're seeing double."

Waldo politely applauded. Then he heard Phosphate's voice.

"Waldo, is that you?" It seemed to be coming from the outskirts of the wooded area which lay a short distance away.

Waldo spotted the top doo-wopper, propped up against the trunk of an elderly tree. Even in the pale light the moon cast from behind its swirling cloud cover, the stoned smile and subdued expression was clearly visible on his face.

"Yes, it's me, Phosphate. What are you all doing out here at this time of night?"

For one who'd spent as many sleepless nocturnal hours as Waldo Billingsly, in far less stimulating environments, this was a ridiculous question indeed.

"Sheeet, you ain't moved your ass outa these cornfields since we got here." Fontaine pointed out in his usual indelicate fashion.

"Actually, Waldo, we followed Brisbane. Have you seen him?" Phosphate was as concerned as someone in his condition could be.

Waldo stamped his cigarette out. "No, I haven't seen him. What do you mean you followed him? Where was he going?"

"He suddenly expressed concern over your welfare, having received telepathic messages indicating you were in grave danger, and ran off to affect your rescue. He was also very high." The sedated head Afro-Anarchist, who was rarely hypocritical, was the last person to throw stones in this regard.

"Yeah man, you know how I saw that hitchhiker vanish right in front of my eyes? Well, I was watching Brisbane..." Bucktooth was interrupted by a sudden commotion in the woods directly behind the tree Phosphate was sitting under.

Before anyone had a chance to become frightened, several "what the fuck's" and "shit's" broke the stillness of the night air and they all knew there wasn't another voice like that in all of Iowa.

"Brisbane!" Everyone exclaimed in unison.

"Where were you, man?" Fontaine demanded. "One minute you're staggering around just ahead of us, and the next you're gone again."

"Shit, man. There is no way you're gonna believe me." Brisbane was out of breath and obviously glad to see them. He looked at Waldo and put his arm around him. "Listen, pal, if I ever make fun of you seeing M.I.B.'s or anything else again, you just punch me right in the nose, okay?"

Waldo ignored the rhetorical question and inquired as to where he had been and why he appeared so shaken.

Brisbane bummed a cigarette from Waldo and quickly lit it. "Damn, that tastes good. Well, I wandered into a section of the woods way over there." The fredneck pointed in the distance towards a location that none of them could see in the dark, but it was apparently somewhere at the farthest end of the property. "You won't believe this, and maybe I was a little high..."

"A *little* high?" Fontaine chuckled, and asked the fredneck exactly what he'd seen.

Brisbane was hesitant. "Well, uh, I don't know. You promise that you guys won't think I'm making it up?"

Phosphate stood up unsteadily. "My friend, we will do nothing of the sort. Now do tell us what it was that you encountered."

"My boy, I think-that is-all of us have experienced the most inconceivable things imaginable since this journey began, so we certainly have no reason to be skeptical at this point." Professor Buckley came striding slowly up the embankment leading to the dirt path, where he'd been reading in the decidedly un-fredneck-like '65 Dodge Dart. "Please tell us..."

"Yeah, don't keep us in suspense, man!" Bucktooth added.

"Alright. First of all, I think I saw a fucking werewolf. As if that wasn't enough, I'm pretty positive he murdered this old dude. It was kinda dark, you know, and those shadows are tricky at night, but that's what it looked like to me. What that old man was doing out in the woods I'll never know, but this-this werewolf or whatever, pounced on him just like, you know, Lon Chaney, Jr. or something, and devoured him. I still can't believe it was real, but it was awful." The fredneck, still extremely rattled, caught his breath before continuing. "Then I heard a thrashing, and it sounded like something really big was coming through the woods. When I looked up, and I really didn't want to, but I did, I saw a green giant. No shit! Just like in those fucking old commercials! He was a real giant, maybe twenty feet tall, I don't know, and he was green! After that I hightailed it out of there, expecting that green giant to crush me at any minute."

Fontaine and Bucktooth stared knowingly at each other with their eyes as wide open as any black Little Rascal's ever were. "You sure you saw that, Bris?" Fontaine asked, sobering rapidly.

"Shit, yeah." The fredneck was as adamant as a U.F.O. abductee, and every bit as affected as one.

"Brisbane," Waldo was starting to tingle slightly again as he nonchalantly glanced at the tops of the trees in the deep woods, half expecting to see a hairless green pate protruding somewhere above them, "Fontaine and Bucktooth told me yesterday that they saw the same kind of giant right here in the cornfield."

"And a werewolf, too." Bucktooth reminded him.

"My friends, I would like to issue a reminder to everyone that our purpose here is not to investigate all these kinds of phenonema, fantastic though they may be, but to locate Waldo's missing grandfather." These words, uttered in a clipped, deliberate fashion by Phosphate, revealed just how drastically the fredneck's homemade herb had altered his personality, as few people on the face on the earth were more interested in the unexplained than the top doo-wopper. "I believe we should initiate our efforts in that regard the first thing tomorrow morning."

Waldo was a little taken aback by the head Afro-Anarchist's abnormal attitude, but dismissed it as being the result of the strong marijuana he'd consumed over the last few hours. "I guess I owe all of you an apology for delaying the search for my grandfather. I'd already planned, though, to definitely go to the Last Chance Relaxation Home tomorrow. The O'Sullivan twins are on duty then, and they said they'll show us around the place. I offered to give them a ride..."

"*What?* You mean they work at that place?" Fontaine verbalized the astonishment all of them felt over this startling coincidence.

"Huh? Oh, I guess I haven't had a chance to tell you yet." Waldo replied.

Brisbane spoke up. "Shit man, I guess you didn't, since we've hardly seen you since you met that chick."

Waldo was a bit embarrassed. "I'm sorry, I didn't mean to forget about all of you."

"That's quite alright, my boy." The Professor ambled over and placed his hand on the nervous young man's shoulder. "I've seen what-that is-*all those endearing young charms*, you know..."

"Well, let's just visit that Hancock dude tomorrow." Brisbane said. "I don't want to spend any more time around here than I have to."

All of the others could concur with those sentiments except Waldo. Despite having encountered more strangeness than the most experienced schizophrenic in the world, he was going to be very reluctant to leave Iowa, with or without his grandfather. Northern Virginia's crop of available women, he felt certain, could never erase the memory of a certain beautiful, underaged girl.

241

13

SAVE THE LAST CHANCE FOR ME

The weary band of revelers soon retired to Central Headquarters, more commonly known as the decidedly un-fredneck-like '65 Dodge Dart, and everyone except Phosphate and the Professor fell asleep shortly thereafter. Having consumed far too much of Brisbane's powerful homemade concoction, the top doo-wopper grew frustrated at lying uncomfortably in the front seat of the cramped vehicle, so he left the car and went for a walk, feeling that the night air and the exercise might clear his head.

He was promptly followed by Professor Buckley, who had reverted back to his customary state of perpetual wakefulness.

"I say-that is-please wait a moment, Phosphate." The eccentric ex-history teacher lengthened his stride and drew abreast of the head Afro-Anarchist. "Do you mind the company?"

"Of course not, Professor." Phosphate smiled, with the sort of sincerity no drug could eliminate. "I'd be honored."

"Just a-that is-I must say," the Professor lowered his voice and gestured nonchalantly back over his shoulder in the general direction of the other side of the dirt path, "I didn't want to say anything in front of your fellow vocalists, for fear of unduly alarming them, but did you notice..."

"That *Grandpa's Place* is no longer there?" The top doo-wopper interrupted. "I did indeed, Professor, the next time I passed the spot after our memorable experience there. I failed to mention it aloud previously because I considered its absence to be self-explanatory. We seem to be in some sort of dematerialization zone; I'm surprised, in fact, that the cornfield itself hasn't evaporated into nothingness."

"Yes, yes, of course." Professor Buckley responded, sheepishly patting down one of his few remaining strands of hair.

As they strolled around the outskirts of the magical cornfield, lost in a typically odd, introspective discussion, Phosphate began to feel somewhat better. He was just thinking of suggesting to the Professor that they return to the car when he saw an unusual light flickering in the sky directly overhead. The top doo-wopper blinked his eyes several times to make sure they were functioning properly, but the light was still there. It was growing gradually bigger and it soon became clear to Phosphate that if he didn't move quickly whatever it was would land squarely on top of him.

"What the..." Professor Buckley was staring up in wonder as well.

Wasting no time, Phosphate ran for the woods in a manner

reminiscent of Waldo Billingsly and/or other frightened doo-wop protest singers, and took refuge behind the first tree he came to. The Professor arrived at an adjoining tree a moment later, breathing heavily and tugging at his yellow tie.

As he cautiously peered around the tree, the top doo-wopper saw that the light was now taking on a visible shape. It appeared to be a one hundred percent, dyed-in-the-wool unidentified flying object. The oval craft, with a row of soothing, hypnotic blue lights circling its bottom, hovered over the cornfield for a brief time, in true classical fashion, then softly touched down. As the now thoroughly shaken leader of the Afro-Anarchists kept his eyes glued to the craft, a portal opened and two tiny figures emerged from the interior.

"Hey you!"

A voice from behind startled Phosphate to such an extent that he jumped as high as a power forward in the back row at a wet tee- shirt contest. The Professor reacted just as strongly, instinctively running from the direction of the voice, and hitting his head on one of the larger, lower branches in the process, knocking himself unconscious. Turning around slowly, so distracted that he didn't even notice the Professor lying prostrate on the ground a short distance away, Phosphate was surprised to find only a small dog there. It was a rather unimpressive creature, of a mixed or "mutt" variety that no self-respecting breeder would ever allow near his pure-breds, and no dog show would grant admission to.

The dog looked at him quizzically. "Yeah, I'm the one who talked." The voice was as clear as any cartoon character's.

Phosphate rubbed his eyes again. Analyzing the bizarre circumstances in his usual calm, dispassionate manner, he questioned the animal. "But you have no vocal chord function. How is it possible for you to speak?"

The dog smiled, or so it seemed to Phosphate. "You ridiculous human. I can do whatever I want. Do you think that we of the superior canine species are bound by your elementary laws of science?"

The top doo-wopper shook his head. "No, I suppose not. But what do you want with me?"

"I want you to come with us." The dog lifted one of his mangy paws and pointed towards the spaceship.

"What?" Whatever narcotic remnants remained in Phosphate's bloodstream had completely dissipated by now. "Are you some sort of alien dog?" The head Afro-Anarchist's extensive knowledge of U.F.O. abductee cases was little cause for comfort at this point.

The diminutive dog was slowly creeping towards him. "As you cliche-laden Earthlings would say, that's for me to know and you to find out."

243

Phosphate, however, was not waiting to find out anything. With a sudden rush of adrenaline, he made a valiant run for it. Taking off on a tear across the cornfield, the top doo-wopper glanced back over his shoulder and saw that the talkative spacedog was right behind him, accompanied by the two tiny humanoids he'd seen leaving the U.F.O. Soon the effects of his lack of physical conditioning, combined with the massive amount of marijuana he'd sucked into his lungs, became evident as he grew weaker and began gasping for breath. His legs were rapidly turning to rubber, and with a final dramatic leap forward, he plunged heavily to the ground. Fully expecting to feel alien fangs ripping into him at any moment, he buried his face in the rich Midwestern soil and awaited the inevitable.

He lay there shaking for several minutes but nothing happened. Pulling his face from the dirt, Phosphate rose up on one knee. He looked all around him, but there were no signs of the spacedog and the humanoids. The U.F.O. had also vanished without the usual impossible mid-air maneuvering, or any fanfare at all. The top doo-wopper positioned himself Indian-style on the ground and tried to quietly assess the situation. Whatever its basis in reality, this incident seemed indelibly linked to all the others which had transpired previously. It was almost comically incomprehensible, and once again, grave danger had been averted at the last moment and no one had been harmed. As he mulled this over, Phosphate suddenly remembered the Professor, and darted back to the woods as fast as his aching legs would carry him.

He found the spot where he'd last seen the one time pride of the local community college, but Hiram Buckley wasn't there. In fact, he didn't appear to be anywhere. Phosphate scoured the edges of the wooded area, shouting out the Professor's name in an increasingly alarmed voice, but there was no reply. Eventually, he paused to rest on a tree stump and castigated himself for what he perceived to be a selfish interest in his own safety, at the expense of his elder comrade. He wasn't as skilled in this field as Waldo, but he managed to make himself feel quite guilty nevertheless. It was nearing dawn when he finally abandoned his efforts to locate the eccentric ex-history teacher.

When he reached the welcome sight of Brisbane's old automobile, the top doo-wopper thanked the Lord that he'd been spared whatever fate Hiram Buckley had met. He also fretted over having to relate to the others, once they awakened, the distressing news that the Professor was missing. Carefully opening the door, he nuzzled into his front seat cubbyhole and replayed the night's harrowing ordeal in his mind over and over again.

While Phosphate was joining the ranks of those irritating witnesses

244

who insist they've sighted something unidentified in the sky (and the even more confounding few who've interacted with the denizens within them), the fredneck was experiencing another of his recurring dreams, "Brisbane's 501st Fat Boy Nightmare":

Fade to a very important Little League baseball game, circa 1967. The winner will be the league champion and go on to the state tournament. There are two outs in the bottom of the sixth and final inning, and the fat but skilled eleven year old Brisbane Wrock is at bat. His team is trailing by one run and there are runners on first and second base. Brisbane prides himself on being a clutch performer and welcomes this situation. After taking two called strikes, he sees the pitch he wants heading for the outside corner of the plate. The future fredneck swings and the bat meets the ball solidly, driving it into the right-centerfield gap, and it rolls all the way to the fence. Both runs score and Brisbane's team wins the championship. He is mobbed by his teammates in the finest moment of his young life, and he understandably exults in the cheers and wants them to last forever.

When he returns home after the game, Brisbane eagerly tells his parents what happened. His mother lovingly congratulates him, but then she thinks everything he does is great. His father, who has ignored Brisbane's repeated requests to attend the Little League games, is not so enthusiastic. He has been drinking, as usual, and in a short time manages to dissect his son's laudable exploit with a critique the world's highest paid ballplayer shouldn't have to endure.

"Well, fatass," he starts out, referring to him with one of his more endearing and favorite nicknames, "did you make any errors?"

Brisbane replies by saying no, but this doesn't deter him.

"I bet you made a goddamn error, didn't you?" He asks, as if there were a choice of answers.

Brisbane has been through this ritual so often that it is second nature by now, and he knows that a failure to admit an error will result in his father taking the belt to him. At least if he lies and tells him what he wants to hear, the abuse will remain merely verbal. And so the chubby youngster hangs his head and untruthfully confesses to this terrible offense.

The elder Wrock laughs with sadistic glee. "Aha! I knew it! What makes you think you can play baseball? If I've told you once, I've told you a thousand times: you're too goddamned fat to play baseball. Why don't you quit and stop making such an ass out of yourself?"

Brisbane hangs his head a little lower and tries not to cry. Despite the many times he's participated in this routine, it never fails to bring him to tears. This is, of course, what his drunken father most desires. As soon as he spots his son starting to sob and sniffle, he smiles that evil, alcoholic grin.

"Now, I hope you're not crying, are you?" With that, he motions Brisbane towards him, then slaps his son's forehead. It stings mightily but the rotund youth resists crying out in pain. "Now, we're not going to cry, are we?"

Brisbane stands there like a miniature soldier until his father releases him. As he goes to his room, he hears his parents begin to argue. It is the same argument they always have, where his mother's attempts to defend him from another imagined offense are disregarded by his father, who berates her until she gives up and ignores him. Burying his head in his pillow, Brisbane tries to muffle all sound so he doesn't have to listen to any more drunken nonsense. When his tears stop, he lies awake all night wondering what it would be like to be skinny and have guys wanting to be your friend, or know that a cute girl liked you, or be able to buy clothes without going to special, embarrassing shops. These are frequent fantasies of Brisbane's.

The next day is a Friday, and Brisbane is planning on attending the sixth grade dance that night. After school, he tells his parents that he would like to go. His mother is excited and supportive, as she always is, but his father simply orders the future fredneck to bring him another beer. After Brisbane gives it to him, he begins asking his son why he wants to go to the dance.

"You think any goddamn girl is going to dance with a fatass like you?" He snorts cruelly. "You can't dance. You'll just look like an idiot."

Brisbane runs to his room and hears a barrage of inebriated cackles behind him. A half hour goes by and his mother knocks on the bedroom door with unexpected news.

"Guess what, hon?" She asks with the kind of smile parents are supposed to wear when they look at their children. "I talked your father into letting you go to the dance!"

Brisbane is so happy that he hugs his mother for a good minute. Then he starts preparing for the dance.

When he arrives at the dance later that night, he is as confident as an overweight child can be. His hair is neatly combed, and he is wearing a nice, fashionable suit with a new tie his mother bought especially for this occasion. As Brisbane walks in, he gravitates toward a group of boys that are his friends. One of them, whom the future fredneck considers a particularly good buddy, draws Brisbane aside and whispers that the girl he's had a crush on all year, Janice Ingraham, likes him. Brisbane's little heart starts fluttering and he feels on top of the world. He can't wait to see her and ask her to dance, but at the same time he fears facing her because he simply can't believe such a pretty girl could like a fat boy. All the other fellows in the group reassure him that the girl really likes him.

Then he sees her. She is wearing a lovely pink party dress and she looks as desirable as Raquel Welch to Brisbane's eleven year old eyes. His chubby knees are shaking and his palms are sweating as he cautiously walks over to her.

"H-h-h-h-hi." Brisbane manages to stutter at her.

She looks at Brisbane and smiles politely. "Oh, hi there."

The chubby youngster licks his lips nervously and finally drums up the courage to ask her if she would like to dance.

She stares at Brisbane as if he'd asked her to remove her dress. Then she starts to laugh. "You actually think I'd dance with...*you?*"

Brisbane turns as red as a beet and hastily makes his retreat. As he passes by the group of boys he'd supposed were his friends, they howl with mean-spirited laughter and shout out derisive and un-original comments. Brisbane doesn't want to afford them any further opportunities, so he runs as fast as his fat legs will carry him until he is out of the building.

Brisbane sits alone on the curbstone in front of the school, his young heart broken and his world devastated. The worst part of it is that he cannot confide in anyone because it's too painful and embarrassing to discuss. Later, when his mother picks him up, she asks if he had a good time, and Brisbane informs her that he did, having danced with all the prettiest girls there. Then the future fredneck asks her if she would mind baking him one of her delicious homemade cakes. After all, that always seems to make him feel better.

The morning dawned cold and clear, with a rare June frost lightly coating the corn stalks. When everyone had awakened, Phosphate inhaled deeply and told the others how he'd seen a U.F.O., conversed with an alien dog, and lost Professor Buckley. Everyone reacted indignantly to the last piece of information.

"Damn, man, how the hell could you sleep after he disappeared?" Brisbane demanded.

Waldo shook his head sadly. "I can't help feeling disappointed, Phosphate. Why didn't you wake us? We could have helped you look."

"Yeah, the trail's probably as cold as a spinster's ass by now." Bucktooth remarked descriptively.

"How could you *sleep*, Phos?" Fontaine echoed.

Phosphate, more accustomed to being lauded by his comrades than criticized, was visibly rattled. "I-I have no real defense. I suppose, like many of our craftiest politicians, I could blame it on an outside influence-in this case unusually powerful marijuana-but I won't stoop to that. I can only apologize profusely and recommend we search the woods again immediately."

247

After a few more moments of castigating Phosphate, everyone raced towards the woods, with the embattled top doo-wopper leading the way. When they reached the general area where the eccentric ex-history teacher had last been seen, the five of them split off in different directions, shouting his name.

"Hey, over here!" Brisbane screamed a few minutes later.

The others rushed over to where the fredneck stood, pointing excitedly at the base of a massive oak tree. Lying there, under the tree, to everyone's horror, was Hiram Buckley's distinctive yellow tie. It was torn and stained with blood.

"Oh, no!" Waldo cried, picking up the tie and running his fingers lovingly across it. "It can't be! Please, not the Professor!"

"And look at this," Fontaine was a few feet away, holding aloft Professor Buckley's beloved briefcase. "It was behind the..."

"Shit man, I-I guess either the werewolf or the green giant..."

"Brisbane, please." Phosphate, as wracked with guilt as he was, still had the presence of mind to interrupt the fredneck's tacky assessment of the situation. "Under the circumstances, I think it would be best to return to the car." The top doo-wopper then took the briefcase from Fontaine, and held it tightly against his bosom, as if he were protecting it from someone.

"Yeah, man, with all the wild shit around here," Fontaine observed, "it's pretty obvious we ain't gonna be seeing him any more."

Waldo remained there for a moment, staring at the Professor's tie, and at the spot of earth where he must have met his demise. He'd questioned the worth of coming to Iowa many times during the course of their rollicking, fantastic trek there, but never more so than now. If Professor Buckley had indeed been murdered by some monstrous creature, or silenced by the same forces who'd abducted his grandfather, then visiting an aged mental patient at the Last Chance Relaxation Home was not likely to be a very productive line of pursuit. Eventually he dropped the tie resignedly back under the tree and exited the woods with Brisbane's arm around him.

"Shit, man," the fredneck spoke as soothingly as he could, "you've known about Them for a long time, dude. If They got the Professor, he sure wasn't the first one."

"I-I know." Waldo sniffled. "But that doesn't make it any easier."

As they approached the car, Waldo's mood temporarily brightened. Jeanne O'Sullivan was waiting for him. The lovely teenager was holding a plate of fresh buckwheat pancakes, but the nervous young man completely ignored their mouth-watering scent, laid his head on her shoulder, and cried like a baby.

Later that morning, everyone gathered at Brisbane's car and made preparations, in spite of the apparently tragic end of Hiram Buckley, to visit the Last Chance Relaxation Home. It was the consensus belief that they'd traveled a great distance for just that purpose, and to leave without doing so would be something the Professor would strongly disapprove of. The Afro-Anarchists, along with Brisbane and Janie, were growing a bit impatient, however, with "America's Favorite Couple," as Fontaine jokingly referred to Waldo and Jeanne. The young lovers had yet to return from the cornfield, where they'd gone soon after Waldo informed her about the Professor, to comfort each other and/or engage in a bit of time traveling.

Brisbane was, for some unknown reason, now exhibiting an aloof attitude towards Janie, who was standing next to him and trying to be friendly. "Shit man, where do you think they are this time?" The fredneck asked no one in particular.

Janie, confused over Brisbane's inexplicably distant demeanor, was somewhat worried herself. "Yeah, if they don't get here soon, we won't have any time to show you guys around the place before we start working."

Brisbane was about to blurt out a cynical comment expressing his disapproval of whirlwind romances when Waldo and Jeanne abruptly materialized in front of them.

"Hi, everybody! I hope we're not too late!" Jeanne was, in fact, concerned that they were.

"Not if we leave right now." There was more than a trace of sarcasm in her twin sister's voice.

Waldo was too preoccupied with other concerns to care about punctuality. The grief and remorse he felt about Professor Buckley had been greatly assuaged by the morning's activities, which consisted of a journey back to the Egyptian age, where they'd made love in the shadow of the Great Pyramid of Cheops.

"Shit man, where were you?" Brisbane inquired in a bellicose tone.

Waldo lit a cigarette. "I'll tell you later. We better get going, or else the girls will be late for work."

Everyone piled into Brisbane's decidedly un-fredneck-like '65 Dodge Dart. It was taken for granted that Jeanne would sit on Waldo's lap, but it was with a great deal of hesitation that her sister finally placed herself gingerly on top of Brisbane, permitting the cramped old vehicle to accommodate them all.

Bucktooth started the engine. "You know, it just don't seem right, going off without the Professor."

"My friend," Phosphate began to pontificate, "in the struggle between the forces of good and evil, about which Professor Buckley wrote so eloquently, there have been a great many casualties. I can't imagine he could have devised a more fitting end for himself. That is, *if* it was the end."

"What do you mean, Phos?" Fontaine asked. "Damn, you saw that blood on his tie, and you know what kind of wild things we saw around those woods."

"I realize that, Fontaine," Phosphate replied, "but I am merely keeping in mind the other misadventures we've all been a part of, and how nothing has heretofore harmed us. In that vein, perhaps we'd better not bury the Professor just yet, until we reach a more definitive answer to other questions, like who or what was responsible for Waldo's grandfather's disappearance."

Waldo felt somewhat comforted by the top doo-wopper's postulation, and he squeezed Jeanne's slender waist a bit tighter.

They drove on for several miles, down the dirt path, without encountering another automobile, and in almost total silence. All of them were anxious at being so close to the midwestern mental institution they'd come so far to see, and busily pondering what might await them there. At length, the path turned into a paved road, but still there weren't any other vehicles in sight.

"Uh...ain't there usually more traffic around here?" Bucktooth asked suspiciously.

"It does seem a little deserted today." Jeanne answered innocently.

Waldo's heart began racing as a sign, which wasn't purple, came into view indicating that the Last Chance Relaxation Home was imminent. Then he saw it.

Rising all at once over the tops of the trees which lined the right side of the road was a huge, ten story building that appeared displaced amidst the scenic rural setting. It was obviously an old structure, judging by the thick ivy clinging to the sides and the dreary black iron fence that surrounded it. Every brick in its frame was dull and lifeless, and the individual air conditioning units which protruded from each window clearly belied any commitment to comfort, technology, and convenience. It was easy to gaze upon the enormous, intimidating building and picture the strait jackets and bruised fists within it, as well as hear the demented cries from the padded rooms.

"Well, shit, Waldo, take a good look-there it is!" The fredneck's investigative juices were beginning to flow.

"Damn, that place looks awful big and creepy!" Fontaine expressed everyone's feelings nicely.

Waldo nodded and grasped Jeanne's hand for support.

They drove through the imposing front gates, which might have adorned the facade of any classic haunted house, and were directed towards the left, where the visitors' parking was, by a gangly young female in a yellow rain coat. Distracted as they were, none of them noticed the peculiarity in this, for it wasn't raining. There were only a few cars parked in the huge lot, and Bucktooth was able to find a space close to the building.

Waldo's knees were trembling as he unsteadily pulled himself from the car. "You know, I'm a little frightened." He whispered to Jeanne.

She kissed him tenderly on the cheek. "You have nothing to worry about, silly."

As they began walking up the sidewalk towards the main entrance, a man was coming out of the place. Waldo only caught a glimpse of his face before he jumped into a black Cadillac that was waiting in front, but that was enough to make him shudder. He looked exactly like the hitchhiker.

The Last Chance Relaxation Home's lobby was large, with expensive Persian rugs ornamenting the hardwood floors, typically uncomfortable hard back chairs with blue velvet cushions, evenly spaced sofas with impressionistic designs woven into the conservative padding, finely polished cherry desks and tables with white marble tops, and soft, recessed lighting. Immediately upon walking through the heavy wooden doors, which weren't automatic, an overpowering aura of depression, as well as a respectful silence, hit them all.

Waldo led the way, with a great deal of trepidation, towards the information desk, which was situated directly in the center of the lobby. Behind its shining marble veneer sat a pretty young girl with dirty-blonde hair and a marvelous tan.

"Hi. Can I help you?" She asked when Waldo was within ten feet of the desk.

"Uh, well, I-I-I wanted to," Waldo was overwhelmed at finally being *there*, and might easily have been mistaken for someone who was being committed, "well, uh, ask, you know..."

"Relax. We want to do our best for everyone here." The girl smiled, displaying a set of polished white teeth that contrasted nicely with her bronze skin.

"Uh, sure, but I-I, well..."

"Who's responsible for him?" The girl gestured towards the babbling Waldo and glanced around at the others with her eyebrows raised and her lips pursed in a businesslike demeanor.

"Madam," Phosphate stepped forward to clarify matters for his rattled friend, "I believe you have formed a mistaken impression of our purpose here. The young gentleman who has been addressing you would like to visit a patient, and that..."

"Oh, I'm sorry." The girl instantly reverted back to her bubbly receptionist mode. "I don't make that kind of mistake often. What was the patient's name?"

Waldo swallowed, but the lump in his throat was still there. "Uh, Sam Hancock."

"Hancock, hmmm." The girl played with her computer terminal for a few moments, then shook her head with a phony air of disappointment. "There doesn't seem to be anybody here by that name."

"Oh, well," Waldo was numbed by the realization that he'd traveled such a great distance to see someone who wasn't there, "he was admitted here a-a long time ago, and I-I guess it was kind of unlikely..."

"How long ago?" The girl asked with a renewed bit of enthusiasm.

"1969."

"Oh, well, in that case," she jotted something down on a piece of paper and handled it to Waldo, "he'd be in Old Files. It's down at the end of the main hallway on the left. All of his records would be stored there."

Waldo accepted the slip of paper and, without reading it, began walking absentmindedly in the direction of the main hallway.

"I don't recognize that girl at the desk." Jeanne declared. "Do you think she's new?"

"I've never seen her either." Janie replied.

"Hey man," Brisbane grabbed him by the shoulder, "what did that chick write?"

Waldo shrugged and glanced at the slip of paper in his hands. Written upon it, in a characteristically young feminine hand, was: *There are several openings in the Central Supply department.*

A general debate ensued over whether or not, considering the cryptic, unprofessional nature of the note, they ought to leave at once. After a brief exchange, it was decided that they'd come too far to allow yet another odd incident to drive them away, and they marched off down the main hallway.

Old Files was exactly where the young girl had said it would be. Waldo opened the door and they entered a small office with a potent mildew smell wafting through it.

A young man with a clean shaven head looked up from the *Mad* magazine he was reading. "What can I do for you?"

"Well," Waldo spoke with a bit more confidence, "you see, the girl at the front desk told us that I could find the records of a certain patient here..."

"Patient's name?" The bald young man intoned mechanically.

"Sam Hancock."

The young man with the shaved head rifled through several folders which were stored in the bottom drawer of his desk, then pulled one out and laid it in front of him. "I can't give you any information about that patient. It's confidential."

"What?" Waldo licked his lips nervously. "I-I don't understand. If he's a patient, can't he receive visitors?"

"Lots of patients here aren't allowed visitors." The bald young man grinned, revealing two missing teeth in front. "There *is* a way you can see any patient, however."

"And how is that?" Phosphate inquired.

"Work here." The bald young man answered with an even larger grin on his pock-marked face. "Personnel's the next door down."

Fontaine led the charge of the unemployed brigade, and they burst from the office, as much from the mere mention of work as from any fear or suspicion over the staff of the institution being strangely interested in their finding jobs there.

When they were safely out in the hall, Bucktooth began striding back towards the entrance.

"Man," he called out over his shoulder, "you all can have this place!"

"Bucktooth, please stay with us." Phosphate urged, and found, after a few tense moments, that his powers of persuasion over his doo-wopping cohorts were still intact. Throwing his arm around Bucktooth in a fatherly manner, he smiled at the others. "I believe that we should obtain employment here."

"What?" Brisbane cried. "Shit man, you sound crazy enough to have your own room here!"

"Damn, Phos, you can't be serious!" Fontaine's mouth had dropped open in shock. "I mean, it's one thing to visit this weird place, but to work..."

"Alright, gentlemen. Let me explain." The top doo-wopper lowered his voice, so that the handful of passersby in the hallway couldn't hear him. "It seems apparent that *someone* or *something* wants us to find positions here. A logical assumption would be that the same *someone* or *something* was responsible for the disappearance of Waldo's grandfather. I feel strongly that, if we are ever to solve that mystery, which is the ostensible reason for our being here, then we must play by *their* rules, at least for now. Remember, Old Hoss Highway brought us to this facility by a most unlikely route, in an impossibly short period of time."

"That's true." Waldo admitted. "But, still..."

"Ah, come on, honey." Jeanne tugged at his arm with a child-like innocence. "You guys are making too much out of everything. I think it would be really neat if you worked here."

"You know," Fontaine observed, "I never thought I'd say it, but we sure need the money."

"Shit man," the fredneck nodded, "that's right. One paycheck for each of us would more than pay for the trip home."

With that, the O'Sullivan twins reluctantly left them to report for duty at Volunteer Services, and the five less than intrepid would be-rescuers, each of them blessed with a powerful love of freedom and an extremely poor work ethic, tentatively headed for the door marked "Personnel."

The relatively young woman with the anonymous business appearance didn't bother to look up from her crossword puzzle as they entered the Personnel department.

"Excuse me, madam, but we would like to inquire into the matter of employment." Phosphate, with his sporadic work record, was not as adept in discussing this topic as he was most others.

The woman, whose dark brown hair was drawn into a tight, unattractive bun on the top of her head, peered over her eyeglasses, which were perched halfway down her pointed nose in a style once popularized by librarians, and handed the head of the Afro-Anarchists a number of applications.

"Fill these out," she instructed, "then return them to me when you're finished."

Waldo, whose stomach was churning from a combination of hunger and anticipation, sat down in one of the desks, which were identical to those used in public schools, and scanned his application.

"Hey man, what am I supposed to put where it asks for the names of your previous employers?" A befuddled Bucktooth wondered aloud. "Ain't nobody gonna hire me if I put down that shit."

Fontaine elbowed him from the adjoining desk. "Shut up, Buck! You think that's the kind of stuff they want to hear in the Personnel office?"

The woman seated at the desk only a few feet away kept working on her crossword puzzle as if she didn't hear.

They were not the most industrious lot, and each of them had a checkered past, to say the least, as far as jobs were concerned. As they struggled to fill out the forms in an appropriate fashion, they all dealt with their respective employment records:

Employment History-Woodrow "Bucktooth" Johnson:
1976-*McSpeedy's*. Position- French Fry Boy. Reason for leaving-became tired of cooking french fries.
1977-*Burger World*. Position- Senior French Fry Boy/Secret Sauce Mixer. Reason for leaving- couldn't stand the pressure of not divulging the secret sauce ingredients.
1978-1979-*J-Mart*. Position- Stockboy. Reason for leaving- caught smoking dope on the job.
1981-*Hardly's*. Position- Assistant Supervisor of French Fries.

Reason for leaving- felt it was time to branch out from the world of french fries.

1982-*Stillman's Department Store*. Position- Janitor. Reason for leaving- conducted unsuccessful sit-down strike over management's refusal to change job title to the more professional sounding Sanitary Engineer.

1983-*Humans Drug Store*. Position- Soda Jerk. Reason for leaving- job was not challenging enough.

1984-Becomes member of the Afro-Anarchists.

Employment History-Fontaine Washington:
1975-1979-*Fairfield Hospital*. Position- Sanitary Engineer. Reason for leaving- due to having to clean isolation rooms, he contracted many rare diseases over the years. Eventually his fear that one of these might prove fatal motivated him to quit.

1980-1982-*Barlow Hospital*. Position- Laundry Aide. Reason for leaving- was fired for attempting to smother his supervisor with a pile of contaminated linen.

1982-1983-*Danny Lou's Chinatown*. Position- Cashier/Junior Toilet Cleaner. Reason for leaving- was fired for striking supervisor with a tray of hot egg rolls.

1983-*Lone Ranger's*. Position- French Fry Boy. Reason for leaving-fired for striking an unruly customer with a "Tonto" commemorative cup.

1984-Becomes member of the Afro-Anarchists.

Employment History-Phosphate Jefferson:
1974-*Dino's*. Position- French Fry Boy. Reason for leaving- left to pursue a new job with more career potential.

1975-1978-*Little Creek Nursing Home*. Position- Orderly. Reason for leaving- discovered smoking dope with several patients.

1979-1981-*U Buy Us Realty*. Position- Realtor. Reason for leaving-found it hard to obtain the connections necessary for successful real estate career, due to his status as a poor black homeless person.

1983-*Big Man's House Of Red Meat*. Position- Butter and Bun Boy. Reason for leaving- persistent lectures to customers on healthy eating habits were not appreciated by management.

1983-Decides to enter the field of doo-wop protesting, founds the first group devoted exclusively to such music, and names them the Afro-Anarchists.

Employment History-Brisbane Wrock:
1974-*Dino's*. Position- French Fry Boy. Reason for leaving- was discovered smoking dope in employee restroom.

1974-*Burger Barn.* Position- Secret Sauce Boy. Reason for leaving-was discovered smoking dope in employee restroom.

1975-*Sheepsdale Inn.* Position- Dishwasher/Toilet Cleaner. Reason for leaving- discovered smoking dope in employee restroom.

1978-*Rubetown Animal Shelter.* Position- Caretaker/Janitor. Reason for leaving- discovered feeding dope to the animals.

1979-*McSpeedy's.* Position- Assistant Manager in Charge of Quarter Pounders With Cheese. Reason for leaving- fired for telling female customer to "fuck off, bitch" when she complained about her quarter pounder without cheese.

1980-*Clem's Fat And Grease Haven.* Position- Butter and Bun Boy/Toilet Cleaner Crew Leader. Reason for leaving- discovered sprinkling marijuana on various buns.

1981-*Big Eb's Gas And Go-* Position- cashier/service station attendant. Reason for leaving- failed to meet his quota of false directions to unwitting motorists.

1981-1983-*Sunflower Record And Head Shop.* Position- Cassette Boy/ Bong Boy. Reason for leaving- discovered stealing drug paraphenalia.

1985-*Grit Newspaper.* Position- Newspaper Carrier. Reason for leaving- unable to sell the product.

Employment History-Waldo Billingsly:
1974-*Wagon Wheel Restaurant.* Position- Butter and Bun Boy/Bus Boy. Reason for leaving- left to obtain better, cleaner job.

1974-*Seven Shadows Amusement Park.* Position- Big Dipper Operator. Reason for leaving- fired for allowing the rides to last too long.

1975-1979-*Pinecrestview Golf Course.* Position- Range Ball Boy/ Sand Trap Raker. Reason for leaving- had been employed steadily (albeit in a seasonal capacity) for four years, felt he needed a few years off.

1981-1985-*Shimmering Tranquil Mental Health Clinic.* Position- Part-Time-Aide/Orderly. Reason for leaving- became sick of being smashed in the forehead by overaggressive patients during highly competitive ping-pong games.

Bucktooth, with a dubious grin on his face, was first to hand his completed form, filled with impressive but incorrect information on it, to the woman at the desk. The others followed suit within a few moments of each other.

After they'd each turned in their applications, the woman peered over her glasses without even reading them and astonished them by asking simply, "when can you boys start?"

"Well, uh, whenever..." Waldo was startled by this unchecked, blanket approval.

"Fine, then." The woman answered crisply. "It just so happens that there are five openings on the day shift in the Central Supply department. The starting pay is quite good for this area- $8.00 an hour. You will report as soon as possible to the basement and ask for Mr. Duck Hung."

"Pardon me, Madam," Phosphate said, "but as I understand it, a physical examination of prospective employees is usually a requirement in all places of business. Then, of course, the time to process the paperwork..."

"You look fine to me." The woman replied sarcastically. "If you don't want jobs, then say so."

"We want jobs, but it seems a little odd that there are five openings at one time in the same department on the same shift." Brisbane remarked.

The woman winced noticeably at this, and patted the bun on top of her head. "It is a bit unusual, but I assure you that they are legitimate positions. What do you think we are here- some sort of voodoo, alien vampires?" With that, she began laughing hysterically in a way that made them anxious to leave the employment office.

"No, no, that's fine, really." Waldo's forced smile stopped the woman's maniacal laughter. "We'll report at once to Mr..."

"Hung. Duck Hung. In the basement. Elevators are down the hall and to your left."

"Thank you." They all exclaimed and exited quickly.

From the notorious Diary of Mad Millard Billingsly, May 18, 1917:

It is so lovely up here in the mountains...I seem to be able to think more clearly. Summon the Kaiser at once! No? Well, then where are the strange beasts that supposedly inhabit these ranges? I have seen none and I want my money back! Today I found a lonely woman nearby and I have christened her Mona Lisa. We shall sail together for Rome as soon as I accomplish my work here. But so much work! Tomorrow is rock collection day, the next will be count the cloud formations, then sweep out the cave day, and so on. Even as I sit here writing this, They are outside listening to the sound of the pen gliding across the paper. They fear me almost as much as I fear Them. The light shows in these parts are fantastic and every night I am privileged to meet another little creature from some different place. The whole batty world can be laughed at from this altitude, and I am just the one to do the laughing. I am so sorry to be missing out on civilization, but that is the price you pay for having this kind of fun. Well, the Mona Lisa will be coming over shortly for some midnight bird-watching and...what is *that?* Oh, dear, I don't believe it! They are here...

"You the new guys? Take this goddamn shit up now!"

Waldo stared at his new boss, Duck Hung, a diminutive Vietnamese gentleman who had no sooner introduced himself than he began issuing profane and ungrammatical orders.

"Shit man, we don't know where anything is." Brisbane stated the obvious.

"Goddamn shit! Just take up to fourth floor and leave at nurses' desk!" It did not appear to Waldo that Duck Hung, who was slightly overweight and looked to be in his early forties, possessed an overabundance of tact or patience. "You and you go. Rest of you goddamn guys stay here."

Their high strung supervisor had pointed to Waldo and Brisbane, so they each took a cart of supplies and headed for the fourth floor. Duck Hung had already presented their nametags to them, upon which the title of Junior Material Handler was proudly engraved, and lectured them about the tremendous responsibility involved in delivering all supplies, both medical and otherwise, throughout the facility.

Brisbane was still marveling that the time-traveling O'Sullivan twins just happened to be volunteer candy-stripers at the Last Home (Jeanne and Janie had informed them that all the doctors and nurses repeatedly used this morbid abbreviation in front of the patients). It was a coincidence unbelievable enough to make a Warren Commission apologist blush with embarrassment. As they walked through the endless halls of the basement, however, Waldo's interest was being drawn more towards the institution itself.

It was becoming increasingly clear that the Last Chance Relaxation Home was more like a conventional hospital than a mental health facility. It was certainly bigger than most mental institutions, and Waldo questioned whether such a large place could be full of mentally ill people. Could there be that many disturbed Iowans? There was, after all, he wittily mused to himself, only a limited number of dispossessed farmers who'd been foreclosed upon and driven unbalanced in the process. And of course there was the point Waldo tried hard not to ponder: why had Sam Hancock been sent all the way to the heart of the Midwest? More importantly, who had committed him there? Waldo was well aware that Hancock had no family to speak of, his only known friend had been Old Hoss, and there were obviously a great many mental institutions between Virginia and Iowa.

"Hey man, I think this job is going to suck." Brisbane's voice brought Waldo back from the depths of speculation.

Waldo, distracted by his fears and a recurring grief over Professor Buckley, unconsciously nodded in agreement with the fredneck's terse assessment.

They located the elevators, and wheeled their carts into one that was available.

As the elevator door closed, Brisbane initiated the popular, time-tested ritual of denigrating the boss. "Shit, dude, how did that guy ever get to be supervisor?"

"How does anyone get to be supervisor?" Waldo sardonically but effectively closed the subject.

Seconds later, the door opened to the fourth floor, and Waldo and Brisbane were promptly greeted by a most incredible sight. Seated in front of the nursing station, which was straight ahead of them, only ten to fifteen feet away, were two elderly male patients. Both were clad in the standard, regulation hospital gowns and nothing else.

There was a long line of people waiting in front of both old men, which wound around one side of the nursing station and extended far down that corridor, consisting of doctors, nurses, various other employees, and even a few younger patients. They were visibly restless, and growing unruly, reminding Waldo and Brisbane of concert-goers standing in a beer line at intermission. As the two new employees remained frozen just outside the elevator, they saw that what each person was relishing so much was a turn at tweaking the old men's penises.

Waldo was flabbergasted. He knew from past experience visiting friends and relatives in hospitals that a sizable chunk of the doctors and nurses were uncaring and inefficient, but never in his wildest dreams could he have pictured them rounding up helpless, confused senior citizens and abusing them in some bizarre, sexual game.

"Shit man," Brisbane whispered, "are they trying to kill those poor old dudes or what?"

"No, my dear."

Both Waldo and Brisbane were startled by the voice from behind them. Standing there was a very professional looking young nurse, in a radiant white, freshly pressed uniform, who had evidently just arrived on the floor.

"You boys didn't hold the elevator for me- I had to wait for the next one. I hope I'm not late." Staring past them at the barbaric festivities going on in front of the nurse's station, her bottom lip began to tremble. "Damn them! Playing the Degradation Of The Deficient when I'm on break!" She shrieked, and rushed forward to take her place in line.

"Come on, Brisbane, let's deliver these supplies and leave." Waldo urged.

Not wanting to disturb the activities in front of the nursing station, the two new Junior Material Handlers dropped the supplies off at the unoccupied side of the nursing station, and no one even noticed their presence. As they hurried back towards the elevators, everyone suddenly started applauding and stomping their feet. Waldo turned around and saw that all the excitement was resulting from the fact one of the unfortunate souls had been fondled into an orgasm. Staring transfixed like gawkers at a bloody accident site, Waldo and Brisbane watched two orderlies lift the apparently dead old man and carry him away into a room at the farthest end of the hallway to their left. From their vantage point, they could clearly see a sign above the door of the room which read *Staff Lounge.*

"Shit man, what are they..."

The fredneck stopped in mid-sentence as all heads spun at once in their direction. Fortunately, an elevator happened to open at that moment, and the two of them wasted no time in boarding it.

"Man, what kind of fucking place is this?" Brisbane remarked as soon as the door was closed.

Waldo was trembling again. "I-I don't know, Brisbane."

"That shit with the old dude, I mean if he was dead, what the fuck were they doing taking him into their lounge?"

Waldo felt himself beginning to hyperventilate. "It sure doesn't seem like they were following normal hospital procedures for handling a dead body."

"Shit man, they were jacking him off!" Brisbane exclaimed.

"I know." Waldo replied sadly.

"Man, the way those people were acting, you'd think they were at a fucking football game!" The fredneck shook his head in disgust.

"Yes, just like football." Agreed an equally sickened Waldo.

The rest of their work day went by quickly and was filled with other unsettling occurrences. Fontaine and Bucktooth reported seeing, during a delivery to the fifth floor, a nurse who appeared to be the same woman who'd taken their applications in the employment office. Phosphate observed a nurse hitting an elderly patient on top of her head with a bedpan. He also witnessed orderlies entering a room and removing a body which was in an obvious state of rigor mortis. The top doo-wopper had once been an orderly himself, and was aware that such a condition took several hours to develop. He was consequently appalled to think of how infrequently that patient must have been attended to. Waldo and Brisbane encountered additional instances of patient abuse as well, albeit none of them on a par with "The Degradation of The Damned." They saw many older patients, as they traveled throughout the facility with their carts of supplies, who were left out in the halls shivering beneath their undignified gowns, with their private parts exposed for anyone to see.

Then there were the constant cries of "help me!" which emanated from certain rooms on every floor. Waldo noticed that the calls always went completely unheeded by the nursing staff, but it was Brisbane who overheard a nurse respond (which most of them actually seemed trained not to do) to a particularly vocal sufferer by muttering aloud "I wish he'd hurry up and die!" All in all, each of them beheld their share of shabby and unethical treatment.

Duck Hung proved to be a tough taskmaster, watching them relentlessly should they pause in their endeavors, and never hesitating to unleash a barrage of curse words in broken English. Since they were the only five workers in Central Supply, and their Vietnamese supervisor refused to elaborate about the Junior Material Handlers they'd replaced, the question of how the department had been run prior to their convenient arrival that morning, and how it would have functioned without them, was one they all pondered throughout the day.

Waldo was suspicious, naturally, about the whole institution. Actually, the average person who viewed such bizarre goings-on as "The Degradation of The Damned" would undoubtedly have fled in terror and/or contacted the local authorities. Due to the extraordinary nature of their recent experiences, however, Waldo was content to store such things alongside the rest of the large mass of unexplained data accumulated in his brain and turn his concentration towards finding Sam Hancock.

When his lunch break came, Waldo immediately went searching for Volunteer Services. He was able to locate it without too much difficulty and, as luck would have it, Jeanne happened to walk through the door just as his hand was reaching for the knob.

"Hi, sweetie." She kissed him on the cheek. "I was just going to come down to the basement and visit you."

"Oh, really?" Waldo smiled. "Well, I'm on my lunch break."

"Great!" Jeanne exclaimed. "Come on, let's go to the cafeteria. My treat."

Waldo shook his head. "No, I can't let you do that. And besides, I want to use my lunch break to go back to Old Files and see if they'll tell me something about Sam Hancock now that I'm an employee. The nervous young man stared hypnotically into her beautiful green eyes. "Of course, I wanted to see you first because, you know..."

"Yeah, I know." The pretty teenager giggled. "You're sweet. But you're also silly. You have plenty of time to find out about Sam Hancock. You didn't eat those pancakes I brought you this morning, and if you don't get something in you soon, you're going to make yourself really sick."

"Well, I suppose I could eat a little something." Waldo admitted. "But let's hurry. I still want to drop by Old Files."

"Okay." Jeanne said with transparent satisfaction in her sweet voice.

Waldo and Jeanne strolled off hand in hand to the cafeteria. When they arrived there, Waldo refused to order anything more than a sandwich, despite the protests of his underaged girlfriend. Jeanne, meanwhile, in the finest feminine tradition, was having only a diet soda.

"Listen, I really appreciate your buying me this." Waldo said, with an earnest expression on his face. "I'll pay you back as..."

"Don't be ridiculous." Jeanne waved her hand. "It only cost $1.29."

"Yes, but still, just the same..."

"I wanted to do it, silly." The lovely teenager interrupted him again, sipping her diet soft drink daintily through a straw. "It's nothing."

Waldo wolfed down the sandwich in rapid fashion, and they exited the cafeteria before their seats were lukewarm. Jeanne led him through the winding halls of the basement until they came to the elevators. Despite his haste in eating, and his previously expressed desire to visit Old Files before returning to Central Supply, it wasn't easy for Waldo to keep pace with the petite, fast-moving Irish lass as she glided along. As volunteers, Jeanne and Janie were not fortunate enough to possess fringe benefits like the unpaid, half hour lunch break that all Junior Material Handlers enjoyed, and so she was even more rushed than the nervous young man.

A few moments later, they were standing in the first floor lobby.

"Well, you know where it is." The lovely candy-striper pointed towards the main hallway. "I've got to get back now. We'll meet you guys here at four o'clock, okay?" Jeanne then simultaneously flattered and embarrassed him by planting a big kiss on his lips.

Waldo smiled modestly and glanced around the lobby to make sure no one had been watching. "Sure, I'll see you then. Thanks again for the lunch."

Jeanne blew another kiss in his direction, then hurried back to Volunteer Services.

Waldo watched her walk away, then proceeded down the main hall to the Old Files office. When he opened the door, the mildew smell was still in the air, but the young man with the shaved head had been replaced by a plain, middle aged woman who strongly resembled the lady from the Personnel department. Her eyeglasses were balanced on the tip of her nose, as well, although her brown hair was cropped close and wasn't gathered into a bun on the top of her head.

"Excuse me," Waldo gazed at her intently, "but I can't help noticing that you look familiar."

The woman, who'd been reading a cheap romance novel, peered up over her glasses. "Really? Well, I imagine we all tend to look alike after we've been here awhile. How can I help you?"

"I'd like to know the status of a patient." Waldo's palms were sweating. "His name is Hancock, Samuel Hancock."

"You are an employee, I presume?"

"Yes. I just started today, in the Central Supply department."

"Let's see." She rifled through some files in a lower drawer, much as the bald young man had done earlier. "I'm afraid there's no patient here by that name. When was he admitted?"

"A long time ago, 1969 to be exact." Waldo replied, ignoring the fact that the young man with the shaved head had pulled a file that was presumably Sam Hancock's and indicated it was confidential. "I guess it was crazy to think he would still be here."

"Crazy is a term we use sparingly at the Last Home, young man." The woman chastised him in a tone of voice familiar to small children everywhere. "Many of our patients have been with us for a very, very long time."

"Well, do you have any records on him in your files, that might at least show when he was released?" Waldo asked hopefully.

"We are not permitted to release any information about our former patients. This is a *very* private place, you know."

Waldo frowned. "Uh...okay. Well, could you tell me, anyhow, where the Extremely Unreachable Ward is? I know he was originally admitted there."

The woman's face grew noticeably pale. "It is against official policy to discuss the cases in that section." Then, leaning conspiratorially towards Waldo, she whispered, "by the way, have you met our administrator?" Opening the middle drawer of her desk, the woman held up a photograph of a man in a business suit. Waldo felt himself starting to faint, and grabbed onto the desk for support. The woman was laughing at him in the same maddening fashion as her counterpart in the Personnel office, and waved the picture aloft to torture him further. In spite of himself, Waldo was unable to resist another glance at the photo, and satisfied that it was indeed a perfect likeness of the strange hitchhiker they'd encountered during their journey to Iowa, he ran from the room as fast as he could.

14
THEY FOOL ALL THE PEOPLE ALL THE TIME

From *Why My Existence Is Unverified*, an unpublished pamphlet by Abner Billingsly, pg. 17:

"I have come to the conclusion that there has never been an honest investigation by any authoritative body in the history of the world."

Waldo and Jeanne were lying in the cornfield once again. After his nonsensical experience in the Old Files office, Waldo had sprinted back to Central Supply in a most distressed state of mind, and only an arduous collective effort by his fellow Junior Material Handlers persuaded him to remain there for the remainder of the work day. He'd finally had his fill of giants, werewolves, lonely men hidden in forests, names connected to the Kennedy assassination, and that unreal Hitchhiker, and was on the verge of turning around, on foot if necessary, and heading for Virginia with his tail between his legs. Eventually, however, his comrades prevailed upon him to stay the course, with Phosphate earnestly imploring him, in his best paternal manner, to be strong for his grandfather's sake. When he informed the others about the Administrator's photograph, and who appeared to hold that lofty position, none of them seemed too surprised. Having endured the harrowing road trip to Iowa, they all knew there were obviously some very uncanny things going on around them, particularly at the Last Chance Relaxation Home, but they were understandably becoming more desensitized with each additional perplexing development.

The O'Sullivan cornfield, despite its time warps and odd creatures, was a welcome sight that afternoon to Waldo. As he lay there cradled in the bosom of his beautiful, underaged girlfriend, however, he nearly wished that he'd never met her. Their love was mutual and strong, but it was also impossible and illegal. Within a week or two, at most, he would be gone, and Jeanne O'Sullivan would return to being just an average high school junior with a penchant for traveling through time. Brooding over these disturbing thoughts, Waldo sadly sighed and fumbled in his pocket for a cigarette.

"What's wrong, sweetie?" Jeanne was growing enamored with various 'cutesy' terms, and her concern over a mere sigh reflected the extent of her attachment to Waldo.

"Oh, nothing." Waldo took a long drag on his cigarette.

"Are you still thinking about what happened in Old Files?" Jeanne asked.

"No, to tell you the truth, I was thinking about us."

The pretty teenager giggled. "Oh, yeah? What about us?"

Waldo sat up and exhaled his smoke in the general direction where even now the Forest Of Injured Egos was undoubtedly preparing for another cold and bitter night. "Well, I was just wondering, uh...what's going to happen when I leave. I have to, you know."

Jeanne stared at the ground. "I-I-I don't know. I guess I was hoping that maybe you wouldn't."

Waldo suddenly felt a rush of adrenaline, fueled by his considerable supply of impractical optimism. "If I did stay, would there be any future for us?"

"All I know is that I'll always love you, Waldo Billingsly." Jeanne spoke directly into Waldo's ear, much like young Mary had done to her future husband George Bailey in their favorite film, *It's A Wonderful Life*.

Unlike George Bailey, both of Waldo's ears functioned perfectly, and he was delighted by what he heard. He enveloped Jeanne's supple body in his arms and kissed her soft brown hair. They agreed to discuss the matter further, but not at that moment. They were too busy making love for the first time in the present age, right there amid the magical corn stalks.

That night, Waldo elected to forego the comfort of the decidedly un-fredneck-like '65 Dodge Dart once more, braving the unseasonable chill to slumber in the cornfield again. As he stared up at the stars, reclining on the particular spot of land he'd grown so attached to, he drifted off to sleep and dreamt of pleasant, unlikely things:

You are in the wilds of Africa. You are Tarzan. As you begin your day by swinging leisurely through the vines, you spot a lovely young girl walking through the jungle. You quickly land and race to her side.

"Who you?" You realistically grunt.

"Why, I'm Jean." She replies sweetly, with a slight British accent.

"Oh...me Tarzan, you Jean."

"Do you live in the jungle?"

"Umgawa. Me live here with Cheetah."

"Oh, is Cheetah your wife?"

"Bwana. Cheetah monkey."

"Oh, well, is there someplace around here for a girl to freshen up?" Jean bears almost as much similarity to Maureen O'Sullivan as to Jeanne O'Sullivan.

"Umgawa. You pretty girl. You want to swim?"

"Why, alright. But where will I find a bathing suit?"

You reach into one of those handy closets that are so frequently found in jungle dream scenes. "Juju. Here, put on."

It is the same skimpy loincloth Maureen O'Sullivan wore in the first two Tarzan films before the censors forced her to cover up the slits in the sides, which left little to Depression-era imaginations. She coyly hides behind some bushes and changes.

"Ahhhh!" Jean screams suddenly and you see a lion approaching her. As it is your duty to fight all savage beasts and ignorant natives with only your trusty knife, you rush the lion and jump on its back. It is a long and rugged battle, but your quick reflexes and superior intellect win out in the end.

As you are dusting yourself off, Jean giggles and yells, "Come on, silly, bet you can't catch me!" Thus her conversion from English debutante lost in the heart of Africa to submissive sexpot willing to spend her life among the beasts accompanied only by her illiterate lover is complete.

You chase after and follow her as she dives into the crystal clear waters that are part of the fantastic scenery of this Florida wild land (like the M.G.M. Tarzan movies, this dream is actually set somewhere in Florida, and not in deep, dark Africa). You both swim and frolic happily in the peaceful setting, until the serenity is shattered temporarily by the arrival of a pesky crocodile, which you must dispose of. Soon this is accomplished and you resume your fun.

Waldo woke up. For once in his life, he wasn't happy to. It was certainly disappointing to leave a tropical paradise for a lonely, frosted cornfield, however magical it was. Waldo felt the unusual weather was appropriate, all things considered. He was so cold, in fact, that he decided to walk back to the car and share some of the body heat being generated by the others.

As he moved briskly along through the stalks of corn, blowing on his hands to keep warm, he suddenly noticed the sound of footsteps behind him. He didn't turn around, even when the voices started.

"*Waldo, Waaaallllldddooooo...go back home...*"

Waldo kept moving. The voices persisted in their spooky refrain until the nervous young man could stand it no longer. He whirled around and stood face to face with the infamous Hitchhiker and the three M.I.B.'s he'd seen outside of the convenience store a few days earlier. For once, an untapped source of fortitude emerged from the depths within him and Waldo held his ground, expressing himself in a strong and confident manner.

"What do you want from me? Who are you and why do I see you everywhere?" He directed his ire specifically at the enigmatic figure in the gray trench coat and matching fedora hat.

The Hitchhiker grinned and responded in a deceptively tranquil tone. "It isn't wise for you to worry about my identity. I am only here to warn you not to take your activities any farther than you already have."

Waldo continued his courageous stance. "What activities? Who are you?"

The Hitchhiker replied in song, backed by the three M.I.B.'s:

"Please go home and forget it all
You're all alone and much too small
To ever hope to take us on
For we move King and Queen and pawn
We've been around a long, long time
We make justice, we make crime
Others have wished we'd go away
But now they're gone and still we stay
You couldn't stop us if you tried
Many hoped to but they all died
So if you find you have the urge
Take my advice and heed my words
There are things you are not meant to know
So don't upset the status quo."

Waldo didn't like their sleazy, Las Vegas style of singing. He also didn't appreciate what they were saying. "Look, I asked you a couple of times, and I won't ask you again. I know you're not any Administrator, you weren't invited to sit down at the O'Sullivan's dining room table, and you sure aren't just another hitchhiker. If you won't tell me who you are, then I have nothing else to say to you."

The Hitchhiker glared at Waldo. "Very Well." He motioned to his three M.I.B. lackeys and they all began walking away. The Hitchhiker looked back over his shoulder and issued a final warning. "I have been informed that if you don't return immediately to your home in Virginia, then you are a marked man, and *we* don't miss our marks." He then abruptly went into a sales pitch, like some interdimensional insurance agent. "Look, I can tell you that you're not going to find your grandfather, so give it up. I assure you that you can't win- no one ever has. He is now where you cannot possibly reach him, so forget about doing that. You're still young, and it would be senseless to throw your life away for a cause that was lost centuries ago."

Waldo retained his bravery. "Listen, you can tell whoever sent you that they can stop all of this. I came here to find my grandfather and I intend to do just that. If I can't locate him here, then I'll keep looking somewhere else, everywhere I have to, until I know what happened to him."

The Hitchhiker shook his head in disgust. "You fool. All the precious pamphlets in the world can't prepare you for what you're about to face." With that, the four menacing figures started to vanish.

As they did so, Waldo was moved to shout at their dematerializing images, "fuck you and all your kind!" He did it as well as any fredneck could have, and he felt much better afterwards.

The next morning Waldo didn't even bother telling the others about his late-night encounter with the Hitchhiker and the M.I.B.'s. He did confide in Jeanne, however. The happy couple had started another day off by lovemaking in the past, this time choosing the storming of the Bastille during the French Revolution as their romantic backdrop. As they frolicked in the shadows cast by the crude eighteenth century partisans clashing over the momentous issues of the day, Waldo had to laugh at the five criminals and mental patients who were "freed" by the heroic revolutionaries.

Now, back in 1987, everyone was preparing for another day's work at the Last Chance Relaxation Home. None of them were anxious to return there, but a desperate desire to determine the truth about all that had occurred since they'd left northern Virginia, and in the process uncover the fate of Old Hoss Billingsly, was steadily beginning to override any concerns they felt for their personal safety.

Brisbane, who was sitting on the hood of his trusty old vehicle, slapped Waldo heartily on the back. "Shit man, we all came out here to help you look for your grandfather and we haven't done anything to find him yet. I know you're trying to find out about this dude Hancock, and that ward he was supposedly in, but what do you want us to do?"

"Yeah, just tell us what to do and we'll do it." Fontaine echoed.

Waldo truly appreciated their support. "Thanks a lot, guys. I can't tell you how much it means to know you all want to help me out. It's just that I can't think of anything for you to do yet. If it turns out that Sam Hancock is no longer at the Last Chance Relaxation Home, or if he's well...dead, then I have to think of other places to look. I'll really need you then."

"You have my services for as long as you desire." Phosphate smiled. "But I must ask you, Waldo, in light of what transpired yesterday in the Old Files department, how you propose finding Sam Hancock now."

Or last night in the cornfield, Waldo thought to himself. "Well, I figured that I would try going to the Registration department next, just to see what happens. Then, if they don't tell me anything, I plan to ask around, you know, kind of slyly, and hope that somebody there knows where the Extremely Unreachable Ward is."

"I don't know, sweetie. I told you that Janie and I have never heard of it." Jeanne had indeed informed Waldo that if such a place existed within the institution, neither her nor her sister had ever been requested to deliver any flowers or gifts there. A candy striper's main function was to wheel patients to their rooms after they'd been admitted, and to pick them up and wheel them from their rooms when they'd been discharged, but neither O'Sullivan girl had been ordered to such a ward for that purpose in the ten months they'd worked at the Last Chance Relaxation Home.

"Yeah man, we delivered shit through that whole damn place yesterday, and I didn't see any signs about no Extreme Unreachable Ward." Bucktooth remarked. "Are you sure that's the name of the ward he was admitted to?" Janie asked.

"Yes, I'm sure." Waldo lit up a Camel Light. "I heard my grandfather mention it by name many times. And the lady in Old Files said something about not being able to discuss the cases in that section when I mentioned it to her, so obviously she knew about it."

"What I don't understand, sweetie," Jeanne cooed tenderly, "is why you keep running into all these strange people. Janie and I don't know a lot of employees there-most of them look down on the volunteers-but the ones we've met have been pretty normal."

"I don't understand it either." Fontaine said. "But we've seen a lot of strange people since we met Waldo."

Janie glanced at the watch on her wrist. "We'd better get going. It's a quarter to eight."

Spurred on, like the rest of the working world, by a fear of being tardy, the entire day shift of Central Supply, along with the two plucky candy stripers, piled into Brisbane's car and sped off for their place of employment.

After a morning filled with more abuse from their capable and nearly understandable superior, Duck Hung, the unpaid half hour lunch break, which all the manual laborers there enjoyed, was welcomed by the five Junior Material Handlers.

During the course of the morning, Waldo had asked virtually every employee he came in contact with about the Extremely Unreachable Ward, but no one seemed familiar with it. The others conducted similar inquiries as they made their deliveries, and achieved the same results. Waldo's previously expressed plans had changed somewhat, as he'd elected to question fellow workers about the elusive ward Sam Hancock had allegedly been in before seeking information from the Registration department. However, when his lunch break arrived, Waldo took advantage of the opportunity, fully realizing that this might be the last avenue there was to explore at the mental institution, and strode briskly towards Registration.

Waldo knew that registration was located somewhere on the first floor, so he took the elevator there and headed for Volunteer Services, hoping that Jeanne could guide him to the right place. The beautiful teenager, who was permitted as a non-salaried employee to go to lunch whenever she pleased, was more than happy to direct him there, and she waited patiently outside in the hall as he walked into the Registration office.

Upon entering, Waldo was greeted by the sounds of Peter Tosh blaring out his anthem, *Legalize Marijuana.* The receptionist, a very young black woman, was bobbing, Caribbean style, to the beat, while the papers on her desk were being strewn about in all directions by the wind from her flailing arms.

"Excuse me." Waldo raised his voice in an attempt to be heard over her boom box.

The woman hesitated a second, then looked up from her desk and turned the music down with visible disgust. "You don't have to shout." She admonished, in a thick Trinidadian accent, sounding almost civil.

"Yes, well, I wonder, could you please tell me if a certain patient is still here?"

"Patient Information, first floor lobby." The memorized lines flowed easily from her lips, and she was reaching for the volume switch on her boom box when Waldo informed that he had already checked there unsuccessfully. "I can't do anything for you if they can't." was her mechanical response.

Waldo spoke again before she could turn the volume back up. "Look, I've checked with the Old Files office too, and I know this isn't the right place to find this out, but you're my last hope. Can you at least tell me if you've ever heard of a wing here called the Extremely Unreachable Ward?"

She wrinkled her nose and stared off into space. "Hmmm. What's the patient's name?"

"Samuel Hancock. I'd like to have his room number, that is if he's still here. It's been eighteen years since he was admitted, so I don't know how likely that would be."

"There are patients who've been here much longer. What's your relationship to the patient?" The woman was acting a bit more professional now.

"He's an old family friend."

"Have a seat and I'll check for you." With that, the woman walked, about as slowly as was humanly possible, it seemed to Waldo, into an adjoining room.

Waldo wondered why this employee, while not actually acknowledging that it existed, didn't dismiss his mention of the Extremely Unreachable Ward with a curt "never heard of it," as most others there had. Her requests for the patient's name and the relationship between them seemed a tacit admission on her part that she was indeed aware of such a ward.

Several minutes went by as Waldo waited impatiently, staring at the mediocre paintings on the walls. It irked him considerably when people took longer than necessary to perform routine tasks that he felt could be completed in far less time; hence his lifelong boycott of all government office buildings. Of course, it really wasn't his place to criticize, seeing as how he was unemployed most of the time, but still he did. Finally, the woman returned and informed Waldo that Sam Hancock was indeed still a patient there, residing in room five of the Extremely Unreachable Ward, which she said was located in the sub-basement.

"The sub-basement?" Waldo had seen, during the course of a single work day, his supervisor Duck Hung carrying broken equipment there several times. "I thought that was a storage area. You mean they keep patients there?"

But the only reply he received was from Peter Tosh, loudly exhorting the world to "legalize marijuana," as the young Trinidadian wasted no time in resuming her regular duties.

Waldo left the office with more hope than he'd had since they'd arrived in Iowa. Jeanne was still in the hallway, leaning against the wall like a high school cheerleader waiting for her boyfriend to get out of class. This wasn't a difficult image for her to convey, as she was still in high school and could certainly have made the cheerleading squad if she'd had an inclination to.

"Well, how did it go, honey?" Jeanne asked optimistically.

"I found out where the Extremely Unreachable Ward is." Waldo paused in order to build the suspense. "Believe it or not, it's in the sub-basement, and Sam Hancock is still there."

A furrow appeared in the teenager's pretty brow. "Are you kidding? There's nothing down there but extra furniture and stuff."

Waldo shrugged. "That's what she said."

"Unless..." Jeanne was still frowning. "I'm not really sure, but I think there's supposed to be another entrance to the sub-basement, on the west wing of the building. There aren't any patients in the basement, you know, so Janie and I don't get down there very much, but maybe they keep some special ones..."

"So you think it's some kind of storage area, but you've never actually been in the sub-basement?" Waldo interrupted her.

"Well, no, I never had a reason to go there. I've just heard that it's

271

used for storage."

Waldo glanced up at the clock on the wall. "Uh-oh. I better go. See you in the lobby after work."

Without further ado, he hurried back in the direction of Central Supply. Something told him that Duck Hung wasn't likely to be understanding when Junior Material Handlers weren't prompt in returning from their unpaid half hour lunch breaks.

Waldo had been correct in his estimation of Duck Hung's tolerance level.

"Goddamn shit! You supposed to get your ass back here on time!" The silver-tongued Vietnamese supervisor was hopping mad.

"You can take it out of my pay, or make me stay five minutes late if you want, okay?" Waldo made the mistake of trying to reason with him.

"Your ass just get to work! Here- take this shit up by yourself! And hurry back!" Duck Hung pointed to a flatbed loaded with large, heavy cases of supplies.

Normally it would require two people to deliver such a load, but Waldo didn't complain. He even grabbed Brisbane by the elbow when he saw that the fredneck was about to. The nervous young man's uncharacteristically cooperative attitude towards this fanatical authority figure could undoubtedly be attributed to his desire to remain in close proximity to Sam Hancock. It seemed a fair assumption, especially in light of the wide spread lack of familiarity about it among the staff of the institution, that the Extremely Unreachable Ward was probably not an area which was readily accessible to visitors, and that therefore he'd have a far greater chance of getting into the unit as an employee. Waldo was already planning to search in the sub-basement the next day during his lunch break, and he wasn't about to let anyone, least of all a jabbering resident alien, stop him.

"Goddamn shit! Move your ass now or I fire your ass!" Duck Hung's shrill voice snapped Waldo out of yet another dreamy stupor.

"Sorry." He responded meekly, and wheeled the heavy supplies away.

Duck Hung ordered the others to pull some trash modules into the General Processing area. The modules weighed a lot and were not easy to maneuver, even when empty. When they were full of trash or soiled linen, the task was doubly difficult. This was unquestionably the hardest, most distasteful part of their job, and although it was only their second day in Central Supply, they all dreaded it. This strenuous physical labor, a relatively minor aspect of their job description, was a particular affront to their dignity, and a blot on the title of Junior Material Handler.

"Shit man, that Duck Hung is a fucking lunatic!" Brisbane declared.

"You ain't shitting, Bris. Old Waldo caught all that hell for being five minutes late!" Fontaine, being generally unemployed, was consistently shocked by the various niceties of the blue-collar world.

Phosphate led them down the dingy corridor that connected the two departments, which was so congested it violated the most permissive fire regulations. "My friends, let us try and be patient. After all, even though we seem to be toiling under a frustrated and unqualified superior, we only have to tolerate such nonsense for a short while."

"Yeah, I guess you're right, Phos." Fontaine shook his head in dismay, but ceased contemplating the kind of violence that had made his past employment record so memorable.

The four of them pulled their modules into General Processing, or G.P., as everyone referred to it. If Brisbane and the Afro-Anarchists thought that steering the trash carts was demanding and laborious, at least they could take some solace from the fact they weren't members of the weary G.P. staff who had to empty and clean them. On the corporate ladder of success, those unfortunate souls whose lot it is to slave in the General Processing departments of medical facilities rank at the very bottom, just below toilet cleaners and high-rise window washers. Aware that the G.P. personnel were just about the only employees at the Last Chance Relaxation Home who stood even lower than they did on the status totem pole, the Junior Material Handlers felt a natural kinship with them. They had, in fact, already struck up a fast friendship with these unlucky laborers.

After parking his trash module, Phosphate gazed at the sweaty men and women who'd paused a second in their sifting of trash, soiled linen, and contaminated instruments to greet them, and decided to salute them in song. Gathering his compatriots, which included Brisbane as a special, guest Afro-Anarchist, the top doo-wopper began a brand new effort:

"I've heard it said in Congress recently
That they can't survive on their salaries
I know they got their perks and they got their power
But try living on five dollars an hour
If they lose re-election they face the specter
Of finding a job in the private sector
I know they have to skimp and they have it tough
Who thought public service could be so rough?
They'll have to give away all their rights up there
Next they'll have to pay for their medical care
They have their parking and their lecture fees
Tax-paid vacations and their haircuts free

273

They have the only job in the U.S.A.
Where the workers can give themselves a raise
So cheer up, Senators, and never fear
They'll vote you in again next year!"

The G.P. workers, all of them either Black or Hispanic, cheered loudly, recognizing the doo-woppers' work as a sort of tribute to them.

"Alright! Shit, holmes! That's great, homeboy!" Were some of the many responses that echoed throughout the dark and dirty department.

Phosphate acknowledged their cheers as gracefully as any classical conductor and then they were off, in search of more trash carts.

Waldo, meanwhile, was busy delivering the flatbed of supplies, and with each step he felt his blood pressure rise another twenty points. He was starting to experience an overwhelming desire, after less than two days as a Junior Material Handler, to curse every nurse he encountered.

For many of the items he delivered, Waldo was supposed to pick up a charge card from the nursing station. It was the maddening difficulty in completing this seemingly simple task that was causing him such distress. Wherever he went, he was accorded the same treatment by the nursing staff, who from floor to floor persistently refused to acknowledge his existence. Waldo didn't anticipate receiving many thank-you's, or even a handful of phony smiles, but he wasn't prepared for the lack of respect his position commanded. At every station, he would be forced to ask one of the nurses for a charge card, and even though they went through the same elementary procedure many times a day, none of them would ever initiate the actions required of them. Invariably, they would react more like vapid rock groupies than alleged college graduates and stare at him as if he'd demanded their money. They never seemed to have the slightest idea that their patients needed any of the items he left at the various units. In contrast, Waldo noticed that whenever an intern, be he bald, fat, or disabled, passed by a nursing station, he would inspire the kind of cheerful, pseudo-sexual attitudes that public relations firms dream of. Waldo was well aware that the world operated in such shallow ways, but still recoiled in disbelief at every first hand experience.

As he unloaded his last box at the seventh floor nursing station, he finally reached the boiling point. No one was in sight, and Waldo heard more than the usual number of old and infirm patients crying out in futility for assistance. He wanted to obtain the charge card quickly and leave, as his shift was almost over. Seeing none of the nurses out front, he wandered around to the side of the station, where the pantry door was. Waldo knocked lightly, and a voice responded by calling out, "come in, Dr. Edlestein!" The nervous young man was definitely no doctor, but he entered anyhow and gazed about him in astonishment. The pantry was small and tidy, with a full sized refrigerator, a sink, and adequate counter and cupboard space, and it adjoined a comfortable lounge area, which was equipped with everything from cable t.v. to the latest video game system. Waldo could see nurses stretched out everywhere, on the sofa and chairs in the lounge, even on the floor, in varying degrees of relaxation. Some were asleep, but most of them were eating.

It was impossible for Waldo to contain his anger. "Excuse me, I hate to interrupt your busy schedules, but I need a charge card for the supplies I just left at the nursing station."

One of the nurses, apparently a supervisor of some sort, slowly raised her scrawny body from the sofa and glared coldly at Waldo. "This happens to be a private room."

"I knocked." Waldo said.

Despite a physique that resembled a shorter version of Popeye's beloved Olive Oyl's, the nurse strutted up to him and began jabbing her finger in his chest in a display of supreme self-confidence that a ghetto gang leader at a senior citizens' horticulture meeting would be hard pressed to duplicate. "Young man, if you don't leave immediately, I'll have to report you to your supervisor."

"For what? I only came in here because none of you were out there where you're supposed to be. Were you all on break at the same time? Look, I need a charge card, that's all. I work here too, you know." Waldo's frustration was operating against his better judgment. As soon as he'd finished his brief tirade, he realized what a mistake he'd made.

"Who does he think he is, Mildred, talking back to you like that?" A pretty nurse who was probably younger than Waldo exclaimed, as several of the other nurses who were awake stared on in consternation.

"Talking back?" Waldo was incredulous. "You must be mistaking me for an elementary school student. For your information, I'm twenty eight years old. How old are you?"

The pretty nurse turned her nose up in response, looking around her in a manner that expressed the amazement she must have felt over a mere Junior Material Handler daring to speak to professionals like herself as an equal.

"And another thing," Waldo had completely lost his composure now, "what kind of a mental institution is this? All I see on every floor are nurses, aides, and orderlies. Where are the counselors? If this is just a regular hospital, then why don't you say so?"

The diminutive charge nurse stared icily at his name tag. "Waldo Billingsly, eh? Well, Waldo, I'll see that your supervisor hears about this."

Waldo started to exit meekly at this point, as low-wage earners invariably do under such humiliating circumstances. Something- perhaps the three laughing nurses standing next to the sink popping popcorn, or the four intense young medical providers engrossed in a friendly game of *Risk* at the table in the lounge- set him off again, however, and he gave them the tongue lashing they all appeared to desperately need. "Don't any of you hear the screams coming from your patients? What kind of consciences can you have to ignore that? Do you realize how dishonest it is for you to sit in here eating, laughing, and playing games, and being paid a good salary for it, while there are people in need of attention who are paying exorbitant rates for the privilege of being sick? Oh well, don't let me stop your fun. Have a nice day." Waldo could hear a number of stuffy "well, I nevers" and "hmmfs" as he closed the pantry door behind him.

It might have taken her four hours to come and empty a schizophrenic's bedpan, but the charge nurse was much more efficient in calling down and reporting Waldo's impertinence to Duck Hung.

"Goddamn shit!" Duck Hung started in on Waldo the instant he returned to Central Supply. "Jesus Cry! I don't like those goddamn nurse to call down here! You fuck up! If you fuck up one more time, I kill your ass!"

Waldo was becoming accustomed to being berated Duck-Hung style. The crazed oriental supervisor seemed to possess a few choice expressions which he repeated ad nauseam. For instance, it was very clear to Waldo that any punishment from Duck Hung would come in the form of an ass killing. Waldo wasn't sure just what that might entail, but he didn't imagine it to be pretty.

The nervous young man didn't bother to defend himself, and this shortened Duck Hung's rapid verbal barrage. At length, the angry Vietnamese boss left the room shaking his head in disgust and muttering to himself in his native language.

Breathing a sigh of relief, Waldo informed the others of how he'd learned Sam Hancock was indeed in room five of the Extremely Unreachable Ward, which was located in the sub-basement.   .

"The *sub-basement*. That *is* interesting." Phosphate began his rubbing of the chin ritual.

"Shit man, I thought that was a fucking storage area." The baffled fredneck said.

"Yeah, I know I've seen Duck Hung's sorry Oriental ass go down there a lot carrying broken shit with him." Fontaine exclaimed.

"I know, but according to Jeanne," Waldo loved to stoke a paranoid fire, "there's another entrance to the sub-basement on the other side-I think she said the west wing-or at least that's what she's heard."

Brisbane looked up at the clock, which was a persistent habit of his during his infrequent bouts of employment, and declared enthusiastically, "shit, it's four o'clock! Let's go, dudes!"

None of his less than ambitious mates could disobey an ultimatum like that, and they followed the fredneck like the children of Hamlin as he led the way to the lobby and a rendezvous with their two lovely young passengers.

During the ride back to the O'Sullivan property, the five Junior Material Handlers related their various atrocity stories to Jeanne and Janie, who appeared genuinely shocked to hear of such things transpiring under the roof of the Last Chance Relaxation Home.

"I don't understand it at all." Janie remarked. "We've never seen anything like that happen there."

"Believe it, baby." Fontaine assured her. "Some wild shit is going on at that place."

Shortly after everyone had climbed out of Brisbane's trusty old vehicle, which was becoming a sort of un-fredneckmobile to them all, Waldo and Jeanne departed for the magical cornfield and historical parts unknown, and Janie returned to her house to fetch the fredneck a beer.

Phosphate, meanwhile, sat down by himself in the back seat of the car and opened the Professor's battered briefcase, which he'd placed there for safekeeping after retrieving it from the woods. He rifled through the mass of papers until he found one of Old Hoss Billingsly's unpublished pamphlets, *Wild Men Keep Their Own Statistics*, which looked especially interesting, and began reading:

"With all the boondoggles, injustices, and incompetence our leaders threaten to inflict upon us at any given moment, the most frightening everyday problem for most Americans remains the violence of their fellow citizens.

What makes one person want to inflict bodily harm upon another? I can't begin to guess, but then I am hardly qualified to. I have managed the miraculous feat of reaching middle age (perhaps a tad beyond) without ever having been in a real fist fight. Not even as a child. Now that may seem remarkable to most of my fellow countrymen, what with our affinity for the quaint traditions best expressed with a simple 'ya wanna step outside, buddy?' or 'ya shoulda seen the other guy,' but it is true. I just never have been provoked enough, or rather I should say never lost my reason to such an extent that I would be able to hit someone. Even if that person is worthy of being hit (and the Lord knows I've knocked out many with my cutting words), I still could not take the chance that I might damage him, might see his blood flow because of me.

Having explained my own background, or rather lack of one, in this area, I want to state why I believe so many people, Americans in particular, love this evil called violence. I think that upbringing, as in all things, plays a prominent role, but there is more to it than that. I maintain that it is caused in large measure by what we eat. Red meat, or dead animals, as some of my more radical fellow vegetarians like to impolitely call it, is a killer. I am of the opinion that most of the violent, irrational behavior that we see so eloquently portrayed by the group of individuals commonly referred to as rednecks, in particular, can be explained by the food they consume. How many Americans don't love a thick, juicy steak? How many don't love the ground-up feces and left-over body parts that make up the good old patriotic hot dog? How many don't love the chemical crunching snack that we call potato chips? How many don't love the white sugar and chemical mixture we so thoughtfully dole out to our children in pretty packages as candy bars? My point is that the typical American diet is almost totally devoid of any real nutritional value. The bumbling corporate moguls, in their persistent push for profits regardless of the impact on anyone or anything, have forced us to accept appearance and convenience over quality and substance. Consequently, all of us have adopted, insofar as food is concerned, what was once the sole province of the lower classes.

Is all of this somehow connected to the confounding question of why, in spite of billions of dollars expended for just that purpose, a cure for cancer cannot be found? Where was cancer before this century? Did it just suddenly turn up unannounced and become the most fatal disease of modern times? But then, one could just as easily ask where heart disease was, and the silence from the hospitals and research laboratories would be just as deafening. No, I think the answer lies in an increased consumption of red meat, fatty fried foods, and chemical additives and preservatives. Because of this, many Americans will continue to die at early ages from cancer or heart attacks, even though the maladies that most often afflicted their ancestors- polio, the various plagues and fevers- were wiped out long ago by a combination of vaccines, antibiotics, sterile instruments and supplies, and washed hands. The later stands as perhaps modern medicine's greatest contribution to humanity. At any rate, with all the vaunted leaps in medical technology, it is appalling and incomprehensible that America is far down the list of nations in terms of life expectancy. The only logical conclusion to come to, unless one accepts the notion of those even farther out than myself that new diseases are being developed by the conspirators and introduced sporadically into the population, is that we are overseeing our own premature demises. How many of us, during the summer picnic season, emulate our trailer park and inner city brethren; chugging beer and bloating our stomachs, gorging ourselves with chips, soda, mayonnaise, deviled eggs, potato salad, and hamburgers? And then, in the most comical twist of all, when the medical profession suggests we exercise, the activity of choice becomes jogging, an unnatural and painful experience that cannot be proven to have been beneficial to anyone. So, the out of shape American leaves his bacon, sausage, and Tang every morning to pound the pavement come rain or shine, wheezing and sweating in his expensive and fashionable outfit, towards an inexorable grave.

This is, of course, only one man's theory regarding acts of violence, and what may lay behind them. I am sure there are others that make even less sense than mine. However, as for myself, every time I see a crowd cheer a cut opening on the face of a boxer, or witness grown men acting like red-cheeked children on Christmas morning when they gather in sporting packs at the opening of deer season, or watch a man justify hitting his wife and/or children, I think...*I'll take some fresh fruit and vegetables, please.*

I also sometimes ponder the disquieting fact that most of the red-meat-and-violence-lovers consider themselves to be Christians. I am not the most pious man, and I never claimed to be, but I do know that a love of violence is incompatible with *turn the other cheek, let him who is without sin among you cast the first stone,* and *judge not lest ye be judged.* The central message of the New Testament is one of love and tolerance, yet that hardly describes most meat eaters. Or most Christians."

Phosphate sighed in appreciation. *This man,* he marveled to himself, *could have and should have been the foremost philosopher of our times.* Shaking his head sadly, the top doo-wopper went on to the next unpublished pamphlet.

15
THE MAJOR AND THE MINORS

Waldo approached the O'Sullivan house with butterflies in his stomach. Jeanne and Janie had graciously invited them all to dinner, and the hungry pack of pseudo-tourists had, not surprisingly, eagerly accepted their offer. As they followed the Irish twins down the steep embankment which led to the white frame house, the nervous young man struggled mightily against the hyperventilation which seemed to afflict him most powerfully on just these kinds of occasions. Waldo was eager to make a good impression on his underaged love's parents, and had even sworn to utter no controversial political comment for the entire duration of their visit.

"This is really great of you girls!" Brisbane spoke for them all.

Waldo and the others were not in quite as bad a predicament, in regards to their consumption of food, as they had been prior to meeting the O'Sullivan girls, but they still were looking forward to their first full, regulation, sit-down meal since they'd left Virginia. Having eaten like P.O.W.'s during much of their trip, and training their bodies to subsist on the daily caloric intake of an average third-world citizen as a consequence, they had almost reached the point where they understood the kind of spiritual reward Mahatma Ghandi experienced from fasting. The past few days, however, filled with Jeanne and Janie generously bringing them supplies from the O'Sullivan pantry, had resurrected their urge to eat, and stretched their stomachs back to such an extent that they protested vociferously if they weren't filled regularly.

The girls led the way to the front door and opened it. Holding it for them, with a skill any hotel doorman might have envied, was Jeanne. "Come on in!" She invited, sounding like the maitre d' at a budget restaurant.

They entered the modest but inviting foyer and were greeted by Mr. and Mrs. O'Sullivan and a large German shepherd. The dog stared at them suspiciously, bearing the appearance of an animal that would attack at a simple command.

Noticing the anxious looks on their faces, Jeanne laughed. "Relax, Farrah won't bite." Turning to her parents, she introduced them all. "Mom, Dad, I'd like you to meet, from left to right, Waldo Billingsly, Brisbane Wrock, Fontaine Washington, Bucktooth Johnson, and Phosphate Jefferson."

Mr. O'Sullivan, an erect man with closely cropped gray hair and intense, dark blue eyes, stepped forward and smiled. "It's very nice to meet you fellows. The girls have told us so much about you. I'm Bob O'Sullivan- you can call me Major, everyone does- and this pretty lady is my wife Anna."

Mrs. O'Sullivan was a petite, kind looking woman whom Waldo could tell had been a knockout in her day. She waved them all into the dining room with demonstrable concern. "Now, come on boys, let's all sit down. We don't stand on ceremony in this house. There's plenty here, and I want you to eat everything you can. The twins tell us that you haven't been eating enough to keep a flock of birds alive. Don't you all know how important a healthy diet is?"

Mrs. O'Sullivan had once been a clinical dietician, before she'd given birth to the twins and subsequently retired from the salaried working world. Had she been aware of the true unhealthy extent of Waldo and his friends' diet, and how devoid it actually was of vitamins and nutrients, she would have been astonished.

"Yeah man-uh, ma'am-we definitely should be more careful about what we eat." As Brisbane's eyes widened with every additional delicacy the bustling Mrs. O'Sullivan placed in front of them, it was clear that being judicious about what he consumed was the last thing on his mind.

Phosphate spoke as they were all seating themselves at the table. "May I convey our appreciation, on behalf of everyone, for this lovely meal which you so generously have asked us to share?"

"Well, you're quite welcome. If we'd known you were sleeping in our cornfield, and in your car, without being properly fed, we'd have insisted that you get some homemade food in you before now." Mrs. O'Sullivan, whose daughters had obviously kept her abreast of things, came across in a vaguely June Lockhart-like manner. Seconds after filling their plates up, the five famished friends began digging in like young males will do when they haven't eaten much solid food for several days. Brisbane, Fontaine, and Bucktooth were like men possessed, moving their forks and knives at a pace that brought to mind visions of a trio of Jethro Bodines at a speed-eating contest.

Their behavior clearly embarrassed Waldo and Phosphate, who, despite being every bit as hungry, both had some sense of propriety. Waldo initiated a conversation in order to divert attention away from their three starving cohorts. "So, Mr., I mean Major, and Mrs. O'Sullivan, I'd like to compliment you on having two such kind and pretty daughters."

Major O'Sullivan was scrutinizing Waldo carefully. "Well, young man, Jeanne and Janie seem to have a high opinion of you as well."

"Yes, Waldo, Jeanne says that you're some sort of writer. That must be exciting." Mrs. O'Sullivan was curious in that old-fashioned, homespun kind of way. "I'd love to have a talent like that. What do you write about?"

Waldo had to think before he answered, being careful to avoid mentioning that his primary literary interests included such non-appetizing subjects as strange disappearances, U.F.O.'s, and the Kennedy assassination. "Uh, well, I write some poetry, short stories, songs, and I'm working on a novel." Waldo didn't resort to lying as often as most people, but in this case he undeniably was being deceptive. He was not working on a novel, had only attempted and never completed a short story, hadn't written a song in years, and could hardly be considered a prolific poet. Most of his literary output was, in fact, in the same field of unpublished pamphlets that his missing grandfather had been such a pathfinder in.

"Excuse me, sir, but you mentioned that everyone refers to you as Major. Are you still in the military?" Phosphate knew precisely what to say to nearly everyone, and Jeanne's father was no exception.

"That's right, young man." The Major beamed proudly. "I'm a career man. I've been in the Army for 22 years now. Any of you fellows ever been in the service?"

Fontaine held his eating utensils in mid-air, hesitating long enough to confirm, through a mouthful of roast beef, that he was the only one present who'd served his country in that capacity.

"Oh, is that right?" The Major's interest was piqued. "Where'd you serve, son, in 'Nam?"

Fontaine finished swallowing. "No, man, I just was in, you know, basic training and then I worked the rest of my stint at the base hospital."

"Dad, why don't you tell them how the government left behind those prisoners of war and everything?" Jeanne knew the sort of subject matter Waldo and his friends were likely to find interesting, and attempted to bait her father into a scathing lecture on what he considered to be the most scandalous betrayal of modern times.

"Oh, I see." The Major, completely ignoring his daughter's invitation to expound about his pet peeve, was obviously a bit disappointed with Fontaine's uneventful military history. Spreading a healthy amount of butter on his corn muffin, he looked at Waldo as he spoke. "I understand you're from Virginia, near Washington, D.C."

Since Waldo had just spooned some potatoes into his mouth, and everyone else was maniacally inhaling their food, Phosphate felt obliged to respond. "That's correct, sir. I don't know, by the way, if your daughters mentioned it or not, but Waldo recently suffered the loss of his grandfather."

"Oh, I'm so sorry to hear that." Mrs. O'Sullivan, who was seated on one side of Waldo, patted his hand sympathetically.

"Perhaps I've confused you. I mean that he literally lost him- he vanished without a trace." The top doo-wopper explained. "We happened to meet Waldo and Brisbane recently, and I was so moved by his sorrow over this mysterious occurrence, and his determination to find his grandfather, that I offered my assistance- along with Fontaine's and Bucktooth's, naturally- in the matter."

"That was very commendable of you." Major O'Sullivan remarked, as he went for the butter again. "Son, what do you think happened to your grandfather? Surely, you must have some idea. Weren't there any clues?"

Waldo swallowed and dabbed his mouth daintily with his napkin, in the polite manner of a dinner guest. "No, not really. All I had to go on was a short, strange note that he left behind for me."

"But dear, why did you come all the way to Iowa? Did your grandfather come from here, or have some connection to our fair state?" Mrs. O'Sullivan was a proud Iowan, and it showed.

Waldo played with his food as he fumbled his words. "I, uh, he had a-a very good friend who is, uh, out here in Iowa."

Jeanne stepped in instinctively and expanded on a subject that was a bit embarrassing to Waldo. "What Waldo is trying to say, Mom, is that this friend of his grandfather's was committed to the Last Chance Relaxation Home."

Mrs. O'Sullivan gave Waldo an understanding look. "Oh, honey, you don't have to be embarrassed about that. Mental illness isn't anything to be ashamed of. My goodness, we all have our problems, and it isn't as if *you'd* been committed there."

"We all know that, Mom." Jeanne rolled her eyes in a timeless adolescent gesture of exasperation with parental foibles. "Really!"

"I'm sorry, dear." Mrs. O'Sullivan replied. "I'm sure Waldo knows what I meant."

Waldo smiled and nodded.

Major O'Sullivan, although it seemed apparent that neither he nor his wife suspected the extent of Jeanne's involvement with Waldo, then brought up the one question, even in the late twentieth century, that fathers invariably ask their daughters' prospective suitors. "So, son, what do you do for a living?"

Waldo gulped. The Major was staring directly at him again. *How can I answer that without sounding like a lazy, worthless bum*, he wondered. "Uh, I-I hope to pursue writing professionally."

The wily father whipped out the classic paternal follow-up. "Oh, are you going to school?"

Waldo was again mulling his reply over carefully, and taking what must have seemed to Jeanne's father to be an inordinate amount of time in doing so, when the plucky teenager came to his rescue.

"Puleeeese, Dad!" She exclaimed in a semi-valley girl lingo. "That's kind of rude!"

"Jeanne, honey, I was only..."

Mrs. O'Sullivan interrupted her husband. "Jeanne's right, dear.

Waldo and his friends are our guests, and they're very hungry, so why don't we let them enjoy their meal without having to answer a lot of personal questions?"

Major O'Sullivan, who certainly hadn't badgered Waldo, bore the countenance of a man who'd just been mildly berated by his wife in front of company. "I'm sorry, dear. Waldo, I didn't mean to cross-examine you." He suddenly began to chuckle. "Heck, I guess it must have seemed to you like I thought a grown man like yourself was, I don't know, interested in my little girl. Now, what could be crazier than that?"

Mrs. O'Sullivan laughed along with her husband, and Waldo noticed Jeanne forcing a few phony ha-ha's out. He thought he saw tears welling up in her beautiful green eyes as she spoke in a low voice which barely masked the pain within her. "Yeah, what could be crazier?"

Farrah, the O'Sullivan's German Shepherd, was making the rounds of the table begging for scraps. When she came to Waldo, she struck pay dirt. The nervous young man loved animals of all kinds, and they seemed to sense that. Waldo thoroughly enjoyed sneaking pieces of his roast beef to Farrah under the table, and the grateful animal licked his hands lovingly and curled up at his feet afterwards. As the warmth from the dog's body crept up his lower extremities, and he shoveled a few more forkfuls of food into his own mouth, it became obvious to Waldo that Jeanne was upset over her father's comments.

"Mom and Dad, I have something to tell you." Jeanne announced, in a louder and more authoritative voice than usual.

Waldo felt a tingle on the tip of his spine, but this time it had nothing to do with Francis Scott Key or Lee Harvey Oswald.

Overcoming her last little bit of hesitation, the pretty teenager took a deep breath and looked at Waldo. "Waldo and I are in love. He may be older than I am, but we care for each other deeply, and I think that we both feel like we want to spend the rest of our lives together."

Waldo could feel four very inquisitive, parental eyes turn in his direction. He didn't know what to do, so he stared intently at the pattern on his now empty plate, hoping that it would hypnotize him so he wouldn't have to face this uncomfortable situation.

Finally Major O'Sullivan spoke up. "Son, what is this all about? Do you mean to say that you and my daughter really..."

"Yes, Daddy, we're lovers!" Jeanne's strident stance betrayed a latent immature urge to confront her parents.

At this moment Janie, who had been conspicuously quiet all through the dinner, aided her twin and revealed more unwelcome news for her parents to digest along with their meal. "Yeah, and Brisbane and I have strong feelings for each other too, at least I think he does. We haven't gone that far yet, but if I have any say about it, we probably will."

Waldo could feel the anger and tension building up in the twins' parents.

When Mrs. O'Sullivan broke the uneasy silence, her voice was strained and any similarity to June Lockhart no longer existed. "Boys, I think you'd better leave our house right now." She rose from the table in a huff and ran off crying.

Major O'Sullivan's reddening complexion reflected the image of a battle-scarred veteran who couldn't bomb his way out of a distasteful set of circumstances, and he fought mightily to keep his temper under control. "Waldo, and you too, Brisbane, I can't imagine why you'd be interested in girls who aren't even of legal age, and I don't really care to know. I just want you to stay away from my daughters. Do you understand? And I want your car out of here and off my land. If you're still here tomorrow morning, I'll call the police. Is that clear?" Without waiting for a response, he threw his napkin on his plate and followed his wife out of the dining room.

Waldo looked at Jeanne, who seemed more scared than defiant now. "Uh, I guess we better leave." He didn't know what else to say.

Jeanne reached across the table and took his hand. "I'm sorry, Waldo. I just don't think there's anything wrong with the way we feel about each other. I guess I should have kept quiet."

"Neither do I, obviously, but your parents, and more importantly, the law does." Waldo conjured up as much of a smile as he could muster and then stood up unsteadily. "Let's go, you guys."

At this, Bucktooth, who'd been so engrossed in consuming mass quantities of food that he'd missed out on all the drama, looked up from his plate with a dazed expression on his face. "Hey man, what's going on?"

Phosphate shook his head sadly at his befuddled fellow doo-wopper, then turned to the O'Sullivan twins. "Jeanne and Janie, do not worry. Your parents are merely momentarily upset and you must try and reason with them later. As for us, we have a specific mission here, and I don't think I'm overstepping my boundaries by stating that none of us came here pursuing anything other than that. Forgive me for interfering, but..."

"Thanks, but we'll work this out ourselves, Phosphate." Waldo interrupted testily. "Do you all mind leaving Jeanne and I alone for a minute, please?"

Everyone complied and walked outside. Left by themselves in the dining room, Jeanne spoke first. "Waldo, I do love you. I don't care about our ages. You're interested in history- you must know how young most wives once were, especially in the country. It hasn't been that long ago when there were lots of legally married girls, with husbands older than you, who were two or three years younger than me. I would have been considered an old maid in some towns! I want to stay with you forever, and I don't care who knows that."

Waldo looked at her. She really was almost physically perfect. "Jeanne, I love you too and I want to stay with you, but..."

"I'm only sixteen. In two years I'll be eighteen and no one will say anything. Okay, maybe you'll be cruising back through Iowa then. Maybe I'll see you if you are. Until then, goodbye." The heartbroken teenager ran from the room and left Waldo standing there in a familiar, dejected pose.

Waldo slowly walked out of the house. All of the others were standing on the lawn. When she saw him, Janie immediately headed inside. As she passed by the nervous young man, she grabbed his arm and whispered, "she really does love you, you know."

Waldo nodded and joined the rest of the group. "Well," he said in an artificially upbeat voice that fooled no one, "now that we've eaten, why don't we all get as drunk as humanly possible tonight?"

"That's a great idea, man," Fontaine observed, "but what are we gonna get drunk on? There ain't any more beer, and we don't have enough money..."

"Relax." Brisbane lit up a cigarette. "I happen to keep a few bottles in the trunk, under the spare tire, in case of emergencies."

"You mean...bottles of liquor?" Bucktooth asked excitedly.

"Jack Daniels, dude." The fredneck announced proudly.

Everyone agreed that becoming inebriated was the thing to do. Since this was apparently going to be their last night in or near the magical cornfield, they aimed to make the most of it. In fact, if Waldo was successful the next day in making contact with Sam Hancock, it could very well be their last night in Iowa.

As the five comrades paraded away together, a very beautiful and melancholy young girl was watching them from her bedroom window and shedding some adult strength tears.

Out in the cornfield, things had become interesting. The whiskey was flowing and Fontaine, Bucktooth, and Brisbane were rapping incessantly:

> "Who they, who us, who you, who me
> I ain't in the habit of saying 'we'
> I'm single and I wanna be free
> I ain't married now, ain't gonna be
> I ain't gonna spend a whole lot of money
> So you can show your ring off, honey
> You think that you can win my respect
> By getting your hands on my paycheck
> If I see a lady that I want to do

286

Better stand aside and let me through
If you want to play house, then that's okay
But I'll throw you out on your ass one day
You'll be crying and want me back
But I'll have someone else in the sack
So get out of my face and move your butt
And watch your pretty ass when the door slams shut!"

The three rappers bowed to the stoic, unresponsive corn stalks and took a break. "Phos, man, how come you never want to rap with us?" Fontaine asked the head Afro-Anarchist.

Phosphate was sitting under a tree (in recent days, a favorite position of his) drinking a cup of Jack Daniels and Coke. He took a swallow and thought for a second before responding. "Fontaine, as I told you when you joined the Afro-Anarchists, doo-wop is a way of life. I know no other kind of music or lifestyle. I have chosen to express my creative urges through doo-wop protest songwriting. I realize that it is not a financially lucrative field, but it is one that I have all to myself. If you want to branch out into other areas, then by all means do so. I would never dream of holding you back. But as for me, I simply have no desire to. I hope you understand."

Fontaine simply shrugged at the top doo-wopper's long-winded reply to his simple question. "Alright. Shit, Phos, I just thought you might want to join in."

Waldo, meanwhile, had wandered away from the others, as he had been doing so often recently. He was drinking the same no-frills cocktail as Phosphate, and smoking a cigarette as he walked along the edge of the magical cornfield, dangerously close to where the entrance to the Forest Of Injured Egos lay. Eventually he stopped and reclined on the ground, staring at the stars and fantasizing in his uniquely vivid fashion about what life might be like married to Jeanne O'Sullivan. It was quite easy to envision a lovely little house, filled with romping children and animals, and brightened by the presence of his darling little underaged hostess, mother, and wife waiting in the doorway.

"Waldo, is that you?"

Snapping out of his romantic stupor, Waldo gazed towards the entrance to the deep woods, where the voice seemed to originate. In the shadows, he could barely distinguish the figure of Jeanne O'Sullivan, standing there like a vision from the fevered mind of Edgar Allan Poe.

"Come here." She said, with a strange inflection in her voice. "It's your last night on our land and we have a lot to talk about."

The tree limbs were swaying in the night breeze, and the moonlight was peeking through their nooks and crannies in such a way that the gorgeous young girl appeared both frightening and irresistible in the illumination. Waldo was spellbound and followed her motioning finger like a puppy dog.

As he reached her side, she turned her face away from the shadows and into the full glare of the Iowa moon. Waldo felt faint, but the figure placed a pair of unfeminine hands upon his shoulders and steadied him. The girl was not Jeanne O'Sullivan, but the woman from the Last Chance Relaxation Home who'd taken their applications in the employment office, then later been identified as a member of the nursing staff by Fontaine and Bucktooth.

Waldo, under the effects of a giant surge of adrenaline, pulled away from the woman's surprisingly strong grasp and ran off into the magical cornfield with her chilling laughter echoing in the woods behind him.

"I-I-I was not defeated
And you-you-you were so conceited
May I-I-I repeat it
You-you-you-you don't need it
So you think you're gonna make it in the white man's world
Well, straighten your hair, put on your contacts, girl
You're a quota and a token in the land of the free
And that's all your black ass will ever be
You're just a substitute in the home of the brave
And you sweat a little less than you did as a slave
Now you don't pick cotton but you play the lottery
And you're as happy as a second class citizen can be
You don't have to turn Muslim with a ring in your nose
To wear your dashiki and be punished for your clothes
So grow your afro back and stop living a lie
Respect yourself, I might give you a try!"

Fontaine and Bucktooth finished another number in their all night cornfield rap session. Brisbane was no longer participating, having drunkenly stumbled off by himself earlier on in the festivities. The three of them had thought up a name for their group- Fontaine E. and the Steady Heady Boyz. Although Fontaine and Bucktooth were still nominally Afro-Anarchists, it was becoming increasingly apparent that the doo-wop trio was falling prey to the internal creative conflicts that had plagued so many bands before them.

"Shit, Fontaine E., you want to rest a minute or what?" Bucktooth was growing weary.

Fontaine E., as he now requested that everyone call him, looked offended. "Look, Buck, you want to be my main Steady Heady boy or not?"

Bucktooth shrugged resignedly and they prepared for another song.

Before they could begin, however, a bewildered-looking Waldo came running past them out of nowhere at a pace that indicated he was being chased by M.I.B.'s or something similarly unearthly again.

As the one present and two possibly ex-Afro Anarchists scratched their heads in befuddlement, Fontaine spoke. "Shit, I ain't seen a white boy move that fast since the last time I watched Babe Ruth trotting around the bases in one of those old film clips on t.v."

Waldo was moving quickly, alright, heading straight for the O'Sullivan house and a certain young lady's bedroom window.

Waldo stood there with a handful of pebbles. He was, in the finest romantic tradition, throwing the stones at Jeanne's window. Waldo had seen this strategy employed successfully in countless movies and t.v. shows, and only the absence of a ladder in the yard prevented him from resorting to the ultimate hackneyed device.

After hurling three or four of them at her window with admirable aim, he succeeded in rousing her. The light in her room went on and seconds later the beautiful teenager approached the window. Upon seeing Waldo standing below in the pale light of the moon, Jeanne's tender heart was instantly touched. She thrust open the bedroom window, and in a voice just loud enough to be heard whispered, "Waldo, you crazy, sweet fool! What are you doing here? If my parents catch you, they might not wait until tomorrow to call the police."

Waldo answered, probably a bit too loudly. "Jeanne, I love you. Please come and meet me in the cornfield as soon as you can. I need to talk to you and I can't wait. I'll be in the usual place." With those few simple, unmemorable words, the nervous young man dashed away like a gallant prince.

Jeanne, certainly as lovely as any fairy tale princess, wanted to call out after Waldo, but refrained for fear of awakening her family. She knew that she had to go to him, and so she began dressing.

Fontaine E. and the Steady Heady Boyz (still minus Brisbane) continued to rap away by moonlight in a nearly uninterrupted fashion that no spoiled pop star could have matched. Phosphate had passed out beneath yet another tree, so the two still energetic song stylists sang to no one but the lovely Iowa countryside:

"Hey, yo, mister you, on the radio
You say you ain't never seen a U.f.O.
Don't tell me you know what it's like to pretend

289

'Til you've ridden on a spaceship with little green men
I know such things are hard to untangle
Atlantis, Easter Island, the Bermuda Triangle
But when you see those flashing lights in the sky
You better get ready to kiss your ass goodbye
It could be the boogie man coming for you
Or maybe some zombies and that old voodoo
I don't believe in Stonehenge or Nostradamus..."

"Shit, dudes!" Brisbane staggered towards them, out of breath and evidently still inebriated.

"Yo, where you been, my number two Steady Heady boy?" Fontaine E. was growing enamored of the various terms popularized by the latest generation of inner city dwellers.

Brisbane looked flustered. He bent over at the waist, took several deep breaths, then straightened himself up and started talking. "I'm telling you, man...I'm not walking around these cornfields at night again. I'm glad the Major is kicking us out of here."

"What'd you see this time, Bris?" Bucktooth asked.

Despite being short of breath, the fredneck lit a cigarette. "Well, I was near the woods and I saw this old dude and...hey, where is Waldo?"

"I don't have any idea, man. Buck and I saw him running past us a little while ago like some damn madman." Fontaine bent down and picked up his whiskey and Coke, which had been lying among the corn stalks for quite a while.

"Shit, I wonder what that was all about." The fredneck mused. "I really wanted Waldo to hear this, but since he's beamed out again...what the fuck. The old man I saw told me his name was Ambrose Bierce."

At the mention of the cynical master's name, Phosphate awoke with a start. In one swift movement, he was on his feet and at Brisbane's side. "What did you say about Ambrose Bierce?"

"Shit man, you're a light sleeper. I was just saying that I met this old dude and he told me he was Ambrose Bierce."

"Do you happen to know what Bierce looked like? Did this stranger seem to resemble him at all?" The excited top doo-wopper inquired.

"Well, I'm not really sure what Ambrose Bierce looked like- I'm not Waldo, man-but this dude was old and pretty hairy." Brisbane drew deeply on his Marlboro. "What scared the shit out of me was when he asked if we got out of Snortin' Reformatory okay."

Phosphate's face lit up. "The peculiar old man who placed bail for us! But...if this is true, it stretches reality to the breaking point!"

"Sheeet!" Fontaine exclaimed. "With everything we've seen lately, I think my reality has already been stretched as far as it can go!"

"Well, shit man, where the fuck can Waldo be?" Brisbane, anxious to impart this new information to his friend, gazed out into the night, which was gradually becoming blanketed by a dense fog, but the magical cornfield and deep woods offered no answers.

"Indeed." Phosphate, sobered by the ramifications of Brisbane's discovery, reflected somewhat nervously. "I wonder where he could be?"

Jeanne crept up behind Waldo. He was lying on his back in his favorite spot of the large cornfield, a good distance away from where the others were speculating about his whereabouts, gazing dreamily upwards, oblivious to the imposing fog which was completely blocking his view of the sky.

"Waldo?" She called out.

Waldo jumped up anxiously, and seeing it was his beloved teenage sweetheart, ran over and embraced her. "Oh, Jeanne, I knew you'd come." The nervous young man kissed her repeatedly on both cheeks, like an uncle at an Italian wedding. When he finally stopped, he took her by the hand. "Come sit down. I have to talk to you."

They sat down and Waldo looked at her intently. "Jeanne, I had another strange experience here tonight, just before I came and threw rocks at your window. There was a girl out there, at the edge of the woods, who I thought was you. She sounded like you, and looked like you from a distance, but when I came close to her, I saw that she was really the lady from the Last Chance Relaxation Home's personnel office who took our applications."

"Wow." Jeanne placed her hand on his shoulder. "What do you think she was doing out here?"

"That's just it, Jeanne." Waldo lit up a cigarette. "I guess the reason I ran to your house right afterwards was to make sure it wasn't you. And...to ask you what is going on around here."

"What do you mean?" The Irish beauty asked innocently.

"I mean, all of us have seen things on your property- a green giant, a werewolf, a U.F.O. I saw the Hitchhiker that we picked up on our way out here, first in your house, then in your cornfield. And well, I promised not to reveal this, so let's just say I ran into something pretty interesting in the deep woods over there."

Jeanne appeared confused. "You wanted me to come out in the middle of the night so you could ask me *that*?"

Waldo, still prone to the errors that had long marked his relations with the opposite sex, ran his fingers through his hair in frustration. "Look, I'm sorry- I didn't mean it to sound like...anyhow, I-I didn't come and throw rocks at your window because..."

"It's okay, silly." Jeanne smiled sweetly. "All I know about what you

291

said-the strange creatures and everything-is that I've never seen any of them, and neither has Janie. Like I told you, lots of times we get a stray Civil War soldier or Pilgrim popping into the cornfield, or even in the house, but never anything like a green giant or a U.F.O."

"You know," Waldo ventured to reach out and caress her hair, "even if I hadn't seen that lady, I was still planning to come and wake you. I couldn't sleep because of what happened."

"I wasn't sleeping either." Jeanne hugged Waldo tightly. "Please, let's figure something out. I don't know what I'll do if you leave."

"I don't want to, but your parents obviously aren't about to give us their blessing. I just figured that we'd ride to work together again tomorrow, and after I visit the Extremely Unreachable Ward, I might know a lot more about the future." Waldo gazed wistfully out into the fog. "You know, Jeanne, I-I might not, well, with everything that's happened so far, uh, I just have kind of a feeling that..."

"Relax, sweetie." The underaged beauty reassured him. "You have nothing to worry about."

"What if I don't...come back from the Extremely Unreachable Ward?"

"You're silly!" Jeanne replied. "Why wouldn't you come back from there?"

"I-I don't know." Waldo ground out his Camel Light in the rich Midwestern soil. "There has to be some reason for all the weird things that have happened since my grandfather disappeared. I just can't help but be a little scared that this place, well..."

"I told you not to worry." Jeanne mildly scolded him. "Now...since this is your last night staying in the cornfield... why don't we..."

With no further conversation necessary, they grabbed each other and began rolling around in the corn stalks, happily frolicking and making love with as much innocence as the act allows.

"Ambrose Bierce? *Here*?" Waldo stared at his four friends in utter disbelief.

After their late night dalliance had ended, Jeanne had hurried back to her house, and Waldo had drifted around aimlessly until he stumbled upon the others, who were still abuzz with excitement and busily consuming more cornfield cocktails.

"I'm not shitting you, man. The old dude claimed he was Ambrose Bierce." Brisbane said.

Waldo was flabbergasted. "Exactly where was he?"

The fredneck thought for a moment. "Well, he was over by a big old oak tree, down where the woods begin. He didn't say much else, and I didn't feel like asking him a lot of questions."

At the mention of the oak tree, Waldo formed the notion in his mind that perhaps the bitter one had joined his fellow cynicists in the Forest of Injured Egos. Waldo almost laughed out loud at the thought of Ambrose Bierce gathered around a campfire, singing songs of disenchantment with Fred O'Grady and the other members of his pathetic organization.

"Well, right now, I'm very tired and I need some sleep." Waldo responded, surprising the others with his nonchalance.

Actually, Waldo desperately wanted to search for and confront the man who claimed to be Ambrose Bierce, but he feared his suspicions about where he might be were correct. He remembered well The Injured Egos' affinity for privacy, and he felt sure the others would want to follow him. If Waldo brought his comrades there, assuming he was able to locate the elusive band of luckless men, Fred O'Grady would certainly not allow them in, and he would lose any chance he had of speaking to the alleged author of the timeless masterpiece *The Devil's Dictionary*. The strongest reason for Waldo's hesitance to approach the area in the company of others, however, was his vow to O'Grady that he would keep their presence there a secret. The nervous young man took his commitments far more seriously than the majority of his fellow human beings, and therefore was not likely to break such a promise.   "Well, shit man, okay. I just thought that you'd want to try and talk to the old dude right away. He could still be there. But, if you want to sleep, then..." Brisbane simply shrugged.

"I must admit, Waldo, that I too am amazed you aren't more anxious to look for this individual, who after all may very well be the long-lost Ambrose Bierce himself, your grandfather's hero." Phosphate was understandably perplexed by Waldo's attitude.

Waldo attempted a logical explanation, which wasn't easy.   "Look, I do want to see this guy, but it's very late and I've had a long day. Besides, judging by the way things happen around here, whoever that old man is, he's probably long gone by now. Try to understand- right now all I'm thinking about is finding Sam Hancock tomorrow. After I do that, then I'll start searching for imaginary Ambrose Bierces."

As he spoke, Waldo saw by the looks on their faces that his friends found his words even less convincing than he did. Tired and unable to mockingly defend his untenable position any longer, he lay down on the ground and turned his back to them, and lost himself in rapturous thoughts of young Jeanne O'Sullivan.

16

RED ROVER, RED ROVER, SEND WALDO RIGHT OVER

Waldo opened his dew-covered eyelids, after a brief and fitful sleep in the cornfield. Almost instantaneously, as he fumbled in his pocket for a Camel Light, his apprehension about the prospect of contacting Sam Hancock and/or Ambrose Bierce began to wind its way around his delicate emotional system, until it was brimming over in every nerve ending and ready to burst through the skin itself. Before he'd finished his cigarette, Jeanne arrived and greeted him in her usual fashion, with an abundance of hugs and kisses, and the nervous young man readied himself for a quick trip back in time, which was becoming a morning ritual with them. The lovely Irish lass surprised him, however, by requesting that she be given the opportunity to witness what he had been like as a teenager. Waldo, reluctant at first to extend their adventures into such personal domains, eventually agreed, and they were able to observe his participation in a pickup basketball game at the age of fifteen. Jeanne was suitably bubbly and over-enthusiastic, cheering every basket that the less than athletic Waldo scored.

At length, they returned to the present age, and hurried back to Brisbane's decidedly un-fredneck-like '65 Dodge Dart. Suspecting that they would be greeted by a chorus of shaking heads and "we're gonna be late, man's," they discovered instead that Fontaine, or rather Fontaine E., and his full contingent of Steady Heady Boyz had not lost any of their rapping fervor. They were picking up, blood shot eyes and all, where they'd left off a few hours before, putting everyone in the proper frame of mind for their work at the Last Chance Relaxation Home with a catchy new number:

"You know they call me rapmaster Fontaine
I never been to Mars or even flown in a plane
But I've seen enough of planet Earth
To feel I've gotten my money's worth
I've seen hungry kids, seen fat ones too
Probably see a lot more before I'm through
I've always been the baddest one on my block
I got more twists than Alfred Hitchcock
When you play with me, you'll get your fingers burned
And the hardest lesson that you ever learned
Will be when I forget the good times we had
And send you to Jamaica or Trinidad

Sometimes I get those two confused
'Cause I don't read the papers or watch the news
So shake your sexy body and use your brain
And turn yourself over to big Fontaine!"

Phosphate, for one, was growing tired of being constantly serenaded by rap music. "Fontaine, why don't you please 'just say yo' for a minute? Would you and your cohorts grant us at least a temporary respite from that infernal rapping?"

Fontaine might have been expected to adopt his macho Fontaine E. persona, or perhaps point out the similarities between rap music and Phosphate's beloved doo-wop, but instead he apologized. "Okay, Phos-I'm sorry. We'll cool it for awhile. I guess we're all just about rapped out by now, anyway."

Waldo and Jeanne led the others into the car. The excess intake of air into his lungs, along with the tingling fingertips and light headedness, were sure fire indications of just how much Waldo was worrying about his anticipated encounter with Sam Hancock. Jeanne positioned herself on his lap, and the jittery young man placed his trembling arms around her waist. As he did so, the pretty teenager turned around and smiled reassuringly, aware that his mind was preoccupied with thoughts of sub-basements and Extremely Unreachable Wards.

As the five friends who made up the sole staff of the Central Supply day shift reported to their department, Waldo attempted to temporarily forget his concerns by reflecting upon some of the lighter aspects of working at the Last Chance Relaxation Home. For instance, there were the "classics," as Brisbane had quickly dubbed them. "Classics" were those employees who presented a particularly odd or eccentric appearance and behaved just as unusually. They were, in fact, nearly indistinguishable from those Waldo referred to as "Unreals." They looked unique, had their own little catch phrases, and could be relied upon to spout them out consistently. One of the most noticeable things about them was their ageless quality; it was next to impossible to determine how old a "classic" was. They seemed genuinely harmless, unlike some of the employees they'd encountered at the institution, and Waldo and the others immediately took an interest in each one they met. Even after a few days, it was obvious that the Last Chance Relaxation Home was full of them.

Fontaine and Bucktooth especially enjoyed the antics of the supervisor of the Laundry, an older black gentleman by the name of Harvey. Harvey resembled, more than anything else, an African-American version of Popeye. Many years of hoisting heavy bags of dirty linen in the air and dumping them into giant washers had left Harvey with a well-developed set of forearms, but his comical, high pitched, lisping voice belied his impressive physique. Fontaine and Bucktooth rapidly discovered that Harvey was a human parrot; whatever they said to him, no matter how ridiculous it was, he repeated it. He had a penchant for saying "how many baskets" and laughing uproariously whenever he did, and Fontaine and Bucktooth would respond with such variations as "how many women" or "how many drugs," and the supervisor would echo their words without hesitating for a moment in his strenuous labors.

Phosphate, meanwhile, was impressed with a Filipino warehouse worker named Ernesto, whom everyone called "Flames." This nickname derived from his habit of setting fires daily in his department. Evidently, "Flames" was separated from his wife, and was forced to obtain what little rest he could in his car, and thus was constantly falling asleep on the job, usually with one of his ever-present cigarettes in his hand. Waldo's favorite classic was Mr. White, a gregarious pharmacist who looked and sounded a great deal like Hugh Beaumont, the actor who portrayed the legendary Ward Cleaver in the television show *Leave It To Beaver*. Mr. White was evidently very interested in conspiracies, and appeared to be a right-wing extremist in his beliefs, but Waldo refrained from discussing anything of a truly significant political nature with him, because of his general distrust of the mental health facility and all those who worked there. At any rate, Mr. White was a nice, friendly fellow, and was the only employee there with any status who acted civil towards the lowly Junior Material Handlers.

Undoubtedly, the most classic of them all was the legendary housekeeper Otto Motto. Brisbane, especially, tried desperately during his every spare moment to locate and meet him, but he proved to be extremely elusive. In fact, the intense investigation the fredneck conducted brought forth no hard information at all about him from his fellow low-income laborers. Brisbane was able, however, to uncover a single disturbing point: Otto Motto had never actually been seen by anyone he questioned. All of the employees simply knew of him from reputation and none seemed to think it queer that he was apparently capable of mopping and buffing floors without being noticed by those around him. Brisbane had vowed to continue his fruitless inquiry, but for now was content to simply enjoy the talent that made Otto Motto the #1 star classic- his proficient and prolific efforts at graffiti. Otto Motto's graffiti consisted mainly of clever little lists, and it covered virtually all wall space on the basement floor, which was full of other common laborers who could appreciate his observations. It was rumored that Otto Motto was a frustrated writer who'd turned for some reason to the field of sanitary engineering, and, as the saying goes, writers write. The fredneck found himself pausing frequently to gaze at the walls during his sojourns through the winding corridors of the basement, relating to the housekeeper's radical philosophy and raving about such works of art as:

People Not Involved In The J.F.K. Ass. Conspiracy
1. Robert F. Kennedy
2. John-John and Caroline
3. Jackie Kennedy
4. John Wilkes Booth
5. Arnold Ziffel
6. Anyone making less than $25,000 per year
7. Otto Motto
8. Lee Harvey Oswald

Jobs With Less Career Potential Than A Sanitary Engineer's
1. Coal miners
2. Illegal alien migrant farm workers
3. Leaders of white supremacist groups
4. Creative writers, musicians, or painters
5. Plain-looking female newscasters, musicians, or actresses
6. Political conspiracy theorists

Reasons Why The Nursing Staff Needs The New 15% Pay Raise
1. They only got 12% last year
2. Rising cost of all weight loss programs
*3. Necessity of maintaining aura of superiority over other
    employees who received 4% raises*
4. They make a lot less than doctors

Requirements For The Position Or Registered Nurse (R.N.)
1. Ability to consistently ignore patient requests for assistance
*2. Ability to have no recognition of the reality of any other
    employees except management and physicians*
*3. Ability to feel no guilt when assigning all work other than
    hourly rounds to aides, orderlies, and L.P.N.'s*
*4. Ability to join in the coordinated public relations campaign
    to be portrayed constantly as "under-staffed and under-paid"*

Fringe Benefits Of Working In The Basement
*1. You get to meet many cute nurses who just love to associate
    with guys in your profession*
*2. You feel a sense of satisfaction, self-worth, and
    accomplishment
    that is hard to duplicate in any career*

*3. You get to wear a nifty uniform that rivals the highest quality
   prison outfits for style and comfort*
4. You get a half hour (unpaid) lunch break

Phosphate tended to agree with Otto Motto's bleak assessment of
the basement. He called it the ghetto, and as he carefully folded the posey
vests, which was the antiseptic term the institution used to describe the
strait jackets, he quickly churned out a new doo-wop song, *Rock Bottom
Rag*, which was an anthem of sorts about it. It was a solo effort, due to
Fontaine E. and the Steady Heady Boyz' obsession with their own music:

"Down in the basement everything is black
The pay is low and you break your back
The manager walks by in his coat and tie
He moves real fast but he don't know why
The secretary comes and she wiggles past
She hangs her head and shakes her ass
There's a lot of offices with men in ties
And there's always something to supervise
When you pull the trash, no one is smiling
We're like the inmates on Devil's Island
There are plenty of white men in authority
And most of the workers are minorities
We have no union, so we'll never strike
Or tell the bosses what we would like
Like air conditioning when it's hot
Which every director's office has got
My coffee break's over, I have to run
Who says unskilled labor isn't fun?"

"What kind of goddamn shit is that?" Duck Hung was standing in
the doorway of the equipment room, stomping his foot in the finest
supervisory tradition.
"Oh...I, well, I suppose I should be working." The top doo-wopper,
seldom flustered or tongue-tied, hurriedly grabbed some isolation carts
and attempted to "look busy," a talent highly regarded in the business
world, but one that he was neither experienced nor skilled at.
Phosphate's song helped put Duck Hung in an even nastier frame of
mind than usual, and he began spitting out his incorrect and vulgar
English with machine gun-like rapidity.
"Goddamn shit! I kill your ass! You fuck up!" All of the Vietnamese
madman's choice expressions were repeated over and over again,
interspersed among a few random words of non-profanity. Due to his foul

mood, the five of them were on the run all morning long without a moment's rest.

As Waldo made his deliveries, he began to feel increasingly anxious about his imminent lunch break, and what those thirty unpaid minutes might hold in store for him. Even the various indignities inflicted on him by the non-productive and insensitive nursing staff couldn't take his mind off of the sub-basement and the Extremely Unreachable Ward.

Around ten o'clock, he wheeled a cart full of pharmacy medications into the Central Supply elevator, which was for the exclusive use of the Junior Material Handlers and made their job a great deal easier, but was generally out of service. Waldo sensed something amiss as he pressed his floor button and the door closed. Suddenly a voice behind him called out his name and the elevator stopped.

"Waldo...we've been waiting to talk to you."

Slowly he turned around and saw that the Hitchhiker was standing there, along with an old gentleman. Waldo recognized, beneath the long gray hair and beard, the unmistakable features of Ambrose Bierce. "What do you want now?" He asked, his nerve a bit more fortified with each new strange encounter.

The Hitchhiker laughed. Pointing to the old man, he said, "Waldo, why do you refuse to heed my advice? Don't you know who this is?"

Waldo nodded. "It looks like Ambrose Bierce."

"That's right. And do you know how old he must be by now?"

Waldo thought for a minute. "Around 140 or so."

"My, my, you *are* up on things. He is indeed well over 140 years of age. And how, you might ask, can that be? My friend, he is an example of what I've been telling you about. The powers I represent can make so many things possible you cannot begin to imagine them all." The Hitchhiker patted the alleged Bierce on the back.

Waldo looked at them both and became angry. "I thought I told you before to leave me alone! I don't care who you are, but I do know that this old man is not Ambrose Bierce. He may look like him, but the real Bierce would never join forces with someone like you."

The old man instantly became transformed before Waldo's eyes. He went in a split second from being one elderly Ambrose Bierce-clone to the three M.I.B.'s that Waldo had run into on earlier occasions.

The Hitchhiker began laughing hideously. "Very well, Waldooooo...you should have listened to me. It is now officially too late."

The elevator started moving again, and as the door opened at Waldo's intended destination, the Hitchhiker and the three M.I.B.'s chanted in unison, "see you in the sub-basement!"

Waldo left the elevator and passed rapidly through the clean holding area. Clean holding was a standard feature throughout the facility, which was utilized to store each floor's supplies, and it separated the Central Supply elevator from the nursing stations. As Waldo approached the nursing station, he was so distracted with his own thoughts that he didn't even notice that there was quite a commotion in front of it.

A young male patient was waving his arms and yelling at the top of his lungs. "I'm not insane! I don't want to be here! I did not seek any help! This has to be against the law!"

Waldo's attention was finally captured by this loud and moving plea. As he listened, he thought that the patient was making his point clearly and concisely.

"Now, now, Mr. Biggs, calm down and take your medicine." A middle-aged nurse bearing no resemblance to Florence Nightingale was creeping towards him.

The young man lunged forward and grabbed a female security officer, who had been summoned to the floor to help quell the disturbance. He picked her up and lifted her above his head like a barbell. Surprisingly, none of the other dozen or so security officers there, who were in the habit of accompanying each other everywhere, attempted to help her. Waldo, slowly recovering from his latest unsettling experience, was growing interested in the situation. The fact that the majority of the security personnel were women caught his attention immediately. The nervous young man was as sensitive and enlightened as they come, but he still found this extremely peculiar.

"Mr. Biggs, put the young lady down or I'll..."

"Call security on me?" The patient, who was tall and solidly built, with a badly receding hairline that clashed with his round baby face, began laughing at the same nurse who'd tried to reason with him before. "I told you what my demands were. Now meet them, or I'll let this...officer go. If you don't do what I say, I swear I'll toss her out the window."

The nurses and the security guards were abuzz over this, and their lack of response indicated that they were probably unaccustomed to dealing with such a serious crisis. The young lady being held over his head, however, with a great deal at stake personally, anxiously inquired as to what his demands were.

The patient smiled, and turned to the security officers. "Excuse me for not looking her in the face as I respond, that would be very awkward. As I informed these nurses earlier, all I want is for them to gather up every bit of medicine on this floor and allow the patients to stomp on it until it is crushed and worthless."

The nurses, realizing the potential financial losses, obviously were reluctant to accede to this rather unusual request. They were also fearful of the repercussions that would result once the administration was alerted to the names of those responsible for allowing it to happen. The security officers, on the other hand, were in disagreement with the nursing staff now that one of their own was in a precarious position, and they started urging the nurses to do what was asked of them.

"Young man, do you understand how much money this facility would lose if we let you have your way?" An older nurse with a worried look on her wrinkled brow asked.

The young patient grinned, in the learned manner of one who is presumed insane. "Yes, the pills are very expensive, aren't they?"

The nurses, exasperated and undoubtedly seeing more activity than they had in a long time, huddled together briefly behind the station in the pantry. They then broke the huddle like a beginner's league flag football team, it seemed to Waldo. The nurse who'd been serving as a sort of spokesperson looked at the patient with an air of resignation and announced that they had decided to grant him his wish.

Waldo had to stifle a tremendous urge to applaud. He was still standing just outside the door of the clean holding area, unnoticed by anyone, transfixed by the events in front of him.

The nursing staff slowly began dumping out all of the pills on the floor in front of the station. It took quite a bit of time for them to do this, partially because there was such a large supply in stock, but mainly due to the fact their atrophied muscles weren't used to lifting anything heavier than a can of soda or a sandwich. It was hardly strenuous labor, but there were a great many trips to be made back and forth from the locked area behind the pantry where the drugs were kept. Gradually, most of the nurses dropped down exhausted in various locations, and the bulk of the work was left to a few sturdy younger ones. Finally, huffing and puffing as if they'd just run in the Boston Marathon, the nurses who'd survived the ordeal deposited the last load and crawled towards the safety of the pantry.

When the job was completed, there was an impressive amount of pills there, covering the entire width of the nursing station, and piled to a height that was above most of their heads.

The young patient turned out to be a man of his word. He placed the female security officer gently down, and then began shouting to his fellow patients to come and join him because "the fun was about to begin." Waldo didn't surmise that the patients on this or any other floor in the Last Chance Relaxation Home were used to having any fun at all, thus it was no surprise to him that they responded by hurrying out of their rooms as if they'd been shot by cannons. It really was quite a spectacle to behold so many disheveled, confused, and tranquilized people jumping up and down on a gigantic mound of brightly colored pills.

As they stomped about in their innocuous glee, their leader screamed out at the top of his lungs that they were not going to take any more downers. Many of the others followed the young man's lead and shouted things of their own, such as, "No more dirty sheets! No more turning the t.v. off at eleven o'clock! No more fingerpainting in group therapy!" and similar sentiments.

By this time, Waldo realized that he'd been there observing the odd goings-on for much too long, and remembering Duck Hung's nasty disposition, he slipped gingerly past the high-stepping celebrants and dropped off the supplies.

No sooner had he done this, than their young leader surged all at once towards the counter on the side of the nursing station, pointing wildly at the bags Waldo had placed there.

"Look, more pills! Crush them!" He cried ecstatically.

As Waldo hurriedly retraced his steps back to the Central Supply elevator, he gave a thumbs-up salute to the happy mental patients, but they were all too busy to notice.

Waldo was fortunate that Duck Hung did not kill his ass upon his arrival back in Central Supply. Of course, he threatened to, but Waldo was slowly starting to discover that the unstable Vietnamese supervisor's bark was worse than his bite.

After berating him for taking so long on his deliveries, Duck Hung ordered Waldo to go to the lobby and pick up a package at the front desk. For once, Waldo was eager to comply, as the volunteer office was located nearby and he wanted to see Jeanne before his lunch break.

He took the stairs to the lobby floor, in as swiftly a fashion as his non-athletic legs would allow, so he would be able to spend more time with Jeanne. He reached the volunteer office very quickly, and as luck would have it, his true love was there all by herself.

"Waldo, what are you doing here?" The underaged beauty asked in astonishment.

"I have to pick up a package at the front desk, and I thought since I won't get back this way before my lunch break..." The nervous young man stared at her, and tears began welling up in his eyes. "Listen, I don't have long, I have to get back, but there's something I want you to have." He pulled a folded piece of paper from his shirt pocket. "This is a poem I wrote for you."

"Oh, Waldo!" Jeanne, her romantic spirit enthralled by such a gesture, threw her arms around him.

"I-I-I saw the Hitchhiker again in the elevator." Waldo hugged her as tightly as he could without injuring her. "And, if something happens where, well, I..."

"Don't even think it!" Jeanne was becoming all too familiar with the thought processes of a paranoid.

"No, I have to be realistic. I wanted you to understand how I feel, just in case..." He gazed directly into her bright green eyes. "If you don't want me too, I won't go down to the sub-basement."

Jeanne's bottom lip was trembling slightly. "I don't want you to go if you're frightened, silly, but if you didn't you'd always wonder about it and never know. And what about your grandfather? Besides, you're worrying about nothing. You'll be just fine, sweetie."

Waldo handed her the poem. "Yeah, sure. Here, take this now."

Jeanne took the paper and started to unfold it.

"No, please wait until I leave." Waldo looked up at the clock on the wall, and ran his fingers through his hair. "Which really should be now. I love you." He kissed her passionately and walked towards the door.

"I love you, too." Jeanne smiled sweetly. "And I'll tell you again at four o'clock in the lobby. Don't worry, okay?"

"Sure. I love you."

Jeanne laughed. "You just said that, silly. And like I just said, I love you, too. Now you better get back before that boss of yours throws a fit."

Waldo nodded and waved goodbye pathetically, like a young father going off to war.

As soon as the door was closed and he was gone, Jeanne squelched her own apprehensions, opened the paper and read the poem Waldo had written for her:

One taste of Jeanne and out I flew
Wildly, madly, in no direction
But hers, and yet so straight and true
I fly towards her with no protection
It feels so strange to move this way
Though I should land, desire it seems
Moves in strange circles and so I stay
Disoriented beyond my wildest dreams.

By the time she reached the closing line, Jeanne's tender little heart was more touched than it had ever been before. She placed the paper carefully in her purse and wiped her moist eyes with a tissue. Revealing fears of her own that she had camouflaged so well in Waldo's presence, she began sobbing softly. As visions of sub-basements and wards that may or may not exist danced in her head, the beautiful teenager wondered if she should have tried to stop him from going, and all at once she shivered at the prospect of Waldo wandering about on his own in a secluded part of the building, glancing nervously behind him and anticipating more unusual, otherworldly encounters around every corner.

Speaking in a low voice to no one, but with a girlish romantic notion that Waldo could somehow hear her, she said, "that's the most beautiful poem I've ever read. I'll love you forever."

It was nearly lunchtime. There was a momentary lull in the activities at Central Supply. Duck Hung had been trotting off to the bathroom all day, and the five overworked members of his staff took full advantage of his discomfort. Since the Vietnamese supervisor had once again hurriedly departed to relieve himself, Brisbane instantly dropped his work and seized the opportunity to question Waldo, who looked worried.

"Shit man, what's on your mind? You aren't upset about going to the sub-basement, are you?" The fredneck inquired.

Phosphate jumped in before Waldo had a chance to respond. "My dear Waldo, if you wish, any or all or us would be happy to accompany you to the Extremely Unreachable Ward."

Waldo smiled weakly. "Thanks, but this is something I have to do myself." Waldo hadn't been able, between his deliveries, to tell the others of his encounter with the hitchhiker and the fake Ambrose Bierce earlier that morning, and he started to now. "Listen, about that old man..."

"Damn, Waldo, you better be careful when you go down there, you hear?" Fontaine, displaying an unlikely motherly instinct, didn't allow him to finish his sentence.

Waldo was appreciative of the new rapmaster's feeble attempt to assuage his fear. "I'll be okay, but if something does happen..."

"Don't dwell on the negative, Waldo. I do believe that may have contributed to all the other..."

Brisbane interrupted Phosphate. "Shit dude, just be cool and you won't run into any M.I.B.'s or U.F.O.'s."

At that moment, the clock hands were turned straight up to the noon hour, which was their allotted time for lunch. While the others were looking forward to some good, nutritious cafeteria food, Waldo tried to weather a massive onslaught of trepidation and force himself in the direction of the west wing, where the other entrance to the sub-basement was rumored to be. All four of his fellow Junior Material Handlers slapped his back and wished him luck before they left for the cafeteria. This was hardly comforting to Waldo, as it seemed to indicate a realization on their part that he needed some. Just then Duck Hung burst back into the room, with his fiery temperament intact behind his wan exterior.

"Goddamn shit! What the hell you still doing here? Get your ass out and eat some lunch!"

Waldo obeyed and slowly walked away in search of something other than food.

Waldo walked down the stairs to the sub-basement. He had found the other entrance in a seldom-used hallway near the west bank elevators, just where Jeanne had indicated it was supposed to be. The sub-basement's lack of access was reflected by the fact no elevator stopped there, and this only intensified the aura of remoteness that seemed to emanate from the very walls of the dimly lit stairwell. He was filled with anticipation, but as he reached the door that led into the sub-basement itself, he stopped and hesitated a moment before opening it.

As he entered the sub-basement, he saw that it did indeed appear to be a huge storage area; there were extra beds, tables, and chairs everywhere. What really grabbed Waldo's attention, however, and caused him to unfasten the top two buttons on his shirt, was the intense, overpowering heat. The nervous young man had once, several years previously, been a member of a health spa for an extremely brief period of time, and had stepped into the sauna during one of his infrequent visits there. The stifling, oppressive heat in that room had caused him to exit quickly, leaving the sweaty bodies to laugh derisively at him from underneath their towels, but the temperature in the sub-basement was every bit as high, and it was all Waldo could do to maintain his consciousness as he stumbled along gasping for air.

As Waldo passed by what seemed like miles of excess furniture, he gradually became acclimated to the omnipresent heat, and began to feel that perhaps the place did contain nothing more than stored supplies. He wasn't certain if he'd be relieved or distressed by that. Then, all at once, he saw a sign that made his pulse race and his heart pound even faster. It said simply, *Extremely Unreachable Ward*, with an arrow pointing to the right.

Brisbane, meanwhile, had located Otto Motto. Shortly after returning from his unpaid half hour lunch break, the fredneck had been pushing a cart of posey vests down a deserted corridor in the basement when he suddenly saw a diminutive figure swinging a mop directly in his path. As he excused himself for rolling his delivery cart across the wet floor, he happened to glance at the housekeeper's employee nametag. The name Otto Motto leaped out at him, and Brisbane lost all sense of reality by dropping to his knees and asking the graffiti master for his autograph.

"I beg your pardon?" Otto Motto didn't seem as surprised as the average sanitary engineer might be over a stranger requesting his autograph. The housekeeper bore a strong resemblance to the late actor Wally Cox, and he raised his eyebrows in a manner indicating he considered it likely that the fredneck was merely one of the more interesting patients there.

"Man, I've only been working here a couple of days, but, oh yeah, by the way, my name's Brisbane Wrock. Anyway, even though I haven't been here long, I've been admiring your graffiti. It's fucking awesome!" Brisbane exclaimed.

Otto Motto appeared to be slightly embarrassed. "How do you know I'm the one who wrote it?"

"Shit, are you kidding? I heard about you my first day here. Everyone knows who you are. You're a fucking legend!"

"Well, that's nice. Now I really must get back to work." Otto Motto started mopping again.

Brisbane, however, had expended too much time and energy in finding this #1 classic, and he wasn't about to let him out of his sight until he'd had the chance to talk with him awhile. "Listen, dude, how is it that you're so hard to find? I mean, no one that I've met here has ever seen you."

The legendary Housekeeper's countenance hastily changed from a Wally Cox-like placidity to one of seething hostility that would have caused humble Shoeshine Boy to bow his head in shame. "Why don't you leave me alone?" His voice had turned into a hiss. "By the way, have you heard from your friend in the sub-basement yet?" Otto Motto threw back his head and began laughing hysterically in nearly the same fashion as the Hitchhiker and the lady in the employment office/fake nurse/Jeanne O'Sullivan imposter had.

"How did you know I had a friend that was in the sub-basement?" The fredneck felt a Waldo-special starting to tingle at the tip of his spine.

"You've always loved drugs. Why don't you go to the Pharmacy and ask them for a valium? They hand them out to everyone; it seems to help if you're bothered by...the extracurricular activities in here. You're going to need *something*." Otto Motto kept laughing. "I think I'll go speak to Sam Hancock now, in case he needs any preparation."

Brisbane's mouth started to drop open even before the housekeeper suddenly vanished, mop and all. The fredneck then lost his composure completely, running repeatedly around in circles, in a manner emulating his hero Barney Fife, until his terror straightened him out and set him on a course for Central Supply. There was one predominant thought in his mind as he ran like a deer with a lot of drug residue in its system...*fuck this job!*

The freshly reunited Afro-Anarchists were preparing to perform a new number for their appreciative fans in General Processing. During their thirty minutes of eating, a large number of bulky, poorly maneuverable trash modules had built up in the hallway, patiently waiting for them upon their return from the cafeteria. The Junior Material Handlers pulled the carts down the hall to G.P. as cheerfully as possible, digesting their lunch as they went. Fontaine had unexpectedly grown weary of rap music, and was relieved to be free from the pressures of leading his own group. Therefore, just plain Fontaine joined ex-Steady Heady Boy Bucktooth and lead man Phosphate on *G.P. Is Where I Wanna Be*:

"I've been picking up trash bags for so long now
If I could do something else, I wouldn't know how
It's true this is not the greatest career
No money, prestige, or atmosphere
I'm black and I have to think it's groovy
There's enough of us here to make a Tarzan movie
The work is hard and always the same
No one in Administration knows my name
We discuss the great issues of the day
We're just like yuppies, except for the pay
We all watch sports, just like they do
And some of us graduated from high school
Here in G.P. we are into trash
We don't own stocks and we don't watch 'M.A.S.H.'
We also have to clean all the used food trays
Our hands are dirty, none of us are gay
So come on by when you get a chance
And boogie to the doo-wop sanitation dance!"

The G.P. workers applauded wildly. The Afro-Anarchists felt so gratified by the ovation that it made them ponder what it must be like to have thousands cheering you. Phosphate always tried to remember that whenever he became incredulous over the magnitude of celebrity egos.

"Hey man, you all should have a fucking record out!" Hector Hispania, the supervisor of General Processing, shouted gleefully.

There were several other G.P. employees offering similar suggestions and reviews, and when the three of them left to return to Central Supply, the warm reception they'd been given made it significantly easier to face the wrath of Duck Hung.

Waldo was amazed. The place was very dimly lit, and it resembled the set of *The Munsters* more than a mental health unit. There was a sign hanging slightly askew on the front of what was apparently a nursing station which read *The Extremely Unreachable Ward- Keep Quiet*, and the very sight of it stirred up a fusillade of shivers throughout Waldo's overworked spine, and converted his semi-regular breathing pattern back to its familiar hyperventilation mode. The sign, like everything else around it, was covered with menacing cobwebs.

307

The nursing station was situated in the middle of a large open area, which Waldo had stumbled across shortly after seeing the sign and following the arrow pointing to the right. Six rooms, three on either side of the station, were marked with a number above each door. Directly behind the nursing station was a larger, bright red door with no number above it. Waldo wondered about its peculiar conspicuousness as he knocked down the cobwebs in his path.

There didn't appear to be anyone on duty, and the more he explored the place, the more uneasy he began to feel. There was dust everywhere, along with the cobwebs, and Waldo knew that whatever its faults, the Last Chance Relaxation Home would never allow its Housekeeping staff to leave a unit in such abysmal condition. He also sensed, much as he had in the queer little general store he'd frequented shortly after the beginning of their sojourn to Iowa, a distinct ambiance of the past all around him, almost as if the entire ward had been transplanted there from the 1940's. With this in mind, he started searching for a calendar, having seen more than his share of *Twilight Zones*, and with the incident at the O'Sullivan house still fresh in his memory, but no such tidy or dramatic evidence presented itself.

As the nervous young man cautiously circled the nursing station, he noticed that one of the rooms was numbered five. Waldo forgot his trepidation for the time being as he approached it. He was on the literal threshold of speaking with the man he'd undertaken such a long and tumultuous journey to find. In the tense exhilaration of the moment, Waldo ignored his usual courteous nature and turned the doorknob without knocking. He opened the door and there, lying in bed, was Sam Hancock.

Waldo stared at the man in the bed. Sam Hancock looked exactly the same to him. Considering the fact that twenty years had elapsed since he'd last seen him, Waldo found his appearance astonishing. Hancock had always seemed younger than his years, but the individual in front of him now didn't look to have aged a day since 1969. Judging by the healthy glow in his cheeks, the full head of dark hair, and the youthful, unwrinkled skin, one might have mistaken him for a long time resident of a health resort, more accustomed to soaking leisurely in mineral baths and frolicking at various games with rich, attractive partners, than suffering for two decades behind the locked doors of the Last Chance Relaxation Home. Waldo was well aware that mental institutions were rarely noted for their powers in retarding the aging process.

Waldo nervously approached the bed. "Uh...Mr. Hancock?"

Sam Hancock had been staring straight ahead, like a statue, or one with an incision in a vital part of the brain, without reacting in the least when Waldo entered the room. When Waldo spoke, however, he turned his head towards his visitor in the mechanized manner of a robot. "Why, Waldo, this *is* a surprise! Come in and sit down!"

Feeling quite awkward, Waldo sat down in one of the chairs near the bed. "H-how are you, sir?"

"Oh, pretty good for an old man, I suppose. But tell me how you found me. I haven't had anyone come to see me for, oh, I don't know how long." Hancock's voice was stilted and artificial.

Mindful of the fact that the strong medication given to patients at the Last Chance Relaxation Home could easily be responsible for such unnatural speech, Waldo tried to be tactful and understanding. "Well, you see, I knew from my grandfather that, uh, well, you know, he explained when you stopped coming around that you...were here."

"Old Hoss! My greatest friend! How is he? He isn't with you, is he?"

Waldo's heart sank. Obviously, the elderly patient possessed no information about his grandfather. "No, that's why I came here. He mysteriously disappeared recently, and after checking out everything I could think of back in Virginia, without any leads at all, I couldn't begin to guess what happened to him. That's when I figured, well actually it was after discovering what I thought was possibly a clue in your journal, that he might have come to visit you. I guess it was a crazy idea."

Hancock's eyebrows raised at the mention of his journal. "My journal? Now I wonder how that old thing came to be at your house?"

Waldo noticed that the old man was sporting a rather odd smile. "Uh, I don't know, I just thought that my grandfather..."

"Stole it?" Hancock interrupted him. "He always was jealous of that journal. Do you know he never once visited me in all those years? I would like to have it back. Do you have it with you?"

"Uh, no, I'm sorry." Waldo was taken aback. "I-I didn't think of that."

Hancock sighed. "Well, if you didn't, you didn't. I never expected to see that collection of garbage again, anyway."

Waldo slid uncomfortably to the edge of his seat, cognizant of the fact he might be forced to end this less than cordial encounter at any moment. "Garbage? From what I've read of it, Mr. Hancock, I thought it was great."

The elderly patient smiled in the same odd fashion again. "Well, first of all, Waldo, you shouldn't be reading other people's journals without their permission. And secondly, don't believe everything you read."

"I could hardly have asked for your consent." Waldo was growing increasingly wary of Hancock's behavior. *They must have him on some really powerful drugs*, he thought to himself.

"There's no need to get testy. I would like to help you, Waldo, but I haven't seen your grandfather, as I told you, since they brought me here many, many years ago."

"Yes, well, I knew it was a wild hunch." Waldo prepared to depart politely.

Hancock was playing absentmindedly with his sheets. "Tell me, Waldo, you didn't swallow any of that opinionated nonsense in my journal, did you? And when am I going to get it back?"

Waldo was clearly alarmed now. He remembered Sam Hancock as being kind and pleasant, and it would certainly seem logical to expect him to be overjoyed at seeing his best friend's grandson, whom he'd been especially fond of, after such a long time. Of course, it was possible that a lengthy stay in such a facility had severely altered his personality, but Waldo found it difficult to trust the crotchety old figure in the bed, and couldn't rid himself of the impression he was being toyed with. Gazing at Hancock's tranquil face, Waldo couldn't discern a trace of the man who had so eloquently castigated the materialistic world and those who rule it.

"You haven't answered me." Hancock said impatiently. "When am I going to get my journal back?"

"Uh, I suppose when I'm out this way again." Waldo finally replied, unwilling to divulge that Sam Hancock's journal was actually in the back seat of Brisbane's decidedly un-fredneck-like '65 Dodge Dart, safely ensconced in the Professor's briefcase.

"And when will that be, the next time someone disappears?"

Waldo realized that it would be best for him to leave now. "I really should be going, Mr. Hancock. I'm sorry again about your journal. It was, uh, nice to see you."

The old man started smiling in an even stranger way than before. "Waldo, I don't think that would be a wise idea. You see, I'm expecting some more company and they would love to speak with you. And, as you can tell by the looks of this place, we don't have many visitors around here."

"Yes, where *are* the nurses, anyway?" Waldo ventured to ask.

"It does look rather old and deserted, eh?" Hancock began playing with the sheets again, in a frenzied, furious fashion. "How about the cobwebs? Aren't they a scream?"

"W-what happened to you?" Waldo started slowly backing away towards the door.

Instead of answering him, Hancock laughed. It was the same hideous laugh that had been unleashed by so many of the characters Waldo had met recently. "I really think you'll want to stay. Actually, you're already acquainted with the people who'll be arriving here any minute now. I believe you and your friends gave one of them a ride..."

Waldo made a run for the door, but Hancock laughed again, quite loudly for a feeble old man.

"You won't get very far, Waldo. As you observed, there are no nurses here, and there are no patients either. There is, in fact, no way out of the Extremely Unreachable Ward. But consider yourself lucky- very few people can find it."

Waldo now felt the hopelessness of a prisoner on death row being served his last meal. "But...why *you*? I worshiped you almost as much as my grandfather. And your writings..."

Sam Hancock didn't thank him for the compliment. "You might as well sit down and relax, son. You don't have anywhere to go, and we have a lot of catching up to do."

"I'm telling you, man, I think we ought to leave this place now." Brisbane was still unnerved over his encounter with Otto Motto.

"But what about Waldo? Surely you want to wait for him." Phosphate replied.

"Look, man, I never thought I'd say this, but maybe we should call the cops or something." That the fredneck would consider contacting his arch-enemies in law enforcement for any reason at all was a powerful indication of how desperate he felt.

"My friend, do you actually think they'd believe us?" The top doo-wopper almost chuckled at the fredneck's naivete. "Let's be patient. I must confess that I am astounded by your attitude. After everything we have seen thus far, can the disappearance of this...Housekeeper hero of yours really have seemed that remarkable to you?"

"Well, shit man, he knew where Waldo was and everything, even Sam Hancock's name!" Brisbane exclaimed.

"Brisbane," The head Afro-Anarchist responded calmly but firmly, "do you recall the magistrate back at Snortin' Reformatory uttering an enigmatic comment about Waldo's grandfather? These sorts of things have plagued us from the beginning. We can't turn back now, my friend."

Brisbane and Phosphate were wrapping bedpans, one of the many challenging activities Duck Hung had dreamed up to keep them occupied between deliveries. Waldo was nearly two hours late returning from his lunch break, and the Vietnamese supervisor was furious. He'd recovered nicely from his morning bout with diarrhea, and his pale complexion and queasy stomach didn't stop him from ranting and raving about the poor work ethics of all Americans. He was driving the others twice as hard as usual in order to satisfy his sadistic lust to punish Waldo for his unexplained absence.

The four remaining day shift Junior Material Handlers were

311

growing more distraught by the minute. They had all been somewhat apprehensive about Waldo visiting a unit in the sub-basement that was unknown to virtually everyone there, but now they were officially worried. What concerned them more than anything was the fact that Duck Hung had been so upset over Waldo's tardiness that he'd had him paged twice over the loudspeaker system, and there had been no response. Obviously, he was not in the building, or at least any known part of it, as the speakers were located everywhere throughout the facility. Unless, of course-and this fear was foremost in all their minds-he was unable to answer.

"Shit man, I don't understand this." Brisbane was so distracted he'd been wrapping and unwrapping the same bedpan for several minutes. "What the fuck could be going on down there?"

Sounding even more serious than usual, Phosphate stroked his chin. "I'm afraid that what we all secretly feared happening may actually have occurred. Waldo would certainly have rushed back here and informed us of everything that transpired in the sub-basement, if he could."

At that moment Fontaine and Bucktooth strolled into the equipment room, fresh from a mercury spill cleanup on the fifth floor. "Damn, Waldo still isn't back?" They declared in unison.

The top doo-wopper was lost in deep contemplation, as he was most of the time. "I believe that there is nothing else for us to do but attempt to find him."

Bucktooth's eyes grew as big as a black Little Rascal's, as they invariably did in times of crisis. "You mean we're gonna go down to the sub-basement?"

"Sheeeet! And look for a ward that everybody says ain't there?" Fontaine chimed in.

Brisbane merely rolled his eyes and shivered at the prospect of meandering through a dark and secluded area, encountering all kinds of unmentionable horrors.

"Waldo is our friend, and it is apparent that he is in danger. Wouldn't you want us to try and assist you in a similar situation?" Phosphate was adamant, and it was clear that nothing was going to prevent him from performing what he saw as his duty.

"But what about our jobs? Old Duck Hung sure as hell ain't gonna let us off early." Bucktooth could almost feel the texture of a paycheck in his hands, something he was quite unaccustomed to, and was afraid of losing the minuscule amount of money he was entitled to for his brief career as a Junior Material Handler.

"Goddamn shit! You all get to work before I kill all your asses!" Duck Hung suddenly walked into the room.

Brisbane's ire, as well as an ancestral trace of gallantry, rose to the surface, and he told Duck Hung off in classic fredneck fashion. "Listen,

312

you refugee from a rice patty, I've had about all I can take of your shit. I quit, and if the rest of you have any self-respect, you will too." Although he was hardly a "badass" by anyone's standards, Brisbane, like all frednecks, understood the importance of intimidation. Thrusting his chest out belligerently, he utilized the most universal method of confrontation, positioning his face only inches away from his supervisor's. "And if we catch any shit about getting paid for the time we've been here, I'll know whose ass to kick, won't I?"

The Vietnamese boss lamely tried to convince them that he was some sort of martial arts expert, but they remained unimpressed.

"Man, that don't play here. I'm hip to that game and your phony shit. The first thing you all learn when you set your tiny feet down off the boat is to say you know some damn karate or judo. Well, I can see right through your ass and I know you don't know nothing." Fontaine wasn't about to fall victim to the scare tactics that coerced so many large Americans into picturing much smaller orientals as imposing physical specimens.

With that, all four of them stalked off in a manner befitting young men with the kind of employment records they'd spent years establishing. Duck Hung was speechless for once, and seconds later dashed off for the bathroom, having experienced a reoccurrence of his morning affliction.

As they left Central Supply, Phosphate became visibly energized, quickening his step and adopting a determined, uncharacteristically competitive tone of voice. "Duck Hung will undoubtedly not hesitate to call Security, who will consider it part of their job description to remove us forcibly from the premises. We therefore haven't a moment to lose. I realize that it will be an extremely perilous undertaking, but I feel we must head for the sub-basement immediately. Are you all with me?"

His three cohorts were as enthusiastic as a junior varsity football team, their initial reluctance to tred into the uncharted waters of the sub-basement evidently assuaged by Phosphate's Knute Rockne-like charisma, and as there were no young men in different colored uniforms to knock down, they channeled their energetic camaraderie into the potentially hazardous assignment of finding and/or rescuing Waldo.

Fontaine suddenly thought of something. "Hey, what about little Jeanne? She might want to come with us."

Phosphate shook his head emphatically. "No, there's no need for that. I don't think she could aid us to any great extent, and we haven't the time to inform her; the Security officers may very well be unusually fast and efficient here. Besides, it would only unnecessarily alarm her."

They scurried through the depressing corridors of the basement, in the general direction of the west wing, until they came to the hallway where Brisbane had spotted Otto Motto a short time earlier. The fredneck pointed this out to everyone, and also stated his suspicion, which was based primarily on the fact a dematerializing Housekeeper had been ostensibly patrolling the area, that the seldom-used entrance to the sub-basement was close by. Brisbane's fear for his own safety had subsided completely, and he was now interested exclusively in delivering Waldo from whatever unimaginable forces held him.

All at once, the hall became noticeably colder and the fluorescent lights in the ceiling flickered several times. The frail, Wally Cox-like figure of Otto Motto then abruptly appeared before them, earnestly mopping the floor.

"Wet floor, watch your step, folks." He called out, and then his eyes met Brisbane's. "Oh, it's *you*." Otto Motto then unleashed the now familiar blood curdling laugh.

"Shit, that's him!" The fredneck was more brave than wise at this point, and he lunged towards the Housekeeper. "Where's my buddy, you sack of shit?"

But Brisbane plowed into nothing but thin air, as the classic graffiti artist had vanished as suddenly as he'd come. The fredneck hit the floor with a resounding thud, but fortunately was not seriously injured.

As he got up and brushed himself off, Brisbane had tears in his eyes. "Come on, dudes, we better hurry up and find that place in the sub-basement. I got a bad feeling that something has happened to Waldo."

They started moving even faster in the direction of the stairwell which led to the sub-basement, and Phosphate was left to utter one of his patented cryptic comments, "It should be apparent by now, my friends, that anything can happen."

"Try and make yourself comfortable, Waldo. I too fought at first, but eventually I accepted things as they are. You aren't up to the challenge of confronting your captors, believe me. The sooner you understand that, the easier it will be on you." Sam Hancock, who'd left the confines of his bed to pace about the room with surprising spryness, patted the nervous young man on the back.

Waldo simply pressed his face further against the wall in utter despair.

They were still in room five, Sam Hancock's room, of the Extremely Unreachable ward, but they were not alone. The Hitchhiker was there, and so were the three M.I.B.'s and the lady from the employment office who had been known to impersonate nurses and sixteen year old girls. For what seemed like hours to Waldo, they had been interrogating him about a number of things, from what he knew of his grandfather's disappearance to his views on various social and historical matters. The Hitchhiker was obviously the one in charge, and he made it abundantly clear that the organization he represented was displeased with Waldo and aimed to change, convert, or destroy him. The nervous young man was having difficulty grasping any of the paranoid highlights of the lecture, however, due to a disturbing new difference in the Hitchhiker's appearance. The enigmatic figure, who'd been dull and colorless enough in his bland gray attire, had been transformed into a grainy, literally black and white character. Looking at him, Waldo saw the ghost of every old cinematic private detective, businessman, and gangster rolled up into his grim, fuzzy facade.

"Did you actually think, Waldo, knowing everything you do, that we would allow you to keep writing and talking about us?" The Hitchhiker was taking on the air of the character O'Brien in Orwell's novel *1984,* which was, naturally, one of Waldo's favorites. "We are in control, young man. Do you understand that? I don't just mean politically, either- that is obvious even to some college graduates. We can make virtually anything happen. Financial success, love, sex, power, whatever you want- we can give it to you. Or take it away. Our strength is such that even the smallest details can be taken care of, if necessary. Did you ever have a pimple pop up unexpectedly at the wrong time? Or feel the overpowering urge to use the toilet in a crowded and dirty bathroom? Ever try to get a company to honor a warranty? What causes traffic? Remember the old saw about the other line moving faster? Murphy's law, indeed!" The Hitchhiker was beaming with pride. "And, of course, tumors and plane crashes are our specialties."

Waldo was not responding to any of the questions. Having adjusted somewhat to the Hitchhiker's new bleached persona, he was staring into space and attempting as best he could to keep his mind jumping from one disjointed thought to another. He had stumbled across the outlandish theory, somewhere in one of the countless obscure extremist tracts he'd read, that doing this made mind control impossible.

Apparently recognizing Waldo's curious efforts, the Hitchhiker looked almost sympathetic. "Waldo, you have spent far too much time absorbing useless speculation from unreliable sources. We're not aiming to brainwash you. We seldom do that anymore. We have other plans for you."

Waldo stopped his futile mental marathon, and looked the Hitchhiker straight in the eye. "Why do you care what I think? I'm no threat to you."

The faintest trace of a smile curled about the corners of the Hitchhiker's cruel lips. "For many centuries, we didn't bother with common nobodies like yourself. But as time went by, it was gradually determined that since we were so close to absolute power, it was desirable to crush all dissent, no matter how small or insignificant. Therefore, your protests against us could no longer be tolerated the way they might have been a few decades ago."

It was now clear to Waldo that he was in the hands of those responsible for the disappearance of Old Hoss Billingsly. "You have my grandfather, don't you?"

"Yes, your grandfather is now with us. As I told you already, some attacks against us were permitted, as long as they didn't receive a wide circulation. Certainly your grandfather's massive amount of unpublished pamphlets qualified in that regard." The Hitchhiker chuckled snidely. "I don't mean to criticize the quality of his work, his writings were always in great demand at International Headquarters. Actually, he was once considered as a candidate for admission to our Universal Academy, but was eventually deemed undependable and thus never approached. Every indication was that he would be allowed to continue his unproductive pursuits, but then the orders arrived from Elite Command..."

"Can I see him?" Waldo asked.

"If you cooperate with us, perhaps that can eventually be arranged." The Hitchhiker replied. "But first, there are other activities planned for you."

"Well, what happens next? What are you going to do with me?" Waldo was beyond fear now, in a state of complete surrender.

However, before the nervous young man had finished his question the Hitchhiker abruptly vanished along with his sinister companions, leaving Waldo alone with Sam Hancock.

"Wh-what happened to them?" Waldo, though thoroughly used to this kind of thing by now, was still caught off guard.

Sam Hancock sighed. "They do that all the time. They'll be back, I can promise you."

Waldo walked towards the door.

"I told you, Waldo, that's no use. They aren't going to let you out." Hancock said.

"Is this what happened to you back in 1969?" Waldo wondered. "Did they bring you here and put you in this ward to keep you from talking?"

Hancock stared down at his feet. "Yes, I suppose that was their reasoning."

"So was that whole story about you suddenly going crazy and firing the gun just made up?" Waldo inquired. "You were abducted against you will, like my grandfather, weren't you?"

Hancock's eyes met Waldo's. "I'm sorry, Waldo. I'd love to be able to help you, but I ceased being able to help anyone a long time ago."

Now that it appeared perhaps Sam Hancock was still on the side of truth, justice, and the American Way, Waldo kept peppering him with questions. "I know you're here involuntarily, but you seem to be happy. You even let out one of those hideous laughs I've been hearing so much lately."

Hancock walked over to Waldo and embraced him. "Trust me, Waldo, I'm still the same man I always was. I appear happy because I've been here for so long it seems like home to me now. And they do make it quite tolerable for me. If I want to watch anything at all, from Tex Avery cartoons-remember how much Old Hoss loved him?-to the actual suppressed movies of the Kennedy assassinations, then all I have to do is request it and it is provided, promptly and with no questions asked. The same thing is true of the reading matter here. There is nothing that has ever been published by anyone anywhere, no matter how extremist or controversial, that their library does not contain. And the food is gourmet quality."

"Yes, that seems nice, but is all that worth your freedom?" Waldo was already trying to picture himself adjusting to such a situation.

"Of course not, but I have no choice. What I said to you applies to me as well; I can never leave here, either." Hancock's voice was sad and resigned.

Waldo bit his lip nervously. "But what about my grandfather? Do you know where he is or not?"

Hancock's head whirled around in all directions, scanning the room for bugging devices and/or strange creatures, thereby proving he still possessed an admirable supply of paranoia. Apparently satisfied, he motioned Waldo to come closer. He then spoke in a conspiratorial whisper. "You see, Waldo, your grandfather..."

"What about his grandfather?"

All at once, the Hitchhiker reappeared, and this time he was accompanied by more than M.I.B.'s and Personnel employees. Standing behind him were Waldo's would-be rescuers- one frightened fredneck and three trembling Afro-Anarchists.

"Janie, I'm really worried. I just know something awful's happened to Waldo." It was 4:15, and the O'Sullivan twins were still waiting in the lobby for their chums in Central Supply. With each passing minute, Jeanne grew more concerned about her sweetheart.

"Yeah, I agree that Waldo must have run into *something* down there, but what could it be? And where are the others? I thought you said he was going to the sub-basement alone." Janie was mystified on a less personal level than her sister.

"He was definitely going alone. They must have gone down to look for him themselves and..." Jeanne left her worst fears unspoken.

"You know, Jeanne, they're really nice guys and I do like Brisbane a lot, but...they're into some very weird things. Maybe that has something to do with this. They were always talking about U.F.O.'s and stuff like that; Brisbane even told me he saw green giants or something in the cornfield." Janie appeared to forget that she and her sister regularly went time-traveling in the same cornfield, an activity that certainly qualified as abnormal.

Jeanne was somewhat miffed at her twin. "Janie, I can't believe that you would sit there and analyze them at a time like this. I know more than you do about their beliefs-I've heard enough of them from Waldo-and while I think some of them are too pessimistic, they aren't weird." She was keeping her eyes glued to the clock on the wall behind the information desk. "If they're not here by 4:30, I'm going to look for them myself."

"Jeanne, you can't! If something happened to them, what would happen to you?" Janie was horrified by this proposition. "Besides, we're not even sure where this other entrance to the sub-basement is. Why don't we call Security?"

"Have you seen our Security staff? Even if I thought they *would* help us, I doubt if they could. Look, if you don't want to come with me, I'll go alone." The expression on Jeanne's pretty face was not unlike the Gary Cooper-James Stewart look of determination that all Frank Capra heroes, as well as her true love Waldo Billingsly, were noted for. "After all, Janie, I love Waldo. If I don't try and save him, who will?"

Janie shrugged. "Okay, sis. I'll go with you, but I won't like it."

"Brisbane! Phosphate! Fontaine! Bucktooth!" Waldo was so astounded to see his friends that he shouted out each of their names individually, much like Judy Garland did after waking up back in her Kansas bedroom in *The Wizard Of Oz*. "What are you all doing here?"

"It seems that your friends were suffering from valorous delusions. They actually thought they could rescue you, as if the world of Hans Christian Andersen had any basis in reality." The Hitchhiker snickered. "Of course, I had to remind them that this place is full of heroes."

Waldo looked at the four disgruntled faces and felt a great deal of remorse over the fact his misguided mission had now trapped them as well. "I-I'm sorry, guys." He tried to apologize.

"Now, Hancock, why don't you share with all of us the information you were about to impart to young Waldo regarding his grandfather, before I so rudely interrupted you?" The Hitchhiker was reasserting his dominance over the once proud old man, who was now reduced to a quivering basket case.

"Uh, you see, sir, I, uh..." Sam Hancock was behaving like a grammar school student in the principal's office, and wore his submissiveness openly, without the lash marks that some require.

This was too much for Waldo to take. "Look, you gym teacher-reject, why don't you stop this little power game of yours and leave the old man alone? Isn't being here enough punishment for him?"

The Hitchhiker stared at Waldo with all the warmth of a concentration camp commandant. "No. You, like Mr. Hancock and everyone else here, will listen and obey or you will be sent to the Siberian Solitary Confinement Center."

Hancock's face grew contorted in horror at the very mention of this. "No, no, not that! Please, anything but that!" He then threw himself down on the bed and began sobbing into his pillow like a child.

The Hitchhiker seemed pleased with this reaction. "There you are, Waldo- your rabble-rousing man of protest reduced to tears; your darling iconoclast with the rigid set of principles, who dared to vent his wrath against us, whimpering like an abandoned puppy. All of you take heed and watch your step. I'll be back to check on you soon." With that, he vanished again.

As soon as he'd gone, Sam Hancock stopped crying and sat up in his bed. "Okay, Waldo, why don't you introduce me to your friends. It'll be nice to have some company around here."

"Damn, old man, what kind of drugs they got you on?" Fontaine spoke up. "And do you have any more?"

Waldo eyed Sam Hancock warily. "That was a wonderful

performance you put on there. Or was it?"

Sam Hancock smiled as he rose to his feet. "Waldo, you are a bright boy- you always were. But, alas, you are here now. I would love to stay and chat with you some more, but I really must go." He strode towards the door with a peculiar spring in his step, and spun around just as he reached it. "You see, I have an important engagement." He then left the room, but he didn't use the door. He dematerialized in the same manner as the Hitchhiker.

With this startling new development, Brisbane, Fontaine, and Bucktooth were temporarily pushed over the edge. They began running around the room in circles, hooting and shouting out gibberish at the top of their lungs.

Considering that they were in the midst of three freshly created lunatics, Waldo and Phosphate displayed awesome powers of concentration in conversing intelligibly.

"Waldo, I'm the one who should apologize to you." The top doo-wopper spoke above the maddening din. "If we hadn't acted so impulsively, and had formulated a better strategy..."

"Listen, you were incredibly brave to even try it. I'm just sorry that all of us are stuck here now." Waldo responded.

"I suppose it's counterproductive to dwell on that at this point. Determining a means of escape would be a more appropriate area of inquiry, I would think." Phosphate's voice was growing louder, in order to be heard above the inane cries of Brisbane, Fontaine, and Bucktooth.

Waldo lit up a cigarette. Amazingly enough, considering the current anti-smoking craze, smoking was permitted throughout the facility, undoubtedly due to the fact that mental patients were known to be rivaled only by bingo players in terms of tobacco consumption. The nervous young man leaned a little closer to Phosphate. "What do you make of Sam Hancock?"

"I was about to ask you the same question." Phosphate lapsed into his famous stroking-of-the-chin routine, and the Freudian image provided a bit of poignancy in light of the surroundings. "I really did not have much of a chance to evaluate anything, but his disappearance was most unusual. He certainly appeared to be a helpless prisoner. In view of all the assorted oddities we've encountered recently, I'm not sure I trust my senses about anything at this point."

Waldo nodded. "I know exactly what you mean. Sam Hancock acted strange from the moment I entered his room. I was just a kid when he left, yet he recognized me right away, and he even became upset about his journal being found in my grandfather's house. Then he lectured me, saying I should accept staying here, and that it really isn't so bad. He told me that he had fought at first, but it was useless, and that he still felt the same way about things. He almost had me believing him at..."

"Then he acts just as an unstable mental patient might be expected to, sobbing hysterically, and finally vanishes in front of us after vaguely hinting that he is in league with Them." Phosphate added. "Most remarkable."

"Right." Waldo inhaled deeply on his Camel Light. "I don't know whether he's just an innocent victim or maybe not even..."

"Real? You may have a point there." The top doo-wopper completed Waldo's sentence for him. "But what puzzles me most is the condition of this ward, regardless of its purpose. What is the meaning of all the cobwebs and dust? If this truly is some sort of underground penal colony for dissenters, where are all the nurses, or guards, or whatever you choose to call them? Surely the conspirators can afford to adequately staff their facilities."

"I tried to ask Sam Hancock about that, because I..."

Waldo was interrupted again, this time by the desperately out of tune rapping of Fontaine E. and The Steady Heady Boyz, apparently reunited in their confused psyches:

"Hello out there, we are here inside
The walls are thick and the bars are wide
We are all so happy in the asylum
Just give us a t.v. and some librium
Three square meals and a soft, warm bed
At least it's better than being dead
Where can all the doctors and the nurses be?
White linen coats and group therapy
Four padded walls in a room for one
Where all the most effective counseling is done
I'm disappointed 'cause I want to be treated
It doesn't matter whether or not I need it."

As soon as the song ended, the three rappers hugged and congratulated each other, and it was evident to both Waldo and Phosphate that they were slowly being released from the momentary madness that had enveloped them.

"Shit, Phos, what the hell's going on?" Fontaine stumbled back against the wall with a confused expression on his face. His less than eloquent but seemingly rational question indicated that rapping had somehow served as a cathartic to release him, along with Brisbane and Bucktooth, from the throes of temporary insanity.

"Shit yeah, man, let's get the fuck out of this place before that hitchhiker dude or whatever he is gets back here." Brisbane confirmed that he also was back to normal, or a reasonable facsimile thereof.

Waldo was relieved to have his friends returned to the land of the relatively sane, but his uneasiness returned with the sudden, chilling, and all too familiar voice of the Hitchhiker.

"Alright, gentlemen, follow me to room four immediately." The stark black and white figure in the trench coat and matching fedora materialized simultaneously with his words, just inside the doorway. It was obvious to everyone that there was no point in disobeying him.

Room four of the Extremely Unreachable Ward was quite a bit larger than Sam Hancock's room. Actually, it appeared to be some sort of movie theater. There were a great many red velvet-cushioned seats and a full-sized screen in the back. The walls and ceiling were covered with brilliant murals depicting a variety of occult themes. Phosphate, a great admirer of art, recognized the unmistakable hand of his favorite painter, Hieronymus Bosch, behind some of the work. There was even an exit sign lit up over the entrance. All that was missing were the concession stands.

The five of them were ushered in and seated together in the middle row of seats. The Hitchhiker, who had matter-of-factly informed them that his real name was Mr. St. Helen, walked to the front of the room and began setting up a projector. This scene reminded them all of happier times, when the boredom of school was diminished briefly by the knowledge that a darkening classroom permitted tired young heads momentary refuge on their uncomfortable desks. Of course, it also meant excitement to rare students like young Phosphate Jefferson, who truly looked forward to educational films and actually watched them.

Now, many years later, fully grown Phosphate attempted to converse with Mr. St. Helen. "Excuse me, sir, but what movie are we going to see?"

St. Helen looked at them and smiled. "At least one of you has some manners. That's an important asset, young man, in any situation. Ah, but I have a very special feature indeed lined up for you. And the wonderful thing about it is that you are sitting beside the star." He placed his hand on Waldo's shoulder. "You see, all of our guests here are shown a movie featuring themselves shortly after their arrival. It's our way of welcoming newcomers. It is usually a private screening, but in your case, we've decided to allow your associates to enjoy it with you."

Brisbane squirmed in his seat. "What's the title of the film?"

St. Helen glanced in Waldo's direction. "The Death Of Waldo Billingsly."

Waldo's nervous system no sooner had begun responding to this in its customary fashion than the lights went out and the picture started:

The Death Of Waldo Billingsly

The film opened back in room five of the Extremely Unreachable Ward, where Waldo and Sam Hancock were engaged in conversation:

W.B.- So why did you do what you did back in 1969?

S.H.- Well, I guess I must have been insane to shoot at my t.v. set and the cars like that.

W.B.- But you seem normal now.

S.H.- What is normal? But they have helped me a great deal here at the Last Home.

W.B.- I'm a little amazed by your attitude.

S.H.- How so?

W.B.- Can you be the same man whose curiosity led him to charge all over the world searching for answers to baffling mysteries? Whose journal skewers our most powerful leaders and organizations so effectively? I thought you were sent here against your will because you knew about Them. I was under the impression that you were being punished because of your extensive knowledge of the Great Conspiracy and your opposition to it, but you seem to be content with your situation.

S.H.- I am happy to be, period, young man.

W.B.- But how can you say they've helped you when there's no one even working here? Haven't you noticed the cobwebs? And where are all the other patients? Surely they didn't create a unit just for you.

S.H.- Waldo, I'm sorry but I'm feeling a little faint. Would you mind leaving, please?

W.B.- But I haven't even had a chance to ask you...

S.H.- I know. Waldo, listen to me; your grandfather was a wonderful man, but his inquisitive nature finally got the best of him.

W.B.- You know where he is, don't you?

S.H.- Yes, but you'll never find him.

W.B.- Where is he? Tell me, now!

S.H.- He is with all the other misguided ones; Ambrose Bierce, D.B. Cooper, Amelia Earhart...

W.B.- Look, I don't know what you're saying. I just want to know how to find my grandfather.

S.H.- Waldo, there is only one way, but you must give up the most precious thing in the world.

W.B.- Tell me!

S.H.- You'll find out- just open the red door behind the nursing station.

Fade out. Fade in to the O'Sullivan cornfield.
At this point in the film, the voice of a narrator, sounding identical

to the renowned Edward Everett Horton, best remembered for his work
with Rocky and Bullwinkle, began explaining the action on screen in an
odd, wordy style. This served to lend a cartoon aspect to the film, which
began to resemble some sort of black "Fractured Fairy Tale."

It was nearly dark and the beautiful but agonizing sunset reflected the despair felt by the remaining members of the Old Hoss Billingsly search party. They were gathered in the magical cornfield, and the twins had been kind enough to stay and try to reassure them Waldo was alright. This was especially magnanimous of Jeanne, in that she was more personally distraught than any of the others. Brisbane was very upset, as well, bearing the appearance of a man who wanted to punch the world out.

They had remained at work long after their shift had ended, but despite a thorough search by Security officers (which the fredneck maintained was half-hearted at best), no trace of Waldo Billingsly could be found.

It was growing darker by the minute in the cornfield, and Jeanne and Janie tried to convince the four dejected friends to join them in their parents' house for some food and shelter.

Brisbane answered for the group. "Thanks anyhow. You two go in, your parents will be worried about you if you don't." The crude young fredneck method actor threw his arm around Jeanne. "I know we're going to find him." Then, shamelessly hamming it up at a level exceeding the great Brando's finest efforts, he hugged Janie. "If you don't mind, we'd like to stay right where we are. Waldo will be coming back soon, and when he does, I'm sure he'll look for us here."

"We'll all be waiting." Added a sad, overtly histrionic Phosphate.

Fade out. Fade in to Waldo approaching the red door.

He was trembling more than a coffee cup in an earthquake. He wondered what Sam Hancock had meant by saying that he would lose the most precious thing in the world. Was he merely alluding allegorically to the old Faustian theme of selling one's soul to the Devil? There were many questions racing through Waldo's mind. Why had Hancock seemed so resigned and even pleased to be in such a God-forsaken place as this? Why was he so unconcerned about the welfare of his best friend Old Hoss Billingsly? Why were there no other patients and no employees on duty in the Extremely Unreachable Ward? Why wasn't the old man more surprised to see Waldo? Had he been expecting him? Most importantly, why wasn't Waldo allowing these and many other doubts to sway him from listening to Hancock? But, alas, the young hero, romantic and naive as he was, moved his left hand towards the doorknob. He made the sign of the cross and boldly opened the door.

Fade out. Fade in to a park in Georgetown, Washington, D.C.

It was late afternoon and a lonely figure was mindlessly feeding the squirrels. The sky was cold and bleak and Waldo Billingsly sat by himself on a chilly park bench, oblivious to the sounds of crunching acorns and whirling leaves. There were no yuppies or government workers jogging, and no homeless indigents sleeping there. A few furry animals were the only audience for the symphony of self-pity that Waldo was conducting with the aid of the largest wind section in the world. Waldo seemed to be waiting for something that was terrible but inevitable.

All at once, two little girls appeared out of nowhere and walked directly in front of his park bench. Waldo knew immediately that this was it. He stared transfixed as a dark shape leaped from the shadows and savagely, within seconds, stabbed the poor children to death. He wanted to run, but was completely powerless as a slew of police officers arrived shortly thereafter, as if on cue. Handcuffs, Miranda rights, rough shoving, laments about what a "sickass" he was, and then the squad car pulled away with a forlorn Waldo Billingsly in the back seat.

Fade out. Fade in to Jeanne and Janie O'Sullivan at home watching the local television newscast with their parents. A report was just being aired about the brutal slayings of two little girls in Washington, D.C.

"My God, that's horrible!" Exclaimed an outraged Mrs. O'Sullivan. She hugged both of her daughters. "I thank the Lord my children are safe at home."

"Whoever would do a thing like that ought to have his...well, you know." Remarked Major O'Sullivan.

"Those poor little girls! Why would anyone want to harm innocent creatures like that?" Mrs. O'Sullivan, as a longtime resident of rural Iowa, was genuinely perplexed by such things.

"Because," explained Major O'Sullivan, "they're nuts."

"Waldo!" Jeanne and Janie suddenly shouted in unison.

Waldo Billingsly's face was superimposed on their television screen. They all listened to the reporter's words:

"The suspect in this vicious double murder has been identified as unemployed 28 year old Waldo E. Billingsly, who is being described by authorities as a loner. D.C. Police are claiming to have caught him in the act, and say the evidence is stacked against him. At present, no motive has been ascribed to him, but officials are painting a picture of a troubled young man with a long history of erratic behavior and psychological problems.

The lights in the room came back on.

"Well, gentlemen, what did you think?" St. Helen asked.

"It was too damn short, had a contrived plot, and I didn't have any lines." Fontaine could find levity in almost any situation.

"How the fuck did you film that? None of it ever happened, and yet that was definitely us in it." Brisbane was one puzzled fredneck.

St. Helen smiled with the air of a celebrity holding the envelope for Best Picture of the Year. "How about you, Waldo? Doesn't our title character have an opinion to share? You usually do."

Waldo was numb all over. This whole scene was so fantastic that he was beyond trembling or running fifty yard dashes. "I-I am amazed. Like Brisbane said, how could you possibly have made it?"

St. Helen laughed, but in not quite as hideous a manner as he had previously. "Come now, do you expect me to give away any trade secrets? Did Houdini reveal how he made an elephant disappear? As I explained to you earlier, we control *everything*, Waldo, and are capable of doing anything we wish."

"Damn, you can say that again!" A flabbergasted Bucktooth was sitting there with his mouth agape, still staring at the blank screen. "Who was that narrator and how..."

"Sheeet!" Fontaine interrupted his fellow Afro-Anarchist. "Bris, I don't know about anybody else, man, but you were shamelessly overacting."

"I have to vehemently disagree with you, dude." The fredneck tried to defend his performance. "At least I had a speaking part."

Phosphate abruptly stood up. "Frankly, I don't care about any of that. I feel it is more important to leave this place than issue second-rate reviews about productions that are metaphysically impossible. I am going now. If any of you wish to accompany me, please feel free to do so." With that, he marched towards the door.

All of the others were too frightened of the possible repercussions to follow, and besides, such an action clearly seemed futile.

St. Helen's countenance turned grim. "You fool! There is no way out of here once you enter. You can hold your head high and strut out of this room, but I assure you that you'll never leave this ward. Go ahead and try-it will be quite an instructive experience for you. We'll see you again shortly."

Phosphate left the room and walked back in the direction of the stairwell. The heat was just as oppressive as he made his way through the ostensible storage area, past the rows of excess furniture, but the top doo-wopper handled it with the zeal of a missionary. Eventually, he spotted the door leading back into the stairwell. As he approached it, he was suddenly struck by their collective stupidity. How could they have so dutifully accepted St. Helen's ominous boast that there was no way out of the sub-basement? The head Afro-Anarchist grabbed the doorknob confidently and turned. It was at this point that his impetuous surge of optimism vanished. The door was locked.

Phosphate silently cursed this disagreeable turn of events and sat down on the floor for a moment to gather his thoughts. He stroked his chin for several minutes, then all at once a novel but simple idea came to him. Rising up Phoenix-like from the sub-basement floor, he closed his eyes and concentrated with all his might. Then he tried the doorknob again. It turned and the door opened.

"Welcome, new arrivals, to the Court Of No Appeal." St. Helen waved his hand at the antiseptic legal chamber they now found themselves in. "A fascinating trial is about to begin."

After they'd finished their supernatural film festival in room four, and Phosphate had boldly departed, St. Helen had led them through a hidden door behind the movie screen, down a narrow, winding passage into the empty courtroom. There were paintings here as well, although none were as macabre as the surrealistic murals in the movie theater. The art consisted of portraits of several stately looking figures, caught in a variety of impressive legal poses. Waldo, even with his penchant for the historically esoteric, was unable to identify any of them.

Sensing this, St. Helen chuckled. "Recognize anyone, Waldo? Well, it's probably better that you don't. All of them were quite harsh arbiters of jurisprudence, willing to inflict severe penalties on the guilty and innocent alike. That's why their memories are enshrined here. Of course, we know how much you dislike those strict sorts of authority figures, Waldo."

Ignoring St. Helen's swipe at his merciful nature, the nervous young man gazed at all the empty seats, the jury box, and the judge's stand. "Wh-what did you mean, when you said a trial..."

"Yeah man," Fontaine interrupted, "I already had to sit through a boring movie, now what?"

St. Helen's smile, as always, was dripping with lust and insincerity. "Be patient. In just a few moments, you will be...oh, here he is now!"

A hooded figure was led into the room by two large, brawny men and tossed rudely onto the witness stand. A split second later, a modest young man, with blond hair and blue eyes, strode in wearing the traditional robes of authority, and placed himself in the position of prominence, gavel in hand.

"Who's the prisoner?" The judge demanded, with a slight southern twang in his voice.

"Remove the defendant's hood, Edgar and Jimmy." St. Helen

instructed the two henchmen who'd roughly escorted the figure in.

Edgar and Jimmy slowly slid the hood up, and revealed the latest defendant in the Court Of No Appeal to be none other than Professor Hiram Buckley!

"What's the charge, St. Helen?" The Judge inquired.

"Profane and utter disregard for the established order, your honor." St. Helen approached the bench. "I aim to show that the defendant has written, edited, and published a subversive little newsletter for years, in which he has freely and openly criticized his natural rulers."

"Another critic, eh?" The young Judge raised an eyebrow. "That don't sound like a fair deal to me."

"It most certainly isn't, your honor." St. Helen replied. "Especially if you happen to on the receiving end of some of Mr. Buckley's poisonous barbs."

"That's *Professor* Buckley." The eccentric ex-history teacher, absent his yellow necktie, but otherwise none the worse for the wear, corrected the Hitchhiker.

"Oh, I'm sorry." St. Helen's voice was full of sarcasm. "I believe you were once a professor of history, weren't you? Let's see, what institution of higher learning were you employed by? Was it Yale? Harvard? Notre Dame? U.N.L.V.? Of course- how could anyone forget- the prestigious local community college!"

The Professor, having no tie to nervously tug at, was biting his fingernails.

"Alright, present your evidence, Mr. St. Helen." The Judge instructed.

"Very well, your honor." St. Helen produced a pile of papers from underneath his trench coat. "I would like to read into the record, with your permission, some examples of this distasteful periodical."

"That sounds like a fair deal to me." The Judge responded.

"Alright. Mr.-I mean *Professor* Buckley's publication is entitled *Force of Habit.* The bulk of every issue consists of letters to the editor from alleged readers, and the resultant long-winded responses of the distinguished Professor." St. Helen waved a copy in the air. "I offer into evidence Exhibit A, your honor- the February 1986 issue. May I read a few particularly offensive letters?"

"Yeah. That sounds like a fair deal." The Judge answered in his curious, rather uneducated fashion, with what was clearly his favorite expression.

"Thank you, your honor. Here is the first letter:

Dear H.B.,

Recently I saw a film starring Whoopi Goldberg. This was a mistake and a waste of money. First of all, it was obvious after her first few lines that Goldberg is the farthest thing from funny since Robert Klein. Secondly, and more to the point, there was a scene in the movie where her character beat up a man. Now, I don't mean that she did this by hitting him over the head with a frying pan or some other weapon, nor did she kick him where it counts and render him defenseless. This woman got into a fistfight with a large man and defeated him easily. The man didn't lose because he was afraid to hit a woman, either; Goldberg took his best shots in the face and didn't blink, then proceeded to punch him out. I swear, using nothing but her fists, no martial arts or anything, she knocked the guy out! How can anyone believe this? I realize this is only Hollywood, but from what I understand now, this actress has punched out a man in every movie she's made. I have begun a small personal protest and will spend no more money on the film industry until someone, somewhere, explains this to me. You seem to be the best man for the job.

Feeling Wimpy In Fresno

Dear Wimpy: Thanks for bestowing upon me the honor of analyzing this for you. I'm sure the motion picture industry would want me to reassure you that what you seem to have perceived is of no significance, and urge me to advise you to resume supporting its products immediately. However, I think instead that I'll treat you to one of my patented lengthy responses. You raise an excellent point. As someone who closely scrutinizes the media, I can tell you that, particularly over the last thirty years, Hollywood has consistently cast women in a dominant, assertive light. From Lily Munster punching out her seven-foot tall husband Herman to Sigourney Weaver grabbing men's lapels and banging them against walls to Whoopi Goldberg decking half of the character actors in tinseltown, to one degree or another this has been a perpetual theme throughout the history of film and television. When something is portrayed relentlessly over the course of time in the same way, almost without exception, it becomes no longer a vehicle for comedy but a political statement. Evidently, the aim is to make men weaker and women stronger and more self-assured. I don't mean to sound chauvinistic, but are that many disparate writers, who are almost exclusively male, actually arriving at the curious conclusion that females are able to intimidate men physically and beat them up at will? Even if this were somehow true, what is humorous about it? What is the point of this same device showing up repeatedly in movies and television? Isn't there a saturation level to be reached, just as there was for pies in the face? But now with every powerful Whoopi Goldberg blow, a few more men accept the possibility that the fairer sex is the physically superior one, and a few more women take heart and decide to try out their newly discovered confidence on the face of an unsuspecting male. Then there is the accompanying but seemingly contradictory phenomenon, with every woman under sixty climbing out of the closets and onto the stages of talk shows to relate their tragic tales of childhood molestation at the hands of their fathers/brothers/stepfathers/uncles/close male family friends and/or physical abuse from their husbands. I don't mean to make light of this all too frequent, inexcusable behavior, and I certainly recognize the terrible scars it must leave, but I must question its sudden preponderance in present day America, and the message inherent in its epidemic proportions. Is this picture of brutish, insensitive males (which is no doubt an accurate portrayal of most men, I will be the first to admit) compatible with the counter images found in movies and television of passive males unable to defend themselves against smaller, presumably weaker females? Can the picture of victimized women clinging to their children in the shelters, rightfully outraged at the genuine abuse inflicted upon them, be reconciled with the aggressive characterizations of actresses, which seem to glorify feminine violence through repeated assaults upon their hapless male counterparts? Hopefully the viewpoint I'm expressing here will serve a greater purpose than exciting the small band of women-haters out there, for I am of the firm opinion that no one should want to beat anyone else up. All men and women need to give this issue serious deliberation before the damage to male-female relations grows into something a lot more serious than Elly May Clampett "whomping" her larger male cousin Jethro Bodine.

Dear H.B.,
Four years ago, I went to Redskins Park, our N.F.L. team's practice facility, to boo the pro football players who were at that time conducting a strike that was only slightly less absurd than the previous year's walkout by the major league baseball players. What most astounded me, other than the sight of very rich and arrogant young men posturing as common laborers, was the unimpressive physical stature of the players. What with the media constantly harping on the fact that modern players are so big and well-conditioned, sculpting their bodies in arduous, year-round workouts, it was quite a shock to witness a group of average sized guys carrying the picket signs. At first I mistook them for love-starved fans, so desperate to serve their heroes that they were hoisting the signs aloft for them, but when a contingent of boosters drove up in a van and delivered coffee and doughnuts to the unemployed athletes, I realized I was wrong. Most of the receivers and backs were tiny, very slim males,

and most of the linemen were dumpy and fat. I remember in particular standing next to one Redskins' lineman, who is listed at 6'2 and 260 pounds in the team press guide. I am 5'10 and weigh 185 pounds, and I swear there wasn't a noticeable difference in size between us. I came with a good friend of mine, who is a former high school football star and stands a legitimate 6'1 and weighs in at 255 pounds. He was bigger and stronger-looking than nearly anyone there, and he spends the majority of his time in local bars. Many of the players actually seemed frightened of him, and moved to the other side of the street when he passed by. Now, I ask you- how can they lie about all this?
  Startled In The Suburbs

Dear Startled: They can lie about anything they want. The reason the media wildly exaggerates the size and strength of pro football players is obvious: they want to build an image of greatness so the fans will swallow their shameless displays of what we used to impolitely refer to as "jock-sniffing." If the truth were told, many big-boned fans could play in the N.F.L. with a little practice, and they would be a great deal more appreciative of the fantastic lifestyle and financial rewards bestowed upon them. This is why the sportscasters fall all over themselves to portray these whining young members of the upper class as mere working stiffs, not a whole lot different from West Virginia coal miners. Perhaps they do this because they are the beneficiaries of quite an enviable position themselves. If the lie that pro athletes have a hard time of it- blessed with the highest standard of living America can offer through their propensity at playing games, and vacationing for fully half of the year- were ever exposed, then what could be said about the relative merits of those who 'cover' (in other words, attend games at no charge) sporting events and are paid a hefty salary to do so?

"Well?" St. Helen lowered the stack of papers in his hand dramatically. "Have you ever heard such impertinence, your honor?"

"No, I haven't." The judge shook his head disdainfully. "It sure don't sound like a fair deal to me."

"The odd thing, your honor," St. Helen walked over to the witness stand and placed his hand against one side of it, as he sneered at the trembling Professor, "is this man's obsession with belittling the abilities of entertainers in all fields. Consider, for example," St. Helen held another issue of *Force Of Habit* aloft, "his comment, in response to a ridiculous inquiry from one B.O. Roosterbuck concerning whether rock stars really cared for the starving children of Ethiopia, that: *...I simply agree that if the situation bothered them that much, then all of the celebrities who are so quick to play benefits in protest over it would instead dip into their* own *gigantic bank accounts. They shouldn't need television cameras to film their good intentions for posterity. Any fans who send some of their hard-earned money to support one of the causes so dear to celebrities' hearts should immediately check into the Barbra Streisand School For The Hearing Impaired for intensive therapy.* Then there is his reply, to a reader cleverly referring to himself as 'A Non-Member of The Academy,' who is complaining about, of all things, Robert Redford's hairdo in the movie *The Natural: ...A review of recent Hollywood period pieces reveals a single flaw; the modern actor will not wet his hair. The Redford case is a perfect example of this egotistical absurdity. While spending millions of dollars on vintage antique automobiles, while going to the trouble of finding the right style of clothes for each member of the cast, while recreating whole towns into authentic period models, the production team is not capable of providing a jar of Vitalis for its male lead. This is not an isolated case, however; in television, who can forget the hairstyles of the male youngsters on 'The Waltons,' an otherwise unusually good t.v. show. It may have been set during the years of the Great Depression, but those boys could have waltzed into any disco in 1970's L.A. and blended right in. Of course, this show couldn't hold a candle to 'Happy Days,' which was so inaccurate in almost every detail (and grew increasingly more so the longer the show stayed on) that it became embarrassing to watch, even for American audiences. To see Chachi, Potsie, Ralph, Joanie, and their hairdos in 1950's America, one would have had to be at the drive-in watching one of those great science fiction films that era produced, as they resembled aliens more than any teenagers of the Eisenhower years. It became so ludicrous that eventually the writers lost all sense of reality and had Fonzie uttering such things as 'don't hassle me,' as if that phrase had been around in the 1950's. They had Joanie calling some boy a 'hunk,' as all girls did back then, I suppose.* Well, your honor, I think..."

"I object!" Professor Buckley cried.

"What's that?" The judge turned his head and stared at the ex-history teacher with a great deal of amazement. "No one gave you permission to speak. That ain't no fair deal in here. You'll have a chance to defend yourself. Proceed, Mr. St. Helen."

"Thank you, your honor." St. Helen continued rifling through the papers and presenting particularly offensive extracts for the record. "Here he castigates entertainers in the music field: *...Ask any old-timer who has a discerning ear to rate Frank Stinkatra against his peers. They will mention forgotten names like Kenny Sargent, Dick Haymes, Eddy Howard, Russ Colombo, Skinnay Ennis, and a whole host of other worthies whom the critics discarded long ago in favor of the immortal Stinkatra. The same thing applies to music today. The Michael*

*Jacksons, the Bruce Springsteens, Whitney Houstons, etc. are promoted
as stars and their records are played every hour on the hour by all of the
top 40 stations. This is how someone achieves a 'hit.' I'm not being
simplistic here, the radio stations hold all the power. If they play any
song enough times, the kids will buy it (remember 'Horse With No Name,'
'Let Him In,' 'Disco Duck,' 'Tiptoe Through The Tulips?') If they don't play
a song, it doesn't matter how catchy it is, it will never sell.* Then,
returning to his obsession with the world of sports, catch this none too
subtle bit of racism: *...Since you hail from Tampa Bay, it's a wonder you
think there are such things as white professional football players. My
view is that the overwhelming preponderance of black pro athletes, out
of all proportion to their percentage of the general population, stems
directly from racism. ...After all, if blacks are naturally superior athletes,
where are all the black place-kickers?*

"He's got a point there." Bucktooth commented, in a voice just loud
enough to be heard.

"Silence!" The judge slammed his gavel down. "You're just
observers here. You can't speak; that wouldn't be a fair deal."

"May I proceed, your honor?" St. Helen glanced in their direction
with a look of triumph on his evil face.

"Please, go ahead."

"Thank you." St. Helen pulled an issue from the center of the pile
and began waltzing about the courtroom, as if posturing for the imaginary
jury. "I would like to read this letter, from July 1983, in its entirety. It
shows, with crystal clarity, the uniqueness of this man's mind, and the odd
and unproductive way he perceives everything. It, once again, concerns
pro sports:

> *Dear H.B.,*
> *Well, here it is that time of year again, and here I am infuriated
> again. Why, oh why, don't the sportswriters and/or broadcasters
> comment critically on the yearly travesty known as the Major League
> All-Star game selection process? True, once in awhile one of them may
> mildly chastise the fans, but never-ever will any of them expose the
> unjust actions of the A.L. and N.L. managers, whose job it is to name the
> reserve players and pitching staffs. They are so consistently wrong as to
> defy belief that the picks could be merely chance, random selections. I
> now, quite irrationally, believe that they choose the wrong pitchers and
> reserves on purpose, that they make their substitutions during the game
> in diametrical opposition to order of merit, and that they play the least
> deserving reserves the longest amount of time- all for some unknown
> and apparently ridiculous reason. Tell me, am I crazy to be possessed by
> this?*

Bedazzled In Bugtussle

Dear Bedazzled:
You must realize that the professional sports world is one of the largest revenue- producing components of modern America. Thus it has become, like all big business, prey to the same confusing and patently absurd kinds of inconsistencies that are a common denominator in the wonderful world of capitalism. I have received many complaints of a similar nature about the terrible job that the fans do in selecting the starting line-ups for the All-Star game. My usual response is a quick and witty 'look at the political leaders they elect.' One must truly wonder how any enfranchised citizenry, short of being held at gunpoint, could vote into public office the Lyndon Johnsons, the Alan Cranstons, the Tip O'Neills, the Howard Bakers, the Jim Wrights, the Jack Kemps, etc. This is not really surprising, however, to those literate, observant types who subscribe to this humble little newsletter. The American people can't even be trusted to vote for the most deserving baseball players in the annual All-Star game, so is it any wonder that they completely bungle their slightly more important voting rights? But to get to your beef- yes, I agree with you that some member of the sports media should mention something about the atrocious selections and replacement procedures by the All-Star game managers. These men are given the responsibility of rectifying all of the idiotic fan errors, which for some reason are to be expected, and defy all logic by compounding those mistakes and in some cases outdistancing them in degree of ineptitude. But then I have thought for years that some member of the sports media would say something about the barely literate 'students' who produce millions of dollars in revenue for the institutions they fraudulently attend. But, in that case as well, the fans play their part, gleefully watching the corrupt productions of the monstrous sweat-shop known as the N.C.A.A., while their own sons and daughters are unable to afford the cost of higher education at universities with much lower academic reputations. Oh well, as they say in Mudville, we wuz robbed.

"Your honor," St. Helen was obviously relishing his work, "I shall only have to submit a few more excerpts. So far, we have heard mainly of the defendant's penchant for finding fault with the popular entertainers he is so visibly jealous of. Now, I will enter into the record some of his views in other areas. In regards to the letter from 'Call Me Yellow,' a pacifist complaining about citizens wanting to die for their country, Buckley answers sarcastically: *...Don't you think you're getting your money's worth from the government that so kindly withholds tribute from each of your paychecks, in this fifth decade of that temporary wartime measure?*

Can't you see your tax dollars at work on our marvelously maintained roads and bridges? In the police protection and criminal justice system that allows us to walk the streets safely at night? In our congressional representative, who is so attentive to our concerns that he is more than entitled to the hefty raise he regularly votes himself? If war was not a bankers' scam, and if honest politicians actually were in charge, then they would send off to do the fighting and the dying those most fit to do it. If it were ever in our interests, which is highly improbable, to fight in the name of the United States somewhere around the world, then I would suggest we send convicted murderers and other violent repeat offenders in our overcrowded prisons to serve in the front lines. Surely these established criminals would make much better soldiers than our innocent sons and daughters, and would probably welcome the excitement. Of course, those commanding the troops should, in all fairness, be those most in support of the military action. It would be grand poetic justice, indeed, to see some of the old warriors in the White House, the Capitol, and in the media, who sadly missed the opportunity to engage an enemy in battle when they were of prime age, leading our illustrious forces. I am fully aware that no one would ever heed my recommendation and I am careful to keep an American flag handy in case the freedom-loving patriots should tap lightly at my door. Or, his thoughts on the justice system: *...We receive more letters on the discrepancies in sentencing than on any other subject. It is a sad fact that all law and order fanatics, such as Mothers Against Drunk Drivers, etc., who seem to think controlling the behavior of motorists is of paramount importance, want to get tough on everyone except pro athletes, politicians, entertainment figures, and any other very rich individual. All you have to do to validate my point is read the papers. They are filled with daily reports of the famous being caught and charged with various offenses. Without fail, all are eventually let off the hook. Mothers Against Drunk Drivers is anything but M.A.D.D. over this, and all of their crusading members who go to the absurd lengths of sitting in court all day to pressure judges into severely punishing first-time offenders are silent and never protest when the local pro football player is apprehended while driving drunk. I don't mean to come out in favor of drunk driving, nor to trivialize the terrible tragedies that so many members of M.A.D.D. suffered, but I believe that no law can be respected or just if it isn't applied equally to everyone. Thus, I find it difficult to believe that every rich and famous person accused of a crime just happens to consistently find what the average citizen rarely does; a merciful jury and a lenient judge.* Consider the eminent Professor's brief and flippant replies to the following questions: *How do you become nominated for a Nobel Prize? ...Be unworthy of the honor. Why do the directions included in nearly everything that requires assembly seem so* *purposefully confusing? ...Because the same people that make the various overpriced and defective products write them. If one man can drink a beer in one minute, and sixty men can drink it sixty times as fast, can sixty men drink a beer in one second? ...I see you've read your Ambrose Bierce.* In other letters too ridiculous to read, he makes mention of Federal agents killing distressed farmers and other "eccentric" citizens for such things as refusing to send their children to public schools. He goes so far as to quote Thomas Edison's absurd and little-known contention that only one percent of the people actually think, and cleverly quips that the great inventor was being unduly optimistic in his formulation. He dances all over the political spectrum; in one letter he expresses deep sympathy for Nazi leader Rudolph Hess, and demands he be released from prison and *"interviewed on the first available talk show,"* while in another he rants against the concept of colonialism, with a nasty swipe at *"the imperialist Bullshit-Moose man Teddy Roosevelt,"* whom he suggests may have had a hand in the assassination of McKinley. In others, he supports financial reparations for the surviving American Indians, and a ban on all guns, *"particularly in the police stations and the Pentagon."* I could go on and on. This man doesn't believe in free trade, or the fluoridation of the water supply, or foreign aid, or immigration, or the income tax. He doubts the official version of almost everything, from the assassination of Abraham Lincoln to Watergate. He expresses a passing interest, from time to time in his writings, in such nonsensical publications as *Weekly World News* and *The Flat Earth News.* Your honor, I believe I've established beyond any doubt that Hiram Buckley is an enemy of the predominant culture, of all elected officials, and of the State itself. I urge the court to act judiciously in this matter, and sentence the defendant to the maximum penalty provided under the law. Thank you, your honor, I rest my case."

"Very well, Mr. St. Helen." The Judge waited an agonizingly long time before reaching over and tapping Professor Buckley on the shoulder. "Alright, you can answer the charges now. Everyone gets a fair deal here."

The Professor, although terribly flustered by the attack on his thoughts and ideas, managed to gather his composure sufficiently enough to muster up some sort of defense. "There has been so much-that is-I don't know where to begin to respond. I suppose I should mention, first of all, that I didn't write much of what has been read here. That letter about the television programs and the hairdos-I have no idea where that came from. You see, I haven't watched any television for a very long time. I threw my set out of the window back in '59. As for all of the references to sports, I must also confess ignorance in that area as well; I was never much of a sports fan, in fact I always despised the competitive spirit that seems so prevalent among Americans. I admit to having many radical and unorthodox concepts about a great many things, and if that's a crime, I am forced to plead guilty. But, if you're going to-that is-I don't really understand what's going on here, and I'd like..."

"You'd *like*?" The judge asked incredulously. "No one in this courtroom has ever had the audacity to tell me what they'd like. That ain't no fair deal. I hereby sentence you to life imprisonment in the Extremely Unreachable Ward."

"No!" Waldo suddenly jumped up and rushed forward.

Whatever foolish notions were in the nervous young man's head, they were quickly dashed when Edgar and Jimmy, the two brutes who'd so forcefully led the Professor into the courtroom, quickly reappeared and subdued him.

"Tsk, Tsk, Waldo." St. Helen smiled. "That won't do at all. If there is another outburst like that, you'll be sent to the Fortress Of Contamination. That's not a pretty place, I can assure you."

Thus, the four of them held their silence as Professor Buckley was hauled away, kicking and screaming in frustration, to parts unknown. The youthful judge followed a moment later, pleasantly reminding them, with an Aryan integrity shining brightly in his blue eyes, how everyone in his court was sure to get a "fair deal."

"Make yourselves at home, gentlemen." St. Helen intoned. "The Extremely Unreachable Ward is very large, and our tour has only begun."

Jeanne was striding briskly down the hallway in the west wing, where the other entrance to the sub-basement lay, and her twin sister was struggling to keep pace.

"Come on, Jeanne, please slow down a little bit." Janie pleaded.

Jeanne glanced back over her shoulder. "I told you to work out to that aerobics tape with me."

"Jeanne, I'm scared." Janie breathlessly confessed. "What if all that weird stuff they're into...is real?"

Jeanne stopped and placed her arm reassuringly around her sibling's shoulder. "All I know is that Waldo wasn't in the lobby when he was supposed to be, and neither were any of the others. If something supernatural, or whatever, really is responsible for that, then it's probably better that we know about it."

As if he'd been listening in on their conversation, a figure suddenly materialized in their path. It was Otto Motto, the legendary graffiti artist/Housekeeper, who was now apparently relegated to being a sort of hall monitor for those operating the Extremely Unreachable Ward. He carefully placed a 'caution-wet floor' sign down and began mopping.

"Afternoon, ladies. Watch your step."

Jeanne and Janie tried to catch their breath. "Where did you come from?" They both exclaimed at once, while scanning the floor and walls for trap doors and secret panels.

Otto Motto laughed in that infamous, terrifying style. "You two really shouldn't be out this late; there are a lot of distasteful things that can happen to teenage girls. By the way, I hear it's especially busy in the sub-basement this evening."

With that, he vanished into thin air, leaving the O'Sullivan twins standing there with their eyes and their mouths wide open.

Before they could recover from this unforeseen event, they heard a voice behind them.

"Young ladies, what are you doing in this part of the building? Perhaps I can help you find something." It was the woman from the Personnel office, her bun intact on her head; the woman of a thousand faces, a female Lon Chaney. "Are you, by any chance, headed for the sub-basement? I can show you the way." She grabbed each of them roughly by the elbows and began escorting them down the hall.

"No! Uh, we weren't going there!" Janie was more frightened than her sister, who had half anticipated something of this nature.   As they approached the stairwell door leading down to the sub-basement, both girls, having ceased fighting to free themselves from the woman's amazingly powerful grip, closed their eyes tightly and prepared for the worst.

"Jeanne! Janie!" They were startled by the shouting, and opened their eyes to find Phosphate standing there, blocking the stairway to the sub-basement.

The female Lon Chaney appeared to be caught off guard by this development, and the top doo-wopper seized the opportunity to snatch the girls from her clutches. The woman of a thousand faces seemed helpless to act and simply watched as Phosphate and the O'Sullivan twins hurried away in the opposite direction.

When they had walked a considerable distance, Phosphate stopped. They were just outside of the General Processing department, which was located in the heart of the basement. He embraced both girls warmly, then waved his finger at them facetiously.

"Do you realize that you two are just about the craziest... bravest girls I've ever had the privilege to know?"

"*We're* brave? You saved our lives, Phosphate! But, why are you by yourself? Were you down in the sub-basement, in the Extremely Unreachable Ward? Is Waldo okay?" Jeanne's questions were coming as fast as job promotions for pretty girls in clinging outfits.

"Please! Slow down!" The head Afro-Anarchist cautioned the inquisitive teen. "Yes, I was in the sub-basement. We located the Extremely Unreachable Ward. I am by myself because none of the others know how to leave yet; they are under the impression that escape is impossible. And, yes, Waldo is unharmed."

"Thank goodness!" Jeanne heaved a massive sigh of relief.

"But why can't the others leave?" Janie asked. "What do you mean about escaping? I don't understand."

"It's quite complicated and our time is limited, so excuse me for not elaborating." Phosphate knelt on the floor in the manner of a quarterback in a huddle. "Listen carefully to me. It is our responsibility to rescue the others. Right now, they are a defeated lot, and their fate is entirely in our hands. They are unaware of the only way out of the Extremely Unreachable Ward. It is actually quite elementary, but can be easily overlooked. I was extremely fortunate to discover it. The place they are trapped in is indescribable, but suffice to say that it may be difficult to even find them. We must act quickly, and this is what we have to do..."

"All of us possess a powerful, untapped weapon. It is called the human brain. The way out of the sub-basement involves mind over matter." Phosphate was instructing Jeanne and Janie, somewhat condescendingly, in how they could assist him in freeing the others from their nefarious foes.

"What do we have to do?" Jeanne was growing anxious.

Phosphate's demeanor was grim but steadfast. "This is their only hope; you two must believe completely that none of what they are enduring is real. Do you understand?"

Both girls, not unexpectedly, shook their heads.

"Very well, perhaps I'm not explaining things properly. For instance, that Housekeeper you told me about, and the woman who was attempting to force you down into the sub-basement; you must believe, with all your heart, that they did not actually exist. If you accomplish that, no phantoms can stand in your way, and the door leading from the sub-basement will open for you. Now do you comprehend?"

"In other words, we have to ignore everything we see and hear and treat it all as some kind of illusion?" Jeanne's innate intelligence, which was far more useful in this situation than a Harvard degree, was demonstrated by her quick grasp of Phosphate's complex and inadequately enunciated theory.

"Yes, but not exactly an illusion. We are dealing with some clever adversaries, and it is the paranoia and the conspiracy mindset that apparently sustains them. That is why they have been so successful in our case; each of us having spent a great portion of our lives thinking that someone or something like them existed." The top doo-wopper placed a hand on each of their shoulders. "You two have the ability to do this. I don't believe that either of you have swallowed our wild ideas in the least

340

bit. Therefore, it should be quite feasible for you to walk calmly into the Extremely Unreachable Ward and lead Waldo and the others back here safely. Assuming, of course, that you can locate them. Are you willing to try?"

"But what if we can't find them?" Janie's bottom lip was quivering. "Then what will happen to us?"

"If my theory is correct," Phosphate declared, "then the two of you would have absolutely no problem whatsoever in leaving the sub-basement, should you unfortunately be unable to discover the whereabouts of our comrades. I would never think of asking you to go if I thought there was a chance you wouldn't return; I couldn't live with myself under those circumstances."

"With you to guide us, how can we fail?" Jeanne was more enthusiastic about the proposition than her sister.

The head Afro-Anarchist looked down and studied his feet. "You don't understand. I-I'm not going with you."

"What?" was their predictable response.

"You see, I was able to open the door earlier, but that was due to the fact that I wasn't fully cognizant of my actions. If I had been, it is highly probable that I would still be trapped down there with the others. I honestly do believe in Them, and in the pseudo-reality of all we've encountered thus far; I could never will myself convincingly enough to fool Them. It is not desirable that I accompany you for several reasons, much as I would love to be your protector. My presence would only endanger the others and my rigid belief system could only diminish your chances of accomplishing an already difficult task. No, you must go alone."

Jeanne looked at her sister. "Okay, Phosphate. One thing I know for sure is that Waldo considers you his friend. If you say you can't go with us, then, well, you must have a good reason."

Phosphate hugged them both again. "Thank you for understanding. And for being so courageous."

Jeanne felt the butterflies awakening in her stomach. "Well, there's no time like the present. Like you said, we haven't any time to spare."

"The sooner you leave, the sooner you can allow them to." Phosphate was growing emotional and both girls saw the tears welling up in his eyes. "It's very important that you place your mind under control as soon as you walk through the stairwell door. They're likely to know you're coming. When you arrive in the sub-basement, simply keep walking and you will run straight into the Extremely Unreachable Ward. You can't miss it; in all probability it will find you."

With that final bit of instruction, the O'Sullivan twins followed the top doo-wopper back down the hallway leading to the sub-basement. Every moral and gallant fiber in Phosphate's body protested against sending two young girls into a hostile, potentially dangerous enviorment like the Extremely Unreachable Ward, and it required all his willpower to resist going with them.

"Okay, Phosphate, from now on, all of your Federal Reserve System-Communists in the State Department-Assassins under manhole covers-stuff is considered garbage and strictly off-limits." With that, and a dramatic flip of her hair, the spunky little Irish lass led the way into the sub-basement, followed closely by her twin sister.

19
IT'S A MAD, MAD, MAD, MAD WARD

After leaving the odious courtroom, wherein the unfortunate Professor Buckley was treated to an even nastier brand of justice than average citizens are accustomed to, St. Helen led them through another dark, imposing corridor and into a bright, massive chamber that was filled with thousands and thousands of video tapes.

Waldo whistled in astonishment. There were more tapes gathered in the gigantic, garishly lighted room than he could have imagined existed. His own extensive collection couldn't hold a candle to it.

Enjoying the wondrous looks on their faces, St. Helen beamed proudly. "Welcome, gentlemen, to The Escaped Voyeur Video Libertyland. Every taste can be satisfied here; every whim, every perversion. There is no censorship in our ward; you will see, as you look around, many selections that you've never heard of. It is particularly ironic that some of the very filmmakers whose work was considered so daring and innovative it had to be suppressed are long-time residents of the Extremely Unreachable Ward. They've found their audience here; everyone loves them and labels them geniuses. Feel free to browse for a short while; we're ahead of schedule."

As Waldo wandered along, gazing at the shelves of tapes that reached to the cathedral ceiling high above, he marveled at some of the titles. There was an enormous selection of x-rated films which covered every possible fetish; a section devoted to obscure, offbeat, and controversial material, with titles like *Hitler Versus The Forces Of Evil, Secret Footage Of The Aliens That Crash-Landed At Roswell Air Force Base, Revenge Of The Fat Guys, Hidden Cameras At The Skull And Bones Society,* and *Truly Amazing Discoveries*; a fantastic array of cartoons; and even an assortment devoted to classified government film of various events, such as both Kennedy assassinations, black masses with high-profile celebrities in attendance, and C.I.A. experiments on involuntary human subjects. The most interesting items of all appeared to be on the top rows, which were only accessible with the use of one of the huge ladders scattered about the room. There were more conventional selections there, as well, including several recent titles that Waldo recognized as still being in the theaters. It was easy to understand why Sam Hancock was so pleased with the entertainment provided there. The overall effect was mind-boggling, and there was truly enough diversity in this cavernous room alone to keep almost anyone occupied for years.

As St. Helen abruptly clapped his hands, with the stern

343

announcement that the tour was about to continue, Fontaine found it difficult to tear himself away from the "Suppressed Black Films" section, one of the many specialized categories on display, and Brisbane was just as reluctant to leave another entitled "X-Rated Home Movies From The Golden Age Of Hollywood." With long sighs, they reluctantly followed St. Helen out into what was evidently the main corridor of the Extremely Unreachable Ward. There were a great many miniature light bulbs jutting out from the cinder block walls and the white paneled ceiling, and they lent a casino-like atmosphere to the wide hallway. It was paved, curiously enough, and featured a yellow line painted down the middle. Each of them could only imagine, as they stared in wonder at this displaced feature, what sort of traffic might be found on a paved road in the bowels of a mental institution.

St. Helen was a knowledgeable tour guide, with a knack for sophistication and flair that would have endeared him to the management of many a museum or art gallery. The aura of supreme confidence that he projected obviously was essential in running a secluded mental ward which catered to unwilling patients.

As they proceeded along the main corridor, which St. Helen gleefully referred to as Unconstitutional Avenue, they noticed there were rows of closed doors, for as far as the eye could see, along either side. Their black and white guide in the nondescript trench coat explained that only the most distinguished patients in the ward were entitled to a room on Unconstitutional Avenue, and that many of the rooms were in fact empty, due to a shortage of qualified candidates. Apparently, it was an honor of the highest magnitude to be granted a tiny dwelling that bordered the paved strip, and St. Helen exulted in pointing out various doors, behind which the ward's celebrities were lodged.

"Ah, room 104. The last abode of Mary Reeser, probably the most famous of all victims of spontaneous human combustion. I'm sure you, Waldo, at least, must have read of her case- it is one of the most baffling on record. Behold, room 107, home to little Scotty Beckett, perhaps the cutest member of 'Our Gang.' It's really a pity the way he ended up- found beaten on someone's doorstep late at night; the tragedies never seem to cease for child actors. Then, we have the renowned inventor of the engine that bears his name- Dr. Rudolph Diesel, next door in room 108. Strangely little has been publicized about his disappearance from a steamer crossing the English Channel in 1913. He was seen at dinner the night before, but the following morning, he could not be located. You are familiar, I am sure, with all of the baffling particulars that are a standard feature in these cases; his cabin berth had not been slept in, the discovery of his neatly folded hat and coat on deck, etc." Suddenly, they all heard the beautiful strains of a clarinet, which appeared to be emanating from behind a door with the number 111 above it. St. Helen cocked his head to one side, cupped his hand to his ear, and smiled. "That would be perhaps our most famous resident, Mr. Glenn Miller. He's soloing this evening, as always, on *Moonlight Serenade*. He never seems to tire of it."

"B-but...all those people are dead, man." A baffled Brisbane remarked.

"Yeah, how can someone who was last seen on a boat in 1913 be alive now?" Fontaine wondered.

"How could baseball players from another century be carousing in a bar?" St. Helen replied. "How could you converse with them?"

Waldo walked along with the others in stunned silence, wishing desperately that his beautiful teenaged lover was there to comfort and reassure him.

At length, Unconstitutional Avenue veered to the left, and they found themselves on a strip of lush grass that led into an enormous gray building. There were two glorious fountains in front, from which red, gold, green, and blue colored streams of liquid were pouring forth, with an awesome statue of Sir Walter Raleigh between them.

St. Helen approached the building and held open its thick wooden doors, revealing its massive stone columns and golden busts of literary figures such as Oscar Wilde, Jonathan Swift, Emily Bronte and George Bernard Shaw, which glistened with an almost electrical aura.

"Emily Bronte." A wistful Waldo caressed the shiny bust of one of his favorite poets. "She lived such a short life, and yet she wrote such beautiful..."

"There are far more impressive things behind *this* door." St. Helen gestured towards a bronze and smoked glass aperture, with a row of sparkling red rubies running horizontally across it. It opened automatically at the touch of St. Helen's black shoe. "And now, gentlemen, let us step into the library, or as we call it here, the Little Home Of Loud Voices And Unfettered Reading Materials."

As they gingerly entered the library, which was more ancient and breathtaking than any ruins yet uncovered by archaeologists, they saw the hand carved bookcases, lined along the white marble walls by the hundreds, the crystal chandeliers that provided the proper reading light, and felt their feet sink into the deep blue carpet. If the Escaped Voyeur Video Libertyland was large, then there would have to be a new adjective invented to describe the size of the Little Home of Loud Voices And Unfettered Reading Materials. In addition, the scope of the subject matter there, having a much longer history to draw upon, was wider as well, encompassing every viewpoint and "ism" that the spellbound new patients could think of, and they were capable of thinking of a great many.

"Shit man!" Brisbane held up an old battered paperback entitled,

Why I Hate Everybody And Everything by one Omar O'Shaunessey.
Finding a fascination in nearly every book he came across, the fredneck
continued picking up various volumes with such titles as *I Went On a
Blind Date With Satan* by Ida Mae Willoughby, *The Notorious History Of
The Evil Order of The Wild Tuna* by Shucks Saberstein, *Sexual Secrets of
The Vatican* by Earley Pugh, and *The Royal Family Needs a Public
Whipping* by one D.D. Lufenfauver.

"Do you see how foolish your friend was to try and leave us?" St.
Helen asked, referring to Phosphate, whom they'd been informed had
been apprehended and taken to the Radioactive Quiet Corner following
his unsuccessful escape attempt. "You will enjoy every comfort here. I
know, for instance, that Waldo is a voracious reader. Picture yourself
choosing books from this collection, my friend."

Waldo had been snapped out of his awe by St. Helen's reference to
the top doo-wopper. Why had he tried something that was doomed to
failure? When St. Helen had notified them, shortly after the trial of
Professor Buckley, that the head Afro-Anarchist had been quickly
captured and carted off to an ominous-sounding detention center, Waldo's
remaining spirit was crushed. Relegated to making the best of an
intolerable situation, the nervous young man was rather ashamed of how
well he had been doing just that. But St. Helen's mention of Phosphate's
plight had jarred him back into a realization that he was not in some
dingy, dust-covered utopia, but a hidden ward for very special mental
patients.

"You could have everything my grandfather ever wrote in here and I
still wouldn't like this place." Waldo felt better reverting back to his more
natural defiant posture.

"You'll soon discover, young man, that it doesn't pay to be
uncooperative in the Extremely Unreachable Ward." St. Helen intoned
menacingly. "Let us proceed to the next stop on our little tour."

They exited the library and walked down Unconstitutional Avenue
for a short distance. St. Helen, apparently perturbed by Waldo's
comments, remained silent and didn't bother to point out any more
attractions among the patient rooms they passed.

All at once, Unconstitutional Avenue turned into a steep incline and
there appeared in the distance, through a thick blanket of fog, a large
foreboding structure that resembled a castle.

"What the hell..." Bucktooth's eyes were growing wider.

St. Helen turned around and grinned maliciously. "Gentlemen, we
are going to pay a visit to the Factory of Displaced Persons. It is the prime
attraction of our tours."

As they continued walking uphill towards the structure, it became
increasingly clear that it was indeed a castle.

"But, how could a castle be inside the basement of a..." Waldo was flabbergasted.

"Tsk. Tsk. It only makes things more difficult for you new arrivals when you dwell on unanswerable questions." St. Helen advised.

They reached the top of the incline, which was evidently the end of Unconstitutional Avenue as well, and stared at an old, rickety wooden bridge, which they obviously were going to have to cross in order to enter the castle.

Seeing the looks of fear on their faces, St. Helen snickered. "Relax. The bridge is nearly as safe as it appears. But, do be careful; if you fall, you'll land in the Moat of The Maladjusted, and that is never a pleasant sight."

Waldo peered down through the fog into the moat, and saw that it was literally filled to the brim with the largest, most ferocious-looking crocodiles he'd ever seen. They were snapping their giant jaws playfully at each other, diving up and down in the frothy water, and their red eyes seemed to be gazing directly up at him. Averting his gaze for a moment, Waldo scrutinized the castle itself, which stood tall and gray against a black backdrop which hardly appeared to be part of the foundation of the Last Chance Relaxation Home. There were sculpted dragons, lizards, unicorns, wolves, and other un-sundry creatures adorning the facade of the structure.

"Sheeet! Man, there ain't no way I'm crossing that thing!" Fontaine remarked adamantly.

St. Helen stared at him unsympathetically. "You have a choice, young man. If you wish to forego this part of the tour, a substitute selection can be arranged for you. Let's see, I would wager that you'd find the Last Confederate Plantation to your liking. The patients there love to entertain young blacks."

All vestiges of pride and radicalism had been shaken from Fontaine's system, and he stood there placidly. "O-o-okay, man. I'll go with you all."

"That's a very wise decision." St. Helen flashed his trademark sinister smile. "Follow me. It's much easier if you don't look down."

St. Helen then led the way confidently across the unstable bridge, which began creaking terribly when a sudden wind was whipped up from somewhere.

"What the fuck?" Brisbane grabbed the rusted chain railing which lined both sides of the bridge. "We're indoors, man. Where's the wind coming from?"

"Y-y-yeah. How do you fit all this shit down here, man?" Bucktooth asked incredulously.

St. Helen merely chuckled in response, as he stepped off the bridge and marched the short distance to the front door of the castle. He readjusted his fedora hat, which had been blown a bit askew by the wind, as he stood there waiting for them, enjoying every precarious stride they undertook.

The wind was rocking the bridge back and forth, and Waldo closed his eyes and held onto the flimsy chain rails for support. He was never so relieved, or surprised, when he gingerly placed his foot on the other side. The others stumbled off alongside him, and Waldo could hear them mumbling thanks to a higher power for having guided them safely across.

"Everyone make it? Excellent." St. Helen's finger was poised on what was apparently a doorbell, not normally a standard feature of gothic architecture. They didn't hear any ringing, but shortly thereafter the door slowly opened.

Standing there was a tall, odd-looking bald man. "Right on. What do you want, you ex-Illuminati reject?"

St. Helen appeared slightly embarrassed at this jibe, which was obviously directed at him. "I have a few newcomers with me, and they are taking the usual tour. Gentlemen, meet John, better known as Right On. He is the doorkeeper to the Factory of Displaced Persons. Right On, why don't you stand aside..."

"Why don't you get a haircut as short as mine?" Right On interrupted with a childish cackle. He then grabbed his right elbow with his left hand, and swung his arm from side to side like an ape.

Fontaine and Bucktooth burst out laughing at this character who, had he been seen on any of the upper floors of the facility, would have been instantly labeled a "classic."

"You're really getting to be a big problem." Right On cackled in the manner of a giant parrot, egged on by their laughter.

"Right On, move out of the way and let them see inside." St. Helen was growing visibly impatient with the strange doorkeeper.

"Right on, I like that. These tours of yours are really getting to be ridiculous." Right On was still swinging his arm, as well as subjecting the uncomfortable St. Helen to more unorthodox insults, but he obeyed and stood aside.

"You may not enter the Factory Of Displaced Persons. The tour goes no farther than the front entrance." St. Helen cautioned them. "Once you step inside, you can never leave again. Even I would be unable to release you."

St. Helen stepped aside, permitting them to look into the castle. There was a great deal of steam in the air, and they could feel the intense heat, even before they saw the massive furnace in the center of the room, from which it was emanating. The place wasn't well-lit, but Waldo could discern several figures scurrying about with shovels in their hands.

"Come closer, gentlemen. Allow me to point out a few prominent Displaced Persons." St. Helen grinned wickedly. "There- do you see that tall, distinguished-looking fellow with the curiously small head? That happens to be the foreman of the Factory, the honorable Joseph Force Crater."

"Do you mean the famous Judge Crater?" Waldo, being a devotee of unsolved mysteries, instantly recognized the name of one of the world's most celebrated missing persons.

"The one and only. Last seen entering a taxi on August 6, 1930. He stepped directly from there into the Extremely Unreachable Ward."

Waldo could see that Judge Crater was the only figure not carrying a shovel, and he was shouting something unintelligible at a tiny form who was stooped over from the weight of his load.

"Waldo, I can feel your tender heart breaking from here for that unfortunate child. He happens to be famous in his own right. Little Charlie Ross is his name, and he was the first known individual in American history to be kidnapped for ransom. Poor Charlie! The Judge is so very hard on him. The little chap was only four years old when he vanished from a lane behind his house, in a suburb of Philadelphia, on July 1, 1874."

Brisbane whistled. "Shit man, this is too much! How can a kid that was four years old in 1874 still be alive, and still be a kid?"

"How can highway exits appear and reappear? How can hitchhikers do the same thing?" St. Helen threw back his head and laughed uproariously, with a dash of the maniacal fervor they'd come to know so well.

Waldo was incensed. "You've gone too far this time, St. Helen. What right do you have to force that helpless child into hard labor? That was outlawed a long time ago."

"True, true." St. Helen seemed slightly amused. "Frankly, Waldo, I'm amazed at your simplistic ideals. This ward is filled with fantastic things, and most of them are far more unbelievable than a minor working in a factory. I can see you take your Dickens' seriously."

Waldo swallowed nervously. He truly loved children, and always winced whenever the callous adult world showed its insensitivity towards them. Witnessing the scope of the cruelty heaped upon poor Charlie Ross, Waldo forgot the incredible situation he found himself in, and raised his voice in protest.

"This is an outrage! One day, I swear, the people are going to..."

"The *people?*" St. Helen threw his head back and roared with laughter, and had to grab ahold of a gruesome sculpture of a gargoyle in order to avoid losing his balance. "Oh, please- how naive can you get? Your grandfather is a pragmatist compared to you, young man. How much evidence do you need? The people are idiots, Waldo- you've lived long enough to know that. They do exactly as they're told, and always have. They can be convinced their taxes have been cut while they're staring at a paycheck that tells them otherwise. They can be whipped into a war hysteria almost overnight. They'll mutilate their bodies to pay homage to the ever-changing whims of the fashion world. The old line about bread and circuses is one of the most profound ever uttered. Actually, they don't even require much supervision anymore. There are a few especially cruel spirits in the Comedy Of Errors Brigade who have been proposing for years that we start a propaganda campaign to make human feces edible. I only half doubt their observation that the masses would be fighting to the death for this new delicacy in a matter of weeks. Even if they had the will, what would they use against us? The Beatitudes? *Blessed are the meek*, indeed! You've seen far too many movies, young man; in real life, the bad guys always win."

There were tears of frustration on Waldo's cheeks when the black and white figure had finished his lengthy attack upon the common folk. "Well, I don't care- I've had enough of your tour. And of you. Whoever or whatever you are, I think you're a sick, evil..."

"Did you learn nothing from the trial of your friend- the illustrious ex-instructor of history?" St. Helen sighed. "Very well, then. If you insist upon being rebellious, I can play that game too. Hancock, come here."

Sam Hancock materialized out of nowhere at St. Helen's side.

"Take them to the Brig of First Offenses. That ought to create a nice attitude adjustment."

They were quickly led around the side of the Factory of Displaced Persons by Sam Hancock, and all of them sensed that their punishment would be even greater if they resisted and overpowered the old man, which they could easily have done.

Waldo stared at his grandfather's one-time best friend. "Mr. Hancock, how can you do this? You know it's wrong. Please, help us get out of here."

Hancock stopped and glared at Waldo. "You stupid kid! Haven't you figured out what's going on by now?" With those words, he was instantly transformed into the three M.I.B.'s that Waldo had been encountering so frequently.

Waldo shook his head and turned to the others. "There has to be some way out of this place." All at once, he was struck by a stray, incidental notion, and his mood began to brighten. "You know, I just might have the answer! Yes, that could be it! Do you remember that old story by that French author..."

"Voltaire?" Brisbane mentioned the only French author he was in any way familiar with.

350

"No, not him. I can't recall his name right now, but he wrote a story about a prisoner trapped in a cell with only one way to escape. The guy tries all kinds of things- digging tunnels, exploring secret panels in the wall, but nothing works and finally he gives up. The King, I think it was, who had imprisoned him then says something like, 'I didn't lie to you- there is a way out of this cell.' The prisoner gets mad and tells him that's impossible, he's tried everything. And then the King points to the door of the cell. It was never locked."

"That sounds like a cool story, Waldo." Bucktooth said. "I'd like to read it some time."

"Yeah, right, Buck." Fontaine rolled his eyes in exasperation at his fellow Afro-Anarchist, much as Phosphate had done so many times in reaction to his own antics. "What does that story have to do with us, Waldo?"

"Well," Waldo smiled slyly at the three M.I.B.'s, "let's just say that maybe our cell door was left unlocked."

The M.I.B.'s laughed at Waldo as they replied, as always, in unison. "You'll be lucky if you ever get out of the Brig Of First Offenses. It'll make you wish you'd never left the Factory Of Displaced Persons, and beg for a chance to work there."

All at once, they rolled down an unseen embankment, and came to rest in the middle of Unconstitutional Avenue. They were then whisked away, uninjured but still dazed from their fall, down another hallway, off to the right of the main corridor, which was much darker and gloomier. At length, the M.I.B.'s opened a door and revealed a room which was dimly lit by a row of candles that were placed sacrilegiously on one side. There was a smell of gasoline in the air, and in the flickering candle light, they could see several open holes in the floor, spaced evenly apart from each other.

The M.I.B.'s now launched into their version of a collective tour guide, describing with great delight an even more unpleasant part of the Extremely Unreachable Ward than they'd already encountered. "Okay, kiddies, welcome to the Brig of First Offenses. Actually, we don't know why they call it that, because no one has ever gotten the opportunity to visit the second. The open holes you see are filled with an acid strong enough to reduce a human body to nothingness in an instant. And, oh yes, the floor is coated with the most slippery oil."

Sensing the fact their captives were not going to enter the room willingly, the M.I.B.'s snapped their fingers and the two large, Neanderthal-like men, whom St. Helen had referred to as Edgar and Jimmy, suddenly appeared.

"Remember Edgar and Jimmy? I'm sure they'll be able to persuade you to cooperate. Have fun!"

There was no time to react as the giant henchmen shoved them into the room and slammed the door behind them.

Professor Hiram Buckley awoke to find himself in the magical O'Sullivan cornfield. It was nearly dark, and a light rain was falling. Opening his eyes, he felt groggy, as if he'd been knocked senseless, and distinctly heard the sound of voices singing off in the distance somewhere. Disoriented as he was, he didn't have time to chastise himself for his inexcusable lapse in consciousness. The last thing the one time pride of the local community college remembered was being rudely escorted from that hideous courtroom in the sub-basement of the Last Chance Relaxation Home. As to what happened afterwards, and how he'd arrived back in the cornfield, he was completely mystified.

Slowly rising to his feet, the eccentric ex-history teacher brushed himself off and straightened out the collar on his colorful sport coat. The voices were growing louder, and he found himself being drawn inexorably towards them. He strode off in the direction of the deep woods, where they seemed to be coming from, as if guided by an unseen hand.

"Shhh. Here he comes." Fred O'Grady whispered to his fellow members of the Forest Of Injured Egos, who were clustered together in the bushes just behind the ancient oak tree which advertised their existence. "Don't frighten him- he's been through quite an ordeal."

Professor Buckley approached the woods and maintained his composure when a slight figure emerged from within.

"Hiram Buckley?" O'Grady stepped forward from the shadows.

"Who-that is-what do you want?" The Professor, greatly relieved that the figure wasn't a werewolf or a green giant, anxiously inquired.

"My name is Brady O'Grady. You can call me Fred." O'Grady was holding the Professor's beloved, battered briefcase. "Here you are, Professor Buckley- this *is* yours, isn't it?" The leader of the Forest of Injured Egos was compelled to force the briefcase into the numbed hands of the stupefied ex-history teacher. "I would like you to follow me, please."

The Professor, so traumatized by recent events, possessed little power to resist, and amiably meandered along after him.   Pausing by the old oak tree with his organization's name carved into it, O'Grady smiled at the Professor. "Relax, friend. You're finally, at long last, among your true peers."

"But who are you?" Professor Buckley asked.

"I told you, my name's Fred O'Grady. I happen to have a lot of associates in these parts, and we're very happy here. No one bothers us, or makes fun of us, or fires us, or leaves us. We commiserate together, friend, every day and every night. We sing songs, we swap outlandish theories, we tell each other about the cruel people who've hurt us so much. You'll love it here."

352

They made their way through the woods, with the other Injured Egos following surreptitiously behind them. When they eventually arrived at the clearing, with the old-fashioned gas lights hung in the trees, and the roaring campfire in the center, Professor Buckley instinctively felt a great burden lifted from his shoulders, and he turned and smiled at Fred O'Grady, in a way he hadn't done since his days as a history instructor at the local community college, when he'd return from work each evening to the hugs and kisses of his wife and children. Then all of the members of O'Grady's troupe- Tarzan Whelps, Lucky Chesterfield, Narley Butterfields and the rest of them- came out of the underbrush and rushed up to greet their newest arrival.

"I say there," Lucky Chesterfield exclaimed, "this is an honor indeed! Please, sir, do read some of those marvelous letters from your newsletter."

O'Grady patted Hiram Buckley on the shoulder, then ladled some of the Forest Flaming Special into a cup and handed it to him. "Here you go, Professor, this is for you..."

"This is only a storage area. None of the other stuff is real." Jeanne was thinking out loud in the hope it would strengthen her resolve.

The O'Sullivan twins had just entered the Extremely Unreachable Ward. Having persevered through the intense heat of the initial, more legitimate part of the sub-basement, it took them awhile to adjust to a normal temperature again. They were still shivering as they stood together near the deserted, dust-infested nursing station.

"Jeanne, how can we deny what we see?" Janie was not as adept as her sister at this mental exercise. "Look at those cobwebs!"

"Listen, Janie, if you don't try harder, Waldo and the others could be in tremendous danger! Do you want that on your conscience?"

"Okay, I'm sorry. I'll try harder." Janie bore down and concentrated with all her might, but it was evident that she would continue to require reinforcement from her sister.

The girls daintily sidestepped the cobwebs and made their way further into the ward. They had nearly reached the red door behind the nursing station, which Jeanne intuitively felt held some significance, when Mr. St. Helen made one of his patented unannounced entrances.

"May I assist you lovely young ladies with something?" St. Helen was taking the debonair approach.

"What..." Janie was startled.

"I don't see or hear anyone, do you?" Jeanne chided her twin sister for her mental lapse.

"Don't you think we're aware of what you're up to?" St. Helen laughed. "Do you actually imagine it to be conceivable that two little girls could stop the forces I represent?"

Janie had to bite her tongue, but her sister was so confident by now that she kept walking, right through the apparently solid figure of St. Helen, without any trouble whatsoever.

St. Helen was not amused. "You are more clever than I gave you credit for. But you're too late. All of your friends are no doubt mere components in an acid compound by now."

Janie, spurred on by her sister's example, was astounded to find that she too was able to pass right through St. Helen. "Wait for me, Jeanne!" She shouted, now more frightened of her newly discovered powers than of what lay ahead of them in this extraordinary place.

Jeanne reached for the knob on the red door. "I have a hunch, sis, that wherever the guys are, the way to them leads through here."

Janie urged caution. "Listen, Jeanne, I'm really trying hard to do what you say, but this door is bright red and you can't tell me it isn't. Now that is kind of weird and I think we ought to check the other rooms first."

Jeanne smiled. "Just remember, even if I open this door and some killer beasts are on the other side, that it isn't real. As long as you do that, nothing can harm you." She was a firm believer in Phosphate's hypothesis now, and her determination would have been remarkable in anyone, let alone a sixteen year old.

Janie smiled back at her sister, but not quite as assuredly. "Alright, I trust you. Go ahead- I'll try my best."

Jeanne took her hand and squeezed it affectionately. "That's all anyone can do." Then, with one swift motion, she opened the red door.

They entered a dark room that was empty except for a rocking chair, which was in the far corner. An old man was sitting there, and he squinted at the unaccustomed light peeking in through the open door. When he focused his eyes and spotted the girls, he immediately jumped to his feet and started dancing some sort of ridiculous version of an Irish jig. After celebrating in this manner for a few moments, he abruptly stopped and approached the twins.

"Young ladies," he spoke in a booming voice, "I want to thank you for coming to my rescue." Then all at once he frowned. "Wait a minute- you're not with Them, are you?"

Jeanne shrugged. "Who are They?"

Janie tapped her sister on the shoulder. "Hey, I thought you said we were supposed to ignore everything."

"Yeah, I know, but I have a feeling about this." Jeanne stared at the old man. "For some reason, I think he's real."

The old man's face lit up in a broad smile and he bowed like a true old fashioned gentleman. "This is a terrible place and I can't imagine how you two found it, but I'm mightily pleased to meet you both. Allow me to introduce myself- I am Abner Billingsly."

Phosphate wasn't paying attention to Hector Hispania. The supervisor of the General Processing Department was chattering away about his great new singing group.

"Yeah, Phosphate, we were really inspired by you all, man." Hector said excitedly.

"I beg your pardon? Oh, I'm sorry, Hector, but I have a great many things on my mind. What were you saying?" In spite of the fact his friends were in grave danger, the top doo-wopper still remembered his manners and could, as always, actually feel remorse over unintentionally snubbing a fellow human being.

"That's okay, man. I was just saying that hearing you and your homeboys sing gave us the idea to start a group of our own- Hector and the Contaminated Waste Disposer Boys. Would you mind listening to our first song, man?" Hector eyed the head Afro-Anarchist like a child looking up at a dime-store Santa Claus.

Phosphate smiled and decided that a little entertainment would ease his mind. "Certainly, Hector, I'm sure I speak for the other Afro-Anarchists in saying we always welcome competition in the field of doo-wop protesting."

"Well, we're really more of a rap group, man." The G.P. supervisor appeared a bit embarrassed. "I hope you like that kind of music."

"To each his own, my friend." Phosphate, who was abnormally open-minded about most things, didn't bother to lecture the enthusiastic young man about the drawbacks of this latest musical rage. "Please proceed."

Hector seemed slightly on edge as he gathered his group behind him, but warmed up nicely as the song wore on:

"We are just some lonely underpaid homeboys
We would rather be doctors if we had a choice
All of us have labored in this place so long
And the work has made our muscles very big and strong
It's cheaper than an exercise video
Trash, blood, bedpans, and food trays to go
Yes, there is the chance we could catch a disease
But none of us cover our mouths when we sneeze
Still we have a lot of fun among the grease and grime
And very few of us have turned to lives of crime

We show off for the nurses but they never watch us
And so we holler at them and we grab our crotches
But we will never harm you, we don't kill or steal
We have open cans of soda and half-eaten meals
Sometimes we lift the trash bags and we don't take heed
Of the dirty needles jabbing us and making us bleed
There is no time to go and have it analyzed
But most of us are lucky, very few have died
With dirty laundry piled up high like drifts of snow
We have to keep it shoveled or it overflows
So come on down when you have nothing else to do
We'll fix a meal and have a blanket waiting for you."

Phosphate applauded heartily. "If my humble opinion means anything, I think that Hector and the Contaminated Waste Disposer Boys have a bright future ahead of them."

"You really think so, man?" Hector's wide grin revealed his unbridled joy over this bit of flattery, coming as it did from someone with the stature of a Phosphate Jefferson.

"Hector, what is the meaning of all this?" The loud, confident voice belonged to Jerome Jones, the manager of General Processing and Hector Hispania's immediate boss. "Do you have enough spare time to be doing some bad rapping when there's trash, and linen, and food, and instruments piled up in here?"

Hector and his crew quickly exchanged their rudely interrupted dreams for some good, old-fashioned elbow grease.

Phosphate gave them all a sympathetic look and then unceremoniously left the department, denying Jerome Jones the pleasure of ordering him out. As he walked away down the corridor, he glanced at a clock on the wall. Jeanne and Janie had been in the sub-basement for nearly an hour, and the top doo-wopper was starting to worry. If they'd been able to follow his instructions, and had kept their minds under control, then they should have returned with the others by now. He tried not to speculate on what was delaying them.

"*Shitttttt!*" Was the exclamation shouted out in harmony by the four sole inmates of the Brig Of First Offenses. Waldo, Brisbane, Fontaine, and Bucktooth went flying across the floor with breakneck speed, and just missed crashing into one another on several terrifying occasions. Edgar and Jimmy, the two behemoth bouncers who'd flung them into the room so harshly, must have used some sort of supernatural "English" in doing so, as they bobbed and spun like an ace billiard player's finest trick shot. Sliding so haphazardly with their arms and legs flailing, they resembled four screaming human pinballs. When all of them finally came to rest safely against the same wall, it was the kind of unlikely stroke of good fortune that devoted readers of the Hardy Boy stories would have sneered at.

"Shit man, I can't believe none of us slid into that acid!" A dumbfounded Brisbane was gasping for air.

"Yeah, but what are we gonna do now? You know damn well that we ain't gonna be that lucky again, and we have to cross the floor to get out of here." Fontaine was shaking like a leaf, and only the exhilaration of their escape from the jaws of death was keeping him from impersonating a modern version of "Sunshine" Sammy Morrison again.

Waldo was hyperventilating. He caught his breath long enough to express his thoughts. "I-I simply can't understand how we avoided all those holes filled with acid. But I guess you don't question a miracle."

"That's what it was, alright." The fredneck agreed. "But now we have to figure out a plan of escape. Any ideas, Waldo?"

"I'm afraid not. I think I've determined how to exit the Extremely Unreachable Ward itself, but first we have to leave this room, and I really don't know how we're going to do that." Waldo was gradually regaining both his composure and a more regular breathing pattern.

"Uh, I just noticed something, fellas." Bucktooth's eyes were growing larger. "Is it my imagination, or is that acid bubbling up a lot in that hole over there? Don't it look like it could... overflow?"

The others stared at the hole in question and it did appear to everyone as if the deadly fluid was on the threshold of spilling out over the edge and onto the oil-coated floor.

"I don't know about you dudes, but I think we better put our heads together and come up with some way out of here- and fast!" Brisbane declared.

As they fidgeted and squirmed on the floor, in the flickering light of the blasphemous candles, it wasn't difficult to picture St. Helen grinning broadly somewhere.

"You mean you're...*Waldo's grandfather*?" Jeanne was astonished.

The old man smiled at the twins, and it was such a sincere, friendly one that any doubt remaining in their minds about the prudence of interrelating with him instantly dissolved.

"Yes, I'm Waldo's grandfather. Call me Old Hoss." He replied in his hearty, booming voice. "But now I have to ask- who are you and how do you know who I am?"

Jeanne recounted how Waldo and his friends had ventured onto their property (without informing him of its magical powers, seeing no need to confuse the old man at this point) during the course of their search for him. She didn't mention the romantic nature of their relationship either, but Old Hoss was easily able to decipher that the beautiful teenager must feel strongly about his grandson to risk entering the Extremely Unreachable Ward in an effort to save him.

"So you see, he came here to try and contact Sam Hancock, your former best friend." Jeanne expounded further. "But apparently he and the other guys-well, actually there's one that's upstairs-are now trapped down here with no way out."

"Wait a minute, young lady," Old Hoss scratched his wise gray head, "if you knew you couldn't get out of here, then why in Heaven's name did you enter?"

Jeanne giggled, one of the few adolescent mannerisms she still possessed. "There was one member of the search party-I told you he was upstairs-who was able to escape. He told us how to do it, and that's why we came here, to bring back Waldo and the others, because they don't know..."

"Are you saying that there *is* a way out of here?" Old Hoss was incredulous.

"He was down here, and he came back." Jeanne replied. "If his theory is right, then we know the secret of leaving this place."

"Are you sure you know how to get out of here?"

"Well, as sure as we can be without doing it."

Jeanne's answer seemed to satisfy Old Hoss. "Alright, ladies," he said, "I'll put my fate in your hands. I was told if I ever left this room that...well, you don't want to hear such things. Please take me with you."

Jeanne and Janie both smiled and declared that it would be an honor to be accompanied by a gentleman they had heard so many wonderful things about.

Taking him by the hand, Jeanne turned to Old Hoss and adopted the tone of a scout leader. "You just follow us. We don't have much time."

With that, Old Hoss boldly exited the room behind the red door and pointed to a hallway between rooms three and four that neither girl had noticed before.

"There," he said, "I think that, wherever they are, we have to walk down that hall to get to them."

The three of them bravely approached the corridor, which was dark and imposing, pausing only briefly to shiver a bit at the sign over the doorway leading into it; *You Are Now Entering The Hallway Of Lost Hopes.*

Fontaine looked at Brisbane and Bucktooth. "Hey fellas, how's about my Steady Heady Boyz joining me in a little rap?"

Waldo stared at him as if he were a visitor from another galaxy.

"Are you crazy, Fontaine? The acid is on the verge of spilling over and disintegrating us! We need to concentrate on getting out of this place."

"Yeah, Fontaine." Bucktooth agreed, "Besides, I thought you were through with that rapping stuff."

"I'm sorry, fellas, I must have lost my mind for a second." Fontaine pleaded modern man's most popular defense.

"Shit man, I got it!" Brisbane exclaimed. "We can crawl across the floor on our stomachs like worms!"

"Yeah, that's a great ideaa!" Bucktooth started to leap up in excitement, and was fortunate that Fontaine caught him before he lost his footing and became a harmonic bit of deadly, bubbling liquid.

Waldo was mulling Brisbane's suggestion over. *It just might work*, he thought to himself, and at any rate, they needed to act quickly and it was the only plan any of them had formulated. He was about to speak out in favor of the fredneck's idea when suddenly a loud voice reverberated out from somewhere above them.

"When are you going to stop disobeying me?"

St. Helen's distinctive tone was as clear and menacing as ever, although none of them could see him. "I think it's time for you to take the next step, in a manner of speaking, in the art of learning subservience. Edgar! Jimmy!"

The door to the room opened at once and standing there outlined in the sacrilegious glow were the large, nightmarish figures of Edgar and Jimmy. The two bodyguards snapped their hairy fingers simultaneously, and Waldo and the others were no longer in the Brig Of First Offenses.

They found themselves instead in a tranquil, lush setting that resembled a Hollywood hackwriter's vision of paradise. There were flowing streams of crystal clear water; lovely wild, multicolored flowers blooming plentifully; succulent fruit trees providing an inviting shade as well as a plethora of natural delights; tender deer dozing peacefully on the grass; and exotic birds chirping merrily and flitting from tree to tree.

"Damn, this sure beats that oil and acid shit!" Bucktooth, as usual, went right to the heart of the matter.

Waldo blinked in disbelief. Was this supposed to be some sort of punishment? He turned to Edgar and Jimmy, who were standing with their arms across their chests and blank, intolerant looks on their faces in the finest stereotypical fashion.

"Excuse me, uh, Edgar and Jimmy, but is this place supposed to be worse than the Brig Of First Offenses?" Waldo timidly asked.

Edgar laughed crudely. "Welcome to the Garden Of Old Movie Monsters. Good luck with your hunting." He vanished an instant after the words left his ugly lips, along with his equally distasteful companion.

"Garden of Old Movie Monsters? What the hell is that huge dude talking about?" Fontaine shook his head, chuckling to himself.

"Uh...I think he's talking about something like *that*." Brisbane's eyes were raised upwards, and as wide as flying saucers as he pointed behind them with an unsteady hand.

Waldo's spine sprung into action again, readily accommodating the shivers racing up and down its length. He turned around slowly, and then looked up. He both saw and heard the angry roar of a giant ape that was the mirror image of the legendary King Kong.

"Mr. Billingsly, what do you think that sign meant by *The Hallway of Lost Hopes*?" Janie wondered anxiously.

"Please, call me Old Hoss." He gently corrected her. "I really don't know. It seems that whoever runs this place is smitten with those kinds of preposterous titles."

The three of them were creeping cautiously down the Hallway of Lost Hopes, which was illuminated solely by the torches which blazed brightly in certain niches chiseled into the stark stone walls. The air was dank and filled with an unpleasant odor, which reminded them of rotten eggs. All in all, the dreary atmosphere it projected was well suited to its name.

"Roy W. Parker. My records indicate that he's in room 223."

Old Hoss and the O'Sullivan twins were startled by a sudden voice coming from directly in front of them. Straining their eyes in the pre-electrical light, they could see two figures sitting together in the middle of the hall.

"And why would he be here, Shoestring?"

"He pitched in two games with the St. Louis Cardinals in 1919, then completely disappeared."

As they approached the two figures, Old Hoss and the twins saw that one of them was a thin young boy with a brightly colored hairdo, and the other was a plump, spectacled woman. Of course, they couldn't have known that these characters, Shoestring and Dr. Xmaster, had been encountered on two earlier occasions by Waldo and the others.

Dr. Xmaster looked up at the three of them. "Do you have an appointment to see someone in the Unit Of Missing Major Leaguers?"

Old Hoss shook his head.

"Perhaps they'd like to visit with Andy Varga." Shoestring ran his fingers lovingly across the pentagram which covered his bare chest. "He pitched for the Cubs in '50 and '51, but he's been missing for over 30 years now."

Dr. Xmaster patted him on the knee. "Oh, Shoestring, you *are* marvelous!"

Jeanne squeezed Old Hoss's hand. "Remember, nothing here is

real."

Dr. Xmaster laughed at the tenacious teenager. "Oh, my dear, that is truly precious!"

"How about George William Scott? He, like Parker, also pitched in two games for the St. Louis Cardinals, in 1920. There is no trace of him after the mid-1920's."

Jeanne ignored Shoestring and forged ahead, walking right through him.

Shoestring appeared to be deeply offended by this. "What lack of manners our youth today have, Doctor. I bet a few minutes alone with Charles Carroll Uhlir would straighten them out. He was a Chicago White Sox outfielder in 1934. He vanished sometime shortly thereafter, and his sister strangely filed a delayed birth certificate for him in 1940."

"Come on, Mr. Bill...I mean Old Hoss." Janie grabbed the old man, who as an aficionado of old-time baseball was enthralled by these obscure references, by the hand and they passed through the quirky duo and joined Jeanne on the other side.

They could hear Shoestring and Dr. Xmaster loudly protesting their insolence as they hurried away, without glancing behind them, deeper into the Hallway of Lost Hopes.

"I must commend you, young lady." Old Hoss was breathing heavily, but valiantly striving to keep pace with the teenaged twins. "That was the finest demonstration I've ever seen of mind over matter."

Jeanne giggled. "I wouldn't talk if I were you. You did it perfectly yourself on the first try!"

"Mr. Billingsly, what are you doing out of the Discarded Revolutionaries Chamber?" St. Helen materialized all at once directly in their path. "Didn't we warn you what would happen if you left there?"

Jeanne squeezed Old Hoss's hand again and whispered in his ear. "He isn't real, remember?"

Old Hoss nodded and the trio walked through St. Helen, who cursed and stamped his feet in frustration. The old man's satisfaction was evident in his face, and he turned to Jeanne and lightly bussed her cheek as an expression of his appreciation.

No sooner had that obstacle been surmounted than another one sprung up, however. Edgar and Jimmy, the two most visible members of the supernatural security force in the Extremely Unreachable Ward, abruptly appeared out of the shadows. Acting in an expeditious fashion that permitted their victim no time to react, they grabbed Old Hoss by the collar and flung him violently up against the cold stone wall.

"Old Hoss, remember- they're not real!" Shouted a desperate Jeanne.

With advanced age having dulled his senses, the old man was having trouble focusing on the unreality of the two large brutes, which was understandable inasmuch as both of them were applying intense pressure to his neck with their huge, un-manicured fingers. Even a younger man with superb concentration might have been overwhelmed by the scent of their foul breath wafting into his nostrils.

"Beam out, you Unreals!" Jeanne, acting like some sort of exorcist, unwittingly utilized Waldo's favorite term. "You aren't really there, and we know you can't hurt us! Just walk away from them, Old Hoss! Concentrate! They can't harm you!"

Old Hoss garnered up all of his considerable willpower and, in a matter of seconds, had dismissed Edgar and Jimmy from his mind as mere illusions. He then simply walked past them, right out from under their strong hands, which had been so firmly encircled around his elderly neck. The marks left upon his tender skin disappeared instantaneously as well.

At that point, there appeared to be nothing further to impede their progress, but a short time later all of them heard a lovely, feminine voice cry out from someplace unseen.

"Old Hoss! Help me, Old Hoss! I've waited so long to be with you again!" Stepping into view, in the glare of the torch lights, was a beautiful, raven-tressed young woman, clad only in a badly-dated white nightgown.

"Cora!" Old Hoss yelled in glee. "My Cora! But...how..."

"Never mind, darling. Let's go in here where it's private, and I'll tell you everything. We have so much to talk about!" The woman took Old Hoss's hand and led him toward a door on the left hand side of the hall.

"No, Old Hoss! Don't go with her!" Jeanne cried out desperately, but the woman's delicate fingers were already turning the doorknob.

"Run for your lives!" Brisbane shouted, inciting his petrified compatriots to follow him into the dense woods to their right.

There wasn't any clear path in the woods, and as they ran precariously through the thickets and underbrush like a pack of frightened rabbits, they could hear the thunderous thud of the King Kong-like creature's footsteps behind them.

"Oh shit, I don't want to end up like no native in a dinosaur movie!" Bucktooth had shifted swiftly into his Harriet Beecher Stowe-mode, stereotypically rolling his eyes and moaning out various old-time spiritual sayings.

Fontaine, too, was acting absurdly, arms and legs flailing as if he was on fire, and screaming out "ahhhhh!" at the top of his lungs, over and over again. Finally, he veered off to one side like a derailed train and burst off running by himself in no particular direction until the others lost track of him.

362

There was little time for his companions to worry about Fontaine, however, with a gigantic gorilla on their trail. Waldo felt as if his feet would fail him at any minute, causing him to fall down in the classic Hollywood tradition and allow King Kong to use him for a toothpick.

"Look, over there!" Brisbane had sighted a cave up ahead, and the terrified trio turned on their afterburners, desperately struggling to reach its safe confines before the huge ape caught up with them.

They arrived at the cave and ran inside just seconds ahead of the beast. It was not really an actual cave, just a hollow that permitted them enough shelter to avoid the enormous gorilla's hand, which pawed away in vain a few feet from their helpless bodies.

Eventually, the ape gave up, and with an indignant roar, marched off into other parts of the Garden Of Old Movie Monsters.

"Shit, that was close!" Brisbane wiped his brow in relief. "Did you dudes notice how similar that was to the scene in the original *King Kong* where Kong has a guy holed up like we were but can't quite reach him with his hand, the same way that big monkey out there couldn't?"

Waldo, as a great fan of that particular film, had indeed recognized that, and even reflected upon the seemingly planned nature of the whole chase. "You know," he said slowly and evenly, "that monster should have been able to catch us."

Brisbane was intrigued by this observation. "Yeah, I know what you mean, dude. It does seem strange that King Kong- clone wasn't faster than us."

"Doesn't it? None of us are remotely close to being track stars, and even if we were, something that big and strong, with that large a step, should have caught up with us in no time." Waldo was growing more and more assured of the theory he'd begun formulating back outside the Factory of Displaced Persons, which had been temporarily placed on ice during their ordeal in the Brig Of First Offenses.

"But what does that all mean?" The fredneck was baffled.

"I don't know- why the same hitchhiker vanishing and reappearing all the time? Why the roads and people with names relating to the Kennedy assassination? Why giants and werewolves in the cornfields?" Waldo rattled off some of the many unexplainable things they had encountered during the course of their search.

"Shit yeah, why did that fucking St. Helen mention some of that shit to us, like that bizarre bar with the old baseball players, unless it was all connected to this?" Brisbane, while acknowledging the obvious threads running from Old Hoss's disappearance to their present plight, was becoming enthusiastic over a hypothesis he didn't fully comprehend.

"It's pretty clear that Mr. St. Helen knows about everything, from that bizarre gypsy and his skinhead friend we met outside the convenience store after the accident on the beltway..."

"Shit man, I'd forgotten about the gypsy dude!" Brisbane exclaimed. "And remember how he paid a visit to that Arab-dude in his barber shop right before we left?"

Waldo smiled. "Good old Big Abdullah. It's a wonder he hasn't shown up somewhere."

"Well, all that reminiscing shit is fascinating, but what do we do now? I mean, how do we get out of here?" Bucktooth, recovered from his Swing Low Sweet Chariot-syndrome, tried to steer the conversation away from such misty, speculative areas.

"He's right, man. We can't stay in here forever, and we know King Kong's cousin is out there, probably waiting for us." Brisbane agreed.

"I'm not worried about that giant ape." Waldo, for once, was not the One Most Likely to run fifty yard dashes and be rendered speechless. "Like I was just saying, he could have stomped us into the ground without any trouble at all. The fact that he didn't indicates to me that we have no reason to fear him. I'm presuming a masculine gender, of course."

"I don't know about the sex, but what do you mean, dude?" The fredneck still wasn't grasping Waldo's notion.

Realizing this, Waldo, one of the world's most notorious procrastinators, decided to act boldly. "Okay, I'm confident enough to lead us out of here!" Without elaborating anymore to the trusting but still puzzled fredneck, the nervous young man strode out dauntlessly, back into the Garden of Old Movie Monsters.

Brisbane peered out of the hollow hesitantly. "I don't see anything, man, but how do you propose that we leave here? That fucking St. Helen can whisk us around from place to place at his convenience."

"Trust me, Brisbane." Waldo began striding forthrightly towards the thick wooded area. "Are you two coming?"

Bucktooth stuck his head out of the hollow at this point. "Yoo-hooooo, o' mister monster! Are there any of you out there?" The disoriented doo-wopper was now being more idiotic than ever, acting in a manner that would have shamed "Sunshine" Sammy Morrison himself.

Waldo shook his head sadly at the Afro-Anarchist's antics. "Come on, let's go. If we can just get back to the main part of the Extremely Un..."

Waldo's sentence was broken by the sound of someone or something making its way through the nearby underbrush.

"Oh, shit..." Bucktooth appeared to be on the verge of belting out some more old cotton-picking songs.

Waldo watched and waited, still unafraid of what was traveling through the bushes and the undergrowth. He was starting to feel close to solving everything...

"Damn, man!" It was only Fontaine, making an inordinate amount of noise as he tripped and stumbled out into the clearing.

All of them instantly felt a bit ashamed that their own fear had rendered them unaware of Fontaine's absence.

Brisbane sensed that they should at least display a pretense of concern. "Fontaine! Where, oh where, have you been? We were so worried about you, weren't we, guys?"

"As a matter of fact, we were just setting out to search for you." Waldo, although he rarely resorted to such measures, stretched the truth a bit more smoothly than his fredneck cohort.

"Sheeeet, you ain't even gonna believe what's out there!" Fontaine pointed towards the horizon. "Man, what I saw..."

"Shit, come on, dude- tell us!" Brisbane demanded.

"Alright...well, I went to a lot of monster pictures when I was a kid, you know, loved 'em. Well, don't you know that King Kong isn't the only monster from a movie that's right here in this place!" Fontaine was visibly excited, and owing to his self -professed passion for the genre, it was difficult to determine whether he was pleased or disturbed by the population of the Garden of Old Movie Monsters.

"What monsters did you see?" Waldo suspected that any creature there, no matter how hideous or mutated, would prove to be harmless.

"Well, there's this valley, I guess you'd call it, down past the end of the woods, and let me see, there was that giant bald dude- *The Amazing Colossal Man*, right alongside the chick who gets pissed off at her cheating husband in *Attack Of The Fifty Foot Woman*, and some big-ass insects there, you know, like in the movies- ants, spiders, praying mantises. Then there was Godzilla, and a whole lot of dinosaurs. They were all wrestling around, you know, and I ran off before they noticed me standing there looking at 'em."

Fontaine's tale, in light of the name given to the garden they found themselves in, was not as incredible as it sounded, and none of the others doubted it for a second.

"When you say dinosaurs, do you mean like...*that*?" Bucktooth was about to revert back to his blubbering impersonation of a minstrel show-stopper, but still possessed the wherewithal to wag a trembling finger in the direction where Fontaine had just come from.

"Shit!" The fredneck was off and running again, and everyone else except Waldo followed.

The nervous young man bravely and inexplicably walked directly towards the gargantuan Tyrannosaurs Rex that was eyeing him hungrily from the edge of the woods.

Jeanne rushed towards Old Hoss and grabbed his hand, just as he was about to enter the room. "No! Please don't go in there, Old Hoss!"

She implored.

"My, my, Abner." The woman cast her devious eyes in Jeanne's direction. "As you've gotten older, it appears that your women have gotten much, much younger."

"I'm sorry, child, but I've waited a lifetime to be with her again, and I don't intend to wait any longer." Old Hoss said adamantly, recalling her grisly murder and the anguish that followed.

"Alright, if she was real, would I be able to do this?" Jeanne plunged unhesitatingly forward and passed right through Cora's body, emerging unscathed behind her.

The temporary twinkle was removed from Old Hoss's eyes, and he hung his head in sorrow as he realized what this meant. "Cora, Cora, Cora..." He cried out mournfully, inadvertently satirizing the old Japanese war code.

"She's gone now." Jeanne tenderly placed her hand on his shoulder. "I'm so sorry."

Old Hoss looked up slowly. The vision of loveliness he had thought was his long-lost Cora- the delicate novelist struck down so tragically in her youth- was no longer there, only the O'Sullivan twins and the deserted, dimly lit Hallway of Lost Hopes. "I should know better than to be taken in that easily." He was upset over the extent of his own gullibility. "After all, I found her body."

"You mean she was dead?" Janie asked.

"Murdered." Old Hoss spoke softly, with a distant look in his eyes. "They never found out who did it, either."

"Wow...I didn't know." Jeanne gasped.

"She was the only woman I ever truly loved, and when she died I discarded that aspect of life forever..."

"But you must have married someone." Janie reasoned. "After all, you are Waldo's grandfather."

"Ah yes, indeed I did." Old Hoss sighed. "And perhaps I shouldn't be taken literally, for I did love my wife, too, but I must confess that it was not in quite the same way."

"What happened to your wife?" Jeanne was curious.

Old Hoss stared off into the distance again. "She died. Come on now, we've wasted enough time on ancient history. We still have to find Waldo and the others." He began striding off down the hall.

Jeanne and Janie gave each other a look of resignation and sprinted off after him.

"Stop! Are you crazy or something?"

Waldo averted his gaze from the Tyrannosaurs Rex long enough to discover that the voice shouting at him belonged to a diminutive black

366

man wearing a sleeveless white shirt with matching short pants, orange sunglasses and a safari hat.

"Who are you?" Waldo inquired.

"My name is Dr. L.N. Carr." The man extended his small, bony hand. "But we have no time for pleasantries. Come, quickly!" He yanked on Waldo's hand, which he had been shaking, and off they went.

"Wait..." Waldo protested, permitting himself to be dragged along although he felt certain he could have torn away from the little man with minimal effort. "That T-Rex can't hurt us, let me explain..."

"You can explain all you'd like to at my office." Dr. Carr, whose attire was more suitable for jungle terrain than any sort of civilized medical facility, testily replied.

"Your office?" Waldo, having finally grown suspicious, attempted to break free of the small man's grasp, but found himself unable to do so.

The doctor's response was to strengthen his grip on Waldo as he whisked him along into the thick underbrush. Waldo tried repeatedly to pull his hand away, but eventually submitted. After seemingly traveling through miles of twigs and thistles that slapped his legs with maddening precision, they eventually came to another clearing.

Directly in front of Waldo was an odd-looking little building that was shaped roughly like a pyramid.

Waldo brushed himself off. "Is that your office?"

Dr. Carr put his finger to his lips and motioned Waldo to enter the building. The nervous young man, still steadfast and confident in his new belief that nothing there could harm him, and in spite of his curious inability to disengage himself from the grasp of this tiny man, smiled and complied.

Walking up to the building, he hesitated for a moment, but then marched on. As he reached the door and placed his hand on the doorknob, Waldo turned around to find Dr. Carr standing back and observing him from a safe distance. "Say, doctor, aren't you coming in with me?"

Dr. Carr merely tipped the brim of his safari hat, in the manner of a big leaguer doffing his hat to the fans, and flashed a dazzling smile that exposed a mouth full of gold-capped teeth.

"But it *is* your office...oh, forget it." Waldo obviously felt there was no possibility of danger, or he certainly would have questioned the strange doctor a bit more thoroughly about his reluctance to accompany him. With a shrug and an air of mild amusement, he opened the door and fearlessly stepped inside.

Waldo walked into a large room that seemed to be occupied exclusively by the many oversized pillows which were scattered all over the floor. As soon as he'd entered, the door slammed shut behind him of its own volition, in the usual dramatic way.

"Hello, Waldo." Sam Hancock suddenly appeared, sitting on one of the pillows near the center of the room. "Have a seat, son."

Waldo was struggling to maintain his nonchalant attitude, but a creeping fear was starting to gnaw at him.

The door to the room opened again and Dr. L.N. Carr strolled in. "Okay, class, please sit down on one of the pillows that have been provided for you. Today we are going to discuss the problem of acute paranoia."

All at once, as if turned on by the flick of a paranormal switch, the room was filled with the sound of voices. Waldo stared at the crowd of people which were now lying on the pillows. They were babbling among themselves in a quite realistic fashion, and Waldo, growing less assured, rubbed his eyes. He was the only one standing, and he noticed that Dr. Carr was tapping his foot and gazing at him with the intensity of a junior high school vice- principal.

"Well, Waldo, are you going to take a seat so we can get started?" Dr. Carr asked impatiently.

"Over here, Waldo, we've saved you a pillow."

Waldo turned his head and his mouth dropped open to his navel. The sweet voice calling out to him belonged to his mother, who was sitting in a corner next to his father.

"Shit man, Waldo's gone!" Brisbane declared.

The fredneck, Fontaine, and Bucktooth hadn't noticed that Waldo wasn't running with them until they were far away from the Tyrannosaurs Rex.

"Man, this shit is getting ridiculous! Every damn minute one of us is disappearing or something!" Fontaine's pointed observation was especially ironic, in that he had wandered off on a brief sojourn of his own, to a valley brimming with Hollywood's finest grade-b creatures, only a short time before.

They had found their way back, through no geographical skill of their own, to the idyllic spot where they'd first landed, with the abundant fruit trees, and streams, and colorful birds.

Brisbane sat down on a large rock and lit a cigarette. "I gotta tell you guys, I've had enough of all this shit. I just want to get out of here and go home, wherever that is."

"Come on, Bris, what about Waldo? And his grandfather?" Bucktooth attempted to wring some compassion out of the disheartened fredneck.

This strategy worked, as Brisbane's face grew sheepish and he stared down at the ground. "Yeah, Buck, I don't know what I'm saying anymore. I didn't mean...I still want to help Waldo, if we find him, look for his grandfather. It's just all this incredible stuff that's happened, and now we're in some kind of mental ward that has different worlds in it or something. I came to Iowa to search for Waldo's grandfather, not run from any fucking dinosaurs!"

"Well, Brisbane, here he is." Janie's voice caused all three of them to attain their highest vertical leaps ever.

Brisbane looked on in astonishment. The O'Sullivan twins were coming out of the underbrush, and they were being led by an old gentleman with long gray hair and a sprightly step.

Waldo nearly fainted, but as he always did on such occasions, he shook his head defiantly and remained conscious. He stared at the figures who appeared to be his parents. He rationalized that naturally they couldn't be the tangible, flesh and blood role models he'd lost when he was a boy, but the illusion was extremely powerful and he remained transfixed under its spell. He shook his head again, as if the whole scene was some kind of other-worldly Etch-A-Sketch that could be eliminated in that manner. It didn't work, however, as his smiling parents were still there, beckoning to him.

"Alright, you!" He wheeled around and faced Dr. L.N. Carr. "Who are you? One of St. Helen's imaginary assistants?"

"Young man, sit down this minute." The doctor sounded like a geometry teacher, but in his absurd safari outfit and sunglasses, he hardly looked the part. "Are you going to ignore your parents?"

"That's exactly what I mean." Waldo was bristling. "My parents were killed in a plane crash when I was very young. What kind of beings are you that you would stoop so low as to bring my memories of them into all of this?"

Dr. Carr smiled sardonically, the fluorescent lights above him reflecting off his dazzling gold teeth. "Mr. Billingsly, we have been very tolerant of your behavior over the past several weeks, but this has gone far enough. What will it be next- more giant strawberry patches? Or gas station attendants that want to kill you? Perhaps you've seen that phantom hitchhiker again? If you will not sit down and join in group therapy, instead of ranting on and on about these imaginary experiences of yours, then I will have to suggest to Dr. Clemons that you be moved into another group that may prove more beneficial to you."

Waldo laughed. "Oh, no you don't. You're not going to play that old game with me. I am fully aware that I'm not a mental patient."

"Of course, my boy, of course." Dr. Carr spoke in the condescending manner that psychiatrists train long and expensively to master. "None of the others here are either."

"And don't think that you're scaring me with your name and that-

that phony Dr. Clemons." Waldo was beginning to take on the countenance of a mental patient. "I know perfectly well that you just named yourself after Richard Carr, who saw someone other than Oswald exit the Book Depository building that Friday afternoon in Dallas. And as for your make-believe colleague, Acquilla Clemons witnessed two gunmen at the scene of Officer Tippit's murder shortly after the J.F.K. assassination on November 22, 1963, and neither of them was Oswald. Okay, are you satisfied?"

"Grab him, men!" Dr. Carr's order was directed at the versatile, quick moving bouncers Edgar and Jimmy. They had crept up from behind Waldo during his outburst, and the nervous young man was in no position to offer much resistance as they grabbed him firmly under the armpits and dragged him away kicking and screaming in the classic style of the unjustly accused.

"I'm not crazy, I tell you! Just because I was walking up to that dinosaur? He wasn't going to hurt me, he wasn't real! And none of you are either! Now let me go before you make me start believing it!" All vestiges of Waldo's hypothesis regarding the reality of his captors, and how to escape them, had become unraveled now.

Dr. Carr shook his head in dismay as well as any traditional practitioner of medicine. "Take him to the Cave Of Coincidence."

Waldo was placed on a stretcher and immediately began banging his head against it. "Just because I keep running into all these people and places with names related to the Kennedy assassination? That makes me crazy? It's not me, I tell you, it's all your doing!" The nervous young man then suffered the ultimate indignity, as Edgar and Jimmy restrained him in one of the posey vests, or strait jackets, that he may very well have wrapped himself as a Junior Material Handler in Central Supply.

"You'll find the Cave of Coincidence to be quite helpful." Dr. Carr said. "Especially considering that your own brother is the guardian there."

"Jeanne! Janie! You mean this is..."

"Abner Billingsly." Old Hoss thrust out his big right hand and shook Brisbane's heartily. "Glad to meet you, son. I understand that you and my grandson are good friends. I can't tell you how much your coming all this way to help him means to me. That goes for you fellows, too." Old Hoss smiled at Fontaine and Bucktooth, who were both nearly as mesmerized as the fredneck over meeting the focus of their search so unexpectedly.

After everyone had been formally introduced to each other, Jeanne tried not to sound worried as she inquired about what was foremost in her mind. "Where...is Waldo?"

Fontaine and Bucktooth cleared their throats in an exaggerated fashion, making it painfully obvious that something was amiss. It was left for Brisbane to attempt an explanation. "Uh, Jeanne, well, Waldo is...uh, not here."

Old Hoss was standing as erect as a Civil War statue. "What do you mean, young fellow?"

Brisbane swallowed hard. "Uh, we saw this, well, dinosaur, and all of us ran away from it. We stopped here, and that's when we noticed that Waldo wasn't with us."

Jeanne was beginning to sob and Old Hoss took her in his arms to comfort her. "Now, now, sweetheart, don't cry. Ever since you told me about that...what's his name again?"

"Phosphate." The pretty teenager sniffled.

"Yes, well, remember his theory, Jeanne. You're the one who has been quoting it to me so often and, I must say, utilizing it to such great effect. Waldo cannot be harmed by what is not real, can he? We must concentrate on leaving this place, and you are the most proficient one among us at blocking all of these frightening diversions from the mind. Don't worry, we'll find Waldo. We need you to lead us out of here."

Jeanne moved her tear-stained face away from Old Hoss's paternal shoulder and smiled weakly. "I-I guess you're right."

"Of course I am." Old Hoss turned to Brisbane, Fontaine and Bucktooth. "Now, you three, why don't you attempt to lead us back to where Waldo was last seen."

"Sure." Brisbane began walking, then stopped and looked at Old Hoss. "What was that you were saying about Phosphate's theory?"

"Yeah, shit, they told us old Phos was in some place worse than us, for trying to escape." Fontaine said. "How did you... I mean, where is he?"

"He's fine." Janie explained. "He's waiting for us in the basement."

"But, how..." Brisbane stammered.

"He simply walked out the same stairwell where he entered, once he told himself that he could, and once he believed that none of the crazy stuff in the Extremely Unreachable Ward was real." Jeanne dabbed her eyes.

"Why didn't he come back with you?" Bucktooth asked.

"Because he thinks that Janie and I have the best chance of opening the door and getting all of you out of here." Jeanne was growing restless and itching to rescue Waldo.

"Sheeet, why can't we just open the door ourselves?" Fontaine was perplexed.

"I don't mean to sound like a retired military officer, but you can move a lot faster when you're not talking." Old Hoss, as anxious as Jeanne to find Waldo, reprimanded the others in his gentle fashion.

"Hmmmm." Brisbane was thinking as he ambled along. "You know

371

something, I think that was what Waldo was talking about back in the cave."

"What?" Old Hoss forgot his admonition against conversing.

"Well, he was kind of hinting at something like that, I think." The fredneck struggled to recall the details of their discussion. "And way back there, when we'd just left the Factory Of Displaced Persons, he mentioned some story by a French author about their being only way out of a prison cell, and it turns out that the cell door was unlocked or something."

"Ah, that's my grandson!" Old Hoss exclaimed with a great deal of pride. "He knows, alright."

"But what if that dinosaur got to him before he truly believed it?" Jeanne was becoming upset again.

"Now, now, I told you not to worry. We'll find him." They were still in the beautiful section of the Garden Of Old Movie Monsters, and Old Hoss stopped by one of the streams of crystal clear water. "Here, sweetheart, splash some water on your face. It does look refreshing, doesn't it?"

Everyone had to agree that it did indeed, and they all bent down beside him to slake their parched throats. In all the excitement they'd been through, none of them had noticed how thirsty they were, nor how inviting the flowing streams they'd passed had looked.

"This water sure tastes real." Bucktooth commented as he wiped his mouth.

"Ah, breathe that serenity." Old Hoss's bulbous nostrils expanded. "You must admit, they've come up with a pretty..."

"Remember!" Jeanne softly scolded the old man. "The nice parts aren't real, either."

"A momentary lapse, my dear." Old Hoss shook his head again at his forgetfulness. "A momentary lapse."

They drank their fill, without dallying any further, and then rushed off from the placid setting towards other, more nefarious parts of the Extremely Unreachable Ward.

Waldo could hear water dripping. He was in total darkness, and he was shivering from the cold. Edgar and Jimmy had thrown him into what was presumably the Cave Of Coincidence, and the inhospitable climate provided a suitable backdrop for his fevered mind.

Waldo was trying to analyze his situation with a modicum of rationality when he suddenly heard the sound of footsteps approaching.

"Waldo Billingsly?" He heard a masculine voice say.

Waldo, sheltered by the darkness, felt it prudent to remain silent, and even held his breath to prevent anyone from hearing that.

"Come, come, Waldo. We know you're here. Holding your breath like a child won't help. Besides, you're a very heavy smoker- your lungs have a limited capacity for such escapades. Please pay attention so the lesson can begin."

There was not a great deal of fight left within him, so Waldo sighed heavily, indicating he was present and accounted for.

"Ah, excellent. May I introduce myself? I am your long-lost brother Rupert."

"Y-y-you c-can't be." Waldo whispered shakily. "I-I was an only child."

"That's what they told you. I was abandoned at birth a few years before you arrived."

"That's a lie! My parents would never do such a thing!" Waldo, despite feeling as servile as most authentic mental patients, was still capable of becoming outraged.

"Alright, dear brother, no need to become upset. The truth is quite often unpleasant and difficult to accept. But, let's start our lesson, shall we?"

Waldo noticed that the voice belonging to his supposed brother sounded uncannily like his own. "Say, uh, your voice..."

"Sounds familiar, doesn't it?" Rupert chuckled. "Well, dear brother, after all, that isn't uncommon among siblings."

Waldo was biting his lip nervously and aching to see this so-called relative. "Why can't I see you?"

"The Cave of Coincidence is a very special place, Waldo. The proceedings here are always conducted in the dark. We find it to be the best arrangement for all concerned."

Waldo was extremely disconcerted by now, and his grand theory about escaping from the Extremely Unreachable Ward had been driven deep into his subconscious. "But...if you are really are my brother..."

"*We* ask the questions here. Let the lesson begin."

Waldo heard more footsteps.

"Billingsly! It is useless to fight us." There was a new voice, and it sounded deep and ominous, like a narrator of war-preparedness films. "Your actions indicate that you cannot be trusted. However, in the interests of fair play, we have been instructed to test you."

"W-w-what?" Waldo stuttered in confusion.

"Silence! You will speak only when asked to respond to a specific question." The narrator-like voice boomed. "And now, to begin your test, please answer the following with a yes or no: in your opinion, should the Justice Department's Office of Special Investigations, which tracks down alleged Nazi war criminals, have been created in the late 1970's?"

Even in a situation as horrifying as this one, Waldo wasn't reticent about expressing his views. "No, of course not. The whole concept of victors..."

"Silence! A simple yes or no is all that is required of you. We do not desire to hear your long-winded social commentary. Your second question: should the United States draft young people for the military and/or some other alternative form of community service?"

"No." Waldo didn't elaborate this time.

"Number three: is it your belief that much information about the period of time commonly referred to as the 'dark ages' has been suppressed?"

"Yes."

"Number four: do you believe that 85% of the people have to constantly lose at everything, in order for the top 15% to continue to win?"

"Sure, look at casinos..."

"Silence! You will not be warned again about limiting your replies to yes or no. Number five: do you think the Bible has been altered over the course of the centuries for devious purposes?"

"Yes."

"Number six: do you feel that secret experiments are being performed on unwilling subjects at various prisons and mental institutions?"

"Yes."

"Number seven: are you aware of the notorious Bilderbergers- the most powerful leaders from every country- who meet once a year at a secluded spot somewhere in the world to the total silence of the establishment press?"

"Yes."

"Number eight: do you believe that the government has a squad of hitmen that it regularly employs to silence its critics?"

"Yes."

"Number nine: do you think that a few large conglomerates hold a virtual monopoly over everything in the so-called open marketplace?"

"Yes."

"Number ten: if you were offered everything you wanted in life, without exception, would you waive any or all rights in the next world?"

"No."

"Your test is complete." The narrator paused dramatically. "We regret to inform you that you have failed. In fact, you received the lowest score possible. Thus, it is clear that you can never successfully be assimilated into mainstream society. You must pay the consequences."

Waldo gulped. "W-what do you mean?"

"The penalty for failing our test is death. Ironic, isn't it- you being such a vociferous opponent of such drastic measures? Meet your executioner."

"I'm sorry, brother." Rupert was speaking again. "This isn't something I enjoy."

All at once, a spotlight shone on a figure bearing an identical likeness to Waldo, and he was holding a large knife.

Waldo closed his eyes and screamed as his alleged brother Rupert lunged forward with his long, sharp knife glistening in the spotlight. However, he felt no excruciating pain, the anticipated result of a blade entering his body. Cautiously opening his eyes, he found himself lying back on the stretcher.

"This patient is growing more deluded by the minute. There is only one choice- we must perform emergency brain surgery. Take him immediately to the Electro Shock-Lobotomy Postscript Division. He should forget all his problems when they finish with him." Dr. L.N. Carr was standing over him.

Waldo, now out of his mind, heard the good doctor begin laughing in the same cold, hideous manner that so many others had recently.

"Don't worry, they'll leave enough in your head for you to know how much you hate it here!" Edgar slapped his fellow bodyguard Jimmy on the back and they both joined in the hysterical laughter.

Phosphate was pacing up and down in the hallway that led to the sub-basement. A man of action by nature, the top doo-wopper was not one who could easily stand by and wait for events to transpire. At the rate he was pacing back and forth, he seemed ready to race for the gold medal in the expectant father olympics. Then all at once a very simple notion came to him. *Wait a minute*, he thought to himself, *that's too easy, it can't work.* But the more he pondered it, the more he realized that even a certified intellectual like himself had overlooked the obvious- he was out! That was it! Since he was out of the Extremely Unreachable Ward already, all he had to do was walk down the stairs and open the door to the sub-basement, then wait for Waldo and the others to approach it. Why, he could call out to them and make it even easier!

The head Afro-Anarchist wasted no more time in private exultation over his cleverness, and strode confidently down the hall. As he opened the door leading to the stairwell, he again hesitated for a second, still doubting that the solution could be such a simple one, but it was only a split second, and then he bounded down the stairs.

He reached the door that led into the sub-basement in record time, and his hand curled around the doorknob. Hoping with all his might, he tried it. It was locked.

Then he heard the now familiar maniacal refrain, and through the small pane of glass at the top of the door he saw St. Helen slapping his knees in ecstasy.

"Are you sure this is the way, Brisbane?" Jeanne asked in exasperation.

Jeanne, like the others, was rapidly growing impatient, due to the fact they had been trampling about aimlessly in the underbrush for quite some time, without making any visible progress. They were also becoming increasingly affected by the heat, as the area they found themselves in, unlike the bucolic climate in another part of the Garden of Old Movie Monsters, was terribly oppressive, with steam actually rising from the ground and limiting their fields of vision.

"Yeah, it has to be." Brisbane, like all frednecks and a majority of males, was proud of his sense of direction and easily offended when it was questioned. "It can't be much farther. Don't you think this is the right way, guys?"

He directed his question at Fontaine and Bucktooth, and the former replied. "Yeah, it seems like it to me, man."

Janie was shaking her head, still skeptical that a unit within a mental institution, imaginary or not, could contain such things as prehistoric creatures. "You really saw a dinosaur?" Her reluctance to accept their story was hard to comprehend, considering that her own cornfield possessed truly unbelievable powers, including the ability to transport one back to the very age of dinosaurs.

"I believe they did, because that looks suspiciously like one over there." Old Hoss pointed to his right, far enough away that none of them panicked, towards the long distinctive neck of the Brontosaurus that was clearly protruding above the tops of some trees. Despite the intemperate mist, and the distance between them, they could distinguish the mass of leaves in the extinct vegetarian's huge mouth, which it was gratefully chomping on.

Each of them quickened their step, and before long they exited the dense underbrush and emerged into some sort of clearing. A cool breeze caressed their overheated frames, and they all sucked the fresh air into their lungs appreciatively.

"I wonder what could possibly live there?" Janie pointed to a pyramid-shaped building, standing out distinctly amid the thick, tropical surroundings.

"I don't know, but let's find out!" Jeanne wiped her brow with renewed enthusiasm.

"Wait a minute. Let's think about this." Brisbane cautioned her. "It could be dangerous."

"Bris is right, man." Fontaine agreed. "You don't know what kind of wild stuff we've seen, Jeanne. Sheeet! Gas stations with attendants that want to rape and kill you; restaurants where first they want to lynch you, then they offer you a free meal, then they throw you out; prison wardens showing up in another part of the country a few days later running a motel..."

Jeanne was resolute. "I know about most of that, Fontaine- Waldo told me. Are you all forgetting Phosphate's theory again? I told you we'll be okay if we just keep in mind that nothing we encounter here is real. Can everybody please try to do that?"

Brisbane and the two Afro-Anarchists didn't appear totally convinced, but Janie stood up for her twin sister. "Look, I saw her go right through a solid physical body. And Mr. Billingsly did the same thing. I wasn't sure about it either, until I passed through one myself."

"It's our only chance." Old Hoss reminded them.

Brisbane trusted Jeanne, and he certainly had a healthy respect for the intellect of Phosphate Jefferson, so he suddenly felt ashamed of his initial hesitance. "Shit, come on, you guys, we all know that Phosphate wouldn't tell them to do something if it wasn't gonna work."

Old Hoss smiled at the fredneck's exuberance. "As I said when I left the red room, my dear, I place myself in your hands." He grabbed Jeanne's right hand and kissed it with all the adeptness of a medieval prince. "I trust you implicitly, young lady. Lead on."

Jeanne, with this impressive show of faith, forged ahead and without further ado opened the door to the pyramid-shaped building.

Waldo was being wheeled into the Electro Shock-Lobotomy Postscript Division. He was babbling away nonsensically in the manner of a tried and true, involuntarily institutionalized mental patient.

"I've seen lots of movies- *The Snake Pit, One Flew Over The Cuckoo's Nest*- and you're not going to do that stuff to me!" He cried out in desperation. "Just because I keep seeing M.I.B.'s? Look, I promise- I won't tell anyone about you! Please, just let me go!"

"Ah, we've been waiting for you, Waldo." A beefy man in a white coat grinned at him lustily. The coat was stained with enough blood to make a butcher envious. "I'm Dr. Clemons. I'll be performing the operation."

Waldo eyed him warily. "I know you're not real. But I can't make you go away. Why?"

Dr. Clemons chuckled. "Why, heavens, Waldo, what could possibly give you an idea like that?"

Waldo was unstrapped from his posey vest, in which Edgar and Jimmy had so cheerfully and unceremoniously restrained him, and instructed to sit up on the stretcher. He rubbed his arms and legs, which had grown numb from being bridled in such a fashion, and gazed at his surroundings. The room had all the trappings of an old studio set from the classic age of horror films. It would be easy for anyone in such an atmosphere, especially a distraught individual such as Waldo, to picture a mad scientist darting from beaker to beaker and interacting with the monstrosity that resulted from his experiments. The place looked like the sort of laboratory where such things could happen, with lots of Frankenstein-style electronic devices of dubious feasibility flashing on and off in the background. Dr. Clemons even had a short male assistant, although he wasn't a hunchback.

"What is all this?" Waldo laughed in a low, queer manner, bringing to mind the picture of many an unfortunate before him who'd been humored by things unnoticed and unseen.

"Please relax, Waldo." Dr. Clemons said. "The procedure is a very simple and minor one. Afterwards, you will feel no pain."

Waldo was unable to stop his demented laughter.

Dr. Clemons smiled again, and for the first time Waldo noticed there was blood on his teeth as well as his coat. "In fact, after the surgery, you will have no more problems at all."

"No!" Waldo shouted, his survival instinct propelling him to jump off the stretcher. His heart beating like a turkey's on the night before Thanksgiving, he bolted for the door and was out and racing down the hall before anyone reacted.

"Edgar! Jimmy! After him!" He heard Dr. Clemons yell behind him.

He emerged into a hallway that appeared indistinguishable from any on the upper floors of the Last Chance Relaxation Home. The only difference was there were no nurses sleeping or eating anywhere, and no patients crying out for help. In fact, it looked completely deserted, and the sound of Waldo's tennis shoes pounding the tiles echoed hauntingly off the antiseptic walls.

Waldo was not normally a fast runner, but whenever he saw a supernatural creature, or if someone was about to perform a frontal lobotomy on him, then he could move at a pretty fair clip. He ran without looking back, and he was starting to feel like he had outrun Edgar and Jimmy when suddenly a gaggle of figures materialized just ahead of him. Applying the brakes as well as any cartoon character, Waldo whirled around, only to discover an odd- looking group there also.

A tall man in a black cape with extraordinarily pale skin stepped forward.

Waldo stared at him and started giggling hysterically. "Oh, come on, don't tell me you're going to try the vampire bit!"

The man in the cape opened his mouth in a terrifying smile and Waldo saw quite clearly that his teeth were a good deal sharper than the average human's.

"Yes, my friend, allow me to introduce myself." The vampire sounded like a poor imitation of Boris Badanov. "I am Count Loren Zulich."

Waldo closed his eyes and concentrated, in an effort to resuscitate a theory he was now unsure of, but when he opened them he saw the Count leaning towards him with an open mouth, and a terrible thirst in his bloodshot eyes.

Jeanne struggled to remain composed. The scene before her sorely tested her convictions. After entering the pyramid-shaped building, they'd found themselves in a room full of mourners, which appeared for the entire world to be representative of a small country church. The people in the pews, dressed in their Sunday finest, were weeping unashamedly, and an organist was playing *Crown Him With Many Crowns* softly in the background. All at once, a preacher with a head full of flawlessly coiffed silver hair, and clad in a conservative dark blue suit, approached the pulpit and began speaking in a southern cadence.

"And so, my friends, we remember young Waldo Billingsly as a fine, charitable man who considered it improper and unthinkable to harm any living thing. Misguided as he was in his mad quest to expose a group he could never precisely define or identify, he was still a credit to the community. Let us bow our heads now and say a prayer for the repose of his soul."

Jeanne was trying to drown out his awful monotone, but temporarily lost her own self-assurance in Phosphate's theory. "Shut up!" She shouted indignantly. "At least make it realistic! Waldo was raised a Catholic- he'd never..." Before she could charge over and really tell the preacher off, Old Hoss grabbed her and held her back.

"Now, now, Jeanne." He spoke in a calm and patient voice. "You were just telling us only a few moments ago to keep in mind that nothing here is real."

"But they went too far this time!" Jeanne was breathing heavily and obviously very upset. She stared into the old man's twinkling eyes and couldn't stop from smiling. "I-I'm sorry. I-I guess it's pretty easy to forget, isn't it?"

"You won't anymore." Old Hoss took her hand and motioned for the others to follow him. "Everyone just walk confidently with the firm conviction in your minds that everything you see and hear is a mere illusion."

The preacher and the mourners attempted to distract them with a spirited version of *Praise Him From Whom All Blessings Flow*, but Jeanne and the others held their heads high and refused to even glance in their direction.

As they filed nonchalantly out of the would-be church, they entered a long corridor, which was much less imposing than the sinister Unconstitutional Avenue or the Hallway of Lost Hopes. It seemed identical to most of the patient floors far above them, as there were stretchers and wheelchairs scattered along the walls, and rows of closed doors on either side of them.

"Shit man," Brisbane was gazing all around him, "how do they construct all of this, I mean if it's not real?"

"Brisbane, please." Old Hoss cautioned him. "Don't question anything or it may jeopardize Waldo's chances of survival. Just try your best to ignore everything we encounter."

"Okay, I'll try." The fredneck promised.

Suddenly three figures jumped out of nowhere into the middle of the hallway.

"Phosphate!" Everyone but Old Hoss exclaimed, as the one in the middle was undeniably the top doo-wopper himself.

"Alright, hit it, boys." Phosphate signaled his two suave male companions, and they began rapping:

"Welcome to the ward where things become extreme
You might just imagine this is all a dream
All of us are occupied with things to do
And we've been working hard on something just for you
Medicine is hard to find when it is free
But we will treat you to your very own lobotomy
Or we could turn your brain into a frying pan
And you'll be much more current than the average man
We're sure you'll be amazed by all the things you find
We'll be happy to discuss what may be on your mind
There is no Sherlock Holmes, you won't find the solution
The only thing to do is join the institution
Our tranquilizers will get rid of all your fear
So turn to your right and follow us in here."

With that, Phosphate opened a door and beckoned them to enter.

"Say Phos, that was alright! I thought you weren't into rap, though." Fontaine was impressed.

"Come on, Fontaine!" Jeanne had regained all of her ability to place mind over matter. "Did you listen to those lyrics? You know very well that he couldn't be Phosphate."

"It sure looks like Phos!" Bucktooth stared intently at the would be-top doo-wopper. "Sings like him, too."

"No way, man." Brisbane agreed with Jeanne. "The real Phosphate is upstairs in the basement waiting for us."

Old Hoss nodded his head. "We are dealing with some extremely clever adversaries. Remember, too, that Phosphate is the one who formulated..."

"You are all very wise cats." The alleged Phosphate smiled unnaturally. "But there's a lot more where I came from." Then he and his two anonymous backup vocalists vanished into thin air, leaving behind only a faint strain of the familiar blood-curdling laughter.

Brisbane seemed inspired. "Shit man! We just beat them- they had to disappear! And you didn't even have to walk through them!"

Old Hoss grinned. "He's right. Obviously our minds were working very effectively and cohesively that time, and as a result the apparitions weren't nearly as powerful."

Jeanne resumed walking down the hallway in a plucky manner. "Come on, you guys. I know we can get Waldo out of here now."

The real Phosphate walked up the stairs leading out of the sub-basement with a heart almost as heavy as Lyndon B. Johnson's once was. He had tried to help his friends, and now there was nothing for him to do but wait and hope for the best. He was losing confidence in his hypothesis that none of the countless supernatural diversions parading about the Extremely Unreachable Ward were real, for if that were so then he certainly should have been able to open the door that led into the sub-basement. He also realized that everything depended now upon a youngster that society wouldn't trust at the liquor store or the ballot box.

Sitting down on the top step, the nearly listless head Afro-Anarchist slumped over and literally cringed in frustration. In his anxiety and his involuntary idleness, a corner of the top doo-wopper's imagination had been freed for the unconstructive purpose of weighing and measuring his personal sense of presumed loss against that which parents of missing children experience, and it was little consolation to reflect upon how insignificant his agony was in comparison. Preoccupied as he was with these morbid thoughts, Phosphate didn't hear the footsteps creeping up behind him.

"You're wanted in the sub-basement!"

Phosphate jumped up and spun around. Otto Motto was standing in the doorway that led back into the hall, grinning like the proverbial

Cheshire cat.

"Come on, you know you'll never get them out this way." The illusionary Housekeeper said.

"Right on! You're getting to be a big problem, you Coasters- reject."

The top doo-wopper looked back down the stairs to find the tall, bald creature who served as the doorkeeper to the Factory Of Displaced Persons sticking his head out of the now open door to the sub-basement.

Phosphate quickly bounded down the stairs, in a brave effort to enter the place, but the odd, bird-like entity known as Right On cackled loudly and slammed the door in his face. Phosphate could see him peering out from the other side with an idiotic expression on his face.

"Right on. I like that! I really fixed you for good this time."

"Hey, Right On, why don't you let him in?" Otto Motto shouted from the top of the stairs. "Let's have a little fun."

"Why don't you get a haircut as short as mine?" The absurd creature cackled in a muffled voice from behind the door.

The top doo-wopper was tired of conversing with non-existent personnel, so he shook his head in despair, charged up the steps, brushed past Otto Motto, and resumed his steady pacing in the hallway outside the stairwell.

Waldo reacted rapidly. Falling back on his days in catechism, he made the sign of the cross and spoke to the Count. "The Lord is my shepherd, I shall not want."

With those words, the Count instantly retreated to a convenient wheelchair, where he sat down, apparently just as susceptible to the trappings of Catholicism as any celluloid members of the undead. The other dark, vaporous figures in the hall, whom Waldo surmised were fellow vampire cronies, huddled together in front of him like some kind of outlandish basketball team. Waldo seized this opportunity to dash deftly past the squad of ghouls, and seconds later they were on his tail. Over his shoulder, he could hear the Count shouting, "vait, vait, ve're not through vith you!" in a Transylvanian dialect as realistic as the average late-night horror movie host's.

Waldo thought that he was outrunning them until he looked to one side and saw a large gray wolf sprinting along beside him.

"Give up, Valdo." Evidently the wolf possessed the same ridiculously unnatural accent. "Ve vant you to be one of us."

Waldo's legs were growing tired, being that he had not covered this must distance since the junior high school gym teachers inflicted the 600 yard torture test on him. Still he kept moving, with a substantially greater degree of effort than he'd shown back in those physical education classes of yore.

Abruptly, the phony Phosphate darted out from one of the many mysterious rooms which lined the length of the incredibly long corridor.

"Waldo, quick- in here!" He signaled frantically.

Waldo, ecstatic to see his friend, naively ran inside and the fake top doo-wopper closed the door.

"Wow! Phosphate, are you ever a lifesaver! I thought they'd taken you away for good after you tried to escape." Waldo leaned against the wall and tried to catch his breath.

"Well, Waldo, so glad you could join us."

Waldo gazed around the room for the first time. The voice belonged to Sam Hancock, who was sitting on a loveseat with St. Helen. Waldo felt his heart drop to his knees. "*Et tu, Phosphate?*" he thought as he stared at the Afro-Anarchist imposter who'd betrayed him.

The phony Phosphate's only reply to Waldo's unspoken bit of imagery was a cheap chuckle and a fast exit into nothingness.

"Sit down, Waldo." St. Helen smiled in a curiously suggestive manner. He patted the frighteningly small space between Hancock and himself. "There's always room for one more."

Waldo's legs may have been aching, but still he wasn't ready to adopt any alternative lifestyles, particularly with non-existing partners, so he bolted out the door and resumed his lonely, untelevised marathon, deep in the heart of the Extremely Unreachable Ward.

Jeanne, Old Hoss, and the others were marching down the hallway with the kind of singleminded purposefulness that has made telemarketing representatives so loved and admired.

"This is the longest damn hall I've ever seen!" Fontaine remarked.

They'd been strolling along the extensive corridor, which was developing the disagreeable habit of winding back and forth in different directions like a supernatural maze, for quite awhile, and everyone's patience was wearing thin.

"Yeah, and think of all the closed doors we've passed- I wonder what's behind them?" Brisbane pondered.

"I don't want to know, but one thing's for sure- I bet there ain't no Monty Hall or a sexy model asking you to trade for what's behind curtain number one!" Bucktooth was amused at his own humorous aside.

"Mr. Billingsly, how much longer do you think this hallway can possibly be?" Janie asked impatiently.

"Please, my dear, I told you to call me Old Hoss." The king of unpublished pamphlets responded. "I wish I knew. All I can advise is to keep moving forward and telling yourself it isn't real."

Jeanne patted her sister on the back. "Janie, it doesn't matter. We've got to be really close to Waldo by now."

383

Just as the beautiful and feisty little teenager had finished reassuring her twin sibling, Waldo Billingsly rounded the corner, and it was only great reflex action on his part that prevented a head-on collision with his underaged sweetheart, who was walking a step faster than the others.

"Waldo!" Jeanne cried out, and her exhilaration propelled her into his arms with such force that his tired legs almost buckled from the impact. "Oh, Waldo! I just knew we'd find you!"

Waldo appeared to be stunned, and for a moment almost uncertain of their reality. Then he saw Old Hoss, and immediately became alarmed. "Alright, why don't you ridiculous Unreals just beam out and leave me alone!" He yelled.

Jeanne was shocked. "Waldo, honey, we're real! It's everyone and everything else down here that isn't."

Old Hoss ran to his grandson and embraced him. "Now, does that seem like a genuine show of affection?" He asked.

Waldo stared into the old man's eyes, and, just as Jeanne had earlier, instantly became convinced of the sincerity behind them. *No unreal factory could reproduce that*, he thought to himself as he hugged his grandfather warmly.

"I can't believe it's you!" The tears were flowing down the nervous young man's cheeks. "Where were you? What happened? How did they find you?" Waldo rattled off some of the questions that had been stored in his mind since the disappearance.

Old Hoss began walking back down the hall. Placing his arm around his grandson's shoulders, he whispered in his ear. "There'll be plenty of time for me to explain everything to you, at least all that I can. But now, I think you should pay some attention to a certain little lady. She's the one who found me, and she kept us going whenever we wavered. She is very special and she certainly does love you."

Waldo looked over at Jeanne, who smiled at him and then averted her eyes in an embarrassed fashion, as if she'd heard Old Hoss's compliments. He walked over and threw his arms around her. Then they strolled off ahead of the others, lost in the secretive giggles and private sweet nothings of young love.

As they undertook the long journey back to the legitimate part of the sub-basement and the door to the stairs that might or might not open, they ran into the gang of vampires Waldo had encountered only moments before. It was a testament to the will and fortitude the group now possessed that they did not react at all, barely even noticing the pathetic imaginary creatures.

Fontaine turned to everyone excitedly. "Hey, how about Fontaine E. and The Steady Heady Boyz doing one last rap for all these damn illusions?"

No one objected, so Bucktooth and Brisbane took their places behind rapmaster Fontaine:

"We are so doggone glad that we are leaving this place
We want to say we liked it but that isn't the case
There are far too many things in here that do not exist
And even though they never were, they will not be missed
Vampires, giants, and the Hitchhhiker too
We are happy that we have to say goodbye to you
Don't think that in Iowa we haven't had fun
We enjoy the cornfields as much as anyone
But we must return now to Washington, D.C.
Where every street corner has at least one vacancy
We'll be just like the Pope when we kneel and kiss the soil
But we'll never forget the time we spent in Cornoil."

All of them applauded, even Old Hoss, who was predictably lukewarm in his attitude towards rap music.

"Shit man, I can't believe we really found your grandfather!" Brisbane was lost in wonderment as he stared at Old Hoss as if he were a genuine, conventional celebrity. "I love your writings!"

"Where did you have a chance to read them?" Old Hoss inquired.

"Waldo showed me some of them over at your house, after we met at the accident." Brisbane explained.

"Accident?" Old Hoss raised an eyebrow.

"On the beltway. Don't worry, no one was seriously hurt." Brisbane said. "Shit man, if it hadn't happened, Waldo and I wouldn't have met, and I might never have set foot in the fair state of Iowa."

Everyone chuckled at this, and as they proceeded along down the seemingly endless corridor, Old Hoss found himself in the unaccustomed position of expounding upon his work to a gushing fredneck fan.

"Did you ever do any stuff about Albert DeSalvo? Shit man, I know he wasn't the Boston Strangler. Or Lizzie Borden? That's another fascinating case, dude."

"Yes, well I'll keep that in mind." The king of unpublished pamphlets blew his nose, loudly and heartily. "There are so many misconceptions about so many subjects it's difficult to correct them all, even if you devote your life to it."

Fontaine was strutting like a seventeen year old kid who'd just been named captain of the varsity football team. "Well, I never thought I'd say it when we were in that damn Brig of First Offenders, or being chased by dinosaurs, but it looks like we're gonna get out of this place after all!"

Everyone agreed wholeheartedly with his sentiments.

Brisbane pointed to the Little Home of Loud Voices and Unfettered Reading Materials. "Have you been in there?" He asked Old Hoss. "It's awesome!"

Old Hoss smiled at the breathtaking fountains. "No, my young friend. Remember, no matter how smitten you were with the reading matter there, that the place isn't real."

"Oh, yeah, I almost forgot." Brisbane admitted.

They had finally left the lengthy corridor and were now proceeding along Unconstitutional Avenue, the main passageway of the Extremely Unreachable Ward.

"It really is an incredible place." Waldo added. "We weren't in there that long, but I saw some titles..."

"Hey, you guys!" Jeanne scolded them. "If you don't continue believing everything down here is an illusion, then maybe you'll get the chance to spend a long time reading all those great books."

Waldo felt like a reprimanded schoolboy. "I don't know what I was thinking." He squeezed Jeanne's hand. "If we ever get out of here, I owe it all to you. You're the only one who never forgets..."

Jeanne interrupted his apology by planting her lips passionately on his. "Now, don't you do that again! And, it's not *if* we get out of here, it's *when*. Okay?" She turned towards Brisbane. "And that goes for you too, Brisbane!"

"Keep your eyes off all the distractions, and concentrate on reaching the stairwell door." Old Hoss chipped in.

"That's right." Jeanne said, and they moved on at an even brisker pace.

An instant later, St. Helen materialized directly ahead of them, straddling the yellow line in the center of Unconstitutional Avenue like an otherworldly median strip. To his side, a few feet away, was Sam Hancock.

"Well, well, well." He intoned dramatically, sounding as well as looking like a cardboard cutout version of a villain from an old black and white television series. "You know that you shouldn't be out of the red room, Abner."

"Old Hoss, how could you be so stupid?" Sam Hancock pleaded with his old friend. "You and I could live here forever, surrounded by every convenience. Have you seen their video collection? It's astounding. And comic books, Old Hoss- there's a special section just for them. They have all your favorites- *The Golden Age Flash, Dial H For Hero, Forbidden Worlds, Herbie Popnecker.* Please stay!"

Old Hoss ignored the phantom Hancock and stared intently at St.

Helen. "You are not real. And as for your imaginary companion, he is not my old friend Sam Hancock." He turned to Waldo. "That figure looks exactly like Sam, but it just isn't possible, I'm afraid. You see, Sam Hancock died here back in 1977. He never really lived at all after they brought him to this place."

"What do you mean?" Asked a befuddled Waldo.

"Well, they performed a frontal lobotomy on him soon after his arrival." Old Hoss's face grew very sad. "He was completely out of it, as you might expect, after that. I came and visited him once- back in '72- secretly, because I didn't want you to know what had happened to him, Waldo. He wasn't able to recognize me at all."

As Old Hoss spoke, the phony Sam Hancock gradually faded away. St. Helen seemed to wear a defeated expression. "Alright," he said, "you are all very clever and you can congratulate yourselves on that. But just remember," he smiled hideously at Jeanne, "if the girl can't open the door, then... you're all mine!" The old familiar refrain of blood-curdling laughter rang out once more, and St. Helen disappeared.

"But I don't understand." Waldo was more confused than ever. "If Sam Hancock died back in '77, why were you taken here? And what about the note saying 'room five' that you posted in his journal?"

"I never left you any note in his journal." Old Hoss shook his head. "I suppose that was placed there to lure you to the Last Chance Relaxation Home."

"How about the farewell letter I found on the morning you disappeared?" Waldo lit up a cigarette. "Did you write that?"

"When I was... escorted away from Virginia, I didn't have time to write anything." Old Hoss explained. "I'm afraid I can't claim credit for that either."

"Shit, man!" The fredneck exclaimed. "But, if that Hancock dude died here that long ago, was this place a real mental institution then? And who brought *him* here?"

Old Hoss sighed. "There are many things that I don't understand either, Brisbane. Even the sharpest intellects have trouble in this territory. I can only..."

"You all are not exactly creating the right atmosphere for us to leave this place, if you know what I mean." Jeanne implored them to cease their conspiratorial chatter.

Old Hoss looked a bit sheepish. "Young lady, please forgive us. Once again it appears that you are truly the wisest one here."

Waldo apologized once more as well, and they turned off of Unconstitutional Avenue when they saw a sign directing them to the Hallway of Lost Hopes. They all increased their strides with the realization that it wouldn't be long before they reached the stairwell door.

Phosphate had temporarily flipped out. He was so distraught over his friends' failure to return from the sub-basement that he'd taken leave of his senses and commandeered the Central Supply delivery elevator. On the rare occasions when it was operational, Duck Hung zealously guarded against its unauthorized use, but the top doo-wopper fearlessly hopped aboard the elevator without anyone seeing him.

The top doo-wopper proceeded to stop at every floor and inquire at the nursing station as to whether or not anyone had seen Waldo and the others. In the course of doing this, many patients followed him, unnoticed by the nurses, who were busy at other tasks than watching them, and joined him in the elevator. When Phosphate finally finished his irrational and unexplainable expedition, there were a good twenty-five mental patients squeezed into the Central Supply elevator like tranquilized sardines.

Exiting back at the basement, Phosphate led his charges through the General Processing department, to the astonishment of Hector Hispania and the rest of the G.P. workers.

"Follow me, you unheralded Army Of Unrecognized Crowd Extras!" He shouted like a demented General, bestowing a title upon them in a blaze of inspiration.

They marched down the west wing hallway leading to the sub-basement, and Otto Motto didn't even bother to register an appearance. No one in this bizarre group was likely to display the desired reaction.

Phosphate eventually halted, like Douglas MacArthur on the brink of victory in Korea, just outside the door leading to the stairwell. The top doo-wopper actually considered storming the sub-basement with his freshly emancipated squadron, like paratroopers liberating the residents of a faraway land, but the tiny sliver of sanity remaining within him dissuaded him of such a notion.

"There-" he pointed dramatically to the door, "just down that flight of steps lies the Waldo Billingsly party. A more noble and courageous one you couldn't find." He was overacting shamelessly, but his performance was wasted at any rate, for his audience was off in its own confusing, medicated world and unable to appreciate such theatrics.

One of the Army Of Unrecognized Crowd Extras was Mr. Biggs, the young man whom Waldo had witnessed holding a female security officer aloft and demanding that the patients be permitted to trample on their pills. He was sitting down on the floor, engaged in a fierce imaginary chess match with an elderly man who was still spry enough to cross his legs Indian-style.

The other mental patients were pursuing activities along the same line. One of them, an attractive young girl, was performing some kind of belly dance for a drooling middle-aged bald man, who'd obviously had a great deal of experience tucking large bills into the g-strings of topless dancers. The bald man, whose attention to the girl's midsection could only be diverted by his eyeglasses, which were repeatedly sliding down his nose, bore the look of one who'd spent a lot of money on such worthless matters, always returning home to relieve his sexual frustrations alone. An older man and woman, not related to each other but presenting the image of a normal married couple, were dancing romantically as the man hummed *Memories of You* with an intensity that would have made Mitch Miller proud. One young man was standing with his face to the wall and jabbering away about anything and everything. Nearly all of them were smoking cigarettes, and the smoke-filled hallway soon began to resemble a cheap bar more than a corridor in a mental facility.

"Excuse me, ladies and gentlemen." Phosphate clapped his hands crisply, demanding their attention. "I would like to lead all of you now in a rendition of *Let Me Call You Sweetheart*. It is a traditional favorite of mine, and I am sure it would please Waldo and the others if we were singing it when they return from the sub-basement." Resembling a cross between Leonard Bernstein and Lawrence Welk, the top doo-wopper began waving an invisible baton. *"Let me call you sweetheart, I'm in love with you..."*

The cascade of off-key voices droned away, and it would have been apparent to any rational person, had there been any within earshot, that the Army of Unrecognized Crowd Extras was no threat to the Mormon Tabernacle Choir.

"Let me hear you whisper that you love me too..."

The patients were warming up to the task at hand, and their singing grew increasingly louder and more boisterous, if no more melodic, with every line of the old sentimental tune.

"Keep the lovelight burning in your eyes so blue..."

Phosphate was in a mad, mad, mad, mad world of his own now, waving his arms violently, and throwing in some nonsensical doo-wops between the lines.

"Let me call you sweetheart, I'm in love with you."

The group repeated the simple, touching lyrics over and over again, and they were on their eighth go-round when the door to the stairwell opened.

"Jeanne!" Phosphate ran to the O'Sullivan girl, who was the first member of the lost party to appear. The head Afro-Anarchist was behaving more like Fontaine or Bucktooth than his normal detached, introspective self, but his emotional outburst fit more into the mold of a 1980's-style mentally disturbed individual than a 1930's-era racial stereotype. "Oh, I just knew you'd make it!" He hugged her enthusiastically. Then over her shoulder he saw a weary Waldo trudge through the door. "Waldo! Oh, my Waldo! I'm so happy that you're safe!"

Waldo stared at the wild-eyed top doo-wopper, who was acting in such an uncharacteristically strange manner. "Are you okay, Phosphate?"

But Phosphate didn't reply, as he was busily greeting all of the others as they emerged from their subterranean nightmare. "Fontaine! My man! Bucktooth! Good to see you! Janie! Brisbane! I'm so glad all of you made it..." The top doo-wopper paused in mid-sentence, staring open-mouthed at Old Hoss Billingsly, the last one through the door.

"Phosphate Jefferson, I'd like you to meet my grandfather, Abner "Old Hoss" Billingsly." Waldo proudly introduced them.

The shock of encountering face to face the man responsible for their long, perilous journey to Iowa was so great that, like a bolt of lightning, it seemed to retrieve the old Phosphate from the land of insane doo-woppers and restore him to his humble and lovable self.

"You are... Waldo's grandfather?" Phosphate asked reverently. Then straightening up into a more proper posture, he extended his hand. "It is an honor of the highest magnitude to make the acquaintance of such an able and learned man, sir."

Old Hoss grinned broadly. "I should be calling you learned, my friend. If it wasn't for you and your magnificent theory, I might have been stuck in that horrible place forever."

The top doo-wopper, completely back to normal now, turned to Jeanne. "You are the real heroine. I merely formulated a plausible hypothesis- you are the one who had to carry it out. Tell me- you were gone for quite some time- did you have a great deal of trouble opening the door?"

Jeanne laughed. "No, not really, it opened right away. But we had some crazy adventures before we got a chance to open it."

"Crazy? Did I hear someone say *the word*?" Mr. Biggs suddenly spoke, tearing himself away from his imaginary chess game.

Waldo and the others now noticed the ragged group of patients that represented the Army Of Unrecognized Crowd Extras for the first time. Apparently they were so relieved to be free of the Extremely Unreachable Ward they had totally blocked out the strains of *"Let Me Call You Sweetheart,"* with which they were still being serenaded as they exchanged greetings with Phosphate. Had any novice Hollywood director been present, he might have filmed a spectacular scene of the some twenty five mentally confused individuals buzzing around the hallway, belting out the oddest version of the old standard on record, while Phosphate met Old Hoss, and all of the others embraced and thanked the leader of the Afro-Anarchists for deciphering an escape route out of the sub-basement.

"Say, aren't you..." Waldo knew he had seen the young mental patient before.

"Yes, I am." Mr. Biggs' eyes grew sufficiently wide to serve as an indicator of his probable mental instability. "And, may I ask, where are you folks headed now?"

Brisbane, as always, thought like a fredneck. "Say, dude, can you get me some of the drugs they have you all on?"

Mr. Biggs ignored the inane question and turned to the other mental patients. "I think that all of us would like to accompany you, wherever it is you're going. Is that alright?"

Evidently Mr. Biggs was not accustomed to a group as unique as Waldo and the others undeniably were, at least not any from outside the walls of the facility, and he found it difficult to comprehend any attitude from the mentally stable other than the "take your medicine and go back to your room" kind.

Old Hoss, however, walked up to Biggs and placed the first reassuring hand he'd felt on his shoulder in many, many years. "Why, anyone is welcome to leave with us. I'm not sure that we all know precisely where we're going, but if there's room, you're certainly free to come."

Biggs became as excited as a child on Christmas morning, and most of his fellow band of Unrecognized Crowd Extras began acting likewise.

Old Hoss then started walking steadfastly towards the lobby. "Come on, now," he gently prodded a few of the more eccentric patients, who in their exuberance were displaying an especially noticeable odd streak, "if you act like that, you won't get any farther than the Information desk. Just don't say or do anything to draw attention to yourselves until we leave the grounds."

Waldo was strolling hand in hand with lovely little Jeanne, and he couldn't help feeling that he was participating in a worthwhile cause- an emancipation of sorts- by assisting the Army Of Unrecognized Crowd Extras in escaping from their keepers in the Last Chance Relaxation Home. Even prior to his harrowing personal ordeal in the bowels of the institution, he had always harbored a special empathy for the plight of those committed to such facilities.

"There they are! After them!"

The Last Relaxation Home's Security Force all at once rounded the corner at the end of the hall and came racing towards them. The lone male employee, whose frail frame barely filled out his impressive black and orange uniform, was leading the charge of officers. At his heels were several female guards, some of them appearing to weigh over two hundred pounds.

It was easy for Waldo and the others to outrun the Security

personnel, especially considering that the many strange creatures and forces they'd been fleeing from so often in recent times had served to hone their cross-country skills. Even considering the nebulous nature of their status in reality, however, it was still a severe indictment against the Security staff that they couldn't keep pace with the octogenarian king of unpublished pamphlets, who hadn't won a foot race since the roaring twenties. As for the mental patients, even the most sedated among them were operating with intense desperation, and this naturally accentuated their adrenaline levels, causing their athletic prowess to improve accordingly. Soon the deep breaths and gasps of the red faced, out of shape Security officers were barely audible far behind them in the basement corridor, and everyone was able to relax a bit.

Having conserved their energy during the final stretch of hallway, they dashed up the stairs and into the lobby in a flash. While they slowly and nonchalantly moved across the lobby towards the exit doors, every member of the Army of Unrecognized Crowd Extras did an admirable job of behaving inconspicuously. As they neared the doors, Waldo turned and observed the crack Security staff gazing all about in confusion and then running off at length in the opposite direction towards the heart of the facility. When they walked out the doors of the Last Chance Relaxation Home, a few of the newly freed mental patients could hardly be blamed for whooping with joy.

"Thanks for helping us escape. Goodbye and good luck!" Mr. Biggs was running even as he uttered his snappy farewell, and the other Unrecognized Crowd Extras were right behind him, shaking their fists in the air and shouting out various crude epithets at the building where they'd been so involuntarily confined.

"No can do!"

Everyone turned in alarm towards the sound of this familiar voice, which some of them had last heard in the lobby of the motel behind Taco Bull on Old Hoss Highway.

"You must be go home now. You cheat their heart." The rotund Chinese gentleman, with his expansive stomach still protruding out from his undershirt, seemed much mellower than he had on the previous occasion. He was sitting on a bench to the left of the entrance doors, munching on a piece of bacon as he spoke. "You work so hard, man. I must be go back now and make clean like sunshine."

"What is this, man?" Fontaine was starting to hyperventilate as well as Waldo ever did. "I thought we were through with all this stuff."

"Doesn't matter, man. You must be all sit down and delax." The elderly ex-desk clerk approached them with a sincere smile on his face and placed a hand, which contained his ever-present piece of toast, on Waldo's shoulder. "I must be go back to work now, man. Thank you, man. No can do!"

With that, he spun around and entered the Last Chance Relaxation Home, but as he did so each one of them noticed his conspicuous nametag. Although his name was indecipherable, his title was crystal clear: *Senior Material Handler*.

"Perhaps a parting gift from St. Helen? Let's not even discuss it." Phosphate glanced at Waldo's startled expression. "I recommend we locate Brisbane's car immediately."

Waldo merely nodded and squeezed Jeanne's hand.

It was dark outside, and the light from the Iowa moon lent a deceptive tranquility to the massive facade, with its clinging ivy and black iron gates. Waldo and the others proceeded swiftly down to the employee parking lot, and the nervous young man kept an eye on the woods that bordered the sidewalk, half expecting to be treated to some final supernatural shenanigan.

"Shit, those dudes didn't waste any time in forgetting us, did they?" Brisbane was referring to the Army of Unrecognized Crowd Extras, who'd collectively dashed into the same woods an instant after the Chinese ex-desk clerk had so mysteriously appeared and were now nowhere to be seen. There was genuine sadness in the fredneck's voice, as he was undoubtedly regretting the fact they hadn't provided him with any drugs, either.

"My friend, I'm sure they never really wanted to travel with us. All they wanted was their freedom." Old Hoss remarked.

Noting the silence all around them, Bucktooth mumbled in a barely audible voice, "they found that freedom pretty fast."

"Yeah, it sure feels good to know we helped them." Janie said, ignoring Bucktooth's quirky aside.

"Who could ask for a better reward than that?" Old Hoss poignantly observed.

"Waldo, it is my considered opinion that we should leave as soon as possible." Phosphate solemnly intoned. "After all, our mission here is accomplished, and we can now bring your grandfather safely back to Virginia."

"Yeah, and I sure don't want to spend no more time in this crazy state." Fontaine was anxious to see his beloved urban street corners again.

Waldo glanced at Jeanne and saw that she was staring sadly off into the distance. "Well, I don't know..."

"Shit man, we've been through so much here- you ought to be happy to leave in one piece." The fredneck lit up a cigarette. "What do you want to wait for- Satan himself to show up?"

"That's right, Waldo." Bucktooth chimed in excitedly. "You all say that those dudes in the sub-basement weren't real, but I ain't looking forward to spending another night here and giving them a chance to do something else to us."

They located Brisbane's decidedly un-fredneck-like '65 Dodge Dart, which was still parked securely in its spot, and approached it eagerly.

Waldo looked at Jeanne again. "Well, I guess if all of you want to leave tonight, then we will." He licked his lips nervously. "But I'd like to see the magical cornfield one more time."

Brisbane laughed. "Shit man, we have to drop Jeanne and Janie back home, remember? Unless you want to transport the girls across state lines, that is. You'll see the cornfield, dude."

Old Hoss wore a puzzled expression. "What's this about a magical cornfield?"

"Please, sir, allow me to explain it to you..." Phosphate began.

"Shit man, look at this!" Brisbane, who'd just unlocked the car door and was preparing to slide behind the wheel, held a piece of paper aloft. "It was under the windshield wipers."

The fredneck handed it to Waldo, and the nervous young man read it aloud by the light of the moon:

FAREWELL

It is with deep regret that I must inform the loyal readers of my modest little newsletter that *Force of Habit* will cease publication as of this issue. I cannot thank you all enough for the support you've given me over the years. It is not an easy decision to make, nor a pleasant one, but it is unfortunately a necessary one.

I have commented, through scathing editorials and sharp replies to readers' queries, on nearly every aspect of our times, as well as on matters of historical significance. Despite my incomparable wisdom, the world remains virtually the same. I have overturned no injustice, and eradicated no evil, but I have judged. Oh, how I have judged.

I was, until very recently, a typical Christian with little knowledge and no broad perspective about the teachings of Jesus Christ. After chancing to meet a group of acquaintances who fit the precise definition of good Samaritans, I quickly settled down in their quaint community and set a goal for myself: to read the entire New Testament. Well, I have rapidly finished doing so, and it has drastically altered my perceptions of the world.

There are four main themes, in my way of interpreting it, that stand out most distinctly in the teachings of Jesus Christ:

1. Love of God and the next world over the pleasures in this life
2. Love of neighbor.
3. Leave the judging to God.

4. Do unto others, and treat your enemies with kindness.

As I read the New Testament, I realized not only how far off the mark most supposed Christians are, but how misguided I was myself. During the course of the many years I have been writing and editing *Force of Habit*, I have not only judged, I have made a career out of it. I have not only not loved my enemies, I have berated them incessantly. So I have determined that it is no longer in line with my personal faith to publish this periodical, as it is impossible to do so without continuing along the course I have been following for far too long.

Once again, I apologize to the wonderful subscribers who will miss this monthly newsletter, but I trust you will understand that some things are of greater importance. I truly hope that each of you can find the same peace that I have in our Lord and Savior Jesus Christ.

Waldo's voice was cracking to such an extent that he barely was able to finish the closing paragraph. "I-I-I can't believe I forgot all about the Professor." He moaned as the tears flowed down his cheeks.

"What is this?" Old Hoss grabbed the paper from his grandson. "Do you mean that Hiram Buckley..."

"The Professor accompanied us on the trip out here." The top doo-wopper interrupted. "He met an undetermined fate in the woods surrounding the O'Sullivan property."

"Shit man, he was down in the Extremely Unreachable Ward!" Brisbane exclaimed. "You'd already left, man, when we sat through this fucking trial..."

"Yeah man, they accused the Professor of all kinds of crimes." Bucktooth broke in. "And then they sentenced him to life in that damn place."

"His briefcase is missing." The top doo-wopper, who'd retrieved it from the woods and placed it there himself, was peering into the back seat of the car.

"We have to go back and rescue him!" Old Hoss declared.

"He's not down there." Waldo blew his nose. "I-I-I know where he is." The nervous young man knew intuitively, by some unexplainable method, that an enterprising member of the Forest Of Injured Egos, perhaps even Fred O'Grady himself, had placed the final issue of *Force of Habit* under the windshield wiper blades of Brisbane's car and removed the battered briefcase from the back seat. In his mind, the eccentric ex-history teacher was unquestionably now a part of that very exclusive band of societal castoffs.

"What do you mean, Waldo?" Old Hoss inquired.

"Come on, let's get in the car." Waldo replied. "I'll explain it all on the way."

With that, everyone somehow squeezed into Brisbane's trusty old vehicle and they drove back to the O'Sullivan cornfield one last time.

There was hardly a dry eye amid the swaying corn stalks that night. Following their return from the Last Chance Relaxation Home, the teenage twins had rushed home to assure their parents they were safe and sound, blaming their tardiness on some vague complications with the bus schedule. After a quick dinner, the girls were able to sneak outside again. Brisbane was busy saying goodbye to Janie, and Fontaine and Bucktooth were finding it surprisingly difficult to part with the magical cornfield. The two of them were sitting together, pointing out various locations where they had rapped in the moonlight, joined in a time-traveling adventure, or seen such things as green giants and werewolves.

Old Hoss had demanded to be allowed at least one trip back in time, once he'd been informed of the unique powers of the cornfield. Since Jeanne and Waldo were preoccupied spending their last few moments together in a secluded part of the property, Janie agreed to temporarily leave Brisbane and take the king of unpublished pamphlets to a destination of his choice. Old Hoss, after considering the myriad of great events at his disposal, settled at last on witnessing the surrender of Cornwallis at Yorktowne. Afterwards, he marveled continuously over the abilities of their land, making sure to mention repeatedly how fortunate Janie and her sister were to have access to such things.

"You must promise, dear Janie, that you will grant me another experience like that soon." Old Hoss implored.

"Sure, Mr. Bill... I mean, Old Hoss." Janie corrected herself. "Anytime you're around here again, or whatever, just drop by and we'll take you wherever you want to go."

Once he'd calmed down from his exhilarating trip, Phosphate was able to engage Old Hoss in an earnest discussion. "So, then you accept my premise that even the mental patients who left with us were unreal?"

Old Hoss nodded. "I have to. As you pointed out, they were all wearing patient identification bracelets, and most of them were dressed in such a way that someone would surely have approached them in the lobby. The Security force, also undoubtedly non-existent, had to have seen all of us there, yet they ran the other way. The entire facility is probably a mere illusion."

Phosphate stroked his chin thoughtfully. "Sir, if I may be so bold, one thing has baffled me above all, and I must ask you- did the same forces, unreal though they may be, compel both you and Mr. Hancock to come to the Last Chance Relaxation Home?"

Old Hoss patted the top doo-wopper on the back. "You are one of the brightest fellows I've ever met, Phosphate. Although the incidents were separated by nearly twenty years, I do believe that the same... forces, as you call them, were responsible for bringing us both here." The old man gazed longingly at the night sky. "My only regret is that my friend Sam didn't have someone as clever as you to aid him. If he had, we might still be planning our trips together. Unfortunately, he suffered horribly at the hands of those apparitions, and died an agonizing, lonely death."

"I'm so sorry. From the excerpts I've read of his journal, he seemed to be a fascinating, brilliant man." Phosphate saw the agony in Waldo's grandfather's eyes. "You miss him quite a bit, don't you?"

"Terribly." Old Hoss said, his voice breaking. "But... life goes on, Phosphate. You have to forget..."

"Certainly, I understand." Phosphate attempted to steer the conversation away from the subject of Sam Hancock, as the old man obviously was melancholy over his inability to save his friend. "Sir, if I may ask you another question regarding your journey here..."

Old Hoss blew his large nose. "Phosphate, I've already explained to you that the same powers which you fellows kept encountering were responsible for my disappearance."

"I don't know why, but I have the distinct impression that you're not telling me everything about your... abduction. Am I correct?"

"Yes, once again you are, Phosphate." Old Hoss sighed resignedly. "But... I can't even tell Waldo everything. Maybe I will sometime in the future, I just don't know. Until then, however, I must respectfully decline to elaborate."

Phosphate was disappointed, but smiled in an understanding way.

Waldo and Jeanne, meanwhile, were walking alone together in a remote part of the magical cornfield.

"Well, what are we going to do?" Jeanne's lovely green eyes were moist.

Waldo looked crestfallen. "Why does it... Jeanne, I love you, but I don't know how I can avoid leaving you." He took her hand. "I'm more scared of losing you than I've ever been of anything in my life, and I guess you know how easily I scare. I'd love to run away with you, but sometimes I, well... act with my emotions and not my mind. You're sixteen and your parents hate me. I'm amazed they aren't out here with the police, as a matter of fact. I would love nothing more than to take you with me, but if we wait just a little while longer, until you're of legal age, then it won't matter what your parents think, and I won't have to be afraid of a jail sentence."

Jeanne put her head on Waldo's shoulder and spoke between sobs. "I just don't understand it. Life isn't fair when two people who love each other as much as we do have to part because of some stupid law."

Waldo, whose heart was quietly breaking, hugged her reassuringly.

"We'll write to each other, and you can call me collect, as much as you want. And in less than two years you'll be eighteen, and then we can... well, maybe... get married. That is, if you want to."

Waldo's less than scintillating proposal prompted Jeanne to plant a long and passionate kiss on his lips. Pulling her mouth away, she wiped the tears from her eyes. "Do you know how much I'm going to miss you?"

Waldo nodded. "As much as I'm going to miss you, I hope."

They started walking backhand in hand to where the others were. It had finally warmed up in Iowa, and the cloudless night, with the moon and stars glimmering in the sky, provided a suitable backdrop for the occasion.

"Jeanne..." Waldo stared at the ground. "I want to thank you again, you know, for saving me. That was about the bravest thing I've ever seen."

The pretty teenager smiled. "You're welcome again. Waldo..." Jeanne spoke softly, "did you really mean what you said about... us?"

"Of course I did." Waldo replied, and bent down on one knee. "You didn't answer me, so I guess I better do this more officially." Clearing his throat and looking like a late twentieth century version of Sir Walter Raleigh kneeling there in the cornfield, he was very specific. "Jeanne O'Sullivan, would you do me the honor of becoming my wife, as soon as I can get here, on your eighteenth birthday?"

Jeanne was going through the traditional feminine ritual of alternatively laughing and crying. "Oh, Waldo! I'd marry you if I had to wait ten years!" She threw her arms around him, and they made love illegally for the final time.

"Hey, what about our damn paycheck?" It had suddenly dawned on Fontaine that they hadn't received their money for the time they'd spent as Junior Material Handlers at the Last Chance Relaxation Home.

Phosphate stared at him in disbelief. "Fontaine, are you being serious? Do you honestly expect us to return to that house of unreality, just toclaim a few dollars? And even if we did, do you imagine they'd give it to us?"

"Shit yeah, Fontaine!" The fredneck echoed the head Afro-Anarchist's sentiments. "I didn't like putting up with that Duck Hung's bullshit for nothing either, but the last thing I'm thinking about now is a lousy paycheck. Shit, I'm just glad to be out of that place!"

Fontaine, suitably chastised, hung his head in shame and walked away.

Bucktooth followed him and tried to provide some comfort. "It's okay, Fontaine. Hell, I was wondering about the money, too." He stared tentatively back over his shoulder at Brisbane and Phosphate. "But I'm glad I wasn't the one to say something about it."

Old Hoss had been admiring the beautiful star-studded sky and the corn stalks swaying in the warm, gentle breeze. He strolled back to where Phosphate was standing. "Ah, have you ever seen such a sight? It may not be as awe-inspiring as if we were standing in the midst of the Greek ruins, but it is spectacular. How can anyone look at that, my friend, and not see a divine influence?"

The top doo-wopper nodded in appreciation. "It is fantastic. I have to admit that after only a few days here, I was beginning to take for granted such delightful workings of nature. But, I'm puzzled, sir, by your reference to a divine influence. It was my understanding that you were an agnostic."

"No, I am simply not a follower of any organized religion." Old Hoss explained. "There's a substantial difference."

"Indeed there is." Phosphate, as always, refused to expound upon his own very deeply held Christian beliefs.

Brisbane and Janie were talking together by the car. "Well, I'm going to miss you, even if we didn't get as close as I thought we would." Janie remarked wistfully.

The fredneck shuffled his feet as he struggled to express his feelings. "Uh, I-I don't know why we didn't, uh, get closer."

Janie smiled tenderly at the shy fredneck. "Why, Brisbane, I think you really do like me, don't you?"

Brisbane was slowly turning red. "Well, uh...yeah." He kept his eyes glued to the ground, in a style reminiscent of his fellow tongue-tied comrade Waldo. "You see, Janie, I-I never really had many girlfriends. I don't know, they just never seemed to like me. And so I have a hard time, you know, talking to girls, even when they're as nice as you."

Janie hugged him. "You're sweet, Brisbane." She took a pen and a piece of paper from her purse. "I know you don't really have a permanent home right now, so I won't ask for an address or a phone number, but I'll write mine down here for you. Who knows, maybe we can get together again someday. At least I'd like to."

Brisbane smiled broadly at this scrap of hope, as only one used to a lifetime's worth of romantic rejection can. "Yeah, that sounds great."

"Hey, there's Jeanne and Waldo!" Janie pointed towards the couple, who were approaching in the distance.

Phosphate and Old Hoss were continuing their philosophical feeling-out process. "Did you ever question," the head Afro-Anarchist asked, "whether perhaps Thomas Hobbes was correct in his thesis that mankind formulated a pact among themselves, eons ago, to remain miserable and unfulfilled?"

"Young man," Old Hoss responded, "I question *everything*."

"Hmmm." The top doo-wopper stroked his chin reflectively.

"Another thing, sir, that I am wondering about is, frankly, how you could have made a fortune on Wall Street. It has always been my impression that it is impossible for the common man to win there, particularly in such a spectacular fashion as yourself."

Old Hoss chuckled softly. "My young friend, that has been the case for a number of years now, but back then it was still feasible for the average person to come out ahead, providing he was blessed with financial acumen and a good deal of luck. Joseph Kennedy, for instance- J.F.K.'s father-accumulated a far greater fortune than I ever dreamed of, and it was primarily through the stock market. He came from a poor background. I do agree, however, that the common man is unable to compete there now."

"Well, I guess you guys are just about ready to leave." Jeanne said, as she and Waldo lingered near Brisbane's car. They had reconciled themselves to separating until the young girl's eighteenth birthday, and it was a certainty in both their hearts that they would be capable of successfully resisting the charms of Iowa farm boys and eccentric Virginia women to eventually spend a lifetime of happiness together.

"Ladies, I don't know how to thank you." Old Hoss hugged both of the O'Sullivan twins. "I wish we had more time to get to know each other, but I trust you'll understand how these young fellows feel. From what little I know of their experiences, and with all that we encountered in the sub-basement alone, I can't blame them for wanting to leave as quickly as possible. I do hope to see you both again under more pleasant circumstances." With that, he climbed into the back seat of the car next to Fontaine and Bucktooth, who had recovered completely from their inexplicable sadness over parting from the cornfield. As he settled in beside them, he winked at Jeanne. "I suspect, young lady, that I'll definitely be seeing more of you."

Phosphate walked up and embraced Jeanne and Janie. "Goodbye. If it hadn't been for you, I might be returning home alone." The top doo-wopper hurriedly opened the driver's door and slid behind the wheel before he started crying.

"Thanks for getting me out and for having such a cool sister." Brisbane hugged Jeanne and then embraced Janie with a bit more fervor. "I hope we'll see each other again."

He whispered in her ear. "I really do care for you and I'm just sorry that I was too ridiculous to show it. I'll be sure to write you." The fredneck then repeated Phosphate's performance of dashing off before the girls could see his tears, and sat down next to the sniffling top doo-wopper in the front seat.

It was now Waldo's turn to say goodbye. He hated farewells of any kind, but this one was particularly painful. He uttered a perfunctory "I

400

wish you luck, hope to see you again, great to know you," etc., to Janie, then felt a gigantic lump growing in his throat as he faced Jeanne.

"Uh, well...I guess this is it."

"Shhh." Jeanne grabbed the stammering young man and pulled him close to her. In a seductive whisper she left him plenty to yearn for over the course of the next two years. "Waldo Billingsly, I think you're the best looking, smartest, kindest, all around greatest guy in the world. And you better come back for me in two years, 'cause I'll be waiting for you."

Waldo squeezed her tightly, not wanting this goodbye to end. "I love you." He whispered back. "And, believe me, I'll be back here before you blow out the candles on your eighteenth birthday cake. I'll call you as soon as we get home." The two of them had, like Brisbane and Janie, exchanged addresses and phone numbers earlier, and Waldo checked his wallet now to make certain they were there. He then kissed the lovely teenager and entered the car without looking back.

Waldo slid into the front seat next to Brisbane, and Phosphate started the engine.

"Well," the top doo-wopper sighed, "is everyone ready?"

All of them were feeling choked up and unresponsive, so Phosphate took their silence as an affirmation and slowly pulled the decidedly un-fredneck-like '65 Dodge Dart away from the magical O'Sullivan cornfield.

Jeanne and Janie watched them drive off with tears in their eyes.

"I hope that Brisbane writes me." Janie said. "I'm going to miss him a lot."

Jeanne put her arm around her sister. "I have a feeling you and Brisbane will see each other again. I know that Waldo and I will be together in two years, and even though it's going to be hard, it'll be worth the wait." She smiled at her twin. "Come on, sis, let's get back to the house. Mom and Dad must be worried. I think we have enough stuff to talk about for a long, long time."

In the car, Fontaine rubbed his stomach. "Damn man, I'm hungry!"

"Shit man, me too!" Brisbane exclaimed.

Old Hoss blew his nose. "Gentlemen, I understand that your financial resources are extremely limited. Fortunately, no one in the Extremely Unreachable Ward expressed an interest in my possessions." He held up a large wad of bills. "Please allow me to treat you to the full-course meal you all so clearly deserve."

None of the five famished friends were about to argue with him.

Moments later, Old Hoss made a typically off-the-wall suggestion, undoubtedly due in part to his romantic streak, but also in large measure because of his affinity for Frank Capra films.

"Why don't we join together in a few choruses of *Auld Lang Syne*? I think that, under the circumstances, it would be most appropriate."

He then began singing the old favorite of countless New Year's Eve celebrations, and one by one the others joined in. It was a shamelessly sentimental display, but as they rode away from the land of corn and magic, of time travel and Unreals, they thoroughly enjoyed it.

Donald Jeffries has been researching the JFK assassination and related issues since the mid-1970s. *The Unreals* was initially published in May 2007. His first nonfiction book, *Hidden History: An Expose of Modern Crimes, Conspiracies, and Cover-Ups in American Politics,* was published in November 2014. He lives in Virginia with his wife and two children.

CPSIA information can be obtained at www.ICGtesting.com
Printed in the USA
BVOW08s1649220315

392693BV00011B/90/P